Early del Rey

Early del Rey

LESTER DEL REY

DOUBLEDAY & COMPANY, INC.

GARDEN CITY, NEW YORK

"The Faithful," copyright 1938 by Street & Smith Publications, Inc., for *Astounding Science Fiction,* April 1938
"Cross of Fire," copyright 1939 by Weird Tales, for *Weird Tales,* April 1939
"Anything," copyright 1939 by Street & Smith Publications, Inc., for *Unknown,* October 1939
"Habit," copyright 1939 by Street & Smith Publications, Inc., for *Astounding Science Fiction,* November 1939
"The Smallest God," copyright 1940 by Street & Smith Publications, Inc., for *Astounding Science Fiction,* January 1940
"The Stars Look Down," copyright 1940 by Street & Smith Publications, Inc., for *Astounding Science Fiction,* August 1940
"Doubled in Brass," copyright 1940 by Street & Smith Publications, Inc., for *Unknown,* January 1940
"Reincarnate," copyright 1940 by Street & Smith Publications, Inc., for *Astounding Science Fiction,* April 1940
"Carillon of Skulls," copyright 1941 by Street & Smith Publications, Inc., for *Unknown,* February 1941
"Done Without Eagles," copyright 1940 by Street & Smith Publications, Inc., for *Astounding Science Fiction,* August 1940
"My Name Is Legion," copyright 1942 by Street & Smith Publications, Inc., for *Astounding Science Fiction,* June 1942
"Though Poppies Grow," copyright 1942 by Street & Smith Publications, Inc., for *Unknown Worlds,* August 1942
"Lunar Landing," copyright 1942 by Street & Smith Publications, Inc., for *Astounding Science Fiction,* October 1942
"Fifth Freedom," copyright 1943 by Street & Smith Publications, Inc., for *Astounding Science Fiction,* May 1943
"Whom the Gods Love," copyright 1943 by Street & Smith Publications, Inc., for *Astounding Science Fiction,* June 1943
"Though Dreamers Die," copyright 1944 by Street & Smith Publications, Inc., for *Astounding Science Fiction,* February 1944
"Fool's Errand," copyright 1951 by Columbia Publications, Inc., for *Science Fiction Quarterly,* November 1951
"The One-eyed Man," copyright 1945 by Street & Smith Publications, Inc., for *Astounding Science Fiction,* May 1945
"And the Darkness," copyright 1950, by Avon Periodicals, Inc., for *Out of This World Adventures,* July 1950
"Shadows of Empire," copyright 1950 by Columbia Publications, Inc., for *Future Combined with Science Fiction Stories,* July–August 1950
"Unreasonable Facsimile," copyright 1952 by Columbia Publications, Inc., for *Future Science Fiction,* July 1952
"Conditioned Reflex," copyright 1951 by Columbia Publications, Inc., for *Future Combined with Science Fiction Stories,* May 1951
"Over the Top," copyright 1949 by Street & Smith Publications, Inc., for *Astounding Science Fiction,* November 1949
"Wind Between the Worlds," copyright 1951 by Galaxy Publishing Corp., for *Galaxy Science Fiction,* March 1951

Printed in the United States of America

To the memory of

John W. Campbell,
a great editor, who taught me to write.

And to Howard DeVore,
who proved himself a friend.

Contents

Part I

The Early del Rey

I never had any serious intention of being a writer until I found that I was one by a sort of slip of the lip. And for thirteen years after I made my first sale, I never considered myself a professional writer. Putting words on paper was just a (sometimes) lucrative hobby to fall back on when I wasn't doing something else. Even today, after thirty-seven years of selling stories, with about forty books and several million words in print, I can't get as compulsive about writing as I should.

I am a compulsive reader, however, and always have been. That began during my first year of schooling when a marvelous teacher taught me to read well before I could even pronounce many of the words correctly. There were no extensive magazine stands or good libraries in the little farming community of southeastern Minnesota where I grew up. But I was lucky. My father had an excellent home library. I ploughed my way happily through the complete works of Darwin, Gibbons' *Decline and Fall*, and the marvelous works of Jules Verne and H. G. Wells. I learned to enjoy Shakespeare without really knowing the difference between a play and a novel. And I spent about equal time going through the Bible several times and reading the collected works of Robert Ingersoll.

By all the standard criteria, I should have had a miserable childhood. We often moved from one poor farm to another—acting as northern sharecroppers, if you like—and there were plenty of times when we didn't have much to eat. I was expected to do most of a man's hard manual labor in the woods and fields from the age of nine. But the truth is that I look back on it all as a very happy period. And reading had a lot to do with that, along with a deep sense of emotional security given by my father. Also, there were many times when the dollar-a-day wage I earned when working with my father was supplemented by the kind loan of some popular work of fiction from the farmer for whom we worked. I read a lot of books after I should have been sleeping, with no light other than full moonlight! People also saved their used magazines and gave them to me.

In 1927, when I was barely twelve, my father moved to a small town where I could have a chance to attend high school, and my horizons were suddenly broadened by the availability of books and magazines from quite a good local library. It was there I discovered the works of Edgar Rice Burroughs, as well as quite a few early works that could be called science fiction. Then when a friend lent me a 1929 copy of *Wonder Stories Quarterly*, I became a total addict to that branch of literature. I left the familiar Earth behind and explored the craters of the Moon and walked the dead sea bottoms of dying Mars—and I never fully returned from those trips.

This isn't going to be a biography. I intend consistently in these introductory and commentary passages to skim over things and avoid a lot of names and events that aren't relevant to my purpose—which is to show the development of a writer of science fiction. But I have to state that my life wasn't all introverted seclusion and reading; that pattern seems to fit a number of those who did become science fiction fans and writers, but it never applied to me. I had my circle of friends, and sports were as much a part of my life as reading and working. I was always small and thin, but I managed to be chosen pitcher in baseball or quarterback in football for our informal back lot games. In winter, skating and skiing were constant sources of pleasure. And I managed to indulge in at least the normal amount of damfool youthful follies!

In the last year of high school, I began writing—but hardly for the usual reason. I had managed to save up ten dollars for an old Remington #2 typewriter—the kind that required the typist to lift the cylinder to see what was written underneath. And the company that sold it had graciously included a ten-cent manual of touch typing, which I mastered in a few weeks. That left me with the problem of finding something to do with the machine I'd coveted so long. I solved it by inventing stories to type out—including a very long novel. But I never took them seriously, or bothered to submit them. I'd read too much good fiction not to know that my results were pretty dreadful, despite what my friends dutifully told me. The stories were fun and they improved my typing. That was enough reward.

But they led to some surprising other results. I never expected to go to college. Few people from my background in those days went beyond high school. Besides, while my grades were good, they weren't exceptional. But my old friend, the librarian, had seen some of my fiction. She was determined that I must go on to further education. I have no idea how long she worked at her project, but she succeeded. She traced down a long-forgotten uncle of mine who edited a weekly labor newspaper in Washington, D.C., and secured his ready promise that I could live with him. Then she managed to secure a partial scholarship for me at George Washington University. So, in 1931, at the age of sixteen, I headed eastward in search of higher education. I never went back, as it turned out.

I'm afraid the eventual outcome must have disappointed that rather remarkable lady. Living with my uncle was an altogether happy experience, and I enjoyed being in Washington—particularly when I discovered that the Library of Congress had all those books that had been only titles to me before. There were also newsstands near me where I could get all the gaudy, marvelous science fiction magazines. But my college education fizzled out.

I simply dropped out after two years. Except for the science courses, I found most of the studies just a repeat of what I'd learned in high school. And generally, I discovered that it took me a year in school to learn what I could master by myself in a few weeks. So I quit and went to work as a junior billing clerk for a plumbing company —a decision which I still regard as one of the best I've ever made.

I wasn't exactly a success as a billing clerk. I got along fine with the use of the Comptometer, as with any machine; I wasn't as seriously devoted to the rest of the job. But I coasted along for a few years before the company caught up with me and let me go. Then I drifted along, selling magazines, working in restaurants, and so on. My major achievement was becoming a well-known science fiction fan, for whatever that was worth. I wrote long letters to the editors of the magazines, pointing out the errors in science and criticizing the stories, and had the joy of seeing them all printed and commented on by other fans. Thus I achieved my first taste of petty fame!

So we come at last to December 1937—a period of hiatus between the Great Depression and World War II. I was twenty-two years old and feeling a lot older, since my health had been miserable for some time, though it was now finally improving. I was living in a tiny rented room near Washington Circle, for which I paid three dollars a week. My closet was outside the room, the bathroom was down the hall, and my typewriter had to sit on a makeshift desk on the window-sill. My income was erratic; I made perhaps ten dollars a week on the average, mostly from research on the history of music at the Library of Congress.

But I had a lot of leisure for all the things that I most enjoyed. (I think my chief hobby at the time was working on a system of machine shorthand which would produce notes that could be read by almost any typist—unlike Stenotypy. Eventually, I perfected it, too, though I never did anything with it.) I also managed to get all the science fiction magazines as they came out.

I was busy reading one of those a few days before Christmas when my girl friend dropped by to see me. She lived a couple of blocks away, and the landlady knew her and liked her enough to let her go up to my room unannounced. So she appeared just as I was throwing the magazine rather forcibly onto the floor. I still do that sometimes when a story irritates me, though I'm somewhat more tolerant now.

I can't remember why I was so disgusted. The story was one by Manly Wade Wellman, "Pithecanthropus Rejectus," in the January 1938 issue of *Astounding Stories*, in which normal human beings were unsuccessfully imitated by an ape; I suspect my dislike was at the unsuccessful part of the idea. (Sam Moskowitz, in a profile of me, listed an entirely different story by the same writer, though I told him the correct title. I suspect he assumed it couldn't have been a story in the January issue if I read it in December—but he should have known that magazines normally came out long before their date of issue.)

Anyhow, my girl friend wanted to know what all the fuss was about, and I responded with a long and overly impassioned diatribe against the story. In return, I got the most irritating question a critic can receive: "What makes you think you have the right to judge writers when you can't write a story yourself?"

My expostulations on the great critics who couldn't write fiction got nowhere.

"So what makes you think I can't write?" I wanted to know.

"Prove it," she answered.

That was something of a stopper. But I couldn't back down at that stage. So eventually, I talked her down to admitting that maybe even successful writers couldn't sell every story, and that if I could get a personal letter from the editor, rather than a standard rejection slip, I would win the bet.

When she left, I sat down to do a little hard thinking. I was pretty sure I could win, partly because I knew that John W. Campbell had just been made editor of the magazine; I'd written some very nice things about his stories in my letters to the editor, and I was sure he'd remember my name, which would help. That was cheating, a bit, but I still didn't think the challenge was fair, either. Anyhow, I'd stuck my lip out, and now I had to make good: I have always enjoyed challenges, and I meant to enjoy this one.

Well, I'd read an amazing number of articles on how to write fiction in the old *Writers' Digest*—splendid articles by many of my favorite pulp writers. I'd read them because it helped me to enjoy their fiction even more, but I must have learned something out of them. And I'd also come up with a number of ideas for stories during the years of reading. I hadn't written any of them down, even in notes, but I remembered the best of them.

In the end, however, I decided that the best idea was to rebut the story I'd disliked by writing one in which man failed and some other animal took over. Wellman had used an ape, so I chose dogs as my hopefuls. So far as I could remember, few science fiction stories had used dogs, though a lot had messed around with the apes.

During that evening and the next day, I figured out what I hoped was a plot. Then I sat down at my old three-row Oliver and began writing steadily. It took me about three hours to finish. And looking at the results, I wasn't at all happy. It was too wordy in style, and too long. I knew that editors get too many long stories and are usually most interested in fiction that is under five thousand words in length. Mine ran to eight thousand. So I sat down with a pencil and began slashing out and shortening. When I finished, I had only four thousand words left, but the results were much better. I'd also learned a tremendous amount about the art of writing fiction—so much that I never had to resort to that business of slashing again; thereafter, I slashed mentally as I went along.

So I shoved the old 1909 Oliver under the bed and dragged out my modern four-row Woodstock. (There was something about the old machine that suited it for composing; but the Woodstock made much neater copy.) I retyped the story neatly in approved form, put it in an envelope with the required stamped, return-address envelope, and mailed it off to John W. Campbell the day before Christmas, 1937.

The story was entitled "The Faithful," and I thought it a little too simple to sell, but good enough to get a personal letter.

1.

The Faithful

(by Lester del Rey)

Today, in a green and lovely world, here in the mightiest of human cities, the last of the human race is dying. And we of Man's creation are left to mourn his passing, and to worship the memory of Man, who controlled all that he knew save only himself.

I am old, as my people go, yet my blood is still young and my life may go on for untold ages yet, if what this last of Men has told me is true. And that also is Man's work, even as we and the Ape-People are his work in the last analysis. We of the Dog-People are old, and have lived a long time with Man. And yet, but for Roger Stren, we might still be baying at the moon and scratching the fleas from our hides, or lying at the ruins of Man's empire in dull wonder at his passing.

There are earlier records of dogs who mouthed clumsily a few Man words, but Hungor was the pet of Roger Stren, and in the labored efforts at speech, he saw an ideal and a life work. The operation on Hungor's throat and mouth, which made Man-speech more nearly possible, was comparatively simple. The search for other "talking" dogs was harder.

But he found five besides Hungor, and with this small start he began. Selection and breeding, surgery and training, gland implantation and X-ray mutation were his methods, and he made steady progress. At first money was a problem, but his pets soon drew attention and commanded high prices.

When he died, the original six had become thousands, and he had watched over the raising of twenty generations of dogs. A generation of my kind then took only three years. He had seen his small backyard pen develop into a huge institution, with a hundred followers and students, and had found the world eager for his success. Above all, he had seen tail-wagging give place to limited speech in that short time.

The movement he had started continued. At the end of two thousand years, we had a place beside Man in his work that would have been inconceivable to Roger Stren himself. We had our schools, our houses, our work with Man, and a society of our own. Even our independence, when we wanted it. And our life-span was not fourteen, but fifty years or more.

Man, too, had traveled a long way. The stars were almost within his grasp. The barren moon had been his for centuries. Mars and Venus lay beckoning, and he had reached them twice, but not to return. That lay close at hand. Almost, Man had conquered the universe.

But he had not conquered himself. There had been many setbacks to his progress because he had to go out and kill others of his kind. And now, the memory of his past called again, and he went out in battle against himself. Cities crumbled to dust, the plains to the south became barren deserts again, Chicago lay covered in a green mist. That death killed slowly, so that Man fled from the city and died, leaving it an empty place. The mist hung there, clinging days, months, years—after Man had ceased to be.

I, too, went out to war, driving a plane built for my people, over the cities of the Rising Star Empire. The tiny atomic bombs fell from my ship on houses, on farms, on all that was Man's, who had made my race what it was. For my Men had told me I must fight.

Somehow, I was not killed. And after the last Great Drive, when half of Man was already dead, I gathered my people about me, and we followed to the North, where some of my Men had turned to find a sanctuary from the war. Of Man's work, three cities still stood—wrapped in the green mist, and useless. And Man huddled around little fires and hid himself in the forest, hunting his food in small clans. Yet hardly a year of the war had passed.

For a time, the Men and my people lived in peace, planning to rebuild what had been, once the war finally ceased. Then came the Plague. The anti-toxin which had been developed was ineffective as the Plague increased in its virulency. It spread over land and sea, gripped Man who had invented it, and killed him. It was like a strong dose of strychnine, leaving Man to die in violent cramps and retchings.

For a brief time, Man united against it, but there was no control. Remorselessly it spread, even into the little settlement they had founded in the north. And I watched in sorrow as my Men around me were seized with its agony. Then we of the Dog-People were left alone in a shattered world from whence Man had vanished. For weeks we labored at the little radio we could operate, but there was no answer; and we knew that Man was dead.

There was little we could do. We had to forage our food as of old, and cultivate our crops in such small way as our somewhat modified forepaws permitted. And the barren north country was not suited to us.

I gathered my scattered tribes about me, and we began the long trek south. We moved from season to season, stopping to plant our food in the spring, hunting in the fall. As our sleds grew old and broke down, we could not replace them, and our travel became even slower. Sometimes we came upon our kind in smaller packs. Most of them had gone back to savagery, and these we had to mold to us by force. But little by little, growing in size, we drew south. We sought Men; for fifty thousand years we of the Dog-People had lived with and for Man, and we knew no other life.

In the wilds of what had once been Washington State we came

upon another group who had not fallen back to the law of tooth and fang. They had horses to work for them, even crude harnesses and machines which they could operate. There we stayed for some ten years, setting up a government and building ourselves a crude city. Where Man had his hands, we had to invent what could be used with our poor feet and our teeth. But we had found a sort of security, and had even acquired some of Man's books by which we could teach our young.

Then into our valley came a clan of our people, moving west, who told us they had heard that one of our tribes sought refuge and provender in a mighty city of great houses lying by a lake in the east. I could only guess that it was Chicago. Of the green mist they had not heard—only that life was possible there.

Around our fires that night we decided that if the city were habitable, there would be homes and machines designed for us. And it might be there were Men, and the chance to bring up our young in the heritage which was their birthright. For weeks we labored in preparing ourselves for the long march to Chicago. We loaded our supplies in our crude carts, hitched our animals to them, and began the eastward trip.

It was nearing winter when we camped outside the city, still mighty and imposing. In the sixty years of the desertion, nothing had perished that we could see; the fountains to the west were still playing, run by automatic engines.

We advanced upon the others in the dark, quietly. They were living in a great square, littered with filth, and we noted that they had not even fire left from civilization. It was a savage fight, while it lasted, with no quarter given nor asked. But they had sunk too far, in the lazy shelter of Man's city, and the clan was not as large as we had heard. By the time the sun rose there was not one of them but had been killed or imprisoned until we could train them in our ways. The ancient city was ours, the green mist gone after all those years.

Around us were abundant provisions, the food factories which I knew how to run, the machines that Man had made to fit our needs, the houses in which we could dwell, power drawn from the bursting core of the atom, which needed only the flick of a switch to start. Even without hands, we could live here in peace and security for ages. Perhaps here my dreams of adapting our feet to handle Man's tools and doing his work were possible, even if no Men were found.

We cleared the muck from the city and moved into Greater South Chicago, where our people had had their section of the city. I, and a few of the elders who had been taught by their fathers in the ways of Man, set up the old regime, and started the great water and light machines. We had returned to a life of certainty.

And four weeks later, one of my lieutenants brought Paul Kenyon before me. Man! Real and alive, after all this time! He smiled, and I motioned my eager people away.

"I saw your lights," he explained. "I thought at first some men had come back, but that is not to be; but civilization still has its followers, evidently, so I asked one of you to take me to the leaders. Greetings from all that is left of Man!"

"Greetings," I gasped. It was like seeing the return of the gods. My breath was choked; a great peace and fulfillment surged over me. "Greetings, and the blessings of your God. I had no hope of seeing Man again."

He shook his head. "I am the last. For fifty years I have been searching for Men—but there are none. Well, you have done well. I should like to live among you, work with you—when I can. I survived the Plague somehow, but it comes on me yet, more often now, and I can't move nor care for myself then. That is why I have come to you.

"Funny." He paused. "I seem to recognize you. Hungor Beowulf XIV? I am Paul Kenyon. Perhaps you remember me? No? Well, it was a long time, and you were young. Perhaps my smell has changed with the disease. But that white streak under the eye still shows, and I remember you."

I needed no more to complete my satisfaction at his homecoming.

Now one had come among us with hands, and he was of great help. But most of all, he was of the old Men, and gave point to our working. But often, as he had said, the old sickness came over him, and he lay in violent convulsions, from which he was weak for days. We learned to care for him, and help him when he needed it, even as we learned to fit our society to his presence. And at last, he came to me with a suggestion.

"Hungor," he said, "if you had one wish, what would it be?"

"The return of Man. The old order, where we could work together. You know as well as I how much we need Man."

He grinned crookedly. "Now, it seems, Man needs you more. But if that were denied, what next?"

"Hands," I said. "I dream of them at night and plan for them by day, but I will never see them."

"Maybe you will, Hungor. Haven't you ever wondered why you go on living, twice normal age, in the prime of your life? Have you never wondered how I have withstood the Plague which still runs in my blood, and how I still seem only in my thirties, though nearly seventy years have passed since a Man has been born?"

"Sometimes," I answered. "I have no time for wonder, now, and when I do—Man is the only answer I know."

"A good answer," he said. "Yes, Hungor, Man is the answer. That is why I remember you. Three years before the war, when you were just reaching maturity, you came into my laboratory. Do you remember now?"

"The experiment," I said. "That is why you remembered me?"

"Yes, the experiment. I altered your glands somewhat, implanted certain tissues into your body, as I had done to myself. I was seeking the secret of immortality. Though there was no reaction at the time, it worked, and I don't know how much longer we may live—or you may; it helped me resist the Plague, but did not overcome it."

So that was the answer. He stood staring at me a long time. "Yes, unknowingly, I saved you to carry on Man's future for him. But we were talking of hands.

"As you know, there is a great continent to the east of the Americas, called Africa. But did you know Man was working there on the great apes, as he was working here on your people? We never made as much progress with them as with you. We started too late. Yet they spoke a simple language and served for common work. And we changed their hands so the thumb and fingers opposed, as do mine. There, Hungor, are your hands."

Now Paul Kenyon and I laid plans carefully. Out in the hangars of the city there were aircraft designed for my people's use; heretofore, I had seen no need of using them. The planes were in good condition, we found on examination, and my early training came back to me as I took the first ship up. They carried fuel to circle the globe ten times, and out in the lake the big fuel tanks could be drawn on when needed.

Together, though he did most of the mechanical work between spells of sickness, we stripped the planes of all their war equipment. Of the six hundred planes, only two were useless, and the rest would serve to carry some two thousand passengers in addition to the pilots. If the apes had reverted to complete savagery, we were equipped with tanks of anesthetic gas by which we could overcome them and strap them in the planes for the return. In the houses around us, we built accommodations for them strong enough to hold them by force, but designed for their comfort if they were peaceable.

At first, I had planned to lead the expedition. But Paul Kenyon pointed out that they would be less likely to respond to us than to him. "After all," he said, "Men educated them and cared for them, and they probably remember us dimly. But your people they know only as the wild dogs who are their enemies. I can go out and contact their leaders, guarded, of course, by your people. But otherwise, it might mean battle."

Each day I took up a few of our younger ones in the planes and taught them to handle the controls. As they were taught, they began the instruction of others. It was a task which took months to finish, but my people knew the need of hands as well as I; any faint hope was well worth trying.

It was late spring when the expedition set out. I could follow their progress by means of television, but could work the controls only with difficulty. Kenyon, of course, was working the controls at the other end, when he was able.

They met with a storm over the Atlantic Ocean, and three of the ships went down. But under the direction of my lieutenant and Kenyon, the rest weathered the storm. They landed near the ruins of Capetown, but found no trace of the Ape-People. Then began weeks of scouting over the jungles and plains. They saw apes, but on capturing a few they found them only the primitive creatures which nature had developed.

It was by accident they finally met with success. Camp had been made for the night, and fires had been lit to guard against the savage beasts which roamed the land. Kenyon was in one of his rare moments of good health. The telecaster had been set up in a tent near the outskirts of the camp, and he was broadcasting a complete account of the day. Then, abruptly, over the head of the Man was raised a rough and shaggy face.

He must have seen the shadow, for he started to turn sharply, then caught himself and moved slowly around. Facing him was one of the apes. He stood there silently, watching the ape, not knowing whether it was savage or well disposed. It, too, hesitated; then it advanced.

"Man—Man," it mouthed. "You came back. Where were you? I am Tolemy, and I saw you, and I came."

"Tolemy," said Kenyon, smiling. "It is good to see you, Tolemy. Sit down; let us talk. I am glad to see you. Ah, Tolemy, you look old; were your father and mother raised by Man?"

"I am eighty years, I think. It is hard to know. I was raised by Man long ago. And now I am old; my people say I grow too old to lead.

They do not want me to come to you, but I know Man. He was good to me. And he had coffee and cigarettes."

"I have coffee and cigarettes, Tolemy." Kenyon smiled. "Wait, I will get them. And your people, is not life hard among them in the jungle? Would you like to go back with me?"

"Yes, hard among us. I want to go back with you. Are you many?"

"No, Tolemy." He set the coffee and cigarettes before the ape, who drank eagerly and lit the smoke gingerly from a fire. "No, but I have friends with me. You must bring your people here, and let us get to be friends. Are there many of you?"

"Yes. Ten times we make ten tens—a thousand of us, almost. We are all that was left in the city of Man after the great fight. A Man freed us, and I led my people away, and we lived here in the jungle. They wanted to be in small tribes, but I made them one, and we are safe. Food is hard to find."

"We have much food in a big city, Tolemy, and friends who will help you, if you work for them. You remember the Dog-People, don't you? And you would work with them as with Man if they treated you as Man treated you, and fed you, and taught your people?"

"Dogs? I remember the Man-Dogs. They were good. But here the dogs are bad. I smelled dog here; it was not like the dog we smell each day, and my nose was not sure. I will work with Man-Dogs, but my people will be slow to learn them."

Later telecasts showed rapid progress. I saw the apes come in by twos and threes and meet Paul Kenyon, who gave them food, and introduced my people to them. This was slow, but as some began to lose their fear of us, others were easier to train. Only a few broke away and would not come.

Cigarettes that Man was fond of—but which my people never used—were a help, since they learned to smoke with great readiness.

It was months before they returned. When they came, there were over nine hundred of the Ape-People with them, and Paul and Tolemy had begun their education. Our first job was a careful medical examination of Tolemy, but it showed him in good health, and with much of the vigor of a younger ape. Man had been lengthening the ages of his kind, as it had ours, and he was evidently a complete success.

Now they have been among us three years, and during that time we have taught them to use their hands at our instructions. Overhead, the great monorail cars are running, and the factories have started to work again. They are quick to learn, with a curiosity that makes them eager for new knowledge. And they are thriving and multiplying here. We need no longer bewail the lack of hands; perhaps in time to come, with their help, we can change our forepaws further, and learn to walk on two legs, as did Man.

Today, I have come back from the bed of Paul Kenyon. We are often together now—perhaps I should include the faithful Tolemy—when he can talk, and among us there has grown a great friendship. I laid certain plans before him today for adapting the apes mentally and physically until they are Men. Nature did it with an apelike brute once; why can we not do it with the Ape-People now? The Earth would be peopled again, science would rediscover the stars, and Man would have a foster child in his own likeness.

And—we of the Dog-People have followed Man for fifty thousand years. That is too long to change. Of all Earth's creatures, the Dog-People alone have followed Man thus. My people cannot lead now. No dog was ever complete without the companionship of Man. The Ape-People will be Man.

It is a pleasant dream, surely not an impossible one.

Kenyon smiled as I spoke to him, and cautioned me in the jesting way he uses when most serious, not to make them too much like Man, lest another Plague destroy them. Well, we can guard against that. I think he, too, had a dream of Man reborn, for there was a hint of tears in his eyes, and he seemed pleased with me.

There is but little to please him now, alone among us, wracked by pain, waiting the slow death he knows must come. The old trouble has grown worse, and the Plague has settled harder on him.

All we can do is give him sedatives to ease the pain now, though Tolemy and I have isolated the Plague we found in his blood. It seems a form of cholera, and with that information, we have done some work. The old Plague serum offers a clue, too. Some of our serums have seemed to ease the spells a little, but they have not stopped them.

It is a faint chance. I have not told him of our work, for only a stroke of luck will give us success before he dies.

Man is dying. Here in our laboratory, Tolemy keeps repeating something; a prayer, I think it is. Well, maybe the God whom he has learned from Man will be merciful, and grant us success.

Paul Kenyon is all that is left of the old world which Tolemy and I loved. He lies in the ward, moaning in agony, and dying. Sometimes he looks from his windows and sees the birds flying south; he gazes at them as if he would never see them again. Well, will he? Something he muttered once comes back to me:

"For no man knoweth—"

I'd read enough about manuscripts from unknown writers to expect a long delay before I received any notice of my story. But to my surprise, there was an envelope from *Astounding Stories* in the mail of January 8. And it was a small envelope, instead of the large return one I had sent to hold my manuscript. There was no personal letter from the editor—but there was a check for $40.

It's a little hard to find the right word to describe my reaction. Perhaps ecstatic delight is the best description; and from other writers, I've heard that this is a sort of standard, normal feeling. There seems to be something about having one's first work of fiction accepted for publication that is not equaled by any other success on earth!

Naturally, I called the girl friend, who agreed that I'd won the bet—and who never again questioned my right to throw a magazine across the room! Then I called my uncle, who had sold a lot of pulp fiction himself; I think his reaction was fully the equal to mine when he finally figured out what I was saying.

But I was far too practical to frame the check; that got cashed at once, leaving me with more money in one lump than I'd had for several months. And then the second reaction began. How long had all this been going on? Forty dollars was a lot of money in those days; and I'd earned it for only a couple of days of fairly easy work that had been fun. Aha! Mr. World, here I come!

So I finished my fiddling with my current hobby in a few more days—I never seem to have believed in letting important things interfere with even more important ones—and settled down to work.

Naturally, I wasn't content to do another nice, simple, direct story. As a man who'd sold a story, I was ready for tougher duty. So I scrounged around in my old ideas and picked the worst possible choice. It was that of a man who comes back in a time machine to take his younger self into the future to steal a machine which that future credits to him. Then he returns to wait thirty years and go pick up his younger self. Both the invention and time machine can't ever have been built in the first place, since they go round and round in time. And to top it all off, I'd figured the idea out as one which could be told in second person, instead of the normal third person or occasional first-person style.

It took a lot of hard thinking, and I even made a bunch of notes and wrote down quite a few paragraphs in advance to keep it logical. Then I sat down and spent three days writing and recopying it. (For years, I always typed things out and then retyped them on another typewriter, correcting minor slips, but never rewriting.) As an established writer, I used the maximum usual length of a short story, 6,000 words. Then I sent it out, fairly sure that its ingenuity and difference would insure its sale.

This time, a personal note from the editor came back—along with the story. Campbell said it was well written, but he wasn't interested in stories that just went around in a circle of time. (This was before Robert Heinlein did his superb "By His Bootstraps," which was at least as circuitous as my story, but a lot better.)

So I threw the story in a drawer and largely forgot it. Why I never sent it—or any rejects, before I got an agent—to other editors, I don't really know. Perhaps because I considered *Astounding* the best magazine, I wasn't interested in selling to any other. But I've found that most young writers make the same mistake of not exhausting all markets. Every article on writing offers one piece of invaluable advice to writers: When a story comes back, send it out immediately to the next market, and keep sending it until there are no possible markets left. But few writers obey the rule, and I was one of the first-degree offenders.

Eventually, the manuscript was lost, along with eleven others. But in 1950, much to my surprise, I found an envelope among my old papers which contained those notes and preliminary paragraphs. With those, I rewrote it; and since it had been a very careful job in the first place, I feel sure that I remembered it well enough to make it almost identical to its first form. I titled it "And It Comes Out Here," from the song "The Music Goes Down and Around," and sent it to *Galaxy* magazine, where Horace Gold immediately bought it. If anyone is curious, it can be found in the Ballantine collection of my stories entitled *Mortals and Monsters*. (Ballantine published four of such collections of my works, as indicated in the Appendix. The stories I am including here are the ones which were not so collected.)

Campbell also suggested that I try him again. That seemed like a good idea, so I set about it. But nothing so simple as a short story this time; I decided on a novelette of 12,000 words, long enough to make up for the one that didn't sell. It was entitled "Ice" and dealt with men who mined for water ice under the frozen carbon-dioxide snow of the Martian poles—replete with tiny Martians and a giant Martian who was a rather sympathetic menace.

It took more than a week for that to come back, and the letter from Campbell was highly complimentary. "I like the way you write," he commented. And that was highly flattering to me, since I'd been more worried about style than content, along with most beginners.

But I figured that was all, thank you. I'd heard too often of the one-story writer—the man who could sell one story and no more. Quite possibly, such writers outnumber those who can repeat, and the tragedy of their continual attempts is very real. So I'd adopted a simple rule, to which I clung for years: Three strikes are out! Any time I received three rejections in a row, I would quit writing. And this time, while there had been only two rejections, one of them counted double because of its length. There was no point in bothering myself or Campbell with further efforts.

So I turned back to other things. It was a pleasure to see my story in print, of course, and I read every word of it. I still read every story when it first comes out in print. Somehow, things always read differently from what they do in manuscript, and I've learned a good deal about my faults and virtues from such rereading. But my previous poor health was improving, as was my income slightly, and I put the idea of being a writer behind me without too many regrets.

Then came a letter from Campbell, which I can almost quote from memory: "Your story was darned well received, del Rey, and it's been moving up steadily in the readers' choice. But as I look through my inventory, I don't find anything more by you. I hope you'll remedy this."

Well, when an editor sends a very nice note with a rejection, he may be only softening the blow. But when he takes the trouble to ask for another story, maybe that's something else. Still, I checked up in the *Anlab*—a department where the preference of the readers was tabulated. I came in fourth, which wasn't too good. I debated the matter with myself for several days, but finally decided the letter gave me enough excuse for one more try!

This time, I was a little more cautious and sensible. I went out and bought a copy of the *Writers' Digest* where I could find the requirements Campbell listed for his magazine. It wasn't much help, except for a few lines: "I want reactions rather than actions. I want human reactions. Even if your hero is a robot, he must have human reactions to make him interesting to the reader."

Okay, what was the most human thing a robot could do? Obviously, fall madly in love. I picked a female robot—because most mechanical robots were treated as male—and a human male, who would be repelled by her mad crush on him; but if I made her good enough, he couldn't keep resisting her. It was a sentimental idea, and I chose an old-fashioned sentimental ending where the narrator admits he also loved her.

I called the story "Helen O'Loy" and carefully kept it down to 4,500 words.

About a week later, I got a check for $45. That was quite a lot then, along with the satisfaction of proving I could please the editor. Much later, the initial payment turned out to be only a tiny portion of the reward. The story is considered by many—including myself—as one of my two or three best. And hardly a year goes by now in which I don't receive four or five times the original price in reprint rights. I have no clear idea of how much the story has paid me altogether, but the sum is more than that earned by most of the old slick stories.

I felt somewhat better about writing, though I was too busy to give it much time. (I forget what I was busy with, but it took all my attention then.) And one disturbing factor plagued me. I had sold two stories to Campbell; but there are such things as writers who can sell one editor, but no others. Was I one of those?

To find out, I went outside the science fiction field. I'd read *Weird Tales* for years, so I decided to try a story for them. I mulled over a vampire story, and finally decided I had fresh enough an angle. Late in 1938, I wrote it, taking a little less than one day to do the job. It came to only 3,000 words, but that was my best bet, judging from the average length of short stories in the magazine I checked. I sent it off to the editor, Farnsworth Wright, without any covering letter, and waited to see what happened.

It came back, together with a little note pointing out that it was an interesting idea and well written, but seemed to have certain flaws that made it useless to him. They were well-taken points, and I felt grateful to Mr. Wright, who was already so stricken by Parkinson's disease that he could barely scrawl his initials. I sent him a brief note of thanks, and sat down to rethink the story. There had been no suggestion that I try to rewrite it; I suppose most editors have found that unknown writers can rarely handle a rewrite. But I was sure I could correct the flaws. And a couple of weeks later, I sent him the revision, with a note explaining that I realized no rewrite had been requested, but that his criticism had enabled me to do what I hoped was a satisfactory revision. It was entitled "Cross of Fire."

2.

Cross of Fire

(by Lester del Rey)

That rain! Will it never stop? My clothes are soaked, my body frozen. But at least the lightning is gone. Strange; I haven't seen it since I awoke. There was lightning, I think. I can't seem to remember anything clearly, yet I am sure there was a fork of light in the sky; no, not a fork; it was like a cross.

That's silly, of course. Lightning can't form a cross. It must have been a dream while I was lying there in the mud. I don't recall how I came there, either. Perhaps I was ambushed and robbed, then left lying there until the rain brought me to. But my head doesn't hurt; the pain is in my shoulder, a sharp, jabbing ache. No, I couldn't have been robbed; I still have my ring, and there is money in my pocket.

I wish I could remember what happened. When I try to think, my brain refuses. There is some part of it that doesn't want to remember. Now why should that be? There . . . No, it's gone again. It must have been another dream; it had to be. Horrible!

Now I must find shelter from the rain. I'll make a fire when I get home and stop trying to think until my mind is rested. Ah, I know where home is. This can't be so terrible if I know that. . . .

There, I have made a fire and my clothes are drying before it. I was right; this is my home. And I'm Karl Hahrhöffer. Tomorrow I'll ask in the village how I came here. The people in Altdorf are my friends. Altdorf! When I am not trying to think, things come back a little. Yes, I'll go to the village tomorrow. I'll need food, anyway, and there are no provisions in the house.

But that is not strange. When I arrived here, it was boarded and nailed shut, and I spent nearly an hour trying to get in. Then my feet guided me to the cellar, and it was not locked. My muscles sometimes know better than my brain. And sometimes they trick me. They would have led me deeper into the cellar instead of up the steps to this room.

Dust and dirt are everywhere, and the furniture seems about to fall apart. One might think no one had lived here for a century. Perhaps I have been away from Altdorf a long time, but surely I can't have lived away while all this happened. I must find a mirror. There should be one over there, but it's gone; no matter, a tin pan of water will serve.

Not a mirror in the house? I used to like my reflection, and found my face fine and aristocratic. I've changed. My face is but little older, but the eyes are hard, the lips thin and red, and there is something unpleasant about my expression. When I smile, the muscles twist crookedly before they attempt my old cockiness. Sister Flämchen used to love my smile.

There is a bright red wound on my shoulder, like a burn. It must have been the lightning, after all. Perhaps it was that cross of fire in the sky I seem to remember. It shocked my brain badly, then left me on the soggy earth until the cold revived me.

But that does not explain the condition of the house, nor where old Fritz has gone. Flämchen may have married and gone away, but Fritz would have stayed with me. I may have taken him to America with me, but what became of him then? Yes, I was going to America before . . . before something happened. I must have gone and been away longer than I look to have been. In ten years much might happen to a deserted house. And Fritz was old. Did I bury him in America?

They may know in Altdorf. The rain has stopped and there is a flush of dawn in the sky. I'll go down soon. But now I am growing sleepy. Small wonder, with all I have been through. I'll go upstairs and sleep for a little while before going to the village. The sun will be up in a few minutes.

No, fool legs, to the left! The right leads back to the cellar, not the bedroom. Up! The bed may not be the best now, but the linens should have kept well, and I should be able to sleep there. I can hardly keep my eyes open long enough to reach it. . . .

I must have been more tired than I thought, since it's dark again. Extreme fatigue always brings nightmares, too. They've faded out, as dreams do, but they must have been rather gruesome, from the impression left behind. And I woke up ravenously hungry.

It is good that my pockets are well filled with money. It would take a long time to go to Edeldorf where the bank is. Now it won't be necessary for some time. This money seems odd, but I suppose the coinage has changed while I was gone. How long have I been away?

The air is cool and sweet after yesterday's rain, but the moon is hidden. I've picked up an aversion to cloudy nights. And something seems wrong with the road to the village. Of course it would change, but it seems to have been an unusually great change for ten years or so.

Ah, Altdorf! Where the Burgermeister's house was, there is now some shop with a queer pump in front of it—gasoline. Much that I cannot recall ever seeing before, my mind seems to recognize, even to expect. Changes all around me, yet Altdorf has not changed as greatly as I feared. There is the tavern, beyond is the food store, and down the street is the wine shop. Excellent!

No, I was wrong; Altdorf has not changed, but the people have. I don't recognize any of them, and they stare at me most unpleasantly. They should be my friends; the children should run after me for sweets. Why should they fear me? Why should that old woman cry out and draw her children into the house as I pass? Why are the lights turned out as I approach and the streets deserted? Could I have become a criminal in America? I had no leaning toward crime. They must mistake me for someone else; I do look greatly different.

The storekeeper seems familiar, but younger and altered in subtle ways from the one I remember. A brother, perhaps. "Don't run away, you fool! I won't hurt you. I wish only to purchase some vegetables and provisions. Let me see—no, no beef. I am no robber, I will pay you. See, I have money."

His face is white, his hands tremble. Why does he stare at me when I order such common things? "For myself, of course. For whom else should I buy these? My larder is empty. Yes, that will do nicely."

If he would stop shaking; must he look back to that door so furtively? Now his back is turned, and his hands grope up as if he were crossing himself. Does he think one sells one's soul to the devil by going to America?

"No, not that, storekeeper. Its color is the most nauseating red I have seen. And some coffee and cream, some sugar, some—yes, some liverwurst and some of that brown sausage, but not too lean—I want only the fat. Blutwurst? No, never. What a thought! Yes, I'll take it myself, if your boy is sick. It *is* a long walk to my place. If you'll lend me that wagon, I'll return it tomorrow. . . . All right, I'll buy it.

"How much? No, of course I'll pay. This should cover it, if you won't name a price. Do I have to throw it at you? Here, I'll leave it on the counter. Yes, you can go."

Now why should the fool scuttle off as if I had the plague?

That might be it. They would avoid me, of course, if I had had some contagious disease. Yet surely I couldn't have returned here alone, if I had been sick. No, that doesn't explain it.

Now the wine-dealer. He is a young man, very self-satisfied. Perhaps he will act sensibly. At least he doesn't run, though his skin blanches. "Yes, some wine."

He isn't surprised as much as the storekeeper; wine seems a more normal request than groceries, it would appear. Odd. "No, white Riesling, not the red. And some of the tokay. Yes, that brand will do if you don't have the other. And a little cognac. These evenings are so cool. Your money . . . Very well."

He doesn't refuse the money, nor hesitate to charge double for his goods. But he picks it up with a hesitant gesture and then dumps the change into my hand without counting it out. There must be something in my looks that the water did not reveal last night. He stands staring at me so fixedly as I draw my wagon away. Next time I shall buy a good mirror, but I have had enough of this village for the time. . . .

Night again. This morning I lay down before sunrise, expecting to catch a little sleep before exploring the house, but again it was dark before I awoke. Well, I have candles enough; it makes little difference whether I explore the place by day or night.

Hungry as I am, it seems an effort to swallow the food, and the taste is odd and unfamiliar, as if I had eaten none of it for a long time. But then, naturally the foods in America would not be the same. I am beginning to believe that I was away longer than I thought. The wine is good, though. It courses through my veins like new life.

And the wine dispels the lurking queerness of the nightmares. I had hoped that my sleep would be dreamless, but they came again, this time stronger. Some I half remember. Flämchen was in one, Fritz in several.

That is due to my being back in the old house. And because the house has changed so unpleasantly, Fritz and Flämchen have altered into the horrible travesties I see in my dreams.

Now to look over the house. First the attic, then the cellar. The rest of it I have seen, and it is little different except for its anachronistic appearance of age. Probably the attic will be the same, though curiosity and idleness urge me to see.

These stairs must be fixed; the ladder looks too shaky to risk. It seems solid enough, though. Now the trapdoor—ah, it opens easily. But what is that odor? Garlic—or the age-worn ghost of garlic. The place reeks of it; there are little withered bunches of it tied everywhere.

Someone must have lived up here once. There is a bed and a table, with a few soiled dishes. That refuse might have been food once. And that old hat was one that Fritz always wore. The cross on the wall and the Bible on the table were Flämchen's. My sister and Fritz must have shut themselves up here after I was gone. More mysteries. If that is true, they may have died here. The villagers must know of them. Perhaps there is one who will tell me. The wine-dealer might, for a price.

There is little to hold me here, unless the table drawer has secrets it will surrender. Stuck! The rust and rotten wood cannot be wrong. I must have been away more years than I thought. Ah, there it comes. Yes, there is something here, a book of some sort. *Diary of Fritz August Schmidt*. This should give me a clue, if I can break the clasp. There should be tools in the workroom.

But first I must explore the cellar. It seems strange that the doors should have been open there when all the rest were so carefully nailed shut. If I could only remember how long I've been gone!

How easily my feet lead me down into the cellar! Well, let them have their way this once. Perhaps they know more than my memory tells. They guided me here well enough before. Tracks in the dust! A man's shoe print. Wait . . . Yes, they match perfectly; they are mine. Then I came down here before the shock. Ah, that explains the door. I came here, opened that, and walked about. Probably I was on my way to the village when the storm came up. Yes, that must be it. And that explains why my legs moved so surely to the cellar entrance. Muscular habits are hard to break.

But why should I have stayed here so long? The tracks go in all directions, and they cover the floor. Surely there is nothing to hold my interest here. The walls are bare, the shelves crumbling to pieces, and not a sign of anything unusual anywhere. No, there is something; that board shouldn't be loose, where the tracks all meet again. How easily it comes away in my hand!

Now why should there be a pit dug out behind the wall, when the cellar is still empty? Perhaps something is hidden here. The air is moldy and sickening inside. Somewhere I've smelled it before, and the association is not pleasant. Ah, now I can see. There's a box there, a large one, and heavy. Inside . . . A coffin, open and empty!

Someone buried here? But that is senseless; it is empty. Too, the earth would have been filled in. No, there is something wrong here. Strange things have gone on in this house while I have been away. The house is too old, the villagers fear me, Fritz shuts himself up in the attic, this coffin is hidden here; somehow they must be connected. And I must find the connection.

This was an unusually fine coffin once; the satin lining is still scarcely soiled, except for those odd brown blotches. Mold, perhaps, though I've never seen it harden the cloth before; it looks more like blood. Evidently I'll not find my connection here. But there still remains the diary. Somewhere there has to be an answer. I'll break the clasp at once, and see if my questions are settled there. . . .

This time, reading and work have given me no chance to sleep through the day as before. It is almost night again, and I am still awake.

Yes, the diary held the answer. I have burned it now, but I could recite it from memory. Memory! How I hate that word! Mercifully, some things are still only half clear; my hope now is that I may never remember fully. How I have remained sane this long is a miracle beyond comprehension. If I had not found the diary, things might . . . but better this way.

The story is complete now. At first as I read Fritz's scrawl it was all strange and unbelievable; but the names and events jogged my memory until I was living again the nightmare I read. I should have guessed before. The sleeping by day, the age of the house, the lack of mirrors, the action of the villagers, my appearance—a hundred things—all should have told me what I had been. The story is told all too clearly by the words Fritz wrote before he left the attic.

My plans had been made, and I was to leave for America in three days when I met a stranger the villagers called the "Night Lady." Evil things had been whispered of her, and they feared and despised her, but I would have none of their superstition. For me she had an uncanny fascination. My journey was forgotten, and I was seen with her at night until even my priest turned against me. Only Fritz and Flämchen stayed with me.

When I "died," the doctors called it anemia, but the villagers knew better. They banded together and hunted until they found the body of the woman. On her they used a hartshorn stake and fire. But my coffin had been moved; though they knew I had become a monster, they could not find my body.

Fritz knew what would happen. The old servant sealed himself and Flämchen in the attic away from me. He could not give up hopes for me, though. He had a theory of his own about the Undead. "It is not death," he wrote, "but a possession. The true soul sleeps, while the demon who has entered the body rules instead. There must be some way to drive out the fiend without killing the real person, as our Lord did to the man possessed. Somehow, I must find the method."

That was before I returned and lured Flämchen to me. Why is it that we—such as I was become—must prey always on those whom we loved? Is it not enough to lie writhing in the hell the usurper has made of our body without the added agonies of seeing one's friends its victims?

When Flämchen joined me in Undeath, Fritz came down from his retreat. He came willingly if not happily to join us. Such loyalty deserved a better reward. Wretched Flämchen, miserable Fritz!

They came here last night, but it was almost dawn, and they had to go back. Poor, lustful faces, pressed against the broken windows, calling me to them! Since they have found me, they will surely be back. It is night again, and they should be here any moment now. Let them come. My preparations are made, and I am ready. We have stayed together before, and will vanish together tonight.

A torch is lit and within reach, and the dry old floor is covered with rags and oil to fire the place. On the table I have a gun loaded with three bullets. Two of them are of silver, and on each a cross is cut deeply. If Fritz were right, only such bullets may kill a vampire, and in all other things he has proved correct.

Once I, too, should have needed the argent metal, but now this simple bit of lead will serve as well. Fritz's theory was correct.

That cross of lightning, which drove away the demon possessing my body, brought my real soul back to life; once a vampire, again I became a man. But almost I should prefer the curse to the memories it has left.

Ah, they have returned. They are tapping at the door I have unfastened, moaning their bloodlust as of old.

"Come in, come in. It is not locked. See, I am ready for you. No, don't draw back from the gun. Fritz, Flämchen, you should welcome this. . . ."

How peaceful they look now! Real death is so clean. But I'll drop the torch on the tinder, to make doubly sure. Fire is the cleanest of all things. Then I shall join them. . . . This gun against my heart seems like an old friend; the pull of the trigger is like a soft caress.

Strange. The pistol flame looks like a cross. . . . Flämchen . . . the cross . . . so clean!

Farnsworth Wright sent a charmingly gracious letter shortly after receiving the manuscript, telling me he was happy now to accept it, and that it would appear in the April 1939 issue of *Weird Tales,* at which time I would receive a check for $30. He was better than his word, since the check reached me several days in advance of publication.

But that idea of such a delay ruined the magazine as a market for me. I couldn't blame anyone; I should have checked up and seen that they regularly paid on publication, not acceptance. But I had no desire to sit around waiting for money. Maybe I'd been spoiled by the previous promptness of payments, but I still think a writer deserves payment when his goods are bought.

A good many writers agree to the point where they will often send a manuscript to a lower-paying market rather than wait for their payment. Publishers refuse to believe this, unfortunately, but a lot of magazines would do much better in the market if they would pay promptly.

However, in justice to *Weird Tales,* I must say that they were among the better magazines of their day in their treatment of writers. Some of the early science fiction magazines paid rates as low as one quarter of a cent a word, and then long after the story was published—"payment on lawsuit," as some writers claimed.

However, I'd satisfied my doubts about being able to sell to other editors and could now return happily to considering Campbell as my market. And early in 1939, he sent me a letter that not only asked for a story, but suggested the general idea to me. He was, as I came to know, a great and creative editor. Nobody has any idea of how many of the stories in his magazine came from ideas he suggested, but a group of us once determined that the figure must be greater than half. He had a remarkable ability to pick just the right idea for a particular writer, or to throw out the same general idea to several writers and get back entirely different stories from each of them. Part of his success probably came from the fact that he gave just enough of an idea to inspire, but not so much as to stifle the writer's own ideas. This was my first example, and it moved me to a quick response, early in 1939.

The idea was that maybe Neanderthaler wasn't killed off fighting Cro-Magnon, but rather died of frustration from meeting a race with a superior culture. I didn't exactly accept it as good anthropology, but the story took shape easily, and I think the 6,000 words of "The Day Is Done" came out of my typewriter in less than two hours. It won a check for $60 and a note from Campbell saying it was exactly what he'd hoped I'd do, and why didn't I plan on doing a lot more for him in 1939?

Curiously, this story—which was never supposed to be very scientifically accurate—has won considerable praise and blame for its picture of early man. The latest example of that came when Isaac Asimov used it in a book meant for discussion by schoolchildren. He listed a number of points, and commented on the fact that I'd erroneously picked up the long-discarded idea that Neanderthal man couldn't speak. Now actually, I'd straddled that issue with great finesse, neither having him speak nor indicating he could not. But to my delight, a few days after the book was published, an article in the New York *Times* presented a new theory to show that Neanderthal man really couldn't speak! Naturally, I called Isaac up to inquire whether he'd read it. Sorrowfully, he admitted he had and had been sitting there hoping I wouldn't see it!

A couple of days after my sale of the story, my chief source of other income came to an end when the research job was finally finished. I suppose there were other jobs where my ability to read the Romance and Teutonic languages adequately would have been useful, but I didn't look for them. Campbell's letter had been most encouraging, and my wants were fairly small, though I had finally moved to a larger room in the rooming house. This cost me five dollars a week, but it was worth it, since it was at least four times as large as my previous one.

To make things even happier, Campbell sent me down a sample copy of another magazine he was about to edit. This was to be *Unknown* (later *Unknown Worlds*), and to be considered by most readers as the best fantasy magazine that was ever printed. I read through that first issue with complete delight. I'd always preferred real fantasy—as opposed to horror and weird stories—over anything else, even science fiction. And I could hardly wait to try my hand at writing for it.

The result was more haste than taste, I'm afraid. I wrote something called "A Very Simple Man," dealing with a nobody who gets mixed up with mermaids and whatnot and gives it all up in the end for his sense of duty to his wife—and has his wife magically changed to a more pleasant person by the understanding mermaid. Campbell didn't like it very well, but indicated that it might be salvaged. It was the first letter suggesting revision from him I had received, and was really a short course in how to write fantasy fiction. I wish I still had it. He had a great gift for analyzing the elements of fiction and making them plain to others.

I read it several times, and learned at least some of the lesson, but not the part about the difficulties with that story. I tried rewriting it, and found it incredibly hard. That should have warned me.

By nature, I seem to be what one might call a "glib" writer. I sweat out a plot slowly—or used to, though it comes much more easily with practice. Mostly, I walk around the room, thinking desperately, and hoping that the back of my head will come up with something. This back-of-the-head part of me is a person I've come to know as Henry, who sits at all the memory files and handles all of the putting of things together. He's lazy, but very capable. When I demand an idea of him, he always tosses the first cliché he can find forward. But by constantly rejecting the obvious, I can usually get him to figure out some fairly new combination; eventually, when he finds it more work to evade than to co-operate, he'll start filling in details for me. Then I go over everything in my head until it all falls into place and I know precisely what I want to write. Once I have my story firmly in mind, it should move rapidly, after the first false opening paragraphs. Once I have found the right key paragraph to set the mood for me, I like to write steadily as fast as I can type comfortably. Generally, the faster I write, the better the results. This won't work at all for some writers, who sweat it out line by line with constant revision; and as a result, some of them think I don't care about quality. I do—and I begin worrying seriously when my head can't keep ahead of my fingers.

Anyhow, I reworked it and sent it back. This time Campbell simply suggested that maybe I should drop the idea, and that he could use a novelette for *Astounding Science Fiction* (as it was now called).

"A Very Simple Man" is lost for all time, along with ten other stories Campbell rejected. I kept the manuscripts for years, but they were all in a box that was supposed to be sent to me in New York when I moved from St. Louis in 1944. The box never arrived, so I can't include any of my unpublished stories in this book. Frankly, I'm glad of that. With one exception, they were all pretty bad, though I might have been able to sell them during one of the boom periods. If I still had them, I suppose honesty would have compelled me to include them here—and that would have been a bad thing for everyone except those who enjoy serious study of every word a writer puts on paper.

Anyhow, I turned to the novelette. I'd had one in mind—an old idea which started off as an adventure story about a dog that brought a sailor bad luck. Somehow, over several years of ripening, the dog had turned into a little creature from Venus, which brought very bad luck outside its native swamps, but good luck there. I called it "The Luck of Ignatz" and it came to 12,700 words.

Campbell returned it to me, pointing out that I'd violated my own hypothesis. I'd taken Ignatz back to the swamps and still plagued him with incredible bad luck. He was right, of course. Every writer needs a good editor for just such occasions—and if he can find one, as I did, he's incredibly lucky. I straightened that out and got my $127. It came at just the right time to save me from having to look for work, too.

Then I went back to *Unknown*. This time I turned to Anderson's "Little Mermaid" for inspiration. She was a good kid, and the idea of her walking in agony forever after had bothered me for years. I'd always wanted to rewrite that ending to a more logical one. Now I had a chance to. So I stood it on end, took out the essential elements, and took a dryad as my heroine. In the end, I think she had to pay a more logical price for her love—and I like to think it was a price she was willing to accept. It ran to 5,000 words under the title of "Forsaking All Others."

Campbell took it and sent me a check for $62.50. At the regular rate of one cent a word, that didn't work out. So I held the check and queried him. (My God, we were young and honest and naïve once upon a time!) He told me that he was now able to pay a bonus of a quarter cent a word on stories he really liked. So I went off to cash it in a mild aura of euphoria.

But there was more to his letter. Included was another of his ideas, this time for *Unknown*. Suppose, he suggested, that the elves weren't dead, but merely sleeping because they couldn't stand something in modern life. But one wakes up. Now the elves were tinkers, fixing copper pots and pans—of which there are few today. Most things are of aluminum and stainless steel—and the old solder flue won't work on them! Poor little elf. What does he do?

I added the idea that it was the fumes of coal and gasoline from factories and cars the elves couldn't stand. Then the one job he could find soldering copper might be fixing car radiators—thereby adding to pollution. (No, Virginia, pollution isn't a new thing to us who wrote science fiction back then!) I called it "The Coppersmith" and Campbell paid me $75 for 6,000 words—another bonus.

Unknown was obviously a promising market. I went out and bought myself a badly needed new suit and got back to work in a hurry for me—which meant a couple of weeks or so.

But this time I was trying something a little different. The other two stories of fantasy which he had liked had been pretty sentimental. (Sam Moskowitz calls all my early work sentimental; Campbell referred to it as mood writing once or twice. I think Sam is right about much of my fantasy; but, aside from a little deliberate schmaltz at the end, most of my science fiction depended more on creating a mood than on outright sentimentality.)

Now I wanted to do a story that I considered somewhat cynical. I knew small towns pretty well, and had lived in several. Generally, I like them. But some seem to develop a pattern that I dislike intensely, and this was a story in which I would extract all that was bad and forget the good. It wouldn't be a "del Rey" fantasy. (If two stories can be said to create a type!) So I hunted around for a pen name and came up with the first of many I would use. I like something that looks a trifle unusual, so it can be remembered, and yet falls trippingly off the tongue. Philip St. John seemed to meet those requirements, so I settled for that. The story went out and the check came back—$70 for 5,600 words. The title was appropriately "Anything."

3.

Anything

(by Philip St. John)

Until Anything came to Carlsburg, I thought I knew the town like the back of my hand. A small-town paper is built on knowledge of the people it serves, rather than news value, and I'd been editing the weekly *Union Leader*, unofficially known as the Onion, for eight years. But the rumors I heard of the Man in Brown refused to fit into the picture.

In common with most small farming communities where the population is falling instead of rising, gossip was the leading rival of the newspaper; and in Carlsburg, it had been raised to a high art. From Aunt Mabel's dizzy spells to Uncle Tod's rheumatism, everybody's business was common property, and a stranger should have been dissected and analyzed within three days.

The Man in Brown wasn't. There were rumors, of course, but they all boiled down to practically nothing. Apparently, he'd first been seen about a week before, looking for work, and vouchsafing no information about himself. For some reason, nobody had thought to ask him who he was or where he came from—which was the mystery of the affair.

Jim Thompson dropped into the *Union Leader*'s office one morning, to talk about some advertising and to relay his wife's orders. Jim was the owner of the local lumberyard and hardware store, and one of the best advertisers I had, even if he did wear himself bald trying to save pennies.

"Now, Luke," he told me, "it's up to you to find out about this here Brown Man, and Molly don't want any nonsense. That's what you're supposed to be doing, running a newspaper like you are. Molly swears she'll drop her 'scription and get the club to do the same, if you don't find out about him. He's been in town over a week now, ain't he?"

"Uh-huh." Molly ran the Carlsburg Culture Club, and I'd had trouble with her before. "I've been trying to get the facts, Jim, but the lack of information is stupendous. Anyhow, I heard yesterday that your wife has already met the fellow, which is more than I've been able to do. What'd she say about him?"

"He come to the door asking for work, seems like; said he didn't want no pay. Now I ask you, don't that sound half-cracked?" Thompson reached over for my tobacco and filled his pipe, fishing around for a match until I handed him one. "Molly give him the mower and told him to cut the lawn, which he did right smart and proper. Seems like she no more'n stepped back inside when the job was done. So she give him the bowl of bread and milk he wanted—that's all he'd take—and away he went."

It was the same story with minor variations that I'd heard all week; he was continually searching for odd jobs, and taking his pay in bread and milk, or a place to sleep for the night. "But didn't she ask him where he was from and what he intended doing?"

"That's the funny part of it all. You know how Molly is?" Jim grinned and I nodded. Even in Carlsburg, Molly's nose for scandal enjoyed a large reputation. "Somehow she never got around to asking him. They kinda talked about the weather and then begonias, but all the questions just slipped plumb out of Molly's mind. Matter of fact, she didn't even get his name."

Thompson took out his fountain pen and turned to the bench where I kept the ink, but stopped halfway. "Speak of the devil," he muttered, pointing across the street. "Here he comes now, headed right this way. Now see what you can make of him."

The man crossing the street was ordinary enough in appearance, a little over average height, with a weathered brown hat and wrinkled brown suit hanging loosely on him. His very lack of distinction made description impossible, except for the easy humor of the smile he was wearing. With a loose springy stride, he came up the steps and leaned against the door facing me.

"Good morning, gentlemen. You're Luke Short, the editor here, I believe?" The voice was soft and casual. "I'd like to run an advertisement in the paper if you'll let me pay in work. I haven't much use for money."

"Know anything about typesetting?" I asked. My regular one-man staff had been sick, and I needed a man to replace him in the worst way. "If you do, I'll run your item and pay regular wages."

He sauntered in. "Anything. I'm sort of an all-around worker, from baby-minding to house building. Only I don't work for money; just give me a place to stay and a couple of meals a day, and we'll call it square. That's what I wanted to say in the ad. You want the setting done now?"

"This afternoon." I pulled out a galley proof and held it out as a rough test; most people, I've found, don't know six-point from great primer. "What size type is this?"

"Pica, or twelve-point on the caption; the rest's brevier, or eight-point, upper and lower case. I told you I did anything—use a stick or linotype, run a job press, make cuts, write copy—anything. What'll I do this morning and where'll I sleep?"

Jim Thompson had finally succeeded in filling his pen and was sticking a few blotters and envelopes in his pocket. He piped up. "You say you do building work?"

"Anything." The Man in Brown laid peculiar stress on the word whenever he used it.

"Well, I'm putting a new lumber shed up at the yard, and we're a mite shorthanded." The truth of that matter was that Jim had lost his workers because they asked more than he was willing to pay, and because his fat wife tried to run their private lives. "If you want work so bad, you can lay asbestos shingles, whenever Luke don't want you. Sure you don't want money? Okay, there's a cot in the back office where you can sleep. That okay?"

"Perfectly. And you'll find me a rapid worker, I'm sure."

They were almost out of range before I remembered enough to shout after him. "Hey, you! What'll I call you?"

He grinned back over his shoulder. "Anything," he answered, and it struck me as being appropriate, at that.

I had to cover the Volunteer Fire Department's proposed drive for money that noon, and it wasn't until I neared my office that I remembered Anything. I also remembered that the old secondhand linotype was out of order as usual, and needed a new cam installed before it could be used. Well, the paper had gone to bed late often enough before, so there was no use worrying.

Anything had his feet cocked up on the desk when I came in, and a pile of galley sheets lay beside him. "Setting's all done," he said. "Want me to make it up while you finish that story you've been out on?"

I looked at my watch and calculated the time needed to set the work I'd left for him. It didn't work out right, and a linotype refuses to be hurried, but there was no disputing the galley sheets; the work was done. "What about the linotype?"

"Oh, I fixed that. Had a little trouble finding whether you had a new cam, but my nose led me to it. By the way, your former helper called in to say the doctor says no more work for him. I stuck a 'faithful service' notice in the editorial column."

"I suppose you finished laying Thompson's shingles this morning, in your spare time?"

The sarcasm didn't register. "I finished about eleven-thirty—he only had eight thousand to lay. I spent my spare time over at the garage helping Sam White tear out and overhaul a tractor engine. How about that makeup?"

I gave up. "Okay, just as soon as I proofread these sheets."

"No need. They're all perfect now. I found a few broken-face type when I ran off the proofs, and fixed that up." There was no hint of boasting, and his voice was casual; but I'd punched ETAOIN SHRDLU myself, so I had no faith in perfect typesetting. I went over the proofs carefully—and there were no errors!

We put the paper to bed ahead of schedule for the first time in a year, and I took Anything home with me to the bungalow I was renting on the edge of town. For the benefit of subscribers, he'd written a quarter column on himself that gave no information but would fool the readers into thinking they knew all about him. Anything was a master of vague phrasing.

"Look here, Anything," I opened up on him as he began cooking the supper, at his own insistence. "You might fool the others with that story you wrote, but just what is the truth? All you said was that you'd come from somewhere, done something, were somebody, and meant to stay here as long as you felt like it."

He grinned and began dishing out the meal. "At least it wasn't a lie, Luke. You like catsup with your meat?"

"I take meat straight. Better try some yourself."

"Bread and milk's all that agrees with my stomach. Let's say I'm on a diet. How long you been running the Onion?"

"About eight years. Um, that's good!" Anything was more chef than cook, and I appreciated a meal that wasn't thrown together. "I've been trying to get on the regular papers in Chicago or Minneapolis, but there's not much hope. I'd have to quit here and take potluck in the city; they don't think much of small-town editors."

He finished his frugal meal and accepted a cigarette. "You're a pretty good man, Luke; maybe some paper'll take you yet. In the meantime, you might do worse than the Onion. Thanks, I will take a piece of cheese, at that. You know, I think I'll like it here."

"Expect to stay long?"

"Maybe. It's sort of hard to say, the way things go. I had a pretty fair job on a farm upstate, but the farmer was Scotch."

I hoped for more information, but he gathered up the dishes and carried them out to the sink in silence, refusing my help. "Thanks, but I can do them faster alone. I suppose I can't blame people for suspecting me, at that. Anyone who works for room and board nowadays is supposed to be crazy; but I happen to have a dislike for money. The Scotchman got the idea I was a brownie."

The word should have meant something to me, but not very much. I was sure it had something to do with superstition, though; something about little men who went around doing things for people until somebody tried to pay them, or they were driven away.

"Sort of an elf?" I hazarded.

"Sort of; you might call them Scotch elves. They tended cows or children, cleaned up the house of a woman who was sick, and made themselves useful in any way they could, though hardly anyone ever saw them work. Mostly they worked at nights, and all they wanted was a cranny in a barn where they could sleep and a bowl of food left for them once or twice a day. If anyone tried to force other payment on them, they had to leave."

"That doesn't sound like the sort of person a farmer should object to."

"Well, there's more to the superstition than that. It seems that they could do ill as well as good. Make the milk turn sour, cause a cow to go dry, and the like. Anytime they were displeased, it was bad business. Sometimes the people got together and drove them away, and that was always the wrong thing to do. So when I come around dressed in brown and working for their wages, a few people get worried."

I could see where he'd worry some people, but more from curiosity than fear. "But the brownies, if I remember right, were supposed to be short little fellows. And I never read about their smoking or doing work in the newspaper line."

"Oh, I'm not suggesting I am one." He grinned with a hint of puckish amusement. "That sort of superstition has pretty well died out, anyway, and sensible people—like us—know there couldn't be such things. Still, if there were, I imagine they'd be modernized by now. They'd have to be more human looking to mix with men, and they'd have to adapt themselves to city life, perhaps. Of course, some of the old rules might still apply."

I wondered whether he was telling me all that in the hope of discouraging further questions, or whether he had some other purpose in mind. But that was his business. "Maybe they would change, if there were such things," I agreed. "How about staying here tonight? That cot of Thompson's won't be overly comfortable."

"It'll be all right. Anyhow, Thompson's putting me to work making general repairs tomorrow morning, so I'll be up early. See you in the afternoon, Luke."

As he disappeared toward the yard, I had a crazy idea that he'd do more than sleep during the night. Maybe it was what he'd been saying that caused it.

Jim Thompson came in the next morning with a smile that was so genuine it had to mean money for him. "That Anything's what

I call a worker," he greeted me. "Does more work than any six men I ever had, and I don't have to stand watch over him, neither. Just goes off by himself and first thing I know, he's back asking for more."

"He's the best helper I ever had," I agreed. "How'd your wife like the article I ran on him in this week's paper?"

"Oh, fine, fine. 'Bout time you got it out, too. She says it's just what she wanted to know."

I'd had other compliments on the item, too. Anything had succeeded beautifully in telling everybody what they wanted to know without actually telling a thing; but I didn't explain that to Jim.

He drew some wrinkled sheets out of his pocket, covered with what he called writing, and I knew there was more advertising to be had from him. "Got a little job for you, Luke. Want you to run some handbills for me, like it says here."

"Which is—"

"When you ever gonna learn to read?" He snorted at that for the hundredth time. "Okay, just say I'm willing to contract for repairs around town to cost only the price of the lumber and hardware. I'll furnish the labor free for this week to anyone wanting work of that kind done. Town sorta needs a lot of repairs, I guess, and it's a good thing for 'em."

When Jim offered free labor, it meant it *was* free—especially to Jim. "You'll get your value out of your cot out of Anything, won't you?" I asked.

I had to admit that Anything was a good worker. When I'd opened the office that morning, I'd found an envelope inside the door with half a dozen news items in it; as I'd guessed, Anything hadn't wasted the night. "Sam White's figuring on cutting in on it, too. He called up this morning wanting Anything to help with a couple of cars when we're not using him."

"Sam's a chiseler, always has been." He rounded up a scratch pad and eraser and pocketed them. "You make him fork over for Anything's board, or you'll be a fool. By the way, you hear about Olsen's sick horse?"

"No. The vet finally succeeded in curing it?"

"Vet didn't have a thing to do with it, though he claims he done it all. Olsen woke up this morning and there the horse was, raring to go." Thompson filled his pipe and picked up a couple of red pencils. "You get the handbills out right away, Luke. I'm expecting to sell a smart bit of lumber this week."

Jim sold more than a smart bit. By the time the week was almost up, there wasn't a house in town that didn't have some of Anything's work in it, and several houses were practically made over. Where he found time for the work was a mystery that puzzled everyone except Thompson.

Anything worked when people were away from home, and there were rumors that he had a staff of assistants, but no one ever saw them. Molly Thompson had started that idea and the rumor that Anything was a millionaire come to town to rebuild it secretly; somebody else added that he was planning on opening a factory there, which explained his interest in Carlsburg. There were other contradictory rumors, too, but that was the normal course of events in the town.

All I knew was that Anything could do more newspaper work in part of an afternoon than any other man could turn out in a week, and better work, at that. If he stayed in town long enough, paid subscriptions should be doubled at the end of the year. Sam White felt the same about his garage business.

And then the Carlsburg Culture Club held its monthly meeting, and the rumors that had been drifting around were focused in one small group. As a clearinghouse for scandal, the Culture Club acted with an efficiency that approached absolute. But since it was purely for women, I had to wait for the results of the meeting until the sound and fury were over and Molly Thompson brought in the minutes for publication.

She usually came in about nine in the morning, but this time she was late. It was nearly ten when Anything opened the door and walked in, and I was still waiting.

"Good morning, Luke," he said. "Is that bed over at your place still open to me?"

I nodded. "Sure is, Anything. What's the matter with the cot and why aren't you working for Jim this morning?"

"Carlsburg Culture Club," he answered. But his grin was a little sour, and he sat back in the chair without offering to do anything around the place. "Molly'll be calling you up in a couple of minutes, I guess, and you'll hear all the dirt then. Got a cigarette, Luke?"

When Anything asked for something, it was news good for two-inch type, purple ink and all. I handed him the cigarette and reached over to the phone that was beginning to ring. "Carlsburg *Union Leader*; editor speaking."

Molly's shrill voice tapped in over the wire, syllables spilling all over each other. "Don't you 'editor' me, Luke Short; I know your voice. You want them minutes, or don't you?"

"Of course I do, Mrs. Thompson. People always want to know what happened at the Culture Club." Personally, I doubted whether ten people, club members excepted, cared enough to know they were printed; I'd always begrudged the ink that put them on paper.

"You ain't fooling me with that soft soap. But you do want our 'scriptions, don't you? There's over forty of us, and we can make a lot of other people stop 'scribing, too. You want our 'scriptions?"

The line was old; I usually heard it six times a year, and in eight years, the words hadn't changed. "Now, Mrs. Thompson, you know I want your subscriptions. What can I do for you this time?"

"Humph! Well, you better want 'em." She stopped for a dramatic pause and drew in her breath for a properly impressive explosion. "Then you get rid of that Anything, Luke Short! You hear me, you get him outta there today. You 'n' that husband of mine, mixing up with him like you had a bargain, just 'cause you're too stingy to hire honest workers. I'll tell you, I put a bug in Jim's ear, and he won't try *that* again. And that Anything—a-telling me he was a millionaire trying to build up the town! Humph!"

I tried to calm her down and be patient. "Now, Mrs. Thomspon, I'm sure you'll remember he never said that. I knew, of course, that several rumors were going around, but I can assure you he was responsible for none of them."

"Like fun he wasn't. Every member of the club had a different story, and every one of them heard it *personal* from him. They told me so themselves. Wasn't no two alike!" Which was undoubtedly true; rumors in Carlsburg always were heard "personal" from the person concerned, according to reports. "And look what he done!"

Anything had come over and had his ear within a few inches of the receiver—as near as his eardrums could stand. He was grinning. Molly Thompson went on with a truly religious zeal.

"Going around doing all that work. It don't fool *me*. He had a *purpose*, and you be sure it wasn't for nobody's good. Besides, look at Olsen's horse. And Turner's boy that got bit by a hyderphoby dog and never even felt it. And look at them gardens where nobody ever finds any weeds or quack grass anymore. Fanny Forbes saw him working in her garden one night. He's up to everything funny that's going on in this town, doing free work just to fool you men into thinking he's your friend. It's a good thing us women keep our eyes open, or you'd all wake up with your throats cut some morning."

I remember another stranger who'd come to town before and shut himself up in a house, hardly coming out. The Culture Club had decided he was a famous swindler and tried to instigate tar-and-feather proceedings. They almost succeeded, too, when it was learned he was a writer trying to fulfill a contract for a book. Everything that was mysterious was evil to the club.

But I still tried to keep the peace. "I can't see any wrong in what has been done. He merely told us he could do anything, and kept his word. Surely that's nothing against the man."

"Anything! I'd like to see a person who could do anything at all. If I couldn't name a hundred things nobody could do, I'd eat my shoes. And him saying he could do anything!"

"So far, he's done what he claimed, Mrs. Thompson, and I'm not firing him for that."

She choked on it, and then snickered in greasy nastiness. "I'll just show you whether he can do anything. If he'll do just what I want him to, you keep him and I'll not say another word. If he don't, you fire him. That a bet?"

Anything nodded, but I didn't like the sound of it. "Lord knows what she's got in mind," I warned him. He nodded again, emphatically, and there was little humor in the smile.

"It's a bet. You tell him what you want," I answered, handing Anything the phone.

She must have lowered her voice, because I couldn't hear what she said next. But Anything's smile grew sharp and pointed, and there was something on his face I'd never seen before, and didn't want to see again. His usual soft voice was low and crisp as he finally spoke into the instrument.

"As you wish, Mrs. Thompson. It's already done."

There was a sudden shriek over the phone, and he put the receiver back on its hook. "Come on, Luke," he said. "I'm afraid I got you into trouble that time, and I'm sorry about it. Let's go home and see what happens."

Well, the paper was all made up, ready to be turned out the next day, and there wasn't much left to do. During the week I'd learned to respect Anything's judgment, and I had a hunch that this was one of the times to follow his advice. In five minutes, the shop was closed, the curtains down, and we were heading back to my bungalow.

"You won't believe it, Luke, so don't ask questions" was all he would tell me. "She asked something she thought impossible, and

I did it. Matter of fact, you ought to kick me out and not be seen with me again."

That shriek over the telephone had suggested the same; but, hell, I liked the fellow. "I'll stick," I told him. "And when you get ready to talk, I'll listen. How about a little work in the garden this afternoon?"

We didn't do much work, and at Anything's suggestion, we made an early supper of it, leaving the dishes unwashed and sitting around smoking. He seemed to be waiting for something, or listening to something.

"You got any good friends in town, Luke?" he asked finally. "I mean, somebody you can really depend on in a pinch?"

"There's Sam White. He'd lend me his last clean shirt. And he's a pretty good friend of yours, if I'm not mistaken."

"He seemed pretty square. You and he were the only ones who treated me like a white man." Anything stood up and began pacing around uneasily, going out to the door and back. "Why doesn't that messenger come?"

"What messenger?"

"Special delivery letter for you. Don't ask me how I know, either." He was standing on the porch, staring down the street. "Ah, there he is now. Go out and sign for it, Luke."

"Special delivery for Lucian Short," the man said. He avoided my eyes, though I'd known him for years, seized the signed book, and scurried back to the car. I grunted and went back inside.

The letter was short:

> Your letter requesting a chance to work with us has come to my attention. At present, we are looking for a man to fill the position of City Editor, soon to be vacated. We have checked your references and examined your previous work, and believe you are particularly qualified for this position. Please report at once.

It was signed by the managing editor of the Chicago *Daily Blade*, a paper I'd been trying to get on for years; but I hadn't tried for the City Desk.

I grunted, holding it out for Anything's inspection. "Dammit, they don't hire men that way—not for jobs like that on a Chicago paper."

He chuckled. "It seems they did. Maybe that will solve the problem. You'll be leaving on the seven-ten bus, I reckon. Better answer the phone, Luke, while I pack up your things. It's been ringing a couple of minutes now."

With clumsy hands, I stuffed the envelope into my pocket and made a dash for the phone, buzzing its head off. Sam White's voice answered.

"Luke, for the love of Pete, is Anything there?"

"He is."

"Well, get him out of town! Get out of town yourself until this blows over. You're mixed up with him, and they're crazy enough to do any fool thing."

"What's up?" I'd expected something, and the expectation had been growing all afternoon, but nothing that justified the frantic urge in Sam's voice.

"The town's gone gaga, Luke! Absolutely nuts! Molly Thompson, the two Elkridge sisters, the whole damned Culture Club and some besides, have been stirring up people since before noon. Nobody's in his right mind. They're talking about a lynching party!"

That *was* strong. "Lynching party? You're drunk, Sam. We haven't killed anybody."

"Worse than that. They've gone back to the Middle Ages, I'll swear they have. I don't know nor care how he did it, but Anything's gone too far for them. They're talking about witchcraft and his either being Satan or a substitute for him. I thought this was a civilized town, but it's not. They're all drunk on superstition and fear."

"Sam, in heaven's name, slow down and make sense!" His words were jumbled together until I could hardly understand him. "What happened?"

Sam caught his breath and slowed down a little. "Seems Anything hexed Molly and the Elkridges. You know how fat they were? Well, they're the thinnest, scrawniest women in town now. Molly doesn't weigh over eighty pounds! You've got to leave town before they really get stirred up. You can still make it, but give them another hour, and hell's gonna pop! Get out, Luke!"

So that was what the screech over the phone had meant. At heart, I knew, people hadn't changed much in the last thousand years, and I could imagine what was going on. "Okay, Sam, and thanks," I said cutting off his expostulations. "I just got a job in Chicago, and I'm going there. *Daily Blade*."

Relief was heavy in his voice. "That's fine, Luke. I'll see you in Chicago. My brother has a garage there, and he wants me to join him. Just got a special delivery from him. After tonight, I don't want another thing to do with this crazy bunch. Make it as quick as you can."

"I'm leaving now." Anything had just come down with the bags. The furniture was furnished with the house, and I hadn't acquired much except a few books. "See you in Chicago."

The line went dead, and I grabbed for a bag. "We're leaving, Anything. Sam says the town's out for blood."

He nodded and shouldered the two heaviest bags. "I kind of thought that might happen. But when she asked me to make her thin, I couldn't resist the opportunity. Hope you're not mad?"

I wasn't. The whole thing struck me as funny—if we got out all right. The bus station, really only a covered platform, was on the other side of town, and I'd have to catch it to Winona and transfer to a Chicago train there. No train would pass through Carlsburg before ten o'clock. But the whole main street lay between my house and the bus stop.

We walked along in silence. There were people ahead, crowded into little groups, talking in low voices with excited gestures. As they saw us coming, they drew back and dispersed quickly. For a half block on each side of us, the street was deserted, but they re-formed their groups after we had passed. Watching them do that, I quickened my steps, but Anything pulled me back.

"Take it easy," he urged. "They haven't reached the boiling point, but they're pretty close to it. If we take our time, we'll make it, but let them think we're running from them, or afraid of them, and they'll be on us in a jiffy."

It made sense, and I calmed down, but cold shocks kept running up and down my backbone. Even the dogs around us seemed to slink with their tails between their legs. When a whole town turns on a man in one day, it isn't the pleasantest thing in the world.

Anything grinned easily, and his voice was mocking. "Somehow, Luke, I don't think people will like living here much anymore. The town seems sort of dingy and dinky, doesn't it?"

I hadn't noticed, but now I did. Up ahead, things were still looking reasonably well kept and attractive, but as we drew nearer, I noticed that the paint seemed dirty and about to scale off, the buildings seemed about to crumble in, and there was an air of gloom and sickness about the town. Behind us it was worse. There was no real difference that I could see, but the change was there. No, people weren't going to enjoy living in Carlsburg.

We came up to Sam White's garage, now closed for the night, but there seemed to be nothing wrong with the place. Anything nodded. "Cheerful here, isn't it? Well, each town has its own bright spots. And there's your office. Own any of the paper, Luke?"

I shook my head and noticed the same desolation fall on the *Union Leader* office. Even the people on the street behind seemed different. Before, they had been ordinary people, but now they looked older, more frustrated, like ghosts come back to haunt a place after its use was done. The dogs were howling dismally, and I could see none on the street now.

It was a relief to see the bus stop come into view and then feel its platform under my feet. It lacked two munutes of being time for the bus, but topping a hill in the distance, I could make out the amber glow of its lights in the growing dusk.

I turned to Anything. "Where are you going now?"

"Think I'll take that side road there and head west this time." It might have been a weekend trip for all the emotion he showed.

"Better come with me; maybe we can get you a job on the *Blade*. You're too good a printer and newspaperman for small towns."

He grinned. "I'll be all right, Luke, but thanks for all you've done. Someday, maybe, I'll look you up in Chicago."

I nodded and glanced off toward the approaching bus. "So long, Anything, and good luck." Then the question that had been bothering me for a week finally came to my lips. "Just what kind of a man are you, anyway?"

But as I turned back, there was no need of an answer. Where he had been, a little brown man, stocky and with a large head, was walking down the road. His clothes were fashioned like something out of a child's storybook, and he carried a little bag on a pole over his shoulder. As I looked, he turned his head back, and there was a purring chuckle in his answer.

"A brownie. So long, Luke."

Then the bus pulled up and cut off my view of the best newspaperman that ever hexed a town.

In those days, the magazine had a large section at the back devoted to the letters from the readers. This section was probably the first read by any writer, as well as by most fans. A good many of the comments were quite good criticism, and sometimes a writer could learn quite a bit from reading them; I know they offered me a chance to learn more about myself.

But there were moments when the letters were amusing for their lack of judgment, or for their rather extreme self-assurance. In the case of "Anything" I was agreeably surprised to find that a reader who had objected strongly to my stories in both *Unknown* and *Astounding* was now wild with enthusiasm. "I didn't know who Philip St. John was," he wrote, "but now that I know, I must say he's my favorite author." I have no idea whose identity he knew lay behind the masquerade—probably L. Sprague de Camp—but I had a hard time resisting the urge to write him a note, thanking him, and admitting my true identity.

Well, as a writer I was now seemingly in the groove. But one should never question the ability of a writer to get out of the groove as soon as he finds it. My next try had to be something of a fable, of course. Now, nobody was publishing fables, but I had to do this one. And strangely, I still believe I had to do it; it was one of those things that were really done for myself, and I don't resent the time I spent on it.

It was a story called "Hands of the Gods," laid supposedly in the far future, when a man has gone off and left his few animals behind. They can talk, and they have breeding vats, but they have to find their own future. And step by step we see most of them sink back to savage wildness, while the ape begins evolving. There were five episodes, each with the elephant somehow helping the man-ape. Finally, questioned by the lion, the elephant says it is because man must be replaced, and the ape alone has the all-important hands of the gods. And in the end, there's a section laid in what might be any zoo where a child is asking his father why men are really so much superior to animals. The elephant there is listening, and his little eyes twinkle as they move on.

It doesn't sound like much, but I probably wrote that better than anything else I've ever done, and the parts fitted together very well. I thought it might go, since it was only 5,000 words long.

Campbell returned it with a long letter in which he said he was really grateful to me for letting him see it, and that he'd enjoyed it more than anything for a long time. But he couldn't use it. It was a "Just-So" story (he was right about that) and very few grown-ups were mature enough to read such stories.

He must have liked it, since he mentioned it several times over a period of years. And the few people who read it told me it was the best thing I'd ever done. But it went into the box with the other rejects and was lost. I'm sorry about that one, since I could have found a market for it much later. I've sometimes thought of rewriting it. But common sense prevails. Somehow back then I did it just right; and while I might be more skillful in some ways now, the original enthusiasm behind it would be stale. I'm still glad I wrote it.

After that, I went back to more routine flights of fancy and spent 4,800 words on a bit of space wrangling. The story was called "Habit" and won me another $60.

4.

Habit

(by Lester del Rey)

Habit is a wonderful thing. Back in the days of apelike men, one of them invented a piece of flint that made life a little easier; then another found something else. Labor-saving ideas were nice, and it got to be a habit, figuring them out, until the result was what we call civilization, as exemplified by rocket racing.

Only, sometimes, habits backfire in the darnedest way. Look at what happened to the eight-day rocket race out of Kor on Mars.

I was down there, entered in the open-class main event, with a little five-ton soup can of rare vintage, equipped with quartz tube linings and an inch of rust all over. How I'd ever sneaked it past the examiners was a miracle in four dimensions, to begin with.

Anyway, I was down in the engine well, welding a new brace between the rocket stanchion and the main thrust girder when I heard steps on the tilly ladder outside. I tumbled out of the dog port to find a little, shriveled fellow with streaked hair and sharp gray eyes giving the *Umatila* the once-over.

"Hi, Len," he said casually, around his cigarette. "Been making repairs, eh? Well, not meaning any offense, son, she looks to me like she needs it. Darned if I'd risk my neck in her, not in the opens. Kind of a habit with me, being fond of my neck."

I mopped the sweat and grease off the available parts of my anatomy. "Would if you had to. Since you seem to know me, how about furnishing your handle?"

"Sure. Name's Jimmy Shark—used to be thick as thieves with your father, Brad Masters. I saw by the bulletin you'd sneaked in just before they closed the entries, so I came down to look you over."

Dad had told me plenty about Jimmy Shark. As a matter of fact, my father had been staked to the *Umatila* by this man, when racing was still new. "Glad to meet you." I stuck out my hand and dug up my best grin.

"Call me Jimmy when you get around to it—it's a habit." His smile was as easy and casual as an old acquaintance. "I'da known you anywhere; look just like your father. Never thought I'd see you in this game, though. Brad told me he was fixing you up in style."

"He was, only—" I shrugged. "Well, he figured one more race would sweeten the pot, so he blew the bankroll on himself in the *Runabout*. You heard what happened."

"Um-hm. Blew up rounding Ceres. I was sorry to hear it. Didn't leave you anything but the old *Umatila*, eh?"

"Engineering ticket that won't draw a job, and some debts. Since I couldn't get scrap-iron prices for the old soup can, I made a dicker for the soup on credit. Back at the beginning, starting all over—and going to win this race."

Jimmy nodded. "Um-hm. Racing kind of gets to be a habit. Still quartz tubes on her, eh? Well, they're faster, when they hold up. Since you aren't using duratherm, I suppose your soup is straight Dynatomic IV?"

I had to admit he knew his tubes and fuels. They haven't used quartz tube linings for ten years, so only a few people know that Dynatomic can be used in them straight to give a 40 percent efficient drive, if the refractory holds up. In the new models, duratherm lining is used, and the danger of blowing a tube is nil. But the metal in duratherm acts as an anticatalyst on the soup and cuts the power way down. To get around that, they add a little powdered platinum and acid, which brings the efficiency up to about 35 percent, but still isn't the perfect fuel it should be.

Jimmy ran his hand up a tube, tapped it, and listened to the coyote howl it gave off. "A nice job, son. You put that lining in yourself, I take it. Well, Brad won a lot of races in the old shell using home-lined quartz tubes. Must have learned the technique from him."

"I did," I agreed, "with a couple of little tricks of my own thrown in for good measure."

"How about looking at the cockpit, Len?"

I hoisted him and helped him through the port. There wasn't room for two in there, so I stood on the tilly ladder while he looked her over.

"Um-hm. Nice and cozy, some ways. Still using Brad's old baby autopilot, I see, and the old calculator. Only that brace there—it's too low. The springs on your shock hammock might give enough to throw you against it when you reverse, and you'd be minus backbone. By the way, you can't win races by sleeping ahead of time in your shock hammock—you ought to know that." He held up my duffel and half a can of beans. "And that isn't grub for preparing a meteor dodger, either."

"Heck, Jimmy, I'm tough." I knew he was right, of course, but I also knew how far a ten-spot went on Mars.

"Um-hm. Be like old times with a Masters in the running. Got to be a habit, seeing that name on the list." He crawled out of the port and succeeded in lighting a cigarette that stung acridly in the dry air. "You know, Len, I just happened to think; I was supposed to have a partner this trip, but he backed down. There's room and board paid for two over at Mom Doughan's place, and only me to use it. We'd better go over there before her other boarders clean the table and leave us without supper. Eating's sort of a habit with me."

He had me by the arm and was dragging me across the rocket pit before I could open my mouth. "Now, Jimmy, I'm used—"

"Shut up. You're used to decent living, same as anyone else, so you might as well take it and like it. I told you I'd paid for them already, didn't I? All right. Anyhow, I'm not used to staying alone; sort of a habit, having somebody to talk to."

I was beginning to gather that he had a few habits scattered around at odd places.

Jimmy was right; shock cushions and beans don't make winners. With a decent meal inside me, and an air-conditioned room around me, my chances looked a lot rosier. Some of the old cocksureness came back.

"Jimmy," I said, lying back and letting the bed ease my back lazily, "I'm going to win that race. That hundred-thousand first looks mighty good."

"Um-hm." Jimmy was opening a can of cigarettes and he finished before answering. "Better stick to the second, kid. This race is fixed."

"I'll change that, then. Who told you it was fixed?"

He grinned sourly. "Nobody. I fixed it myself." He watched my mouth run around and end up in an open circle. "Maybe Brad forgot to tell you, and it's not common news, but I'm a professional bettor."

It was news to me. "But I thought Dad—did he know?"

"Sure, he knew. Oh, he wasn't connected with it, if that's what you're wondering. When he switched from jockeying to dodging, I left the ponies to handicap the soup cans. Learned the gambling end from my father, the best handicapper in the business. It's a habit in the family."

There was pride in his voice. Maybe I was screwy; after all, some people have a pretty low opinion of rocket dodgers. I decided to let Jimmy spill his side without foolish questions.

"Um-hm. Natural-born handicapper, I am. I won twice every time I lost. Never cheated a man, welshed on a bet, or bribed a dodger to throw a race. Anything wrong with that?"

I had to admit there wasn't. After all, Dad used to do some betting himself, as I should know. "How about the race being crooked?"

Jimmy snorted. "Not crooked—fixed. Don't go twisting my words, Len." He stretched out on the bed and took the cigarette out of his mouth. "Always wanted to be famous, son. You know, big philanthropist, endow libraries and schools. Got to be a habit, planning on that; and you can't make that kind of money just handicapping. Your dad ever tell you about that fuel he was working on?"

I began to see light. "We knew he'd been doing something of that sort, though the formula couldn't be found. Matter of fact, he was using it in the *Runabout* when it went out."

"That's it." Jimmy nodded. "A little bit of the compound in the fuel boosts the speed way up. There was a couple of kinks in the original formula, but I got them straightened out. I pick the winner—the fellow who needs to win most, if that's any comfort to you—and sell him on the new fuel. Only the thing won't work in quartz tubes—burns 'em out."

"I won't need it. I'll win this race fair and square." All the same, that did mess things up; I knew Dad had thought a lot of that fuel.

"No rules against better fuels. A man can pick the fuel he wants, the same as he can travel any course he wants to, no matter how long, if he goes past the markers." He grunted. "Brad didn't want you racing, so he sent me the formula. Had a hunch about going out, I guess; dodgers get a habit of hunches."

"And we Masterses have a habit of winning. Better change your bets, Jimmy."

"It's all fixed, too late to change, and the odds are long. After this race, I'm going back and get the habit of being a big philanthropist. Look, kid, you're not sore about my using Brad's formula?"

"If he gave it to you, that was his business." I pulled the sheet up and reached for the light switch. "Only don't blame me when you lose your bets."

But the morning of the start, I had to confess I wasn't feeling so cocky, in spite of living high on Jimmy for a week. I'd seen the favorite —*Bouncing Betty*—and Jimmy's fix, the *Tar Baby*, and both looked mighty good to me.

"What's the *Tar Baby* pulling?" I asked Jimmy. "Or do you know?"

"Olsen says he's driving her at better than two G's all the way. The *Bouncing Betty*'s pulling straight two, which is tough enough, but Olsen thinks he can stand the strain at two and a quarter."

I looked them over again. An extra quarter gravity of acceleration, even if it is only an extra eight feet per second, uses a lot of additional fuel, even for a sixteen-ton soup can. "How about that mixture, Jimmy? Does it pep up the efficiency, or just the speed—combustion rate and exhaust velocity?"

"She'll throw out a fifty percent, mixture I gave Olsen; optimum is good for eighty." Something began to click in my head then, but his next words sidetracked it. "You'd better draw out, kid. An eight-day race is bad, even if you can hold two G's. How's your supplies?"

I was worried a little myself, but I wouldn't admit it. "They'll last. I've stocked enough soup to carry me to Jupiter and back at two G's, if I had to, and the marker station is forty million miles this side of the big fellow, on a direct line from here. I've got plenty of oxygen, water, and concentrates."

They'd given out the course that morning. We were to head out from Kor, point straight at Jupiter with a climb out of the plane of the ecliptic, drive down and hit a beacon rocket they were holding on a direct line with the big planet, forty million miles this side of him; that made about an even three-hundred-million-mile course from Mars, out and back, figured for eight days at a constant acceleration and deceleration of two gravities. It had been advertised as the longest and toughest race in rocket history, and they were certainly living up to the publicity.

"That's a tough haul on a youngster, Len," Jimmy grumbled. "And with quartz lining, it's worse."

"I've had plenty of practice at high acceleration, and the tubes are practically safe for six days' firing. I think they'll last the other two."

"Then you're matching the *Bouncing Betty*'s speed?"

I nodded grimly. "I'll have to. The *Tar Baby*'ll probably run into trouble at the speed she's meaning to make, but the *Betty*'s built to stand two."

The starter was singing out his orders, and the field was being cleared. Jimmy grabbed my hand. "Good luck, Len. Don't ride her harder'n she'll carry. You Masterses make too much of a habit of being crazy."

Then they forced him off the field and I was climbing into the cockpit, tightening the anchor straps of the shock hammock about the straitjacket I wore.

And I expected to need them. Two gravities mean double weight, during eight days, fighting your lungs and heart. If you take it lengthwise, it can't be done, but by lying stretched out on the hammock at right angles to the flight line, it's just possible.

The *Betty* roared up first, foaming out without a falter. Olsen took the *Tar Baby* up a little uncertainly, but straightened sharply and headed up. Finally, I got the signal and gave her the gun, leaving Mars dangling in space while I tried to keep my stomach off my backbone. The first ten minutes are always the toughest.

When that passed, I began feeding the tape into the baby autopilot that would take over when I had to sleep, which was about three quarters of the time, under the gravity drag. There wasn't anything exciting to the takeoff, and I was out in space before I knew it, with the automatic guiding her. I might have to make a correction or two, but she'd hold at the two-G mark on course for days at a stretch.

I'd been fool enough to dream about excitement, but I knew already I wasn't going to get it. By the time I was half an hour out, I was bored stiff, or felt that way. The automat ran the ship, space looked all alike, and the only sensation was weight pressing against me. I looked around for the *Betty*, and spotted her blast some fifty miles away, holding evenly abreast of me. The others were strung out behind in little clusters, except for Olsen. His blast was way up ahead, forging along at a good quarter gravity more than I could use. At the end of an hour, he was a full ten thousand miles away from me; there was no mistaking the harsh white glare of his jets. Olsen had decided to duck over the ecliptic, as I was doing, but the *Bouncing Betty* had headed below it, so it was drawing out of sight. That left me out of touch with what I hoped was my leading competitor.

Of course, the radio signals came through on the ultrawave every so often, but the pep-talk description of the thrilling contest for endurance racing didn't mean much when I put it up against the facts.

A racing ship in space on a long haul is the loneliest, most God-forsaken spot under the stars. For excitement, I'll take marbles.

Having nothing better to do, I turned over and went to sleep on my stomach. You can kill a lot of time sleeping, and I meant to do it.

The howler was banging in my ear when I woke up. I reached over and cut on, noting that the chronometer said sixteen hours out of Kor.

"Special bulletin to all pilots," said the ultrawave set. "The *Bouncing Betty*, piloted by James MacIntyre, is now out of the race. MacIntyre reports that, in cutting too close to the ecliptic, he was struck by a small meteoroid, and has suffered the loss of three main tubes. While out of the running, he feels confident of reaching Kor safely on his own power.

"This leaves Olsen of the *Tar Baby* and Masters of the *Umatila* in the lead by a long margin. Come in, Olsen."

Olsen's voice held a note of unholy glee that the obvious fatigue he was feeling couldn't hide. "Still holding two and a quarter, heart good, breathing only slightly labored; no head pains. Position at approximately twenty-two and a half million miles from Kor; speed, two million eight hundred thousand per hour. Confident of winning."

"Report acknowledged, Olsen. Come in, Masters."

I tried to sound carefree, but I guess I failed. "Acceleration at two, holding course beautifully on autopilot, rising over ecliptic. Body and ship standing up okay. Pyrometer indication of tube lining very satisfactory. Position, twenty million miles out, speed, two and a half million. No signs of meteoroids up here. Can you give next highest acceleration below me?"

Already it took time for the messages to reach Kor and return, and I tried to locate Olsen with his two-and-a-half-million-mile lead. Even if he cut down to two now, the race seemed a certainty for him—unless something happened. Finally the report came back.

"Burkes, on the *Salvador*, reports one and three quarters, refuses to try higher. No others above that except yourself and Olsen. Are you going to match the *Tar Baby?*"

Match the *Tar Baby*, indeed, and run short of fuel or blow up! "No chance. Still expect to win, though."

Well, at least it would sound nice back home, and it might worry Olsen a little. He was too conceited about his speed. But I couldn't see myself making good. Even if I cut closer to the ecliptic, it wouldn't save enough time to count, and the risk wasn't worthwhile. I dug into my store of concentrates and satisfied a raving hunger—

double weight takes double energy, just as it does sleep. The only thing I could think of was to wish I could maintain acceleration all the way, instead of just half.

That's the trouble with racing. You accelerate with all you've got half the way, then turn around and decelerate just as hard until you reach your goal; then you repeat the whole thing in getting back. The result is that as soon as you reach top speed, you have to check it, and you average only a part of what you can do. If there were just something a man could get a grip on in space to slew around, instead of stopping dead, every record made would go to pieces the next day.

I checked over the automat, found it ticking cheerfully, and fiddled around with the calculator. But the results were the same as they'd been back in Kor. It still said I'd have to decelerate after about forty-four hours. Then I messed around with imaginary courses to kill time, listened to the thrilling reports of the race—it must have been nice to listen to—and gave up. Setting the alarm, I went back to sleep with the announcer's voice concluding some laudatory remarks about the "fearless young man out there giving his ship everything he's got in a frantic effort to win."

But I was awake when the next bulletin came in from Kor at the end of the forty-hour mark. "Special bulletin! We've just received word from Dynatomic fuels that there's a prize of fifty thousand additional to any and every man who makes the course in less than eight full days! Olsen and Masters are now way ahead in the field, and about to do their reversing. Come on, Masters, we're pulling for you; make it a close race! All right, Olsen, come in."

"Tell Dynatomic the prize is due me already, and give 'em my thanks. Holding up fine here, fuel running better than I expected. Hundred and forty million out; speed, seven million. Reversing in two hours."

By a tight margin, I might make it, since it applied to as many as came in within the time period. "I'll be in the special field, Kor. Everything like clockwork here, standing it fine. Pyrometer still says tubes okay. Position, one-twenty-five millions; speed, six and a quarter. Reversing in four hours."

"Okay, Masters; hope you make it. Watch out for Jupiter, both of you. Even at forty million miles, he'll play tricks with your steering when you hit the beacon. Signing off at Kor."

Jupiter! Right then a thought I'd been trying to nurse into consciousness came up and knocked on my dome. I dug my fingers into the calculator; the more the tape said, the better things looked.

Finally I hit the halfway. Olsen had reversed a couple of hours before with no bad effects from the change. But I was busy dialing Mars. They came in, after a good long wait. "Acknowledging Masters. Trouble?"

"Clear sailing, here and ahead, Kor." It's nice to feel confident after staring second prize in the face all the trip. "Is there any rule about the course, provided a man passes the beacon inside of a hundred thousand miles? Otherwise, do I have free course?"

"Absolutely free course, Masters. Anything you do after the beacon is okay, if you get back. Advise you don't cut into asteroids, however."

"No danger of that. Thanks, Kor."

I'd already passed the reversing point, but that wasn't worrying me. I snapped off the power, leaving only the automat cut into the steering tubes, and gazed straight ahead. Sure enough, there was Jupiter, with his markings and all; the fellow that was going to let me maintain full speed over halfway, and make the long course the faster one. I was remembering Jimmy's remark that put the idea into my head: "A man can pick the fuel he wants, the same as he can travel any course he wants, no matter how long."

With power off, I was still ticking off about seven million miles an hour, but I couldn't feel it. Instead, I felt plenty sick, without any feeling of weight at all. But I couldn't bother about that. Kor was calling again, but I shut them off with a few words. If I was crazy, that was my business, and the ship was doing okay.

I set the buzzer to wake me when I figured I'd be near Olsen. Looking out, when the thing went off, I could see his jets shooting out away off side, and a little ahead. But he was cutting his speed sharply, while I was riding free, and I began sliding past him.

I was all set to gloat when his voice barked in over the ultraset: "Masters! Calling Masters!"

"Okay, Olsen."

"Man, decelerate! You'll crack up on Jupiter at that rate. If something's wrong, say so. We're way out ahead, and there's plenty of time. Give me the word and I'll try to cut in on you. The *Tar Baby*'s strong enough to hold back your soup can. How about it, Masters?"

That was the guy I'd been hating for a glory hound, figuring him as out for himself only. "No need, Olsen, but a load of thanks. I'm trying out a hunch to steal first place from you."

The relief in his voice was as unquestionable as his bewilderment. "It's okay if you can do it, mister. I'll still make the special. Why not let me in on the hunch? I won't crib your idea."

"Okay, but I don't know how it'll work, for sure. I'm going around Jupiter at full speed instead of cutting to the beacon."

"You're crazy, Masters." The idea didn't appeal to him at all. "Hope your tubes hold up under the extra eighty million miles. So long!"

Sixty-seven hours out of Kor I passed the beacon at the required hundred thousand miles—which isn't as wide a margin at full speed as it sounds—and headed out. Olsen must have called ahead to tell them what I was doing, because the beacon acknowledged my call, verified my distance, and signed off without questions.

I caught an hour's sleep again, and then Jupiter was growing uncomfortably close. I'd already been over my calculations twenty times, but so darned much depended on them that I wasn't taking chances. I ran them through again. The big fellow was coming up alongside like a mountain rolling toward an ant, and I was already closer than anyone I'd ever heard of.

But it worked out all right, at first. I grazed around the side, was caught in his gravity, and began to swing in an orbit. That's what I'd been looking for, something to catch hold of out in space to swing me around without loss of momentum, and that's what I'd found; Jupiter's gravity pulled me around like a lead weight on a swung rope.

Which was fine—if I had enough speed to make him let go again, as close as I was to his surface. Fortunately, he hasn't any extensive atmosphere to speak of—beyond that which creates his apparent surface—in proportion to his diameter, or I'd have been warmed up entirely too much for pleasant living. In no time I was coming around and facing back in the general direction of Mars; and then two things happened at once.

Jupiter wasn't letting me go on schedule; he seemed to think he needed a little more time for observation of this queer satellite he'd just caught. And Io swung up right where it shouldn't have been. I'd forgotten the moons!

That's when I began counting heartbeats. Either Jupiter pulled me too far, or he threw me square into Io, and I didn't like either prospect. The steering tubes were worthless in the short space I had at that speed. I waited, and Jupiter began to let go—with Io coming up!

Whishh! I could hear—or imagine, I don't know which—the outer edges of the moon's atmosphere whistle briefly past the sides of my soup can, and then silence. When I opened my eyes, Io lay behind, with Jupiter, and I was headed straight for the beacon. Dear old Io!

Light as its gravity was, it had still been enough to correct the slight error in my calculations and set me back on my course, even if I did come too close for my peace of mind.

I was asleep when I passed the beacon again, so I don't know what they had to say. It was Olsen's call that woke me up.

"Congratulations, Masters! When you reach Mars, tell them to hold the special and second prizes for me. And I'll remember the trick. Clear dodging!" He was still heading in toward the beacon on deceleration, and less than eighty hours had passed.

Well, there wasn't much more to it, except for the sleeping and the ravings of that fool announcer back on Kor. I reversed without any trouble at about the point where I'd stopped accelerating and began braking down for Mars. Then the monotony of the trip began again, with the automat doing all the work. The tubes, safe for six days, would be used for only about three and a half, thanks to all that time with power off, and I had soup to spare.

Miraculously, they had the landing pit cleared when I settled down over Kor, and the sweetest-looking white ambulance was waiting. I set her down without a jolt, slipped out, and was inside the car before the crowds could get to me. They've finally learned to protect the winning dodger that way.

Jimmy was inside, chewing on an unlit cigarette. "Okay," he told the ambulance driver, "take us to Mom Doughan's. Hi, kid. Made it in a hundred and forty-five hours. That gives you first and special, so you're out of the red. Nice work!"

I couldn't help rubbing it in a little. "Next time, Jimmy, bet on a Masters if you want to go through with those endowments of yours."

Jimmy's face was glum, and the cigarette bobbed up and down in his mouth in a dull rhythm, but his eyes crinkled up and he showed no rancor at the crack. "There won't be any endowments, kid. Should have stuck to the old handicapping, instead of trying to start something new. I'm cleaned, lock, stock, and barrel. Anyway, those endowment dreams were just sort of a habit."

"You've still got your formula."

"Um-hm. *Your* fuel formula; I'm sticking to the old habits and letting the newfangled ideas go hang."

I stopped playing with him then. "That's where you're wrong, Jimmy. I did a lot of thinking out there, and I've decided some habits are things to get rid of."

"Maybe." He didn't sound very convinced. "How'd you mean?"

"Well, take the old idea that the shortest time is made on the shortest possible course; that's a habit with pilots, and one I had a hard time breaking. But look what happened. And Dad had one habit, you another, and you'd both have been better off without those fixations."

"Um-hm. Go on."

"Dad thought a fuel was good only in racing, because he was used to thinking in terms of the perambulating soup cans," I explained. I'd done plenty of thinking on the way in, when I was awake, so I knew what I was talking about. "You had a habit of thinking of everything in terms of betting. Take that fuel. You say it gives eighty percent efficiency. Did you ever stop to think there'd be a fortune in it for sale to the commercials? The less load they carry in fuel, the more pay cargo."

"Well, I'll be—" He mulled it over slowly, letting the idea seep in. Then he noticed the cigarette in his mouth and started to light it.

I amplified the scheme. "We'll market it fifty-fifty. You put up the fuel and salesmanship; I'll put up the prize money and technical knowledge. And if you're looking for fame, there ought to be some of that mixed up in there, too."

"Um-hm." Jimmy stuck out his hand. "Shake on the partnership, Len. But, if you don't mind, I'll use the money like I said. Those endowment ideas sort of got to be a habit with me."

I read "Habit" when it first came out in the magazine and somehow never read it again until I began putting this book together. Now I wonder why Campbell bought it, or why he ever thought it deserved a bonus. He must have been very hard up for short fiction on the day it came in.

I could probably try to excuse it by suggesting that (to my knowledge) it was the first story that pointed out that high acceleration could be tolerated much better in a prone position than when standing or sitting. But that's a minor virtue, and it has a major error in science that renders the whole thing invalid.

At the time, I figured the course of the rocket race very carefully, and the time and distances given are correct enough. But then I have the little ship whipped around Jupiter and brought back to head toward Mars—when the ship is going some seven million miles an hour. This is the result of pure, sloppy carelessness. Jupiter does have a strong gravity, and a ship could be made to turn through 180° when going close to it—but only if the ship was doing less than 100,000 miles an hour. That's an error of seventy times in my figures.

Of course, I didn't bother to figure it out. The formula for centrifugal force is a bit complicated, with a lot of figures beyond the decimal point. So instead of sitting down and calculating it, I took it for granted. And that's pretty inexcusable in science fiction. I've always prided myself on figuring things out, but this story doesn't bear any degree of pride.

There was another error in the magazine version, which seemed to make me suggest that Jupiter had no atmosphere. Even in those days, I knew that Jupiter had more atmosphere than any other planet! On checking with my manuscript when the story was published, I found that several lines had been omitted in setting it.

Well, as Campbell told me at the time, "those things just happen and somehow slip by." But I've tried to restore them in this copy, to reduce the needless errors by one, at least.

So far as possible, incidentally, all the stories in this book are appearing exactly as I wrote them, except for the last one (which will be explained when we come to it). I think it only fair that something meant to show my early writing should show it as I wrote it. And the magazine versions sometimes differ to a considerable amount.

Generally, Campbell made fewer alterations than most editors; he expected his writers to turn in finished copy, not stuff he had to rewrite. But certain changes are necessary, as I've learned from my own experience in editing. Sometimes a story has to be cut slightly because it takes up only a few lines on the last page, leaving too much blank space to be filled in. Sometimes it requires minor changes to get rid of "widows"—incomplete or short lines at the top of a page, which make the page look wrong. There are a number of other legitimate reasons for such changes and deletions in a writer's copy. I don't object to them, but I see no reason to perpetuate purely mechanical changes.

Where I've had originals, I've followed them exactly. In many cases, due to a basement that flooded, my carbon copies were almost useless, but did enable me to check against the published version. And in a few cases, such as "Habit," I've filled in where I clearly remember noting changes in the magazine version when I read it. In any event, these stories will be closer to what I wrote than any other version to appear in print.

I haven't the faintest idea of how good or bad the next story I wrote was. The only information I have on it is a list which shows the order in which it was written, the length, and the title. It was called "Glory," it ran for 5,000 words, and was meant for *Unknown.* It bounced back to me, and even Campbell's rejection must have been pretty routine, since it's one of the few that don't stick in my mind. Generally, hardly a memorable story.

I can remember that both "Habit" and "Glory" were written during my only attempt to write on something like a schedule. The idea is a fine one. Every morning for a certain number of days of the week, the writer is supposed to sit down at his typewriter and stay there for a fixed number of hours. I'd figured out that four hours a day for three days a week would work out very well. If I turned out a thousand words an hour average—allowing for all kinds of bad starts, thinking up new plots, etc.—it would produce something very respectable as an income, even if only half of what I wrote sold. There are lots of fallacies built into that idea, but some writers can make it work.

I can't. When I get a story started, I have to keep with it. I gain momentum as I go along. Ideas seem to pop into my head for its development at a speed that increases slightly faster than my writing speed does. I can even work up a mild fever when I'm really going, and that seems to help. But if I stop, I usually find I'm dull when I return, that the ideas have all flown, and that it's like starting all over again.

I've found that true for novels, too. Once I can get one moving, I stay with it for sixty to eighty pages at a stretch, only breaking when some development will offer a fresh start. And I've turned out 180 pages in one case without ever leaving the typewriter—though that was because I'd gotten myself into a horrible jam and had to finish the book at once. That novel is at least as good as others over which I labored much longer.

Anyhow, that attempt to be systematic came to a sudden end after the fiasco of "Glory." I reverted to my normal sloppy and rather lackadaisical habits, and a feeling of deep peace came over me to exceed any that may have blessed Abou ben Adhem.

When I came back to the typewriter, it was fun to begin writing again, and the result was much better. I wrote my longest story up to that time (14,500 words) and Campbell accepted it and sent a prompt check for $187.50. It was called "The Smallest God."

5.

The Smallest God

(by Lester del Rey)

I

Dr. Arlington Brugh led his visitor around a jumble of machinery that made sense only to himself, and through a maze of tables and junk that occupied most of his laboratory.

"It's a little disordered just now," he apologized, glad that his assistant had been able to clear up the worst of the mess. "Sort of gets that way after a long experiment."

Herr Dr. Ernst Meyer nodded heavy agreement. "Ja, so. Und mit all dis matchinery, no vunder. It gives yet no goot place v'ere I can mit comfort vork, also in mine own laboradory. Und v'at haff ve here?"

"That's Hermes—my mascot." Brugh picked up the little, hollow rubber figure of the god Hermes; Mercury, the Romans called him. "The day I bought him for my daughter, the funds for my cyclotron were voted on favorably, so I've kept him here. Just a little superstition."

Meyer shook his head. "Nein. I mean here." He tapped a heavy lead chest bearing a large *Keep Out* label. "Is maybe v'at you make?"

"That's right." The physical chemist pulled up the heavy cover and displayed a few dirty crystals in a small compartment and a thick, tarry goo that filled a half-liter beaker. "Those are my latest success and my first failure. By the way, have you see Dr. Hodges over in the biochemistry department?"

"Ja. Vonderful vork he makes yet, nicht wahr?"

"Umm. Opinions differ. I'll admit he did a good job in growing that synthetic amoeba, and the worm he made in his chemical bath wasn't so bad, though I never did know whether it was really alive or not. Maybe you read about it? But he didn't stick to simple things until he mastered his technique. He had to go rambling off trying to create a synthetic man."

Meyer's rough face gleamed. "Ja, so. Dot is hübsch—nice. Mit veins und muschles. Only it is not mit life upfilled."

Brugh sifted a few of the crystals in the chest out onto a watch glass where they could be inspected more carefully. Then he put them into an opened drawer and closed it until the crystals were in a much dimmer light. In the semidarkness, a faint gleam was visible, hovering over the watch glass.

"Radioactive," he explained. "There is the reason Hodges' man isn't filled with life. If there had been some of this in his chemical bath when he was growing Anthropos—that's what he calls the thing—it would be walking around today. But you can't expect a biochemist to know that, of course. They don't keep up with the latest developments the way the physical chemists do. Most of them aren't aware of the fact that the atom can be cracked up into a different kind of atom by using Bertha."

"Bert'a? Maybe she is die daughter?"

Brugh grinned. "Bertha's the cyclotron over there. The boys started calling her Big Bertha, and then we just named her Bertha for short." He swung around to indicate the great mass of metal that filled one end of the room. "That's a lot of material to make so few crystals of radioactive potassium chloride, though."

"Ach, so. Den it is das radioagdivated salt dot vould give life to der synt'etic man, eh?"

"Right. We're beginning to believe that life is a combination of electricity and radioactivity, and the basis of the last seems to be this active potassium we've produced by bombarding the ordinary form with neutrons. Put that in Anthropos and he'd be bouncing around for his meals in a week."

Meyer succeeded in guessing the meaning of the last and cocked up a bushy eyebrow. "Den v'y not das salt to der man give?"

"And have Hodges hog all the glory again? Not a chance." He banged his hand on the chest for emphasis, and the six-inch figure of Hermes bounced from its precarious perch and took off for the watch glass. Brugh grabbed frantically and caught it just before it hit. "Someday I'll stuff this thing with something heavy enough to hold it down."

The German looked at the statue with faint interest, then pointed to the gummy mess in the beaker. "Und dis?"

"That's a failure. Someday I might analyze a little of it, but it's too hard to get the stuff out of that tar, and probably not worth a quarter of the energy. Seems to be a little of everything in it, including potassium, and it's fairly radioactive, but all it's good for is—well, to stuff Hermes so he can't go bouncing around."

Brugh propped the little white figure against a ring stand and drew out the beaker, gouging out a chunk of the varicolored tar. He plopped it into a container and poured methyl alcohol over it, working with a glass rod until it was reasonably plastic. "Darned stuff gets soft, but it won't dissolve," he grumbled.

Meyer stood back, looking on, shaking his head gently. Americans were naturally crazy, but he hadn't expected such foolishness from so distinguished a research man as Dr. Brugh. In his own laboratory, he'd have spent the next two years, if necessary, in finding out what the tar was, instead of wasting it to stuff a cheap rubber cast of a statue.

"Dis Herr Dr. Hodges, you don't like him, I t'ink. Warum?"

Brugh was spooning the dough into his statue, forcing it into the tiny mouth and packing it in loosely. "Hodges wanted a new tank for his life-culture experiments when I was trying to get the cyclotron and the cloud chamber. I had to dig up the old antivivisection howl among the students' parents to keep him from getting it, and he thought it was a dirty trick. Maybe it was; anyway, he's been trying ever since to get me kicked out, and switch the appropriations over to this department. By the way, I'd hate to have word of this get around."

"Aber—andivifisegtion!" Meyer was faintly horrified at such an unscientific thing.

Brugh nodded. "I know. But I wanted that cyclotron, and I got it; I'd do worse. There, Hermes won't go flying around again. Anything else I can show you, Dr. Meyer?"

"T'ank you, no. Der clock is late now, und I must cadge my train by die hour. It has a bleasure been, Dr. Brugh."

"Not at all." Brugh set the statue on a table and went out with the German, leaving Hermes in sole possession of the laboratory, except for the cat.

II

The clock in the laboratory said four o'clock in the morning. Its hum and the gentle breathing of the cat, that exercised its special privileges by sleeping on the cyclotron, were the only noises to be heard. Up on the table Hermes stood quietly, just as Dr. Brugh had left him, a little white rubber figure outlined in the light that shone through from the outside. A very ordinary little statue he looked.

But inside, where the tar had been placed, something was stirring gently. Faintly and low at first, life began to quiver. Consciousness began to come slowly, and then a dim and hazy feeling of individuality. He was different in being a unit not directly connected in consciousness with the dim outlines of the laboratory.

What, where, when, who, why, and how? Hermes knew none of the answers, and the questions were only vague and hazy in his mind, but the desire to know and to understand was growing. He took in the laboratory slowly through the hole that formed his partly open mouth and let the light stream in against the resinous matter inside. At first, only a blur was visible, but as his "eyes" grew more proficient from experience, he made out separate shapes. He had no names for them, but he recognized the difference between a round tube and a square tabletop.

The motion of the second hand caught his attention, and he studied the clock carefully, but could make no sense to it. Apparently some things moved and others didn't. What little he could see of himself didn't, even when he made a clumsy attempt at forcing motion into his outthrust arm. It took longer to notice the faint breathing of the cat; then he noticed it not only moved, but did so in an irregular fashion. He strained toward it, and something clicked in his mind.

Tabby was dreaming, but Hermes couldn't know that, nor understand from whence came the pictures that seemed to flash across his gummy brain; Tabby didn't understand dreams, either. But the little god could see some tiny creature that went scurrying rapidly across the floor, and a much-distorted picture of Tabby following it. Tabby had a definitely exaggerated idea of herself. Now the little running figure began to grow until it was twice the size of the cat, and its appearance altered. It made harsh explosive noises and beat a thick tail stiffly. Tabby's picture made a noise and fled, but the other followed quickly and a wide mouth opened. Tabby woke up, and the pictures disappeared. Hermes could make no sense of them, though it was plain in Tabby's mind that such things often happened when her head turned black inside.

But the cat awake was even more interesting than she was sleeping. There were the largest groups of loosely classified odors, sights, and sensations to be absorbed, the nicest memories of moving about and exploring the laboratory. Through Tabby's eyes he saw the part of the laboratory that was concealed from him, and much of the outside in the near neighborhood. He also drew a hazy picture of himself being filled, but it made no sense to him, though he gathered from the cat's mind that the huge monster holding him was to be both despised and respected, and was, all in all, a very powerful person.

By now his intelligence was great enough to recognize that the world seen through the cat's eyes was in many ways wrong. For one thing, everything was in shades of white and black, with medial grays, while he had already seen that there were several colors. Hermes decided that he needed another point of view, though the cat had served admirably to start his mind on the way to some understanding of the world about him.

A low howling sound came from outside the laboratory, and Hermes recoiled mentally, drawing a picture of a huge and ferocious beast from his secondhand cat's memory. Then curiosity urged him to explore. If the cat's color sense was faulty, perhaps her ideas on the subject of dogs were also wrong. He thrust his mind out toward the source of the sound, and again there was the little click that indicated a bridge between two minds.

He liked the dog much better than the cat. There was more to be learned here, and the animal had some faint understanding of a great many mysteries which had never interested Tabby. Hermes also found that hard, selfish emotions were not the only kind. On the whole, the mind of Shep seemed warm and glowing after the frigid self-interest of Tabby.

First in the dog's mind, as in all others, was the thought of self, but close behind was mistress and master, the same person whom the cat's mind had pictured filling the god. And there were the two little missies. Something about the dog's mental image of one of them aroused an odd sensation in the little god, but it was too confused to be of any definite interest.

But the dog retained hazy ideas of words as a means of thought, and Hermes seized on them gratefully. He gathered that men used them as a medium of thought conveyance, and filed the sixty partly understood words of Shep's vocabulary carefully away. There were others with tantalizing possibilities, but they were vague.

Shep's world was much wider than that of Tabby, and his general impression of color—for dogs do see colors—was much better. The world became a fascinating place as he pictured it, and Hermes longed for the mysterious power of mobility that made wide explorations possible. He tried to glean the secret, but all that Shep knew on the subject was that movement followed desire, and sometimes came without any wish.

The god came to the conclusion that in all the world the only animals that could satisfy his curiosity were men. His mind was still too young to be bothered with such trifles as modesty, and he was quite sure there could be no animal with a better intelligence than he had. The dog couldn't even read thoughts, and Hermes had doubts about man's ability to do the same; otherwise, why should the master have punished Shep for fighting, when the other dog had clearly started it?

And if he hadn't, Shep would have been home, instead of skulking around this place, where he sometimes came to meet the master after work.

Hermes tried to locate a man's mind, but there was none near. He caught a vague eddy of jumbled thought waves from someone who was evidently located there to guard the building, but there was a definite limit to the space that thought could span.

The cat's brain had gone black inside again, with only fitful images flickering on and off, and the dog was drifting into a similar state. Hermes studied the action with keen interest and decided that sleep might be a very fine way of passing the time until a man came back to the laboratory, as he gathered they did every time some big light shone from somewhere high up above.

But as he concentrated on the matter of turning off his mind, he wondered again what he was. Certainly neither a dog nor a cat, he had no real belief that he was a man; the dog didn't know about him, but the cat regarded him as a stone. Maybe he was one, if stones ever came to life. Anyway, he'd find out in the morning when the master came in. Until then he forced thoughts from his mind and succeeded in simulating sleep.

III

A strange noise wakened Hermes in the morning. From what he had seen in Shep's mind, he knew it was the sound of human speech, and listened intently. The people were talking at a point behind him, but he was sure it was the master and one of the little missies. He tuned his mind in on that of the master and began soaking up impressions.

"I wish you'd stay away from young Thomas," Dr. Brugh was saying. "I think he's the nephew of Hodges, though he won't admit it. Your mother doesn't like him either, Tanya."

Tanya laughed softly at her father's suspicions, and Hermes felt a glow all over. It was a lovely sound. "You never like my boyfriends," she said. "I think you want me to grow up into an old-maid schoolmarm. Johnny's a nice boy. To hear you talk, a person would think Hodges and his whole family were ogres."

"Maybe they are." But Brugh knew better than to argue with his older daughter; she always won, just as her mother always did. "Hodges tried to swindle me out of my appropriations again at the meeting last night. He'd like to see me ruined."

"And you swindled him out of his tanks. Suppose I proved to the president who sent those anonymous vivisection letters to all the parents?"

Brugh looked around hastily, but there was no one listening. "Are you trying to blackmail me, Tanya?"

She laughed again at his attempt at anger. "You know I won't tell a soul. 'Bye, Dad. I'm going swimming with Johnny." Hermes felt a light kiss through Brugh's senses, and saw her start around the table to pass in front of him. He snapped the connection with the master's mind and prepared his own eyes for confirmation of what he had seen by telepathy.

Tanya was a vision of life and loveliness. In the fleeting second it took for her to cross the little god's range of sight, he took in the soft, waving brown hair, the dark, sparkling eyes, and the dimple that lurked in the corner of her mouth, and something happened to Hermes. As yet he had no word for it, but it was pure sensation that sped through every atom of his synthetic soul. He began to appreciate that life was something more than the satisfaction of curiosity.

A sound from Brugh, who was puttering around with a cloudy precipitate, snapped him back to reality. The questions in his mind still needed answering, and the physicist was the logical one to answer them. Again he made contact with the other's mind.

This was infinitely richer than the dog's and cat's combined. For one thing, there was a seemingly inexhaustible supply of word thoughts to be gleaned. As he absorbed them, thinking became easier, and the words provided a framework for abstractions, something utterly beyond the bounds of the animal minds. For half an hour he studied them, and absorbed the details of human life gradually.

Then he set about finding the reasons for his own life; that necessitated learning the whole field of physical chemistry, which occupied another half hour, and when he had finished, he began putting the knowledge he had gleaned together, until it made sense.

All life, he had found, was probably electricity and radioactivity, the latter supplied by means of a tiny amount of potassium in the human body. But life was really more than that. There were actions and interactions between the two things that had thus far baffled all students. Some of them baffled the rubber god, but he puzzled the general picture out to his own satisfaction.

When the experiment had gone wrong and created the tarry lump that formed the real life of Hermes, there had been a myriad of compounds and odd arrangements of atom formed in it, and the tarry gum around them had acted as a medium for their operation. Then, when they were slightly softened by the addition of alcohol, they had begun to work, arranging and rearranging themselves into an interacting pattern that was roughly parallel to human life and thought.

But there were differences. For one thing, he could read thoughts accurately, and for another, he had a sense of perception which could analyze matter directly from its vibrations. For another, what he called sight and sound were merely other vibrations, acting directly on his life substance instead of by means of local sensory organs. He realized suddenly that he could see with his mouth instead of his eyes, and hear all over. Only the rubber casing prevented him from a full 360° vision. But, because of the minds he had tapped, he had learned to interpret those vibrations in a more or less conventional pattern.

Hermes analyzed the amount of radioactive potassium in Brugh's body carefully and compared it with his own. There was a great difference, which probably accounted for his more fully developed powers. Something ached vaguely inside him, and he felt giddy. He turned away from his carefully ordered thoughts to inspect this new sensation.

The alcohol inside him was drying out—almost gone, in fact, and his tarry interior was growing thicker. He'd have to do something about it.

"Dr. Brugh," he thought, fixing his attention on the other, "could I have some alcohol, please? My thoughts will be slowed even below human level if I can't have some soon."

Arlington Brugh shook his head to clear it of a sudden buzz, but he had not understood. Hermes tried again, using all the remaining thought power he could muster.

"This is Hermes, Dr. Brugh. You brought me to life, and I want some alcohol, please!"

Brugh heard this time, and swung suspiciously toward the end of the room, where his assistant was working. But the young man was engaged in his work, and showed no sign of having spoken or heard. Hermes repeated his request, squeezing out his fast failing energy, and the master jerked quickly, turning his eyes slowly around the room. Again Hermes tried, and the other twitched.

Brugh grabbed for his hat and addressed the assistant. "Bill, I'm going for a little walk to clear my head. The session last night seems to have put funny ideas in it." He paused. "Oh, better toss that little rubber statue into the can for the junkman. It's beginning to get on my nerves."

He turned sharply and walked out of the room. Hermes felt the rough hands of the assistant, and felt himself falling. But his senses were leaving him, drained by the loss of alcohol and the strain of forcing his mind on the master. He sank heavily into the trash can and his mind grew blank.

IV

A splatter of wetness against Hermes' mouth brought him back to consciousness, and he saw a few drops fall near him from a broken bottle that was tipped sidewise. Occasionally one found its way through his mouth, and he soaked it up greedily. Little as he got, the alcohol still had been enough to start his dormant life into renewed activity.

There was a pitch and sway to the rubbish on which he lay, and a rumbling noise came from in front of him. Out of the corner of his "eye" he saw a line of poles running by, and knew he was on something that moved. Momentarily he tapped the mind of the driver and found he was on a truck bound for the city dump, where all garbage was disposed of. But he felt no desire to use the little energy he had in mind reading, so he fell back to studying the small supply of liquid left in the bottle.

There was an irregular trickle now, running down only a few inches from him. He studied the situation carefully, noting that the bottle was well anchored to its spot, while he was poised precariously on a little mound of rubbish. One of Newton's laws of momentum flashed through his mind from the mass of information he had learned through Brugh; if the truck were to speed up, he would be thrown backward, directly under the stream trickling down from the bottle—and with luck he might land face up.

Hermes summoned his energy and directed a wordless desire for speed toward the driver. The man's foot came down slowly on the accelerator, but too slowly. Hermes tried again, and suddenly felt himself pitched backward—to land face down! Then a squeal of brakes reached his ears, as the driver counteracted his sudden speed, and the smallest god found himself rolling over, directly under the stream.

There were only a few teaspoons left, splashing out irregularly as the bouncing of the truck threw the liquid back and forth in the fragment of glass, but most of them reached his mouth. The truck braked to a halt and began reversing, and the last drops fell against his lips. It was highly impure alcohol, filled with raw chemicals from the laboratory, but Hermes had no complaints. He could feel the tar inside him soften, and he lay quietly enjoying the sensation until new outside stimuli caught his attention.

The truck had ceased backing and was parked on a slope leading down toward the rear. There was a rattle of chains and the gate dropped down to let the load go spinning out down the bank into the rubbish-filled gully. Hermes bounced from a heavy can and went caroming off sidewise, then struck against a rock with force enough to send white sparks of pain running through him.

But the rock had changed his course and thrown him clear of the other trash. When he finally stopped, his entire head and one arm were clear, and the rest was buried under only a loose litter of papers and dirt. No permanent damage had been done; his tarry core was readjusting itself to the normal shape of the rubber coating, and he was in no immediate danger.

But being left here was the equivalent of a death sentence. His only hope was to contact some human mind and establish friendly communications, and the dump heap was the last place to find men. Added to that, the need for further alcohol was a serious complication. Again he wished for the mysterious power of motion.

He concentrated his mental energy on moving the free arm, but there was no change; the arm stayed at the same awkward angle. With little hope, he tried again, watching for the slightest movement. This time a finger bent slightly! Feverishly he tried to move the others, and they twisted slowly until his whole hand lay stretched out flat. Then his arm began to move sluggishly. He was learning.

It was growing dark when he finally drew himself completely free of the trash and lay back to rest, exulting over his newfound ability. The alcohol was responsible, of course; it had softened the tar slightly more than it had been when he made his first efforts in the laboratory, and permitted motion of a sort through a change of surface tension. The answer to further motion was more alcohol.

There were bottles of all kinds strewn about, and he stared at those within his range of vision, testing their vibrations in the hope of finding a few more drops. The nearer ones were empty, except for a few that contained brackish rainwater. But below him, a few feet away, was a small-sized one whose label indicated that it had contained hair tonic. The cork was in tightly, and it was still half full of a liquid. That liquid was largely ethyl alcohol.

Hermes forced himself forward on his stomach, drawing along inch by inch. Without the help of gravity, he could never have made it, but the distance shortened. He gave a final labored hitch, clutched the bottle in his tiny hands, and tried to force the cork out. It was wedged in too firmly!

Despair clutched at him, but he threw it off. There must be some way. Glass was brittle, could be broken easily, and there were stones and rocks about with which to strike it. The little god propped the neck of the bottle up against one and drew himself up to a sitting position, one of the stones in his hands. He could not strike rapidly enough to break the glass, but had to rely on raising the rock and letting it fall.

Fortunately for his purpose, the bottle had been cracked by its fall, and the fourth stone shattered the neck. Hermes forced it up on a broken box and tipped it gingerly toward his mouth. The smell of it was sickening, but he had no time to be choosy about his drinks! There was room inside him to hold a dozen teaspoonfuls, and he meant to fill those spaces.

The warm sensation of softening tar went through him gratefully as the liquid was absorbed. According to what he had read in Brugh's mind, he should have been drunk, but it didn't feel that way. It more nearly approximated the sensation of a man who had eaten more than he should and hadn't time to be sorry yet.

Hermes wriggled his toes comfortably and nodded his approval at the ease with which they worked. Another idea came to him, and he put it to the test. Where his ear channels were, the rubber was almost paper-thin; he put out a pseudopod of tar from the lumps inside his head and wriggled it against the membrane; a squeaky sound was produced like a radio speaker gone bad. He varied the speed of the feeler, alternating it until he discovered the variation of tones and overtones necessary, and tried a human word.

"Tanya!" It wasn't perfect, but there could be no question as to what it was. Now he could talk with men directly, even with Tanya Brugh, if fate was particularly kind. He conjured up an ecstatic vision of her face and attempted a conventional sighing sound. Men in love evidently were supposed to sigh, and Hermes was in love!

But if he wanted to see her, he'd have to leave the dump. It was dark now, but ultraviolet and infrared light were as useful to him as the so-called visible beams, and the amount of light needed to set off his sight was less than that for a cat. With soiled hands he began pulling his way up the bank, burrowing through the surface rubbish. Then he reached the top and spied the main path leading away.

His little feet twinkled brightly in the starlight, and the evening dew washed the stains from his body. A weasel, prowling for food, spied him and debated attack, but decided to flee when the little god pictured himself as a dog. Animals accepted such startling apparent changes without doubting their sanity. He chuckled at the tricks he could play on Tabby when he got back, and sped down the lane at a good two miles an hour.

V

Brugh worked late in the laboratory, making up for the time he had taken off to clear his head. All thoughts of his trouble with Hermes had vanished. He cleared up the worst of the day's litter of dirty apparatus, arranged things for the night, and locked up.

Dixon, head of the organic chemistry department, was coming down the hall as the physicist left. He stopped, his pudgy face beaming, and greeted the other. "Hi, there, Brugh. Working late again?"

"A little. How's the specific for tuberculosis going?"

Dixon patted his paunch amiably. "Not bad. We're able to get the metal poison into the dye, and the dye into the bug. We still can't get much of the poison out of the dye after that to kill our friend, the bacillus, but we've been able to weaken him a little. By the way, I saw your daughter today, out with Hodges' nephew, and she told me—"

"You mean Johnny Thomas?" Brugh's eyebrows furrowed tightly and met at the corners. "So Hodges *is* his uncle! Hmmm."

"Still fighting the biochemistry department?" By a miracle of tact and good nature, Dixon had managed to keep on friendly terms with both men. "I wish you two would get together; Hodges is really a pretty decent sort. . . . Well, I didn't think so; you're both too stubborn for your own good. That nephew of his isn't so good, though. Came up here to pump money out of his uncle and get away from some scandal in New York. His reputation isn't any too savory. Wouldn't want my daughter going with him."

"Don't worry; Tanya won't be going with Hodges' nephew any longer. Thanks for the tip." They reached the main door, and Brugh halted suddenly. "Damn!"

"What is it?"

"I left my auto keys on the worktable upstairs. Don't bother waiting for me, Dixon. I'll see you in the morning."

Dixon smiled. "Absentminded professor, eh? All right, good night." He went out the door and down the steps while Brugh climbed back to his laboratory, where he found the keys without further trouble. Fortunately he carried a spare door key to the lab in his pocket; it wasn't the first time he'd done this fool trick.

As he passed down the hall again, a faint sound of movement caught his ear and he turned toward Hodges' laboratory. There was no one there, and the door was locked, the lights all out. Brugh started for the stairs, then turned back.

"Might as well take advantage of an opportunity when I get it," he muttered. "I'd like to see the creation of Hodges, as long as he won't know about it." He slipped quietly to the door, unlocked it, and pulled it shut after him. The one key unlocked every door in the building and the main entrance; he had too much trouble losing keys to carry more than needed with him.

There was no mistaking the heavy tank on the low table, and Brugh moved quietly to it, lifted the cover, and stared inside. There was a light in the tank that went on automatically when the cover was raised, and the details of the body inside were clearly defined. Brugh was disappointed; he had been hoping for physical defects, but the figure was that of a young man, almost too classically perfect in body, and with an intelligent, handsome face. There was even a healthy pink glow to the skin.

But there was no real life, no faintest spark of animation or breathing. Anthropos lay in his nutritive bath, eyes open, staring blankly at the ceiling and seeing nothing. "No properly radioactive potassium," Brugh gloated. "In a way, it's a pity, too. I'd like to work on you."

He put the cover down and crept out again, making sure that the night watchman was not around. The man seldom left the first floor, anyway; who'd steal laboratory equipment? Brugh reached for his keys and fumbled with them, trying to find the proper one. It wasn't on the key ring. "Damn!" he said softly. "I suppose it fell off back on the table."

But he still had the spare, and the other could stay on the table. With the duplicate, he opened and relocked the door, then slipped down the hall to leave the building. Again a faint sound reached him, but he decided it was the cat or a rat moving around. He had other worries. Mrs. Brugh would give him what-for for being late again, he supposed. And Tanya probably wouldn't be home yet from the beach. That was another thing to be attended to; there'd be no more running with that young Thomas!

In the latter supposition, he was wrong; Tanya was there, fooling with her hair and gushing to her mother about a date she had that night with Will Young. She usually had seven dates a week with at least four different men serving as escorts. Brugh thoroughly approved of Young, however, since he was completing his Ph.D. work and acting as lab assistant. Mrs. Brugh approved of him because the young man came from a good family and had independent means, without the need of the long grind up to a full professorship. Tanya was chiefly interested in his six-foot-two, his football reputation, and a new Dodge he owned.

Margaret Brugh spied her husband coming through the door and began her usual worried harangue about his health and overwork. He muttered something about a lost key, and Tanya changed the subject for him. Brugh threw her a grateful smile and went in to wash up. He decided to postpone the lecture on Thomas until after supper; then she was in too much of a hurry to be bothered, and he put it off until morning.

The old Morris chair was soothing after a full meal—so soothing that the paper fell from his lap and scattered itself over the floor unnoticed, until the jangling of the telephone brought him back with a jerk. "It's for you," his wife announced.

The voice was that of Hodges, his nasal Vermont twang unmistakable. "Brugh? Your latest brainstorm backfired on you! I've got evidence against you this time, so you'd better bring it back." The pitch of the voice indicated fury that was only partly controlled.

The back hairs on Brugh's neck bristled up hotly, and his voice snapped back harshly. "You're drunk or crazy, like all biochemists! I haven't done anything to you. Anyway, what is it you want back?"

"You wouldn't know? How touching, such innocence! I want Anthropos, my synthetic man. I suppose you weren't in the laboratory this evening?"

Brugh gulped, remembering the faint noises he had heard. So it had all been a trap! "I never—"

"Of course. But we had trouble before—someone trying to force his way in—and we set up a photoelectric eye and camera with film for u.v. light. Didn't expect to catch you, but there's a nice picture of your face on it, and your key is in the lock—the number shows it's yours. I didn't think even you would stoop to stealing!"

Brugh made strangling sounds. "I didn't steal your phony man; wouldn't touch the thing! Furthermore, I didn't leave a key. Go sleep your insanity off!"

"Are you going to return Anthropos?"

"I don't have him." Brugh slammed the receiver down in disgust, snorting. If Hodges thought that he could put such a trick over, he'd find out better. With all the trumped-up evidence in the world, they'd still have to prove a few things. He'd see the president in the morning before Hodges could get to him.

But he wasn't prepared for the doorbell a half hour later, nor for the blue-coated figures that stood outside. They wasted no time.

"Dr. Arlington Brugh? We have a warrant for your arrest, charge being larceny. If you'll just come along quietly—"

They were purposeful individuals, and words did no good. Brugh went along—but not quietly.

VI

Hermes spied the public highway below him, and began puzzling about which direction to take back to town. Brugh had never been out this way, and he had failed to absorb the necessary information from the garbage man, so he had no idea of the location of Corton. But there was a man leaning against a signpost, and he might know.

The little god approached him confidently, now that he could both move and talk. He wanted to try his new power instead of telepathy, and did not trouble with the man's thoughts, though a faint impression indicated they were highly disordered.

"Good evening, sir," he said pleasantly, with only a faint blur to the words. "Can you direct me to Corton University?"

The man clutched the signpost and gazed down solemnly, blinking his eyes. "Got 'em again," he said dispassionately. "And after cutting down on the stuff, too. 'Sfunny, they never talked before. Wonder if the snakes'll talk, too, when I begin seeing them?"

It made no sense to Hermes, but he nodded wisely and repeated his question. From the vibrations, the man was not unacquainted with the virtues of alcohol.

The drunk pursed his lips and examined the little figure calmly. "Never had one like you before. What are you?"

"I suppose I'm a god," Hermes answered. "Can you direct me to Corton, please?"

"So it's gods this time, eh? That's what I get for changing brands. Go away and let me drink in peace." He thought it over slowly as he drew out the bottle. "Want a drink?"

"Thank you, yes." The little god stretched up and succeeded in reaching the bottle. This time he filled himself to capacity before handing it back. It was worse than the hair tonic, but there was no question of its tar-softening properties. "Could you—?"

"I know. Corton. To your right and follow the road." The man paused and made gurgling noises. "Whyn't you stick around? I like you; snakes never would drink with me."

Hermes made it quite clear he couldn't stay, and the drunk nodded gravely. "Always women. I know about that; it's a woman that drove me to this—seeing you. 'Stoo bad. Well, so long!"

Filled with the last drink, the god stepped his speed up to almost five miles an hour. There was no danger of fatigue, since the radioactive energy within him poured out as rapidly as he could use it, and there were no waste products to poison his system. His tiny legs flickered along the road, and the little feet made faint tapping sounds on the smooth asphalt surface.

He came over a hill and spied the yellow lights of Corton, still an hour's trot away. It might have been worse. The swishing of the water inside him bothered him, and he decided that he'd stick to straight alcohol hereafter; whiskey contained too many useless impurities. Hermes flopped over beside the road, and let the water and some of the oil from the hair tonic trickle out; the alcohol was already well inside his gummy interior where there was no danger of losing it. For some reason, it seemed to be drying out more slowly than the first had, and that was all to the good.

The few cars on the road aroused a faint desire for some easier means of locomotion, but otherwise they caused him no trouble. He clipped off the miles at a steady gait, keeping on the edge of the paving, until the outskirts of the town had been reached. Then he took to the sidewalk.

A blue-coated figure, ornamented with brass buttons, was pacing down the street toward him, and Hermes welcomed the presence of the policeman. One of the duties of an officer was directing people, he had gathered, and a little direction would be handy. The smallest god stopped and waited for the other to reach him.

"Could you direct me to the home of Dr. Arlington Brugh, please?"

The cop looked about carefully for the speaker. Hermes raised his voice again. "I'm here, sir."

Officer O'Callahan dropped his eyes slowly, expecting a drunk, and spied the god. He let out a startled bellow. "So it's tricks, is it now? Confound that Bergen fellow, after drivin' the brats wild about ventriloquence. Come out o' there, you spalpeen. Tryin' your tricks on an honest police, like as if I didn't have worries o' me own."

Hermes watched the officer hunting around in the doorways for what he believed must be the source of the voice, and decided that there was no use lingering. He put one foot in front of the other and left the cop.

"*Pssst!*" The sound came from an alley a couple of houses below, and Hermes paused. In the shadows, he made out a dirty old woman, her frowsy hair blowing about her face, her finger crooked enticingly. Evidently she wanted something, and he turned in hesitantly.

"That dumb Irish mick," she grunted, and from her breath Hermes recognized another kindred spirit; apparently humans were much easier to get along with when thoroughly steeped in alcohol, as he was himself. "Sure, now, a body might think it's never a word he'd heard o' the Little Folks, and you speaking politely, too. Ventriloquence, indeed! Was you wanting to know what I might be telling you?"

Hermes stretched his rubber face into a passable smile. "Do you know where Dr. Arlington Brugh lives? He's a research director at Corton University."

She shook her head, blinking bleary eyes. "That I don't, but maybe you'd take the university? It's well I know where that may be."

Dr. Brugh lived but a short distance from the campus, he knew, and once on the university grounds, Hermes would have no trouble in finding the house. He nodded eagerly. She reached down a filthy hand and caught him up, wrapping a fold of her tattered dress about him.

"Come along, then. I'll be taking you there myself." She paused to let the few last drops trickle from a bottle into her wide mouth, and stuck her head out cautiously; the policeman had gone. With a grunt of satisfaction, she struck across the street to a streetcar stop. "'Tis the last dime I have, but a sorry day it'll be when Molly McCann can't do a favor for a Little Folk."

She propped herself against the carstop post and waited patiently, while Hermes pondered the mellowing effects of alcohol again. When the noisy car stopped, she climbed on, clutching him firmly, and he heard only the bumping of a flat wheel and her heavy breathing. But she managed to keep half awake, and carried him off the car at the proper place.

She set him down as gently as unsteady fingers would permit and pointed vaguely at the buildings on the campus. "There you be, and it's the best of luck I'm wishing you. Maybe, now that I've helped a Little Man, good luck'll be coming to me. A very good night to you."

Hermes bowed gravely as he guessed she expected. "My thanks, Molly McCann, for your kindness, and a very good night to you." He watched her totter away, and turned toward the laboratory building, where he could secure a few more drops of straight alcohol. After that, he could attend to his other business.

VII

Tanya Brugh was completely unaware of the smallest god's presence as he stood on a chair looking across at her. A stray beam of moonlight struck her face caressingly, and made her seem a creature of velvet and silver, withdrawn in sleep from all that was mundane. Hermes probed her mind gently, a little fearfully.

Across her mind, a flickering pageant of tall men, strong men, lithe and athletic men, ran in disordered array, and none of them was less than six feet tall. Hermes gazed at his own small body, barely six inches high; it would never do. Now the face of John Thomas fitted itself on one of the men, and Tanya held the image for a few seconds. The god growled muttered oaths; he had no love for the Thomas image. Then it flickered into the face of Will Young, Brugh's assistant.

Hermes had probed her thoughts to confirm his own ideas of the wonderful delight that Tanya must be, and he was faintly disappointed. In her mind were innocence and emptiness—except for men of tall stature. He sighed softly, and reverted to purely human rationalization until he had convinced himself of the rightness of her thoughts.

But the question of height bothered him. Children, he knew, grew up, but he was no child, though his age was measured in hours. Someway, he must gain a new body, or grow taller, and that meant that Dr. Brugh would be needed for advice on the riddle of height increase.

He dropped quietly from the chair and trotted toward the master's bedroom, pushing against the door in the hope that it might be open. It wasn't, but he made a leap for the doorknob and caught it, throwing his slight weight into the job of twisting it. Finally, the knob turned, and he kicked out against the doorjamb with one foot until the door began to swing. Then he dropped down and pushed until he could slide through the opening. For his size, he carried a goodly portion of strength in his gum-and-rubber body.

But the master was not in the bed, and the mistress was making slow strangling sounds that indicated emotional upset. From Brugh's mind, Hermes had picked up a hatred of the sound of a woman crying, and he swung hastily out, wondering what the fuss was about. There was only one person left, and he headed toward the little Missie Katherine's room.

She was asleep when he entered, but he called softly: "Miss Kitty." Her head popped up suddenly from the pillow and she groped for the light. For an eight-year-old child, she was lovely with the sleep still in her eyes. She gazed at the little white figure in faint astonishment.

Hermes shinnied up the leg of a chair and made a leap over onto the bed where he could watch her. "What happened to your father?" he asked.

She blinked at him with round eyes. "It talks—a little doll that talks! How cute!"

"I'm not a doll, Kitty. I'm Hermes."

"Not a doll? Oh, goody, you're an elf then?"

"Maybe." It was no time to bicker about a question that had no satisfactory answer. But his heart warmed toward the girl. She wasn't drunk, yet she could still believe in his existence. "I don't know just what I am, but I think I'm the smallest of the gods. Where's your father?"

Memory overwhelmed Kitty in a rush, and her brown eyes brimmed with tears. "He's in jail!" she answered through a puckered mouth. "A nasty man came and took him away, and Mamma feels awful. Just 'cause Mr. Hodges hates him."

"Where's jail? Never mind, I'll find out." It would save time by taking the information directly from her head, since she knew where it was. "Now go back to sleep and I'll go find your father."

"And bring him home to Mamma?"

"And bring him home to Mamma." Hermes knew practically nothing of jails, but the feeling of power was surging hotly through him. So far, everything he had attempted had been accomplished. Kitty smiled uncertainly at him and dropped her head back on the pillow. Then the little god's sense of vibration perception led him toward the cellar in search of certain vital bottles.

A child's toy truck, overburdened with a large bottle and a small god, drew up in front of the dirty white building that served as jail. Hermes had discovered the toy in the yard and used it as a boy does a wagon to facilitate travel. Now he stepped off, lifted the bottle, and parked the truck in a small shrub where he could find it again. Then he began the laborious job of hitching himself up the steps and into the building.

It was in the early morning hours, and there were few men about, but he stayed carefully in the shadow and moved only when their backs were turned. From his observation, men saw only what they expected, and the unusual attracted attention only when accompanied by some sudden sound or movement. Hermes searched one of the men's minds for the location of Brugh, then headed toward the cell, dragging the pint bottle behind him as noiselessly as he could.

Dr. Brugh sat on the hard iron cot with his head in his hands, somewhat after the fashion of Rodin's *Thinker*; but his face bore rather less of calm reflection. An occasional muttered invective reached the little god, who grinned. Arlington Brugh was a man of wide attainments, and he had not neglected the development of his vocabulary.

Hermes waited patiently until the guard was out of sight and slipped rapidly toward the cell, mounting over the bottom brace and through the bars. The scientist did not see him as he trotted under the bunk and found a convenient hiding place near the man's legs. At the moment, Brugh was considering the pleasant prospect of attaching all police to Bertha and bombarding them with neutrons until their flesh turned to anything but protoplasm.

Hermes tapped a relatively huge leg and spoke softly. "Dr. Brugh, if you'll look down here, please—" He held up the bottle, the cap already unscrewed.

Brugh lowered his eyes and blinked; from the angle of his sight, only a pint bottle of whiskey, raising itself from the floor, could be seen. But he was in a mood to accept miracles without question, and he reached instinctively. Ordinarily he wasn't a drinking man, but the person who won't drink on occasion has a special place reserved for him in heaven—well removed from all other saints.

As the bottle was lowered again, Hermes reached for it and drained a few drops, while Brugh stared at him. "Well?" the god asked finally.

The alcohol was leaving the scientist's stomach rapidly, as it does when no food interferes, and making for his head; the mellowing effect Hermes had hoped for was beginning. "That's my voice you're using," Brugh observed mildly.

"It should be; I learned the language from you. You made me, you know." He waited for a second. "Well, do you believe in me now?"

Brugh grunted. "Hermes, eh? So I wasn't imagining things back in the lab. What happened to you?" A suspicious look crossed his face. "Has Hodges been tinkering again?"

As briefly as he could, the little god summarized events and explained himself, climbing up on the cot as he did so, and squatting down against the physicist's side, out of sight from the door. The other chuckled sourly as he finished.

"So while Hodges was fooling around with amoebas and flesh, I made super-life, only I didn't know it, eh?" There was no longer doubt in his mind, but that might have been due to the whiskey. The reason for more than one conversion to a new religious belief lies hidden in the mysterious soothing effect of ethanol in the form of whiskey and rum. "Well, glad to know you. What happens now?"

"I promised your daughter I'd take you home to the mistress." But now that he was here, he wasn't so sure. There were more men around than he liked. "We'll have to make plans."

Brugh reflected thoughtfully. "That might not be so good. They'd come after me again, and I'd have less chance to prove my innocence."

Hermes was surprised. "You're innocent? I thought you'd murdered Hodges." After all, it was a reasonable supposition, based on the state of the physicist's mind the day before. "What happened?"

"No, I haven't murdered him—yet." Brugh's smile promised unpleasant things at the first chance. "It's still a nice idea, after this trick, though. It all started with the key."

"Maybe I'd better take it from your head," Hermes decided. "That way I'll be less apt to miss things, and more sure to get things straight."

Brugh nodded and relaxed, thinking back over the last few hours. He lifted the bottle and extracted another drink, while Hermes followed the mental pictures and memory until the story was complete in his head.

"So that's the way it was," he grunted, finished. "Some of it doesn't make sense."

"None of it does. All I know is that I'm here and Hodges has enough trumped-up evidence to convict me. He wanted to make the charge kidnapping, but they suggested corpse stealing, and compromised on larceny—grand larceny, I guess."

"I still might be able to swipe the guard's keys and attract their attention—"

Brugh gathered his somewhat pickled senses. "No. Your biggest value to me is in your ability to get in places where a man couldn't, and find out things without anyone knowing it. If I get out, I can do no more than I can here—I'm not a detective when it comes to human reactions; just physical or chemical puzzles."

There was something in that, Hermes had to concede. "Then I'm to work outside?"

"If you want to. You're a free agent, not bound to me. Slaves have gone out of fashion, and you're hardly a robot." The physicist shook his head. "Why should you help me, come to think of it?"

"Because I want to grow up, and you might help me; and because in a sense, we both have the same memories and thought actions—I started out with a mixture of dog, cat, and you." He climbed off the bunk and scuttled across the floor. "I'll give Hodges your love if I see him."

Brugh grinned crookedly. "Do."

VIII

Professor Hiram Hodges stirred and turned over in his bed, a sense of something that wasn't as it should be troubling his mind. He grunted softly and tried to sleep again, but the premonition still bothered him. And then he realized that there was a rustling sound going on in his study and that it was still too early for his housekeeper.

He kicked off the sheet and rummaged under the bed for his slippers, drawing on the tattered old robe he'd worn for the last six years. As quietly as he could, he slipped across to the study door, threw it open, and snapped on the light switch, just as the rustling sound stopped. Probably his nephew up to some trick—

But the room contained neither a nephew nor any other man. Hodges blinked, adjusting his eyes to the light, and stared at his desk.

It had been closed when he went to bed, he was sure of that. Now it was open, and a litter of papers was strewn across it in haphazard fashion. Someone must have been there and disappeared in the split second it took to snap on the lights.

Hodges moved over to the desk, stopping to pick up a few scraps of paper that had fallen on the floor, then reached up to close the roll top. As he did so, something small and white made a sudden frantic lunge from among the papers and hit the floor to go scuttling across the room. With startlingly quick reactions for his age, the professor spun his lank frame and scooped up the scurrying object.

Apparently it was an animated rubber doll that lay twisting in his grasp. Words came spilling out, though the tiny mouth did not move. "All right, you've caught me. Do you have to squeeze me to death?"

Some men, when faced with the impossible, go insane; others refuse to believe. But Hodges' life had been spent in proving the impossible to be possible, and he faced the situation calmly. A robot wouldn't have spoken that way, and obviously this wasn't flesh and blood; equally obviously, it was some form of life. He lifted the figure onto the desk and clamped the wire wastebasket down over it.

"Now," he said, "what are you, where from, and what do you want?"

Hermes devoted full energy to picturing himself as a charging lion, but the professor was not impressed.

"It's a nice illusion," he granted, smiling. "Come to think of it, maybe your other shape isn't real. Which is it—my nephew or Brugh?"

Hermes gave up and went over the story of his creation again, point by point, while dawn crept up over the roofs of the adjacent houses and urged him to hurry. Hodges' first incredulity turned to doubt, and doubt gave place to half belief.

"So that's the way it is? All right. I'll believe you, provided you can explain how you see without the aid of a lens to direct the light against your sensory surface."

Hermes had overlooked that detail, and took time off to investigate himself. "Apparently the surface is sensitive only to light that strikes it at a certain angle," he decided. "And my mouth opening acts as a very rough lens—something on the order of the old pinhole camera. The tar below is curved, and if I want clearer vision, I can put out a thin bubble of fairly transparent surface material to rectify the light more fully, as a lens would. I don't need an iris."

"Ummm. So Brugh decided he'd made life and wanted to make a fool of me by bringing my man to consciousness, eh? Is that why he kidnaped Anthropos?"

Hermes grunted sourly. His mind was incapable of the sudden rages and dull hates that seemed to fill men's thoughts, but it was colored by the dislike Brugh had cultivated for the biochemist. "It's a nice way of lying, professor, but I know Dr. Brugh had nothing to do with your creation."

The other grinned skeptically. "How do you know?"

"I read his mind, where he had to reveal the truth." In proof, the little god transferred part of the picture he had drawn from Brugh's mind to that of Hodges.

"Hm-m-m." The biochemist lifted the wastebasket off and picked up the little figure. "That would account for the exposed film. Suppose you come with me while I get dressed and try reading my mind. You might be surprised."

Hermes was surprised, definitely. In the professor's mind there had been complete conviction of Brugh's guilt, shaken somewhat now by the story transferred by Hermes. Instead of being a cooked-up scheme to ruin his rival, the theft of the synthetic man was unquestionably genuine. The god fixed on one detail, trying to solve the riddle.

A note received the night before had first apprised the biochemist of the disappearance of his pet creation and sent him to the laboratory to investigate. "What happened to the ransom note?" Hermes asked.

Hodges was stuggling with man's symbol of slavery to the law of fashion, his necktie. "It's still in my pocket—here." He flipped it across the room, where the other could study the crude scrawl. The words were crude and direct:

> Perffeser, we got yur artifishul man itll cost you 1000$ to get him back leave the dough in a papre sack in the garbaj can bak of yur hows noon tomorer and dont cawl the bulls.

"Obviously the work of a well-educated man," Hodges grunted, succeeding finally with the tie. "They always try to appear too illiterate when writing those notes. That's why I thought Dr. Brugh wrote it to throw me off the trail."

"Hatred had nothing to do with it, I suppose?"

"I don't hate Brugh, and if his conscience didn't bother him, he wouldn't hate me. We used to be fairly good friends. We could still be if we weren't so darned stubborn." The professor grinned as he picked up the small figure and moved toward the kitchen. "You don't eat, do you? Well, I do. Brugh played a dirty trick on me, but I've put over a few of them myself to get money for my department. At Corton, it's always been dog eat dog when appropriations were under debate."

"But did you think he'd leave his key lying around for evidence?"

"People do funny things, and only the department heads are permitted master keys. It had his number." Hodges swallowed the last of a bun and washed it down with milk. "It is funny, though. Let's see, now. Brugh left the keys on the table; and sometime yesterday he lost one of them. Tanya was in the laboratory in the morning, just before a date with that confounded nephew of mine. Hm-m-m."

"But Tanya wouldn't—" Hermes felt duty bound to protect Tanya's reputation.

Hodges cut in on his protest. "It's plain you don't know Tanya Brugh. For herself, she wouldn't take it. But give her a fairly handsome young man with a smooth line, and she'd sell her own father down the river. That ransom note might be some of Johnny's pleasant work."

"Then you think it's your nephew?"

"I don't think anything, but it might be. He's the type. Tell you what I'll do; you try to get some of that potassium salt—oh, yes, I knew about it long ago—from your patron, and I'll help you investigate Johnny."

"If you'll help increase my size." That question was still a major one in the god's mind. "How'll we find out whether young Thomas has the thing?"

"That's your worry, son. I'll carry you there, but from then on, it's in your hands." Hodges pocketed Hermes and turned out of the kitchen.

IX

Johnny Thomas looked reasonably pleasant as he stuck his head out of the door, though the circles under his eyes were a little too prominent in the early morning hours. He grinned with evident self-satisfaction.

"Ah, my dear maternal uncle. Do come in." He kicked aside a newspaper that was scattered across the floor and flipped the cigarette ashes off the one comfortable chair in the room, seating himself on the bed. "What can I do for you this morning?"

Hodges coughed to cover the noise of Hermes slipping across the room to a dark place under the table. With that attended to, he faced his nephew. "You know Anthropos—that synthetic man I grew in a culture bath? Somebody stole him last night, tank and all, and slipped a note under my door demanding a thousand dollars for his return."

"Too bad. But surely, uncle, you don't think I had anything to do with it?"

"Of course not; how could you get into the laboratory? But I thought you might help me contact the man and make arrangements to pay. Of course, I'd be willing to let you have a few dollars for your work."

Thomas smiled, and looked across the room while apparently making up his mind. As he looked, a cat came out from where no cat should be, gravely lifted a bottle of whiskey, and drank deeply. "Excellent, my dear Thomas," the cat remarked. "I suppose when you collect that grand from your uncle, we'll have even better drinks. Smart trick, stealing that thing."

The cat licked its chops, sprouted wings, and turned into a fairy. "Naughty, naughty," said the fairy. "Little boys shouldn't steal." It fluttered over to Thomas' shoulder and perched there, tinkling reproachfully.

The young man swatted at it, felt his hand pass through it, and jumped for the chair. Now the room was empty, though his eyes darted into every corner. His uncle coughed again. "If you're done playing, John—" he suggested.

"Didn't you see it?"

"See what? Oh, you mean that fly? Yes, it was a big one. But about this business I have—"

"I think he'd make a nice meal," said a grizzly bear, materializing suddenly. "So young and succulent."

A shining halo of light quivered violently. "You'd poison your system, Bruin. Go back home." The bear obediently trotted to the window and passed through the glass; the halo of light struck a commanding note, and a face of wrath appeared in it. "Young man, repent of your ways and learn that your sins have found you out. Time is but short on this mortal sphere, and the bad that we do must follow us through all eternity. Repent, for the hour has come!"

Thomas quivered down onto the bed again, wiping his forehead. The idea of getting nervous at a time like this! The things couldn't be real. He turned back to Hodges, who was waiting patiently. "Just a little nervous this morning; not used to getting up so early. Now, as we were saying—"

Click! The sound was in the young man's head, and a soft purring voice followed it. "I know a secret, I know a secret, and I'm going to tell! Johnny, old kid, tell the old fossil what a smart guy you are, putting over a trick like that on him. Go ahead and tell!" There was a hot flicker of pain that stabbed up the backbone, then ran around the ribs and began doing something on the order of a toe dance in Thomas' stomach.

He gritted his teeth and groaned. Hodges became all solicitation. "Something you ate?" asked the professor. "Just lie down on the bed and relax."

There was a whole den of rattlesnakes curled up on the bed, making clicking sounds that seemed to say: "Come ahead, young fellow, it's breakfast time and we're hungry!" Thomas had no desire to relax among even imaginary snakes.

"*Gulp—ugh!*" he said, and an angel unscrewed its head from the light socket and dropped near him. "*Gulp—ouch!*" The angel sprouted horns and tail, and carried a red-hot fork that felt most unpleasant when rubbed tenderly along his shins.

Click! Again the voice was in his head. "Remember that girl at Casey's? Well, when she committed suicide, it wasn't so nice. But that was gas, and she didn't feel any pains. When you commit suicide—"

"I won't commit suicide!" The bellow was involuntary, forced out just as the little devil decided his fork would feel worse in the stomach. "Take 'em away!"

Hodges clucked sympathetically. "Dear, dear! Do you have a dizzy feeling, Johnny?"

Johnny did, just as the words were out. His head gave an unpleasant twang and leaped from his body, then went whirling around the room. A gnome picked it up, whittled the neck quickly to a point, and drew a whip. "Hi, fellows!" called the gnome. "Come, see the top I made." He drew the whip smartly across Thomas' head and sent it spinning as a horde of other little hobgoblins jumped out of odd places to watch. That was a little too much for Johnny, with the addition of two worms that were eating his eyes.

Hodges chuckled. "All right, Hermes, let him alone. The boy's fainted. It's a pity I couldn't see the things you were forcing on his mind. Must have been right interesting."

Hermes came out of the corner, smiling. "They were very nice. I think he'll talk when he comes to. He persuaded Tanya to get him the key by pretending an interest in cyclotrons—said he was writing a story. She wouldn't have done it, except that the key was lying so temptingly within reach. He worked on her innocence."

"Okay, Hermes," Hodges grunted. "She's washed whiter than snow, if you want it that way. Better get back in my pocket; Johnny's coming around again."

It was noon when Hodges came to the cell where Brugh sat. The biochemist dropped the little god on the floor and grinned. "You're free now, Arlington," he informed the other. "Sorry I got you in here, but I've tried to make up for that."

Brugh looked up at the professor's voice, and his face wasn't pretty. "*Arrughh!*" he said.

The smile on Hodges' face remained unchanged. "I expected that. But Hermes here can tell you I honestly thought you'd stolen Anthropos. We just finished putting him back where he belongs, and seeing that young nephew of mine leave town. If you'll avoid committing homicide on me, the warden will unlock the door."

"What about my reputation?"

"Quite untouched," Hermes assured him. "Professor Hodges succeeded in keeping everything hushed up, and it's Sunday, so your absence from the university won't mean anything."

The physicist came out of the cell, and his shoulders lifted with the touch of freedom. The scowl on his face was gone, but uncertainty still remained in the look he gave Hodges.

The biochemist put out a hand. "I've been thinking you might help me on Anthropos," he said. "You know, Arlington, we might make something out of that yet if we worked together."

Brugh grinned suddenly. "We might at that, Hiram. Come on home to lunch, and we'll talk it over while Hermes tells me what happened."

Hermes squirmed as a hand lifted him back into the pocket. "How about helping me grow up?"

The two men were busy discussing other things. The height increase would have to wait.

X

Hermes sat on the edge of Anthropos' tank, kicking his small legs against it and thinking of the last two days. To live in the same house, breathe the same air as Tanya Brugh! He dug up another sigh of ecstasy and followed it with one of despair.

For Tanya regarded him as some new form of bug, to be tolerated since he was useful, but not to be liked—an attitude shared by her mother. Dr. Brugh had the greatest respect for the little god, and Kitty was fond of him. Of them all, Kitty treated him best, and Tanya worst.

Of course, that was due to his height. John Thomas was gone, but there were still Will Young and her other escorts, none less than six feet in height. And Hermes was far from being tall. The consultation, held with Brugh and Hodges, had resulted in nothing; when all was said and done, there was no hope for him.

He sighed again, and Dixon, who was helping Hodges and Brugh with Anthropos, noticed him. "What's the matter, Hermes?" he asked good-naturedly. "Alcohol drying out again? Why not try carbon tetrachloride this time?"

Hermes shook his head. "I don't need anything. The alcohol seems to have permanently combined with the tar—something like water and a crystal, to form a hydrate. I'm softened thoroughly for all time."

Hodges looked up and then turned back to the tank where the synthetic man lay, and Hermes turned his attention to it. As far as outward appearance went, Anthropos was nearly perfect, and a tinge of envy filled the little god's thoughts.

Dixon wiped his forehead. "I give up. When three separate divisions of chemistry can't bring life to him, there's no hope. Hodges, your man is doomed to failure."

"He's breathing, though," the biochemist muttered. "Ever since we injected the potassium into him and put it in his nutritive bath, he's been living, but not conscious. See, his heartbeat is as regular as clockwork." He indicated the meter that flickered regularly on the tank.

Brugh refused to look. "To anyone but a biochemist," he informed the room, "the answer would be obvious. Hiram's created life, yes; but he can't give it a good brain. That's too complex for his electric cell formation determiner. What Anthropos needs is a new brain."

"I suppose you'd like to stick his head full of that gummy tar of yours?" Old habit made the words tart, though good fellowship had been restored between them.

"Why not?" It was Hermes' voice this time. Inspiration had flashed suddenly through his small mind, opening a mighty vista of marvels to his imagination. "Why wouldn't that solve it?"

"I'll bite. Why?" Dixon grinned, sweat rolling from his chubby face. "That's the best suggestion we've had today."

"But he wouldn't be real life then, not organic life. Besides, we can't be sure that another batch of the tar would live—it might be an accident that Hermes contained just the right ingredients. The rest of the tar probably isn't the same."

Hermes wriggled in his excitement. "Organic life is merely a chemicoelectrical reaction, with radioactivity thrown in; and I'm all of that. What difference does it make?" He stretched out a small leg. "Dr. Brugh, will you examine my feet?"

With a puzzled frown, Brugh complied. "They're wearing out," he said. "The rubber is almost paper-thin. You'll need a new body soon, Hermes."

"Precisely. That's what I'm talking about. Why couldn't I be put in Anthropos' brainpan?"

Hodges let out a startled wail that died out and left his mouth hanging open. Finally he remembered to close it. "I wonder—" he muttered. "Would it work?"

Dixon demurred. "It'd be a delicate operation, removing the useless higher part of the brain and leaving the essential vital areas that control the heart and organs. Besides, could Hermes control the nerves?"

"Why not? He can control your nerves at a distance if he tries hard enough. But the operation would need a doctor's skill."

Hermes had that all figured out by now, and he voiced his plan while the others listened carefully. Hodges finally nodded. "It might work, son, and Anthropos isn't much good as is. I promised to help you grow up, and if you can use this body, it's yours. The university doesn't seem to value it much."

Later, the borrowed dissecting equipment from the zoology department was in readiness and the men stood looking on as Hermes prepared for his work. He paused at the brink of the tank. "You know what you're to do?"

"We do. After you open it, we'll lower your temperature until you harden up to unconsciousness, remove your casing, pack you in the brainpan, so there's no danger of nerve pressure, and cover the opening with the removed section of the skull."

"Right. In that nutrient fluid, it should heal completely in a few hours." Hermes dropped into the tank and was immersed in the liquid; his ability to work in any medium facilitated the operation.

And his sense of perception made him capable of performing the work with almost uncanny skill. As the others watched, he cut briskly around the skull, removed a section, and went into the brain, analyzing it almost cell by cell and suturing, cutting, and scraping away the useless tissue.

Blood oozed out slowly, but the liquid's restorative power began functioning, healing the soft nerve tissue almost as rapidly as it was cut. Hermes nodded approval and continued until only the vital centers that functioned properly were left. Then he indicated that he was finished and Hodges pulled him out.

The dry ice was numbing as they packed it around him, and his thoughts began moving more sluggishly. But as consciousness left him, a heady exultation was singing its song through every atom of his being. He would be tall and handsome, and Tanya would love him.

Consciousness faded as Hodges began the relatively simple job of removing his casing and inserting him into the vacancy in Anthropos' head.

XI

Darkness. That was the first thought Hermes felt on regaining consciousness. He was in a cave with no entrance, and light could not stream through. Around him was a warm shell that held him away from direct contact with the world. He started to struggle against it, and the uneasy sense of closeness increased.

Then he remembered he was in the head of the synthetic man. He must open his eyes and look out. But his eyes refused to open. Again he concentrated, and nothing seemed to happen.

Brugh's voice, muffled as from a great distance, reached him. "Well, he's awake. His big toe twitched then." There was another sensation, the feeling of faint current pouring in from one of the nerve endings, and Hermes realized that must be his ears sending their message to his brain.

This time he tried to talk, and Hodges spoke. "That was his leg moving. I wonder if he can control his body." Hermes was learning; the sound and nerve messages co-ordinated this time. Learning to use Anthropos' auditory system would not be too difficult.

But he was having trouble. He had tried to open his eyes, and a toe had twitched; an effort to use his tongue resulted in a leg moving. There was only one thing to do, and that was to try everything until the desired result was obtained.

It was several minutes later when Dixon's voice registered on his nerves: "See, his eyes are open. Can you see, Hermes—or Anthropos?"

Hermes couldn't. There was a wild chaos of sensation pouring in through the optic nerve, which must be the effect of light, but it made little sense to him. He concentrated on one part that seemed to register less strongly, and succeeded in making out the distorted figure of a man. It was enough to begin with, but learning to use his eyes took more time than the ears had.

He gave up trying to speak and sent his thought out directly to Brugh. "Lift me out and move me around, so that I can study which sensations are related to my various parts."

Brugh obeyed promptly with the help of the others, enthusiasm running high. Hermes had the entire job of learning to make his body behave before him, but he brought a highly developed mind to bear on the problem. Bit by bit, the sensation sent up by the nerves registered on his brain, was cataloged and analyzed, and became a familiar thing to him. He tried touching a table with his finger, and made it in two attempts.

"You'll be better than any man when we're done with you," Hodges gloated. "If I'd brought consciousness into Anthropos, I'd still have had to educate him as a child is taught. You can learn by yourself."

Hermes was learning to talk again, in the clumsy system of breathing, throat contraction, and oral adaptation that produces human words. He tried it now. "Let me walk alone."

Another half hour saw a stalwart young figure striding about the laboratory, examining this and that, trying out implements, using his body in every way that he could. It answered his commands with a smooth co-ordination that pleased them all.

Brugh was elated. "With a brain like that, Hermes, and the body you have now, we could make the world's greatest physical chemist out of you. A little wire pulling and a few tricks, examinations, and things, and you'd have your degree in no time. I could use you here."

"He'd be a wonderful biochemist," Hodges cut in. "Think of what that sense of perception would mean to us in trying to determine the effects of drugs on an organism."

Dixon added his opinion. "As an organic chemist, think what it would mean in analyzing and synthesizing new compounds. But why not all three? What we really need is someone to co-ordinate the various fields, and Hermes is ideal." He held out an old pair of trousers, acid-stained, but whole, and Hermes began climbing into them. That was a complication he hadn't thought of, and one which was not entirely pleasant. He saw no reason to conceal the new body of which he was so proud.

Brugh had accepted Dixon's idea. "How about getting yourself added to our staff in a few years? It would mean a lot to science, and the board of directors couldn't refuse the appointment if you'd force a little thought into their empty heads."

Hermes had been considering it, and the prospect appealed to him. But Tanya wouldn't like it, probably. He'd have to see her before he could make any decisions. Of course, now that he was a real man instead of a rubber statue, she couldn't refuse him.

There was an interruption from the door, a small child's voice. "Daddy, Daddy, are you there?" The door swung open and Kitty Brugh came tripping in.

"Kitty, you don't belong here." Brugh faced her with a scowl of annoyance. "I'm busy."

"But Mamma sent me." Her voice was plaintive. "She gave me this telegram to bring to you."

Brugh took it and read it through, his face lighting up. "Great luck," he told Hermes, handing it over. "I never thought Tanya would choose so well."

The telegram was as simple as most telegrams are:

HAVE MARRIED WILL YOUNG AND ON HONEYMOON IN MILLSBURG STOP EVER SO HAPPY STOP LOVE

TANYA

And with it, the newly created man's hopes went flying out into nothingness.

But somehow he felt much better than he should. He handed it back to Brugh, and the sigh he achieved was halfhearted. Kitty's eyes noticed him for the first time.

She squeaked delightedly. "Oh, what a pretty man! What's your name?"

Hermes' heart went out to her. He stooped and picked her up in his strong young arms, stroking her hair. "I'm the little god, Kitty. I'm your Hermes in a new body. Do you like it?"

She snuggled up. "Um-hmm. It's nice." There was no surprise for her in anything Hermes might do. He turned back to the three men then.

"Dr. Brugh, I've decided to accept your offer. I'd like nothing better than working with all of you here at Corton."

"Splendid, my boy. Splendid. Eh, Hiram?"

They crowded around him, shaking his hand, and he thoroughly enjoyed the flattery of their respect. But most of his thoughts were centered on Kitty. After all, she was the only woman—or girl—who had treated him with any consideration, and her little mind was open and honest. She'd make a wonderful woman in ten more years.

Ten more years; and he wasn't so very old himself. There might be hope there yet.

This is another story I hadn't read from its publication until I started doing this book. And in this case, I enjoyed a chance to go over it again, and I found it something of an old friend.

But quite a bit of it surprised me. I couldn't write that story now. I've added some skills since then, and I've learned a great deal more about the business of plotting and writing. But that knowledge would get sadly in the way of shaping up such a story as this. There is too much casual assumption of one thing after another, and Hermes seems to move about far too easily, just to suit the needs of the writer.

There's something to be said for naïveté and young enthusiasm. Maybe one of the troubles with us older writers is that we know too much of what can't be done, and we never try the stories that we often should write. Skill has its place, as has discipline; but the craft of writing can be approached through many doors.

Still, the only thing in it for which I apologize is the cliché picture of the cat. I should have known better. I've had quite a few cats as my friends, and I've found them to be anything but cold and calculating in the affection they can give to a human.

Anyhow, while I liked making another sale and getting a good check for it, I wasn't fully satisfied, because I wanted to write fantasy for *Unknown* far more than science fiction for *Astounding*. So I started in almost at once to try fantasy again. This was something called "Fade-Out," dealing with a rather dull young man who tried to commit some crime by astral projection. Somehow he managed to break the silver cord that bound him to his body, and naturally he then slowly faded out. It was short, which was its only virtue, running to about 3,800 words.

Campbell bounced it promptly. But the story didn't quite achieve the oblivion it deserved. At that time, several of the fan magazines being put out by the readers were trying to use some fiction as well as the articles they usually printed. Harry Warner, one of the leading fans—as he still is—wrote to ask if I had any rejects he could have. So I sent him "Fade-Out," which he wisely shortened before printing. So somewhere in some attic, there may still be a version of it. I don't have one, nor want one. But I wish I'd sent him "Hands of the Gods." Ah, well. It was the only time I submitted a story to a fan magazine, incidentally.

Campbell's letter of rejection had a number of comments about the fact that I was trying to write stories that weren't my type. I was counting too much on gimmicks and trick plots, and should go back to doing characters. (He was very right, though it took me quite a while to learn the lesson.) He also pointed out that he didn't expect to see straight action stories from me; that wasn't my chief ability. There were plenty of other writers who did such things, and what he needed from me was what made me unique.

So I couldn't write an action scene or a good fight scene, eh? That boggled. Who, I asked myself, had been writing him all the letters explaining why artists were drawing the use of a knife all wrong? Who had seen more rough stuff in life? Certainly not most of those who were writing about it, to judge by their idea that a fist to the chin was more effective than the side of the hand to the throat.

At that time, I'd been working up an idea for a conflict in getting rockets out to space. That would be a good chance to show Campbell how wrong he was, I decided. So I immediately recast it to include some good action sequences. And fired with indignation, I wrote 15,000 words, entitled "The Stars Look Down."

6.

The Stars Look Down

(by Lester del Rey)

I

Erin Morse came down the steps slowly without looking back, and his long fingers brushed through the gray hair that had been brown when he first entered the building. Four years is a long time to wait when a man has work to do and the stars look down every night, reminding him of his dreams. There were new lines in his face and little wrinkles had etched themselves around his dark eyes. But even four years had been too few to change his erect carriage or press down his wide shoulders. At sixty, he could still move with the lithe grace of a boy.

The heavy gate opened as he neared it and he stepped out with a slow, even pace. He passed the big three-wheeled car parked there, then stopped and breathed deeply, letting his eyes roam over the green woods and plowed fields and take in the blue sweep of the horizon. Only the old can draw full sweetness from freedom, though the young may cry loudest for it. The first heady taste of it over, he turned his back on the prison and headed down the road.

There was a bugling from the car behind him, but he was barely conscious of it; it was only when it drove up beside him and stopped that he noticed. A heavily built man stuck out a face shaped like a bulldog's and yelled.

"Hey, Erin! Don't tell me you're blind as well as crazy?"

Morse swung his head and a momentary flash of surprise and annoyance crossed his face before he stepped over to the car. "You would be here, of course, Stewart."

"Sure. I knew your men wouldn't. Hop in and I'll ride you over to Hampton." At Erin's hesitation, he gestured impatiently. "I'm not going to kidnap you, if that's what you think. Federal laws still mean something to me, you know."

"I wouldn't know." Erin climbed in and the motor behind purred softly, its sound indicating a full atomic generator instead of the usual steam plant. "I suppose the warden kept you well informed of my actions."

The other chuckled. "He did; money has its uses when you know where to put it. I found out you weren't letting your men visit or write to you, and that's about all. Afraid I'd find out what was in the letters?"

"Precisely. And the boys could use the time better for work than useless visits to me. Thanks, I have tobacco." But at Stewart's impatient gesture, he put the "makings" back and accepted a cigarette. "It isn't poisoned, I suppose?"

"Nor loaded."

Erin let a half smile run over his lips and relaxed on the seat, watching the road flash by and letting his mind run over other times with Stewart. Probably the other was doing the same, since the silence was mutual. They had all too many common memories. Forty years of them, from the time they had first met at the institute as roommates, both filled with a hunger for knowledge that would let them cross space to other worlds.

Erin, from a family that traced itself back almost to Adam, and with a fortune equally old, had placed his faith in the newly commercialized atomic power. Gregory Stewart, who came from the wrong side of the tracks, where a full meal was a luxury, was more conservative; new and better explosives were his specialty. The fact that they were both aiming at the same goal made little difference in their arguments. Though they stuck together from stubbornness, black eyes flourished.

Then, to complicate matters further, Mara Devlin entered their lives to choose Erin after two years of indecision and to die while giving birth to his son. Erin took the boy and a few workers out to a small island off the coast and began soaking his fortune into workshops where he could train men in rocketry and gain some protection from Stewart's thugs.

Gregory Stewart had prospered with his explosives during the war of 1958, and was piling up fortune on fortune. Little by little, the key industries of the country were coming under his control, along with the toughest gangs of gunmen. When he could, he bought an island lying off the coast, a few miles from Erin's, stocked it with the best brains he could buy, and began his own research. The old feud settled down to a dull but constant series of defeats and partial victories that gained nothing for either.

Erin came to the crowning stroke of Stewart's offensive, grimaced, and tossed the cigarette away. "I forgot to thank you for railroading me up on that five-year sentence, Greg," he said quietly. "I suppose you were responsible for the failure of the blast that killed my son, as well."

Stewart looked at him in surprise which seemed genuine. "The failure was none of my doing, Erin. Anyway, you had no business sending the boy up on the crazy experimental model; any fool should have known he couldn't handle it. Maybe my legal staff framed things a little, but it *was* manslaughter. I could have wrung your neck when I heard Mara's son was dead, instead of letting you off lightly with five years—less one for good behavior."

"I didn't send him up." Erin's soft voice contrasted oddly with Stewart's bellow. "He slipped out one night on his own, against my orders. If the whole case hadn't been fixed with your money, I could have proved that at the trial. As it was, I couldn't get a decent hearing."

"All right, then, I framed you. But you've hit back at me without trying to, though you probably don't know it yet." He brushed Erin's protest aside quickly. "Never mind, you'll see what I mean soon enough. I didn't meet you to hash over past grievances."

"I wondered why you came to see me out."

They swung off the main highway into a smaller road where the speed limit was only sixty and went flashing past the other cars headed for Hampton. Stewart gunned the car savagely, unmindful of the curves. "We're almost at the wharf," he pointed out needlessly, "so I'll make it short and sweet. I'm about finished with plans for a rocket that will work—a few more months should do the trick—and I don't want competition now. In plain words, Erin, drop it or all rules are off between us."

"Haven't they been?" Erin asked.

"Only partly. Forget your crazy ion-blast idea, and I'll reserve a berth for you on my ship; keep on bucking me and I'll ruin you. Well?"

"No, Greg."

Stewart grunted and shrugged. "I was afraid you'd be a fool. We've always wanted the same things, and you've either had them to begin with or gotten them from under my nose. But this time it's not going to be that way. I'm declaring war. And for your information, *my* patents go through in a few days, so you'll have to figure on getting along without that steering assembly you worked out."

Erin gave no sign he had heard as the car came to a stop at the small wharf. "Thanks for picking me up," he said with grave courtesy. Stewart answered with a curt nod and swung the car around on its front wheels. Erin turned to a boy whose boat was tied up nearby. "How much to ferry me out to Kroll Island?"

"Two bucks." The boy looked up, and changed his smile quickly. "You one of them crazy guys who's been playing with skyrockets? Five bucks, I meant."

Erin grimaced slightly but held out the money.

II

There was nobody waiting to greet him on the island, nor had he expected anyone. He fed the right combination into the alarm system to keep it quiet and set off up the rough wooden walk toward the buildings that huddled together a few hundred yards from the dock. The warehouses, he noticed, needed a new coat of paint, and the dock would require repairs if the tramp freighter were to use it much longer.

There was a smell of smoke in the air, tangy and resinous at first, but growing stronger as he moved away from the ocean's crisp counteracting odor. As he passed the big machine shop, a stronger whiff of it reached him, unpleasant now. There was a thin wisp of smoke going up behind it, the faint gray of an almost exhausted fire. The men must be getting careless, burning their rubbish so close to the buildings. He cut around the corner and stopped.

The south wall of the laboratory was a black, charred scar, dripping dankly from a hose that was playing on it. Where the office building had stood, gaunt steel girders rose from a pile of smoking ashes and half-burned boards, with two blistered filing cabinets poking up like ghosts at a wake.

The three men standing by added nothing to the cheerfulness of the scene. Erin shivered slightly before advancing toward them. It was a foreboding omen for his homecoming, and for a moment the primitive fears mastered him. The little pain that had been scratching at his heart came back again, stronger this time.

Doug Wratten turned off the hose and shook a small arm at the sandy-haired young husky beside him. "All right," he yelled in a piping falsetto, "matter's particular and energy's discrete. But you chemists try and convince an atomic generator that it's dealing with building-block atoms instead of wave-motion."

Jimmy Shaw's homely, pleasant face still studied the smoldering ashes. "Roll wave-motion into a ball and give it valence, redhead," he suggested. "Do that and I'll send Stewart a sample—it might make a better bomb than the egg he laid on us. How about it, Dad?"

"Maybe. Anyhow, you kids drop the argument until you're through being mad at Stewart," the foreman ordered. "You'll carry your tempers over against each other." Tom Shaw was even more grizzled and stooped than Erin remembered, and his lanky frame seemed to have grown thinner.

"All right," he decided in his twangy, down-East voice. "I guess it's over, so we . . . Hey, it's Erin!"

He caught at Jimmy's arm and pulled him around, heading toward Erin with a loose-jointed trot. Doug forgot his arguments and moved his underdone figure on the double after them, shouting at the top of his thin voice. Erin found his arm aching and his ears ringing from their questions.

He broke free for a second and smiled. "All right, I got a year off, I sneaked in, I'm glad to be back, and you've done a good job, I gather. Where are Hank and Dutch?"

"Over in the machine shop, I guess. Haven't seen them since the fire was under control." Shaw jerked a long arm at the remains. "Had a little trouble, you see."

"I saw. Stewart's men?"

"Mm-hm. Came over in a plane and dropped an incendiary. Sort of ruined the office, but no real damage to the laboratory. If those filing cabinets are as good as they claimed, it didn't hurt our records."

Doug grinned beatifically. "Hurt their plane more. Tom here had one of our test models sent up for it, and the rocket striking against the propeller spoiled their plans." He gestured out toward the ocean. "They're drinking Neptune's health in hell right now."

"Bloodthirsty little physicist, isn't he?" Jimmy asked the air. "Hey, Kung, the boss is back. Better go tell the others."

The Chinese cook came hobbling up, jerking his bad leg over the ground and swearing at it as it slowed him down. "Kung, him see boss fella allee same time more quick long time," he intoned in the weird mixture of pidgin, bêche-de-mer, and perverted English that was his private property. "Very good, him come back. Mebbeso make suppee chop-chop same time night."

He gravely shook hands with himself before Erin, his smile saying more than the garbled English he insisted on using, then went hobbling off toward the machine shop. Shaw turned to the two young men.

"All right, you kids, get along. I've got business with Erin." As they left, his face lengthened. "I'm glad you're back, boss. Things haven't been looking any too good. Stewart's getting more active. Oh, the fire didn't do us any permanent damage, but we've been having trouble getting our supplies freighted in—had to buy an old tramp freighter when Stewart took over the regular one—and it looks like war brewing all along the line."

"I know it. Stewart brought me back and told me he was gunning for us." Erin dropped back onto a rock, realizing suddenly that he was tired; and he'd have to see a doctor about his heart—sometime. "And he's stolen our steering unit, or thinks he's getting it patented, at least."

"Hmmm. He can't have it; it's the only practical solution to the controls system there is. Erin, we'll . . . Skip it, here come Dutch and Hank."

But a sudden whistle from the rocket test tower cut in, indicating a test. The structural engineer and machinist swung sharply, and Doug and Jimmy popped out of the laboratory at a run. Shaw grabbed at Erin.

"Come on," he urged. "This is the biggest test yet, I hope. Good thing you're here to see it." Even Kung was hobbling toward the tower.

Erin followed, puzzling over who could have set off the whistle; he knew of no one not accounted for, yet a man had to be in the tower. Evidently there was an addition to the force, of whom he knew nothing. They reached the guardrail around the tower, and the whistle tooted again, three times in warning.

"Where is the rocket?" Erin yelled over the whistle. There was nothing on the takeoff cradle.

"Left two days ago; this is the return. Jack's been nursing it without sleep—wouldn't let anyone else have it," Shaw answered hurriedly. "Only took time off to send another up for the bomber."

Following their eyes, Erin finally located a tiny point of light that grew as he watched. From the point in the sky where it was, a thin shrilling reached their ears. A few seconds later, he made out the stubby shape of a ten-foot model, its tubes belching out blue flame in a long, tight jet. With a speed that made it difficult to follow, it shot over their heads at a flat angle, heading over the ocean, while its speed dropped. A rolling turn pointed it back over their heads, lower this time, and the ion-blast could be seen as a tight, unwavering track behind it.

Then it reversed again and came over the tower, slowed almost to a stop, turned up to vertical with a long blast from its steering tubes, and settled slowly into the space between the guide rails. It slid down with a wheeze, sneezed faintly, and decided to stop peacefully. Erin felt a tingle run up his back at his first sight of a completely successful radio-controlled flight.

The others were yelling crazily. Dutch Bauer, the fat structural engineer, was dancing with Hank Vlček, his bald pate shining red with excitement. "It worked, it worked," they were chanting.

Shaw grunted. "Luck," he said sourly, but his face belied the words. "Jack had no business sending our first model with the new helix on such a flight. Wonder the darn fool didn't lose it in space."

Erin's eyes were focused on the young man coming from the pit of the tower. There was something oddly familiar about those wide shoulders and the mane of black hair that hugged his head. As the boy came nearer, the impression was heightened by the serious brown eyes, now red from lack of sleep, that were slightly too deep in the round face.

The boy scanned the group and moved directly toward Morse, a little hesitantly. "Well," he asked, "how did you like the test—Mr. Morse, I think? Notice how the new helix holds the jets steady?"

Erin nodded slowly. So this was what Stewart had meant by his statement that he had been hit twice as hard. "You resemble your father, Jack Stewart!"

Jack shifted on his feet, then decided there was no disapproval on Erin's face, and grinned. He held out a small package. "Then I'll give you this, sir. It's a reel of exposed film, shot from the rocket, and it should show the other side of the Moon!"

III

The secretary glided into the richly appointed room, sniffing at the pungent odor given off by the dirty old pipe in Stewart's mouth. "Mr. Russell's here, sir," she announced, wondering whether his scowl was indicative of indigestion or directed at some particular person.

"Send him in, then." He bit at the stem of the pipe without looking at her, and she breathed a sigh of relief. It wasn't indigestion, which was the only thing that made him roar at the office force; at other times he was fair and just with them, if not given to kindliness. Looking at Russell as she sent him in, she guessed the object of his anger.

"Well?" Stewart asked curtly as his right-hand man entered.

"Now look," Russell began, "I admit I sent the plane over before you said, but was it my fault if they brought it down? How was I to know they had a torpedo they could control in the air?"

"Not torpedo, you fool; it was a rocket. And that's bad news, in itself, since it means they're making progress. But we'll skip that. I gave orders you were to wait until Morse refused my offer, and you didn't. Furthermore, I told you to send it over at night, when they'd be unprepared, and drop it on the tower and laboratory, not on the office. I'm not trying to burn people to death."

"But the pilot didn't want—"

"You mean you had your own little ideas." He tossed the pipe into a tray and began picking at his fingernails. "Next time I give you orders, Russell, I expect them to be followed. Understand? You'd better. Now get down to Washington and see what you can do about rushing our patent on the unified control; Erin Morse didn't look surprised or bothered enough to suit me. He's holding something, and I don't want it to show up as an ace. Okay, beat it."

Russell looked up in surprise, and made tracks toward the door. Either the old man was feeling unusually good, or he was worried. That had been easier than he expected.

Back on Kroll Island, Erin Morse settled back in his chair in the corner of the workshop that served as a temporary office. "Read this," he said, handing over a dog-eared magazine with a harshly colored cover to Shaw. "It's a copy of *Interplanetary Tales,* one of the two issues they printed. It's not well known, but it's still classed as literature. Page 108, where it's marked in red."

Shaw looked at him curiously, and reached for the magazine. He began reading in his overly precise manner, the exact opposite of his usual slow speech. "Jerry threw the stick over to the right, and the *Betsy* veered sharply, jarring his teeth. The controls were the newest type, arranged to be handled by one stick. Below the steering rod was a circular disk, and banked around it was a circle of pistons that varied the steering jet blasts according to the amount they were depressed. Moving the stick caused the disk to press against those pistons which would turn the ship in that direction, slowly with a little movement, sharply if it were depressed the limit."

He looked at Erin. "But that's a fair description of the system we use."

"Exactly. Do you remember whether the submarine periscope was patented?"

"Why, Jules Verne . . . Hmmm. Anything described reasonably accurately in literature can't be given a basic patent." Shaw thought it over slowly. "I take it we mail this to the attorneys and get Stewart's claim voided. So that's why you didn't try for a patent on it?"

"Naturally."

Morse picked up the records that had been saved from the fire by insulated cabinets, and ran back over the last few years' work. They showed the usual huge expenditures and small progress. Rockets aren't built on a shoestring nor in the backyard during the idle hours of a boy scientist. "Total cost, five-foot experimental radio-controlled rocket, $13,843.51," read one item. From another book he found that it had crashed into the sea on its first flight and been destroyed.

But there were advances. The third model had succeeded, though the flickering, erratic blast had made control difficult. A new lightweight converter had been tested successfully, throwing out power from the atoms with only a .002 percent heat loss. An ion-release had been discovered by General Electratomic Company that afforded a more than ample supply of ions, and Shaw had secured rights for its use. Toward the last there were outlays for some new helix to control the ion-blast on a tight line under constant force and a new alloy for the chamber. Those had always been the problems.

"Good work," Erin Morse nodded. "This last model, I gather, is the one Jack used to reach the Moon." Under it he penciled the word "success" in bright green. "The boys were quite excited over those pictures, even if they did show nothing spectacular. I'm glad he sent it."

"So am I. They need encouragement." Shaw kicked aside a broken bearing and moved his chair back against the wall. "I suppose you're wondering why Jack's working with us. I didn't know how you'd take it."

"I'm reserving my opinion for the facts." It had been a shock, seeing the boy there, but he had covered up as best he could and waited until information was vouchsafed.

Shaw began awkwardly, not sure yet whether Erin approved or not. "Jack came here about a year ago and—well, he simply told us he was looking for work. Had a blowup with his father over your being sent up for the accident, it seems, back then. Anyway, they'd been quarreling before because Jack wanted to specialize in atomics, and the old man wanted him to carry on with explosives.

"So Jack left home, took his degree with money his mother had left him, and came here. He's good, too, though I wouldn't tell him so. That new helix control is his work, and he's fixed up the ion-release so as to give optimum results. Since Doug and you studied atomics, they've made big progress, I reckon, and we needed someone with his training."

"Any experimental work needs new blood," Erin agreed. "So Greg succeeded in teaching his son that Mars was the last frontier, but not how to reach it."

"Seems that way. Anyway, his father's kicking up a worse fuss with us since he came. Somehow, there's a leak, and I can't locate the source—Jack has been watched, and he's not doing it. But Stewart's getting too much information on what we're doing—like that control. He managed to cut off freighter service and choke our source of supplies until I bought up a tramp and hired a no-good captain."

"He'll hit harder when we get his patent application killed. By the way, are the plans for that air-renewer of Jimmy's still around?"

Shaw nodded. "Sure, I guess so. He never found out what was

wrong with it, though, so we've been planning on carrying oxygen flasks with us." Based on the idea of photosynthesis, the air-renewer had been designed to break down the carbon dioxide waste product of breathing by turning it into sugar and free oxygen, as a plant does, and permit the same air being used over and over.

"All it needs is saturated air around the catalyst." Erin had fished around in the papers from the burned office until he had the plans. Now he spread them before Shaw and indicated the changes. "A spray of water here, and remove the humidity afterward. Took me three years up there, working when I could, to figure out that fault, but it's ready for the patent attorneys now. Dutch can draw up the plans in the morning."

They stuck the papers and books away and passed out of the building into the night. "Stars look right good," Shaw observed. "Mars seems to be waiting until we can get there."

"That shouldn't be long now, with the rocket blast finally under control. What's that?" Erin pointed toward a sharp streak of light that rose suddenly over the horizon and arced up rapidly. As they watched, it straightened to vertical and went streaking up on greased wings until it faded into the heights beyond vision.

"Looks like Stewart's made a successful model." A faint, high whine reached their ears now. "If he has, we *will* have a fight on our hands."

Erin nodded. "Start the boys on the big rocket in the morning; we can't stop for more experimental work now."

IV

The big electric hammer came down with a monotonous thud and clank, jarring against the eardrums in its endless hunger for new material to work on. Hank Vlček's little bullet head looked like a hairy billiard ball stuck on an ape's body as he bobbed up and down in front of it, feeding in sheets of cuproberyl alloy. But the power in the machinist's arms seemed to match that of the motor.

Dutch Bauer looked up from a sheet of blueprints and nodded approvingly, then went back to the elaborate calculations required to complete the design he was working on. The two co-operated perfectly, Dutch creating structural patterns on paper, and Vlček turning them into solid metal.

On paper, the *Santa Maria* was shaping up handsomely, though the only beauty of the ship itself was to be that given by severe utility. Short and squat, with flaring blast tubes, she showed little resemblance to the classic cigar-hulls of a thousand speculative artists. The one great purpose was strength with a minimum of weight, and the locating of the center of gravity below the thrust points of the rockets. When completed, there would be no danger of her tipping her nose back to Earth on the takeoff.

Out on the ways that had been thrown up hastily, gaunt girders were shaping into position to form her skeleton, and some of the outer sheathing was in position. The stubby air fins that would support her in the air until speed was reached were lying beside her, ready to be attached, and a blower was already shooting in insulation where her double hull was completed. Space itself would be insulation against heat loss, but the rays of the unfiltered sunlight needed something to check them, or the men inside the ship would have been boiled long before Mars was reached. Hsi Kung was running the blower, babbling at it in singsong Peking dialect. At a time like this, they were all common laborers when there was work to be done.

Erin pulled on coveralls and reached for the induction welder, while Jimmy Shaw consulted his blueprints. "Wonder why Doug hasn't shown up?" the boy asked. "He usually gets back from the mainland before morning, but it's nine already. Hmm. Looks like Hank's machined enough hull plates to keep us busy until supper."

"It does, though where he finds time is a puzzle. He must work all night. We need other workers, if we're to compete with Stewart's force. Even counting Kung, eight men aren't enough for this job." Erin began climbing up the wooden framing that gave access to the hull, wondering whether his heart would bother him today. Sleep had been slow coming the night before, and he was tired. This work was too heavy for an old man, though he hadn't thought of himself as old before. Certainly he didn't look old.

"Wonder why Doug goes to town once a week?" he asked.

Jimmy chuckled. "Don't you know? He's found a girl friend there, believe it or not. Some woman has either taken pity on him, or he's found his nerve at last."

Doug wasn't exactly the sort that would appeal to women. His short, scrawny figure was all angles, and his face, topped by its thin mop of reddish hair, was vaguely like that of an eagle. Then, too, he usually stuttered around women.

Erin smiled faintly. "It's a shame, in a way, that Doug's so shy around girls. I hope he has better luck with this one than that other."

"So do I, though I wouldn't tell him so. He's been as cocky as a rooster since he found this Helen." Jimmy settled into position with a grunt and began moving a sheet into place as it came up on the magnetic grapple Jack was working below him. "Okay, fire away."

The welder was heavy, and the heat that poured up from the plates sapped at Morse's strength. He was conscious of sudden relief at noon when a shout came up to him. He released the welder slowly, rubbing tired muscles, and looked down at the weaving form of Doug Wratten. One of the physicist's thin arms was motioning him down erratically.

"Drunk!" Jimmy diagnosed in amazement. "Didn't know he touched the stuff."

There was no question of Doug's state. His words were thick and muffled as Erin reached him. "Go 'head 'n' fire me," he muttered thickly. "Fire me, Erin. Kick m' out 'thout a good word. I'm a low-down dirty dog, tha's what."

"For being drunk, Doug? That hardly justifies such extreme measures."

"Huh-uh. Who's drunk? It's tha' girl. . . . I foun' the leak we been worr'n' about."

Erin got an arm around him and began moving toward the bunkhouse, meaning to pay no attention to his mumbled words. But the last ones struck home. The leak of information to Stewart's camp had been troubling them all for the last two months. "Yes?" he encouraged.

"'S the girl. She's a spy for Stewart." His voice stuck in his throat and he rumbled unhappily. "Use'a be his sec'tary, planted her on me. Jus' usin' me, tha's all. Saw a letter she was writin' him when I was waitin' for her to come down. Din't wait anymore. . . . Jus' usin' me; tol' me she was in'rested in my work. Tol' me she loved me. Foun' out all I knew. . . . Better fire me, Erin."

"I think not, Doug. It might have happened to any of us. Why don't you go to sleep?"

Wratten rolled over in the bed as he was released, gagging sickly, and moaning to himself. "I love . . . Helen . . . Damn Helen!" As Erin closed the door, his voice came out, pleading. "Don't tell Jimmy; he'd laugh."

Jimmy stood at the door as Erin came out. "Poor devil," he said. "I heard enough to know what happened. Anything I can do for him?"

"Let him sleep it off. I'll have a talk with him when he wakes up and see what I can do about bolstering his faith in himself."

"Okay," Jimmy agreed, "but it was a dirty, rotten trick of Stewart's, using him like that. Say, Dad's up at the shack swearing at something else Stewart's done, and yelling for you. I just went up there."

Erin grunted, and turned hastily toward the temporary office building they had erected. It was always something, except when it was more than one thing. First the fire, the trouble with the patent, now safely squelched, difficulty in obtaining tools, and one thing after another, all meant to wear down their morale. This was probably one of the master strokes that seemed to happen almost at regular intervals.

Sometimes he wondered whether either of them would ever succeed; forty years of rivalry had produced no results except enough to keep them trying. Now, when success for one of them seemed at hand, the feud was going on more bitterly than before, though it was mostly one-sided. And war was menacing the world again, as it would always threaten a world where there were no other escape valves for men's emotions. They needed a new frontier, free of national barriers, where the headstrong could fight nature instead of their brothers.

He had hoped to provide that escape valve in leading men to another planet, just as Stewart hoped. But would either of them succeed? Erin was sure of Stewart's ultimate failure—explosives couldn't do the trick; though he had enough of a sense of humor to realize that Stewart was saying the same thing about him and his method. If only there could be peace until he finished!

Shaw was waiting impatiently, swearing coldly in a voice Erin hadn't heard since the days when Tom was tricked out of a discovery by a company for which he'd worked as metallurgist, and he joined the men on the island. "The mail's in," he said, breaking off his flow of invectives. "Here's a present from Captain Hitchkins—says he can't get the cargo of beryllium alloy we ordered made up. And here's the letter from the Beryl Company."

Erin picked up the letter and read it slowly. It began with too profuse apologies, then cited legal outs: "—will realize that we are not breaking our contract by this action, since it contains a clause to the effect that our own needs shall come first. Mr. G. R. Stewart, who has controlling interest in our company, has requisitioned our entire supply, and we are advised by our legal department that this contingency is covered by the clause mentioned. Therefore we can no longer furnish the alloy you desire. We regret—"

He skimmed the passage of regret and polite lies, to center on a sentence at the end, which conveyed the real message, and revealed the source of the letter. "We doubt that you can secure beryllium alloy at any price, as we are advised that Mr. Stewart is using all that the market can supply. If such is not the case, we shall, of course, be glad to extend our best wishes in your enterprise."

"How about that?" he asked Shaw, pointing to the last sentence. "Have you investigated?"

"Don't need to. Hitchkins showed more brains than I gave him credit for. He scoured the market for us, on his own initiative, and beryllium just ain't." Shaw passed over the other letters that had come, reverting to his invectives. "Now what do we do?"

"Without beryllium, nothing. We'll have to get it, someway." But Erin wondered. Whatever else Stewart was, he was thorough, and his last stroke had been more than the expected major move.

V

The supper table had turned into a conference room, since news of that importance was impossible to keep. Even Doug Wratten had partially forgotten his own troubles, and was watching Erin. Kung stood unnoticed in the doorway, his moon face picturing the general gloom.

Dutch Bauer finished his explanation and concluded. "So, that is it. No beryllium, no *Santa Maria.* Even aluminum alloys are too heavy for good design. Aluminum—bah! Hopeless." He shrugged and spread his pudgy hands to show just how hopeless it was.

Jimmy grunted and considered. "How about magnesium alloys—something like magnalium?" he asked, but without much hope. "It's even lighter than beryllium—1.74 density instead of 1.8."

"Won't work." Their eyes had turned to Shaw, who was the metallurgist, and his answer was flat. "Alloys aren't high enough in melting point, aren't hard enough, and don't have the strength of the one we've been using. When the ship uses the air for braking, or when the sun shines on it in space, we'll need something that won't soften up at ordinary temperatures; and that means beryllium."

"Then how about the foreign markets?" Jack wanted to know. "My fa . . . Mr. Stewart can't control all of them."

Erin shook his head. "No luck. They're turning all they can get into bombing planes and air torpedoes. They're not interested in idealism."

"I liked that new helix, too." Jack tapped his fingers on the table, then snapped them out flat. "Well, there goes a nice piece of applied atomics. We should have bought our own beryllium plant, I guess."

"And have to close down because Stewart gained control of the new process for getting beryllium out of its ores." Shaw grunted. "We'd have had to fall back on the old process of extracting it by dissolving out in alkalies."

Erin looked up suddenly, staring at Shaw. "When I was first starting," he said thoughtfully, "I considered buying one of the old plants. It's still standing, all the machinery in place, but it's been closed down by the competition of the new process. The owner's hard up, but he can't sell the place for love or money."

Jimmy's face dropped its scowl and came forth with a fresh grin; even the mention of a faint hope was enough to send up his enthusiasm. "So we buy it or get him to open up, start using it, and go ahead in spite of Stewart. How much does the old system cost, Dad?"

"About fifteen hundred dollars a ton, using a couple of tricks I could show them. Going to try it, Erin?"

Erin nodded silently, but the frown was still on his face as he got up and went out to the new office where he could use the visiphone. The plant had a maximum capacity of four tons a week, which was hardly adequate, and there were other objections, but trying would do no harm. The frown was heavier when he came back.

"Sanders will open up," he reported, "but he'll need money to fix the plant up. He agrees to turn the plant over to us, and furnish the alloy at the price Tom mentioned, but we'll have to invest about sixty thousand in new equipment. Add that to the cost of the metal, and it runs to a rather steep figure."

"But—"

"I know. I'm not kicking about the money, or wouldn't be if I had it to spend." Erin hadn't meant to tell them of his own troubles, but there was no way to avoid it now. "Stewart left nothing to chance. The stocks and investments I had began to slip a month ago, and they kept slipping. My brokers advised me that they have liquidated everything, and I have about ten cents on a dollar left; today's mail brought their letter along with the other news."

Jack swore hotly. "Da—Stewart always could ruin a man on the market. Erin, I've got a decent legacy from my mother, and we're practically running a co-operative here, anyhow. It's all yours."

Erin saw suddenly just what the loss of the boy had meant to Stewart, and the last of numbness from his own son's death slipped away. His smile was as sweet as a woman's, but he shook his head. "Did you read your mail today?"

"No, why?"

"Because Stewart would know his own son well enough to take precautions. See if I'm not right."

They watched intently as the letters came out of Jack's pocket and were sorted. He selected one bulky one and ripped it open hastily, drawing out the paper where all could see, skimming over it until it formed a complete picture. " 'It almost seems that someone is deliberately trying to ruin you,' " he read. " 'Our best efforts have failed completely—' Damn! There's about enough left to pay for the new machinery needed, and that's all."

Doug came out of his trance. "I won't be needing my savings for the future now," he said grimly. "It's not much, but I'd appreciate your using it, Erin. And I don't think any of us will want the salary you've been paying us."

The others nodded. All of them had been paid more than well, and had had no chance to spend much of their salary. Their contributions were made as a matter of course, and Erin totaled them.

"It may be enough," he said. "Of course, we form a closed corporation, all profits—if there are any from this—being distributed. I'll have the legal papers drawn up. Perhaps it will be enough, perhaps not, but we can put it to the test. Our big trouble is that we need new workers, men to help Hank particularly. Most of the machining will have to be done here on the island now."

"Mebbeso you fella catchee plenty man." Kung hobbled forward to the table, a dirty leather sack in his hands. "You fella catchee li'l planet, fin' allee same time catchee time makee free." His jargon went on, growing too thick for them to understand.

Tom Shaw held up a protesting hand. "Talk chink," he ordered. "I spent five years there once, so I can get the lingo if you take your time."

Kung threw him a surprised and grateful glance, and broke into a rambling discourse, motioning toward the sky, the bag in his hand, and counting on his fingers.

Shaw turned back to the others.

"He says he wants to join up, putting in the money he's been saving for his funeral when they ship his body back to China. Wants to know if his race will be allowed on the other planets when we reach them?"

"Tell him the planets are big enough for all races, provided ships are built to carry them."

"Very good, boss fella, savvee plenty." Kung lapsed again into Peking dialect.

"He says he can get us workers then, who'll obey with no questions asked, and won't cost us more than enough to buy them cheap food. His tong will be glad to furnish them on his say-so. Since Japan conquered them and they digested the Japanese into their own nation again, it seems they need room to expand.

"Darn it, Erin, with even the Chinese cook behind you, we're bound to beat Stewart."

VI

Captain Hitchkins had left the unloading to the ruffian he called his mate and was examining the progress made on the island. His rough English face was a curious blend of awe and skepticism. "Naow was that 'ere a ship, mitey," he told Erin, "I'd s'y 'twas a maost seaworthy job, that I would, thaough she's lackin' a bit o' keel. 'N' I m'y allaow as she's not bad, not bad atawl."

Erin left him talking, paying as little attention to his speech as the captain would have to a landlubber's comments on the tub of a freighter. Hitchkins was entirely satisfied with that arrangement. The *Santa Maria* could speak for herself.

The hull was completed, except for a section deliberately left open for the admission of the main atomic generator, and a gleaming coat of silver lacquer had been applied, to give the necessary luster for the deflection of the sun's rays. In comparison to a seagoing ship, she was small, but here on the ways, seen by herself, she loomed up like some monster out of a fantasy book. Even with the motors installed and food for six years stocked, she still held a comfortable living space for the eight men who would go with her.

"I've heard as 'aow they've a new lawr passed, mikin' aout against the like o' such, thaough," Hitchkins went on. "Naow w'y would they do that?"

"People are always afraid of new things, Captain. I'm not worried about it, though." Erin turned over the bills of lading. "Have any trouble this trip?"

"Some o' the men were minded the p'y was a bit laow. But they chinged their minds w'en they come to, that they did." He chuckled. "I've a bit o' a w'y wi' the men, sir."

They were back at the dock now, watching the donkey engines laboring under the load of alloy plates that was being transferred to the machine shop. The Chinese laborers were sweating and struggling with the trucks on which these were hauled, but they grinned at him and nodded. He had no complaint with the labor Kung had obtained. If the money held out, things looked hopeful.

Jack Stewart located him, and yelled. "There's a Mr. Stewart at the office," he said flatly. "He came while you were showing Captain Hitchkins the ship, and is waiting for you. Shall I tell him to go on waiting?"

"No, I'll see him; might as well find out the worst." Stewart had visiphoned that he was coming under a temporary truce, so Erin was not surprised. "Carry on, Captain." He turned after Jack toward the shack, wishing the boy would treat his father a little less coldly. It wasn't good for a man to feel that way about his father, and he wished Stewart no personal problems.

Jack swung off toward the ship as they sighted Stewart, and the older man's eyes followed the retreating figure.

"He's a good boy, Greg," Erin said, not unkindly. "I didn't plan this, you know."

"Skip it. He's no concern of mine, the stubborn ass." Stewart held out a newspaper. "I thought you might be interested to know that the law has been passed against the use of atomic power in any spaceship. It just went through the state legislature and was signed by the governor."

"Don't you think it's a bit high-handed? I thought that interstate and international commerce was out of the hands of the state legislature."

Stewart tapped the paper. "But there's no provision against their ruling on interplanetary commerce, Erin. A few scare stories in the Sunday supplements, and a few dinners to the right men did the trick. They were sure the Martians might find the secret and turn atomic power back on us."

"So you had to come and bring me the news. I suppose you expect me to quit now and twiddle my thumbs."

"That offer of a berth on my ship—which will work—still stands. Of course, if I have to get out an injunction to stop you, it will make matters a little more difficult, but the result will be the same."

Erin smiled grimly. "That was the poorest move you've made, Greg," he said. "Your lawmakers bungled. I read the law, and it forbids the use of atomic power in the 'vacuum of space.' And good scientists will tell you that a vacuum is absolute nothing in space—but between the planets, at least, there are a few molecules of matter to the cubic inch. Your law and injunction won't work."

"You've seen a lawyer, I suppose?"

"I have, and he assures me there's nothing to stop me. Furthermore, until I reach space, the law doesn't apply, and when I'm in space, no Earth-made laws can govern me."

Stewart shrugged. "So you've put one over on me again. You always were persistent, Erin. The only man I haven't been able to beat —yet. Maybe I'll have to wait until your crazy ship fails, but I hope not."

"I'll walk down to the dock with you," Erin offered. "Drop in any time you want to, provided you come alone." He was feeling almost friendly now that success was in sight. Stewart fell in beside him, his eyes turned toward the group of laborers Jack was directing.

"I suppose—" he began, and stopped.

"He goes along, according to his own wishes."

Stewart grunted. "You realize, Erin, that one false attempt might set the possibility of the public's accepting rocket flight back fifty years. And the men in the ship would be—well, wouldn't be." He hesitated. "How much would you take to stop it?"

"You know better than that." But Erin realized that the question was more an automatic reaction than anything else. When Stewart asked that, he could see no other solution, and money had been his chief weapon since he made his first fortune.

As the man left in the little boat that had brought him, Erin wondered, though. Was Stewart licked, for once and for all? Or was it only the combination of seeing his son turned against him, and finding his carefully laid scheme hadn't made a decent fizzle? He shrugged and dismissed it. There seemed little more chance for trouble, but if it came, it would be the unexpected, and worry would do no good.

It was the unexpected, but they were not entirely unwarned. The first pale light of the false dawn showed when a commotion at the door awakened them. Doug got up grumpily and went groping toward the key. "Some darned Chinese in a fight, I suppose," he began.

Then he let out a sound that scarcely fitted a human throat and jerked back in. The others could see only two small, rounded arms that came up around his neck, and a head of hair that might have been brown in a clearer light. The voice was almost hysterical.

"Doug! Oh, I was afraid I wouldn't get here in time."

"Helen!" Doug's words were frigid, but he trembled under the robe. "What are—don't start anything. . . . I saw the letter."

They could see her more clearly now, and Jimmy whistled. No

wonder Doug had taken it so hard. She was almost crying, and her arms refused to let him go. "I knew you'd seen the first page—part of it. But you didn't read it all."

"Well?" Only the faintest ghost of a doubt tinged his inflection.

"I wasn't just acting the Saturday before; I meant it. That's why I was writing the letter—to tell Mr. Stewart I was through with him." She groped into her purse and came out with a wrinkled sheet. "Here, you can see for yourself. And then you were gone and I found this in the wastebasket where you threw it, so I didn't quit. I thought you'd never speak to me. Believe me, Doug!"

His wizened little face wasn't funny now, though two red spots showed up ridiculously on his white skin. His long, tapering fingers groped toward her, touched, and then drew back. She caught them quickly. "Well—" he said. Then: "What are you doing here, anyhow, Helen . . . Helenya?"

She jerked guiltily. "Stewart. His lieutenant—Russell—wanted the combination to your alarm system again—forgot it."

"You gave it?"

"I had to. Then I came here to warn you. There are a bunch of them, every rat on his force, and they're coming here. I was afraid you'd be—"

There was something almost wonderful about Doug then. All the silly cockiness and self-consciousness were gone. "All right," he said quietly. "Go back to the cook shack and stay there; you'll know where to find it. No, do as I say. We'll talk it over later, Helen. I don't want you around when it happens. Go on. Erin, Tom, you'll know what to do. I'll wake the Chinese and get them in order." And he was gone at a run.

VII

They didn't stop to dress fully, but went out into the chill air as they were. Doug had the Chinese lined up and was handing out the few spare weapons grimly, explaining while he worked. A tall North Country yellow man asked a few questions in a careful Harvard accent, then turned back and began barking orders in staccato Mandarin. Whether they would be any good in a fight was a question, but the self-appointed leader seemed to know his business. They were no cowards, at least.

Tom Shaw passed Jimmy a dried plug of tobacco. "Better take it," he advised. "When you're fighting the first time, it takes something strong in your mouth to keep your stomach down, son. And shoot for their bellies—it's easier and just as sure."

There was no time to throw up embankments at the wharf, so they drew back to the higher ground, away from the buildings, which would have sheltered them, but covered any flanking movement by the gunmen. Jack stared incredulously at the gun in his hand, and wiped the sweat from his hands. "Better lend me some of that tobacco," he said wryly. "My stomach's already begun fighting. You using that heavy thing?"

"Sure." The gun was a sixty-pound machine rifle, equipped with homemade grips and shoulder and chest pads, set for single fire. It looked capable of crushing Shaw's lanky figure at the first recoil, but he carried it confidently. "It's been done before; grew up with a gun in my hand in the Green Mountains."

Erin rubbed a spot over his heart surreptitiously and waited. Stewart would be defeated only when he died, it seemed, and maybe not then.

Then they made out the figures in the tricky light of the dawn, long shadows that slunk silently over the dock and advanced up the hill toward the bunkhouse. Some movement must have betrayed the watchers, for one of the advancing figures let out a yell and pointed.

"Come on, mugs," a hoarse voice yelled. "Here's our meat, begging to be caught. A bonus to the first man that gets one."

Whing! Shaw twitched and swore. "Only a crease," he whispered, "and an accident. They can't shoot." He raised the heavy gun, coming upright, and aimed casually. It spoke sharply, once, twice, then in a slow tattoo. The light made the shooting almost impossible, but two of the men yelled, and one dropped.

"Make it before sunup," he warned, as the thugs drew back nervously. "The light'll hit our eyes then and give them the advantage." Then the men below evidently decided it was only one man they had to fear and came boiling up, yelling to encourage themselves; experience had never taught them to expect resistance. Shaw dropped back onto his stomach, beside the others, shooting with even precision, while Erin and Jimmy followed suit. The rest were equipped only with automatics, which did little good.

"Huh!" Jack rubbed a shoulder where blood trickled out, his eyes still on the advance.

Erin felt the gun in his hand buck backward and realized suddenly that he was firing on the rushing men.

Jimmy's voice was surprised. "I hit a man—I think he's dead." He shivered and stuck his face back to the sights, trying to repeat it.

Shaw spat out a brown stream. "Three," he said quietly. "Out of practice, I guess."

The few Chinese with handarms attempted a cross fire as the men came abreast, but their marksmanship was hopeless. Then all were swept together, waves breaking against each other, and individual details were lost. Guns were no good at close range, and Erin dropped the rifle, grabbing quickly for the hatchet in his belt as a heavy-set man singled him out.

He saw the gun butt coming at him in the man's hand, ducked instinctively, and felt it hit somewhere. But the movement with the hatchet seemed to complete itself, and he saw the man drop. Something tingled up his spine, and the weapon came down again, viciously. Brains spattered. "Shouldn't hit a man who's down," a voice seemed to say, but the heat of fighting was on him, and he felt no regret at the broken rule.

A sharp stab struck at his back, and he swung to see a knife flashing for a second stroke. Pivoting on his heel, he dived, striking low, and heard the knife swish by over his head. Then he grabbed, caught, and twisted, and the mobsman dropped the metal blade from a broken arm. Most of the fighting had turned away down the hill, and he moved toward the others.

Jimmy spat out a stream of tobacco in the face of an opponent, just as another swung a knife from his side. Erin jumped forward, but Tom Shaw was before him, and the knife fell limply as Shaw fired an automatic from his hip. "Five," Erin heard his dispassionate voice. Beside Shaw, Hank Vlček was reducing heads with a short iron bar.

Erin moved into the fight again, swinging the hatchet toward a blood-covered face, not waiting to see its effects. Two of the Chinese lay quietly, and one was dragging himself away, but none of his other men seemed fatally injured. He scooped up a fallen knife, jumped for one man, and twisted suddenly to sink it in the side of Jack's opponent, then jerked toward the two who were driving Doug backward.

Doug stumbled momentarily, and something slashed down. Morse saw the little body sag limply, and threw the hatchet. Metal streaked through the air to bury itself in the throat of one of the men, and Erin's eyes flashed sideways. Kung stood there, another kitchen knife poised for the throwing. The remaining one of Doug's assailants saw it, too, and the knife and gun seemed to work as one. Kung gasped and twisted over on his bad leg; the knife missed, but Erin's hatchet found its mark. Only a split second had elapsed, but time had telescoped out until a hundred things could be seen in one brief flash.

And then, without warning, it seemed, the battle was over and the gunmen drew back, running for the dock. Shaw grabbed for his gun and yelled, "Stop!" A whining bullet carried his message more strongly, and they halted. He spat the last of his tobacco out. "Pick up your dead and wounded, and get out! Tell Stewart he can have the bodies with our compliments!"

Russell lay a few yards off, and their leader had been the first to fall under Erin's hatchet. Lacking direction, they milled back, less than a third of the original number, and began dragging the bodies toward the dock. Shaw followed them grimly, the ugly barrel of the machine gun lending authority to his words, and Erin turned toward Doug.

The physicist was sitting up. "Shoulder," he said thickly. "Only stunned when I hit the ground. Better see about Kung over there." Then a rushing figure of a girl swooped down, taking possession of him and biting out choking cries at his wound. Erin left him in Helen's hands and turned to the cook.

It was too late. Kung had joined his ancestors, and the big Hill Country Chinese stood over him. "A regrettable circumstance, Mr. Morse," he enunciated. "Hsi Kung tendered you his compliments and requested that I carry on for him. I can assure you that our work will continue as before. In view of the fact that you are somewhat depleted as to funds, Hsi Kung has requested that his funeral be a simple one."

Erin looked at Kung's body in dull wonder; since he could remember, the man had apparently lived only that he might have a funeral whose display would impress the whole of his native village in China. "I guess we can ship him back," he said slowly. "How many others?"

"Two, sir. Three with injuries, but not fatal, I am sure. I must congratulate your men on the efficiency with which the battle was conducted. Most extraordinary."

"Thanks." Erin's throat felt dry, and his knees threatened to buckle under him, while his heart did irregular flip-flops. To him it seemed that it was more than extraordinary none of his friends were dead; all were battered up, but they had gotten off with miraculous ease. "Can some of your men cook?"

"I should feel honored, sir, if you would appoint your servant, Robert Wah, to Hsi Kung's former position."

"Good. Serve coffee to all, and the best you can find for any that want to eat—your men as well." Then, to Shaw who had come up: "Finished?"

Shaw nodded. "All gone, injured and wounded with them. Wonder if Stewart's fool enough to drag us into court over it? I didn't expect this of him."

"Neither did I, but it will be strictly private, I'm—sure." Erin's knees weakened finally, and Shaw eased him to a seat. He managed a smile at the foreman's worried face. "It's nothing—just getting old." He'd have to see a doctor about his heart soon. But there was still work to be done. With surprise, he noticed blood trickling down one arm. Stewart had done that; it was always Stewart.

VIII

The clerks in Gregory Stewart's outer office sat stiffly at their work, and the machines beat out a regular tattoo, without any of the usual interruptions for talk. Stewart's private secretary alone sat idle, biting her nails. In her thirteen years of work, she thought she had learned all the man's moods, but this was a new one.

He hadn't said anything, and there had been no blustering, but the tension in the office all came from the room in which he sat, sucking at his pipe and staring at a picture. That picture, signed "Mara," had always puzzled her. It had been there while his wife was still living, but it was not hers.

The buzzer on the PBX board broke in, and the girl operator forgot her other calls to plug in instantly. "Yes, sir," she said hastily. "Erin Morse, on Kroll Island. I have the number. Right away, sir."

She could have saved her unusual efforts; at the moment, Stewart was not even conscious of her existence. He stared at the blank visiscreen, his lips moving, but no sound came out. There was a set speech by his side, written carefully in the last hour, but now that he had made his decision, he crumpled it and tossed it in the wastebasket.

The screen snapped into life, and the face of his son was on it, a face that froze instantly. At least they were open for calls today, which was unusual; ordinarily, no one answered the buzzer. Stewart's eyes centered on the swelling under the shirt, where the boy's wound was bandaged. "Jack," he said quickly. "You all right?"

The boy's voice was not the one he knew. "Your business, *sir?*"

Humbleness came hard to Stewart, who had fought his way up from the raw beginnings only because he lacked it. Now it was the only means to his end. "I'd like to speak to Erin, please."

"Mr. Morse is busy." The boy reached for the switch, but the other's quick motion stayed his hand.

"This is important. I'm not fighting this morning."

Jack shrugged, wincing at the dart of pain, and turned away. Stewart watched him fade from the screen's focus and waited patiently until Erin's face came into view. It was a tired face, and the erect shoulders were less erect this time.

Morse stared into the viewer without a change of expression. "Well, Stewart?"

"The fight's over, Erin." It was the hardest sentence Stewart had ever spoken, but he was glad to get it over. "I hadn't meant things to work out the way they did, last night. That was Russell's idea, the dirty rat, and I'm not sorry he found his proper reward. When I do any killing, I'll attend to it myself."

Erin still stared at him with a set face, and he went on, digging out every word by sheer willpower. "I'd meant them to blow up your ship, I admit. Maybe that would have been worse, I don't know. But Russell must have had a killing streak in him somewhere, and took things into his own hands. Who was killed?"

"A Chinese cook and two others of the same race. Your men might have done more."

"Maybe. *Men* might have. Yellow river rats never could put up a decent fight against opposition of the caliber you've got!" Stewart checked off a point on a small list and asked, "Any relatives of the dead?"

"The cook had an uncle in China—he must have slipped over the border, since he's not American-born. I'm shipping him back with the best funeral I can afford. The others came from Chinatown."

"I'll have the cook picked up today and see that he gets a funeral with a thousand paid mourners. The same to the others, and ten thousand cash to the relatives of each. No, I'd rather; I'm asking it as a favor, Erin."

Erin smiled thinly. "If you wish. Your rules may be queer, from my standards, but it seems you do have a code of your own. I'm glad of that, even if it's a bit rough."

Stewart twitched his mouth jerkily; that hurt, somehow. Erin had a habit of making him seem inferior. Perhaps his code was not the sporting one, but it did include two general principles: mistakes aren't rectified by alibis, and a man who has proved himself your equal deserves respect.

"I don't fight a better man, anyway, Erin," he admitted slowly. "You took all I handed out and came up fighting. So you'll have no trouble getting supplies from now on, and we'll complete this race on equal footing. How did Jack take it?"

"Like a man, Greg." In all the years of their enmity, neither had quite dropped the use of first names, and Erin's resentment was melting. "He's a fine boy. You sired well."

"Thank God for that, at least. Erin, you hold a patent on an air-reconditioning machine, and I need it. The government's building submarines, and I can get a nice bunch of contracts if I can supply that and assure them of good air for as long as they want to stay under." Stewart's voice had gone businesslike. "Would ten percent royalties and a hundred thousand down buy all but space rights? It's not charity, if that worries you."

"I didn't think it was." For himself, the price mattered little, but here was a chance to pay back some of the money the others had invested with him. He made his decision instantly. "Send over your contracts, and I'll sign them."

"Good. Now, with all threats gone, how about that berth on my ship I offered you? She'll be finished in a week, with a dependable fuel, and there's room for one more."

Erin smiled broadly now at Stewart's old skepticism of his methods. "Thanks, but the *Santa Maria* is practically done, too, using a dependable *power source*. Why not come with me?"

It was Stewart's turn to smile. And as he cut connections, it seemed to him that even the face in the picture was smiling for the first time in almost forty years.

Erin rubbed his wounded arm tenderly and wondered what it would feel like to go ahead without a constant, lurking fear. At the moment, the change was too radical for his comprehension. Things looked too easy.

IX

The *Santa Maria* was off the skids, and the ground swell on the ocean bobbed her up and down gently, like a horse champing at the bit. Not clipper built, Erin thought, but something they could be proud of. Now that she was finished, all the past trouble seemed unreal, like some disordered nightmare.

"Jack and I are making a test run at once," he announced. "It'll be dark in a few minutes, so you can follow our jets and keep account of our success or failure. No, just the two of us, this first time. We're going up four thousand miles and coming back down."

"How many of us go on the regular trip?" Jimmy wanted to know. "Dutch says he'll stay on the ground and design them. Since Doug's turned into a married man, he'll stay with his wife, I suppose, but how about the rest?"

They nodded in unison; though there had been no decision, it had always been understood that all were to go. Doug wrapped his arm possessively around Helen and faced Erin. "I'm staying with my wife, all right," he stated, "but she's coming along. Why should men hog all the glory?"

Erin glanced at the girl hastily. This had not been in the plans. "I'm going," she said simply, and he nodded. This thing was too great for distinction of sex—or race. He motioned to Robert Wah who stood in the background, looking on wistfully, and the tall Chinese bowed deeply.

"I should be honored, sir, by the privilege." Pleasure lighted his face quickly, and he moved forward unobtrusively, adding himself to their company. That made eight, the number the ship was designed for.

Jack was already climbing into the port, and Erin turned to follow him, motioning the others back. There was no need risking additional lives on this first test, though he felt confident of this gleaming monster he had dreamed and fought for.

"Ready?" he asked, strapping himself in. Jack nodded silently, and Erin's fingers reached for the firing keys. They were trembling a little. Here under them lay the work of a lifetime. Suppose Stewart was right, after all? He shook the sudden doubt from himself, and the keys came down under his fingers.

The great ship spun around in the water, pointing straight out toward Europe. The ground swell made the first few seconds rough riding, but she gathered speed under her heels and began skimming the crests until her motion was perfectly even. All the years Erin had spent in training, in planning, and in imagining a hundred times every emergency and its answers rose in his mind, and the metal around him became almost an extension of his body.

Now she was barely touching the water, though there was a great wake behind her that seethed and boiled. Then the wake came to an end, and she rose in the air around her, the stubby fins supporting her at the speed she was making. Erin opened up the motors, tilting the stick delicately in his hand, and she leaped through the air like a soul torn free. He watched the hull pyrometers, but the tough alloy could stand an amazing amount of atmospheric friction.

"Climb!" he announced at last, and the nose began tilting up smoothly. The rear-viewer on the instrument board showed the waves running together and the ocean seemed to drop away from them and shrink. At half power she was rising rapidly in a vertical climb.

"Look!" Jack's voice cut through the heady intoxication Erin felt, and he took his eyes from the panel. Off to the side, and at some distance, a long streak of light climbed into the sky, reached their height, and went on. Even through the insulated hull, a faint booming sound reached them. "Stewart's ship! He's beat us to the start!"

"The fool!" The cry was impulsive, and he saw the boy wince under it slightly. "There might be some small chance, though. I hope he makes it. He'll follow an orbit that takes the least amount of fuel, and we'll be cutting through with at least a quarter gravity all the way for comfort. He can't beat us."

The course of the other ship, he could see, held true and steady. Stewart knew how to pilot; holding that top-heavy mass of metal on its tail was no small job.

Jack gripped the straps that held him to his seat, but said nothing, his eyes glued on the blast that mushroomed down from the other ship, until it passed out of sight. Behind the *Santa Maria*, the pale-blue jet looked insignificant after seeing the other. Something prickled oddly at Erin's skin, and he wondered whether it was the Heaviside layer, but it passed and there was only the press of acceleration.

He opened up again as the air dropped behind, and the smooth hum of the atomics answered sweetly. Jack released himself and hitched his way toward the rear observation room, then fought the acceleration back to Erin's side. "Jets are perfect," he reported. "Not a waver, and they're holding in line perfectly. No danger to the tubes. How high?"

"Two hundred miles, and we're making about twenty-five miles a minute now. Get back to your seat, son, I'm holding her up." He tapped the keys for more power, and grunted as the pull struck them. By the time they were a few thousand miles out, most of Earth's gravity would be behind them, and they wouldn't have that added pressure to contend with. Acceleration alone was bad enough.

At the two-thousand-mile limit, Morse twisted the wheel of the control stick and began spinning her over on her tail. Steering without the leverage of atmosphere was tricky, though part of his training had taken that into account, to the best of his ability. He completed the reversal finally, and set the keys for a deceleration that would stop them at the four-thousand-mile limit.

Jack was staring out at the brilliant points made by the stars against the black of space, but he gasped as Erin cut the motors. "How far?" he asked again. "There seems to be almost no gravity."

"Earth is still pulling us, but only a quarter strength. We've reached the four-thousand mark we planned—and proved again that gravity obeys the laws of inverse squares." The novelty of the sensation appealed to him, but the relief from the crushing weight was his real reason for cutting power. Now his heart labored from weight and excitement, and he caught his breath, waiting for it to steady before turning back.

"Ready?" he asked finally, and power came on. They were already moving slowly back, drawn by the planet's pull. "Hold tight; I'm going to test my steering." Under his hands the stick moved this way and that, and the ship struggled to answer, sliding into great slow curves that would have been sudden twists and turns in the air. All his ingenuity in schooling himself hadn't fully compensated for the difficulties, but practice soon straightened out the few kinks left.

His breath was coming in short gasps as he finished; the varying stress of gravity and acceleration had hit hard at him, and there was a dull thumping in his chest. "Take over, Jack," he ordered, holding his words steady. "Do you good to learn. Half acceleration."

But the thumping went on, seeming to grow worse. Each breath came out with an effort. Jack was intent on the controls, though there was little to do for the moment, and did not notice; for that, Erin was grateful. He really had to see a doctor; only fear of the diagnosis had made him put it off this long.

"Reversal," Jack called. He began twisting the control, relying on pure mathematics and quick reactions to do the trick. They began to come around, but Erin could feel it was wrong. The turn went too far, was inaccurately balanced, and the ship picked up a lateral spin that would give rise to other difficulties. Here was one place where youth and youth's quick reflexes were useless. It took the steady hand of calculating judgment, and the head that had imagined this so often it all seemed old.

He fought his way forward, pressing back the heart that seemed to burst through his chest. Jack was doing his best, but he was not the ship's master. He welcomed Erin's hand that reached down for the stick. Experience had corrected the few mistakes of the previous reversal, and the ship began to come around in one long, accurate blast. When it stopped, her tail was steadily blasting against Earth.

"I'll carry on." Erin knew he had to, since descent, even in an atmosphere, was far trickier than it might seem. To balance the speed so that the air-fins supported her, without tearing them off under too much pressure required no small skill. He buckled himself back in, and let her fall rapidly. Time was more important, something told him, than the ease of a slower descent. He waited till the last moment before tapping on more power, heard the motors thrum solidly, and waited for the first signs of air. The pyrometer needles rose quickly, but not to their danger point. The tingling feeling lashed through him again, and was gone, and he began maneuvering her into a spiral that would set her down in the water where she could coast to the island.

He glanced back at the boy, whose face expressed complete trust, and bit at his lips, but his main concern was for the ship. Once destroyed, that might never be duplicated. Time, he prayed, only time enough. The ocean was coming into view through thin clouds below, but it still seemed too far.

"God!" Jack's cry cut into his worries. "To the left—it's the other ship."

Erin stole a quick glance at the window, and saw a ragged streak of fire in the distance. Stewart's ship must have failed. But there was no time for that. The ocean was near, now.

He cut into a long flat glide, striving for the delicate balance of speed and angle that would set her down without a rebound, and held her there. A drag from the friction of the water told him finally that she was down. More by luck than design, his landing was near the takeoff point, and the island began poking up dimly through the darkness. He threw on the weak forward jets, guessing at the distance, and juggled the controls.

There was a red knot of pain in his chest and a mist in front of his eyes that made seeing difficult, but he let her creep in until the wood timbers of the dock stood out clearly. Then the mist turned black, and he had only time to cut all controls. He couldn't feel the light crunch as she touched the shore.

Erin was in bed in the bunkhouse when consciousness returned, and his only desire was to rest and relax. The strange man bending over him seemed about to interfere, and he shoved him away weakly. Tom Shaw bent over him, putting his hands back and holding them until he desisted.

"The ship is perfect," Tom's voice assured him, oddly soft for the foreman. "We're all proud of you, Erin, and the doctor says there's no danger now."

"Stewart?" he asked weakly.

"His ship went out a few thousand miles, and the tubes couldn't stand the concentrated heat of his jets. Worked all right on small models, but the volume of explosives was cubed with the square of the tube diameter, and it was too much. We heard his radio after he cut through the Heaviside, and he was trying to bring her down at low power without burning them out completely. We haven't heard from the rescue squad, but they hope the men are safe."

The strange man clucked disapprovingly. "Not too much talk," he warned. "Let him rest."

Erin stirred again, plucking at the covers. So he finally was seeing a doctor, whether he wanted to or not. "Is there—" he asked. "Am I —grounded?"

Shaw's hand fell over his, and the grizzled head nodded. "Sorry, Erin."

X

Erin stood in the doorway of the bunkhouse, looking out over the buildings toward the first star to come out. Venus, of course, but Mars would soon show up. He had not yet told the men that the flight was off, and they were talking contentedly behind him, discussing what they would find on Mars.

A motorboat's drone across the water caught his attention and he turned his eyes to the ocean. "There's someone coming," he announced. "At least they seem to be headed this way."

Jimmy jumped up, scattering the cards he had been playing with his father. "Darn! Must be the reporters. I notified the press that tonight was supposed to be the takeoff and forgot to tell them it was postponed when you came back from the test. Shall I send them back?"

"Bring them up. There should be room enough for them here. Have Wah serve coffee." Erin moved back toward his bunk, being careful to take it easy, and sank down. "There's something I have to tell them—and you at the same time."

Helen brought him his medicine and he took it, wondering what reception his words would have with the newspapermen. Previous experience had made him expect the worst. But these men were quiet and orderly as they filed in, taking seats around the recreation tables.

Even though it had failed, Stewart's flight had taught them that rocketry was a serious business. Also, they were picked men from the syndicates, not the young cubs he had dealt with before. Wah brought in coffee and brandy.

"Your man tells us the flight has been delayed," one of them began. He showed no resentment at the long ride by rail and boat for nothing. "Can you tell us, then, when you're planning to make it, and give us some idea of the principle of flight you use?"

"Jimmy can give you mimeographed sheets of the ship's design and power system," Erin answered. "But the flight is put off indefinitely. Probably it will be months before it occurs, and possibly years. It depends on how quickly I can transfer my knowledge to a younger man."

"But we understood a successful trial had been made, with no trouble."

"No mechanical trouble, that is. But, gentlemen, no matter how perfectly built a machine may be, the human element must always be considered. In this case, it failed. I've been ordered not to leave the ground."

There were gasps from his own men, and the tray in Wah's hands spilled to the floor, unnoticed. Shaw and Jack moved about among the others, speaking in low voices.

Among the newspapermen, bewilderment substituted for consternation. "I fail to see—" the spokesman said.

Erin found it difficult to explain to laymen, but he tried an example. "When the Wright brothers made their first power flights, they had already gotten practice from gliders. But suppose one of them had been given a plane without previous experience and told to fly it across the Atlantic? This, to a much greater extent, is like that.

"Perhaps later, if rocketry becomes established, men can be given flight training in a few weeks. Until then, only those who have spent years of ground work can hope to master the more difficult problems of astronautics. This may sound like boasting to you, but an immediate flight without myself as pilot is out of the question."

Jack struck in, silencing their questioning doubts. "I tried it, up there," he told them, "and I had some experience with radio-controlled models. But mathematics and intelligence, or even a good understanding of the principles involved, aren't enough. It's like skating on frictionless ice, trying to cut a figure eight against a strong head wind. Without Erin, I wouldn't be here."

They accepted the fact, and Erin went on. "Two men, to my knowledge, spent the time and effort to acquire the basic ground work —Gregory Stewart and myself. Even though he crashed, killing two of his men, he demonstrated his ability to hold a top-heavy ship on its course under the most trying conditions. To some extent, I have proved my own ability. But Stewart has no ship and I have no pilot. Mars will have to wait until one of my own men can be given adequate preparation."

The spokesman tapped his pencil against a pad of paper and considered. "But, since each of you lacks what the other has, why not let Stewart pilot your ship? Apparently he's willing to give up his interests here and try for some other planet."

"Because he doesn't consider my ship safe." Erin knew that it might prove detrimental to their acceptance of his design, but that couldn't be helped. "Stewart and I have always been rivals, less even in fact than in ideas. Now that his own ship proved faulty, he'd hardly be willing to risk one in which he has no faith."

A broad man in the background stirred uneasily, drawing his hat farther down over his face, which was buried in his collar. "Have you asked him?" he demanded in a muffled voice.

"No." It had never occurred to Erin to do so. "If you insist, I'll call him, but there can be only one answer."

The heavy man stood up, throwing back his hat and collar. "You might consult me before quoting my opinion, Erin," Gregory Stewart stated. "Even a fool sometimes has doubts of his own wisdom." The eyes of those in the room riveted on him, but he swung to his son, who was staring harder than the others. "Will the *Santa Maria* get to Mars?" he asked.

Jack nodded positively. "It will get there, and back. I'm more than willing to stake my own life on that. But you—"

"Good. I'll take your word for it, Jack, with the test flight to back it up. How about it, Erin?" He swung to his rival, some of the old arrogance in his voice. "Maybe I'd be glory-hogging, but I understand you're in the market for a pilot. Like to see my letters of reference?"

Strength flowed back into Erin's legs, and he came to his feet with a smile, his hand outstretched. "I think you'll prove entirely satisfactory, Greg." It had been too sudden for any of them to realize fully, but one of the photographers sensed the dramatic, and his flashbulb flared whitely. The others were not slow in following suit.

"When?" a reporter asked. "Expect to be ready in the near future?"

"Why not now? The time's about right, and my affairs are in order. Is everything ready here?" Judging from their looks that it was, Stewart took over authority with the ease of old habit. "All right, who's coming? A woman? How about you, Jack?"

Jack's voice was brisk, but the cold had thawed from it. "Count me in, Dad. I'm amateur copilot."

"Me, I think I go too," Dutch Bauer decided. "Maybe then I can build better when I come back."

Erin counted them, and rechecked. "But that's nine," he demurred. "The ship is designed for eight."

Tom Shaw corrected him. "It's only eight, Erin. I've decided to let Jimmy carry on the family tradition. Shall we stay here and watch them take off?"

There was a mad rush for the few personal belongings that were to go, and a chorus of hasty good-byes. Then they were gone, the reporters with them, and the two men stood quietly studying each other. Erin smiled at his foreman, an unexpected mist in his eyes. "Thanks, Tom. You needn't have done that."

"One in the family's enough. Besides, Dutch wanted to go." His voice was gruff as he steadied Erin to the door and stood looking out at the mob around the spaceship. The reporters were busy, getting last words, taking pictures, and the Chinese laborers were clustered around Wah, saying their own adieus. Then Greg's heavy roar came up, and they tumbled back away from the ship, while the men who were to go filed in. The great port closed slowly and the first faint trial jets blasted out.

Confidence seemed to flow into the tubes, and they whistled and bellowed happily, twisting the ship and sending her out over the water in a moonsilvered path. Erin saw for the first time the fierce power that lay in her as she dropped all normal bounds and went forward in a headlong rush. Stewart was lifting her rather soon, but she took it and was off.

They followed the faint streak she made in the air until it was invisible, and a hum from the speaker sent Shaw to the radio. Greg's voice came through. "Sweet ship, Erin, if you hear me. I'll send you a copy of *Gunga Dhin* from Mars. Be seeing you."

Erin stayed in the doorway, watching the stars that looked down from the point where the *Santa Maria* had vanished. "Tom," he said at last, "I wish you'd take my Bible and turn to the last chapter of Deuteronomy. You'll know what I mean."

A minute later Shaw's precise reading voice reached him. "'And the Lord said unto Moses, This is the land which I sware unto Abraham, unto Isaac, and unto Jacob, saying, I will give it unto thy seed: I have caused thee to see it with thine eyes, but thou shalt not go over thither.' "

"At least I have seen it, Tom; the stars look different up there." Erin took one final look and turned back into the room. "Until the reporters come back here, how about a game of rummy?"

Campbell accepted the story and paid a bonus on it, though he failed somehow to notice that I was a great action writer. At least no note from him acknowledged the fact. But I was delighted to find, when it finally came out, long after it was bought, that it had a most beautiful cover painting by Hubert Rogers. Somehow, having a story illustrated on the cover of a magazine was very sweet to us newer writers in those days.

It wasn't the first cover I'd had, to be truthful. "The Luck of Ignatz" had also been a cover story. But that was such a bad one that I couldn't quite accept it. It was by Virgil Finlay, too, who was one of my favorite artists up till then. It wasn't until I met Finlay, thirty years later, that I learned why it was so bad. He drew most of his art the same size as it would be when reproduced, rather than two or three times as large. But the art director had decided that only a small corner of the painting should be used, for some idiotic reason. So that little area was blown up to many times the size it should have been —and naturally, it couldn't stand the enlargement for which it had never been intended.

I guess I cherished "The Stars Look Down" (the title was original, I thought, until I learned that A. J. Cronin had used it for a book) for years because I thought I'd proved my ability to handle action with it. I included it in my first hard-covered collection in 1947 as one of my best. But much time has passed, I've since done a great deal of real action writing as well as science fiction, and I wish now that I'd written it as I meant to originally.

It was supposed to be a conflict of ideology between the two men, without all the melodramatics. It should have been. And I wanted to show that the usual science fiction idea of two men building a spaceship in a few months was utter rubbish. Engineering such projects must take many years, a lot of money, and a large crew of men. (We hadn't yet learned that only governments could fund them.) Some of that remains in the story, but without sufficient emphasis.

Also, if I'd been busier thinking instead of trying to prove a needless point, I might have avoided a stupid error in science. I knew perfectly well that there is no feeling of gravity inside a ship falling freely in space. But here I have them with the rockets off talking about weighing a quarter as much as on the surface of Earth! I guess that mistake had been in so many stories that it had become accepted science fiction. Campbell knew his physics very well, but he didn't catch the error, and no reader complained. I wonder why.

I also wonder why I did such a bad cliché portrait of the Chinese cook. I knew better, since a couple of my friends in college were Chinese. All I can guess is that Henry in the back of my mind must have been getting even for my overworking him by spewing out the banal junk from all the bad stories in his files.

By now, I'd been writing fiction fairly steadily for seven months in 1939, and not doing too badly at it. I'd made more than a hundred dollars a month, which wasn't a bad income for me in those days. I could probably have gone on and established a fair reputation and been able to call myself a professional. But I wasn't ready for that kind of prosperity, and I still wasn't thinking of writing as anything more than a pleasant interlude.

The end to my zeal for fiction came when I happened to find a real bargain in a camera store. It was a lovely little camera, a sort of fake reflex with a good f:4.5 lens, but without a focusing viewing lens—which I didn't need, anyhow, since I knew how to focus. I'd learned my photography before anyone thought of range finders and exposure meters. There are tricks for estimating distance very closely and for measuring the true light with only one's eyes, as I have proved at times to those who claim it can't be done. So I bought the camera and assorted darkroom chemicals and equipment and went home, planning how I'd turn my closet into a darkroom and build an enlarger that would use the lens of the camera.

Since the closet was only about two feet deep and four feet wide, that involved a great deal of planning to leave me enough room between the enlarger and the developing trays for my body. But it all worked out, as did the homemade enlarger. And then, of course, I had to use all the stuff I'd spent my time on.

I take miserable pictures—technically excellent but totally uninteresting. But I am a good darkroom worker, and I have a pretty fair knowledge of photochemistry. And there were wonderful new developers, papers, and all kinds of things that had been put on the market since my last experience with photography. All of that happened to be expensive, too.

So I went about making it pay for itself, which is fairly simple in any hobby, if a man thinks about it. In those days, almost every parent had a favorite photo of a child taken on one of the automatic machines in the five-and-dimes. Kids always looked better in those little pictures, somehow. And the pictures themselves were often very sharp and capable of considerable enlargement.

So I went out looking. I could take one of the pictures, copy it onto film, and then enlarge it up to 8 by 10 on a nice heavy portrait paper with an ivory tint instead of unflattering white. Then I could sepia tone the blacks. After that, the picture could be colored easily with transparent colors, and it would look remarkably good. A lot of people were willing to pay ten dollars for one such enlargement plus a few smaller uncolored prints. And the whole operation took maybe a couple of hours and cost about half a dollar for supplies.

Then there were all kinds of experiments. I had to learn how to process film well in a darkroom that often reached a temperature of a hundred degrees, for instance. Life was full of fun and challenge again.

I did remind myself that I was supposed to be writing. I was still bugged by my difficulty in selling to *Unknown*, too. So I finally tore myself out of the darkroom and back to the typewriter. The first story was something about a fortune-teller and how her prediction came true "by coincidence, of course"—named "Coincidence," and stretched out somehow to 5,000 words. Campbell bounced it with a little note that said: "We take prediction for granted in *Unknown*. And why don't you give up your gimmick stories when they have no characters in them?" Looking it over, I began to see what he meant.

So I sat down and deliberately came up with a character. That isn't normally the way I write. I begin with an idea of some kind, and gradually build up a series of events around it to form a plot. The character of any central figure in the story evolves somehow by itself as the story gets developed and as I come to know him. How it happens, I don't know; but I get acquainted with the people in my stories in the same way I learn to know real people—by watching what they do. In this case, character was to come first, before plotting.

So I picked a characteristic and created a character from that. He was a reporter who was always late. One day he was late getting to interview a mobster and was killed along with the gangster. But he did even better. He managed to be late for the wagon that picks up souls, so he got stranded here as a ghost. And so on. I called it "The Late Henry Smith" with great cleverness, and it wrote fairly easily to 6,000 words. It came back with a very short note from Campbell: "I said characters, del Rey, not character tricks." And that was my last try at creating character in a vacuum. From then on, I let them grow by themselves.

By then, photography was moving along fairly well, and fiction obviously wasn't moving at all.

When I look through the profile written about me—which is probably the standard source of information about me in most libraries—I find that from this period on, for a couple of years at least, I was despondent and frustrated, wanting to write but somehow unable. It's probably a good guess as to the mood of anyone who seriously wants to be a writer, but I can't remember anything like that happening to me. Years later, when I ran into a prolonged writer's block (where nothing goes well, and every word looks worse than the one before, until you can't write even a note to the milkman), I suppose I should have felt that way; I was calling myself a full-time writer by then. But somehow, the despondency never came, except at those rare times when I had to write some short piece. Somehow, there were always too many other things that I wanted to do to worry about the block, which would eventually wear itself out. And during the period beginning in 1939, I had no trouble selling a fair amount of what I wrote. I was just too wrapped up in other things to bother with fiction.

In fact, during this period when I was writing almost nothing for Campbell, I did get in a bind where I needed a lot of money in a hurry. I solved it by writing confession stories. They paid much better than science fiction, were easier to do, and the magazine bought every story of that type I wrote. But once I had the money I needed, I went happily back to whatever I was doing and never wrote another confession story.

Campbell sent me a couple of ideas during the next month or so, but I returned them to him. Then he sent one that did look attractive. Apparently my "Coppersmith" had been very well liked, and the readers were asking for a sequel. One reader who collected information about myths and folklore had even made a suggestion. This was a gentleman named James Beard, with whom both Ted Sturgeon and I later collaborated.

I had never tried a sequel before. Somehow, when I was finished with a story, I never felt like going back and trying to use the same characters or background again. But this time, the idea seemed interesting, and I felt it was about time I had at least one sequel to my credit. So the little elf, Ellowan Coppersmith, was resurrected for another 6,400 words in a story called "Doubled in Brass."

7.

Doubled in Brass

(by Lester del Rey)

Ellowan Coppersmith stopped outside the building and inspected the sign with more than faint pleasure. It was a new one, gleaming copper letters on a black background catching the first rays of the sun, and showing up clearly against the newly painted walls. It read:

> DONAHUE & COPPERSMITH
> Blacksmithing—Auto Repairs
> All Work in Copper:
> RADIATORS A SPECIALTY

To be sure, it was not his idea to join Michael Donahue in partnership, but the smith had insisted when the shop was remodeled, and the elf's protests had not been too loud. Now that the sign was up, he found the sight a pleasant one. But there was work to be done, as usual, and Ellowan was not one to waste his time. He unlocked the shop and went back to his workroom, the little bells on his shoes tinkling in time to his whistling.

"Eh, now," he chuckled at the sight of the radiators waiting his work. "It's a fortune we'll be making yet, and never the need of hunting my work. I'll be wanting no more than to stay here."

The elf picked up the first radiator and placed it in the clamps on his worktable, arranged his charcoal brazier and cunning little tools, and raised his three-foot body up onto the stool. Things had indeed changed since the day when he awoke in the hills where his people had retired in sleep to escape the poisonous fumes of coal. He had found that there was little use for his skill in copper and brass; the people no longer used copper utensils, and it had been hard with him until he drifted into this town and found the smithy.

Michael Donahue had given him a copper radiator to mend, and the excellence of his work had suggested a permanent job working on the brass and copper parts of the autos and making little ornaments for the radiator caps. And though the fumes of the autos were as bad as the coal smoke which had poisoned his people, he had found pleasure in the thought that someday all the coal and gas must be used up, and his people could once more come out into the world.

As his skill had become known, more work was found. Donahue bought old radiators, Ellowan mended them better than their original, and they resold them for an excellent profit. Now the shop had been repaired, and the elf had a workroom to himself. His old clothes had given place to a modern style of dress, except for the little turned-up sandals with their copper bells; modern shoes hurt his feet. And the people of the town had become used to him, and accepted him as merely a pleasant little midget who did unusually fine work.

Under his hands, the twisted shell of the radiator which had been smashed in an accident became whole again. His little tools straightened the fins, and the marvelous flux and solder he used made the tubes watertight once more, until it was gleaming and perfect. He set it aside, and the bright glow of his brazier sank instantly into blackness as its work was done. The clock, whose hands pointed at seven, indicated it was breakfast time, and his cereal and milk would be waiting in the little lunchroom down the street.

Ellowan was coming from his own workroom to the smithy when he saw the battered little car drive up. A red-headed young man one size too large for the car climbed out. His face was pleasant and open, and he wore a wide smile, but still managed to convey the impression that whatever he had to do left him highly uncomfortable.

"Is Mr. Donahue here?" he asked of the elf.

"That Donahue is not. He'll not be coming in until the hour of eight." Ellowan studied the other and decided he liked what he saw. "And you should be the one to know that, too, Patrick."

"So you recognize me? I suppose you're Ellowan Coppersmith that my father wrote me about?"

"Aye, I'm Ellowan. Eh, now, it's thinking I was that you'd be at the college studying to be the great engineer."

"Uh-huh." The grin was distinctly sheepish now. "I couldn't stand the math. As an engineer, I'm a fine machinist, and that's all; so they told me I could come home. Now I'll have to face the music and tell Dad what happened to his plans."

"Eh, so? Now that's a shame, indeed, but not one that a good breakfast won't make better." Ellowan locked the shop carefully and started down the street, his short, stubby hand plucking at the boy. "A man takes things best at his work, and your father isn't the one to spoil a good rule. It's hungry you must be after the night of driving, and a pretty waitress to serve the food will do you no harm."

Patrick fell in behind. His face was incapable of looking anything but good-natured, nor could his worry ruin his appetite. But the waitress failed to draw more than a casual glance from him. The elf watched him carefully for signs of the normal male curiosity, then searched through his memory of Donahue's conversations for some clue.

His brown eyes twinkled as he found it, and his rough bronzed skin crinkled up until his beard threatened to stand out straight before him. "Now I'm minded that young men have a habit of not coming home when there's trouble they're in," he said calmly. "And it's not the like of what you'd do except for good reason, when there's work to be found at all. Now who might the girl be, Patrick?"

"People call me Pat, Ellowan." He took three times too long in eating the food on his fork, then answered indirectly. "I heard that Mary Kroning was seeing quite a lot of young Wilson. I don't like him, and—well, I do like her. Know them?"

"Eh, that I do. A sweet lass, and a pretty one. It's a shame, to be sure, that her father can work no more from the stroke that he had. And Hubert Wilson has the money, though I'm not saying he's the man for the girl. It's nothing but trouble we've had since his car came to the shop for our work."

Pat nodded heavy agreement. "Wilson's a swine, and looks like one."

"That may be. But I'd not be telling the girl of that," the elf advised. He counted out the price of the breakfast and carefully left the proper tip for the waitress. It had taken time, but he had finally learned that money was much cheaper than that he had used a hundred and twenty years before. Then they headed back to the shop, and the elf returned to his workbench.

But this time he did not glance at the radiators, nor did the little brazier glow brightly as he sat down. Ellowan liked the smith for his broad common sense and good-humored fellowship, and he owed him gratitude for the work and the partnership. From what he had seen, he liked the boy as well—certainly better than the greasy superiority of Hubert Wilson.

Eh, well, there was only one answer. Pat must win Mary, and to keep her, he must secure work from which he was sure of a good living. The elf chuckled suddenly, and dropped down to go over to his bag that still hung on the wall of the smithy. From within it, he produced an ingot of brass that had retained its luster through the years of his sleep, and sped back into his workshop.

There were new tools there, in addition to the old ones he had carried, tools that he polished and cared for as if they were living things. Now he switched on the motor and inserted the brass bar into a small lathe, working it deftly into the rough shape he desired. Always to him, the turning lathe partook of magic, though he understood the mechanical principles well enough. But that men should make metal serve them so easily was in itself magic, and good magic that he did not hesitate to use.

Satisfied with the rough form, he climbed back on the stool and began cutting and scraping with his instruments, breaking the bar apart in the middle to make two identical pieces. Donahue came into the smithy as he worked, and he could hear the mutter of voices after the first surprised exclamation. His sharp ears made out most of their speech, but it was the same in nature as what Pat had told him, and he went on with his work, paying them little attention. The metal was shaping up beautifully.

Again he put them on the lathe, shaping up the base of the figurines and cutting threads on them. Completed, they were little statues, a few inches high, molded above a conventional radiator cap. But they were unusual in lacking the conventional streamline greyhound or bird; instead they carried small replicas of Ellowan himself, as he had looked in the old jerkin and tights when he first came to town, and the eyes seemed to twinkle back at him. He chuckled.

"It's neat copies you are, if I do say it myself, and it's good material you have in you. I'm thinking there were never yet better ornaments —nor more useful," he told them. "Almost I'm sorry to silver the one of you."

Donahue and Pat came into the room as he finished the silvering. "The boy's staying with us for the time," Donahue informed the elf. "But I'll not be moving you; he's taking the guest room until he finds a job. When might you be done with the Wilson car?"

Ellowan was unscrewing the old cap and putting the silvered copy of himself in its place. "Finished it is now, all new wires. And a free cap I'll give him for the money it costs." He looked at the ornament in place and nodded, well pleased. Surely Hubert Wilson would like it. It was novel and shiny enough to please his love of display.

Pat examined the copper one thoughtfully. "You're an artist, Ellowan. But I prefer this to the other; the color suits you better, and I think the face is more cheerful. Who's this for?"

"Who but yourself, lad? There's never a bright spot on the car that you drive, and this will serve, I'm thinking."

"And more than he deserves," Donahue said. "Now be off, you young fool, and don't bother honest men at their labors. There's food in the icebox, and your credit will be good at the store. Since it's loafing you'll be, loaf at home." When Pat had gone, he winked at Ellowan and grinned.

"Now there's a boy for you, Coppersmith. And it's glad I am that he'll be wasting no more time at school. *Foosh!* 'Twas time and money wasted, that it was." The ways of a father and son change little with the passing of time.

Ellowan nodded silently and went back to his work, while Donahue stepped into the smithy and began hammering out iron on the anvil. If a man had work, there was little more he needed, save a wife for the young and a son for the old.

The moon was full and the air was cool and sweet. Ellowan sat on the back porch with Donahue, each smoking thoughtfully and saying little. Out in the garden there was a sudden rustling sound, then a faint *plop-plop* on the grass before them. The smith looked down.

"More rabbits," he said. "Now where would they all be coming from, this near the town? *Shoo!* Go along with you! I'd have no rabbits eating my vegetables."

The rabbits looked up at him, and one of them thumped a hind leg nervously on the ground, but they refused to move. Ellowan caught Donahue's arm as he started to rise. "They'll not harm the garden." He made a little clucking sound in his throat and the rabbits drew closer. "It's to see me they've come, and there's not a leaf of the place they'll touch, except such weeds as they like."

"Friends of yours?"

"Now that they are, as you should know. Haven't the Little People and rabbits been friends since they hid together in the same burrows from the giants? But I'll send them away and let you say the words you'd be thinking." Again he made the clucking sounds, and the rabbits kicked out a little thudding chorus on the grass, then turned and hopped peacefully away—all except one that went out into the yard to examine some weeds that looked edible.

Donahue watched it for a few minutes, then turned back to the elf. "I'm sorry for the boy. His heart's set on the girl, but it's only right that she'd be thinking of her father needing care and the mother with hardly enough to live on. And money comes hard to a young man here. Never a chance does he have."

"Eh, so; but there's many a girl who thinks of money but doesn't choose it. I'd not be worrying about the boy." The elf picked up a package at his feet and brought out three small articles that looked like dust filters to be worn over the nose. "What might ozone be?"

"Eh? Oh, ozone. Have you smelled the air close to the big electric motor? Well, that'll be the stuff. Why, now?"

"I bought these at the drugstore and the clerk was telling me they settled the dust, cleaned the air, and gave off ozone. See, there's a battery that's to be worn on the waist, and a wire to run to the thing. Do you think it might make bad air good?"

"It might that. But precious little ozone you'll get from those batteries, though some there might be. I've seen the like of it used for hay fever."

"Aye. That he told me. And that there were big machines to make more of it for an office. I was for trying it on, and he let me. 'Tis a wonderful invention, I'm thinking."

"Maybe." The smith rose, stretching his big frame. "Though there's more interest in bed, to be sure, that I have. A good night to you." He turned into the house.

Ellowan whistled softly, and two rabbits stuck their heads out of the bushes and came closer.

"Now, maybe you'd like a ride?" he asked them, and listened to the thudding of their feet. "So? Then come along." He headed for a shed, their little bodies following quietly. For a second he disappeared, while they waited patiently, to come out with a small-framed bicycle. Since the time when a boy had carried him into the town on a wheel, the elf had been fascinated with such an easy way of traveling, and his first money had gone into the purchase of one, built specially to fit him, and equipped with a three-speed device.

He put his bundle into the basket and picked up the rabbits. They were familiar with such rides and made no protest as he put them beside the bundle. He chuckled. "Now, it's a longer ride you'll get this night. I've five hours before the boy'll be coming home, or he's not what I'm thinking, and there's more than a little road to be covered in that time."

They flattened out, little noses quivering with excitement, and he mounted quickly. There were strong muscles in his corded short legs, and the speed that he made would have surprised the boys who saw him riding only around the town. The road slipped by him smoothly and silently, his faint whistling broken only by a few muttered words. "And they'll be filling the air with poison when there's the like of this to be ridden. Eh, well."

Ellowan's guess as to the time of Pat's return was a shrewd one. The little elf had barely put his bicycle away and turned the rabbits loose when the battered car came chugging along. He settled back on a seat and watched the auto, paying no attention to the rabbits that scampered back and forth across the driveway.

Nor did Pat; his thoughts were not on the driving, and his eyes were only focused enough to enable him to reach the garage. Sure of the elf's protection, the rabbits gave no more thought to the car than the man did to them.

Since no one else bothered, the car seemed to take matters into its own hands. A rabbit sat placidly chewing a leaf until the wheels were within a few feet of it. The little car jerked, bucked sideways, and left the driveway for the lawn, only to run toward another squatting there. Again it bucked, seemed to consider, and found no opening. The motor roared, and it darted forward, straight toward the animal. Then the wheels left the ground abruptly, front first, followed by the rear, and the auto headed for the garage, leaving the rabbit eating steadily where he had first been.

Ellowan chuckled as Pat came out of the garage, swearing under his breath. "'Tis a pleasant car you have, methinks," the elf observed.

"Must have hit a rock somewhere. I thought sure I'd hit one of those silly animals, but it seems I didn't." Pat pulled at one ear and stared back at the garage. "I've had trouble with the car all evening. First it backfired; almost seemed to pick the times when Mary and I started to quarrel. Then it stopped out in the country, and I couldn't start it for an hour."

"Now it's little trouble I'd call that. Was she minding the stop?"

"Well," the boy admitted, "she didn't seem to. But it's no go, Ellowan. She even told me she wished I'd never come back."

"Eh, so? Now there are many reasons she could have for that, indeed. When a girl likes a boy, and there's money she needs that he'll not be having, perchance she'd welcome him less because of the liking she has." The elf smiled at some joke of his own.

Pat nodded slowly. "Maybe you're right, at that. But money doesn't grow on trees."

"It depends on the man who owns the tree. There's a wonderful demand for ornaments of brass, wrought by true craftsmen. I'd a letter from a man who'd been seeing some of the work I do, and it was wanting me to make more for his trade, and at good prices, too. Now, if you were to start a small factory for the making of hinges and doorknobs, ashtrays and fruit bowls, there'd be money for you."

"Uh-huh. I thought of that when I saw your radiator cap. But it takes money to start, and workmen in brass are rare. I'd need money, some machinery, a building, and men—even if you know of a market. That's a tall order."

"Mayhap. Don't be worrying your head with it, lad. The sleep's more needed than the money. And I'll be getting a bit myself." Ellowan nodded good night as they passed inside and turned to his own room, still chuckling over the action of the car. Eh, now, that was good brass in the ornament, and unusual, too.

It was another night, and the elf had finished supper and gone to his own room. From a bureau drawer he drew out a handful of thin sticks and tossed them on the floor, studying them thoughtfully until they made sense to him. "Now, they're not the equal in prediction to the future itself, but they seem sure enough," he muttered. "And the boy's been telling me his Mary was seeing the Wilson pup this night. I'm thinking a ride might do me no harm."

He pocketed the runes, hoping their information might be accurate, as it sometimes was, and went out to his bicycle, tossing a small bag in the basket. Rabbits hopped around, thumping out their desire to go with him, but he shooed them off and set out alone. He slipped out of the town in short order, and out through the pleasant moonlit country around, until he came to a little winding lane that led back through a wooded section. There was a tiny clearing a way farther on, and tire marks on the dirt indicated that it was not unknown to the boys of the town.

Ellowan turned back into the woods, some distance below the clearing, and concealed his wheel. From the bag he pulled out a large cloth and tied it about his face, over his nose. Then he whistled shrilly, and sat down to wait until the rabbits could respond, studying the runes again. Satisfied with them, he looked up at the circle of gray bodies and bright eyes around him. Little muttered words came to his lips, while the noses of the rabbits twitched excitedly.

They started off obediently, if somewhat reluctantly, each going in a direction slightly different from the others. There was another wait before two returned. Then he whistled the others to cease and followed the first rabbit, the second hopping along behind. They passed through most of the woods before they reached their objective.

A small animal with a bushy tail was sedately looking under a log for insects, and the stripes along its back identified it clearly. Ellowan muttered unhappily, and the rabbits refused to go farther. The elf sidled in cautiously, careful not to make a hostile move, and began dropping the food from the bag to the ground, making a trail back toward the clearing. Watching him carefully, the skunk moved over and investigated the line of food, moving along slowly, in no haste to go anywhere.

The second rabbit led off a short distance to another skunk, and the process was repeated until both trails joined and were connected to the clearing. There the elf scattered the remainder of the bag's contents and moved hurriedly away, seeking a position upwind from the spot, but well within range of his sharp eyes and ears.

He felt nauseated and cursed his own dumbness for being unable to plan a better scheme. "*Aghh!*" he grunted. "It's bad enough the fumes of coal may be, but this smell is worse. If I'd not met one once before, I'd never believe there'd be such beasts. In that, the Old Country is better than the new. *Ehu!*"

The wait was longer this time, and the moon crept up until its light shone full on the clearing. Ellowan tossed the runes again, but they were still in the same pattern, and he muttered. Three times should be proof enough, but their prediction had still not come true. Then the faint sound of a car came from down the lane, and he watched tensely until it appeared.

It was the right one, with the little silvered figure shining on the top of the radiator. A low, heavy convertible it was, chosen with the obvious bad taste and love of display that were typical of the Wilsons, but money in goodly quantity had gone into its purchase. Inside, the elf made out the fat, smirking face of Hubert Wilson, and the troubled face of Mary Kroning.

Wilson swung it up in a rush, braked sharply where the wheel marks were thickest, gunned the motor, and cut it off. Out of the car came words in Wilson's pompous voice.

"Runs pretty sweet now. But the way Donahue fixes cars, I suppose it'll go to pieces again in a week. Charged me sixty bucks for the work, and probably palmed off the shoddiest material he could find. I told him so, too."

Mary's weak protest sounded tired and Ellowan guessed that there had been little sleep for her the night before. "I don't think Mr. Donahue would do that to you. He's always been very careful in the work he did for us, and his prices are lower than we can get elsewhere."

"Sure, why wouldn't they be when it's the only way he can get work? Anyway, he's crazy enough to think you'll marry that dumb son of his." Wilson moved slightly on the seat and Mary drew back into a corner. "And that reminds me; I heard you were out with him last night, and I don't like it. Probably got in trouble and kicked out of college, so he comes sneaking back here to his father. You keep away from him, understand? I don't want my girl going with such people."

"He's not dumb, and he didn't get in trouble. I think—" She checked the words quickly and deliberately softened her voice. "I'm not engaged to you yet, Hubert, and I don't think you should try to dictate my choice of friends. I've known Pat for years. Why shouldn't I see him when he returns?"

"Because I don't like it and won't have it! I used to think you were sweet on him, but that's all done. Anyway, he couldn't take you to the movies now, even the cheap ones. His old man's spent most of his money fixing up the shop and just paid back the loan from our bank."

"Let's not argue, Hubert. I'm tired, too tired for another quarrel. I wish you'd take me home."

"Aw, it's only eleven. Stay here a little while and we'll go over to the Brown Pudding Inn. It's the most expensive place around, and they've got an orchestra that's really hot!"

"I'm tired, Hubert, and I don't want to go to the inn. I've been looking for work all day. Take me home and I'll see you tomorrow and let you take me to the inn if you want."

"If that's the way you feel." He straightened up slowly, a petulant frown on his face. "Anyway, I told you you didn't need work; I'll send your dad to the hospital and take care of you if you'll promise to marry me. Oh, all right. But why don't you let me get you a job in the bank? All I gotta do is say the word and you're hired."

Ellowan saw that Wilson was making slow signs of giving in and leaving, and he decided it was time to act. The big rabbit at his feet thumped heavily at his orders, then loyalty conquered instinct, and it moved off. As it left, the elf saw two pairs of eyes shining in the underbrush, and the skunks poked sharp little heads through to gaze at the quantity of food nearer the car. They moved forward slowly, uncertain of the auto, but fairly confident of their natural protection.

Wilson was grabbing for the brake when the rabbit scampered out of the woods into the clearing and headed for the car. With a bound, it hopped to the running board, jumped from there to the hood of the engine, and cleared the windshield to land in Wilson's lap. His clawing hands missed it, and it was in the back seat, leaving a streak of mud on the newly laundered suit and a scratch from a sharp toenail on his forehead. The words he said were ones no lady should hear from a man.

Again it bounced, landing on his head, then thumping down on the hood again. Wilson sprawled out, diving for it, and the rabbit hit the ground and began circling the man, just out of reach. "Get out of that car and help me catch this thing!" he shouted at Mary. "For the love of Peter, don't sit there like a bump on a log! Aren't there any brains under your hair?"

"Leave it alone and come back to the car. You can't catch it, and I want to go back."

"I don't care what you want; I'll fix this fellow." He stopped his frantic attempts and climbed back in the car. "Maybe I can't catch it, but we'll see what the car can do."

Ellowan's eyes turned back to the skunks, moving along toward the manna from heaven they saw and smelled in the clearing. They knew perfectly well that the insane hoppings of the rabbit were harmless, and took no notice of them.

Wilson gunned the motor and threw the machine into second savagely. It jerked forward, straight at the rabbit—and straight for the skunks. This was a new menace to them, and they jerked their heads up and erected the danger signal of their tails. Wilson did not see them, nor did he notice a sudden change in the radiator cap. The two brass hands were creeping slowly up over the little nose.

The car bucked and backfired, and the wheels seemed filled with life, trying to drag the car to the right. The gear lever suddenly shifted to neutral and the car stopped. Alert and poised for action, the skunks were waiting on a hair-trigger balance; the rabbit decided it was time to leave.

But now Wilson's anger was transferred to the car, and he fought it fiercely, jamming it back into gear. It backfired again, and the skunks decided they had waited long enough. With a unison of action that seemed preplanned, they opened fire and the wind favored them. Mary took her frightened eyes off Wilson and tried to hide her nose from the stench. Wilson let go of the wheel, and his face turned pale and sick.

But the car, left without a guiding hand, took matters onto itself. The front end jumped up and twisted around, and the machine bobbed in a crazy circle, streaking away from the skunks. It slowed and the engine sputtered and coughed, then seemed to decide things could be no worse than they were, and stopped.

Wilson opened his mouth and spilled out words, first at the car, then at Mary. She bore it in stolid silence for a few minutes, but there are limits to all things, even the need of money. Ellowan grinned as she reached for the door and climbed out, turning down the lane toward the general highway and leaving young Wilson ranting to himself.

Then a vagary of the wind let a few whiffs of the air from the clearing reach the elf, and he ran back toward his bicycle. His work was done, and it was an excellent time to leave.

Business in the smithy was slack the next day, and Donahue was across the street, playing billiards, when Pat came into the shop in the early afternoon, looking much more cheerful than previously. "Mary's given up Wilson," he announced, as he might have spoken of discovering perpetual motion. "She called me up this morning, and we've been talking things over since then. I don't know what happened, but she's through with him."

"Eh, now, and it's glad I am to hear that." Ellowan dropped his work and squatted on a bench across from the boy, wondering how well she had rid herself of the smell of skunk. "And did she tell you she'd be marrying you?"

Some of the joy went out of Pat's face. "No, but she practically did. I've got to get a job, though, paying enough to support her and help the family along. She'll probably find work for a while, and it won't take so terribly much. They've almost enough to live on. But I'll need at least twice as much as I can make here."

"There'd be money in the selling of handmade brass trinkets," the elf pointed out again. "A very good sum, indeed, and immediately. Now, I've been doing some work with figures, and I'm thinking you'd be making more than you need, and could pay back the expense of the shop in little time, if your craftsmen knew the knack of the material."

"I figured it up too, from the letter you got giving prices, and there's a gold mine in it for a plant with a few workers. But where can I get men who can do the type of work you turn out? That's where the money is. And where would I get the initial outlay?"

"All in good time now." Ellowan filled his pipe and puffed at it thoughtfully. "It seems that the Wilsons have arrived as they telephoned. A bit of business and we'll talk this over afterwards, lad."

The Wilsons had indeed arrived, Hubert's car in front, driven by the chauffeur, and the banker driving his own car at a good distance off. Hubert Wilson stood on the front bumper of his auto, looking more miserable than seemed possible; his hand rested on the silvered radiator cap, and his thumb was caught between the little brass arms. The boys along the street added nothing to his comfort.

The older Wilson came bristling in, growling gruff words. "I'll slap a suit on you that'll make your ears ring," he threatened. "Hubert's caught in that thing you made, and can't get loose, unless we amputate his thumb. The metal simply can't be cut, for some reason."

"That suit now," the elf answered. "It might not help the thumb, and there's little fault I have in the matter. 'Tis his own carelessness. You should know that."

Since bluffing didn't work, Wilson tried the only other argument he knew. "All right, but get him loose. I'll give you fifty dollars for it and forget the whole thing."

Ellowan demurred. "There's a most unpleasant odor about the car," he pointed out. "I'm overly sensitive to such an odor, and there's fear in my heart that it might be poisonous to me. But if you'll come into the garage, I'll be glad indeed to talk of the matter with you."

Back in the building, the banker stormed and ranted, but it did him no good. The quiet words of the elf, inaudible to Pat, conquered in the end. "And I'll have it in cash, you understand," he finished. "I'm not used to these checks, nor liking of them."

Wilson looked through the window at the sight of his son caught in that humiliating position and gave in. "Robber!" he growled. "I'll send a boy with it, and to fetch your note." He stalked out of the shop quickly, climbed into his car, and drove off toward the bank.

Ellowan waited until the boy showed up, and exchanged a package for a piece of paper from the elf. Then he wrapped his face in moist cloths and took his tools out where Hubert Wilson stood. With a direction of purpose that gave no heed to the swearing and pleading of the man, he applied his little pinchers and pulled the arms loose from the thumb; the brass responded easily to his tug.

"And now," he said, unscrewing the cap and substituting one with a greyhound on it, "you'd best be off. We'll not be wanting your trade hereafter." He swung quickly into the shop, unmindful of the retort that reached his ears, and watched the car pull away. When the sickness from the stench left him, he turned back to Pat.

"Now as I was saying, there's money in copper artistry. And there's a building down the street that'll be lending itself perfectly to the work. It's quite cheap you could get it. As for the tools you'd need, they'd be few, since handwork is better for this than the cleverness of many machines."

"It would take at least three thousand dollars to start, and I'd have to get workers and pay them." Pat shook his head sadly. "Better forget it, Ellowan."

"Eh, so? And it's mistaken you are. In this pile you'll find the sum of five thousand of your dollars, which should start the shop and let you marry the girl when she will." He tossed the package over casually.

Pat grinned, but shoved it back. "So you blackmailed Wilson, did you? That's a high price for letting the youngster loose."

"It's not too high, I'm thinking, since it's but a loan. You'll be paying me, and I'll give it to him—with five percent interest, to be sure. And perhaps you'd turn up your nose at a chance to marry the girl when it's only a business agreement?"

Pat pocketed the money. "That way, I'll take it, provided you let me pay you at six percent. How long does your note run?"

"Five years, and you'll pay me but five percent, as I pay the banker. I'm tired indeed of the arguing you'd be doing." Ellowan turned back to his workroom. "Now it's workers you need, eh?"

"And it's workers I won't find, probably. Where can brass craftsmen be found who can do any amount of work by hand?"

The elf grinned and disappeared into the shop. He whistled once and reappeared, but not alone. Behind him were three others like him, differing but little, and all clearly of the Little People. They were dressed in brown leather clothes of a cut older than the mechanical age, but about their noses were filters with wires leading down to little batteries at their belts. Ellowan chuckled.

"Here, now, are the workers I brought back for you," he told Pat. "You'll find them quick with their hands and good workers, not greedy for money. But you'll be needing one of those machines that'd make ozone for the whole shop—only a little, but enough to counteract the poison of the air. 'Tis a marvelous invention. Now be off with you, and leave me with my friends. I'd have none of your thanks."

As Pat went out, shaking his head but smiling, the four elves turned back to the workroom, and Ellowan knew his task was well done. The boy would have the girl and his work would prosper, while the elf would no longer be alone in a world of men.

One of the others drew off his filter and tested the air. "Bad," he grunted. "But now that you've wakened us, there seems little enough harm in it. Perchance the years of sleep have given us strength against the poison fumes."

More likely it was the call to work, Ellowan reflected, stronger even than the poisons of the air. And someday when the boy's plant expanded, the call would be greater, and others might be awakened until the Little People could come into their own again. They were sleeping in the hills now, but not for long.

The rabbits were James Beard's idea. He wrote me that back in the days when the giants invaded the land, the Little People were given sanctuary in the holes of the rabbits, and that since then there has been a close relationship between them. But skunks were never seen there. So what would an elf think of a skunk? The rest of the story was mine.

Campbell and the readers were apparently satisfied with it, but I wasn't sure. It seemed to me that Ellowan was more sympathetic in the first story, and that I might better have left him as he was. I still feel the sequel was a slight mistake, though not a bad one. And since then, I've deliberately avoided writing sequels, except much later when publishers demanded them for juvenile books. I've had a number of ideas for stories to follow others, but I've put them firmly aside.

Still, for personal reasons, I'm glad I wrote the story. I'd been vaguely deciding to go up to New York to see Campbell for a while before, and the story gave me a good excuse. I put it into an envelope, dug out some other stuff, and went up by bus.

Street and Smith published *Astounding* then, from headquarters in an old building at the corner of Seventh Avenue and Fifteenth Street. (I always study maps before I go anywhere, and I have a good memory, so I had no trouble getting about by subway, which conveniently went from near my hotel to where I was going.) The building was old, and the elevator was one that had seen better days. Isaac Asimov writes of the smell of printing paper, but I never noticed it, though great bales of it were stacked about. My nose was probably deadened by smelling it too often in a newspaper office. But I did smell a kind of moldy odor. I didn't find it very exciting.

Nor was the entrance to Campbell's office anything to rave about. It was down one twisty little hallway after another, with the door skillfully hidden by more paper in bales.

But there was no hiding the man behind the desk as he stood up to welcome me. He was huge, and he seemed to lift the even huger barrel of his chest ponderously, as if by effort. A head with a stiff bristle of close-cropped hair seemed balanced precariously on heavy shoulders. The nose was sharp, the eyes piercing. Then the face broke into a smile, and he suddenly looked like some overgrown pixie. That was my first view of John W. Campbell.

"We-e-ehlll, del Rey," he said in a rather high voice. The tone was somewhat amused at the specimen before him, but warm in spite of that. "Take a chair. You're not at all what I pictured."

I'd had that reaction before. I stretched to five-feet-five early in the morning, and then weighed exactly the eighty-nine pounds that was synonymous with a weakling in the ads. So I grinned back and admitted that he wasn't exactly what I'd expected.

He chuckled at that and settled back, stuffing a fresh cigarette into a holder. He took my manuscript, tossed it aside negligently, and nodded to a pile of magazines. "Seen the latest *Astounding*?"

I had, and we immediately went into a long discussion of the stories in it, followed by his account of the great stories he had lined up for future issues. He'd apparently just accepted either an outline or the finished story by A. E. van Vogt with the strange title of "Slan" and was bubbling with enthusiasm for it. (It deserved his praise.) He told me enough to whet my appetite, then leaned back and grinned. "And now can you guess where the supermen are hiding?"

"Did you say this dictatorship had a palace?" I asked.

For a second, he frowned. Then he nodded slowly and chuckled. "Okay. Suppose you drop back here about five, and I'll take you out to my place for supper," he suggested, dismissing me.

He hadn't said a word about my writing, and didn't during the whole visit. But somehow, he'd made a lot of points about what he wanted, and had managed to teach me more than I realized until I had time to digest it.

When I went back, he had the check waiting for me. I know that John hated to bother the front office, but this was only the first of many times when he did so to get me a quick check. He was like that.

That evening, after supper, we inspected his fuel battery. He had written a story about one once, but I didn't know he'd actually built one. It didn't work very well, but it was a prototype of the fuel cells later developed for work in space, and he had every right to be proud of it. Then we talked mostly like good fans about the old days of science fiction—all the way back to 1930!

The next day, I went in to see another editor. Frederick Pohl had just begun working for Popular Publications, editing *Astonishing Stories* for them at some minuscule salary. What a contrast! Here, everything was efficient and busy, with well-laid-out offices, a standard receptionist, and all the trappings of business. Only Fred seemed out of place, sitting behind a desk with his shoes propped up on it. We talked briefly about business, and he took the copies of "It Comes Out Here" and "Ice" I'd brought along as an excuse to see this famous science fiction fan. Then we spent some time talking about our real interest—fans and fandom.

I had one other visit to make. I'd corresponded in a sort of mutual admiration with L. Sprague de Camp, and he'd invited me by postcard (he never used anything but postcards, so far as I knew) to drop in. We had a marvelous visit, discussing phonetics more than science fiction, and then he invited me to go down with him to see the Naval Games. I'd read about these mock sea battles with tables of statistics and model ships, but wasn't the least interested. However, I was interested in the men who would be there. I was still enough of an unabashed fan to be a bit in awe of a room that contained Fletcher Pratt, L. Ron Hubbard, and I forget how many other writers. (This was before Dianetics, when Hubbard was a writer of numerous pulp stories; in those days, he was a big genial redhead who could tell whopping good stories about all the adventures nobody believed he'd had.) And when Sprague finally let me off outside my hotel, I was in something of a daze. I was also filled with inspiration—any visit to Campbell seemed to produce that—and eager to get back to the typewriter.

I got over it fairly quickly. I'd figured out an incredibly clever idea about a man who comes down from heaven on a visit, equipped with enough miracles to take care of the trip. Unfortunately, they're all second-class ones, because he chose by quantity instead of quality. I knew it was a great idea as I began it. Somehow, by the time I had put 6,400 words on paper, I was less sure. But I sent "Miracles, Second Class" off to Campbell. Its speedy return somehow dampened all my writing enthusiasm, and I went back to having fun with other business.

But in December, there was another idea for a story from John—or this time, really from Willy Ley through John. It suggested a very good story, but I was busy then with stuff I was supposed to deliver well before Christmas. As a result, I rushed the story through the typewriter without taking enough time to think it over. I finished writing and retyping the 11,000 words of "Reincarnate" in one day, once I had the basic idea worked out, and waited, half expecting it to be returned. But instead, I got a prompt check for $137.50, which made my year's total come out to a little over $1,000. It was the most I was to make from writing for a long time.

8.

Reincarnate

(by Lester del Rey)

I

Thorne Boyd lay in a dark tarry pit under black stars that threw out hot blinding points of jagged lightning. And the lightning was aimed at him, crashing down in a steady tumult of sound that shattered into his mind and kept him from fainting. Where the pinpoint lightning struck, pain lanced out with soul-tearing force that threatened to sear his flesh from his bones. It was hot and cold, and all the sensations of a lifetime seemed determined to pile up on him in one malefic swoop.

The sensation was too much for his body; it tore itself away from him, leaving his brain stranded in the pit, and went tearing off through the turgid blackness. Without senses, his mind yet followed it, striving to draw it back.

"Come back, body!" he yelled at it, but there was no sound save the thundering yammering of the lightning. That seemed in some mysterious way to sense his ultimate nakedness, for it crashed down more fiercely, and the black stars threw off their veils, revealing themselves as vultures soaring in a murky sky. With inexorable precision, they wheeled slowly down toward him, beady red eyes feasting on the sight of his naked brain.

Wild thoughts ran through his mind. "Poe'd love this—only they aren't ravens." Then there was no time for thought. The monsters were so near that their wings beat a brazen cacophony in his ears. He had to leave. In a frenzied struggle, he thrust out wisps of matter from his brain to serve as legs and began running, running—but the smooth surface of the pit held him fast, and his false legs were too weak. The birds sank lower. One of them came to rest.

A strong beat, as of a heart, pulsed madly through his mind, and he let out one frantic cry that reverberated in a pitch too high for sound. Then his mind tore free and went soaring down and away, through Stygian depths that went on endlessly, toward some unknown goal. Something snapped.

"Crazy dream," he thought. Or was it? He was still in darkness, set with jagged flashes of light that formed no pattern, and sound that rushed on in a muffled discordant roar. Pain was all about him. But the insanity of fear was gone, and he began groping for a rational solution.

He could not feel his body, though that was due to the pain, probably. There had been an accident—or was that a part of the dream? And today was to be his wedding day. He struggled to get up, but his only response was a fresh stab of pain. Well, if he had to lie there, there was no other solution. Maybe there had been an accident, fatal—and this might be Hell. It certainly wasn't the other place.

Boyd settled his mind into rough order and subdued the larger part of the fear. The immediate past was still clouded, but perhaps if he went back over it, starting at the beginning of the day, some clue would come. If nothing else, a chronological review would take his mind off his present condition.

It had been the big day toward which they had been working. The smokestacks were throwing out their columns of inky oil smoke, telling of power feeding into the turbines that furnished the station with a steady, dependable supply of high-voltage, direct-current electricity. Allan Moss, old and bent, but still with the hot fire that had made him the world's greatest mathematician and physicist, was helping Boyd inspect the safety suits.

"Lot of good they'll do if anything happens in there," he grunted. "You better let me go in alone, Thorne."

Boyd shook his head, and his eyes traveled past to a figure motioning for him around the corner. Moss followed his gaze and chuckled. "Go on, son, don't keep her waiting."

Joan Abbot's dark hair was flying in the wind, her eyes filled with bubbling deviltry that seemed never to leave them. "Meany," she greeted him. "I'll bet you forgot that tomorrow was to be our day. You and your old work."

He grinned at her awkwardly, not quite sure of her banter, but pleased by it, as always. He needed her lightness and gaiety, her willingness to find the sunnier side of everything in direct contrast to his own character. Seen through her eyes, life must be a wonderful thing. Time had taught him that under the effervescence and impulsive enthusiasm there was a mind he could meet and respect.

"I haven't forgotten. Moss has agreed to drive us away as soon as he can get rid of your father, and I have the license in my pocket. Only I wish you'd let me tell your father we're being married."

"No, you can't do that. Wait till it's over and I'll spring it on the old dear. Mmm, and won't he growl, though! But it never does him any good." She gurgled and stretched herself up on tiptoes to grab for his neck. "Let's run away now! Let's, Thorne."

"No can do." He scraped his unshaven face down against hers, grinning slowly as she slapped at him. "Anyway, you're only teasing me."

She crinkled her nose up at him. "How'd you guess? Mmm." The pause that became necessary was definitely not unpleasant. "All right, Pickleface, you can go back to your work, but if you leave me at the altar—"

Moss looked up at them and tucked an almost paternal smile away in the corner of his mouth. "Been poking your nose into things that were none of your business again, youngster?" he asked her.

She nodded, peering over his shoulder at the suits. "Mm-hmm. One of the men opened the casing around your atom-smasher and let me look inside. I promised him I wouldn't tell you who he was."

"And did you understand anything you saw?"

"A little. I've been studying lately, so I'd know what Thorne is doing. He'll talk about his work all the time, and a good wife should understand, shouldn't she? What's a restrictive field, Dr. Moss?"

Moss shoved the work aside and sat down opposite her. He was always willing to answer her eternal questions, and managed somehow to make it clear. Something inside the old scientist went out to the insatiable curiosity that filled her. "A restrictive field is just what its name implies. It's a field of force generated around something and designed to hold that something within certain limits or patterns. You might say that a magnet exerts such a field on iron filings to keep them from scattering and line them up in definite patterns. Only we're using a field to hold neutrons in the uranium 'fuel' and not let them dissipate uselessly as they try to. Understand?"

"Mm. Well enough." She ran curious fingers inside the suit and examined it. "What's this for?"

"In case there's trouble inside. Just an added precaution." Boyd picked her up and set her out of his way while she squeezed his nose with a little hand. The cooing sound she made embarrassed him, but he wouldn't have made her stop it for an extra arm. "Dr. Moss and I aren't taking any risk, you see."

She appealed to Moss again, a serious note in her voice. "Why do either of you have to go? Couldn't you control it from outside or use automatic machinery?"

"Not well enough. Automatic machinery can't do things it isn't designed for. When we start ripping atoms to pieces, we'll have to expect the unexpected. That's what men were built for—emergencies."

She brushed her hair away from troubled eyes, and a frown had taken the place of her impish deviltry. "Thorne, I'm scared. Call it a sudden premonition, if you like, but don't go in there. Or let me go with you. Please."

"You stay out here and it'll be over before you know it. There's no real danger," he assured her. "If we thought there were, we wouldn't be going in, would we?"

"But if there's no danger, why can't I go in with you?"

"Because—" Feminine logic was too direct at times. "Well, your father . . ."

"Speaking of me?" The voice came from behind them, thin and crisp, that of a man used to giving orders without the need of backing them up with anything but money. They saw the tall, heavy figure of John Abbot entering the doorway.

Moss covered quickly. "Just warning your daughter not to go fooling around while the experiment's in progress. She's a science bug, you know, poking her nose into everything. Ordinarily, I like it, but not today."

"Okay, meanies." Joan grinned at them, though it looked a little forced, and kissed her fingers at Boyd with her back toward her father, then went tripping out, an odd look of determination on her face. Abbot squatted down on a box and watched them dourly.

"Better work," he grunted. "Some of the men are complaining about the money we've invested in this, with no results for two years. I still don't see why you needed all this for an experiment."

"I warned you it'd take five years, maybe." Moss had the patience with work and men that necessity develops in scientists. "And in dabbling with atoms, there is no small-scale experiment. The results gained then mean nothing. Finished, Thorne?"

"Yeah, the suits are in good condition. Mica's clear and the asbestos hasn't been damaged."

"Good." Moss picked up one and Boyd followed with the other, leaving Abbot staring after them. They slipped through the doors of the great barnlike experimental building and began donning their suits by the control table at one side of the forty-foot shell encasing the atom-blaster.

Boyd looked at Moss and voiced the question that had been troubling him for months. "How'd you ever pry the money out of Sourpuss in the first place?"

"I didn't. He heard the government was planning to finance my experiment and came after me on double-quick. Had visions of what government control of atomic power would mean to his utilities, and got the other financiers in with him. It's the first time he's had an employee whose orders had to be followed, and he doesn't like it." Moss chuckled. "Wonder what he'll say when you run off with his daughter?"

"Lord knows. Probably try to fire me, but I'm counting on you and her to pull me through that, if our work succeeds; anyway, if it does, he won't kick too hard. What are you planning to do after this is over?"

"Publish my monograph on restrictive fields and mathematical concepts of atomic disruption—the one with the new type of math I've spent two years teaching you." His heavily gloved fingers found the zipper on the suit finally and pulled it up, muffling his words. "After that, I'll probably visit Norman Meisner at City Hospital. Haven't seen him for years, and he's invited me down to see his latest miracle."

Thorne grunted as the zipper on his own suit slid up. "I was reading about that miracle; something about his taking a dog's brain and putting it in some mechanical body where it learned to wag its tail, wasn't it? The newspaper account gave practically no information."

"Something like that. Ready?"

"Ready!" Boyd watched the indicators as Moss turned on power into the restrictive fields that would limit the spread of neutrons and stabilize atomic breakdown. For a split second he imagined he caught a flash of movement in one corner of the building, but there was nothing there when he looked. He turned back to the panel. Power was already swelling out.

Moss leaned over, yelling above the sound of the machinery. "Looks good, eh?" A sudden flash of red sent him darting back, and his hand groped for a switch. Then a roar of light, heat, and sound cascaded out from the big shell!

For a fraction of a second, there was a scream in Boyd's ear, and he felt his hands clutch at the control switch. Then his mind blacked out, leaving only a numb nightmare of agony.

It could have been only a few seconds later when the agony brought consciousness back again. He made groping movements that sent cold throbs up to join the killing pain, and from the motions, a picture of his own condition sprang into being. His arms were half gone, there were no legs, and the body of which he had been so sure was only the withered hulk of a man—a cinder left miraculously behind to mark the fury of the atom flame! From the pain, part of his face must have been torn away, and sight and sound were gone.

Desperation killed the pain temporarily, and he fought to shout. He was on something that gave like sand, and the dull thuds around him could be only the earth vibrations of footsteps coming at a run. The blast must have thrown him free of the building, out onto the ground, and the other men were just coming up.

A faint idea was in his head, though the torture of existence fought against it. Sand below him, the stump of an arm—and no other means of telling what he wanted.

A convulsive heave threw him to what should have been his knees, and the right stump of his elbow bit down into the sand. He had only muscular memory to guide him, and the letters would have to be big. "MEISNER," the stub scrawled, and he fought backward against restraining hands that were meant to soothe him. Then: "CITY HOSP—N—" The "Y" was only half completed when his body refused to stand more and collapsed.

Now he was here—wherever here was—with only a dim idea that too much time had passed. The review of the past had only suggested that he was dead and in Hell—or in City Hospital. And that would mean—

The brain of a dog in a metal case, wagging a tail. Meisner of City Hospital, with the charred body of what had been a man, and only the first few experiments to pave the way. Boyd writhed mentally in the fantastic horror to which he had awakened and hoped suddenly that he was dead and in Hades. That at least would give him a background of familiarity. The other possibility was beyond the imagination.

II

Norman Meisner had left Germany as a boy. Had he remained, he might have become a great engineer, as he had planned. Instead, by a long chain of circumstances, he now held the reputation of being the greatest experimental surgeon on the American continent, and his word was law in the newly built experimental wing that had been added to City Hospital. Medicine was finally learning the value of "abstract" science.

"Morning, Papa Meisner," a trim nurse greeted him, and he chuckled amiably at the surprised expression that crossed the face of his companion.

"Discipline is not good, eh? But when it is brains that are needed, should a man bother with so small things? No, I think not. It is when they are happy they work best."

Dr. Martin nodded in half agreement. "You seem to get results, anyway. That's all the board's interested in. It isn't official yet, but they've decided to vote you the money you've been asking to continue this latest thing of yours."

"I don't need their money now. It is recently I have acquired a new donation—for experimental work only—from a rich man. I have work from him to do, as you shall see after this." He led the way down the hall to his private laboratory and smiled at the tall young man waiting outside. "The reporters all here, Tom?"

"All here. Hello, Dr. Martin."

Martin nodded at him. "Finished your course yet, Tom?"

"Full-fledged engineer now. But I've been helping Dad with the mechanical end of this new work—sort of ex officio."

They followed Meisner in and worked their way through the representatives of the press until they were standing beside a gleaming metal box that lay on a bare table, with only a small magnetic speaker in front of it. Its smooth surface was broken by a hole at one end and a short rubber tube that projected from the other. From inside came a faint hum and a regular muffled thudding.

"Good morning, gentlemen," Meisner greeted the reporters. "Now if you'll let me run this little show to my satisfaction . . . Rex, wake up!"

The tube at the rear came to sudden life and began twitching in a haphazard fashion, and a rough whining sound was emitted from the speaker. The reporters stared at it curiously, though they knew roughly what it was.

One of them started to ask a question, and the tube stopped its beating at the new sound; the speaker made a hoarse, sharp noise, almost like a bark. The barking continued until Meisner made soothing sounds that quieted it. The plump little physician patted his stomach fondly, opened the top of the box, and pointed inside.

"Life," he began, "must have food and air for energy, water to serve as a liquid medium, no? Good. And it must have blood to carry them, and something to remove the waste matter from the cells, or the blood. Also, to survive is needed white corpuscles or some other defense to kill destructive organisms, such as bacilli. Here, I have them all. When my Rex is run over, I fix him up a new body for his brain—not good, maybe, but better than nothing.

"See, here is the brain case and the big blood vessels are connected to this mechanical heart—a refinement I make on the Lindbergh-Carrel pump which you know, maybe. Here is a jet air infuser for a lung; blood goes in, loses carbonic acid gas, and picks up oxygen. So. Then up through the brain, down into this glass kidney —the same that Lindbergh also worked on—and the life-poisons come out and are a trouble no more. This is the stomach, where predigested food enters the blood by osmosis."

The newspapermen were impressed, but hardly amazed. Most of them had seen pieces of chicken's heart kept alive by the use of the Lindbergh pump and kidney before. This was merely a refinement of that, though the use of an entire brain was a big forward step. "I suppose you put in new blood as the old red corpuscles break down?" one of them asked.

"Ach, that is the beauty of this; blood I do not use." Meisner waited for their reactions until satisfied that they were properly curious. "I have a new substitute for blood. It carries food, air, and water, just as does the real, but there is no breaking down. That is the great advance."

Dr. Martin stared at him with sudden interest. "How about its effects on the cells? I suppose it's some nontoxic organic compound with a loose affinity for oxygen, but do the cells work well with it?"

"Perfectly. And—" He tapped a small chamber that had been overlooked. "Here it is sterilized. With real blood, that could not be, no? Real blood has white bodies that fight disease, but my blood washes the germs through this and *poof*—they are dead. I have given my brain all that is needed for life."

"Yeah, but how'd you get the brain in there without letting it die? And what starts the magnets that wag its 'tail'?"

Meisner shrugged. "Have you no imagination? First the blood vessels are opened and reconnected one by one, so life does not stop, until the artificial heart does all the work. Then my liquid replaces the blood, and the brain is moved to its new case—not before. And the nerve endings, which conduct faint currents of electricity from the brain, are hooked up to platinum filaments. So. And their so faint electric impulse is boosted in relays to operate the magnets and the speaker which is connected to two modulators, one for the whine and the other a bark."

He held up his hands to silence their instant protests. "So, you know nobody can trace out individual nerves, eh? That is true. But I can locate nerve *bundles* that lead to the ears, throat, and tail, and separate the sensory nerve bundles from the motor impulse bundles. I attach the bundles on the right places, not separating nerves, and hope maybe the brain gets some sensation—and it does. Two months Rex has had to learn in, and already he knows my voice and his name. Rex!"

Again the speaker whined and the tube that served as a tail twitched. It beat in a hopelessly disordered fashion, but apparently any beat seemed better than none to the dog's mind. The reporters examined it again, checked up on their information, and began filing out.

"Going to use it on a man sometime?" one of them asked as a parting shot.

"Why not, maybe?" Meisner turned to his son as they left and he grinned. "Maybe we use it on a man, eh? Tom, shall we honor the fine Herr Doktor Martin with our latest efforts?"

Tom's grin answered him. "If it won't shock the esteemed Dr. Martin."

Martin stared from one to the other, making no sense of their expressions. "Why so darned mysterious?"

Meisner took his hand on one side, and Tom marched around

him to the other. "You now have the honor, Dr. Martin, of seeing—oh, skip it, come on and see for yourself. It really isn't funny, after all."

Dr. Charles Martin followed along meekly enough, as they led him, and light began to dawn. Unless he was mistaken seriously, what he was about to see had something to do with the reporter's last question.

III

Boyd fought against himself in the crazy world of chaotic sensation to which he seemed doomed, and sudden darkness rolled down over him, cutting off the disordered jumble of varicolored light that had been torturing his eyes—or where his eyes had been. With a sense of pride he realized he'd done the equivalent at least of closing his eyelids.

But the dark emphasized the solitude of the place. There was still a rushing confusion of sound, but the hours he had lain there had dimmed his consciousness of it until it formed a hazy pattern in his mind. The pains were less sharp now, mercifully.

But there was no mercy for him. In spite of himself, his mind insisted on speculating on death, though the more rational thoughts insisted that this could not be death.

A sudden torrent of fresh sound struck down on him, not loud but raucous in disorder. The sounds grew louder and changed, and he guessed that something or someone was coming closer to him. He tried to see, and again his eyes acted without his knowledge of how. Stronger light lanced out, flickering for a moment, and then burning hotly. His struggles to close his eyes again only resulted in a harsher glare, as if his pupils had dilated.

The confused sounds kept on, and there was something in the rise and fall of them that suggested speech. They were clearer than the other noises. Boyd cried out, or tried to, and was startled to hear a grating jangle. It couldn't have been his voice, yet he was sure it had come from him.

The other noises stopped momentarily, and then the sound he had made was repeated, slightly changed but recognizable. Surely no human throat could have imitated it—a hyena, perhaps, but not a man. He tried again, getting a different noise this time, and it was repeated by the other.

There was a silence for a moment, and a clear tone broke in, different from the rest. It was hoarse, but lacked the confusion of all former sounds. "Dit-dit-dit-dit," it said in short clicks. Then there was a slight pause, and it began again, this time in longer signals mixed with the short ones. "Dit . . . dit-dah-dit-dit . . . dit-dah-dit-dit . . . dah-dah-dah."

The short clicks and longer ones resembled something he had heard. He groped around in his mind, seeking the answer, and finally found it. The irregular frequency was that of a telegraph sounder, and the clicks must be code. It came again, and he listened more closely, piecing out the letters. "H . . . E . . . ? . . . ? . . . O."

"Hello!" That was what they were saying. But his knowledge of code was too limited. As a boy, he had known a friend who operated a ham station, but all he had ever learned were the symbols for THE, I, and SOS. That gave six letters out of twenty-six. He started to return the signal they sent with whatever noise his throat chose to make, depending on the length instead of articulation of sound, but thought better of it. If he made no reply, they might realize he could not understand.

There was a conference of noises, and the clicking again, all short this time. One click, space, two clicks, space, three— They were running over the numbers in the simplest of codes. Clumsily he repeated, and the numbering left off. Then the clicker reverted to a series of mixed short and long sounds, with spaces coming in irregular order. He counted the sounds between spaces and made out twenty-six. As the signals started again, he checked. The fifth was E, the eighth H, and the others fitted in. They were sending the alphabet for him to memorize. He selected four of the most necessary letters and concentrated on them until he was sure he could make an intelligible sentence.

"Where am I?"

There was an excited buzzing of sounds, and the clicker broke out quickly. "–o– are i– the –it– hos–ita– to –et we–." So he was in City Hospital and they were trying to patch up what was left of him. But how much was that. Something was wrong with his sight, his hearing, and his voice, and he had no ability to move any other part—or at least could feel no response.

The alphabet was running through again, certain letters emphasized by longer space between them this time. He made a sound when satisfied that he knew them, and the sounder began picking out words slowly and carefully.

"This is Meisner. You are making out well. You must rest now. We will make you well. We must leave now. The machine that makes ABC will stay to keep teaching you. You must not worry."

Even the simple sentences brought half comfort, suggesting as they did the possibility of communication. Boyd made the proper sounds for "yes," and the noises that were voices began to fade away. The machine kept up its alphabetical discourse.

They were almost gone when Boyd remembered the questions he must ask and shouted. There was a series of increasing sounds, and a voice answered.

"Moss?" he spelled.

"Dead!"

"How long?"

"A month," the answer came. "No worry. All is well."

Then the voices receded again, and he knew he was alone. So Moss was dead, and it was a month since he had been conscious. They must have kept his mind drugged while the pain of healing was going on, and the ache he was now experiencing must come from muddled sensations. A month, while he had lain here in a fog, and the world had gone on without him.

It must have been hell for Joan, he thought. Next time the men came to see him, he'd ask about her, if he wasn't too horrible for her to see. Perhaps it would be better if she never visited him. As a future husband, he was a washout.

The clicking of the machine called his mind back, and he turned his thoughts to the code, glad for a reason to forget all the troubles that were looming up for the future. Hours sped by, and the machine buzzed on, leaving the alphabet for simple primer sentences. He seemed to have no desire for sleep, and the light flashes finally disappeared, leaving him in darkness that was soothing. Some of the noises in the background disappeared, and he realized it was night.

The machine went back to simple words, and there was a new element. "Man" it spelled out. "M." The letter was followed by a different noise, then "A" and another. Finally the whole word was spelled in completion and a longer noise that resembled the voice sounds of the men. They were trying to teach him to speak!

The sounds that followed the letters seemed all alike at first, but slowly he noted minor differences that clarified as he studied them. They bore no resemblance to speech as he remembered it, being a jumble of whistles, buzzes, and things for which there was no name. Dutifully, he tried to imitate them, but the response was disheartening. In the hours that followed he learned there were just thirty-one sounds he could make, and that making them in any logical order was going to take education. His voice refused to respond to the old patterns of speech in any sensible fashion. And some of the sounds he had regarded as primary were now made up of more than one. A vowel might require two or more sounds blended in rapid order.

But slowly the distinctions between the sounds he could hear became plainer, and he was able to grasp in a dim way the meaning of a few words out of each simple sentence before the code form was spelled out. It was slow, grim work and only the desperate urge for knowledge of himself drove him on.

Light was streaking back again as he made his last efforts at speech. Surprisingly enough, at the twentieth time ordered sound came out. "I am." The words that man had first spoken in the dim past when consciousness of self was new. Now they marked a milestone in his progress as great as that first effort.

He could not repeat them, though he tried. But what he had done once could be done again, in time; he might learn even to recognize the weird conglomeration that constituted speech for him with a semblance of ease. At least he would not be doomed forever to solitude.

He was! For the time, that would have to suffice.

IV

"The prince kissed her lightly," oozed the telegraphone with nice unction, "and Sleeping Beauty opened her eyes and smiled at him. Then they were married and lived happily ever after."

Boyd swore mentally at the recording. It wasn't bad enough to stay awake twenty-four hours a day in Hell, but they had to furnish recordings to remind him of his sleepless condition. Not that he needed sleep, apparently. But a little merciful oblivion would have been welcome. Still, the machine was familiarizing him with the hoots and gargles that represented spoken language.

Grumbling to himself, he turned his attention to the chart that hung over him. By a series of manipulations that normally would have made his eyes act in a distinctly abnormal manner, he finally focused on it and began piecing out the characters. They all looked like blobs of wax that had been left too long in the sun, but careful study was bringing some sense out of them.

He could recognize the straight lines now, and a few letters of the alphabet, though he had to take their words about the beauty of the girl's face in the central picture. So far, motion was the only thing that registered properly, when he could keep it in focus.

"Like using the faceted eyes of an insect," he growled. Then it didn't sound right; he repeated it. That was better. His new voice still insisted on getting the whistle that went with "k" mixed up with the rushing cough that stood for "e."

Someone was at the door, coming toward him, from the sound. He waited until a moving blob registered on his eyes, looked for what he had come to know as a beard, and decided from its absence that his visitor was Tom Meisner. There was another figure with him, thinner, and also without a beard.

"Hello, Boyd." Tom's clear-cut English identified him further. "I've bought you a visitor—Mr. Abbot."

Looking at the other, Boyd decided it did look something like Abbot. Careful inspection revealed the bald spot on the man's head, and he felt a sudden glow of pride at his achievement. Then it disappeared into the usual gloom. "Hello," he said slowly. "I didn't expect to see you, Mr. Abbot."

"And why not?" From the speed of the words, the question was probably meant to be good-natured, though the fine nuances of tone failed to register. "You've been costing me a small fortune, Thorne, so I figured I might as well see what was coming of it."

"You've been paying for me?" It was news to Boyd, though he had wondered about the financial end of it. "Why?"

Something that might have been a chuckle came from Abbot. "Not from sentimental reasons, as you've guessed. I've been paying because I need your memory and knowledge. When I saw what you'd scrawled in the sand, I figured you'd learned something that might prove the solution to the problem of power, and took you to Meisner. What was it?"

"Mostly nothing. Instinct of self-preservation, I guess, made me write that. You've had experts go over the wreck?"

"Naturally, and they don't understand it. Some of Moss's notes are incomplete, and the equipment is pretty well ruined. The other investors in the work are yelling about the money they've put in, and I've got to show results." Abbot paused, and Boyd guessed which one of the investors was most worried about the money. "At least, you can supply the information in the missing notes."

"It wouldn't do any good, sir. All I know is that the field we'd built up collapsed just after it started, and the experiment went wild before the neutrons were dissipated enough for the reaction to stop.

Theory doesn't explain that, and another test might give you more things like me. If I could go over the wreck and try again, I might find the trouble. But—"

"Good." Abbot picked up his hat and started to leave. "Hurry up and learn to use your arms and legs, and I'll see you don't lose if it works." He motioned Tom back and went out the door alone, leaving Boyd's mind in a state of numbed shock.

Learn to use his arms and legs! He'd been thinking of himself as a brain in a box, with nothing but the senses of sight and hearing, but that was apparently false. Now, perhaps he wasn't like the dog in the newspaper item. Perhaps— Fifty wild conjectures ran through his mind in the half second it took him to call Tom.

Young Meisner sat down within range of his sight, and his voice was low and calm. "I know, Boyd. Take it easy. We didn't tell you about it because we wanted you to spend all your time learning to see and talk. But you're about as complete as we can make you. Ever read any of those robot stories?"

"Yes, but—"

"Well, in a rough way, that's what you are now. There wasn't enough of your body left to save, so we gave you a new one. In some ways, it can't equal the old one, but it has points of superiority. The blood system insures your brain against disease and fatigue. You'll never need sleep because all poisons are removed as they form. You'll never have to worry about your body wearing out, because new parts can be added. And you'll probably live longer than Methuselah, since your brain cells are perfectly fed and cared for. For instance, the thermostatic controls that keep your brain and spinal cord at the right temperature are far more sensitive and dependable than the normal bodily methods."

Some of those, Boyd decided, weren't assets. He'd have given a lot for one night's sleep and forgetfulness, and the idea of living a long time might prove a mixed blessing. But there was no use of complaining about that. "How'd you do it?"

"By combining Dad's surgical skill with what I know of engineering, and getting a lot of outside help," Tom answered. "Your ears are vocoders, breaking down sound into its basic elements. For a voice, you have the opposite, a voder, that takes the basic elements and recombines them. We couldn't hope to re-create anything like the original, since nature, working with millions of unified cells, is devilishly complex. But the substitutes will serve fairly well.

"You have a television scanner for eyes, connected to the optic nerves, and the nerves governing your eye muscles are hitched on to change the focus tubes and move them about. We used a photoelectric cell to govern the iris setting, but you can control that to some extent. Incidentally, our biggest trouble was getting a television hookup that would work properly with lenses having a focal length short enough to give sufficient depth of field to your sight, and the wide-angle f:1.0 lenses had to be made specially.

"Most of the apparatus is located in your torso, of course, along with the new high-power accumulator coils to furnish power. Not having your atomic energy yet, that's the best we could do, so you'll need recharging regularly."

"Mmm." In a hazy way, Boyd had figured out part of that for himself, but his chief interest was in motility. "What about the muscles in arms and legs?"

"Magnets. Dad planned on using motors and sliding shafts, but that would have taken a body the size of an elephant. We used thin disk magnets with a one-tenth-inch gap between them. A hundred of them equal a ten-inch gap, and there's no comparison between the two when it comes to pull exerted. Where the big gap might not work, the series of small ones pack in plenty of power. The old inverse-square law that applies to all force fields, you know."

The door opened again with a faint creak, and Meisner's thick pronunciation broke in on them. "So?" He moved over beside his son. "So you tell our Mr. Boyd all about himself, eh? All I hear is how good an engineer you are to make a body like this. How you feel, Boyd?"

"A little better, now that I won't be cramped down in a box all my life. What about the sense that governs muscular movements?"

"You see, Dad, he wants to know. You can boast about your part when I'm finished." Boyd made out that Tom and Meisner were grinning at each other as the younger man went on. "We used piezoelectric crystals as pressure detectors in the muscle piles. They should gauge the effort applied by the magnets and serve as a fair kinesthetic sense. Temperature sense isn't so important to you, but we used thermocouples for that, and gyroscopes attached to the balance-organ nerves supply a sense of balance."

Meisner nodded. "And so you are a man again. A brain and spinal cord from nature taken, a body made from skill. We hook the nerves to wire filaments, indiscriminately, and they learn again. Maybe then you are once more complete."

"Sounds like a horrible mess to me," Boyd stated.

"Maybe. But it is nature that makes the so horrible mess. One million cells she puts in a muscle, and makes them work as one. A hundred little habits of thought that you don't know about she gives you by experience, to work those million cells. No, that we could not duplicate. We've simplified, instead. That you could do all that you did before would be impossible, but that you could approximate normal activity—yes. Good, eh?"

"If I learn. But all the sensations I get are completely distorted."

Again Meisner disagreed. "Not distorted, but different. You are again a baby. Are the eyes of a baby incomplete? No. But he has learned no habits of understanding the messages sent by his eyes, and he cannot fully see. Even a boy of five may draw a picture that to him looks like his mother, and to you or me, like nothing.

"It is the old senses that lie as much as the new. You must forget the old habits and new ones acquire. In his head, man sees upright, but the message on the nerves is reversed. Glasses have been built to reverse this, and for a time sight seems upside down; then, in a few weeks, the brain corrects, and all looks normal. Now it is without the glasses that sight is wrong. So.

"I could sort afferent nerve bundles from efferent. I could trace the ones to the ears, to the eyes, to other parts. But the separate nerves? No, never. And they would not work with the new sensors and motors, anyhow. So the message is sent to the brain—without any system it is sent. And the brain, that great organizer, it must learn to find habits that work with them. It will. In time new habits you will learn, and then your senses will no longer distort."

Boyd turned it over in his mind, and partly agreed. Already sound was beginning to seem more natural to him, and there was some promise of his eyes working properly. He tried to see his body, but the movement of his eye tubes was too limited for that. Meisner seemed to sense his desire.

"There is a mirror here." He moved away for a few seconds, and came back carrying something. Tom helped him adjust it. "So. Now look, if you must."

Boyd looked. At first, he saw only a vague blur, but as he analyzed it part by part, some meaning began to come out of what he saw. That was a straight line, that a curve, and another straight line at a forty-five-degree angle. His mind built up a picture from the separate messages sent to it.

He was big, far bigger than any normal man; probably the problems of structure had necessitated that. And his head was too large even for his body. They had made little effort to copy the human form accurately. Tubes stuck out in front of his face for eyes, and there was no nose or chin. He realized quickly that he looked less human than the various robots that had been built for stage exhibition purposes.

And in that body he was supposed to move about among the normal people of the world! There could be no concealing it in coats and hats, no hope of being anything but a freak for people to stare at. Men distrust the unknown, and he would have few if any friends. No home, no social life—no wife!

Surely he couldn't expect Joan to marry him in such a form. Perhaps that was why they had kept her from seeing him. He was a monster, a creation that even Frankenstein would have shunned as unholy. All that was left to tie him to the world of men was a job to be finished.

"All right," he said. "Help me sit up and put that mirror where I can watch myself. I've got to learn how to handle these muscles you gave me, if I can start the things twitching."

V

The razor blade was absolutely steady in the big hand and the hair moved toward it surely until it was split smoothly down the center. The other hand picked up one of the pieces, and this time the blade moved against the half hair, splitting it into quarters of the original.

Boyd tapped one finger against the palm of his hand in a clicking sound he used to express satisfaction; some of the old habits had been redesigned to work with the new body. Being made of metal made for steadiness, at least, as the split hair proved, and the auxiliary lenses changed the focal length of his eyes to his optional telescopic or microscopic sight. Now he slipped the lenses off and put them in the fur-lined pouch that was attached to his body.

Tom Meisner opened the door of the office and came in, his lips blue with the cold, beating his hands together to warm them. "All set, Boyd," he said. "The transformers just came in. Want I should start the men on them?"

Boyd grunted. "Guess so. Abbot's still climbing on me for being so slow. I'll go along and help with the installation." Tom had been doing good work since the return to the station, and he was glad to have the young engineer as an addition to his staff. He rose from his seat, a little jerkily as the faint giddiness of motion hit him. His balance sense still wasn't in perfect tune, and a slight dizziness usually accompanied any change of position. For a second, he moved his legs carefully, then sureness came back.

"The X-ray plates for the transformer cores they sent okay?"

"Yeah, seem to be. I can't find a trace of flaw in any of the stuff this time. *Brr!* It's colder than Billy-be-damned. How you can stand it without an—" He caught himself suddenly. "Skip it!"

Even though he had been largely responsible for Boyd's body, Tom still made those little mistakes. And his acceptance of Boyd as a man at such times bothered more than the frank stares of the others. It was bad enough to be an object of ridicule, but to have the other man start treating him normally and suddenly realize the difference was worse.

"I wouldn't get much good out of an overcoat," Boyd answered his unfinished question. "It's a good thing you chose chrome steel for the foot plates, though, with all this slush on the ground."

His heavy feet made harsh plopping sounds in the muck that served as a constant reminder of his strangeness. One of the men stopped his work to stare as he passed, wonder still written large on his face, though Thorne had been at the station nearly a month now. Then the man turned quickly and too obviously back to his work, avoiding Boyd's eyes.

The men were uncomfortable, he could see, as they worked under his orders, setting the big transformers in place, coupling them up, and adjusting them. Some of them had worked with him before, on easy terms of camaraderie, and it was hardest for them. They tried their best to act toward him as if nothing had happened, and their efforts failed miserably.

Some of the new men made jokes about him behind his back and called him "Frankie," derived mistakenly from Frankenstein. That did not worry him; if men could treat his new body as a joke and be serious about the brain in it, life would be tolerable. But they pitied him, instead, and looked down at him from superior normality. They were a little too quick to accept his orders, to address him as "Mr. Boyd," to laugh at his attempted jokes.

He caught up one end of a beam the men were working with and twisted it around to the position they wanted. For a minute, they looked up with surprise and admiration, then it faded. Boyd's sharp ears caught the remark one of them made. "Why shouldn't he be strong? Automobiles got strong engines, too. He don't need to show off in front of us."

"Shut up, dammit!" the other growled, but there was the same hint of dislike in his voice.

That's how it was. If he did what they couldn't, they resented it; if he failed to do anything they could, they were condescendingly pitying. He was a freak, something hashed together from an accident, which should have killed him, and they had to take orders from him. There was no way he could win their respect or friendship, since those were reserved for men with human bodies and limitations.

Tom came back as the last transformer was being swung up and in by the donkey engine hoist. "Dad phoned he was coming out this afternoon to check up on your progress," he said. "Should be here any minute."

"Good." Thorne liked Tom's father better than anyone else he'd seen since the accident; the physician worked on bodies but respected only brains. "Abbot's dropping over, too, to let me understand just what each day's delay costs him."

"He would, of course. He was decent enough about it all when we still had you back at City, but now he thinks there's no more excuse." Tom glanced back toward the door and waved. "There's Dad now—hey! Watch it there!"

The friction clutch on the hoist holding the transformer was slipping and the mass of metal began to fall, wobbling sidewise. At Tom's yell, Hennessy, who was waiting for it, started to jump back quickly, but the awkwardness of fright tripped him. He sprawled flat, clawing wildly, and the transformer began slipping more rapidly.

Boyd had no time to think of the signals his brain must send out. He shot full power into the magnets and jumped forward in two twenty-foot leaps that brought him under it, his arms up to catch it. His head spun with sudden giddiness, but the weight in his arms slowed reluctantly, came to a stop, and he stood straining at the pull of it. It threatened to carry him down, but the full strength of the body they had given him resisted, fighting to hold it and retain his balance.

The other men shut their mouths and darted in now, pulling Hennessy out from under; the man had fainted. Then they came forward to catch at the transformer and help Boyd, but Tom's quick voice barked out. "Stop it! You'll do more harm than good."

Slowly Boyd moved it, edging his way forward half an inch at a time until it came to rest over its supports. He let his knees flex slightly as it settled, then it was still, ready to be bolted in. As he let go, a sick weight seemed to leave his mind. A few pounds or seconds more would have been too much.

He stopped to examine the metal on one arm, looking for dents or scratches, and finding none. For the first time, the full realization of the strength that was his came to him; four ordinary men would have buckled under the load. But there was no pride in it—the achievement was really that of the Meisners, who had built the body, not of himself. And the other men could hardly admire him for doing a mechanical job well with a machine for a body.

But the remarkable recuperative powers of his synthetic circulation system came into play almost at once, freeing his brain of the toxins of its efforts in commanding full power from the muscle piles, and he felt no ill effects. Meisner stood beside him, raging at him hotly.

"Nincompoop! Maybe it's mountains you'll move next, eh? Is it no gratitude that you should try to destroy the life I gave you? One slip and—*ploosh!*—it squashes you flat on the thin abdominal walls, and your nice new heart is *kaput!* Maybe you could live without a heart, eh? So? I think not!"

Boyd looked at the surgeon and there was a grin in his mind, though no change could show on his face. "Why all the fuss? You wanted to test me; there's your test."

"So. Maybe it is. And there is nothing now wrong with you but that you think too much about yourself and how different you are. You should forget that."

One of the men tapped Meisner's shoulder. "Did you mean the accident might have killed him?" he asked.

"And why not? The brain he has—maybe—is as soft as yours, the fool. Did you think he was solid iron?"

"No. No, I guess not." The man shook his head doubtfully and moved back to his fellows, where the unconscious Hennessy was slowly coming around.

A voice coughed from the doorway, and they turned to see Abbot standing there.

"Nice work, Thorne," he commented. "Those transformers cost money, and having a man killed here might cause trouble."

"As much as a day's delay?"

"More." Abbot chuckled. "All right, no talk of money today, then. How's it coming?"

"Most of the new stuff is in. Be ready to make a trial next week," Boyd decided. "And I'm glad you let me hire Tom, here. He's been doing some fine work, and the men do well under his instructions."

Abbot frowned slightly. "Mm-hm. A week, you say? But— All right, I said I wouldn't say anything about it today, and I won't. There's someone I want to bring out when you go through with it. This . . . person insists on being present."

Meisner glanced at him quickly. "You mean— Maybe it should be. The—person might benefit by it, even."

"It's dangerous enough for me alone, without a stranger."

Tom stuck his oar in, shaking his head at Boyd. "It's okay. I know whom they mean, and I think you should do it, danger or not."

"Anyway, I'm still in charge of the station," Abbot pointed out smoothly. He took Boyd's reluctant consent for granted. "Good, it's settled then. Want to ride in with me, Dr. Meisner?"

"I think so, yes. I'm not needed here. And Boyd, I shall expect to be present here when already you start the test." Meisner slapped the metal chest and followed Abbot out. Tom and Boyd turned back to the men who were finishing their work.

One of the men gestured, and they stopped. "Well, Hennessy?"

Hennessy hesitated, looking uncomfortable, but another man urged him on. "Look, boss, I— Well, some of us are going to town tonight, boss, to take in a show, and we thought . . . well—want to come with us?"

For once Boyd was glad that his face was expressionless as he looked at the others and saw that they were all in on the invitation. But it wouldn't do to embarrass them in town with his presence, especially now that they had suddenly thawed. "Thanks, boys," he answered. "I appreciate the offer, but there's a full night's work waiting for me. I'm on a twenty-four-hour schedule this week."

There was no look of relief on their faces, as he had expected, but only the look to be found whenever a friendly invitation is turned down for good reason. "Any idea what happened?" he asked Tom as they moved away.

"A little. For one thing, you saved Hennessy when they couldn't, at some risk to yourself. They heard Dad say you could be killed, and men are funny that way; they're just selfish enough to dislike anyone who can't be hurt, because they'd like that ability themselves and can't get it. Now, because you stand about as good a chance of getting killed as they do, they're back on even footing with you."

Whatever the reason, it would be a blessing to work with them as a man again, even though their social life was in another world. Boyd had a mental picture of himself at a show, and it didn't appeal to him. Companionship, even when offered, was impossible for him.

VI

There was a hint of snow in the air, and the temperature outside was so low that Boyd had been forced to wear heavy rubbers to keep the dampness from getting onto his feet and freezing the joints stiff. He clumped around in them now, thoroughly enjoying the ribbing the men were giving him about catching pneumonia. They had loosened up remarkably in the last week.

Now preparations for the test were complete, and they were waiting for Abbot and Meisner to arrive before starting. Tom was still begging to go in with him while the test was run, but Boyd was firm.

"No soap, Tom. Having this whosit of Abbot's is bad enough. I wanted to take the risk alone, since I could probably stand another explosion fairly well, but I don't want three in there. You'd be needed anyway to build me a new body if this one gets wrecked." He wiggled his shoulders uncomfortably and scratched at his back. "Darn it, there's a place on my back that itches."

Tom grinned, then saw that he was serious. "How could it?"

"I don't know, but it does. Every time I get cold, it itches. You must have put a defective thermostat in there, or gotten some nerves mixed up." He tapped his back sharply. "There, that does it. A light blow works sometimes."

"I'll have a look at you later when Dad's around," Tom offered. "Maybe I'd better increase your foot heaters at the same time. Anyhow, it's a good thing we fixed it so you had electrical heat over your whole body if you insist on running around in the cold. Otherwise, your lubrication might stiffen up."

Boyd grunted, looking down the road. "Here comes Abbot, and your father must be with him—there are two in front, and it looks a little like someone behind. I'd rather not talk to them now, Tom, so I'm going inside, and you meet them here. Send in whosit, if Abbot still insists. By the way, is he dry behind the ears yet?"

"Partly. Had a little science in college and been studying since, but it's mostly scientific curiosity. You'll have no trouble, though." Tom grinned at him, but Boyd could see nothing funny as he went into the experimental building. Even a well-trained helper might be a nuisance, and sending in a greenhorn was as idiotic a thing as he could think of.

He couldn't help thinking of another person filled with incessant craving to know. Work and the need of relearning himself had filled his time until Joan had been pushed into the background, but now her image came surging up, bringing futile longings to his mind. Always in the background, he had missed her prying eyes and bubbling saucy grin. But they still told him that Joan was sick, too sick to see him. That was probably an excuse to spare his feelings.

Love, he supposed, was gone, since that was basically a physical sensation, but respect, fondness, and desire for her company persisted. He needed her now, more than ever.

Meisner had been right; he did think too much of himself and his own differences. Life to him was a serious thing at best, and in his new body it had assumed a tragic mood. He knew it, but with the queer twist of his brain, the knowledge only made it worse. He needed someone to laugh at him, to love him, and to show him the gaiety and humor that lay all about him, someone like Joan who could lend him her eyes and let him forget his own brooding.

To a lesser extent, Allan Moss had done the same, and he was another that Boyd missed. The old physicist's theories and plans were familiar to him now, but he still would have welcomed the firm guidance of the scientist, now more than ever. Instead of that, they were sending a science bug to add to his troubles.

Then a metallic clanking behind him broke through his thoughts, and he swung quickly away from the control panel toward the door. Cold wonder caught at him as he saw the creature moving toward him. It was larger than a man, its shiny metal body topped by a head without either chin, neck, or face, save for tubes to serve as eyes. In every line and pattern, it might have been a mirror image of himself!

The figure moved forward calmly, holding out a hand. "Tom Meisner told me you were all ready to begin. It's good to see you, Thorne!"

Thorne! Boyd groped numbly, hunting some streak of light. Only Moss and a few others had used his first name, and now— It had to be Moss! If he had escaped, the physicist might have also, though in little better shape. Since it had apparently taken long to recuperate and relearn, he must have been even worse hit. And Abbot had made them say he was dead so that Boyd would be willing to rush things through before the other could come out. That made sense.

He stretched out a metal hand quickly, feeling confidence again for the first time since his return to the station. "And I can't say how glad I am to see you, sir. I've been trying to carry on, but you're needed here. Want to take over?"

A funny choking sound came from the other. "I'm afraid you'll have to do it all this time, Thorne. I'm not . . . I won't be much help to you. Any idea of what caused the failure before?"

"Some idea," he said doubtfully, taking the control seat and pulling out the chair for the other. Obviously, Moss hadn't entirely recovered from the shock, but his mere presence helped. "It doesn't entirely suit me, and I'd rather not mention it until I find out whether it was purely mechanical defects that caused the field to collapse. Ready?"

"Ready."

Boyd closed the switches and watched power drain into the big shell, his eyes glued to the indicators that shifted erratically before he could balance them accurately. Then they found their marks and held. Nothing seemed wrong there. One second went by, then others followed it. He counted slowly to fifty, and still there was no sign of failure. The power needle that indicated energy release within the shell quivered and began to climb, and all was still in balance. Boyd settled back somewhat, relief spreading through his mind. It was working.

Plop! A thin red light cut on quickly and the needles quivered suddenly, crazily. He tensed himself for movement, wondering whether he could make the switch in time, and looked down. His hand was resting quietly on the switch and every needle was dead! His new arm had moved before the thought was more than beginning in his mind.

Quick reactions and no damage! That had been the trouble before; the ordinary motor impulse had traveled along Moss's arm at a comparatively slow speed, in common with all neural impulses, and things had happened before he could reach the switch. But Boyd's nerves were filaments of silver and the electrical impulse traveled down them with almost the speed of light, while the muscle packs threw the hand forward faster than the eye could see, before the field had entirely failed.

His companion stirred uneasily. "Is it over?"

"That test is, and a failure. Thank heaven, not a fatal one, this time." He gathered up the kit of high-tension testing meters they used and moved from the control seat toward the shell. Now he was more than willing to have the other here. Of all the men he could have chosen for a helper, Moss in his new body alone had reaction time quick enough for the work.

"You'll have to watch the board, sir," he said. "It's in balance now, so just throw the switch on when I signal, and keep your eyes glued on the panel. If a red light comes on or the needles bob, cut it off. You'll be able to do it in time."

He set up the meters quickly, cutting in through the insulation around the transformers and the box to the shell. At his motion, the switch was thrown, and his pointers began pouring out their messages, registering the surprisingly delicate balance of current on his dials. Then, while he was still analyzing them, they went dead.

"Failure again," the other reported. "Find out what the trouble was?"

Boyd assorted the results in his head until the jigsaw pattern shaped up. "Yes. It's simple enough, though we'd never have guessed it before that first attempt because of that simplicity. Back E.M.F. of a sort, you might say. When power starts feeding in, it induces a back pressure in our field coils, like the back current generated in a running electric motor. That current gets into the transformers and throws the balance of power feeding into the field off kilter, with the results we've seen. I think I know where the trouble starts."

"But can we fix it today?"

"Why not? I suspected it, and there's everything here to work with. We can do it together in half an hour and not bother the men." It was strange to be explaining things to Moss and be giving orders, but the other seemed to expect it. Boyd motioned as the robot came down. "We'll yank this section of the shell out. If my idea works, we can shunt it around harmlessly."

Again he was thankful for the presence of his companion. Mechanical bodies, he was finding, had very definite points of superiority. They had prevented disaster twice already, and now they promised to save the necessity of making room for a crew of men and machines that would have been needed for the job. Even with Moss's odd hesitation and uncertainty, sheer brute force coupled with good mental co-ordination could work wonders.

The half hour was only slightly past when he pulled the control chair up and cut the switch in again. There was the usual lag, and then the power needle began climbing, took a sudden lurch, and settled down at the highest mark on the dial. There was a smooth high drone in the air that continued minute after minute, spelling out power in unbelievable quantities and fully under control.

"Okay, sir," Boyd said finally. "We've done it, and I'm glad you were where you could see it."

The other figure stirred uncomfortably, then looked up at him with a sound that held amusement. "Are you, Pickleface? You didn't seem to want me where I could see it before."

Something that should have been the pit of Boyd's stomach went numb, and his eyes shifted erratically out of focus. Gulping sounds came from his vocal apparatus, but they made no sense. Why should they? There was no sense left in the world itself.

Something that approximated a soft laugh came from the other. "Dad told me I wasn't to let you know until after the experiment and warned me you might think I was Dr. Moss. You should have heard the fight I put up to get here!" Again she giggled. "Poor old Pickleface. Don't you like me, now that I'm hairless and ugly?"

"Joan!" The numbness left him in a rush, and he dived for her, only to realize what the loss of lips meant. "Joan, you crazy little fool! So that's what I heard before the explosion?"

Her voice was flat, as usual, but he sensed mockery and guilt in her words. "Mm-hmm. I sneaked in and hid before it began, behind the transformer bank. That's what saved me, I guess. From what they told me, we landed not three feet apart, though I didn't come to until I was in City Hospital. Father thought that if you had a chance at life, I should have the same. Mad at me, Thorne?"

Even without lips, he showed her he wasn't.

Later, when some of the shouting was over and Abbot had gone in to stand over the big shell and gaze fondly at the power indicator, they found Meisner alone in the office. The doctor made room for the two big bodies, grinning at them paternally.

"So it's married my model patient and my not-so-model one shall be, eh? Abbot has told me already."

Boyd relaxed on the seat, realizing that his mind had refused to rest and be peaceful for months. It was almost a novelty. "Married we shall," he answered, "though I suppose it's mostly a formality with us. Funny thing, Abbot seems willing enough now, for some reason."

"That isn't so funny, is it, Papa Meisner? Dr. Moss left you his interests in this, and you're almost rich now. Anyway, just picture poor Dad trying to get anyone else to marry me now!" Joan twisted one of his big fingers possessively. "This time, Mr. Thorne Boyd, there'll be no convenient accidents to save you. I won't let you out of my sight until it's over."

Meisner patted Boyd's metal chest. "Me, I think I shall also see there are no more delays. So. And be maybe your best man. Life is not so bad, eh?"

"With twenty-four hours a day for years and years together and never a gray hair or a wrinkle?" Joan kicked her heels together and giggled. "Even Pickleface should be happy now."

The change had made no difference in her, Boyd thought, wondering when she would tire of the nickname; well, if she kept using it, he'd have to learn to like it yet. No, life wasn't so bad. There was work for him now, with men who respected him, a rough friendship with Meisner and Tom, and most important of all, companionship with his own kind.

"I'm growing rather attached to this body," he admitted. "Except for one thing. I can't smoke. A cigarette is too small for my air vents, and any holder I've tried is liable to get stuck in them or else it scratches some of the filters off. If I hold it in front, I get just enough nicotine to tantalize me. Think you can fix it?"

Meisner chuckled and winked at Joan. "Never satisfied, this man of yours, I think. Well, we can fix that, maybe." He held out a silvered case. "Try a cigar."

Boyd grunted. He hadn't thought of that!

The year 1940 began with the return of the two stories I'd left with Fred Pohl. He'd decided that there wasn't anything wrong with them, but that they just weren't what he wanted. I felt rather relieved, since I'd discovered that *Astonishing* was going to pay only half a cent a word. There were many magazines that paid even less, but the writers in their articles for *Writers' Digest* were claiming that one cent a word should be the minimum.

I saw nothing wrong with competing against professional writers for a spot in the market. But I did feel a little uneasy about doing so for what they seemed to regard as "scab" rates—despite the fact that I knew many of them were accepting such rates.

I expected to do a lot less writing during the year. I'd learned from the rather corny ending on "Reincarnate" that forcing ideas was not a good thing, in my case. My ideas needed time to ripen—and if some withered away during the maturing process, they were better left unwritten. I still feel this is true; and many of my later stories would have been improved by being filed away in my head until I felt ready to do them.

But I wrote a little, mostly when the urge struck me without my hastening it. "The Pipes of Pan" was an old plot that had begun with a vague idea that Pan might appear on Wall Street—tied in with the ancient and modern meaning of panic. Eventually, it changed until I was interested in what happened to a god when his last worshiper dies and he has to go to work. It wrote easily to 6,000 words, and Campbell let me know he liked it better than anything I'd done for quite a while.

There was an unexpected bonus, too. Phil Stong wrote to say he'd pay ten dollars for the right to include it in an anthology to be entitled *The Other Worlds*. In those days, the idea of having a story of fantasy put between hard covers was an impossible dream. It was unheard-of. The price didn't matter, but the free copy of the book was enough to make sure I agreed. I had sold all rights to Street and Smith—a normal arrangement then—but they were very gracious about releasing any right for a specific purpose, so I wrote Stong an enthusiastic acceptance.

"Dark Mission" was one of those ideas that didn't seem to require much time to ripen. I think I wrote it within a few weeks after first getting the idea. It involved a man who seems to be injured in some rocket accident and deprived of his memory. But he has two driving urges—one to avoid any skin contact with other men, and the other to find and destroy our first spaceship. In the end, it turns out he's from Mars, where a plague is killing them all off, and he's come here to prevent our going there and contracting the illness. It was a pretty simple idea, but Campbell paid $80 for the 6,400 words.

Then I got trapped into far more work than I expected to do in writing. James Beard, the fantasy fan and myth authority, sent an idea to Campbell which he thought I should try. It was worked out in great detail, and looked easy. So I simply turned the outline into fiction. Campbell promptly sent it back with a long letter saying the story lacked feeling and conviction.

I know now that I should never collaborate. My stories tend to be pretty personal things, and my working methods don't fit well with most other writers. But I had taken on the responsibility; I'd agreed to split the proceeds with Beard, and that meant there had to be such proceeds.

So I sat down and thought it all through, following Campbell's letter. He complained that my lead character was both dull and foolish—and he was right. So I had to pick a more interesting one. This time I picked the safety of a narrator—an old woman who saw what went on, but who could be an interesting character by herself.

That came back with a note indicating the story was now better, but it still didn't have much feeling in the areas where it needed the most intensity.

And so finally, I began to realize a lot about viewpoint in a story —the most valuable lesson I think I ever learned. I hunted through the story to find the one person who was most deeply affected by the events and who was central to them. It came out to 6,400 words, and I split the $80 with Beard, so I didn't make much on it. But even then I knew it was a useful exercise. Since then, I've never had much trouble finding the right viewpoint, so all the work on "Carillon of Skulls" was well worthwhile.

It appeared under the pen name of Philip James, using half of Philip St. John and half of James Beard. Why I didn't simply list both our names is more than I can remember.

9.

Carillon of Skulls

(by Philip James)

Ann Muller ran a pale hand down the massive bole of the single oak, standing out in forsaken grandeur over the ruins of Lefferts Park, and gripped tightly on a shaggy outcropping of its bark. Through a hole in the tattered leaves overhead she saw angry clouds scudding across the sky and watched the last threads of the moon vanish, leaving the park a pit of sordid black. She shuddered and old words slipped through her teeth.

"How long wilt Thou forget me, O Lord? Forever? How long wilt Thou hide Thy face from me? My God, my God, why hast Thou forsaken me?"

"Strange words from you, dearie." The voice piped up from the blackness near her, ending in a cackling hiccup. A thin shaft of moonlight trickled down again, showing an old crone with dirty gray hair and the ragged shreds of former beauty still clinging to the reddened face. "Strange names you're calling on this night, I'm thinking. Hee!"

Ann dropped her hand from the tree and nodded faintly. "Perhaps. You're late, Mother Brian. Did you find the remedy?"

"That I did, and simple enough, too. Dried dust of balsam needles, the book said, and I have it with me. Here's your bag with it, though I'd not open the same, was I you. And the bullet. What you'll be doing, though—"

"Your pay," the girl suggested, stripping a curious green-set ring from her finger. "It's all I have now."

Mother Brian—Madame Olga, the seeress, she called herself now—pushed it aside. "Then you keep it, dearie. I've whiskey money this night, and you used to be a good girl, once. It's a long memory only that brings Madame Olga into this God-forsaken place, not pay. Hee! A sweet girl, if a bit headstrong and foolish before—"

"Yes. Thank you, Mother Brian. What night is it?"

"Friday." She bit the word out reluctantly, and the girl jerked back at it, her fingers trembling as she caught at the oak bark again. In the dark, the old dealer in spells stretched forth a solicitous hand.

"Friday! Are you sure?" Ann's eyes strained against the darkness, and saw truth on the other's face. "Then that's why *he* was with me when I woke. He doesn't trust me now, but whispers his orders in my ear while I'm sleeping."

"Lot of good it'll do him this night. They've a police guard all about the place so only them as know the old tunnel can squeeze through the bulls and get in. It's an empty night for him, the slimy thing. For a thimble of smoke, I'd be—"

"No." Ann interrupted again, wearily. She was strangely tired, and the assurance of Madame Olga failed to bring hope with it. "No, they wouldn't believe you, and he'd—hunt. You'd better leave now, Mother Brian. He might come."

"Hee! He'll be busy still." But she turned away and went creaking out through the gloom with a grunted farewell.

Ann slumped against the tree, noting that the rift in the clouds was only a brief flash this time, and that it promised to be the last that night. But her eyes were accustomed to the dark, and she watched the old figure hobble away, down into a weed-grown hole, and out of sight toward safety.

Then she twitched her shoulders and stepped out from under the tree, picking her way through the tangle around. At one time Lefferts Park had been the mecca of the amusement-minded, with theater, roller-skating rink, picnic grounds, and places where barkers announced the admission price was "only a thin dime, folks, the tay-yenth paht of a dollah." But that had been years before.

Now weeds and sumac had overgrown it, crowding against the few deserted beech-trees. Where the wooden recreation buildings and flashy theater had been, there was only an irregular series of pock-marks in the ground, cellars half filled in by dirty cans, bottles, and general debris, or crumbling foundation walls, overgrown with a mossy fungus of some kind. Charred boards and cinders of old dead fires showed that the last occupants had been bums seeking its weedy privacy for the night.

Ann picked her way with uncannily sure feet through the maze, hardly glancing at the tangle about her. She was thinking of other things, chiefly of *him* and his reasons, and her thoughts were barely rational. If only the control were less complete, so that she could pierce through to his object, or remember details, if— But there were too many ifs. It was Friday night, when his commands were always strongest; what those commands were or had been was hazy, but the repressed memories in the back of her mind filled her with a dread that was greater because of its vague uncertainty.

She skirted the roller-skating pavilion, an area treacherous with covered holes, and slipped quickly past what had been the Apollo Theater. Across town a bell sounded, laboring under the twelve strokes of midnight, and yellowish light began to shine through the back windows of the theater. They were getting ready for another performance, apparently, though the marquee was still either missing or hidden by the shadows. Probably her duties would lead her there before the night finished.

The gateway leading from the park was in front of her then, and she looked out cautiously. Mother Brian had been right; two police were moving slowly up and down in front. Some of their words spilled back to her.

" 'Tis the very broth of hell's kettle in there, MacDougall, I'm thinking. I'd put face to the Old One himself before I'd be sleeping in there, sure as my name's O'Halloran."

"Aye."

"Yet fools there are, and newspapermen, like as not the one under two names. Devil a bit of it do I like."

"Aye."

Back in the park, a shrill burble of sound keened out in what might have been a laugh or a shriek of derision. O'Halloran hunched his big shoulders and scowled in its general direction. "Faith, what a noise, not human at all, at all. Well, 'twas probably the wind a-howling through a hole. No need to be looking again for what made it, d'you think? Better to stick to our beat."

"Aye."

The girl turned back aimlessly, still mumbling over the dark suspicions in her mind. That shriek had been *his* voice, directed at her for loitering. Ann knew, but what good were his orders if no one entered the park? Of course, there was no one there, so she had nothing to fear. He—but who was he? Something probed at her mind, and vanished, leaving her standing there uncertainly. She knew where she was, but how had she got there, and why? What was she doing at night in Lefferts Park? She was sure she had known an instant before, but now the memory eluded her.

Then she was conscious of being cold, and the faint smell of woodsmoke coming to her from the back of the park. Someone must have a fire there that would offer warmth and companionship until her vagrant memory returned. She shivered and moved forward toward it, now picking out her way carefully, and stumbling a little over the tangled ruins under her feet. Down in a hollow beyond her, sheltered by a corner of a wall that still stood, she caught a flicker of yellow light and hastened toward it, drawing the inconspicuous dark suit closer to her thin, small body, and clutching tightly on the odd handbag, decorated with bright beads and closed at the top by means of a drawstring.

There was a man at the fire, she saw now, and hesitated. But he was well dressed and pleasant-faced as he bent over to light his cigarette from the fire and put on more wood. As he straightened, he caught sight of her from the corner of his eye and jerked around in surprise. "Hello, there," he called uncertainly, staring at her doubtfully. But her large gray eyes, contrasting with the white face, must have been reassuring, for he motioned her forward. "Care to join me?"

"Please, yes . . . I hope you don't mind." She shouldn't be here, talking to a strange man, but until the vanished thread of memory returned, there was little else to do. "It was so dark and cold out there alone, and I saw your fire. I'll go away, if you wish."

He smiled quickly at that. "No, glad to have you. Coffee? There. Afraid the rock is the best seat I can offer you." As she settled down beside the fire, he smiled again, and she was no longer afraid of him; only of the dark outside the rim of light thrown by the fire. Then, suddenly he frowned. "How'd you get in here? I thought the police were guarding the whole place."

"Were they? I didn't know. Nobody stopped me. . . . And how'd you get here, then?"

"Oh, they know I'm here; got a permit from the captain to stay here and see what happens for my newspaper—the Kendicon *Daily Leader*. I'm Harry Chapman, Miss—"

"Ann Muller."

"Hmm. Well, anyway, White—the editor—sent me down here. We couldn't find any trace or clue of the heads that have been missing, so he figured it would at least make a good suspense story, and might even trap the maniac who's responsible." At her uncertain look, he stopped. "You know about the missing heads, don't you?"

Was she supposed to? There was something vaguely familiar about it, but nothing clear. "No."

"Don't read the papers, eh? Well, briefly it's like this. Every week for the past four weeks, there's been a man killed here. Every Saturday morning the police find a body—but no head. They've hunted for the missing heads, but there's not even a speck of blood left to show where they went. Either some maniac's loose here, or there's black magic—which we don't believe. But nobody can find any traces."

Ann nodded, poking at the fire with a stick and only half listening. "I must have heard something about it, I guess, but not much. What happened?"

"That's the catch; nobody knows. The first three were bums, probably just hiding out here for the night, but the third was Dean Mallory . . . had an orchestra playing at the Dug-Out. At a guess, I'd say he stumbled here in looking for atmosphere for a modern thing he was writing, and it got him. His head was sheared off as clean as a cut of meat from the butcher. . . . Hope I'm not frightening you?"

"No." Whatever reaction came to her from Chapman's words, it wasn't fear, though there had been a tinge of fright since the moment when she first noticed the park about her. Her eyes wandered out into the shadows and back to him quickly. "They think it's a maniac?"

"All except a drunken old fortune-teller named Olga. She's been pestering the police sergeant with tales of the supernatural. Claims it's a nis. And I think he about half believes her, judging by the stress he lays on the absence of rats from the ruins, and the cross he made me wear around my neck." Harry tapped his shirt to indicate the faint bulge of the tiny object. "You know, it's lucky you found me; running around here alone might be bad. More coffee?"

"No, thanks." Funny the way the flickering light on his face made it seem quixotical and boyish. Ann slipped closer to him. "What's a nis, some kind of evil ghost? I . . . I've heard the name somewhere, I think."

"Mmm. I had to look it up in a book." He bit off the corner of a cigarette package, pulled one out, and lighted it without disturbing the arm on the stones behind her. Where his fingers touched her back, little dancing tingles went tripping up as he continued. "Seems a nis is someone who was too interested in life and too contrary to die, so he turns into a half-demon, decides on what he wants to do and does it, not bothering about normal men anymore. According to the book, there used to be one who stole colors from living people to paint his pictures, leaving them with eyes black as a stoat's and hair like the feathers of a crow. But nisses can't stand sunlight, so it killed him when he tried to steal the colors from the sunlight."

Ann stirred restlessly. "Good always triumphs in the stories, doesn't it? And I think you used the wrong plural."

"Probably. There's another story with a somewhat neater ending, if you'd care to hear it. . . . Mmm. One of them took up lodging in a valley hidden from civilization and went about building up a choir. He swiped the voices from all the yokels around and played on them like an organ, thundering his music down from the hills in a great symphony. Naturally, without voices, the people were struck dumb. Then word got out, and musicians began stemming in from the far corners of the earth to listen. But so many who came left their voices behind in the valley that in time they stopped coming, and even the location of the valley was lost to man's memory."

"Rather horrible, those legends, aren't they?" She stretched out suddenly and got to her feet, restlessness stirring in her. "Let's go somewhere to a show; I'll pay my way. At least, it's more cheerful than sitting out here all night."

Harry glanced at his watch. "It's rather late. What show'd you have in mind?"

"Apollo, I guess." What other show would they see, with the Apollo only a few yards away across the park? There was no point to going clear across town to another. "Just cheap vaudeville, of course, but better than usual this week; at least everybody says so."

Chapman made no comment, but came to his feet quickly, one

hand sliding back to his pocket and clutching at something there; in the flickering light, it looked like the handle of a gun. His actions were suddenly unfriendly and odd. She turned at his motion, leading the way, and he followed a few feet behind. She could feel his eyes riveted on the nape of her neck, and hear him muttering something that sounded suspiciously like "maniac," but she shook her head and stopped puzzling about it, heading toward the theater. From the dark ahead, a gurgling ululation sounded. There was something about it—where had she heard that before?

"Lord!" Harry's gasp behind her cut through her thoughts and brought them back to him. "Look! It's there!"

His fingers were pointing ahead to the building that reared up from the tangled ground, its marquee blazing with light, announcing the stellar attraction of *Loto, the Incomparable.* The lights spelled out Apollo Theater in no uncertain letters.

"Of course it's there. What did you expect?" His odd surprise was amusing, though it annoyed her a little. "Shall we go in?"

"Listen, I may be crazy, but O'Halloran and I went over the grounds this morning, and it wasn't there then. I even dug part of that sign out of the wreckage. There hasn't been an Apollo Theater for forty years. You'll be telling me next I'm the headhunting maniac." He stared about hastily, and his fingers clutched more tightly on the object in his pocket. "What's the game?"

He was being silly about something. Perhaps it would be best to forget about taking him in, she thought, then felt a pressing urgency to have him accompany her. "It's always been there, Harry," she assured him soothingly. "You must have been imagining things by the fire; people do that sometimes."

"Mmm. All right, I'm crazy. . . . I must be, unless I'm asleep 'by the fire.' Okay, in we go. This wouldn't make good copy, but it may be interesting—maybe." He strode forward grimly, glancing back at her once as if expecting her to be gone. She smiled at him, but there was no lightening of his face.

Suppose he was right? He seemed so positive, and there were alarming gaps in her memory. Something had happened before she found herself in the park, but she could recall none of it. And this building, standing in the wilderness about, didn't make sense. She glanced at the sign again, studying the billing. *Loto, the Incomparable.* Who and what was Loto? Harry was back at her side then, and she clutched his arm.

"Let's not go in; I've changed my mind. There's something wrong here; I can feel it."

"You're darned right there is. They aren't charging amusement tax, for one thing. Still trying to tell me I'm crazy?"

"I don't know. I can't remember what I should about all this; there's a blank in my head."

"Mmm. You're a queer kid, Ann, and I should take you to O'Halloran, but I'm going to trust you instead. Maybe there's a cog slipped in your memory—amnesia; we'll see about it later." He took her hand and the friendliness she wanted from him was back, though determination pulled his face in stern lines. "Come on, we're in this now, and whatever it is, I'm seeing it through. It wouldn't surprise me to find the missing heads somewhere at the bottom of it. Game to try it?"

Ann tossed her head, though a prickling of her skin seemed like a warning, and they passed into the lobby. There was a moldy smell in the air, and a look of cheap opulence to the place that dated it. The unsmiling usher greeted them, his face masked in shadows, and led them down the middle aisle and to fancy plush-covered seats at the edge. The place was dimly lighted, probably by gas lamps, and the shadows spewed over the audience and up to the stage, which stood out in a contrasting glare of brilliance, though the curtain was still down. The musty odor was stronger, and the hissing buzz of the audience already seated carried a note that was half familiar, but entirely unpleasant.

Harry nudged her. "Notice anything queer about the audience? No? Well, try and pick out any details. All I can see are dark blobs. I can't focus on them—might as well be a veil over the whole place—and I don't like it, Ann. Maybe you shouldn't be here."

"*Shh.* I'm here now." She caught his hand. It was nice to be worried over. Whatever her past, she was sure there had been too little of that. "Curtain's going up."

"Yeah."

There was a fanfare from the orchestra pit and a blurred announcement from the stage, followed by a quartet, all with long moustaches and dressed in tight pants, who came out and sang sentimental ballads, ending on the sad song of "Nelly, the Bartender's Daughter," unexpurgated. Ann had the impression that it was old to her, even the disgust at the cheap words. Harry grunted, but said nothing.

A team doing stunts on roller skates to jingling ragtime came next, followed by a man who juggled little balls that looked like glass eyes. Ann was still puzzling over the feeling of familiarity with the acts. Harry sat with his eyes glued on the stage, and his nerves sticking out all over. A hush settled over the audience, and the stage lights cut to a center spot, coming from the wings, and leaving two lanes of black around the lighted section.

Offstage a ratty voice announced the main feature with unctuous pride. "The Great Loto, with his Carillon of Skulls, the Delight of the Crowned Heads of Europe, in Person. Rasputin himself was proud to honor the art of the Incomparable Loto. Ladeezngents, we now bring you a new and hitherto Unplayed Symphony of his own composition. I give you—Loto!"

A full roll from the drums brought Loto out, dressed like a clown and carrying a large, covered object that must surely be his instrument. But his chalk-white face and long, red mouth were entirely unfunny, and the tapering fingers of his hands might have belonged to an Inca priest, adept at tearing the living heart out of a sacrifice. When he removed the covering from his instrument, it was revealed to be in truth a long line of skulls, suspended from a shining bar by small chains. The effect was appalling, and a low shudder of expectancy ran through the audience.

Loto was a good showman; the skulls went into the lane of light, so that attention was focused on them and his fingers, which held two small hammers shaped at the ends like teeth. The rest of him was shrouded in shadow, except for the thin white oval of his face. Harry twisted in his seat and caught at Ann's shoulder.

"Third skull from the end!" His breath came whistling between his teeth, harsh against her ear. "Notice the bulge over the eye sockets. If it didn't belong to Dean Mallory, I'll eat it!"

Ann looked, and sickness swept over her as something in her head snapped. She remembered noticing—long ago, it seemed—how Mallory's brow bulged out, and now she saw the same on the skull. So that was what *he* wanted! And now, under his command of the night, shrouded in forgetfulness, she had brought another.

"Harry!" She fought down her qualms and forced out the words. "Now I remember. We've—"

"Hush, he's starting. I've got to think this out." His arm on her shoulder held her down, and the weakness that had engulfed her kept her from throwing it aside. She turned her eyes numbly to the stage, and the first of Loto's music clamped her down completely, leaving only numbness and fear.

Loto was swaying back and forth in the semidarkness behind the skulls, tapping out the notes as on a xylophone. Mostly they were in a minor key, but interwoven with majors in a fashion both fascinating and horrible. This piece was worse than the others she had heard; it should never have been written, but it fitted the instrument, and there was a frightful personality to each individual note that seemed to rouse the audience to a frenzy. Loto ran down to a long wail and began developing a rising crescendo, going higher and higher, until the air seemed to shriek under the torture of the impact.

Suddenly he stopped with one hammer in the air above his head, needing still one savage higher note to complete it; but the last skull was missing. The chain which should have held it dangled there, but there was only a screw and a small shred of bone left. A sigh welled up from the audience, and Loto turned to face them, his hammer still in the air. Slowly his feral eyes swung over the rows of seats, lingering just a moment on each, while he seemed to study.

Ann shuddered, knowing what was to come and powerless to stop it as the eyes swung slowly over the seats and toward them. Harry was staring toward the stage, too tense to notice her efforts to attract his attention. Then Loto's eyes found them and lingered, swept sideways, up and down, and came back to Harry. He nodded, lowered his hammer softly, and strode firmly down the steps into the orchestra pit, while the whole audience swung to keep their eyes on him.

Then her hand slid over the beads on her bag and sudden hope shocked her back to control. It would not be this time! Not this man! She dug her fingers into Harry's arm, tightening her grip until he jerked around. "Quick, before he reaches you. If I help now, will you help me later?"

"Of course," he answered, still studying Loto from the corner of his eyes. "But I can take care of Loto. I'm armed."

She shook her head urgently. "No, you mustn't. The others had guns and knives. Here, take my bag—here! Breathe some of the balsam needle dust into your nose like snuff and throw the rest toward Loto. Meet me the same place tomorrow night. . . . Now, quickly!"

Would he never take it! His hand hovered halfway between the useless gun and the bag while his eyes shuttled uncertainly to her, back to Loto, and then to the purse. But some of her sincerity must have impressed him, for he finally reached out impulsively and opened the bag. Loto was at the row in which they sat as he breathed in on the dust and tossed a handful toward the advancing figure.

There was a strangled sound as it spread out in the musty air, and all the blurred outlines wavered. Ann felt something catch at her breath and go stinging down into her lungs. She crumpled down and lost consciousness with a tired little sigh of satisfaction; tonight there would be no headless corpse in Lefferts Park.

With the contrariness of nature, there was a glorious moon the next night, but Ann was in no mood to appreciate it. *He* had not appeared, and she wondered why, unless the effects of the night before were still on him. Surely he must have seen that it was her bag the balsam dust came from, and he was not the forgiving kind. But she was too tired to care much.

What had Harry thought, and would he keep his appointment? Once, years before, there had been another—but that was past. The Apollo was only a weed-grown basement tonight, but she gave it a wide berth; there was no way of telling where *he* might be hiding. Then a faint smell of smoke reached her, and she half smiled and quickened her pace a little. Harry had remembered.

"*Hiss!* Annie, lass." It was Madame Olga's voice, and Ann stopped to let the hobbling figure catch up with her. "Och, now, I've been chasing you all over the place, I have. I've almost run my legs off my poor old body, dearie."

Half annoyed, Ann waited until the old crone caught her breath. "What is it, Mother Brian?"

"Hee! I'm a fool, dearie—a fool, no less—poking my nose where it's no business a-being. But I looked in on you last night, and a rare sight it was, seeing *him* get the surprise he did. A-standing there on them old stones, making noises fit for the Old One, while the two of you sat like ones bewitched on the dirty old wall. Though I'm sorry you learned of the things he'd have you do; 'twas ever my thought that you'd best never find that out."

She thrust a dirty paper sack into Ann's hands. "Your young man forgot them, and O'Halloran—the dumb mick—never saw a thing but the lad asleeping in the ruins. Most smart and proper was the tongue-lashing he gave the boy, too. Hee! You'll find your bag, your bullet . . . which'll fit; I tried it . . . and his gun there in the bag. I was after them as soon as the sun upped in the early morning."

"Thank you, Mother Brian. You're kind." The girl fiddled uncomfortably with the sack, and stared out toward the source of the smoke. Madame Olga cackled.

"All right, be off with you, dearie, since you're wanting the sight of him. But keep the two ears of you open. I had the cards out this day, and I read things in them that'll surprise you, mayhap."

She chuckled again and made off quickly before Ann could ask what the surprises were. But the girl wasted no time in wondering. Tucking the bag under her arm, she moved forward toward Harry's fire, hastily inserting the cartridge Madame Olga had made into the gun. Unless her plans went wrong, another morning should find release for her. Then, as she neared the fire, she caught the rich voice of O'Halloran and saw two bulky figures beside that of the reporter. Moving soundlessly, she slid into the shelter of a tangle of scrub growth and waited.

"Kept thinking I'd heard the name," O'Halloran was saying, "though where you heard it, devil knows. But sure enough, this morning it come to me. Used to be a girl by that name poking around here, looking for something; claimed she was busy about historical research or something. But that was twenty, twenty-five years ago, and never a word has been heard of her since; disappeared all of a sudden, like she came. Little, dark, queer thing she was."

Harry nodded vaguely. "Probably not the person I'm thinking of, though it fits. . . . I still think the center of what's going on here is the Apollo."

"Might be. I grew up hereabouts, lad, and there was ever men—strong, God-fearing men they was, too—who'd have devil a thing to do with the place, even in broad daylight. Sure, being a kid, I wanted to see for myself, what with the skating rink and all that, but I was never allowed it. Well, don't be dreaming again this night, lad. Come on, MacDougall, we belong outside."

"Aye." They lumbered off, flashing their lights about nervously.

Ann waited a few minutes more, while Harry glanced at his watch and fidgeted on the rough stone seat, then slipped out of her concealment and was beside him before he realized his waiting was over.

"So I didn't dream up this date, then?" For a man of almost thirty, the embarrassment on his face was almost too boyish, but Ann decided it was charming in a way. He suffered from another acute case of fidgets before he went on. "Look, Ann, I feel like a heel for going to sleep on you last night. Darn fool stunt, and I can't even remember what happened."

"Sleep?"

"Yeah. Right after I finished the nis yarn, I guess . . . wasn't it? *Ugh*, and what nightmares I had. Walking around in my sleep and letting O'Halloran find me in the ex-Apollo!" He grimaced sheepishly. "If I hadn't found your footprints around here, I'd have thought the whole thing was imagination. When did you leave?"

The temptation to continue the pretense of his sleeping was almost overpowering, but cold logic choked back the impulse, even as she started to follow it. *He* was still somewhere near, and there was no time for small talk. "After you threw the dust," she answered, holding out the automatic to him. "Here, Mo . . . Madame Olga found this and sent it to you."

"After I—" He disregarded the gun, his face freezing into a tight mask of suspicion. "That's ridiculous! I looked over the Apollo as soon as O'Halloran woke me, and it's in ruins. What's the game?"

"Only the truth, Harry. Would I remember your dreams—the dust, the carillon, how you were unable to see the audience clearly? You saw the Apollo through my eyes, and I'm . . . But you promised to help me."

He nodded reluctantly, only partially convinced. "If it's true, I did. But—hell, what is it you want?"

Ann held out the gun again, trembling a little, now that the moment had actually come. The carefully rehearsed explanation she had planned in advance left her now and she stumbled for words. And from across the park, a quavering shriek keened out, warning her there was no time to waste.

"Well?" Chapman's voice was impatient.

"There's a silver bullet in it now," she began, and hesitated. Then, because she could find no other way, she blurted it out in a rush. This acting as a lure under temporary forgetfulness must stop, and there was no other escape. "I want you to use it on me, Harry! It . . . oh, I can't explain it, but you must. You promised!"

Blankness crowded the grimness and suspicion from his face, only to vanish abruptly. He grabbed her shoulder and began shaking it, shouting at her. "Ann, are you crazy? Of all the damned nonsense! Put up that gun. And if you try to use it yourself, I'll spank you—soundly!"

So she had failed; the human taboos she had almost forgotten were stronger than his promise. But it had seemed so right, so obvious to her! Wearily she slipped from him and back toward the tangled hinterland. "All right. I can't use it anyway; that's part of *his* commands. Good night, Harry!"

"Wait. No you don't!" One of his arms caught her as she turned and swung her back. "You're going to explain this mess before you go. And whose commands are you talking about?"

Her futile struggles against him were cut short as a voice oozed out of the shadows behind them. Still dressed in his clown's clothing, Loto slipped out from a clump of weeds. "I believe," he said unctuously, "that I am the one she refers to. I'm her master, even when she tries to disobey me." He was rubbing his hooked fingers over the edge of a curved saber and there was a sickly grin on his chalky face. "Ah, what a lovely skull shape, man-thing. I admire it."

Ann saw Harry tense for a spring as Loto lifted the heavy blade and knew he would never make it. Up went the blade, twisting a little, curved in the air, and started down! Then the scream that had been stuck in her throat ripped out, and she felt one of her hands, stll clutching the gun, go up to knock against the blade, just as Harry began his leap. But the saber continued down. She heard it thwack as it struck and saw Harry crumple into a heap. Loto moved forward.

"Stop!" Her throat was frozen shut so that the word was only a whisper, but Loto heard it and paused.

His voice was filled with furious arrogance. "You dare! One side, wench! You've been useful, but this is too much for my patience. Drop that harmless toy and leave me!"

"The harmless toy," she warned him quietly, "is loaded with a silver bullet."

Loto checked himself. "Silver! You fool, you little fool! If you dared to use it, you couldn't go back to your place without me, and the morning would find you here. You know what that means?"

"Death, I suppose, when the sunlight touches me."

"Death!" He wrenched the word out and started forward again. "And an unpleasant one, I assure you. Give me that gun."

As he reached for it, her fingers seemed to contract of their own volition, and the automatic coughed once. Disbelief flickered over Loto's face. He threw out one arm, easing slowly to the ground, his eyes boring into her. "You . . . you love the man; I should have known."

Blood was trickling from his mouth, and he coughed his throat clear, forcing himself half erect. "Then, Ann Muller, I give back your womanhood before I . . . die. I revoke the curse. And the man-thing . . . is stunned . . . no more. You—" Something that was either a smile or a sneer slit his thin mouth and was replaced by horror as he pitched forward limply.

Ann stumbled back into the shadow of a tree. The curse was gone, as Loto had said—she had felt the change as he spoke; but the picture of him softening under the shadow of death was too much for her to grasp.

"Harry!" she called, wondering fearfully whether the last words had been truthful.

They had. Harry was coming toward her as she turned, rubbing his temples. "It's all right, Ann. Only the flat of the blade, thanks to you. I came to just as you shot and heard the rest."

"Then you know?"

"Hush, it doesn't matter now. We'll forget all this nightmare." Faintly in the darkness, she saw his eyes smiling down at her, and a glow swept up and enveloped her like a soft wind. "But O'Halloran must have heard the shot and he can't find you here—too hard to explain. Know someplace to hide?"

"There's an old hidden tunnel near the Apollo."

"Good. I'll tell O'Halloran I shot the maniac and phone the paper. Then . . ." His lips brushed light across her forehead and he turned her around and pushed her gently away. "When it's safe, I'll find you. Now, off with you."

Somehow her feet found their way through the tangle, but her thoughts were dancing on ahead, no longer bothered by Loto's strange reversal of manner or the quick telescoping of events. Ahead, the Apollo loomed up, its naked ruins now nothing but a monument to a dead past, and behind the wind brought the faint sound of excited voices. She stopped beside the old oak, caressing its wrinkled bark, then turned toward the tunnel, slowly, as the emotions denied her so long pulsed hotly through her. So intent on them was she that she almost tripped over a dim-burning lantern before she noticed Madame Olga squatting in the tunnel.

"Mother Brian—"

"I know, dearie." The seeress rose slowly to her feet, her eyes on the rotten door that covered the entrance. "I heard, and 'twas a good thing to see him a-dying, may the Old One carry his foul soul away!"

"*Shh!*" Ann couldn't hate him now, not with the curse so newly gone from her. "Mother Brian, I'm a woman again. A woman!"

"That I know, too, and the words you've been hearing from the boy. But did the lad see your face—did he that, Annie child?"

"I don't suppose so; we were in the shadows. But what's wrong with that?" In the old woman's eyes there was a glint of tears before they dropped again, and something that sent a cold lance of fear down her back. Ann clutched at the bent shoulders. "Mother Brian, is there—? There's nothing wrong? There can't be!"

For answer, the crooked old fingers groped in a dirty bag and came out with a broken mirror. "When you've done with it, I'll be waiting at the other end," Madame Olga said gently. "Don't be waiting too long."

She went hobbling off hastily and Ann raised the mirror, studying it with dawning comprehension. There had been no kindness in Loto's last gesture! Even dying, he had planned that time, held in abeyance during the years his trickery had held her, should finally catch up with her. And Harry! But he was young enough to forget, though he might wonder for a time.

The cracked mirror slipped from her fingers and shattered on the floor, its work finished. Then, with a low moan, she turned slowly down the tunnel, away from all she wanted in life. For the face in the mirror had been that of a woman of fifty, without even a trace of youthfulness to match her unchanged emotions.

I started another story almost immediately after the collaboration was finally successful. I suspect that I felt some need to get back on my feet and wanted to get the taste of the previous experience out of my mouth.

I'd read in some book or article on writing that a good way to get an idea is to look for some obvious and accepted truth, and then use the opposite idea as the basis for a story. It's one of the numerous gimmicks to make plotting easier—and like most of them, one that probably is harder to master generally than the art of direct plotting. Most stories based on such gimmicks seem strained and contrived, anyhow. But I remembered it when a crippled friend was complaining that space travel would never mean anything to people like him, because no handicapped person would ever be permitted to enter a rocket.

The story was easy to write, and Campbell bought it. But this time there was no bonus on its 6,400 words. I wasn't writing enough to make my name important, and the story was what he called a standard tear-jerker, which didn't deserve a bonus.

He was planning to run it in the same issue with the long-overdue "Stars Look Down" and he needed a different by-line on it. How about using Philip St. John?

Well, this was a highly sentimental story, and the St. John name was supposed to be used for stories that were not sentimental. But I couldn't think of another name on the spur of the moment.

I now consider the use of multiple pen names bad business for a beginning writer. Generally, a man's own proper name is the best, for a number of legal and business reasons of convenience. But there are sometimes good reasons for adopting something else. Not, however, for a whole raft of names. If a story is below par, a wise beginner should scrap it, or put it aside until he can do it properly. If it's good, he should use his normal writing name on it. He needs all the credit he can get in establishing himself. As in every other business, a good brand name helps sell the goods. I learned that after about the hundredth time someone said to me, "Oh, did *you* write that? Why that's one of my favorite stories."

Anyhow, Philip St. John was credited with the story, "Done Without Eagles."

10.

Done Without Eagles

(by Philip St. John)

The triangulator registered eight thousand miles up from Earth, though naturally we couldn't see the old ball behind us. When they built the *Kickapoo,* they left out all windows and covered her with a new laboratory product to bounce back hard radiations, which is why I have a couple of normal kids instead of half-monsters; cosmic rays just love to play around with a man's genes and cause mutations if they get a chance. Anyway, the spy instruments we used were worth a whole factory of portholes.

Captain Lee Rogers ran his eyes over the raised indicators when I signaled that we'd made one diameter, and found them all grooved where they should be. He pushed back his shoulders and tapped down for normal space acceleration before swinging around to face me. "They all come back, Sammy," he said, for no good reason I could see. "Once a man's been outside the atmosphere, you can't keep him grounded. Remember Court Perry?"

How could I help it, with some of the records he'd made still unbeaten? He'd won his eagles back in the old quartz-window days.

Then, when they built the *Kickapoo* as the first blind ship and made him captain, he'd made history and legends for six years, until even the die-hards admitted spy instruments worked, and every student in navigation school with marrying ideas darned near worshiped him. After that, his landings and takeoffs began to go sour, and got worse for months. They seemed to be improving again at the last, but it was too late then; the officials called him in and yanked his eagles, offering him an office job instead, which he turned down. That had been five years before and nobody had heard a word of the captain since.

"Sure," I told Lee. "It was before I got my copilot ticket on the *Kickapoo*, but they gave us his life for inspirational reading in navigation school. Why?"

He handed me over a hen-scratched paper giving the passenger listings. "Take a look at the angel roll. The steward sent it up for my okay on the use of the superdeck cabin."

"Inspector eyeing our flare?" The superdeck cabin is reserved for officials, usually, and lies right down the hall from the dugout—navigation room—next to the captain and pilot's quarters.

Lee shook his head. "Free-wing angels. We're carrying a full load this trip, and they came aboard with 'any consideration will be appreciated' passes, so I had to okay it. You might read it, you know."

It was an idea, though I was beginning to catch on. All the same, my eyes popped when I saw the names after Cabin O-A. "Captain Courtney R. Perry, Ret., and Stanley N. Perry, M.A., M.M., Ph.D., F.R.P.S., F.R.S.," I read. "Mmm. So he's come out of the hole. Who's the alphabet?"

"Court Perry's son, and that's only part of his degrees and such. One of the hard-radiation mutes." Mutation, he meant, not speechless. "Born while the captain was on the old ships, so don't be surprised when you see him. Claims he's a superman, and maybe he is—Get ready for trouble, Sammy."

"I don't get it." I'd been wanting to meet Court Perry for years, and this looked like a first-class opportunity to me.

Lee grimaced. "Naturally, not knowing him. I was his pilot before they sacked him, though, and I know what he'll think of another man pushing his ship. Inside of an hour, you'll hear a knock on the door there, and won't have to guess who it is."

Lee was wrong, partly. It wasn't more than half an hour before the knock came, and the door opened to show the hugest body I'd seen on a man six feet tall and not fat. It was topped by a head that was simply magnificent; beautiful describes it better than handsome. And below that—well, the man had four arms, all fully developed, and muscled like a gorilla's, with long hands that ended in six tapering fingers apiece. Apparently the double shoulder system left no room for a waist, but ran in a straight line from hips up. I must have gasped, but the mute took no notice of it.

"Hi, Lee. How's tricks?"

Lee gave him a rather troubled grin and came to his feet to grab one of the arms. "Not bad, Stan, though the two of you might have written once in a while. You're looking good. How's Court?"

"All right, I guess." He swung a couple of hands in an uncertain gesture that gave me the heebies. "He wants to join you here for a while, if you don't mind."

"Afraid I can't. The rules forbid passengers—"

"What's that?" The voice rapped out from the hall and swung me around to face a little, thin man with a ramrod down his back and a neat Vandyke on his face. He looked like the sort who'd hit heaven and been routed through hell on the return ticket, but come through it. Pride, authority, and indignation were all mixed, and another expression I couldn't quite place. Something about him made me pull my stomach in and come to attention, even though he wasn't wearing twin eagles on his old space cap.

"What's that, Lee?" he rapped out again, pushing forward to the dugout. "When have I ever been an angel, eh? Don't be an ass!"

Lee's arm barred his way. "Sorry, sir, but technically you're an angel now. The rule clearly states that no passengers are to be admitted to navigation or engine rooms under any circumstances. You taught me those rules were to be obeyed!"

"I taught you not to be a blamed fool! Out of my way, Lee. I'm coming in. I want to find out what's happened to my ship while you've been running it. Stan, make way for me!"

Stan started forward, and I didn't like the look of those bulking shoulders, but Lee waved him back with a sharp gesture. There were little creases torturing his forehead, and the muscles along his jaw stood out sharply. "Sorry, Captain Perry. I'm wearing the eagles on this ship. Return to your quarters!"

For only a fraction of a second, Court Perry winced, and then his face froze into a blank. "Very good, Captain Rogers," he said precisely, coming to salute. He executed a right-about-turn with a snap and marched down the hall, fingering the place where the eagles should have been, Stan following.

I swung to Lee. "Good Lord, man, did you have to—"

"I had to." The cigarette in his hands was mashed to a pulp, and he tossed it away savagely, fiddling with the controls, while the air machine clicked out the only noises in the room and I made myself busy with charts. Finally he shrugged and reached for another cigarette.

"Court Perry dug me out of an orphanage, Sammy, put me through navigation school, and taught me all he knew about running the *Kickapoo.* He's—" Lee stopped and looked to see how I was taking it. "All right, I suppose it does make me seem an ungrateful pup. But if I'd broken that rule or let him override my authority, he'd have hated me for a weakling and himself for having failed with me. Now let's forget it and wait for his next move. He won't give up on the first try."

He didn't. Almost as Lee finished speaking, the etherphone *ikked* from behind the controls and I jumped to answer it. " 'Lee Rogers,' " I read as it came over, " 'Captain, *Kickapoo:* Captain Courtney Perry and son are to have full freedom of ship. Signed, Redman, president—' How'd they get word through without sending on our transmitter?"

"Probably Stan built a sender from the pile of gadgets he always carries along."

"In fifteen minutes?"

"Mm-hmm. He does those things when he wants to. I've seen him take a computator apart and reassemble it in ten." Lee glanced at the clock and slid off the throne. "Take over. So Court still has pull in the office, it seems. Redman had no business interfering; we're in space and my word is supposed to be final. Nothing I can do about it, though. Come in!"

The door snapped open to show Court Perry standing with his feet exactly on the imaginary line of the dugout, Stan behind him. He came to rigid attention and saluted stiffly. Lee returned it. "The freedom of the ship is yours, Captain Perry," he acknowledged. "Sammy, see that Captain Perry is provided with a set of master keys to the lower decks."

"Thank you, Captain Rogers." Court's square shoulders were perhaps a trifle farther back as he stepped over the line and approached the control seat. He reached out as I slid up to let him take it, then hesitated. "With your permission, sir."

"Permission granted." It was the first time I'd seen formality in space, and I felt awkward as a two-tailed comet between them. Lee disappeared around the panel to the etherphone cubbyhole with a handful of miscellaneous and unrelated charts in his hands.

As Court took the seat I had vacated, the huge bulk of Stan moved in front of me, cutting off my view. He was almost too big for the little room. But I could hear the faint sounds of the old man's fingers on the panel, as he tested it bit by bit. He grunted once or twice, and Stan seemed to mutter something, then twitched his arms slightly and looked around. Court got up.

"Copilot—Sammy's the name, isn't it? Good." He nodded faintly at that. "Sammy, where are the testing instruments? I used to keep them under the panel, but apparently they're no longer there."

"We don't have testers, sir; at least, I've never seen any."

"No testers, eh?" He swallowed it carefully, then tossed his voice over the instrument panel. "Captain Rogers, your copilot informs me there are no instrument testers. Is that correct?"

Lee's voice bounced back at him. "It is, Captain Perry. Under the new regulations, we're checked over at both ends, and no tests are made in space. That system has proved entirely satisfactory."

"Hmm. I distinctly remember explaining to you the reasons for space tests. Takeoff accelerations sometimes jar loose a delicate control, and furthermore, ground men are sometimes careless; they're not trained in actual flight conditions, and their lives aren't involved. I advise an immediate test of your instruments. Hall Indicator C responds slowly, and the meteor repeller itself may be at fault instead of the indicator."

"Sorry, sir, that's impossible. We have no testers."

Court grimaced at that. "Your engine-room testers can be adapted. I believe I also taught you how that was done."

"Sorry, Captain Perry," Lee decided positively. "I don't consider such measures necessary under the present regulations."

Seeing the uselessness of arguing, Court shrugged. "Take over, Sammy," he said, relinquishing the controls. "And if he'll listen, you might remind Captain Rogers that Mars lies in the region of the Little Swarm now. Meteors—even peanut-sized ones—aren't pleasant company when the hull repellers are out of order. Now, if I could have those keys—"

When the door closed again, Lee came out of the hole. "Easier than I thought . . . Mmm. Nothing wrong with Indicator C that I can see. It answers to a change in the hull charge perfectly. Wonder what happens next."

Nothing really happened for a while, except that Stan and Court were poking over the ship in a methodless hunt for inefficiency. It was just that something was in the air, an unpleasantness that traveled from the control room down to the crew deck, and finally hit the passengers. But any little thing in space does that, and the old customers of the line shrugged and forgot it, as much as they could. Court wandered about the ship with Stan at his heels, but I could see no particular point to his activities.

I was off duty on a prowl when the first trouble came. Down from the cook's galley came a caterwauling and sounds of some sort of scrap, with the shrill yelps of the little cook predominating. As I bounced around a corner, I saw Tony leave the deck in a flying leap and plunge toward the entrance of his domain.

Then one of Stan's big arms came out carelessly and caught him in midair. "Naughty boy," the mute said softly. "You'll hurt yourself trying that. Lucky I was here to catch you." He held the cook easily, while the little man squirmed and fumed helplessly.

"What's going on here?" I wanted to know. Tony swung away at the sound of my voice and bounced up and down before me.

"Mr. Noyes, you gotta help me, you gotta! They steal my galley; they snoop all over; they won't let me work. How can I cook without I get in? Get 'em out, Mr. Noyes, kill 'em, lock 'em in irons. Oh, Santa Maria, I'll kill 'em so dead! Alla my help's in there and I ain't telling 'em what to do! They'll spoil the dinner. Get away from my galley, you bums, or I'll make soup outa you both! Spoil my dinner, I feed you to pigs! Mr. Noyes, you gotta get 'em out."

Stan grinned at me and winked, which was my first indication that he had a sense of humor of some kind. "Tony's a little overenthusiastic, Sammy. Don't mind him." He caught one of the little man's flailing fists and drew him close, patting his head. "Sh, Tony. Dad decided to investigate the galley, so we dropped down. Tony came in just as we were looking over his pans, and set up a squawk. When he grabbed a butcher knife and came at us, I had to put him out. Finished in there, Dad?"

"All finished." Court appeared in the door. "Tony!"

The tone of voice cut through Tony's indignation and left the cook at limp attention.

"Yes—sir?"

"Tony, you use too much grease, and you don't clean your pans often enough! Look at that!" He held out a frying pan with a thin coat of oil on the bottom. "That carries one meal's flavor over to the next food. I've found grease on your griddles, too, thick enough to come off on my finger and half stale. Anything to say about it?"

"That new helper," Tony suggested weakly. "Musta been the new helper."

"So? Then teach that new helper to keep clean pans. I don't like indigestion. All right, back to your work! Hello, Sammy. Any objections from headquarters?"

"Not this time, sir." I suppose Lee would have objected, but Lee didn't need to know. After all, there had been a slightly off taste to the food this voyage, and I didn't have much use for Tony's treatment of his assistants, anyway.

Court smiled, apparently in the best of spirits after his conquest of the galley. "Fine. I don't suppose Captain Lee has followed my advice, eh? . . . No, I thought not. Thinks I'm a meddling old fool who had no business going over his head. Pigheaded—made him that way, I guess. Needs an accident to teach him good sense—and he'll get it, or I'm mistaken. Damn!"

He caught his foot against a swabber's kit and lurched forward, grabbing at a handrail to regain his balance. "Who left that . . . that bucket in the middle of a man's way? Rollins still bossing the middle decks? A fine way to run a ship! You go on with Sammy, Stan. I'm seeing Rollins."

"Don't want me to go with you, Dad?"

"No, I don't need you. Rollins knows me well enough to behave himself. Swab pails in the middle of the deck!" He went muttering off toward the stairs that led to the crew quarters, carrying himself on parade dress. Stan and I turned up to the superdeck. He began filling his pipe with three hands, while I watched in fascinated silence until it was finished, and he turned back to me.

"Dad's quite a remarkable man, Sammy," he said. "You're not getting a very good slant on him, I suppose, but if you knew him better you'd find it isn't prejudice on my part—I have no prejudices."

"I've seen one thing," I agreed. "He's the only man I ever knew who could be thoroughly provoked with the captain and not take it out on the copilot as well. It's a pity he and Lee can't get together."

The mute threw open the door of his cabin and motioned me in. "Make yourself comfortable. I wouldn't worry about Lee and Dad, fellow. They both put a ship's command above Heaven and Earth, but that'll be finished the minute we dock. Anyway, it's sort of a farewell fling for Dad, so he's making the most of it."

"How do you mean, farewell trip? Thanks, yes." The wine he

brought out of some little gadget was cold and delicious. He sampled his own before replying.

"Heart trouble, they told him. When he found out, he decided to make one more trip in the *Kickapoo* and settle down on Mars. No dying on Earth for him. Keep this under your hat—Lee's not to know—but the chances are all against his living another year. So I left the wife and kids behind and came along."

"The wife and kids?" It had caught me off guard, and I blurted out the question like a darned fool.

There was a grin on his face then. "Sure, I'm married, and there are four children back in Dad's old house—all like me. I'm a true mutation, you know; pass on my differences to any children. It's my duty to continue my strain; otherwise the human race may have to wait a few thousand more years for another superman."

There was certainly no false modesty about him; neither was his tone boasting. About all I could say to that was a grunt.

He grinned again. "It's the truth, Sammy, so why should I deny it? I look strange to you; but you must admit I have advantages physically; among others, I'm practically immune to all diseases. I finished high school and college in the absolute minimum time. I got the 'F.R.P.S.' after my name for working out a process for grinding lenses in a true parabola to an accuracy of one molecule's thickness—using a colloidal abrasive suspended in air, and controlled by the irregularities themselves; that was something they said couldn't be done. Want more proof?"

Something suddenly brought me up out of the seat and toward him, and I could feel a flood of anger running through me at his egotism. I hated the man with a red blood lust that made me crouch in grim determination to clutch and mangle and bite. Then, as quickly as it had come, it was gone, and I found him laughing at me.

"Telepathic control, Sammy, so don't feel foolish. Convinced of my right to call myself super now?"

It was as good an explanation of his ability as anything else, but there were still angles on it. "Okay, you're a superman. But why aren't you out turning the world over? I've never read of a superman in a story where the fellow minded his own business like the average man."

"You won't—it isn't interesting that way. But one superman in a world of normal men isn't enough to do much. His best bet is to raise children and pass it on until only the supermen are left—that's the way nature did it. I learned early to speak and act like a normal man, whatever differences there are in our way of thinking. Anyway, I was brought up by normal men, and I'm somewhat limited by that—my children won't be. More wine?"

I nodded, my head spinning. I'd felt about the same way in training school when I got my first whiff of butyl mercaptan in the chemistry class and was told a living animal could make and use a similar odor. It was a good thing Court came in then.

"Rollins knows better now," he said, satisfaction heavy in his voice. "Sammy, your name's sounding on the caller; captain wants you." And as I slipped out of the cabin toward the dugout, I caught a less-welcome sentence from him. "Think I'll look over the engine room tomorrow, Stan."

All I could do was pray!

Apparently my prayers weren't much good, though. Near the end of Captain Lee's shift the next day, while I was waiting around to take over, the engine phone buzzed and McAllister's voice rattled through it. Lee winced and held it out so we could both hear.

McAllister was in fine fettle. "Captain, there's an old fool down here making trouble, with a freak to help him! Three of my best men have their arms broken and a couple are out. 'Twas a lovely fight, while it lasted, but I've work to be done and no more time for play. What'll I do with 'em?"

"What happened? Where are they now?"

"They're backed in a corner a-waiting for more competition right now, and the old man's using highly uncomplimentary language, so they'll get it. He came down to fiddle around, you might say, over the shininess of my turbines and the dripping of my oil, and I let him have his way with only a word or two dropped about his nose being a bit long. But when the freak found where one of the black gang had hidden some liquor and the old man broke the bottle, the bugger jumped him, and the freak joined the play. Naturally, the others didn't stand by helpless, and I had a bit of a time quieting things down. . . . Shall I shoot them or use a club?"

Lee swore into the phone and then quieted down to make sense. "McAllister, put the fellow with the liquor in the brig! I'll settle with you later. Keep the gang of cutthroats in line and send up the other two—they'll come if you tell them I ordered it. Did any outside the engine crew hear the fight?"

"No, just a little private party that your dainty little angels won't know about. I hated to break it up, but I needed a few sound men to run the engines, and I thought you might have some slight objection. . . . Okay, I've told 'em, and they're on the way up."

"McAllister would!" Lee slapped the phone back onto its cradle and expounded further on the beauties of a captain's life and the virtue of sundry individuals. "If he weren't the best engineer out, I'd sack him—and if there's any more drinking or fighting aboard, I will anyway. He does enough brawling in port—*come in!*"

I don't know what I'd expected; probably some pieces of man and mute, from the nature of McAllister's black gang. Anyway, I was wrong. Court was highly undirty and unscratched, which could only mean Stan had done the actual fighting. The mute's shirt would have made lint, and his general color was that of stale oil; but, except for a few slight scratches, he was untouched. I had a vision of those gorilla arms swinging all together, and began to see why McAllister had called Lee before the fight was completely finished.

"Discipline," said Court, while Lee was still swallowing enough ire to clear speaking space in his throat, "is terrible aboard, sir. Since you will probably insist on retaining the creature that passes for your engineer, I have asked Stan to accept his invitation and meet him after we dock; I hope you'll show better judgment in choosing the new engineer you'll need."

Lee was practically gagging by that time. "Captain Perry, you forget yourself! Only your age prevents me from confining you to the brig, sir! Keep out of my mind, Stan! That goes for you, too. If I suspect you of trying to control me, I'll brig you before I break. Angels running my ship! You will return to your quarters and remain there until we dock. During that time, you may leave to dine, only, and you will refrain from all comments to the other passengers or any members of the crew. And you, Captain Perry, will remove the uniform you wear by courtesy, and dress in civilians!"

"That exceeds your authority, Lee," Stan pointed out softly. Court was radiating a cold white anger that needed no speech. "It's true that there was some trouble below, but we were not unauthorized in our search, and the fight was not of my making; I had no choice, unless I preferred to have my father and myself mutilated. There's no need to strip Dad!"

"Except that he's been scaring the angels with wild tales while his clothes give his words weight! He's ruining my crew and destroying morale—generally making a nuisance or a laughingstock of himself. I won't have the uniform disgraced. To quarters!"

There was a click of heels from Court and the sound of feet slapping down the hall before his door shut. Stan stood a moment longer, spreading his hands at odd angles, then followed. With a glance at the clock, Lee clapped his hands down on the panel and jerked from the throne.

"Seven hours from Mars. Take over! Don't call me unless there's an emergency."

That left me alone at the controls, and the peace should have been welcome, but wasn't. I could still hear echoes bouncing from the walls, and the face of Court Perry kept getting in front of the controls. I never took sides in a ruction in a family or ship, but I'd have given half an eye to see the answer to this one. Grown men, I figured, are worse than kids, and you can't spank them as easily. And when they're hurt, I reckon the sting lasts longer.

If I hadn't been darned fool enough to worry about something that wasn't my business, I might have taken more notice of the slight quiver that touched the ship a couple of hours later, but I put it down to temporary lag in one tube, corrected it automatically, and went on roiling around mentally. In the back of my mind, I heard the door open softly and close, and was glad Lee had returned instead of getting drunk as I feared, but didn't bother to look around. A hand slid across my back and gripped my shoulder before I swung to see Court Perry.

He'd put off his uniform and most of himself with it, and now only a small, beaten old man stood there looking at me uncertainly. There's a certain kind of hell in the back of the best minds, and Court had found it. The fact that there was no pain or bitterness on his face only made it worse, somehow. I slid out of the copilot stool.

"Sit down, sir. Lee's turned authority over to me and won't be back for hours." His look toward the chair was hesitant and I motioned toward it again. "I'm commanding now, and if I choose to request your presence here as an adviser, nobody can do anything about it."

"Don't counter your captain too much, Sammy." But he took the stool, sinking down into it like a half-pricked balloon. "Sometime you may be running your own tick. I felt the ship lurch back there. Know what it was?"

"Tube lag. I've corrected."

"I thought so. You'd naturally make that mistake. It *wasn't* tube lag. That lurch came from Hull Section C, or everything I've learned about the feeling of a ship is wrong—and I don't think so. That means a peanut from the Little Swarm clipped up too close before the repellers functioned, and it was soaked up too quickly for recoil compensation. That's dangerous business, and I couldn't stay berthed with it going on."

"Indicator's registering." I tapped out more current to the hull repeller and watched the pointer. It fluttered a second, and wabbled slowly over—but kept on going instead of stopping at the mark. "Hm-mm!"

"Exactly."

Right then I began to see meteors swarming up as thick as peas in a can. I grabbed the phone, yelled down for the repair crew to jury-rig whatever was wrong. Court tapped me.

"Make an overroll. They strike from the starboard side, and if we turn the weak section to port, it'll help." As he saw me grab for the calculator to figure my thrusts, he brushed my hands aside and laid his on the controls, feeling over the raised indicators with fingers that seemed jointless, then pulled on the firing pins. Spirit ran back over him.

The *Kickapoo*'s thwart tubes muttered obediently, and I could feel the faint press of overroll acceleration. While she was just starting, those long flickering fingers went back to the steering panel and made another lightning reset, twisted the delayed-fire dials, and punched the pins again to check when half-over was reached. I'd heard men claim ships could be handled by conditioned reflexes, but I'd never seen it tried before.

Court leaned back, his hands still playing over the indicators. "Not much chance of two meteors hitting the same spot for hours, anyway, but there's no sense—"

SSSping-awgh-ooOOM! Something burst in front of us, white-hot and flaming hotter as it struck through the etherphone and threw hot metal splattering over the dugout. One of us grabbed the other—which, it wasn't clear—and we lurched toward the door, just as the last sounds subsided. There was a series of rolling slams, and the automatic air gates whammed shut, one, two, three, cutting the dugout in two just behind the panel. The local danger lights went off and we stopped our scramble for the door.

Then the thwart tubes burbled again, stopping the roll of the ship after the damage was done. From below came faint sounds of excitement that meant the angels were milling around with their fear on their arms, like a pack of sheep. Court snapped up and dived for the angel communicator while I began bellowing down for the checking gang to patch the holes in the outer and inner sheaths.

His voice was brisk and confident. "The small meteor you just felt drove into the control room from which I'm speaking," he announced. "No serious damage was done, and there is absolutely no danger. Passengers are requested to continue as before. The slight inconvenience caused will in no way affect them, nor the arrival time at our destination. I assure you, there is no cause for worry."

As they began quieting down under his words and I turned to inspect the panels, Lee came bursting in and thrust himself in front of me. "What happened?"

I told him quickly, and he grunted. "Etherphone gone, of course. All instruments are dead! It must have hit the relay chamber and burned out the connections. We're flying completely blind, without spy instruments! No way of contacting Earth, where the repair ships are; none on Mars at present. Even if we could get a message out, our momentum would carry us to Jupiter by the time they could reach us."

"The controls are all right, though." It was Court's voice, breaking in on the gloom. "The overroll counterset worked. They're not connected with the spy instruments, anyway."

"What good are controls without indicators? You! I thought I gave orders you were to stay berthed! Is this accident more of your work, Captain Perry?"

"Easy, Lee." I caught him just as Stan slid through the doorway, arms and all, and completely filled what was left of the dugout. "Court was helping me, at my request, and he almost succeeded in preventing this. He might still help if you'll calm down and use your head. What next?"

"What can be next? Get Stan to signal Mars with the etherphone he used before and have them contact Earth, I guess—and then wait. There's no chance of fixing the fused mess the meteor would make of the relays."

Court shook his head. "We can't wait. I promised the passengers they'd reach Mars on time, and I mean to see they do. I'll fly it if you can't."

"Without instruments? Captain Perry, return to your quarters and keep this to yourself."

"Without instruments!" Court's voice was flat and positive.

"For the last time, will you get out?"

"No. I'm flying the *Kickapoo* to Mars Junction!"

That was a little strong, even for me. "You can't do it, sir. That would be mutiny." I grabbed for one arm as Lee caught the other, but the old man braced himself and refused to move.

"It *is* mutiny," he said. Then, as Lee let go and grabbed for the phone to summon help: "Stan!"

Stan stood there for a second, then moved toward us, a slow frown creeping up on his face. A flurry of arms came at us—they must have been arms, at least—and I felt myself leave the floor, twist and turn in the air, and hit something. Blackout!

Lee's voice, raging furiously and almost incoherently, was the first thing I knew later, except for the ringing that went on in my head. "—behind bars till the devil catches pneumonia! I'll—"

Stan turned from some problem he was working on, and little furrows of concentration set on his brow. "Shut up, Lee! You'll not say another word until we reach Mars. Understand?"

Lee opened his mouth and worked furiously, but nothing came out of it. Finally, he slumped back and gave up. The mute turned to me. "Sorry, Sammy, but I had to do it. Here, I'll fix that headache for you." Again there was a second of concentration, and the ringing was suddenly gone, though the lump on the back of my head was still there.

"Where are we now?"

"Half an hour from Mars; you've been out quite a while," Court answered me. "Stan plotted a course from the co-ordinates I remembered were on the panel before the crash, and we're using dead reckoning. Of course, there may be a slight error of a few hundred miles, but that isn't much."

Slight error! Technically, it was; but that wouldn't help if we crashed square into the planet or missed completely. Lee writhed in the corner and managed a hissing sound. Well, there was nothing I could do now. Court had the ship and there was no chance of outside help. All I could do was ride along and pray—fervently if not hopefully.

"Get a reading yet?" Court asked. "And better signal Mars to clear the field—I may wobble a little."

Stan picked up a little box with a few loops of wire sticking from it and began twisting a dial; it wasn't big enough to be an etherphone, as I knew one, but a faint whisper from the headset reached me, after a brief pause.

"They say all clear down there, Dad; I told them we were having a little trouble. From the directional angle I get with the loop here, we're about two seconds of an arc too high. Better correct."

"Already done. Now if I can hit into the atmosphere right, and get the feel of the air currents so I can recognize the territory I'm in, we'll be all set." He hunched himself over the panel and sat waiting for a few aeons longer. Finally: "Ah, there's the first layer of thin air—we're still a little too fast! There, that should fix it. We're getting down where the air currents have character now."

"Junction on a line from us, almost," Stan reported. "Correct to port one degree five and a half seconds . . . two minutes . . . eight seconds. Good!"

"Updraft. That puts us over—mmm . . ."

Magic may have its place, but I wasn't used to it aboard the *Kickapoo*. "Good Lord, Stan," I begged, "do something about it! No man can fly a rocket by air currents and the feel of her! I can't even tell an updraft from a hurricane in this heavy shell."

"He can." The calm in his voice was infuriating. "Dad's memorized every square inch and reaction of the whole *Kickapoo*, until he knew every quiver of her hull and pull of her controls. Flew her for a year without using the vision plate. Dad's been blind six years, Sammy!"

"But—" That was too much for even Stan's control, and Lee squeezed the one word out hoarsely.

"This time, I've been his eyes. Telepathy, you know. Dad didn't want people to guess. When his eyesight began failing—probably from the radiation he used to have to take—he put those raised indicators in at his own expense and went ahead. And for your mental comfort, he made his last two landings with eyesight completely gone and without a hitch. If the officers' board hadn't caught on, he'd still be running a regular tick, and Lee would be copiloting without guessing the truth."

Maybe so, but the mental comfort he'd mentioned wasn't there. Those raised indicators weren't helping this trip, and Court hadn't touched a control for five years. He'd been hunched over them while Stan was speaking, but now he broke in again.

"There's Junction, by the feel of it. Test her, Stan; that should be the field."

"I think it was."

"Good! We're high, from the sound of the backblast." The *Kickapoo* veered around in a huge circle, Court fighting the controls to hold her on a level without indicators. Stan apparently was capable of nothing but confidence, which wasn't shared entirely by his father. Sweat began popping out on the old man's face. "Can't make it this time, either!"

"Steady, Dad!"

"I'm steady enough." Again the ship made a tight circle, her vanes shrieking against the air; her speed was low now, and she wobbled uncertainly. Court's hands bleached white, and his face blanched suddenly. One fist jerked away spasmodically, slapped back, and the grim fight with the controls went on. I was cooking in my own sweat.

Then something slithered under us, the rockets died, and silence reigned. From the outside came a rattle, and we went into motion again in a way that meant the field tractors were dragging us in. Safe! Stan was untying Lee and myself, and then Lee was muttering something I didn't try to understand and moving toward Court.

The old captain watched his approach with a tired smile and came slowly to his feet. "It's your throne again, Lee. It's—"

Hell splashed over his face at that moment! Stan barely managed to catch him as the legs buckled and failed him. But the salute he had started continued, and the voice went on faintly. "A very nice landing *you* made, Lee—*you* made, understand? . . . . My cap! . . . Where's my cap?"

Lee caught himself and jerked his own cap up out of the corner where it had lain, making gulping motions in his throat. "Here, Captain," he said, putting it on the old man's head. "Here's your cap."

Some of the agony left Court's mouth as his fingers felt it and groped up the visor. "Eagles!" The smile that suffused his face might almost have been a prayer. "My eagles!"

Then Stan was laying the body down and clutching tight at Lee's shaking shoulders. "Not your fault," he was saying gently. "Not your fault, Lee. His heart—"

I turned and stumbled out of the dugout to oversee the passengers who were landing after another uneventful trip to Mars.

From then on for a long time, writing was the least of my interests. I've often called myself a professional dilettante, with a fair measure of truth. And my interests tend to have long cycles. I'll suddenly get interested in something and drop everything else to rush into it. Eventually, I seem to go as far as I can on that go-round, and it gets put aside until some time in the future when I can attack it with new zeal.

I was busy with the typewriter, however, writing long letters to Campbell. But they had nothing to do with writing, usually. He had gotten interested in photography, and my enthusiasm for a hobby was as nothing compared to his. I'd discovered a new, experimental developer that sometimes gave fantastic exposure speeds to film. I took a picture once of a friend playing the piano, lighted only by two candles. That's obviously impossible for a lens opening of only f:4.5—but the negative was excellent, with good, soft shadows. However, the stuff was tricky and uncertain. Campbell and I must have wasted reams of paper discussing it.

Then my visit to Fred Pohl bore unexpected results. I was suddenly visited by two prominent fans, Milton Rothman and Elmer Purdue. Milt had been one of the great letter writers back when I was filling the letter columns, and we were old friends, even though we'd never met. And now, for the first time, I had an informed fellow fan with whom I could discuss science fiction for hours. We saw a lot of each other, and the friendship has lasted firmly until the present.

But my letters to Campbell and his answers began to arouse an itch in me to visit him again. That meant I'd better do a story to pay for the trip, and I sat down to concoct one.

I called it "The Boaster," and it was all about a braggart who was suddenly granted the gift from the gods of having every bragging lie become sober truth. If he claimed he could speak ancient Aramaic fluently, from then on he could. I'm afraid I didn't have much of an ending, though I patched on something that seemed good at the time. It added another 5,000 words to my reject pile.

Okay, I decided, I should have known better than to try one for *Unknown*. My sales record was much better at *Astounding*. So I plotted out something full of character and rich with something else that wasn't exactly freshness, all about a young man on Mars who's afraid to take strong drink or indulge in other manly arts, but who naturally becomes a great hero when the chips are down. I tucked the 6,400 words of "The Milksop" into an envelope and got on the bus for New York, no longer willing to wait another week for the mail.

It was a time when the war in Europe was heating up sharply, and Campbell was as excited about that as I was—though we were totally in disagreement about what would come of the latest moves.

Almost at once, we got on to that, with Campbell brushing me aside to explain the real facts.

I wasn't going to be brushed. He sat back while I argued, frowning for a moment. Then his whole face lighted up with pleasure and we went at it hot and heavy. His assistant, Miss Tarrant, sat quietly enjoying the whole thing. John Campbell was a formidable opponent in an argument, and he was also the editor who bought stories. Apparently most who saw him were afraid or unable to argue with him. Yet no man ever loved an argument more, and he was delighted when I fought back. I think our real friendship began then. Happily, it continued for a great many years, until the day he died.

In the end, he stopped long enough to inquire where I was staying. I hadn't made arrangements, expecting to take the bus back late that night. He then invited me to stay with him—he'd recently moved into a house in New Jersey, and he'd be glad to put me up on the couch. Meantime, he'd look at my manuscript.

When I came back that evening, there was a strange look on his face, half puckish, half troubled. When I was seated, he reached over to his manuscript pile and extracted my story. Holding it gingerly at the corner between thumb and one finger, he moved it over above the wastebasket. "Do you really want this back?" he asked. "Or should I just drop it in the permanent file?"

I suppose I gulped. "Really that bad?"

He nodded sadly and dropped it into the wastebasket. I think that was the best piece of literary criticism I ever received—and the truest, as I found when I tried to read my carbon copy later. There were times when a point had to be driven home—and he knew when and how to do it.

Later, after a cordial welcome and an excellent dinner from his wife, Doña, we settled back to my first real bull session on working methods and attitudes. John had taught himself to write; I don't think he had a great deal of natural talent, but he had a tremendous ability to analyze and to learn. It was a marvelous evening and full of information for me—particularly after we began analyzing why so many of my stories had failed.

Neither he nor I could pinpoint the main fault at first. But gradually, we worked it out. *Unknown* used a good deal of light, humorous fantasy. And most of my failures had been attempts to write that type of story. I couldn't do it, as many other writers couldn't. "You can get way down inside your characters," John decided. "And that's a gift. But when you're that deep in them, they just don't seem funny to themselves or anyone else." I never tried to write humor again.

There was a bit of clumsy humor, however, when John fitted me out with a pair of his pajamas. He went around taking pictures of me stumbling about in enough cloth to outfit five of me.

It was a good trip, and eventually a valuable one. But I wasn't inspired to try any more writing this time. I got a lot of rough ideas from Campbell, but I filed them away. I didn't have the least desire to pull words out of my typewriter.

Almost a year drifted by. Once in a while, Campbell would add a story idea to one of his letters, and a few times he threatened to find some way of getting me so broke that I'd write again. But I wasn't interested. 1941 came along and spent more than half of itself without any fiction going through the typewriter.

Then my girl friend decided she had to take in the World's Fair in New York. I didn't want to see it, but I agreed to meet her and ride back with her, since it was a good excuse to see Campbell again. And that meant I had to have a story with me.

I worked up a little 4,500-worder called "Hereafter, Inc.," about a man who dies after a life of self-denial and suffering for his faith. But heaven isn't what he expected—it's a place where you go on doing what you've always done. To his atheist boss, it's heaven; to him, it's hell. It was an idea of Campbell's that he'd sent to several writers, but he didn't recognize it—and when I told him, he pointed out that he probably bought it because I'd made it one he no longer recognized.

A couple months later, an old idea suddenly matured and began nagging me until I finally sat down and wrote it. It dealt with the last survivor of a race native to the Moon, and what happened when a spaceship accidentally landed in his covered crater. It came to 6,500 words and was called "The Wings of Night." Campbell didn't pay a bonus, but he suggested that maybe I was back where I belonged, doing just the kind of writing he wanted, and why not try more? I wasn't inclined that way, however, since no other idea seemed ready for easy use.

Then came December 7, 1941, and Pearl Harbor. My uncle called me up to tell me the news. We weren't too surprised; there were sources of information in Washington that had made us pretty certain Japan was going to strike. But we were horrified at the extent of the damage. And we were somehow relieved that America was finally going to fight. Hitler had been anathema to us for a decade, at least.

I was as caught up in the wave of patriotism and war fever as anyone else, I believe. My thoughts all began to center on the coming war. But I couldn't quite stomach the silly stories of Hitler's depravity; his real evil was far more terrible than the petty stories of his madness.

Eventually, I began thinking of a story about what would be a suitable end for a power-driven man like Hitler. I didn't want to make him a clown or a fool, but to show him as I really believed him to be. And somehow, I found the idea that seemed to fit.

It came out as a 10,000-word novelette called "My Name Is Legion," and Campbell loved the idea and added a bonus to the check.

11.

My Name Is Legion

(by Lester del Rey)

Bresseldorf lay quiet under the late-morning sun—too quiet. In the streets there was no sign of activity, though a few faint banners of smoke spread upward from the chimneys, and the dropped tools of agriculture lay all about, scattered as if from sudden flight. A thin pig wandered slowly and suspiciously down Friedrichstrasse, turned into an open door cautiously, grunted in grudging satisfaction, and disappeared within. But there were no cries of children, no bustle of men in the surrounding fields, nor women gossiping or making preparations for the noon meal. The few shops, apparently gutted of foodstuffs, were bare, their doors flopping open. Even the dogs were gone.

Major King dropped the binoculars to his side, tight lines about his eyes that contrasted in suspicion with his ruddy British face. "Something funny here, Wolfe. Think it's an ambush?"

Wolfe studied the scene. "Doesn't smell like it, Major," he answered. "In the Colonials, we developed something of a sixth sense for that, and I don't get a hunch here. Looks more like a sudden and complete retreat to me, sir."

"We'd have had reports from the observation planes if even a dozen men were on the roads. I don't like this." The major put the binoculars up again. But the scene was unchanged, save that the solitary pig had come out again and was rooting his way down the street in lazy assurance that nothing now menaced him. King shrugged, flipped his hand forward in a quick jerk, and his command moved ahead again, light tanks in front, troop cars and equipment at a safe distance behind, but ready to move forward instantly to hold what ground the tanks might gain. In the village, nothing stirred.

Major King found himself holding his breath as the tanks reached antitank-fire distance, but as prearranged, half of them lumbered forward at a deceptive speed, maneuvered to two abreast to shuttle across Friedrichstrasse toward the village square, and halted. Still, there was no sign of resistance. Wolfe looked at the quiet houses along the street and grinned sourly.

"If it's an ambush, Major, they've got sense. They're waiting until we send in our men in the trucks to pick them off then, and letting the tanks alone. But I still don't believe it; not with such an army as he could throw together."

"Hm-m-m." King scowled, and again gave the advance signal.

The trucks moved ahead this time, traveling over the rough road at a clip that threatened to jar the teeth out of the men's heads, and the remaining tanks swung in briskly as a rear guard. The pig stuck his head out of a door as the major's car swept past, squealed, and slipped back inside in haste. Then all were in the little square, barely big enough to hold them, and the tanks were arranged facing out, their thirty-seven millimeters raking across the houses that bordered, ready for an instant's notice. Smoke continued to rise peacefully, and the town slumbered on, unmindful of this strange invasion.

"Hell!" King's neck felt tense, as if the hair were standing on end. He swung to the men, moved his hands outward. "Out and search! And remember—take him alive if you can! If you can't, plug his guts and save his face—we'll have to bring back proof!"

They broke into units and stalked out of the square toward the houses with grim efficiency and rifles ready, expecting guerrilla fire at any second; none came. The small advance guard of the Army of Occupation kicked open such doors as were closed and went in and sidewise, their comrades covering them. No shots came, and the only sound was the cries of the men as they reported "Empty!"

Then, as they continued around the square, one of the doors opened quietly and a single man came out, glanced at the rifles centered on him, and threw up his hands, a slight smile on his face. "*Kamerad!*" he shouted toward the major; then in English with only the faintest of accents: "There is no other here, in the whole village."

Holding onto the door, he moved aside slightly to let a search detail go in, waited for them to come out. "You see? I am alone in Bresseldorf; the Leader you seek is gone, and his troops with him."

Judging by the man's facial expression that he was in no condition to come forward, King advanced; Wolfe was at his side, automatic at ready. "I'm Major King, Army of Occupation. We received intelligence from some of the peasants who fled from here yesterday that your returned Führer was hiding here. You say—"

"That he is quite gone, yes; and that you will never find him, though you comb the earth until eternity, Major King. I am Karl Meyers, once of Heidelberg."

"When did he leave?"

"A matter of half an hour or so—what matter? I assure you, sir, he is too far now to trace. Much too far!"

"In half an hour?" King grimaced. "You underestimate the covering power of a modern battalion. Which direction?"

"Yesterday," Meyers answered, and his drawn face lighted slightly. "But tell me, did the peasants report but one Führer?"

King stared at the man in surprise, taking in the basically pleasant face, intelligent eyes, and the pride that lay, somehow, in the bent figure; this was no ordinary villager, but a man of obvious breeding. Nor did he seem anything but completely frank and honest. "No," the major conceded, "there were stories. But when a band of peasants reports a thousand Führers heading fifty thousand troops, we'd be a little slow in believing it, after all."

"Quite so, Major. Peasant minds exaggerate." Again there was the sudden lighting of expression. "Yes, so they did—the troops. And in other ways, rather than exaggerating, they minimized. But come inside, sirs, and I'll explain over a bottle of the rather poor wine I've found here. I'll show you the body of the Leader, and even explain why he's gone—and where."

"But you said—" King shrugged. Let the man be as mysterious as he chose, if his claim of the body was correct. He motioned Wolfe forward with him and followed Meyers into a room that had once been kitchen and dining room, but was now in wild disarray, its normal holdings crammed into the corners to make room for a small piece of mechanism in the center and a sheeted bundle at one side. The machine was apparently in the process of being disassembled.

Meyers lifted the sheet. "*Der Führer*," he said simply, and King dropped with a gasp to examine the dead figure revealed.

There were no shoes, and the calluses on the feet said quite plainly that it was customary; such few clothes as remained had apparently been pieced together from odds and ends of peasant clothing, sewed crudely. Yet on them, pinned over the breast, were the two medals that the Leader alone bore. One side of the head had been blown away by one of the new-issue German explosive bullets, and what remained was incredibly filthy, matted hair falling below the shoulders, scraggy, tangled beard covering all but the eye and nose. On the left cheek, however, the irregular reversed question-mark scar from the recent attempt at assassination showed plainly, but faded and blended with the normal skin where it should have been still sharp after only two months' healing.

"An old, old man, wild as the wind and dirty as a hog wallow," King thought, "yet, somehow, clearly the man I was after."

Wolfe nodded slowly at his superior's glance. "Sure, why not? I'll cut his hair and give him a shave and a wash. When we're about finished here, we can fire a shot from the gun on the table, if it's still loaded . . . good! Report that Meyers caught him and held him for us; then, while we were questioning him, he went crazy and Meyers took a shot at him."

"Hm-m-m." King's idea had been about the same. "Men might suspect something, but I can trust them. He'd never stand a careful inspection, of course, without a lot of questions about such things as those feet, but the way things are, no really competent medical inspection will be made. It'll be a little hard to explain those rags, though."

Meyers nodded to a bag against the wall. "You'll find sufficient of his clothes there, Major; we couldn't pack out much luggage, but that much we brought." He sank back into a rough chair slowly, the hollow in his cheeks deepening, but a grim humor in his eyes. "Now, you'll want to know how it happened, no doubt? How he died? Suicide—murder; they're one and the same here. He died insane."

The car was long and low. European by its somewhat unrounded lines and engine housing, muddy with the muck that sprayed up from its wheels and made the road almost impassable. Likewise, it was stolen, though that had no bearing on the matter at hand. Now, as it rounded an ill-banked curve, the driver cursed softly, jerked at the wheel, and somehow managed to keep all four wheels on the road and the whole pointed forward. His foot came down on the gas again, and it churned forward through the muck, then miraculously maneuvered another turn, and they were on a passable road and he could relax.

"Germany, my Leader," he said simply, his large hands gripping at the wheel with now needless ferocity. "Here, of all places, they will least suspect you."

The Leader sat hunched forward, paying little attention to the road or the risks they had taken previously. Whatever his enemies might say of his lack of bravery in the first war, there was no cowardice about him now; power, in unlimited quantity, had made him unaware of personal fear. He shrugged faintly, turning his face to the driver, so that the reversed questionmark scar showed up, running from his left eye down toward the almost comic little moustache. But there was nothing comic about him, somehow; certainly not to Karl Meyers.

"Germany," he said tonelessly. "Good. I was a fool, Meyers, ever to leave it. Those accursed British—the loutish Russians—ungrateful French—troublemaking Americans—bombs, retreats, uprisings, betrayals—and the two I thought were my friends advising me to flee to Switzerland before my people—Bah, I was a fool. Now those two friends would have me murdered in my bed, as this letter you brought testifies. And the curs stalk the Reich, such as remains of it, and think they have beaten me. Bonaparte was beaten once, and in a hundred days, except for the stupidity of fools and the tricks of weather, even he might have regained his empire. . . . Where?"

"Bresseldorf. My home is near there, and the equipment, also. Besides, when we have the—the legion with us, Bresseldorf will feed us, and the clods of peasants will offer little resistance. Also, it is well removed from the areas policed by the Army of Occupation. Thank God, I finished the machine in time."

Meyers swung the car into another little-used but passable road, and opened it up, knowing it would soon be over. This mad chase had taken more out of him than he'd expected. Slipping across into Switzerland, tracking, playing hunches, finally locating the place where the Leader was hidden had used almost too much time, and the growth within him that would not wait was killing him day by day. Even after finding the place, he'd been forced to slip past the guards who were half protecting, half imprisoning the Leader and used half a hundred tricks to see him. Convincing him of the conspiracy of his "friends" to have him shot was not hard; the Leader knew something of the duplicity of men in power, or fearful of their lives. Convincing him of the rest of the plan had been harder, but on the coldly logical argument that there was nothing else, the Leader had come. Somehow, they'd escaped—he still could give no details on that—and stolen this car, to run out into the rain and the night over the mountain roads, through the back ways, and somehow out unnoticed and into Germany again.

The Leader settled more comfortably into the seat with an automatic motion, his mind far from body comforts. "Bresseldorf? And near it—yes, I remember that clearly now—within fifteen miles of there, there's a small military depot those damned British won't have found yet. There was a new plan—but that doesn't matter now; what matters are the tanks, and better, the ammunition. This machine—will it duplicate tanks, also? And ammunition?"

Meyers nodded. "Tanks, cars, equipment, all of them. But not ammunition or petrol, since once used, they're not on the chain any longer to be taken."

"No matter. God be praised, there's petrol and ammunition enough there, until we can reach the others; and a few men, surely, who are still loyal. I was beginning to doubt loyalty, but tonight you've shown that it does exist. Someday, Karl Meyers, you'll find I'm not ungrateful."

"Enough that I serve you," Meyers muttered. "Ah, here we are; good time made, too, since it's but ten in the morning. That house is one I've rented; inside you'll find wine and food, while I dispose of this car in the little lake yonder. Fortunately, the air is still thick here, even though it's not raining. There'll be none to witness."

The Leader had made no move to touch the food when Meyers returned. He was pacing the floor, muttering to himself, working himself up as Meyers had seen him do often before on the great stands in front of the crowds, and the mumbled words had a hysterical drive to them that bordered on insanity. In his eyes, though, there was only the insanity that drives men remorselessly to rule, though the ruling may be under a grimmer sword than that of Damocles. He stopped as he saw Meyers, and one of his rare and sudden smiles flashed out, unexpectedly warm and human, like a small, bewildered boy peering out from the chinks of the man's armor. This was the man who had cried when he saw his soldiers dying, then sent them on again, sure they should honor him for the right to die; and like all those most loved or hated by their fellowmen, he was a paradox of conflictions, unpredictable.

"The machine, Karl," he reminded the other gently. "As I remember, the Jew Christ cast a thousand devils out of one man; well, let's see you cast ten thousand out of me—and devils they'll be to those who fetter the Reich! This time I think we'll make no words of secret weapons, but annihilate them first, eh? After that—there'll be a day of atonement for those who failed me, and a new and greater Germany—master of a world!"

"Yes, my Leader."

Meyers turned and slipped through the low door, back into a part of the building that had once been a stable, but was now converted into a workshop, filled with a few pieces of fine machinery and half a hundred makeshifts, held together, it seemed, with hope and prayer. He stopped before a small affair, slightly larger than a suitcase, only a few dials and control knobs showing on the panel, the rest covered with a black housing. From it, two small wires led to a single storage battery.

"This?" The Leader looked at it doubtfully.

"This, Leader. This is one case where brute power has little to do, and the proper use everything. A few tubes, coils, condensers, two little things of my own, and perhaps five watts of power feeding in —no more. Just as the cap that explodes the bomb may be small and weak, yet release forces that bring down the very mountains. Simple in design, yet there's no danger of them finding it."

"So? And it works in what way?"

Meyers scowled, thinking. "Unless you can think in a plenum, my Leader, I can't explain," he began diffidently. "Oh, mathematicians believe they can—but they think in symbols and terms, not in the reality. Only by thinking in the plenum itself can this be understood, and with due modesty, I alone in the long years since I gave up work at Heidelberg have devoted the time and effort—with untold pure luck—to master such thought. It isn't encompassed in mere symbols on paper."

"What," the Leader wanted to know, "is a plenum?"

"A complete universe, stretching up and forward and sidewise—and durationally; the last being the difficulty. The plenum is—well, the composite whole of all that is and was and will be—it is everything and everywhen, all existing together as a unit, in which time does not move, but simply is, like length or thickness. As an example, years ago in one of those American magazines, there was a story of a man who saw himself. He came through a woods somewhere and stumbled on a machine, got in, and it took him three days back in time. Then, he lived forward again, saw himself get in the machine and go back. Therefore, the time machine was never made, since he always took it back, let it stay three days, and took it back again. It was a closed circle, uncreated, but existent in the plenum. By normal nonplenar though, impossible."

"Someone had to make it." The Leader's eyes clouded suspiciously.

Meyers shook his head. "Not so. See, I draw this line upon the paper, calling the paper now a plenum. It starts here, follows here, ends here. That is like life, machines, and so forth. We begin, we continue, we end. Now, I draw a circle—where does it begin or end? Yes, followed by a two-dimensional creature, it would be utter madness, continuing forever without reason or beginning—to us, simply a circle. Or, here I have a pebble—do you see at one side the energy, then the molecules, then the compounds, then the stone, followed by breakdown products? No, simply a stone. And in a plenum, that time machine is simply a pebble—complete, needing no justification, since it was."

The Leader nodded doubtfully, vaguely aware that he seemed to understand, but did not. If the machine worked, though, what matter the reason? "And—"

"And, by looking into the plenum as a unit, I obtain miracles, seemingly. I pull an object back from its future to stand beside its present. I multiply it in the present. As you might take a straight string and bend it into a series of waves or loops, so that it met itself repeatedly. For that, I need some power, yet not much. When I cause the bending from the future to the present, I cause nothing—since, in a plenum, all that is, was and will be. When I bring you back, the mere fact that you are back means that you always have existed and always will exist in that manner. Seemingly, then, if I did nothing, you would still multiply, but since my attempt to create such a condition is fixed in the plenum beside your multiplying at this time, therefore I must do so. The little energy I use, really, has only the purpose of not bringing you exactly within yourself, but separating individuals. Simple, is it not?"

"When I see an example, Meyers, I'll believe my eyes," the Leader answered.

Meyers grinned, and put a small coin on the ground, making quick adjustments of the dials. "I'll cause it to multiply from each two minutes," he said. "From each two minutes in the future, I'll bring it back to now. See!"

He depressed a switch, a watch in his hand. Instantly, there was a spreading out and multiplying, instantaneous or too rapid to be followed. As he released the switch, the Leader stumbled back from the hulking pile of coins. Meyers glanced at him, consulted his watch, and moved another lever at the top. The machine clicked off. After a second or so, the pile disappeared, as quietly and quickly as it had come into being. There was a glint of triumph or something akin to it in the scientist's eyes as he turned back to the Leader.

"I've tried it on myself for one turn, so it's safe to living things," he answered the unasked question.

The Leader nodded impatiently and stepped to the place where the coins had been piled. "Get on with it, then. The sooner the accursed enemies and traitors are driven out, the better it will be."

Meyers hesitated. "There's one other thing," he said doubtfully. "When the—others—are here, there might be a question of leadership, which would go ill with us. I mean no offense, my Leader, but —well, sometimes a man looks at things differently at different ages, and any disagreement would delay us. Fortunately, though, there's a curious by-product of the use of the machine; apparently, its action has some relation to thought, and I've found in my experiments that any strong thought on the part of the original will be duplicated in the others; I don't fully understand it myself, but it seems to work that way. The compulsion dissipates slowly and is gone in a day or so, but—"

"So?"

"So, if you'll think to yourself while you're standing there: 'I must obey my original implicitly; I must not cause trouble for my original or Karl Meyers,' then the problem will be cared for automatically. Concentrate on that, my Leader, and perhaps it would be wise to concentrate also on the thought that there should be no talking by our legion, except as we demand."

"Good. There'll be time for talk when the action is finished. Now, begin!"

The Leader motioned toward the machine and Meyers breathed a sigh of relief as the scarred face crinkled in concentration. From a table at the side, the scientist picked up a rifle and automatic, put them into the other's hands, and went to his machine.

"The weapon will be duplicated also," he said, setting the controls carefully. "Now, it should be enough if I take you back from each twenty-four hours in the future. And since there isn't room here, I'll assemble the duplicates in rows outside. So."

He depressed the switch and a red bulb on the control panel lighted. In the room, nothing happened for a few minutes; then the bulb went out, and Meyers released the controls. "It's over. The machine has traced ahead and brought back until there was no further extension of yourself; living, that is, since I set it for life only."

"But I felt nothing." The Leader glanced at the machine with a slight scowl, then stepped quickly to the door for a hasty look. Momentarily, superstitious awe flicked across his face, to give place to sharp triumph. "Excellent, Meyers, most excellent. For this day, we'll have the world at our feet, and that soon!"

In the field outside, a curious company was lined up in rows. Meyers ran his eyes down the ranks, smiling faintly as he traced forward. Near, in almost exact duplication of the man at his side, were several hundred; then, as his eyes moved backward, the resemblance was still strong, but differences began to creep in. And farthest from him, a group of old men stood, their clothes faded and tattered, their faces hidden under mangled beards. Rifles and automatics were gripped in the hands of all the legion. There were also other details, and Meyers nodded slowly to himself, but he made no mention of them to the Leader, who seemed not to notice.

The Leader was looking ahead, a hard glow in his eyes, his face contorted with some triumphant vision. Then, slowly and softly at first, he began to speak and to pace back and forth in front of the doorway, moving his arms. Meyers only half listened, busy with his own thoughts, but he could have guessed the words as they came forth with mounting fury, worked up to a climax and broke, to repeat it all again. Probably it was a great speech the Leader was making, one that would have swept a mob from their seats in crazy exultation in other days and set them screaming with savage applause. But the strange Legion of Later Leaders stood quietly, faces betraying varying emotions, mostly unreadable. Finally the speaker seemed to sense the difference and paused in the middle of one of his rising climaxes; he half turned to Meyers, then suddenly swung back decisively.

"But I speak to myselves," he addressed the legion again in a level, reasonable voice. "You who come after me know what is to be this day and in the days to come, so why should I tell you? And you know that my cause is just. The Jews, the Jew-lovers, the Pluto-democracies, the Bolsheviks, the treasonous cowards within and without the

Reich must be put down! They shall be! Now, they are sure of victory, but tomorrow they'll be trembling in their beds and begging for peace. And soon, like a tide, irresistible and without end, from the few we can trust many shall be made, and they shall sweep forward to victory. Not victory in a decade, nor a year, but in a month! We shall go north and south and east and west! We shall show them that our fangs are not pulled; that those which we lost were but our milk teeth, now replaced by a second and harder growth!

"And for those who would have betrayed us, or bound us down in chains to feed the gold lust of the mad democracies, or denied us the room to live which is rightfully ours—for those, we shall find a proper place. This time, for once and for all, there shall be an end to the evils that corrupt the earth—the Jews and the Bolsheviks, and their friends, and friends' friends. Germany shall emerge, purged and cleansed, a new and greater Reich, whose domain shall not be Europe, not this hemisphere, but the world!

"Many of you have seen all this in the future from which you come, and all of you must be ready to reassure yourselves of it today, that the glory of it may fill your tomorrow. Now, we march against a few peasants. Tomorrow, after quartering in Bresseldorf, we shall be in the secret depot, where those who remain loyal shall be privileged to multiply and join us, and where we shall multiply all our armament ten-thousandfold! Into Bresseldorf, then, and if any of the peasants are disloyal, be merciless in removing them! Forward!"

One of the men in the front—the nearest—was crying openly, his face white, his hands clenched savagely around the rifle he held, and the Leader smiled at the display of fervor and started forward. Meyers touched his shoulder.

"My Leader, there is no need that you should walk, though these must. I have a small auto here, into which we can put the machine. Send the legion ahead, and we'll follow later; they'll have little trouble clearing Bresseldorf for us. Then, when we've packed our duplicator and I've assembled spare parts for an emergency, we can join them."

"By all means, yes. The machine must be well handled." The Leader nodded and turned back to the men. "Proceed to Bresseldorf, then, and we follow. Secure quarters for yourself and food, and a place for me and for Meyers; we stop there until I can send word to the depot during the night and extend my plans. To Bresseldorf!"

Silently, without apparent organization, but with only small confusion, the legion turned and moved off, rifles in hands. There were no orders, no beating of drums to announce to the world that the Leader was on the march again, but the movement of that body of men, all gradations of the same man, was impressive enough without fanfare as it turned into the road that led to Bresseldorf, only a mile away. Meyers saw a small cart coming toward them, watched it halt while the driver stared dumbly at the company approaching. Then, with a shriek that cut thinly over the distance, he was whipping his animal about and heading in wild flight toward the village.

"I think the peasants will cause no trouble, my Leader," the scientist guessed, turning back to the shop. "No, the legion will be quartered by the time we reach them."

And when the little car drove up into the village square half an hour later and the two men got out, the legion was quartered well enough to satisfy all prophets. There was no sign of the peasants, but the men from the future were moving back and forth into the houses and shops along the street, carrying foodstuffs to be cooked. Cellars and stores had been well gutted, and a few pigs were already killed and being cut up—not skillfully, perhaps, but well enough for practical purposes.

The Leader motioned toward one of the amateur butchers, a copy of himself who seemed perhaps two or three years older, and the man approached with frozen face. His knuckles, Meyers noted, were white where his fingers clasped around the butcher knife he had been using.

"The peasants—what happened?"

The legionnaire's face set tighter, and he opened his mouth to say something; apparently he changed his mind after a second, shut his mouth, and shrugged. "Nothing," he answered finally. "We met a farmer on the road who went ahead shouting about a million troops, all the Leader. When we got here, there were a few children and women running off, and two men trying to drag away one of the pigs. They left it behind and ran off. Nothing happened."

"Stupid dolts! Superstition, no loyalty!" The Leader twisted his lips, frowning at the man before him, apparently no longer conscious that it was merely a later edition of himself. "Well, show us to the quarters you've picked for us. And have someone send us food and wine. Has a messenger been sent to the men at the tank depot?"

"You did not order it."

"What— No, so I didn't. Well, go yourself, then, if you . . . but, of course, you know where it is. Naturally. Tell Hauptmann Immenhoff to expect me tomorrow and not to be surprised at anything. You'll have to go on foot, since we need the car for the machine."

The legionnaire nodded, indicating one of the houses on the square. "You quarter here. I go on foot, as I knew I would." He turned expressionlessly and plodded off to the north, grabbing up a half-cooked leg of pork as he passed the fire burning in the middle of the square.

The Leader and Meyers did not waste time following him with their eyes, but went into the house indicated, where wine and food were sent in to them shortly. With the help of one of the duplicates, space was quickly cleared for the machine, and a crude plank table drawn up for the map that came from the Leader's bag. But Meyers had little appetite for the food or wine, less for the dry task of watching while the other made marks on the paper or stared off into space in some rapt dream of conquest. The hellish tumor inside him was giving him no rest now, and he turned to his machine, puttering over its insides as a release from the pain. Outside, the legion was comparatively silent, only the occasional sound of a man walking past breaking the monotony. Darkness fell just as more food was brought in to them, and the scientist looked out to see the square deserted; apparently the men had moved as silently as ever to the beds selected for the night. And still, the Leader worked over his plans, hardly touching the food at his side.

Finally he stirred. "Done," he stated. "See, Meyers, it is simple now. Tomorrow, probably from the peasants who ran off, the enemy will know we are here. With full speed, possibly they can arrive by noon, and though we start early, fifteen miles is a long march for untrained men; possibly they could catch us on the road. Therefore, we do not march. We remain here."

"Like rats in a trap? Remember, my Leader, while we have possibly ten thousand men with rifles, ammunition can be used but once—so that our apparently large supply actually consists of about fifty rounds at most."

"Even so, we remain, not like rats, but like cheese in a trap. If we move, they can strafe us from the air; if we remain, they send light tanks and trucks of men against us, since they travel fastest. In the morning, therefore, we'll send out the auto with a couple of older men—less danger of their being recognized—to the depot to order Immenhoff here with one medium tank, a crew, and trucks of ammunition and petrol. We allow an hour for the auto to reach Immenhoff and for his return here. Here, they are duplicated to a thousand tanks, perhaps, with crews, and fueled and made ready. Then, when the enemy arrives, we wipe them out, move on to the depot, clean out our supplies there, and strike north to the next. After that—"

He went on, talking now more to himself than to Meyers, and the scientist only pieced together parts of the plan. As might have been expected, it was unexpected, audacious, and would probably work. Meyers was no military genius, had only a rough working idea of military operations, but he was reasonably sure that the Leader could play the cards he was dealing himself and come out on top, barring the unforeseen in large quantities. But now, having conquered Europe, the Leader's voice was lower, and what little was audible no longer made sense to the scientist, who drew out a cheap blanket and threw himself down, his eyes closed.

Still the papers and maps rustled, and the voice droned on in soft snatches, gradually falling to a whisper and then ceasing. There was a final rattling of the map, followed by complete silence, and Meyers could feel the other's eyes on his back. He made no move, and the Leader must have been satisfied by the regular breathing that the scientist was asleep, for he muttered to himself again as he threw another blanket on the floor and blew out the light.

"A useful man, Meyers, now. But after victory, perhaps his machine would be a menace. Well, that can wait."

Meyers smiled slightly in the darkness, then went back to trying to force himself to sleep. As the Leader had said, such things could wait. At the moment, his major worry was that the Army of Occupation might come an hour too soon—but that also was nonsense; obviously, from the ranks of the legion, that could not be any part of the order of things. That which was would be, and he had nothing left to fear.

The Leader was already gone from the house when Meyers awoke. For a few minutes the scientist stood staring at the blanket of the other, then shrugged, looked at his watch, and made a hasty breakfast of wine and morphine; with cancer gnawing at their vitals, men have small fear of drug addiction, and the opiate would make seeming normality easier for a time. There were still threads to be tied in to his own satisfaction, and little time left in which to do it.

Outside, the heavy dew of the night was long since gone, and the air was fully warmed by the sun. Most of the legion were gathered in the square, some preparing breakfast, others eating, but all in the same stiff silence that had marked their goings and comings since the first. Meyers walked out among them slowly, and their eyes followed him broodingly, but they made no other sign. One of the earlier ones who had been shaving with a straight razor stopped, fingering the blade, his eyes on the scientist's neck.

Meyers stopped before him, half smiling. "Well, why not say it? What are you thinking?"

"Why bother? You know." The legionnaire's fingers clenched around the handle, then relaxed, and he went on with his shaving, muttering as his unsteady hand made the razor nick his skin. "In God's will, if I could draw this once across your throat, Meyers, I'd cut my own for the right."

Meyers nodded. "I expected so. But you can't. Remember? You must obey your original implicitly; you must not cause trouble for your original or Karl Meyers; you must not speak to us or to others except as we demand. Of course, in a couple of days, the compulsion would wear away slowly, but by that time we'll both be out of reach of each other. . . . No, back! Stay where you are and continue shaving; from the looks of the others, you'll stop worrying about your hair shortly, but why hurry it?"

"Someday, somehow, I'll beat it! And then, a word to the original —or I'll track you down myself. God!" But the threatening scowl lessened, and the man went reluctantly back to his shaving, in the grip of the compulsion still. Meyers chuckled dryly.

"What was and has been—will be."

He passed down the line again, in and out among the mingled men who were scattered about without order, studying them carefully, noting how they ranged from trim copies of the Leader in field coat and well kept to what might have been demented scavengers picking from the garbage cans of the alleys and back streets. And yet, even the oldest and filthiest of the group was still the same man who had come closer to conquering the known world than anyone since Alexander. Satisfied at last, he turned back toward the house where his quarters were.

A cackling, tittering quaver at his right brought him around abruptly to face something that had once been a man, but now looked more like some animated scarecrow.

"You're Meyers," the old one accused him. "*Shh!* I know it. I remember. Hee-yee, I remember again. Oh, this is wonderful, wonderful, wonderful! Do you wonder how I can speak? Wonderful, wonderful, wonderful!"

Meyers backed a step and the creature advanced again, leering, half dancing in excitement. "Well, how can you speak? The compulsion shouldn't have worn off so soon!"

"Hee! Hee-yee-yee! Wonderful!" The wreck of a man was dancing more frantically now, rubbing his hands together. Then he sobered sharply, laughter bubbling out of a straight mouth and tapering off, like the drippings from a closed faucet. "*Shh!* I'll tell you. Yes, tell you all about it, but you mustn't tell *him. He* makes me come here every day where I can eat, and I like to eat. If *he* knew, *he* might not let me come. This is my last day; did you know it? Yes, my last day. I'm the oldest. Wonderful, don't you think it's wonderful? I do."

"You're crazy!" Meyers had expected it, yet the realization of the fact was still a shock to him and to his Continental background of fear of mental unbalance.

The scarecrow figure bobbed its head in agreement. "I'm crazy, yes—crazy. I've been crazy almost a year now—isn't it wonderful? But don't tell *him.* It's nice to be crazy. I can talk now; I couldn't talk before—*he* wouldn't let me. And some of the others are crazy, too, and they talk to me; we talk quietly, and *he* doesn't know. . . . You're Meyers, I remember now. I've been watching you, wondering, and now I remember. There's something else I should remember—something I should do; I planned it all once, and it was so clever, but now I can't remember— You're Meyers. Don't I hate you?"

"No. No, Leader, I'm your friend." In spite of himself, Meyers was shuddering, wondering how to break away from the maniac. He was painfully aware that for some reason the compulsion on which he had counted no longer worked; insanity had thrown the normal rules overboard. If this person should remember fully— Again Meyers shuddered, not from personal fear, but the fear that certain things still undone might not be completed. "No, great Leader, I'm your real friend. Your best friend. I'm the one who told him to bring you here to eat."

"Yes? Oh, wonderful—I like to eat. But I'm not the Leader; *he* is . . . and *he* told me . . . what did *he* tell me? Hee! I remember again, *he* told me to find you; *he* wants you. And I'm the last. Oh, it's wonderful, wonderful, wonderful! Now I'll remember it all, I will. Hee-yee-yee! Wonderful. You'd better go now, Meyers. *He* wants you. Isn't it wonderful?"

Meyers lost no time in leaving, glad for any excuse, but wondering why the Leader had sent for him, and how much the lunatic had told. He glanced at his watch again, and at the sun, checking mentally, and felt surer as he entered the quarters. Then he saw there was no reason to fear, for the Leader had his maps out again, and was nervously tapping his foot against the floor; but there was no personal anger in his glance.

"Meyers? Where were you?"

"Out among the legion, my Leader, making sure they were ready to begin operations. All is prepared."

"Good." The Leader accepted his version without doubt. "I, too, have been busy. The car was sent off almost an hour ago—more than an hour ago—to the depot, and Immenhoff should be here at any moment. No sign of the enemy yet; we'll have time enough. Then, let them come!"

He fell back to the chair beside the table, nervous fingers tapping against the map, feet still rubbing at the floor, keyed to the highest tension, like a cat about to leap at its prey. "What time is it? Hm-m-m. No sound of the tank yet. What's delaying the fool? He should be here now. Hadn't we best get the machine outside?"

"It won't be necessary," Meyers assured him. "I'll simply run out a wire from the receiver to the tank when it arrives; the machine will work at a considerable distance, just as long as the subject is under some part of it."

"Good. What's delaying Immenhoff? He should have made it long ago. And where's the courier I sent last night? Why didn't he report back? I—"

"Hee-yee! He's smart, Leader, just as I once was." The tittering voice came from the door of their quarters, and both men looked up to see the old lunatic standing there, running his fingers through his beard. "Oh, it was wonderful! Why walk all that long way back when he knew it made no difference where he was—the machine will bring him back, anyhow. Wonderful, don't you think it was wonderful? You didn't tell him to walk back."

The Leader scowled, nodded. "Yes, I suppose it made no difference whether he came back or not. He could return with Immenhoff."

"Not he, not he! Not with Immenhoff."

"Fool! Why not? And get out of here!"

But the lunatic was in no hurry to leave. He leaned against the doorway, snickering. "Immenhoff's dead—Immenhoff's dead. Wonderful! He's been dead a long time now. The Army of Occupation found him and he got killed. I remember it all now, how I found him all dead when I was the courier. So I didn't come back, because I was smart, and then I was back without walking. Wonderful, wonderful, wonderful! I remember everything now, don't I?"

"Immenhoff dead? Impossible!" The Leader was out of the chair, stalking toward the man, black rage on his face. "You're insane!"

"Hee! Isn't it wonderful? They always said I was and now I am. But Immenhoff's dead, and he won't come here, and there'll be no tanks. Oh, how wonderful, never to march at all, but just come here every day to eat. I like to eat. . . . No, don't touch me. I'll shoot, I will. I remember this is a gun, and I'll shoot, and the bullet will explode with noise, lots of noise. Don't come near me." He centered the automatic squarely on the Leader's stomach, smirking gleefully as he watched his original retreat cautiously back toward the table.

"You're mad at me because I'm crazy—" A sudden effort of concentration sent the smirk away to be replaced by cunning. "You know I'm crazy now! I didn't want you to know, but I told you. How sad, how sad, isn't it sad? No, it isn't sad, it's wonderful still, and I'm going to kill you. That's what I wanted to remember. I'm going to kill you, Leader. Now isn't that nice that I'm going to kill you?"

Meyers sat back in another chair, watching the scene as he might have a stage play, wondering what the next move might be, but calmly aware that he had no part to play in the next few moments. Then he noticed the Leader's hand drop behind him and grope back on the table for the automatic there, and his curiosity was satisfied. Obviously, the lunatic couldn't have killed the original.

The lunatic babbled on. "I remember my plan, Leader. I'll kill you, and then there won't be any you. And without you, there won't be any me. I'll never have to hunt for clothes, or keep from talking, or go crazy. I won't be at all, and it'll be wonderful. No more twenty years. Wonderful, isn't it wonderful? Hee-yee-yee! Oh, wonderful. But I like to eat, and dead men don't eat, do they? Do they? Too bad, too bad, but I had breakfast this morning, anyhow. I'm going to kill you the next time I say 'wonderful,' Leader. I'm going to shoot and there'll be noise, and you'll be dead. Wonder—"

His lips went on with the motion, even as the Leader's hand whipped out from behind him and the bullet exploded in his head with a sudden crash that split his skull like a melon and threw mangled bits of flesh out through the door, leaving half a face and a tattered old body to slump slowly toward the floor with a last spasmodic kick. With a wry face, the Leader tossed the gun back on the table and rolled the dead figure outside the door with his foot.

Meyers collected the gun quietly, substituting his watch, face up where he could watch the minute hand. "That was yourself you shot, my Leader," he stated as the other turned back to the table.

"Not myself, a duplicate. What matter, he was useless, obviously, with his insane babble of Immenhoff's death. Or— The tank should have been here long before this! But Immenhoff couldn't have been discovered!"

Meyers nodded. "He was—all the 'secret' depots were; I knew of it. And the body you just tossed outside wasn't merely a duplicate—it was yourself as you will inevitably be."

"You—Treason!" Ugly horror and the beginnings of personal fear spread across the Leader's face, twisting the scar and turning it livid. "For that—"

Meyers covered him with the automatic. "For that," he finished, "you'll remain seated, Leader, with your hands on the table in clear view. Oh, I have no intention of killing you, but I could stun you quite easily; I assure you, I'm an excellent shot."

"What do you want? The reward of the invaders?"

"Only the inevitable, Leader, only what will be because it has already been. Here!" Meyers tossed a small leather wallet onto the table with his left hand, flipping it open to the picture of a woman perhaps thirty-five years old. "What do you see there?"

"A damned Jewess!" The Leader's eyes had flicked to the picture and away, darting about the room and back to it.

"Quite so. Now, to you, a damned Jewess, Leader." Meyers replaced the wallet gently, his eyes cold. "Once though, to me, a lovely and understanding woman, interested in my work, busy about our home, a good mother to my children; there were two of them, a boy and a girl—more damned Jews to you, probably. We were happy then. I was about to become a full professor at Heidelberg, we had our friends, our life, our home. Some, of course, even then were filled with hatred toward the Jewish people, but we could stand all that. Can you guess what happened? Not hard, is it?

"Some of your Youths. She'd gone to her father to stay with him, hoping it would all blow over and she could come back to me without her presence hurting me. They raided the shop one night, beat up her father, tossed her out of a third-story window, and made the children jump after her—mere sport, and patriotic sport! When I found her at the home of some friends, the children were dead and she was dying."

The Leader stirred again. "What did you expect? That we should coddle every Jew to our bosom and let them bespoil the Reich again? You were a traitor to your fatherland when you married her."

"So I found out. Two years in a concentration camp, my Leader, taught me that, well indeed. And it gave me time to think. No matter how much you beat a man down and make him grovel and live in filth, he still may be able to think, and his thoughts may still find you out—you should have thought of that. For two years, I thought about a certain field of mathematics, and at last I began to think about the thing instead of the symbols. And at last, when I'd groveled and humbled myself, sworn a thousandfold that I'd seen the light, and made myself something a decent man would spurn aside, they let me out again, ten years older for the two years there, and a hundred times wiser.

"So I came finally to the little farm near Bresseldorf, and I worked as I could, hoping that, somehow, a just God would so shape things that I could use my discovery. About the time I'd finished, you fled, and I almost gave up hope; then I saw that in your escape lay my chances. I found you, persuaded you to return, and here you are. It sounds simple enough now, but I wasn't sure until I saw the legion. What would happen if I had turned you over to the Army of Occupation?"

"Eh?" The Leader had been watching the door, hoping for some distracting event, but his eyes now swung back to Meyers. "I don't know. Is that what you plan?"

"Napoleon was exiled; Wilhelm died in bed at Dorn. Are the leaders who cause the trouble ever punished, my Leader? I think not. Exile may not be pleasant, but normally is not too hard a punishment—normal exile to another land. I have devised a slightly altered exile, and now I shall do nothing to you. What was—will be—and I'll be content to know that eventually you kill yourself, after you've gone insane." Meyers glanced at the watch on the table, and his eyes gleamed savagely for a second before the cool, impersonal manner returned.

"The time is almost up, my Leader. I was fair to you; I explained to the best of my ability the workings of my invention. But instead of science, you wanted magic; you expected me to create some pseudo-duplicate of yourself, yet leave the real self unaltered. You absorbed the word 'plenum' as an incantation, but gave no heed to the reality. Remember the example I gave—a piece of string looped back on itself? In front of you is a string from some peasant's dress; now, conceive that piece of string—it loops back, starts out again, and is again drawn back—it does not put forth new feelers that do the returning to base for it, but must come back by itself, and never gets beyond a certain distance from itself. The coins that you saw in the pile disappeared—not because I depressed a switch, but because the two-minute interval was finished, and they were forced to return again to the previous two minutes."

Escape thoughts were obviously abandoned in the mind of the Leader now, and he was staring fixedly at Meyers while his hands played with the raveling from a peasant's garment, looping and unlooping it. "No," he said at last, and there was a tinge of awe and pleading in his voice, the beginning of tears in his eyes. "That is insane. Karl Meyers, you are a fool! Release me from this and even now, with all that has happened, you'll still find me a man who can reward his friends; release me, and still I'll reconquer the world, half of which shall be yours. Don't be a fool, Meyers."

Meyers grinned. "There's no release, Leader. How often must I tell you that what is now will surely be; you have already been on the wheel—you must continue. And—the time is almost here!"

He watched the tensing of the Leader's muscles with complete calm, dropping the automatic back onto his lap. Even as the Leader leaped from his chair in a frenzied effort and dashed toward him, he made no move. There was no need. The minute hand of the watch reached a mark on the face, and the leaping figure of the world's most feared man was no longer there. Meyers was alone in the house, and alone in Bresseldorf.

He tossed the gun onto the table, patting the pocket containing his wallet, and moved toward the dead figure outside the door. Soon, if the Leader had been right, the Army of Occupation would be here. Before then, he must destroy his machine.

One second he was dashing across the room toward the neck of Karl Meyers, the next, without any feeling of change, he was standing in the yard of the house of Meyers, near Bresseldorf, and ranging from him and behind him were rows of others. In his hands, which had been empty a second before, he clutched a rifle. At his side was belted one of the new-issue automatics. And before him, through the door of the house that had been Karl Meyers', he could see himself coming forward, Meyers a few paces behind.

For the moment there were no thoughts in his head, only an endless refrain that went: "I must obey my original implicitly; I must not cause trouble for my original or Karl Meyers; I must not speak to anyone unless one of those two commands. I must obey my original implicitly; I must not cause trouble—" By an effort, he stopped the march of the words in his head, but the force of them went on, an undercurrent to all his thinking, an endless and inescapable order that must be obeyed.

Beside him, those strange others who were himself waited expressionlessly while the original came out into the doorway and began to speak to them. "Soldiers of the Greater Reich that is to be . . . Let us be merciless in avenging . . . The fruits of victory. . . ." Victory! Yes, for Karl Meyers. For the man who stood there beside the original, a faint smile on his face, looking out slowly over the ranks of the legion.

"But I speak to myselves. You who come after me know what is to be this day and in the days to come, so why should I tell you? And you know that my cause is just. The Jews, the Jew-lovers—" The words of the original went maddeningly on, words that were still fresh in his memory, words that he had spoken only twenty-four hours before.

And now, three dead Jews and a Jew-lover had brought him to this. Somehow, he must stop this mad farce, cry out to the original that it was treason and madness, that it was far better to turn back to the guards in Switzerland, or to march forth toward the invaders. But the words were only a faint whisper, even to himself, and the all-powerful compulsion choked even the whisper off before he could finish it. He must not speak to anyone unless one of those two commanded.

Still the words went on. "Not victory in a decade, nor a year, but in a month! We shall go north and south and east and west! We shall show them that our fangs are not pulled; that those which we lost were but our milk teeth, now replaced by a second and harder growth!

"And for those who would have betrayed us, or bound us down in chains to feed the gold lust of the mad democracies, or denied us the room to live which is rightfully ours—for those, we shall find a proper place. This time, for once and for all, there shall be an end to the evils that corrupt the earth—the Jews and the Bolsheviks, and their friends, and friends' friends. Germany shall emerge, purged and cleansed, a new and greater Reich, whose domain shall not be Europe, nor this hemisphere, but the world!

"Many of you have seen all this in the future from which you come, and all of you must be ready to reassure yourselves of it today, that the glory of it may fill your tomorrow. Now, we march against a few peasants. Tomorrow, after quartering in Bresseldorf, we shall be in the secret depot, where those who remain loyal shall be privileged to multiply and join us, and where we shall multiply all our armament ten-thousandfold! Into Bresseldorf, then, and if any of the peasants are disloyal, be merciless in removing the scum! Forward!"

His blood was pounding with the mockery of it, and his hands were clutching on the rifle. Only one shot from the gun, and Karl Meyers would die. One quick move, too sudden to defeat, and he would be avenged. Yet, as he made the first effort toward lifting the rifle, the compulsion surged upward, drowning out all other orders of his mind. He must not cause trouble for his original or Karl Meyers!

He could feel the futile tears on his face as he stood there, and the mere knowledge of their futility was the hardest blow of all. Before him, his original was smiling at him and starting forward, to be checked by Meyers, and to swing back after a few words.

"Proceed to Bresseldorf, then, and we follow. Secure quarters for yourself and food, and a place for me and for Meyers; we stop there until I can send word to the depot during the night and extend my plans. To Bresseldorf!"

Against his will, his feet turned then with the others, out across the yard and into the road, and he was headed toward Bresseldorf. His eyes swept over the group, estimating them to be six or seven thousand in number; and that would mean twenty years, at one a day—twenty years of marching to Bresseldorf, eating, sleeping, eating again, being back at the farm, hearing the original's speech, and marching to Bresseldorf. Finally—from far down the line, a titter from the oldest and filthiest reached him—finally that; madness and death at the hands of himself, while Karl Meyers stood by, watching and gloating. He no longer doubted the truth of the scientist's statements; what had been, would be.

For twenty years! For more than seven thousand days, each the same day, each one step nearer madness. God!

The readers were less enthusiastic about my Hitler story than Campbell was. Probably I made a mistake, in the temper of the times, in not making Hitler more grotesque. But I wouldn't change it; to me, the ruthless hunger for power without other purpose for that power is evil enough. I still agree with my friend, Milt Rothman, who told me it was the best piece of writing I'd done in science fiction. He called much of my other writing lackadaisical, and I can see what he meant, though I don't quite accept that word.

By the beginning of 1942, everyone was caught up in a big fervor of patriotism. The magazines issued by Street and Smith were planning to cooperate with others by using nothing but a flag on their July issues. And Campbell asked me to do a story of patriotic fantasy for *Unknown* to go with the cover; I suspect my Hitler story had made him choose me.

I had a hard job rejecting all the obvious ideas. Angels coming down to help the soldiers, as they were supposed to have done in World War I. Merlin coming back to help us. The Little People rising in wrath. There were hundreds of ideas, all bad, and Henry (the little man in back of my mind) tossed every one at me.

The trouble was that most of such ideas get pretty sticky about halfway through and cease being stories by overdoing the propaganda. But I was saved by remembering that the Tomb of the Unknown Soldier lay just outside of Washington. I wanted a fairly quiet, restrained story.

Campbell sent the 12,600-word novelette back for two reasons. First, I wound up with my hero just walking up and down guarding the tomb all by himself, which was a pretty bootless contribution. And second, I indicated that my hero might have an affair with a flesh-and-blood girl. That, Campbell insisted, would be horrible to most readers.

I agreed with the first objection, and set about dragging out other elements I'd buried in the first version to fix it. I didn't agree with the second, and sort of fudged it by taking out only the specific references. Campbell spotted my trick, but let it get by. But the price was $126—with no bonus.

It's dated now, of course, and the world no longer can react properly to the story. But I'm still rather fond of "Though Poppies Grow."

12.

Though Poppies Grow

(by Lester del Rey)

Vaguely he was aware that he should have been some heroic figure, stalking along with his head up and the fire of high devotion in his eyes. His shoes should have gleamed brightly, his chin should have been firm and square, and there should have been a glint of devil-may-care recklessness in his expression, an appealing quirk to the smile he should be wearing. For a few seconds, he tried to simulate the dashing, heroic figure in his mind, but the best he could do was a wry grimace at his own thoughts.

Service shoes, mud-spattered, scratched, and with a hole picked out of one toe, were blunt and heavy on his feet—there'd been no time for polish. The wraparound leggings were correctly done, but somehow they were lacking in any trim smartness. And the dirty suit of khaki was hardly the raiment of a hero, especially when topped by a trench cap roughly mended. A cord around the tight collar supported a grim gas mask, and a lumpy rucksack was on his back, but the holster on his hip was empty; his hands felt lost without a rifle and bayonet in them.

"Lost" was the right word; his whole feeling was one of being lost, of wandering in a dirty fog, slushing through muck and mire, aimlessly, dimly conscious of some high mission, not quite believable. And with that in his mind, it was too much to ask his body to assume heroism. Instead, he trudged along quietly, neither trim nor quite careless, his eyes turning slowly from side to side, but somehow without much curiosity.

He stopped then, to fish for a cigarette, and realized his last butt was already gone. "Wish I had a cigarette, at least," popped into his mind, something someone had said once, while lying down in a muddy hole watching the blood trickle out slowly. For a moment, the scene was crystal clear, then it faded back and was gone, and he turned on with a shrug; he'd been without smokes before, would be again. A thin, average-height youth, with something almost haunted in his eyes, lips tensed a trifle, lost without name or place or knowledge of why he was there.

But there was nothing to do but go on, and the hazy idea that he had to go on was fixed in his mind. Back there in that place, he'd felt it—had been feeling it grow until he could no longer resist, and had risen and come out into a strange world where no guns boomed ominously to suggest a coming drive, and where a clean, well-paved road led down through the early mist to this bridge that ran over a river, somewhere.

It was a clean, white bridge, and beyond it was the suggestion of some building, looming up quietly ahead. There was neither mud nor dust, no shell holes, no barbed wire, no men screaming out their last breaths, just beyond the reach of their comrades—like Tommy. The picture of Tommy out there on the wire, pleading to them to shoot him and get it over with, was the one sharply etched memory that was left. Tommy'd been there for hours, screaming between the roars of the guns and whine of the shells, begging them to finish it off for him; and they'd huddled back behind the bags, risking death at intervals in an attempt to center a rifle on him and grant his wish—uselessly; Death hadn't been ready for Tommy yet.

And then it had been too much. Someone with them had laughed, gripping his head, and dropped his rifle to go out there, over the sandbags, and through the debris of shell holes and mud, running, not bravely but hysterically and crazily to where Tommy was caught and dying too slowly. Twice fragments had hit him, and he'd staggered back to jump forward again. Tommy'd seen the running figure and somehow Tommy'd straightened up a little in the snarl and managed to shake his head, yelling now for the runner to go back, swearing with oaths learned only at the right hand of Death. Somehow, the runner had made it, and groped down with pliers for the wire holding Tommy helpless there, just as a shell burst somewhere with a jar. Then Tommy'd slumped back, silent.

Beyond that, the picture vanished, and the man on the bridge shook his head. He couldn't remember who'd been the crazy fool to run out then, nor what had happened to him; he'd probably been blown into small pieces—if he was lucky. Shells could do funny things. For all he knew, Tommy's would-be rescuer might have been himself. Why not? That had been a long time ago, from the time-sense that had gone on measuring out the passing days and years and was still a part of him, but between the incident and the moment when he'd stirred restlessly and climbed out into the morning mist, he had no pictures, no feeling even that there should be pictures. It fitted his mood that he should be dead. There were no angels around, but his religion had been the rather hazy feeling of a God somewhere who let a man go on after he shuffled off his flesh. Angels would have been nice, but not necessary to the thing. Somewhere in school, he'd been taught of Asgard and the Norse Valhala, where the warriors came up over the bridge Bifrost to enter Odin's halls and fight and eat and die and fight again.

Again he grimaced. Bunk! Under his feet was good cement, and the asphalt on the road wasn't exactly heavenly. Neither were the graceful autos that passed in increasing numbers, low and rounded in lines, and mercifully silent. This was some part of the same crazy world, though he didn't know where, nor how he'd gotten there, nor what he'd been doing in all the time he could feel had passed. He didn't much care.

Ahead of him, another figure appeared, clad in khaki, also, but a khaki that had more green and less yellow in it. In mild curiosity he examined the trim uniform, wondering when they'd issued clothes like that—they looked like a cross between service uniform and civvies. Long pants, no leggings, a well-draped coat and, of all things, an open lapel and soft-collared shirt. Habit led his eyes to the gold bars on the shoulders, and his arm came up in a gesture that was almost pure conditioned reflex, yet still not quite snappy.

The lieutenant returned it smoothly, started on past, and then slowed to stare in a puzzled frown, glancing from the uniform to the boyish face, and back. "Where'd you get it?"

"France, sir. Where else? The ones we got here fitted."

"France? Mister, you're a da—" The lieutenant's eyes caught the boy's then, and he dropped his own, fumbling for a cigarette. "Sorry. You looked so— Anyway, none of my business. Smoke?"

"Thanks, sir." He drew in on the cigarette with a grateful relief from the gnawing little tension that had been in his muscles, saluted again, and went on toward the white building that loomed up closer now, and clearer as the sultry heat of the day began dispersing the fog. At least he knew for sure that this wasn't France—it could only be America. When you've been away long enough, you get to know the walk of a man on foreign land, and the lieutenant hadn't had it. Funny, he'd never expected to get back here, and now he couldn't tell how he'd done it.

Then the bridge came to an end, and he was facing a circular roadway around the building; he knew where he was for sure, now. Few buildings carry the individuality of the Lincoln Memorial, and there could be no mistaking it. Beyond it, in confirmation, was the spire of the Washington Monument, and between them, as he circled, he caught sight of the Reflecting Pool. He'd seen dozens of picture postcards, and there'd been the guide books an aunt had brought back from her trip to Washington, showing an artist's rendering of what it would all look like when finished. Well, he'd meant to see it sometime for himself, and now he was looking at it, wondering only faintly how he'd come to the capital.

He completed the half circle, and stood looking out over the Pool toward the Monument and on to where the dome of the Capitol showed in the now clear air over the trees on the Monument grounds, then swung back to face the statue of Lincoln, sitting calmly gazing over it all, enshrined like the old Greek gods in their temples. There was no thrill, no lift of spirits in the boy's mind, but he stood there for long moments, feeling the calm peace and sure purpose of the masterpiece. And as he looked, the feeling of purpose and some call to duty began to flow through his mind again. There was a reason for his presence here, and it was up to him to find it. Feeling half silly, he brought his arm up in a smarter salute to the statue than the lieutenant had received, turned and headed toward the city proper.

He was walking slightly more slowly, the stride of someone used to exhaustion and no longer capable of feeling fatigued or rested, as he came to the red light. This, he saw, was Fourteenth Street, and he'd been following New York Avenue for the last block; Pennsylvania Avenue, which had carried him past the White House, had vanished somewhere, and he had no desire to trace its windings. As he stood there, the light changed, and he started across, sticking to the general direction he'd been following for the last half hour. Already the streets were filling with people, and he could feel their occasional stares, but by now he'd learned the trick of turning to meet their eyes. Invariably, they dropped their gaze and went on, without looking back.

The girls had bothered him most, at first. He remembered faintly the girls who'd said good-bye to them back home, and was aware more strongly of the time and changes since then. He'd blushed like a fool when he saw the first young woman walking along, her short skirt showing her legs, her sheer blouse concealing all too little of the lace and silken things she wore beneath. But there'd been a freshness and cleanness about her that left no doubts in his head. Now he was becoming used to the cosmetics, the red fingernails, the revealing feminine clothes, and the free, confident carriage. There was an ache inside him somewhere that the French hussies who'd come out to the doughboys had never brought there, a queer tingling pride in this country that could produce such girls. He caught himself reaching out with slightly trembling fingers to touch the arm of one of them, jerked it back, and blushed again, hot with the feeling of his own foolishness. A man who'd get fresh with these deserved shooting or worse.

Sloppy sentimentality, he told himself. What he needed was breakfast. Wonder if he could wangle a little white-bread toast and coffee with sugar? There'd been letters about that in the trenches, and of how fifteen pounds of substitutes had to be bought for one pound of good white flour. He shrugged and turned into a restaurant at

Twelfth Street after jingling his pocket hastily to make sure he had the money. The counter was filled, and he ran his eyes over the booths, wondering whether to wait or take up one of them by himself.

It was then he saw the girl sitting alone, reading a newspaper, and the queer ache came over him again. She wasn't exactly beautiful, but somehow lovely, her brown hair falling softly to the shoulders, her face a trifle gaminish, with a dash of Irish around the mouth, and a smoothness of line that made what might have been thinness seem utterly feminine. You can't describe a girl like that, he thought, knowing it was sloppy and not caring; you just look at her and feel it.

She seemed to sense his gaze, for her eyes met his. That did it. How an impish provocativeness could be blended with naïve innocence and a trace of maternalism, he couldn't have told, but her eyes held all that, even as they registered faint distrust. He started forward, crimson again, but impelled by the craving for feminine words that he'd been feeling for the last hour.

"I . . . sorry if I'm rude—" Her eyes were still on his, and he stopped. He couldn't do it, even though she'd been the first one who hadn't jerked her glance away. He started to turn, just as she smiled, a half-amused, half-puckish lighting of her face. "Oh, darn it, miss, I don't want to be . . . but—"

"Why not sit down? I suppose I should, but I don't mind." She pushed the paper away from her and motioned to the seat opposite. He slid in awkwardly, and she smiled in honest amusement that was less embarrassing than any attempt to cover it would have been. "You act as if you'd never seen a girl before, soldier."

"It's not quite that bad, miss. But—well, over there, things were different. We didn't see the nice ones, and the others—" He dropped it and ordered his toast and coffee. "Seems funny, getting back to America. Over there in France, I thought I'd never make it."

"Over there in France? You were fighting the Nazis?" She'd finished her breakfast and was digging into her handbag. A cigarette came out and she lighted it casually while he stared. But no one else seemed to notice, and there were so many strange things that he decided to forget it.

"What Nazis? All I know is that we were supposed to be fighting the Kaiser, but after we got there, all I ever saw were a bunch of boys on the other side in different helmets. We were too busy fighting to be fighting anyone in particular, even when we called them Heinies."

Her eyes were wide now, and she shook her head, suspicion written large on her face. "Kaiser? Heinies? But that was twenty-five years ago; and you're no older than I am. My father was over there with them; he married Mom after he came back."

The boy made no comment. Twenty-five years! Her paper was still lying open, and he glanced at it, to see her words confirmed. "July 3, 1942." And his world was built around 1918. The girl's father had returned from the World War to marry her mother!

They'd pulled *him* out of college in '17, put him in a camp for hasty instructions, run him across on a troopship, and then there'd been the long months of death and mud. There'd been the starving French girls and Tommy and— Then other men had come back, married, brought up children and put them through college, while he felt that nothing had happened to him. Even the mud spots on his clothes seemed the same old familiar ones, and the stubble on his face was still a yellow down, hardly needing a razor. He was nibbling at the toast and tasting the coffee as he thought it over in his head, but he pushed them back. He had no need of them—there was something wrong with the idea of eating now, and only old habit had driven him to try it.

She was speaking again. "Yet, I guess I believe you—I don't know why. The way your eyes look—Dad always had the same thing in his when he talked about that war. And your uniform doesn't look like a parade getup. There's something about you—as if I knew you, or something. How—"

"I don't know," he answered slowly. "I don't know anything—my own name, even, how I got here, where I'm going, what I'm to do. I can remember the whine of shells one minute, then something made me get up this morning and come out, looking for something I've got to do. I don't even know what a returned doughboy can do in peacetime."

"It isn't exactly peacetime." She looked at the clock, frowned, and turned back to him, holding out the paper. "I shouldn't believe you, but I do. And I'm supposed to be at work in ten minutes, yet I'm going to be late just to tell you what's been going on. I wonder why I'm not surprised, but I'm not."

It was much later when he sat back, nodding. Hitler, Mussolini, Japan—no longer an ally, but an enemy, ruthless and without principles. France, no longer a battleground for democracy, but in the hands of the invaders. And this time they weren't merely Heinies, but something grimmer and uglier, Nazis who devoted themselves to the blood altar of a barbarian racial fanaticism.

"'To make the world safe for democracy,'" he quoted softly. Funny, he'd really believed that, in spite of himself. He'd laughed at it among his cynical college friends, and yet all of them must have been swept up by it, with the old crusading spirit. It had been a bright vision, even in the mud of France, a hope for the world; and a few power-mad idiots had taken only twenty-five years to trample it down into the ground and begin all over again.

"Bitter?" she asked.

He shook his head. "No, somehow I'm not. We were right, then, I think. If there'd been no need to make the world safe for democracy, then all this would never have happened afterward. We just figured we could do it all in one swoop, and it seems to take more doing than that. I should have known; I was majoring in history before it began. No other major conflict was ever finished in five years, or fifty years. You have to keep fighting for your side until someday there isn't any other side, because you've conquered it a little at a time and the grandchildren of the men you fought believe the same as you do. Then there'll be something else to fight about. But the important thing is that little by little things do get ahead that way. We had to fight the Revolutionary War to start democracy, the Civil War to keep it, the World War to save the others who felt as we did and tried to extend it, and this war the same. It's like gold mining, you might say."

"I don't get it."

He didn't entirely himself. Principles were vague things to die for, and yet sometimes they were worth dying and killing for. Usually the direct action was easier than trying to understand clearly why you had to do it. "Well, the prospectors found themselves mines by working harder hunting for it and keeping at it, believing that there was gold there if they'd work for it. They dug it out and began thinking about bringing out their families, and then somebody jumped their claims with a gun in his hand. They had to fight him for it, and probably fight his kind more than once, fight out false claims in court, and maybe at last come through with it, bring out their families and help build up one of our modern cities where others could live and work safely. If anything's worth having—mine, family, flag, country, or democracy—it's worth fighting for, and you'll have to fight for it."

"I never thought of it that way. But you've already fought once—and it didn't seem to do much good, did it?"

He grinned slowly, realizing that her question was not meant as an argument against his, but only a probe for his reaction. "It gave me the chance to fight again—maybe this way we can beat them someday and keep the gold; the other way, we never could. And this time, I'm going to enlist—that's probably what I felt I had to do all the time."

"And I'm going to be bawled out for being two hours late, but I don't care. . . . No, I'll pay my own check." She reached for it, but he had it in his hand already, and was groping in his pocket for the change that had rattled there.

It came out—seven francs and four centimes. There was nothing else, though he groped back again in frantic hope. There were only the eleven pieces, dated from 1904 to 1915, and all coins of France—a France that no longer had any real existence except in the mind of its still rebellious people. He stood there helplessly staring at them, his face reddening slowly, and puzzlement vying with the embarrassment. Even the coins he carried were the same coins that had been in his pocket in France the day that . . . that . . .

He almost had it when she pulled him back to the seat. "Easy, soldier. It's all right. I understand—or I seem to understand, at least. Here." She had her handbag open and was pushing a bill into his hand. He saw that it was about half the size of the bills he'd remembered, and that Lincoln's picture was still on the five-dollar note. And the memory that had almost come to him was gone again.

"But—"

"Shh. You can pay it back someday. Here, I'll take these as security." She was smiling at him, and the maternal part of her eyes was uppermost then as she picked the French coins out of his hand and stuck them into her pocketbook. "And here's my name and address, so you can return it. A soldier needs some money to carry him until payday, you know. Besides, I don't have anyone in the service writing me, and this will give me a good excuse to ask you. You will keep it?"

For an instant, he was afraid he was going to cry in front of her, but he managed to control most of it. "What else can I do, when you make it sound so natural? I—oh, you know what I feel about it."

She smiled and nodded again. "I'm glad. Write often, and good luck!" Then he was paying the checks and buying cigarettes, while she went down the street away from him, her short skirt no longer something strange to him, but a part of the spirit of her. He asked the cashier for directions, and she gave them with eyes carefully away from his. Now to enlist and quiet the strengthened urge to do his part again.

Out on the street, it seemed hard to realize that this was the capital of a nation—his nation—at war. Particularly when he remembered that tomorrow was the Fourth of July, most patriotic of all the national holidays. Oh, there were children with their cap pistols already, and the posters everywhere advertising Defense Bonds, silence to keep secrets from the enemy, and similar things, but there was none of the blatant hysteria of the last war, as he remembered it. And yet, in the quietness with which everyone went about his business, he sensed a determination that was more solidly based than it had been in '17.

The newspapers, he saw, were filled with news, some good and some bad, from what he could tell, and there was bickering in Congress, and accusations of war profiteering, of "too little, too late," and other current cries. But those things had happened before, and this time there was more control than there had been. It was impossible for any large nation to agree on all details, useless to hope that some shortsighted people would not try to turn the general trouble into a lever to use for their own selfish purpose. Those things were a part of war, as much as the fighting. But this was a healthy spirit around him, a calmer, more determined spirit. Before, in America there had been the cries and the shoutings, the loud oratory, and disordered scrambling that had been in severe contrast to the actual frontline spirit. This was no longer a people trying to convince themselves that they should fight for a principle, but a people who knew they had to, just as the soldiers at the front must know. He pushed on toward the recruiting office, more at ease than he'd been since he'd come out of the place in the morning. This would be a better war to fight in.

There were a few men already there, sitting in chairs and waiting their turn. They were ordinary enough young men, mostly, though one oldster was vehemently protesting his ability, and there was a small amount of good-natured kidding going on. The man on his right turned to say something, caught his glance, and settled back quietly. Something about him was different; their looks weren't ones of fear, but of minding their own business, something like the expression of a soldier who'd started to address another familiarly, and then caught the insignia of a major just in time to check it.

They came to him in time, with the inevitable papers that were different but strongly familiar. At least, there was less of the hurried, impersonal treatment here than there had been in the draft center the last time; probably some of the prejudice in favor of enlistment still lasted, though he'd learned that the matter was no test as to a man's courage at the front. He filled in as he came to the questions, pulling his answers out of the air, conscious that a lot of them were probably the correct ones, but sure of none. He stated his age minus the lapse of twenty-five years, and no questions were raised, nor was the matter of his outmoded uniform brought up. Once a new man came into the office and stared for a second before turning on, but he seemed under a blanket protection. Wearing even a last-war uniform should have been a matter for suspicion in an enlistee, but there seemed to be none.

"You forgot to put down your name," he was told. Name? He had none. But his eye fell on the belt of a uniform at the other end of the room and he wrote down "Sam Brown" quietly. "Middle name?"

"None."

"Okay, might as well get your medical over with. In there."

He went in, behind two others who were discussing their surprise at the prompt medicals; they'd expected to have to wait for notice, as in the case of draftees. He was free from expectation or curiosity, his mind almost empty as he waited his turn.

Finally one of the doctors indicated him. "Sam Brown next. Dr. Feldman, take this one."

Feldman took him in tow, into a place where another man was dressing. "Strip." And still there was no comment on his uniform, though he was surprised himself to see the gashed underclothes, stained and muddy. A bath and fresh clothes would have come in handy.

"Step up here; stand straight. Good. Weight, one hundred forty-three; height, five feet nine and one-half inches. A little thin, but not too bad. Bend over." It went on through the old routine, and finally the strap was wrapped around his arm for blood pressure, pumped up, and Dr. Feldman looked at the gauge, which held no meaning for him. "Systolic . . . umm. Wait a minute."

The medico brought out a stethoscope, listened carefully, moved it, and listened again. "Just a minute. Dr. Palz, will you come here?" And again it was repeated, this time by Palz. Feldman looked on carefully. "Well?"

Palz nodded. "If you mean—then I do get the same results. Hmm. All right, young man, if you'll jump from one leg to another twenty times . . . Good." And it was all begun for the third time, now with muttered consultations going on between the two doctors. "We're probably both crazy, Dr. Feldman, but—"

"Yeah." Feldman rubbed his hands against his side. "Yeah. When in doubt— I'm sorry, Mr. Brown, but I'm afraid you won't do. You can dress now."

The boy looked slowly from one to the other, and he drew nothing from their incredulous expressions. He'd been sure there would be no trouble that way—he'd passed the draft physicals with an A-1 rating, and while the fighting at the front had been tough, surely it hadn't softened him—unless there had been something in the years between that he couldn't remember.

"Soldier's heart?" he ventured, remembering talk of men whose hearts raced, weakened, and failed at the first real sign of exercise. "You mean my heart's too fast?"

"Hardly too fast—no." Feldman looked at him thoughtfully and almost fearfully. "If I had time of my own, I'd— You can leave by that door."

That was no answer. "Doctor, what's the reason then? Oh, I gather it's my heart, but what's wrong with it?"

Again Feldman studied him before answering. "Don't you know?"

"No. I wouldn't ask if I did."

"Then feel your own pulse, man. That's all."

He stumbled out, wondering, into one of the little parks that seemed to be all over the capital, drawing slowly at a cigarette. He wasn't sure he wanted to try it—anything that had such a reaction on men who were familiar with all kinds of disorders must be pretty bad. But as he finished the cigarette, he mashed it out under his heel and put his finger to his pulse.

There was none!

Nor was there a sign of heartbeat when he held his hand there; the artery under his neck gave the same answer. Five times he tried it. No heartbeat. Even when he jumped from the bench and ran wildly through the park and down the street to another, he could detect no faintest sign of a pulse anywhere. Yet he was panting, and he had the feeling of hot blood coursing through him and sweat pouring off. He pressed his hand under his armpit and drew it away—dry! His skin showed no slightest sign of moisture anywhere, though the day was as hot and sticky as any he'd known—typical Washington summer weather, he'd gathered from various uncomplimentary remarks.

Curiously, there was no excitement in him. His brain should have been turning frantically from point to point for some rational explanation, but he sought none. Instead, he got up from the bench and went up Eleventh Street with a slow, even stride, across E Street, through the crowds at F, and beyond G toward H, his only thought being the counting off of the blocks as they came. Then a little novelty shop caught his eye, and he went in.

"Do you have a small mirror—anything at all, just something cheap?"

The woman nodded and handed across a small square of glass. "Ten cents," she said, and dropped her eyes hastily to the coin as he looked at her.

He stuck it in his pocket and went out onto Eleventh again, carefully aware that the heat and walking were making him breathe heavily; he was conscious of the fairly rapid rise and fall of his chest, of the slightly choking feeling that comes from too much humidity in the air. He held the mirror up to his mouth, drew it back, and inspected it before tossing it away.

Its work was done. There was no condensed moisture on it from his breath. He'd expected it, and again there was the curious lack of emotional response. Quite calmly he faced the fact that by two standard tests he was dead. But it was a senseless paradox of death that seemed to breathe but didn't—the cigarette smoke eddied slowly from his mouth as he watched, but the mirrow showed no sign of moisture. To hell with it; at worst, it was a highly vital death.

No wonder they'd turned him down, though; the miracle was that they hadn't gone crazy, though he supposed it would take a lot to do that to a doctor—or would it? Weren't they used to certain absolute facts, such as that a living man automatically included a beating heart, and when confronted with a violation of their fundamental law, wouldn't it hit them harder? He didn't know.

And perversely, the feeling that he had been called forth for some job that needed doing was stronger than ever. And the people about him were suddenly strangers, walking in a strange world. That feeling passed, and he felt normal again, except for the urge to do something and the knowledge that he was unable seemingly to find it.

One of the boxes in the shops along the street which were giving out music and speeches—"radios," apparently, since the shop was advertising the things under that name—broke off its news report of some action taking place in the Pacific and began one of the announcements he heard several times already. "Men, Uncle Sam needs your help. If you're a skilled worker . . ." There was more of it, but he stopped listening, turning it over in his mind.

His skill was limited. Before the war, he'd been an unlicked cub of a kid, filled with a kid's idle dreams and hazy desires to do something, but unsure of what. He hadn't even peddled papers; and they'd packed him off to college to a thoroughly impractical education at sixteen. He remembered vague discussions of the typical pseudo-politics with other boys there, something about the United States being able to stay out of all foreign affairs; he'd been for it, as he remembered. Tommy hadn't—that's where he'd met Tommy, and they'd met again over there. Tommy'd enlisted, but he'd been too full of the school twaddle to free his mind from it at first, and he'd been drafted before he could reorient himself. An incomplete major in history, a vague feeling that he'd sometime write a book on the "Dynamics of History," and school politics hardly constituted skills.

His thoughts had been too much in his head for him to notice where he was going or the people around him, but now a vague awareness of something unusual made him look forward quickly. One of the crowd ahead was staring at him with a sickly, whitish-green cast to his skin that made him stand out like a ghost at a wedding. As the boy watched, the man's knees were trembling visibly, and he stood, half turned, apparently rooted to the spot.

Still the soldier's feet moved forward toward the man directly in his path, and sudden fright seemed to galvanize the frozen expression into a grimace of the purest possible fear.

"*Gott, nein! Gott bewahre, so mach' ich nie wieder! Hinweg, um Gottes Willen!* No, back—back! I repent, I surrender, but back! O, *du lieber Gott, schuldig kenn' ich mich—*" German and English spilled out in a quavering admission of treachery and deceit, both carrying an accent, as if the groveling creature had grown up in both and learned neither perfectly.

The bulging eyes were centered squarely on the boy now, and he began to realize that whatever frightened the man was something about himself, but his feet carried him remorselessly forward without direction from his mind. Fear seemed suddenly to pass its ultimate pinnacle, and a convulsive flash of movement brought the man to his feet and sent him off in a wild bound, unmindful that it carried him directly into the arms of an approaching policeman. For a moment the officer stepped backward and then, as the meaning of the babbled words hit him, he pinned the other firmly and looked over the crowd that had collected.

"Anyone see what got into this damned spy here?"

The boy started backward, but none were looking at him accusingly, as he'd expected, save for the frozen eyes of the self-confessed German agent, and they shook their heads, denying any knowledge of the reasons behind the peculiar actions of the captive. The officer shrugged and turned toward the call box on the corner.

"Darned funny. He acts as if he'd seen Old Nick himself. All right, break it up, we'll take care of this guy!"

The boy looked around again at this dispersing crowd, but no eyes were on him, and their curiosity was uncentered. Whatever the German had seen was unrevealed to the rest of them. He went up the street, and there was no more attention paid to him than before. Why?

The question went without answer. Ordinarily, he might have put it down to coincidence and dropped it from his mind, but too many strange things had been forced upon him at once, and it seemed that there must be some connection. The German had looked at him and seen—what? Whatever it was, it obviously had been neither pretty nor normal, unless there was some incident between them in the buried years of which he had no memory. And such stark fear seemed hardly capable of being inspired by anything even as nearly human as he seemed to be.

Having no answer to the riddle, he dropped it as he struck New York Avenue and turned toward Twelfth, that being the only place in the city with any associations in his mind. He hardly expected to find—uh—Anne there, and he was right in that. But he went in out of the heat and sat down in a booth. "Beer."

It came out, cold and amber clear, and his eyes lighted faintly. Whether there was blood in his veins or a heart to pump it, at least the beer slid down smoothly and its taste was unchanged. He had no hunger, no faintest desire for food, which was another abnormality, and the familiarity of the unchanged taste of the liquid was like the presence of an old friend. Three more pennies went for a copy of a newspaper, picked at random, and he glanced over the headlines, mostly without meaning. Some of the stories helped a little to clarify his hazy notion of the world of 1942, though. He was more interested in the comparatively few appeals to the patriotism of the readers; he chuckled wryly at the idea of giving his blood to the Red Cross. But the general idea was far from humorous; if his interpretation of the plasma bank was correct, it would have been a godsend twenty-five years before. He'd seen them lying on the stretchers, white and deathly still, with spilled blood on all sides of them and none available to save them. Now, it seemed, blood from civilians could keep the life going in men three thousand miles or more away. And he couldn't help, even in that.

Somehow, he wanted desperately to help. And his inability only made the need to do so the greater in his mind. They weren't blazoning frantic appeals from the rooftops this time, but the few small advertisements he saw reached out as the wildly painted signs had never done. Then, he'd been a boy, untempered and uncertain about such abstractions as the good of patriotism. The dragging months in France had cured it, had hardened him into a man, and burned a sense of responsibility into him. It seemed that a man picked up an obligation to a country that gave him the right to fight and—well, why not finish the thought?—and die for it.

But would beer sit well in a dead man's stomach? It didn't matter. He turned back through the paper idly, glancing over the sports items, which meant nothing to him, noticing that movie advertisements were still in superlatives, though there was casual mention of "talkies," which must mean the experiments with sight and sound had been perfected, and skipping the local stuff. The cartoon on the editorial page meant no more to him than the sports cartoon, and he swept over the puerile-sounding editorial, then to the column beside it; there his eyes stuck.

The arguments were old; variants of them had been used by a few papers in the last war. Nothing treasonable, of course; the old line of "we agree with you—only we're more patriotic—but . . . Can we trust our allies? Stab Russia when you can before she gets out of hand! Keep the armies at home to defend our own shores, instead of out there fighting for England, who wouldn't do anything for us. The Japs have already got India where they want her, so let's retreat and hold Hawaii!" All the appeals to the festering little fears and hatreds of a great mass of the people were there, to stir up the readers, increase their prejudices, make them doubt, and hinder any forthright offensive. He'd been swayed by those same arguments once, and because of that, and because he'd seen their falsity as he mingled with the men of other nations and saw the grim facts at the front, his swearing was none too gentle as he read it. Better the German agent than the man—managing editor, he saw by the masthead—who'd write such rot in the guise of patriotism while better men were dying for it, without time to talk of the love of right or country. Damned slimy skunk!

Why, or what he hoped to accomplish, he couldn't have told, but anger swelled up in him as he paid his check and moved out into the street and toward the nearby address he'd noted carefully. He was a little ashamed of his anger, and then ashamed of his shame; anger on that subject was justifiable, and if it did no good, it could at least do no harm.

He found the editorial rooms without trouble, and the girl who stood guard outside only looked up once, then went on about her work, raising no objections as he pushed through the door and into the inner office; such minor miracles no longer caught more than a passing notice from him.

The editor threw a quick glance up and back to the work he was doing. "Well? How'd you get in here, and what do you want?"

Anger was still hot in him as he held out the column. "I'd like to make a complete fool of myself by pushing your face in. I should do it, because I don't have the average man's reasons for not doing it, and it's a strong temptation. Man, do you realize what ideas you're trying to put into your readers' minds? Doesn't the responsibility of your job mean anything to you?"

"It means a great deal, young man." The answer seemed sincere enough, surprisingly, though it was hard to tell while the other kept his eyes down. "It means enough that if you and a dozen others who've threatened me were to come up here regularly to push my face in, as you put it, I'd still do all I could to keep us from going down the little end of the horn before the ultimate threat of communism. We did it before, and—"

"Bunk! If you mean to tell me you believe in this unmitigated, treasonous rot—" For a breathing space he paused, and then the words inside him poured out. He couldn't have told afterward just what he'd said, though it had seemed important at the time; partly, he knew, it was an appeal to logic, mostly to emotions, but the words came to his lips almost automatically, while the editor sat quietly, face relaxed after the first flush of anger, slowly raising his eyes. Finally the words were drained from him completely, and still the other made no answer. What was the use? He turned back with half a shrug, out of the office and down to the street.

But he was feeling more cheerful, somehow. The release of his emotions had been better for him than keeping them to himself, at least, and he was no worse off. With new determination, he set off toward an agency on E Street; the small notice he'd seen had indicated they might be able to help him in locating the work he must do. His heart—or whatever served him—was lighter as he headed down Ninth, whistling faintly.

Night found him again in front of the restaurant on Twelfth Street. He stood there, much as he had been on the bridge in the morning, though the gas mask was in some trash can and the rucksack had followed it—the little it held was useless to him. But where he had merely felt empty and lost on the bridge, his feeling now was one of having been emptied—not only emptiness, but the emptiness which follows fullness.

The cigarette dangled from his lips and finally dropped out. He watched the door, seeing the people come in and go out, and could feel himself apart from them—a useless, wasted part of the world. The afternoon had taught him the last meaning of futility. At the agency, they'd been as helpful as they could, but there was nothing for him; he had no skill beyond soldiering, and that one skill "lodged in him useless, though his soul more bent to serve therewith—" Milton, he remembered; but Milton had his work still to do when he wrote that sonnet.

And afterward, tramping the streets, looking everywhere in the faint hope that he could at least replace someone who would be of more use, he'd found a man out of his true time has no place. But there was no room for bitterness, or even for more than the merest stirring of thought. He stood there, watching, and it was later still when he realized that he'd been hoping to catch a glimpse of Anne.

Once he started inside, but he had no need of food, and the beer that would have been welcome could only come out of money which he no longer had a right to use.

Finally he turned slowly, with a last look down the street, and began moving down New York Avenue toward no destination in particular. Behind him was the sound of men's feet, the brusque stamping of workmen on their way to their homes, and the clicking of high, feminine heels. He heard them all objectively, as if he could no longer connect them with people, or the people with himself, but only noises coming through a thick gray mist.

For seconds, one set of foot sounds had been near him, and now it was beside him. He slowed, without looking around, to let the owner of the feet go on, but the sounds slowed also, and he finally turned.

She was smiling, and the first warmth of the evening came into his spirits. "About time, soldier," she greeted him. "I had a hunch you might return there, but you were already going away when I spotted you. Were you look—"

"Looking for you? Yes. Though I had no right to be."

"Shh, soldier. If I could look for you, hadn't you the right to do the same for me?" Her arm went through his possessively, and in spite of himself, unnamed and painfully wonderful things passed through him; she was scarcely shorter than he in her high heels, yet she had the art of making him feel tall and strong and protective—even when it was she who did the protecting. "Did the day go so badly with you?"

He disregarded the last question, choosing to answer the first. "You were looking for me out of pity—you knew what would happen. And I . . . well, I was looking for you to get that pity, I suppose. No man has the right to go hunting for that."

"You weren't; I know that. You'd never turn to a woman for pity, soldier, but only because there are times when a man needs to talk to a girl. But I asked how the day went—and you haven't answered."

He told her of the recruiting station—though not the reason for the rejection—his flare-up at the newspaper, and the agency; the other places he mentioned without bothering to list. And her eyes were troubled as she listened, but there was neither scorn nor pity in them, and when he had finished, she made no immediate comment. For that he was grateful. Sometimes a man needs a woman's silent presence more than any words she can give him. They'd swung off New York Avenue and up one of the numbered streets while he talked, and now she turned him, again, into a lettered street, down a block, and finally stopped.

"Home." The house was one of the innumerable brownstone buildings scattered over the city, but better kept than most. She indicated a great curved window on the first floor. "I've got an apartment there. It isn't as fancy as living in an apartment hotel, but it's comfortable, and I can do as I please. Come on up with me and I'll have supper ready shortly."

With the best of intentions to refuse, he found himself following her up the few steps and into the place. There, at the door, he stopped, conscious of his dirty clothing, the heavy, worn shoes, and the appearance he presented in general. He had no business in the room he saw in front of him, with its graceful furnishings that managed to suggest comfort and hominess without any loss of fineness of line or richness of appointment. She smiled quizzically at his expression, throwing her bag and paper carelessly onto a chair.

"In with you, Mr. X. I'm not holding this door open another minute."

And again he was unable to disobey her as she pushed him down onto a sofa, pulled an apron off a rack, and went out into the little kitchenette to begin supper. He relaxed back on the seat after the first minute, and watched as she moved about, soaking in the grace and motions of her body as he might have basked in sunlight after sleeping in a cold cellar. Apparently the meal was almost entirely prepared already; she must have gone out after him deliberately either on a hunch or a wild chance. He wondered which.

"Hungry?" she asked as she piled the last dish on the table and indicated his chair.

He took it. "Not very. I—" Why go on pretending? She'd earned the truth, or at least a part of it. "I suspect I don't have any need to eat. I've managed to go all day without anything, and I'm still not hungry. Smells good, though."

"Then eat it," she ordered. "There's no fun in cooking unless someone else is around to enjoy it."

To his surprise, he found that there was still a savor to food, and while he felt no need of it, the sensation of eating was as enjoyable as ever. What would a ghost do with food? Or what should a living man do without the beat of his heart? Neither life nor death would serve as a single answer to the conflicting facts of his existence, just as there was no work for him among the living, nor rest among the dead.

Her voice broke in on his thoughts. "You don't need to breathe, either, do you, soldier? You forget to whenever you're thinking about something else."

There was no fear or surprise on her face as he looked up sharply. And as he glanced back at himself, he noticed his breath begin with a little jerk and then go on smoothly. He pushed the food aside and held out his wrist to her.

She touched it for a few seconds and nodded slowly; the whitening of her face was so slight that he sensed rather than saw it, but her voice was still perfectly calm. "I thought so. I noticed the breathing this morning, but didn't realize I'd done so until after I'd left you. Do you know 'In Flanders Field'? No, of course not."

Perhaps no war poem has ever come so close to perfection as that one, and she recited it well: " 'We lived, felt dawn, saw sunset's glow; loved and were loved, and now we lie in Flanders Field. . . . If ye break faith with us who die, *we shall not sleep,* though poppies grow in Flanders Field. . . .' "

But the living had broken no faith here; over there, perhaps. Here they had taken up the quarrel with the foe—not the literal foe of men and arms, but the truer one of hatred and barbaric ideologies—and from what he had seen, none who might lie in Flanders Field could begrudge them their holding of the torch. He, it seemed, was guilty of breaking faith, but that not willingly.

He shrugged off the overlaid feeling of the poem on his own mood and stood up. "I can't bother you anymore, Anne. You know as much about me as I do, and you can see how hopeless I am. Here . . . I spent part of it, but here's what's left. I got it under false pretenses, and I'll probably never pay the rest back, but I have no need for this."

Her eyes were hurt, and then proud. "You need it more now, and I don't need it at all. Father has a home and money, if I want them; and my own work pays more than I can use. Call it a debt that my generation owes yours, and let me pay it. You'll need a room, unless you want to stay here. No, I meant that, soldier, but not as it sounds. There's a room here I never use, and I can trust you. Which will it be?"

"A room, I guess, if I can find one in this overcrowded city."

"There's one up the street somewhere; a friend of mine was telling me about it at work today. I've got the address in my other pocket-book, if you'll wait half a minute." She started back, then stopped at the door. "Darn, I took it out of the bag, now that I remember. No telling where I put it or how long you'll have to wait now. Why don't you look at the paper while I'm hunting. Something on page twelve may interest you, I think."

He picked it up and began to open it, but as she slipped back out of sight, he tossed it aside and did what he knew he must. The rug muffled his footsteps as he dropped the money on the table and passed to the door, which opened silently and closed without a creak. Outside and down the street, he heard her voice raised and a click of heels on the steps, but he was running then with every ounce of energy in his legs, around a corner, through an alley, and in zigzag fashion until she couldn't possibly trail him. The knowledge that she had tried to was oddly comforting, though.

It hadn't been pity, he knew, nor charity, nor any of the other blind and selfish emotions men use to inflate their own egos at the expense of others less fortunate. None of them would have made her accept and trust him or bear the knowledge of what sort of a creature he was without flinching and drawing away from him. That fact only made it the more necessary that he should leave.

He was a failure. How much of a failure, he could only guess as his feet carried him steadily onward through the streets, to Constitution Avenue and beyond. Lincoln Memorial was before him, but he avoided the statue, and was back on the bridge, again partially wrapped in a mist from the river that put halos around the lights. He was to have been a miracle and a symbol, somehow, and instead he was returning to the place from which he came, useless in a world where even the average ordinary failures could serve.

The bridge was more than a quarter of a mile in length, and his feet carried him along slowly, but it was behind him at last, and he was following a curving roadway that led up a hill. Just where he was going he did not know. That morning, beyond the driving need to come out, he had been aware of nothing. All he knew was that he had come from a place and was going back to it, carried by feet that drew him onward surely if slowly.

Yet he was reluctant to return. He halted to smoke and try to think, off the road a ways. In the sky, a premature skyrocket flashed up in zooming arc from somewhere in the city, and he ducked with an instinctive desire to hole up from anything that whined in the sky above him. Then he lay there, smoking and feeling; it could hardly be called thinking. And his emotions were a jumble of dark moods and bluely warm thoughts of the one part of the city that was other than an impersonal goal behind him.

It might have been minutes or hours later when he reached again for a smoke and drew out the last one in the package. But it was time to go on, and there was no sense in turning back. Above him, bright stars dappled the sky, and behind him the lights gleamed through the fog that snuggled against the ground and swirled about his feet. Before him, the road led somewhere.

It ended before his feet stopped and he looked about him to see the outlines of something that might have been a shrine or an amphitheater. Up there a soldier was pacing up and down in rigid military precision, and as he watched, another came forward and went through the high ritual of changing guards. Forward to the end of the stone platform, turn, backward to a stone structure. That caught his eye then, and he studied the eleven-foot object idly, noting the simple beauty of the work and the three figures adorning it. But his feet were moving again, carrying him forward. This was the place, and there was but one thing left to do.

The force of the grip on his shoulder nearly threw him from his feet, and he whirled to see her again beside him, panting hotly, her left fist clenched tightly and her right one still digging into the flesh of his arm.

"Thank God!" It was more than an exclamation as she whispered it through her teeth. "Didn't you hear me shouting? I called, but you were going on, and I thought I wouldn't make it . . . only somehow I did! Soldier, you can't go there! Wait!"

He was dull with the wonder of it, and the fierce, hot, foolish hope that flamed up in him as he gripped her and pulled her around before him. "How'd you find me, Anne? How could you trail me the way I went?"

She stopped to catch some of her breath, and she was limp and trembling from running as she held onto him. "I didn't; I knew better than to try. But I knew where you were going—the only place you could go. So I came after you. You should have waited. It would have been so much easier."

The flame was dying out of him, and he shook his head. "It's no use. You shouldn't have come, you know."

"I don't know, soldier. Do you think I'd have come after you to see you go there, unless there was some hope I could keep you from it? That's why I took so long, telephoning, waiting, arguing, and finally driving out here, afraid to find you already gone, but just praying I wouldn't." She was pulling him back now, into one of the shadows, and out of it again, to where a half-hidden figure was standing. "Father fixed it for me to see him finally and I forced him to come with me."

The figure was moving toward them now, and the boy could make out four stars on the shoulders of the uniform. Anne's father must be somebody, he thought, to arrange an interview at such an hour; and Anne herself had performed no small miracle in bringing a general out here on a crazy mission she couldn't have explained fully.

"Well, young man!" There was a bluff heartiness to the general's voice that didn't entirely cover other emotions. "This young lady tells me you're looking for work to help your country again, and she tells it so well I'm out of my bed and out here to see you. If her story hadn't been so completely insane, I'd have thought she was. I am myself, or I wouldn't be here. Let's have a look at you, over here in the light from my headlights."

He stared for long minutes, silently, nodding faintly to himself, while the younger man could feel his flesh crawl with doubt of the outcome. Finally the general turned away, and he could hear Anne's breath catch.

"Well?" she asked, and for the first time her voice quivered.

The older man shook himself, and his eyes were on neither of them, but directed outward toward the horizon. "For some reason, I believe it. I wondered, riding here, when I was foolish enough to imagine things, what it would feel like if I found you were correct, Miss Bowman. I told myself I'd be afraid, incredulous, and perhaps half mad. Now I find I'm none of those things. If God or whatever other Power rules in this has arranged it as it seems to be, I guess those of us who discover it will be protected by His will. All I can feel is something I've felt when I saw what men can do in battle. . . . My God, what a magnificent propaganda story; and what a pity nobody'd ever believe it. Young man, do you know what that monument is that you were looking at?"

He looked back at it. "No, sir."

"That's the Tomb of the Unknown Soldier. He was one of those who fell in France without any trace to indicate who he was. He was selected and brought back here in 1921, and ten years later they erected that in his honor—or, rather, in honor to all those who fell over there without names that could be honored personally. That monument stands as a symbol of our obligation to the men whose efforts brought us victory before. And you came out of there." The general stopped then, looking for a response, but there was none, and he continued: "You don't owe your nation anything, son; it owes you."

"So I'm a ghost then." He turned it over in his head, but already it was as if he'd received the knowledge long ago. "Or am I the personalization of the thoughts of all the people who've been aware of me—or even a little of each? I'm apparently physical enough—I seem to weigh as much as I did before. I can do anything a living man can, phantom or not. No, sir, the dead can never have claims on the living, except to ask them to carry on. And if I'm returned, it's because there is something I can do. I want to do it—you've honored me, or those I represent, long enough; now you're in the same old struggle, and it's my turn to serve again. If you can help me find something, that's all the honor I—or those others—can ask."

"But if I made you a soldier in the present army, would it be fair for you to take up arms against the . . . the living, if you can carry arms and still fight? Or if we only see you by some trick of illusion that fools even yourself, could you help in a purely physical army?"

He thought it over slowly, silently accepting a smoke from the other; to him, the cigarette answered the last—if it were illusion, such an illusion might kill as easily as consume beer or blow smoke from its mouth. But could the dead be killed again—if he belonged to the truly dead? And if they could not, then surely he had no right to injure those who could not harm him. "Sorry, sir. It was good of you to come out here, but since you've shown me there's nothing I can do—" He began a salute, only to check it as his eyes rested again on the guard pacing back and forth up there.

"Those guards! They're living soldiers, and you could use them in combat. Then, why can't I do their work—there'd be no need to kill in that? And the men . . . How many? Two-hour shifts on and eight off were usual guard hours, with the next day free. The six men I replaced could be used far better than I could as an individual. I have no need of food or sleep or rest; of that I'm sure. Why shouldn't I take that on a full-day, full-week shift, sir?"

"Unthinkable. What's the purpose of having a guard of honor when the dead do their own guarding?"

"Do you think the dead want that guard, sir, when their country needs men? Isn't it only necessary because civilian morale requires that the customs—most of them—of peacetime be maintained?"

"No." The general's voice ended all argument. "No, son, I can't see it. And I'm not going to look at you while you talk, to make sure you don't convince me. . . . That wasn't the work you were cut out for; it would have been far easier to let six who might die of wounds or infection live. And I can think of no more futile work than standing guard twenty-four hours a day over a tomb that we have reason to feel may now be empty, however necessary for morale."

"But, sir—"

The general smiled, but kept his eyes averted. "No. Ten minutes ago, I'd have defied any proof that the dead could walk; I came only to humor the whim of the daughter of a very close friend and because I felt the ride might do me good. Now, just looking at you, I'm taking it for granted that that sarcophagus is empty. That's why I won't look at you, and why I'm willing to let Miss Bowman tell you her idea."

He looked questioningly at the girl, who held out a paper, opened in the middle. "I wanted to show you that, soldier, but you ran off first. I knew, after what you'd told me, that it was the answer. But I knew you'd never listen to me alone."

He took it from her, noting it was a later edition of the same paper he'd bought that afternoon, opened to the editorial page where the same cartoon and editorial struck his eye. But the column between was different, and set in heavy-leaded type. It was titled quite simply, "APOLOGY!" and his eyes caught the first words and led him on.

To the readers of this paper and to a certain energetic young man who broke into this office to "push my face in," I want to apologize. I don't know who he was, nor do I care; I couldn't describe him to you, beyond the fact that he appeared to be a soldier in a rather sloppy uniform. But whoever he was, I'm grateful to him.

He told me with complete candor that I was a fool. I agree. I have been a fool. I've been writing here for the last months as only a paid mouthpiece of the enemy should write, though in my own biased way I thought I was serving my country. I wasn't. The ideas could serve no one save the enemy.

So, after three hours of careful thought, my opinion now is that the decent readers of this paper should know, and probably do know, that all I've written has been lies—sheer, stupid lies. We're in no danger from England, or Russia, or any other ally who helps us in this war. We're in danger only from the knaves and fools who fill our minds with defeatism and the filth of which I have been as guilty as any. This probably means I'll lose my job, and you'll see another name here in later editions.

Why? Because, if you see the truth, you'll know who your real enemies are, and they don't want that. Because some people would rather cling to their own interests, would rather watch this nation perish, than give up one iota of their stupidity or their profits.

There have been too many lies to list here; it were better to refer you to the back columns I've written and tell you simply that the men who repeat them are your enemies. There is no truth in them, only plausibility and cheap emotional trickery. But one I must point out while I still can. You've heard us say, "If you do thus and so, can you face the soldiers when they return again?" and it made a strong emotional appeal for every cheap purpose we were furthering. Now, I refer you to a well-known poem, of which I quote the last lines only:

If you fail us who die, we shall not sleep,
Though poppies grow in Flanders Field.

You know the source, surely. Well, we—this newspaper and myself—have failed those dead, and the dead of this war, grievously. For that no apology is enough, but for the little good it may do, I apologize.

He was silent as he finished it. He'd been so sure he'd failed; he'd said nothing new, surely, that hadn't been said before. Yet, this was the result.

"You see?" the general broke in on his thoughts. "However you do it—by your eyes, or some driving force we lack, you walk around in a sort of aura that makes others believe pretty much what you want them to. My own present belief in you, Anne Bowman's faith—don't they suggest a better job than guarding an empty tomb?"

He nodded slowly, the idea still too new, and Anne picked up. "I'd read this before, and wondered about it; everyone was discussing it, and I couldn't be sure at first, but I suspected you. Then when you told me of seeing the editor, I knew. But you ran off before I could tell you; like a fool, I guess, I was going to surprise you later instead of telling you at once."

He looked slowly from one to the other, still only half believing. "You mean—"

"Nothing else," the general agreed. "You found your own job, because you were meant for it, apparently, only you were too blinded by desire for direct action to realize it. There are still plenty of people in this world of ours who are fighting us from within. Some of them do it deliberately—nothing much you can do about that, I suppose; but the real trouble comes from the sincere men who are blinded by prejudices against which none of our arguments or propaganda can make headway. You'll be a godsend to us, son, if you'll report to me in the morning. We'll give you some official but meaningless commission and let you follow your own impulses, unless you want to take suggestions. Well?"

It was obvious, of course; it should have been obvious from the time he'd first noticed the protection he'd seemed to be under; the willingness of Anne to believe him. Some glamor surrounded him, and he wasn't sure that it worked only on those who were for the same things he wanted—there'd been the German, who'd seen him differently. Maybe, he thought, the general was wrong about his being able to do nothing to the deliberately treasonous, judging by that. He grinned and nodded.

"In the morning, sir. And—did the writer get fired? Umm. Then, perhaps, sir, I know where my first duty will lie." His hand came up in brisk salute, and the officer returned it before starting toward the car door.

"In the morning, then, and do as you like. Coming back with me, Miss Bowman?"

She shook her head. "I think not, thank you. I haven't had a good walk in ages, and it'll do me good."

The lights of the car swung and headed back, leaving them alone in the shadows near the Tomb. He stood awkwardly looking at her, and she was laughing softly at his expression.

"I guessed, soldier; somehow, it wasn't hard to guess, after I saw a small feature story in this afternoon's newspaper about a guard out here who thought he saw a ghost come out of the Tomb. The poor fellow's probably in trouble about it, but that can all be straightened out now. Anyway, the description, what there was of it, fitted you. That satisfy your curiosity?"

"No, Anne; that's unimportant. I'm wondering about you. You know what I seem to be—as much as we can know. And yet— Someday, this war will be over, and when that happens, what becomes of me? Do I go back there? Even forgetting that, how can I fit into the lives of others? Obviously—"

"Shh. Don't say it." Her hand was on his shoulder again, gently this time. "You needn't worry about that—it isn't *that* which I feel for you, soldier. Once, under other circumstances, perhaps, but now it's only a very deep and genuine friendship and a desire to help—nothing more."

"I'm glad, Anne." He meant it. All the things he'd feared she felt were obviously a part of his former life's possibilities, but none belonged to him now. They had been gone twenty-five years, and he couldn't even miss them now. "I'm glad and relieved. I need friends in this strange new world, but . . ."

"Let's forget it," she advised, settling back onto a rock. "A smoke together, and then you can walk me home. It's almost dawn already. Wonder how you'll look in your new uniform?"

It was dawn when they reached the bridge this time, almost the double of the dawn into which he had come out. But this time, as he walked quietly along beside the girl, there was no uncertainty, no shuffle. He had work to do, and a friend to explain the puzzle of his new life to him.

And, once again, he had his country. Already, as they neared the end of the bridge and the mist began fading, he could see flags flying here and there in celebration of the Fourth, anniversary of the country's birth. Perhaps it would be more solemn this year than in peacetime, perhaps not, but certainly to more people its original meaning would be nearer. To the others who did not care for that meaning, perhaps he was at least a partial answer. He was content, as he walked along beside the girl toward his new work, to know that whatever might be her future or his own, it was a part of the future of America; at the moment, he wanted no more.

Well, at the end of the story she told him they'd just be friends, but . . . Does a girl give up a comfortable ride to walk beside a boy for miles through an early morning fog for friendship? Or is something else brewing in her emotions? Let's say I hope the boy got something to make up for all that he'd been denied through his earlier service. Justice wouldn't work in real life, but it's nice to have some of it in fiction.

Naturally, publishing being what it is, there was no flag on the July *Unknown*, and "Poppies" got published in the August issue.

Meantime, the war was getting into full swing. The girl friend worked for a government agency that was soon to be transferred out of Washington to St. Louis. The big question between us was whether I should go along. Of course, if I made my living by writing, there was no reason not to go. But I'd been doing all sorts of other things that I couldn't transfer.

In the long run, I decided to leave the decision up to chance. Campbell had sent me a major idea. Suppose, he suggested, an industrial atomic plant of the future had a big accident and was in danger of blowing up; and now suppose we saw it all through the eyes of the plant doctor; then we could get something of the same mood and feeling that had made Willy Ley's novelette "Fog" so popular.

I liked the idea, though I had no intention of trying to duplicate the total confusion and turmoil that Willy Ley had painted in his story of a petty future revolution in a city. I wanted to do a suspense story, all out and no strings attached.

The reason was a study I'd made on the suspense elements in books and movies. I'd gotten interested in why some suspense stories work and others fail. In fact, I'd wasted several weeks on the project, and I had some lovely charts and rules all made out when the idea first reached me. This would be a chance to put my theory to practice—and maybe pay for all the time I'd spent for the sheer fun of figuring it out.

So I did a lot of deliberate work on a plot, and laid it all out in six carefully drawn chapter outlines. There was also a tremendous amount of background material I didn't intend to use, but which was necessary to give the full feeling to the story in my own head. (I think the mark of a good science fiction story is that the writer always knows ten times as much about it as he is able to use.) It was to run to 30,000 words, twice as long as anything else I'd done; but I needed the space for full development.

My biggest trouble was that I couldn't find a title for it. I tried everything, and nothing seemed to fit. (Titles are important to me. I find it hard to write until I've come up with one that seems to sum up what I have in mind. I also think that a good title has a lot to do with how favorably the readers will remember a story.) This held me up for weeks, and the time for the agency to move came and passed.

In the end, I wound up with something that was only meant to be a working title, but somehow stuck permanently: "Nerves."

After all the preliminary work, I didn't want to rush through this story, and 30,000 words was more than I thought I could do at one stretch. So I decided to write one chapter, let it sit overnight, and retype it the next day before going on to the next chapter. Each chapter was about 5,000 words long, as long as an average short story. And I think the system was an excellent one. If I had had good sense, I'd probably have used it for all subsequent writing. Certainly it worked well in this case, though I got impatient the fifth day and did the final two chapters at one sitting.

One of the chapters involved the use of a big crane and power scoop. Surprisingly, the local authorities must have decided to give me some help, because they began digging up the street in front of my room just as I began writing the story. When I came to that section, I could look out the window and see the big machinery chugging away. Very helpful!

Campbell liked the story well enough to pay a bonus, though he undercounted the length a bit. (Note to beginning writers. Never use elite type. It saves on postage and looks neat, but editors don't quite trust your word count. Stick to pica, ten letters to the inch.)

So the die was cast, and I was going to follow out to St. Louis. I took the time to visit Campbell again, and then began packing everything I could take into a big plywood box. I was leaving the photo equipment behind, with most of my hobby material and stuff for odd jobs. In a new city, I'd have to depend on my writing. I couldn't even join the army if things didn't work out. I already tried to enlist and been turned down; even the draft board had rejected me for extreme tachycardia—a pulse that was much faster than normal.

I probably should have been worried. But all I can remember is getting on the train and losing myself contentedly in the latest issue of *Astounding*.

Part II

The Early del Rey

St. Louis was going through a wartime boom already when I got there in May 1942, but I had no trouble in finding new living quarters. I took a room in a small hotel on Lindell Boulevard, a couple of blocks from the rooming house where my girl friend had located. It cost the large sum of seven dollars a week—but it had a shared bath with the adjoining room and a telephone right in the room. It represented luxury to me then, I guess. I settled in after my box arrived, finding a place for my typewriters. I still had what I considered a fair amount of money, so I rested from my toil of moving, getting to know the local drugstore where I'd be eating breakfast and lunch and learning the city.

During my visit to Campbell before my move, he'd shown me a cover painting by someone name Munchausen (*sic*). It was one of the "astronomicals" Campbell liked to use occasionally, showing a rather crude rocket and several figures standing beside a sort of cliff on the Moon, with Earth above and a flaring sun in the sky. He suggested that I might like to do a novelette around the cover, about 20,000 words. There was plenty of time, and he'd send me a 'stat of the cover. I'd never tried writing a story around a painting before. It wasn't usual for *Astounding* to buy covers first, though it was common practice on other magazines. But I figured it was an interesting challenge.

So I waited for the 'stat, idly turning over vague ideas. It was going to be tough, I realized. Even then, stories of the first landing on the Moon were old hat in science fiction. Finding anything new to write wasn't easy. I rejected a lot of things, and was still pondering when a letter arrived from Campbell.

Something must have gone badly agley in his plans or my understanding, however. There was no 'stat. Instead, the letter began to the effect that he was planning to use the cover on the October issue, and time was growing very late. He hoped it was coming along, because I'd have to have it in his office by the end of the week or he'd be forced to find another writer for the cover.

Naturally, this was one of those times when the letter had taken longer than usual to reach me. He'd mailed it on Monday, but it was already Wednesday—and I probably couldn't expect a manuscript to reach him if I waited until the next day to mail it.

Well, I have a pretty good visual memory, though for some reason my stories rarely show much attention to visual things; I see the background in my mind, but it never gets on paper. I was pretty sure I could remember how many figures were beside the ship. That should be no problem.

But getting a plot was. The mail had reached me about nine o'clock in the morning. I went out to breakfast with my head turning over every banality ever written about the Moon. And somehow, under pressure, I got the first trace of an idea. Was it really the first trip? Or did they just think it was?

With that, I managed somehow to plot out most of it before I finished breakfast, and to begin getting the feel of my major character. The rest of the development would have to come as I wrote. (Some writers like to surprise themselves by beginning with just the beginning of an idea. I hate to start until I know every detail. But in a few cases, I've found that I can work the other way, though the results are rarely as good.)

So I came back to my room, picked up the Oliver, shoved paper into it, and began writing. I never got up until the last of those 20,000 words was down. Then I grabbed a hasty bite to eat and rushed back to switch typewriters and begin retyping it all.

I took the finished manuscript down to the main post office and put it in the mail at ten o'clock that night. It included a short note not quite saying, but strongly indicating, that fortunately only a little work had remained to complete it. And I came back and quietly collapsed.

I don't think Campbell was fooled by my note. He bought the story, but there was no bonus. But knowing what I do now about smart editors (and he was one of the smartest) I suspect that I could have taken more time and done a somewhat better job. He'd almost certainly protected himself from my tendency to do everything at the last possible moment, and I could just as well have mailed it on Saturday to reach him Monday.

Sometimes I think no writer should learn anything about editing or publishing. There seems to be a sort of inherent contest between writers and editors, in which each tries to fool the other. It works very well, too, until the writer becomes sophisticated enough to fool himself.

Anyhow, that was my first lesson in writing under extreme pressure, and it helped me later on many occasions. I no longer would fear a rush assignment, and for that I owe a great deal to "Lunar Landing."

13.

Lunar Landing

(by Lester del Rey)

I

Grey's body was covered with a cold sweat that trickled down from his armpits and collected in little round drops over his body, and he stirred in his bag, crying faintly. The sound of his own voice must have wakened him, for he came out of his dream of falling endlessly, to a growing consciousness. The falling sensation still persisted, and he made an unconscious frantic gesture toward something to stay his fall; then his hands met the loose webbing of the bag, and he grimaced.

Even without the feel of the webbing, the reaction of his motions should have told him where he was, as his body shot back against the opposite surface of the sack; this was space, where gravity had been left far behind, except for the faint fingers of it that were now creeping up from the Moon and pulling him slowly back to the top of the bag. For a few seconds he lay there, grinning slightly at the thought of the stories he'd read in which lack of gravity had set the heart to pounding wildly, or the stomach to retching. Space wasn't like that, he knew now, and should have known before. It was simply like the first few moments of free fall, before the parachute opened; sort of a peaceful feeling, once you realized fully there was no danger to it. And the heart was freed from some of the effort needed, and adjusted to a calm, easy pumping, while the stomach took it all in stride. It hadn't been absence of gravity, but the shifting of it that made seasickness.

Of course, his ears felt odd—there had been a dizziness that increased slowly as the liquids inside were freed from the downward pull, but the hours in the acclimating chamber had done their work, and it soon passed. Mostly it was a matter of mental adjustment that overcame the old feeling that somewhere had to be down, and recognized that all six walls were the same. After that, space was an entirely pleasant sort of thing.

With loose easiness of motion necessary here, he reached up and unfastened the zipper above him, then wriggled out of his sleeping sack and pulled himself down to the floor by means of the ropes that were laced along the walls for handholds. The room was small and cramped, heavy with the smell of the human bodies that hung now in other sacks along the sides, and loud with the snores of Wolff and the hiss of the air-conditioning machines.

"Is that you, Grey?" One of the bags opened, and Alice Benson stuck her head out, smiling calmly at him.

Somehow, looking at her, he could never feel the impatience he should; she was too old and fragile to be making such a trip, especially since there seemed neither rhyme nor reason to her presence, and yet the utter normality of her conduct under the conditions was strangely soothing. In the cramped, stinking little cabin of the *Lunar Moth*, she was still possessed of a mellowed gentility of bearing that concealed the air of urgency he'd sometimes suspected.

"Yes, ma'am." Unconsciously, the few manners he'd learned leaped to the surface around her. "Why aren't you asleep?"

She shook her head slowly, the faintest of grimaces showing in the corners of her mouth. "I couldn't, lad. I've been living too many years with something under me to adjust as well as you youngsters do. But it has its compensations; I've never rested so well, whether I sleep or not. Would you like some coffee?"

He nodded, pulling himself carefully along the ropes that made handholds while she removed a thermos bottle from a locker and replaced the cork with another that had two straws inserted through it. Above her, Wolff went on snoring in a particularly horrible gargling manner, and she glanced up distastefully at his sack but made no mention of it. Grey took the coffee gratefully, drinking slowly through one straw; cups would have been worse than useless here, since liquids refused to pour, but chose to coalesce into rounded blobs, held in shape by surface tension.

"Ralston's already gone out to the engines," she answered his glance at the empty sack. "And June's still in the cockpit. The rest are asleep; I put a sedative in their broth, so they wouldn't be awakened during the landing. I'll take a mild one myself after you start reversing, so you needn't worry about us here."

Grey finished the coffee and handed the bottle back to her, smiling his thanks, then turned down the narrow little shaft that led to the control pit. A pull on the ropes sent him skimming down the shaft, guided by a hand on the walls, before he checked his momentum at the bottom and squeezed open the little door. Inside, he could see June Correy hunched over the observation window, staring down through the small telescope, making notes in a little book, but he slid in silently without disturbing her and settled himself into the padded control seat, pulling out a cigarette.

She glanced up nervously as the first odor of the smoke reached her, and for a brief moment there was more than mere contempt in her eyes. They were nice eyes, too, or could have been if she'd wanted them to be; he'd seen warmth and courage in them when the grueling takeoff had unsettled the others. But for him, there was only a look that reminded him pointedly of his eighty pounds and four-feet-ten height. He grinned at her, raking over her own slender five feet and up to the hair with a hint of auburn in it, mentally conceding her beauty while knowing that she was aware of it, and chose to make the fullest use of it to gain her ends. The fact that he was outwardly immune to her charms added nothing to her liking for him.

Now she turned back with a shrug to the observation window, carefully not noticing the smoke that drifted toward her, though the corners of her nose twitched faintly. She'd been used to a full pack a day, and the five rationed out to them here had probably been smoked within as many hours.

"Smoke, Carrots?"

"I don't chisel, Pipsqueak!" But her eyes turned involuntarily toward the white cylinder he held out.

He tossed it to her. "Landing rations, special to the head pilot. I got a whole pack bonus for the landing, to steady my nerves, if I had any. Technically, you don't rate, but my chivalry won't stand a suffering female. Take it and stop whining."

"Chivalry!" She grunted eloquently, but the cigarette was already glowing, and she settled back, some of the hostility gone from her eyes. "You never found the meaning of the word."

"Maybe not. I never had anything to do with women under sixty before, so I wouldn't know. . . . 'S the truth, don't bug your eyes at me. As long as I can remember, at least, I've been poison to girls, which suits me all right. . . . Nervous?"

"A little." She stared down again through the scope. "The Earth doesn't look so friendly down there from this distance. And I can't help remembering that Swanson must have cracked up. Wonder if he's still alive?"

Grey shook his head. This was both an exploring expedition and a rescue party for Swanson and his two men, if any remained alive;

but they'd set off the double magnesium-oxygen flare indicating a crack-up almost eighty days before, and their provisions had been good for a month only. "If none of their supplies were injured, perhaps. You can go through a lot of hell if you have to; probably depends on how much faith they had in a rescue whether or not they tried to make out till we reached them. . . . I'm going to reverse now. Staying here?"

She nodded, and he reached for the tinny little phone that connected him to the engine hold. "Ralston? Get set, because time's due for a turn. Gyros ready? And power? Okay, strap in." He was already fastening himself down with webbing straps, while Correy came over beside him and began doing likewise. A final glance at the chronometer, and he reached out for the gyro clutches, throwing them in.

Slowly, the *Moth* heeled, dipping her tail reluctantly, and through the small observation window before him, sighted out along the side of the great rocket tubes, the small ball that was Earth slithered away and out of sight. The seconds ticked by slowly as the tiny gyros reacted, one thousand turns or more to make one half turn for the *Moth,* since they were in a ratio of a pound per ton of ship. In space, there was no need for any sudden maneuvering, but the saving of weight was immensely important, even with atomic fuel supplying the energy that activated the tube. Then the rough face of Luna began to peek in at the edge of the window, and Grey snapped off all lights in the cockpit, sighting through the now glaring screen of the telescope. He reached for the gyro controls again, edging the great ship slowly about until the mark he had selected was squarely in the cross-hairs of the screen. Satisfied, he cut out the clutches.

"Nice work, Half-Pint!" She said it with a grudging tone, but he knew it was justified, and accepted the words at face value. "For delicate work, you're not bad!"

"Mm-hm. Suppose you get on the radio there and call Earth; once I cut in the blast, you won't have a chance, with the field out there fighting your signal. Know what you want to say?"

"After working for the news syndicate five long years? Don't be silly. How long can I take?"

"Ten minutes about."

"Mmm. Got any messages to send yourself? Friends, relatives? I'll bug out a few words for you if you like—square the cigarette." She was already pushing the key of the bug back and forth, throwing full power through the bank of tubes and out across space on the ultrashort waves that would cut down through the Heaviside on a reasonably tight beam.

"No friends, no relatives, no messages. I had a dog once, but he died, so we'll forget him, too." Grey was estimating speeds and distances from the few instruments and the rough guide of the image of the Moon, knowing that the calculations made back on Earth would be far more accurate than anything he could arrive at, but still feeling the need of checking for his own satisfaction.

She glanced up from the bug, a glint of curiosity showing. "You're a queer duck, Grey, but I didn't figure you were a misanthrope."

"Not. People just don't think the same way I do, or something; maybe because nobody wrote anything on my blank pages except what I scribbled myself." He thrust up a hand into the steel-gray hair that bushed up on his head, sweeping it back from cold gray eyes, grinning at the mental picture of himself. Even that didn't fit in with normality, since healthy human skin shouldn't be tanned to a dark brown that somehow had gray undertones, making him a complete monotone in harmony with the name he'd chosen for himself. "Don't go asking personal questions, Carrots, because I can't answer 'em any better than you could for me. I'm an amnesiac, had a seventy-year-old psychologist for a mother, an encyclopedia for a father, and the hell of making a living for a school."

He could see nothing of her face, but her voice held none of the expected pity or maudlin slop he'd come to expect when the facts were spilled. "Then how'd you ever decide on this?"

"Dunno even that. Hunch, or something. Finished? Good, then shut up while I start this thing gentling down. Luna doesn't look pretty down there, but I reckon we'll find a level place somewhere to slap down on our tripod. Ralston, here we go. Keep 'em smooth!"

Grey's long, sensitive fingers went out to the vernier and studs that covered the action of the single tube, cutting in the circuits, letting it warm up, then throwing in the high potential needed to start it before normal action could proceed. A small red button on the panel clicked on, and he dropped back, feeding in power slowly, while the edge of the window nearest the tube took on a faint blue glow, and a slight haze showed up near it. The blue streak of inferno that was the rocket blast was blazing out behind—or ahead, really, since the so-called bottom of the ship was always directed toward the destination when decelerating power was on. Rockets at each end, or strung along the sides, would have made the weight unmanageable. The gravitometer needle flickered upward, quarter-gravity deceleration, half, then a full gravity pounding out behind them.

The feeling of weight came back over him, setting his stomach into a belated sickness that he was totally unprepared for, but it was only momentary, and the action of his heart surged up, then settled back into the routine business of fighting to equalize pressure and circulation in spite of the downward pull. He flopped the cigarette package in front of Correy, and she lighted one for him and another for herself; words would have been wasted while the greater roar behind from the tube filtered in, drumming against their ears. Maybe a theoretical rocket should be soundless, but this one certainly wasn't. From now on until the actual landing began, it was simply a matter of sitting quietly and waiting for the blind rush of the ship to slow down and the distance to diminish, with only a cursory attention from him. He settled back, smoking and thinking idly, stirred again into unemotional memories by Correy's earlier words.

No child grown to manhood could remember its earliest infancy, apparently; but a newborn mind in an adult body might still soak up and remember impressions for which it had no name; the eyes still carried their training at separating objects, the ears knew still how to sort and classify sounds, meaningless though they were. And now, even as if it were but a moment before, he could remember waking there on the strange green meadow and stirring without purpose, called by the unrecognized pangs of hunger. Under him, his legs had stirred, but he'd forgotten how to walk, and had resorted to creeping toward a stream that flowed nearby, the call of thirst stronger than blank memories. The farmer had found him there, half drowning from his clumsiness, and by the time he'd been half carried to the farmhouse, his legs were again learning the difficult work of supporting him, though they had felt weak and shaky.

The doctor had turned him over to a psychiatrist. And then, days later, words began to take on meanings, and the first sentences became again familiar to him. Oh, he'd learned rapidly—some faint neural paths were still left, easing the job of learning. He'd heard that it was amnesia—not partial, but complete, wiping out all memories with an utter finality; and during the year that followed, he'd stored into his unfilled mind all the information from the libraries at hand, and all the odd relations of mankind he could glean. He'd been forced to think in his own way, almost without relation to those about him, and with its own peculiar advantages. But there could be no friendships in that frantic chase after knowledge. He'd never realized, until the psychiatrist died, that he was an object of charity, though he found shortly after that living was done by the sweat of a man's brow.

Well, it hadn't been too hard, all things considered. He'd been analyzed before and told that he had an ability for mechanics, so the job in the airplane factory had followed almost automatically. The other men had stared at his strange little figure, and had laughed in well-meant kidding that turned slowly to sullen dislike at his lack of response to what he could not understand; but the work had gone well. Then, the call to run these ships he built had grown in him, and the flying school that followed had grudgingly granted his ability. Learning, to him, was the only known pleasure, and he'd tackled all new things with a set purposefulness that brooked no obstacles.

Three years of flying the great ships had won him a certain half-respect, and even an outward familiarity with the other pilots, as well as a reputation for courage which he felt unjustified; it wasn't recklessness, but a lack of any feeling that he had anything to lose. Life was oddly unvaluable, though he reacted automatically to the old law of self-preservation when faced with trouble.

He'd been flying two years when the first news of Swanson's rocket appeared in the papers. There, he'd thought, was something worth trying, and for the first time he'd felt the common stirrings of envy; Swanson had been a name to conjure with among flying men, and his selection as pilot by the mysterious company building the rocket had been entirely fair, yet Grey had been almost jealous of the man. There was magic in the idea of sailing out beyond the Earth toward the Moon that stirred odd feelings in him, unfelt except in the fantastic dreams he sometimes had.

And then, when Swanson had set off the two flares to indicate a crack-up, there'd been announcements of a second ship on the way, which would be used in a gallant, although almost hopeless, attempt to rescue the three men in the first one. But this time, they had no handpicked candidate for pilot, and it had been conducted on a severely practical series of competitive tests among the pilots flying commercially or privately who volunteered. In the long run, it was his size and weight, along with the smaller amount of air and food he needed, that had turned the scales in his favor; others were as good pilots, as quick in their reactions, and as clever at learning the new routine. But none had been as economical to ship, and the small balance had gone in his favor, just as the same factor had helped all of the rest of the crew's selection, with the exception of Bruce Kennedy, designer of the *Moth*. He stood almost six feet tall, but of the others, June Correy was the tallest with her exact five feet of height; and even among them, Grey was the smallest.

Not that it bothered him; he was apparently lacking in the normal human self-consciousness about such things, and for the weeks that followed, the grind of preparing himself as best he could for the task ahead was to give him no time for thoughts. Swanson and two men were up there on the Moon, short of food and water and the all-important air needed for life, while the mysterious sponsor of the ships operated through its trust company with a frenzied drive that could rush the *Moth* through in too long a time at best, but had to hope that the men would somehow survive.

It had impressed Grey at the time, the struggle to save those *three* men who'd already managed to accrue more glory than a normal lifetime could give them. He'd felt more hopeful for this strange mass of humanity. But to him, the important factor was that the *Moth* must get through, since there could be no more—that had been made clear to them; ships cost fortunes, and not all people were willing to spend the money needed. Now, here he was, and under his fingers lay perhaps the future of all space travel; certainly the life of the queer crew with him. Below him, the hungry pits and craters of the satellite seemed to reach out jagged teeth to swallow this presumptuous bug that insisted on daring what men had never been created to try.

"Strange," Grey muttered, leaning forward beyond the screen to stare directly at the black and white selenography under him. "Logically that stuff down there should be queer to me, but it isn't. Not half as strange as old Earth looked the first time I really saw her. I . . . Huh?"

Correy was clutching his shoulder, gripping at him and trying to attract his attention. The ship's combination radioman, reporter, and assistant pilot was indicating the headset, and he grunted, adjusting the ill-fitting thing reluctantly; there was a lot of equipment on the *Moth* that indicated both the frantic last-minute rush and the depletion of funds, though the important things were well enough done.

Her voice came driving in through the phones, now that some of the thunder of the tube was muffled out. "Wake up from your dreams, Squirt! Listen to that tube! Hard, it isn't obvious; I'm not sure I hear anything, but I think I do, and don't like it!"

He yanked back one earpiece and listened, screwed up into a small bundle of concentration, but at first there was nothing wrong. The thunder came rushing in like an overgrown bee against a microphone, a tumultuous *Sh-sh-sh*, gradually resolving into something faintly but distinctly different, a slightly changing *Sh-sh-zh-zh-sh-sh-zh-zh*, almost unnoticeable. The change had no business there. And even as he strained to catch it, it seemed to become more pronounced.

"Damn! I do hear it, Correy! How long's it been going on?"

"I don't know—I only just noticed it, but that was because I was listening deliberately, trying to find some nice description to write up if we ever get back. What is it?"

"Dunno, but I've got suspicions. Ralston! Hey, Ralson, cut in! Notice anything funny about the tube sound?"

There was a long pause from the engineer, then a grunt came over the phones, which might have indicated anything. Grey called again, but got no answer, and his skin began to feel tight with the one sensation he could clearly recognize as an emotional response to danger. Correy started to get up from the straps, obviously intending to go in person after little Ralston, but he shook his head, and something about him made her sink back quietly. Finally, a faint noise came over, followed by the boy's excited voice, its normal bitterness washed out.

"Yeah, Grey, something's damned funny. I've checked over everything here, and it isn't in my province. Nothing I can do about it. Motors are feeding perfectly, voltage and amperage aren't off a hair, ionizer's perfect, and the whole hookup's about as good as anything can be. Any ideas, or you want mine?"

"I've got 'em, but I'm hoping I'm crazy. That tube's control field tested out one hundred percent, didn't it?"

The boy's voice caught faintly. "So you've been thinking the same! Yeah, it tested okay, and Kennedy told me it was theoretically perfect, but— Grey, do you think that's why Swanson crashed?"

He hadn't thought of it, but it was an idea. "Mmm, could be. But look, how can we check on it?"

"We can't. If it gets worse in geometrical progression, then we're right, and ions are eating through, in spite of the field, working on their own controls, and the more damage they do, the faster it goes. Of course, if you can shut off the rocket, give it time to cool off where there's almost no convection, and let me get out into the tube in a suit, maybe I can fix it; maybe not. I doubt it."

"No use trying. Luna's too close, and we'd hit before you could get inside. Think we could ease up a little? Umm, no. Won't work, same amount of damage in the long run, and we'd have to take a course to make an orbit; that'd give us a longer trip and probably do more harm than good. At this rate, how long should it last?"

"Your guess is as good as mine, Grey, but I'd say about an hour and a half."

June cut in, her voice somewhat relieved. "Then we won't have to worry until we land! We'll be down in half an hour more!"

"At this rate, I said," Grey reminded her brusquely. "If this keeps up, we'll begin to lose efficiency, and fast! Then we'll have to cut in more juice, more damage, more juice, and so on. Right, Ralston?"

"Right. It'll be nip and tuck, though I think you've got leeway. Swanson made it, even if he crashed, and our tube figured against weight and things with a minutely higher safety factor than he had, so we should be good for a little better luck, if that's what failed him. Look, June, you still there? . . . Mm, well, if you can . . . The others—"

Grey chuckled a little, amused at the odd quirks of human thought that could be embarrassed about its other twists, even now, and answered for her. "They'll be all asleep, unless Mrs. Benson's still awake. No use waking them up to worry; nothing they could do. And if you're thinking about Helen Neff, the doctor was snoring a nice soprano when I left. She's as safe as she can be. Go back to your engines and let me worry about the others."

He cut Ralston off, still grinning, and looked across at Correy's frowning face. "Heart's on his sleeve, eh, Carrots? Sometimes I can guess why you women don't like little men—they're too darned intense and obvious. She knows she's got him, so she chases big Bruce Kennedy."

"You're no giant yourself, Pipsqueak," she reminded him absently. "And since when did you take over command of the ship?"

"But I don't feel like a little man—I don't bother thinking one way or the other. That's the difference. As to the command, I took that over when we took off, by my own consent; nobody thought to figure out that somebody had to be boss here, so I'm it. If you've any objections, let's have them, and then I'll forget them."

"You get us down, and I'll argue about it later. Listen, it's worse already."

For a moment, Grey put it down to imagination, but then he realized she was right; it was an obvious whishing now that had no business there, and steadier. He grunted, feeding in slightly more power, and watched while the gravitometer settled back where it should be. The moonscape on the screen was still too far away to suit him—

though it might soon be too close. Be a pity if anything happened to the *Moth*, with all the hopes and dreams that must be in her. Alice Benson's gently faded face with its hidden purpose flashed through his mind, then the perverse warmth he'd seen in June Correy's face, but they were less than the ship to him.

He looked again at the screen, then back to the girl. "I'll get us down somehow, June: I give my word on that, if I have to climb out in the tube and swear against gravity."

"Somehow . . . somehow I can picture that right now." She nodded slowly, a puzzled mixture of worry and surprise on her face. "Nemo Grey, I never believed those stories about your rescue of the group in Canada, but I do now. Don't you know what fear is?"

He shook his head slowly. "Not exactly, I guess. But watch it, Carrots, you're getting soft. You'll be clinging to my shoulder in a minute, just another woman trusting in a man. Scared?"

"Yes. That sound out there, getting worse. And then when I look at the screen— Could I have another smoke, Grey?" She took it, sucking in eagerly on it, suffering from too good an imagination, he guessed. But her sudden about-face surprised him, and aroused a ghost of another emotion he couldn't place. Women were a strange species to him, and his little knowledge of them came mostly from books. "You know, right now I *am* just another woman, I guess, and that scrawny shoulder of yours may look pretty good to me, before we land. You seem so damned sure of yourself and so unruffled."

"Cling if you want; I won't hold it against you after we land. But right now, I'd rather you used that telescope and tried to hunt out the wreck of Swanson's ship, if you can spot it. Reports of the flare indicate it's about there, I think." He pointed to a dot on the screen, now showing a greatly enlarged version of the Moon's face, or part of it.

She seized on the chance, and more confidence came back to her with something to occupy her mind besides the mental picture of a crash. Grey had his hands full, trying to keep the indicator where it should be, against the slowly tapering-off thrust of the rocket. And they were close enough now that another factor began to enter, one on which he'd counted, but for which no amount of "tank" work could fully prepare him. The ship was top-heavy, its center of gravity located a good many feet above the center of thrust, and the feeble gravity of the Moon was beginning to act on that; the top showed an alarming tendency to swing over toward the Moon, away from the straight line of fall.

No rocket impulse could be exactly centered or exactly balanced on both sides at all times, and the faintest off-center effect was enough to start a list. He swore, watching the slight movement of the window over the moonscape, working the gyro clutches to correct it and bring them back to dead center. As long as the tilt was only a slight one, the gyros could do it, but the moment he let it get beyond a degree or two, they'd be too feeble to do the work, and his only chance would be to cut the rocket and let them work without the thrust; that had happened on the takeoff, but there'd been time. Now, with the closeness of the Moon and the deterioration of the tube, he'd have no chance to try it successfully.

Again the tube sound was worse, and there was a rise in temperature inside the room, coming from the rocket side that formed one wall; that meant considerable loss of efficiency. Grey dropped his hand from the gyro clutch, stepped up the power, and jerked it back, just as the tilt decided to take advantage of the one uncontrolled moment. But he was in time, by a slight margin. Correy's face had jerked from the scope and tightened as she took it in, but she nodded, caught herself, and went back to searching.

His estimate indicated their fall was faster than safe, and he snapped his eye from the window to the gravitometer, setting the thrust up to a tenth over one gravity, as corrected against lunar drag by the radio indicator that was now working, giving altitude by signal echo time. Again he had to jerk back to the gyro controls. And the rocket was behaving abominably now, wasting a large part of its energy in fighting itself, while the temperature continued to rise.

June motioned suddenly, switching the scope back to the screen at full amplification, pointing to a tiny spot that gleamed more brightly than the rough ground around it. It was located in the oddly shaped crater to which he was headed, and a careful inspection seemed to show the shape of a broken rocket. "Must be, don't you think, Grey?"

"Must be. Wrong side of the crater, of course. Damn! Leave the scope on and make sure all your straps are tight. We may hit hard. Mmm. Men should have three arms. Yeah, that's it, all right. I caught a gleam of metal that's been polished then." He bent forward, catching the toggle switch in his teeth. "Ralston, get set. Landing in ten minutes. Tube's raising hades, but I think it'll last."

"Okay, Grey." The boy was scared, but determined not to show it. "I'll keep my hand on the main motor switch, try to cut it off as we hit, so that won't get out of control. Luck!"

"Luck, Phil!" The use of the first name was deliberate, since he seldom used one, but it should sound familiar. He released the toggle again with his teeth, his eyes screwed to close focus on the indicators, then slid back. Slowly, cautiously, he let the ship slip over two degrees toward the direction of the wreck, and the ground in the window slid sluggishly aside as it drew nearer. But he couldn't keep it up; too much risk of the tilt getting out of hand. He straightened again, and moved the switch over almost full way; now nearly the last amount of available power was coming from the rocket. Suddenly the tendency to list stopped, and a whine growled out from somewhere in the center of the ship.

"God bless Ralston!" Grey realized what had happened; during the trip, the boy had been piecing out extra gyros, crude and unsafe, from anything he could lay his hands on, knowing that the regular ones had been almost inadequate for the takeoff. Probably they'd burn out his rough bearings, blow up from centrifugal force, or overload their motors in a few minutes, but for the moment they'd work, and it would be long enough. "That's real courage for you, Carrots! The kid's scared sick, but he still bucks it through in time. Well, she's steady, she's pointing to the best spot I can locate, so all I have to fool with is the power control, and I think it'll last. . . . Hey!"

The glance he'd shot at her had spotted her white knuckles and clenched teeth, her eyes set on the screen that showed ground rushing up at them, growing like the face of a monster in the stereoscopic movies, seeming to swallow them up. On an impulse that he recognized as probably normal but still surprising, he reached around her shoulders with his free hand, pulling her over against him, and turning her face from the sight. "Hey, it isn't that bad, Carrots. I said we'd get through, didn't I?"

She nodded, burying her face against him, and her voice was almost too faint to hear. "I'm scared, Grey! I'm scared!" Her arms came around him then, pulling hard at him for the purely animal comfort his solidity could give, and he recognized it as something not related to him personally, but there was an odd pleasure in it, all the same.

He kept his voice level, one hand on the control lever, trying to match the erratic thrust against the gravity, the other patting her shoulder. "Easy, June. It's all right!" But he knew it wasn't. An irregular fading blast was complicating his calculations until a smooth landing would be impossible. Then the ion stream struck the ground below, and the screen became a blue glare. On a guess, he set power to counteract their motion.

For a seemingly endless quarter of a minute or less, he held it there, then jerked his hand away and struck the cut-off switch savagely, just as something caught the tripod landing gear, and his stomach seemed to drop through the seat.

"Landed!" The word leaped through his head as a lance of pain struck and ended in blackness.

II

Grey stirred mentally, his hand groping up to the painful lump on his forehead, and his mind was straining for something that he couldn't reach. The perversely calm part recognized the impulse and the frustration of it, though. Whenever any shock hit him, he unconsciously expected the amnesia to lift, as it did in the books; but it never happened that way, though it wasn't the first time he'd gone through a mental blackout. A hand brushed the thick hair off his face, and he looked up into the troubled eyes of June Correy.

"Hi, Carrots, you got through?"

"We all did." She'd jerked her hand back, and now something like embarrassment passed over her face. "It wasn't a bad landing, Grey; but the combination of me hanging onto you and your own loose strapping threw you against the control panel. Sorry I got so soft."

"Skip it!" He wasn't sorry.

Alice Benson's frail hands were adjusting a cold compress on the lump that ached, and he looked around then to find himself in the main room of the ship where most of the others were making preparations of some sort. She poured something onto a cut that stung sharply, smiling at him. "It was a very fine landing, lad; we hardly felt it through the springs holding our sacks—just enough to waken the others. Feel better?"

"Fine, thanks." His eyes located the bitter little Philip Ralston, and he turned to him. "Did you tell the others?"

"Left it to you." The kid's blue eyes flicked away from Helen Neff, then back again, while his hands went on pulling out the spacesuits. "Go ahead and tell them, Grey."

Grey pushed aside the hands of Mrs. Benson, and pulled himself to his feet against the light gravity, surveying the others as they turned to face him, watching their various reactions. "Okay, then, here it is in a nutshell. We're here, and we spotted the other spaceship quite a ways off. But right now, I wouldn't risk a ten-foot hop with that tube—it's shot! You might look it over, Kennedy, but I don't think there's much we can do unless there's enough left of

Swanson's tube to put the two together and make one good one."

"Shot?" Kennedy scowled, his heavy sullen face looking more aggressive than usual. "Look, Grey, that tube was right—it tested for double the time we took. What'd you do—forget to warm it up? If you ruined it, I'll—"

"Yeah?" Ralston jumped up facing the bigger man, a little blond bantam defying a brunet giant. "You got two to clean up then, Kennedy. Grey did a damned good job and it wasn't his fault your theories couldn't take the actual work."

Grey put a hand to the boy's shoulder, pushing him back gently. "It's okay, Phil, forget it. Kennedy, you know darned well you can't say that tank tests are the same as actual workouts; anyhow, Swanson cracked up, probably the same way. But we can't stop to fight about it now. We've got to get out there, locate the other ship, and find out whether we can work it up from the two tubes. Otherwise—well, there won't be any otherwise. Now get out and into that tube; find out what happened, and how we can fix it. The rest of you get into space togs so we can start outside. Orders! I'm taking command."

"By whose consent?" The ship's designer stood rooted, unmoving, his eyes challenging the pilot, and something unpleasant on his face.

Grey grinned, turning toward the others. Correy made a face at him, along with an overly humble bow, but she nodded and stepped to his right, just as Ralston's quick steps carried him to the left. With a little smile, almost of amusement, Mrs. Benson joined them, leaving Neff and Wolff on Kennedy's side.

Ralston jerked his head savagely. "Come over here, Helen, or I'll drag you back with us!"

The sharp-featured doctor opened her enormous eyes in hurt surprise, her hand going to her thin hair. Grey never had seen what attracted the boy to her. She stared at the big man slowly, found him not looking at her, and back to Ralston. Then, like a spoiled child being forced to its duty, she obeyed. The kid should try those tactics more often, maybe.

Wolff was a dwarf. Now he bobbed his immense head, shrugged his shoulders, which seemed hunchbacked, and ran his tongue over his thin lips. "I . . . ah . . . of course I side with the others, Mr. Grey. I . . . I'll obey orders, to the letter. But . . . umm . . . I'd rather not go out, if—"

"You'll come. It'll take six of us to carry back the three men out there, if they're still alive. We'll get them first, make a second trip for the tube parts needed. Well, Kennedy?"

Kennedy shrugged, his face expressionless, picked up the suit, and began climbing in. Satisfied, Grey reached for his own suit, wondering about Alice Benson. But she was in her cumbersome outfit before any of them, her voice cheerful over the phones as she offered to help Neff. It might have been a pleasant little picnic from her reactions, though there was a suppressed eagerness to her voice that he could not explain. He donned his own outfit, turning to Correy.

"Carrots, what about the radio?"

"Still working—or was when I sent back a report; but two tubes were weakened and they blew out when I switched over for the acknowledgment—the big special ones for which we only stocked one spare. So that's out now, not that it'd do us much good. . . . You know, you look almost like a man in a suit, Half-Pint."

He grinned. "So do you, Redhead, so don't count on feminine wiles out there. Okay, let's go. This is serious business, so no foolishness from anyone. Swanson, Englewood, and Marsden may be dying any minute in their ship; and we're looking out for our own lives, too. Take it easy, remember you're dealing with only a sixth-normal gravity here, don't turn on too much oxygen, and stay together. We'll go over your findings when we get back, Kennedy, and report on the other tube. See you."

"Right." The big man had decided to take it with outward pleasantness, at least, and he managed a smile through his suit's helmet. "Luck!"

Grey should have felt strange as the little lock opened finally and he stepped out, his suit ballooning in the absence of pressure. There was an odd feeling inside, but it was one of homecoming, as near as he could place it. The harsh black shadows and glaring sunlight, with no shadings, looked good to him, and the jagged ground seemed friendly now. He stepped back out of the others' way and let them climb down carefully, staring with them at the ship and the scene around.

They were in a queer valleylike crater, at one side of which a seemingly topless cliff rose upward, sheer and colossal. The great ship thrust up seventy feet from the floor on its three legs, a pointed cylinder that ended finally in the rocket tube and the observation window. Above, the sky was black with a harsh sun shining at one side, a swollen Earth on the other, glowing by the reflected light. It was beautiful in a coldly impersonal way, and he breathed deeply, relaxing. Then, with a shrug, he turned off toward the spot that had shown on the screen, marking the other ship.

Ralston and Correy were having troubles in adjusting to the light gravity, both putting too much effort into it. They bounded along, struggling to keep their balance, fighting where they should have relaxed, and only slowly gaining a mastery of the situation. Neff minced primly, not efficiently, but with fair success, while Wolff hitched himself over the ground with an apparent expectation of instant death. Alice Benson alone seemed to take it easily, relaxed and quiet, staying at Grey's side. They halted, ahead of the others, and he could see her smiling.

"I like this, Grey. It makes me feel young again to walk without effort and actually see myself making progress instead of creeping along. . . . Where are your shoe plates, lad?"

He looked down quickly, then realized he'd forgotten to put on the heavy lead plates that were to compensate partially for gravity. He hadn't noticed the lack, though; the feeling of walking here had seemed completely natural to him. "I guess I don't need them; why not take yours off? You've been taking it easy enough to be safe, I think, ma'am."

She put her foot out, and he found himself stooping to remove the plates. Then she tried it, a little uncertain at first, but soon moving easily. "This is lovely, Grey. It's like those dreams of sliding along above the ground without effort. Do you think perhaps men have been here before, leaving memories with us—that falling dream and this other?"

"Doubt it, ma'am. I'm afraid that's romanticism, though I can't prove they haven't. Next thing, you'll be expecting to find people here."

She smiled again, but he wondered if she didn't expect just that. Oddly, it wouldn't have surprised him either. Then the others were with them, and they began moving down a comparatively gentle slope to the smooth floor of the valley's bottom. Progress was rapid, now that even Wolff was catching the swing of the loose motion needed; they were traveling along at a sort of lope that must have covered ten to twelve miles an hour, and the long decline shortened rapidly.

June tapped on his shoulder and pointed as they neared the bottom. "Look, Pipsqueak! Is that green down there—growing green?"

He stared. It was green—the same green as grass would have been. But it meant nothing, he knew. There were plenty of rocks that could give the same color, and without an atmosphere how could chlorophyll-type plants grow? Then out of the corner of his eye, he caught something, and a crazy hunch formed in his mind. "Bet a cigarette against a kiss we find animals, too!"

"Done! Now you're being silly."

The others had heard, of course, and the stirring of excitement was good for morale, at least. They hurried down, Grey, Correy, and Mrs. Benson in the lead, taking it in long easy jumps of twenty feet at a time, a sort of run that lifted from one foot to the other, as a ballet dancer seems to. A few minutes more found them at the bottom, staring at the ground.

It was covered with domes of some thick cellophanelike material, varying in size from a few inches to several feet across, and under them, definitely, were plants. "Lichens, highly complicated ones, too," Neff said. "They've adapted somehow."

Grey nodded. "Probably four or five different types of life together in symbiosis. One must form the dome—that greenish-brown ring they spring from. Another probably cracks raw material from the rocks, another takes energy from sunlight, and so on. Looks to me as if they grow by budding out a small cell from the main one, and they seem to follow this particular type of rock formation. Carbonates, nitrates, probably gypsum, containing water of crystallization. I suppose they could get all the elements of life that way; the lichens of Earth managed to come out of the water and make soil out of our rocks before the other plants got there. Life insists on going on. Only question is how they evolved to begin with."

He bent down, pricking open the tough skin of one of the smaller domes, watching it deflate rapidly. The air in them was under considerable pressure, probably equal to five or six pounds. "You know what this means, don't you? Well, if worst comes, we could probably pump out a fair quantity of oxygen from these things—there are miles of them. Squeeze water out, too, and maybe they have food value. We couldn't live indefinitely, I feel sure, but they might help."

Wolff stared at them unbelievingly, but with a flicker of interest. "Until . . . ah—"

"Yeah." It was foolish. "Until we died anyway. There'll be no rescue ship for us. Well, Carrots?"

"Animals!" she reminded him, grinning.

"Coming up!" He pointed across the lichen-covered ground toward the motion that had first attracted his attention. At the time it might have been a falling rock, but now, as it approached, it obviously wasn't. Rather it resembled a cross between a kangaroo and a balloonlike bird, two long heavy legs under it, and an elongated beak in front. "Watch!"

The thing had been traveling at a tremendous rate, sailing in bounds. Now it stopped a few yards in front of them, ducked its beak down into one of the bigger domes, and rooted around, gulping up some of the growth there, while the dome deflated slightly as it took up all but a little of the air, leaving enough, probably, for the lichen to continue, and no more; the creature should have swelled up enormously, but there was no outward difference.

"Must have some tricky way of absorbing the oxygen into a loose chemical compound, unless it's got a magnificent pressure tank inside it somewhere. More likely something like a whale uses to store oxygen in its body for a long trip underwater. Notice how he exudes a cement out of that beak as he draws it out—sealing the dome so he won't kill the lichen completely?"

June grunted. "Okay, you win, darn it. Look at him go!"

"Has to—he can't stay on the dark part of the Moon, I'll bet, so he has to travel fast enough to equal the rate of rotation—once around the Moon in a month. It can be done here, rotation, size, and gravity considered. The lichens must spore up during the two weeks of night, grow during the day. And probably that dome has heat-filtering powers, like no-heat glass; he's carrying a bright shell on top to reflect heat, you notice. 'Smatter?"

"I was just thinking of his love life." She giggled again, watching the vanishing creature. "No long courtships here—unless he's like a bedbug, sufficient unto himself."

"Probably is. Okay, gang, we've wasted enough time, though we should make a study of all this. I'll collect later, Carrots."

They turned on, winding among the domes that were everywhere, bits of conversation going on over the radios among the others. The finding of life here had cheered them all, somehow, made them feel that the satellite wasn't as unfriendly as it had seemed. There was a kinship to protoplasmic life, no matter how distant. Grey accepted the fact as a matter of course, wondering if he hadn't expected it, and led on, his eyes peeled for a sight of the other ship.

Mrs. Benson beat him to it, though. She stopped, and pointed to the small part showing, a mere speck across the rough ground. "Grey, June, Philip! See!"

Now their leaps increased, and they straggled out. Correy ripped her sole plates off, dropped them, and staggered before redoubling her efforts to keep up with Grey. But ahead of them, the seemingly feeble legs of Alice Benson sped along, covering the ground with a fluidity of motion that indicated the dancer she must have been once. There was a faint sound of her voice in the phones, and it sounded oddly like praying, but the words were too muffled for understanding. They stopped as she lifted herself to a slight projection and looked down.

"Bill!" It was a shout and a prayer, and the thinness of her voice was suddenly gone, leaving it strong and young. Grey stared at June, shaking his head. There were no Bills in either his or Swanson's crew. But again the cry came. "Bill! Oh, God!"

Then they were beside her, staring down at the ship lying below, on its side, and Grey caught her as she slumped forward. But he had eyes only for the object ahead. It wasn't Swanson's ship. Thirty feet long, or slightly less, it was an even cylinder, blunt fore and aft, one great rocket at one end, and little muzzles stuck out athwart, somehow fragile, but apparently with no damage. Whoever had set it down had done a magnificent job of space jockeying, coming in at an angle and sliding forward on steel runners, instead of making a tail landing. He glanced at Correy, but her look was as dumbfounded as his own.

Mrs. Benson struggled to her feet, a red spot showing under the pallor of her cheeks. "I'm sorry, children. I'm afraid I was overcome for a minute. You see, I know that ship. I helped build it—thirty years ago!"

"Thirty years—just before the Great War?" June looked at her carefully, searching for hysteria and finding none. "But they didn't have fission motors then, nor ion releases. How—fuel rockets?"

"Bill had a fission motor, June; oh, it wasn't a good one, but it worked. And he wasn't using an ion release. He broke water up into monatomic hydrogen and oxygen, then let them explode again. They worked better than any normal oxy-hydrogen jet could have. Thirty years—and I'm finally here. Now do you see why an old lady forced herself into your crew, lad? Come, let's go down!"

They fell in beside her, and now she moved leisurely, telling them the story as she went, while the others caught up. It could have been a colorful story, a great one, but she told it simply, giving only the highlights, and letting them fill in the rest with their imagination.

More than thirty years before, about the time the Great War was starting, when the first uranium fission was discovered, she'd married a boy with a dream. It must have been a wonderful dream, for he wasn't the type, otherwise, to use his wife's fortune, but he'd done so, burning it up carelessly while he applied his own rather remarkable genius toward extracting the elusive U-235 isotope and using it; and he'd succeeded, while others were groping toward the solution. He'd even managed to work out a motor light enough for the dream he had, and to construct two ships, using an adaptation of the monatomic release already known and used in welding, now that he had a reliable source of energy.

"Two ships?" Grey cut in quickly.

"Two, Grey. He had to." She went on quietly. One ship had been fitted for himself—it was impossible for her to accompany him, though they'd tried to make it that way. The other was radio-controlled. Then he'd taken off in one, secretly at night, and she'd sent the other up near him, up until he could fall into an orbit around the Earth, high enough to have conquered part of the drag of gravity. One ship couldn't hold enough supplies for the voyage. But using his own radio controls, he'd somehow brought the second one beside him, joined them, and transshipped supplies and fuel, released it, and waited until his orbit brought him in position for a try at the Moon. She'd seen his supply ship explode into tiny fragments that could fall back to Earth or drift harmlessly in space, and her watcher in one of the observatories had thought he detected the flare that indicated success where Bill had chosen to land.

"There were two other ships being built," she went on. "I was supposed to follow, and we hoped that from the two, and what fuel was left, we could escape the Moon's lighter gravity and return, risking a parachute fall in spacesuits to land on Earth; it might have worked. I think it would, since we could bake our needed water out of the gypsum here. But the war came—and metal became harder to get, and finally unavailable. Our helpers went off to fight, mostly, and the months slipped by—"

Hearing her, Grey could imagine the desperate months going, while she fought vainly to go on, stumbling against the impossible, afraid to tell too much and release the horror of atomic energy for war, unable to get supplies or help otherwise. Three years had been spent in a sanitarium, to come out and find fire had destroyed their shops and the notes that had contained Bill's precious secrets. By then, even she knew that saving him was hopeless. But she'd promised to meet him there.

"Some money remained. And I could remember part of the secrets. New engineers, working from my memory, finally managed to separate the isotopes again, and Wohl perfected the motor for me. After that—well, money wasn't a problem any longer. You see, I own Atomic Power. Nobody knows it, save a few, and Cartwright, who handles it all for me. . . . That's right, Wolff, I'm really your employer, though you didn't know why Mr. Cartwright instructed you to watch over me, as well as report on commercial possibilities, if any. I didn't want it that way, but he insisted, so you know now. . . . Anyway, it took time to work out the problems again, differently this time, but money can hire brains and what has been done can be done again, perhaps better. I wanted to go with Swanson, but it was impossible. Now—" She put out a hand, touching the ship they had reached. "Now, I've kept my promise to Bill, finally. I wish—"

Grey nodded, holding the others back. "Go ahead, ma'am, we'll wait."

She smiled faintly, thanking him silently, and opened the little lock of the ship that bore her name on its side, her hands fumbling briefly. Then she was inside, and the others clustered around, forgetting for the moment even their own and Swanson's plight.

Wolff stirred, and Grey snapped at him.

"Shut up!"

Alice Benson's low voice came over the phones this time, and the few words should have been consecration enough for even the soul of her Bill. They heard her at the lock again, and she came down, calm and collected, a little book in one hand, a thin sheet of paper in the other.

"His body isn't there. It's all here in his diary, which you can read. Bill waited as long as he could, until he knew something had happened; he never thought we'd failed him! Then he went out in his suit—he wanted to see this world he'd found. I think we needn't look for him." She'd labored under no delusions of finding him living, and it had been no shock. Now she shook her white-haired head and smiled at the crew. "Well, shouldn't we try to find Swanson, Grey? I shouldn't have taken up so much time when they might be dying, and so much depends on our finding the other tube. I'm sorry."

Grey stirred, such emotions as he had retreating before her self-possession. "Right, Mrs. Benson. But there's no use searching from here—the ship we saw was this one, and we'll have to get up to higher ground to spot the other, so we might as well go back to the *Moth*. From on top of her we should have a fair view of the area nearby. We'd never find the ship in searching around from here."

She agreed, apparently, and they started back, this time in a solid bunch, exchanging idle comments about the sights around them. By common consent, the story of Alice Benson and her Bill was unmentioned. Slowly, the conversation picked up, mostly in a discussion of the lichens as they came to them again. Others of the birdlike creatures were speeding across the ground now, stopping occasionally, then driving on in their never-ceasing march around the Moon.

Grey caught one, and there was no fear about it, only an impatience to continue. The flesh was abnormally firm, but was obviously protoplasm, covered with some thick, rubbery skin, and it might have weighed forty pounds on Earth. He dropped it again, and it went leaping off after its fellows.

"They have sex," he commented. "Odd, according to our standards, but there are two kinds. See, the females have a pouch, and if you noticed, that one was full. I'd guess they were egg-laying, with the eggs hatching in the pouch. Then the young cling to the little tubes there, drawing air from the mother. She must feed them with lichens drawn from the domes. Nature seems to stick to fairly familiar patterns."

"Wish I'd brought a camera, at least," Correy muttered ruefully. There was one in the ship, but the quarrel before leaving must have jostled it out of her mind, or else she'd figured on being unencumbered during the rescue attempt.

Then they were out of the valley of the lichens, going up the slope, and the rocket ship began to show up above it, climbing slowly into view until they could make out the tube, and finally see the tripod resting on the rocks under it, in the little pit the blast had scoured. Grey flipped a switch outside his suit, and pointed the beam antenna toward the *Moth*.

"Come in, Kennedy. Grey calling Kennedy. Come in."

There was no answer, though he tried again. It wasn't important, but it was odd. Those radios were supposed to be on at all times, and with full power running through the directional antenna, it should have reached in clearly. Or, if the man was inside the tube, the metal might blanket out the signal. In the ship proper, the outer antenna would have shot it through a speaker; the short-distance tubes had been sturdier than the trick experimental ones in the space set, and should still be working.

The little company loped up beside the ship, and Ralston slid under the tube, looking up it, and pounding. There was no response, nor could Grey find anything inside when he flashed the beam of his headlight in through the inky blackness of the shadows, here where no air diffused the light.

"Funny, he must be inside, but why doesn't the fool answer a CQ?" Ralston asked.

Helen Neff glared at him resentfully. "Bruce is no fool, Phil Ralston, and he's probably busy fixing that tube of yours. Don't be so aggressive about everything."

"Umm." Grey didn't like it. Kennedy was supposed to answer—that was one of the rules posted, that all sets should be on when anyone was outside, and answers should be prompt. It might mean life or death, and if the designer was taking things into his own hands, there would be an accounting, pronto. "Okay, inside, all of you!"

They climbed the ladder, slipped into the lock, and let air come in, then out of the suits and removed helmets rapidly. At a gesture from him, they left the suits stacked in the lock, breathing the much fresher oxygen-helium mixture of the ship; here with light gravity demanding smaller energy from them, the ten-pound pressure of the air was ample, though it had seemed thin when he first dropped the pressure in space.

"Kennedy!" The voice boomed through the room, down into the engine well and the cockpit, its echo sounding back metallically. Ralston slid down to the engines, and was up again. "Not there, Grey!"

"Nor in the cockpit," June reported. "Where is the stubborn idiot?"

Alice Benson came back from the hampers, her face tight. "I'm afraid even he doesn't know, now. His suit's in the locker, and he's nowhere in the ship!"

Dumbly, they stared at each other, fear climbing into their faces. The ship had been searched thoroughly, and he wasn't on it. Yet his suit was, and there had been only seven of them, of which six had been used by the rescue gang.

"He couldn't have gotten far enough away from the ship without a suit not to be seen by us. We've got a clear view for hundreds of feet. Phil, get out there and search!" Grey watched Ralston slide through the lock, his skin tight again, but his mind troubled only by the paradox presented.

The boy was back again in fifteen minutes. "Not there! I scoured the whole area."

Bruce Kennedy couldn't go a thousand feet without a suit—yet he had. How?

III

They were no nearer a solution as Mrs. Benson and Neff cleared up the food and disposed of the thin paper plates. It couldn't have happened, but it had. Of course, it was conceivable that Kennedy might have rigged a sort of oxygen flask and breathing nozzle and gone out, but it was utterly reasonless, in the actinic glare of the sun; he wouldn't have gotten far, anyway, and there was no use speculating about it.

"Madness," June suggested, not too positively. "There's life here, so there must be bacteria."

Neff shook her head. "Anything that would affect such life as we saw wouldn't be likely to hit at men; too much difference in body organization. Of course, gangrene attacks almost any flesh, but the more complicated diseases are choosy about their hosts."

There was no answer to that, beyond the useless speculation of a possibility among improbabilities. Grey thrust back and shrugged. "Okay, let's face it. Kennedy didn't leave. He was taken!"

"But—"

"No buts. When there's only one simple solution to a problem, that solution is to be taken as the correct one, unless something else comes up. We found life here—plant and animal life. Neither form would have hurt Kennedy, but we don't know what kind we failed to find. Granted, there's still the problem of that life getting into the air locks and finding Kennedy, without the suit—and the answer to that is intelligence of some sort. So we're dealing with intelligent life —pretty highly intelligent, too—and apparently inimical. We don't have weapons; nobody thought they'd be necessary. Well, we'd all hoped to find intelligent life on Mars, I guess, but we find it here instead."

Wolff licked his thin lips. "When we get back, the government's going to hear of this!"

"Yeah? Why? We ship in a space navy and kill off the natives, I suppose, to pay for Kennedy. What makes you think the government'll be interested?"

"They will. I . . . ah . . . I'm a fair metallurgist, Mr. Grey. There's plenty of raw materials here, just as Mr. Cartwright suspected. These craters and things . . . umm, whatever caused them forced the rarer metals up out of the inner strata; Mr. Cartwright thought it might, even if the Moon is made of much lighter stuff than Earth. We'll tame down these Moon creatures, all right; we'll put 'em to work digging out ore, that's what."

Ralston bristled. "Slavery went out with the Fourteenth Amendment, you slimy snake. Sure there's metal here—I spotted some pretty rare stuff myself, in scouting over nearer the cliffs. But you won't get far in dealing with any natives on that line."

"They're not exactly . . . ah . . . human, you know." Wolff flinched away from the boy's eyes, but held firm. "It isn't exactly slavery to make horses work, is it?"

The boy took a step toward him, to be halted by Grey. "I agree with you, kid, but you can't convince that sort of man; he doesn't know about little things like ideals, such as you have. This whole problem isn't new—Wolff and Kennedy were talking about it back on Earth, and there are plenty who'd agree with them, with that plenty having most of the money for something shown to be commercially worthwhile. To you and some of the rest of us—perhaps even to me—interplanetary trips are an ideal, sort of a dream; to them, it means money, and it doesn't matter how they get it."

"I'm afraid you're right, lad. Bill used to worry about that, too. . . . Wolff, I'm paying your salary, still. You'll tell no tales of what we find here." Alice Benson gave the order firmly, and the man nodded; but Grey saw the look on his face, and knew how much obedience she could expect. There were people who'd pay for information, and Wolff wanted the money.

"Anyhow, that doesn't settle the problem. Right now, the main thing is to find out where Swanson came down and try to get his tube. Ralston, can you make repairs, do you think? Good. Then suppose you go up to the emergency lock at the top and see if you can spot the other ship from there? We'll hope we don't meet any of these hypothetical natives until we get off this place, and the sooner we do it, the surer we'll be. The rest of you might as well get ready to go out again."

Ralston was already swarming up, a small telescope in his hand. Wolff wriggled in his seat. "I . . . ah . . . don't you think someone should stay here?"

"'Smatter, afraid to go out and face those natives you're all set to subdue? Well, Kennedy stayed on the ship. Like the idea?"

"There are locks. I . . . umm . . . that is, if it's locked inside—"

Grey looked at him, his eyes colder than usual, but he shrugged. "Okay, stick around and whimper, then, and if they do get you, I'll be darned sure nobody looks for you! . . . See anything, Ralston?"

"Spotted it in a few seconds, almost in the shadow of the cliff. Must have been too dark when we landed to show up on the screen. About three miles off, is all."

That was better luck than Grey had hoped, for a change. He supervised their entry into and out of the lock, listening to Ralston's description of the location, then sent the boy on ahead, holding Correy back. She looked surprised as he moved toward her.

"You owe me something," he reminded, grinning.

"Darn you! I thought you'd have forgotten. The nerveless wonder, eh? Okay." She turned her face around, the expression halfway between a grimace and a smile. "Collect, Shylock!"

He'd never done it before, and his skin was tighter than when finding Kennedy gone, but movies are instructive, if one is curious enough about human habits. Also he found he had instincts that guided his arms and tightened them for him. Her lips were tense at first, but her own instincts softened them, until some of the analytical calm went out of his. Finally, he drew back to find her face faintly flushed.

"*Woof!* For a nerveless guy, you do all right, Pipsqueak! Where'd you hide those muscles, anyway?" She shook back her hair, seemingly surprised at herself. "Now I need that darned cigarette."

"For an encore—" His grin wasn't as mocking as it should have been, he felt. He was growing soft himself. But it was worth it. Afterward, she dragged at the smoke, studying him with an expression he hadn't seen before, then sharing it with him in a hasty consumption of the cigarette. Outside the lock, someone was pounding out a signal for them to come on, and they moved out, both looking foolish. Alice Benson smiled, and the others were grinning, amusement temporarily stronger than their worries. June avoided his glance and slipped back, leaving the older woman beside him as they started.

It was rougher ground this time, and almost impassable from Earth standards, but they skimmed through easily enough here, leaping over the heavier boulders, or moving from one high spot to another. Going was comparatively slow, since Grey had to pick the trail, but progress was entirely satisfactory. No sign of life showed on any side; there were no trails, no indications of intelligent construction. Only the forbidding cliff loomed up closer, jagged edges of it unshaped by wind or water.

Grey waited for Alice Benson, his eyes admiring her as she made the spring to his side. "I wonder what sort of a girl you were, ma'am? Right now, you're the best man in the bunch!"

"Thank you, Grey. It's nice not to be a nuisance." Then she smiled.

"As a matter of fact, I was a little imp. Just about the same sort as June Correy. That girl's got good stuff in her; all she needs is a bridle!"

June's grunt came in scornfully. "Don't get ideas from her, Half-Pint. It'll take a man to put that bridle on!"

He started to answer, then caught the older woman's warning head-shake, and left it to her judgment. The girl looked up, expecting a reply, frowned when none came, and seemed surprised. Mrs. Benson winked at Grey, as they picked up their way again, leaving him wondering why. Maybe he was soft, but he wasn't fool enough to think he'd have a chance with the girl—even if he wanted to.

Finally, the ship became visible, lying close to the cliffs. It had been hard hit, there was no doubt of that; apparently it had landed on only one leg of the tripod, and had been falling too rapidly. The leg had crumpled under it, letting the whole side of the ship slip over and come crashing down. Where the engines were located, the walls had broken in, though the tripod leg must have soaked up most of the initial shock, leaving a comparatively small blow from the crash.

The fact that the two flares had been set off, however, indicated that the air within must not have been lost; the ships were designed to take a fair blow on their thin outer skin without it breaking the walls of the living quarters. He flipped the switch over, beaming in his call. "Swanson! Englewood! Marsden! Ship *Lunar Moth* calling spaceship *Delayed Meeting!* Come in!"

They hung waiting for an answer, but none came. It meant nothing, though. Any one of numerous reasons could have existed for the lack of response. The men might be dead, or nearly so. Or the antenna outside the ship might have been broken; more probably, the whole radio outfit was smashed, since no signal had been pushed through to Earth. He shortened the distance in long bounds until he was directly under it.

As it lay, the air lock was within reach, and he stretched up and twisted the handle. It came open easily, letting the four climb into the lock behind him; it closed smoothly after them with a sudden hiss of air. He flipped open his helmet, sampling it; he'd expected it to be overused and stale, but beyond the smell of too much passage through the filters, there was nothing wrong, and the others followed his example in taking off his helmet.

Then the inner lock opened to show the living quarters, smaller even than those of the *Moth,* and in wild disarray. Seals had been clamped down over the engine and cockpit tubes, indicating both had lost their air. Inside, there was no one!

Grey shook his head, glancing into the food and water tanks and noting that they were still half full, jerked open the paper drawer, spilled the log out into his hands, and riffled through its pages quickly. The first entries were about the routine preparations, the takeoff, and the coast through space after killing the blast. Then trouble, just as it had appeared on the *Moth*, but worse.

> June 29: Landed somehow last night, expecting the blast to cease entirely every moment. It was crooked, and we tipped sidewise, breaking open the engine room. Poor Englewood didn't have a chance. Buried him today after finding the radio ruined and setting off our flares; doubt they'll be visible from Earth, but we hope somehow they'll be noticed. Marsden is quite confident of a rescue by the second ship. With two of us, we can hold out some time. First men on the Moon!

That, Grey knew now, was wrong, though Swanson and Marsden had every right to believe it at the time. There followed pages of their estimates, their minor activities in going outside, and a gradually dimming hope as they figured more carefully on the length of time needed to complete the other ship.

> July 11: Marsden and I talked it over this morning and decided that one man can easily last until rescue, two almost certainly cannot. We agreed to draw lots tomorrow. Tonight, while the boy's sleeping, I'll go out; I've already seen a fair sample of life, and I'm content. Keep a stiff upper lip, Bob, and when you read this, I hope you'll realize I was right in going.
>
> July 12: Poor Bob Marsden. He must have drugged my food, for I lay down expecting to wait for him to sleep, then slept myself. When I awoke, he was gone, leaving only a note wishing me good luck. I went out of the lock searching for him, but on this ground there is no spoor, and I failed. A fine assistant, a gentleman, and a great guy! God rest his soul. Somehow, I'll last until rescue comes, to make sure he gets the credit he's earned.

After that, entries became rarer, though they were still hopeful. A stray biblical quotation showed how Swanson was filling his time. Then Grey came to the last brief entry.

July 23: I miss having someone to talk to, but I'm fairly cheerful. Tomorrow I must clean up the mess I've made of my living quarters. I took some of the litter out and buried it today. My spade turned up gold—a rich vein of it; thank God, it isn't worth carrying back to Earth, or the Moon might see another bloody chaos such as the other gold rushes have been, and the gold reserves be flushed beyond all value as a monetary exchange. I suspect there are more valuable ores, though.

Beyond that there were only blank pages. Grey looked for any small note, but none was present. "Wish I knew how many suits they had."

Mrs. Benson answered. "Two—they were supposed to leave one man inside at all times, so only a pair of suits were provided. You mean—"

"Probably. There's a well-used suit in the locker, and Marsden must have worn the other. Get all the pictures you can to confirm it, will you, Correy? And we'll take the log along. Something must have taken Swanson out without a suit—again with no sign of a struggle."

He clapped his helmet back on and headed for the lock, out of the way while she snapped the pictures and pulled the finished negative roll out. Then they filed back again toward the rear of the *Delayed Meeting*. Neff, he noticed, was shivering and sticking closer to Philip Ralston, who seemed almost glad of the troubles that confronted them. June was frowning, looking to him for instructions.

He had none. Hunting the missing men was worse than senseless. All they could do now was to remove the necessary parts from the big tube, if possible, and proceed back to the *Moth*. He motioned to Ralston, and the two rounded the ship, proceeding to the tube.

Only the shell was left! The lining had been entirely removed, and as he flashed his light inside, he could see that a few bolts were left, all wires and connecting pipes cleanly snipped off. Someone had removed it before them. "God!" Ralston stepped back slowly, his face falling back to its former bitterness. "Now what?"

Grey dropped to the ground beneath, his light on, searching for some faint clue as to the ones who had done it, but there were none; the hard rock held no imprints, and the coating of dust was undisturbed, though there was no wind to blow it about and remove prints. The whole lining would have been a staggering load for all five of them, even here, but there was no sign as to its removal.

"Now, I suppose we go back to the ship empty-handed again! Six of us left, and with the provisions and air from this ship as well as the *Moth*, we can live for at least two months, by taking it easy. Then, or rather before then, we'll have to try getting air and food from the lichens. Maybe those bird-things are edible, too, though I doubt it. Perhaps we can find ores and materials to make a repair on that *Moth* that will work." He looked at the boy, who made no answer; it was just as well, since Grey knew they had no tools for all that work. But it would leave some faint hope for the others, perhaps.

They spread out again, going slowly this time. Grey wondered whether there was any hope of finding the natives, if such they were. If so, they might not be inimical, but only different, and some contact might be made that would enable an understanding. To himself, though, he still doubted the existence of intelligent lunarities; the birds could exist by keeping in motion—but could intelligence appear from such a life? And it would take a pretty fair civilization to reach the stage where they could survive the long night in one place; until that stage was reached, intelligent evolution seemed out of the question, and without intelligence, the stage was impossible.

Correy was beside him, and he noticed her flip her switch, addressing him over a beam that left the others out. "Curtains, do you think? Give it to me straight, Half-Pint."

He beamed his own answer. "Probably, though we may be able to stave it off for quite a while. And—blooey goes space travel; it was bad without two accidents, but now they'll be surer than ever it won't work! Just the same, we'll try to get back, somehow. Maybe we can get Bill Benson's old machine to working, since it's in good condition, and send one person back with the straight of it, maybe to lead a rescue trip. We've got the fuel he needed, and we can bake out water for his jets. Willing to try it?"

"Me? Chivalry getting the best of you again?" But her eyes carried the same speculative glint he'd seen before. "I'd risk it, if necessary, of course."

"No, but you're the official reporter for this trip, and you've got the connections to put it across; I haven't. The others aren't acceptable, either, that seems like the answer, so far. Anyhow, if I don't get you out from under my feet, I'm likely to find myself beginning to get used to you, sort of. Then you'd probably be insufferable."

"Think so?" He could read nothing in her remark, and put it down to devilishness that wanted to make more of a fool of him. "I'm afraid you'd be, Pipsqueak. I like men, but—"

She snapped back to nondirectional sending, dropping back beside Mrs. Benson and leaving him to lead on alone. But if he was supposed to think about her, she was mistaken. He had other worries, and he turned to them. Right now he'd have been just as happy without the responsibility of the command he'd assumed, though he knew that there was more need of it now than ever. Ahead loomed the *Lunar Moth*, and the best observatory from which to survey the surrounding moonscape for some sign of life.

He leaped ahead of the others, flipping the switch and calling the ship. His fears were justified; there was no response, and Wolff would have been too glad to have them return not to answer. So now Wolff was among the missing! Not that it was any loss, but it added somewhat to the mystery. How did the things know when to strike?

Obviously their method was shaping up. They apparently made no move to seize a group, but chose to pick them off one by one. Bill Benson and Bob Marsden were accounted for. But they'd taken Swanson after waiting—either because of the lock or for reasons of their own—then Kennedy at the first opportunity, and now Wolff. Seemingly, then, if they all stuck together, they might be safe. And again, they might not.

He gripped the outer lock, relieved to find it still unlatched; if they—whoever they were—could unfasten it from the outside, they could fasten it again—and he had no means of forcing his way in. A relieved look came to the others, who apparently assumed that Wolff was opening it, but Grey said nothing, waiting until he was inside and the facts were confirmed before adding to their troubles. Then his suit was off and he was pushing open the inner seal to finish inspection.

A gentle snore answered him, and the body of Kennedy rolled back from the door as Grey pushed it, the man sleeping heavily, but apparently untouched! Wolff was nowhere to be seen, and there was no answer to Grey's shout. Kennedy did not awaken, but went on snoring easily, relaxed, sliding slowly aside as the pilot pushed the lock the rest of the way and stepped into the room.

Neff stared as Grey picked up the big designer and dumped him into a more convenient place, her mouth open and her eyes threatening to pop out of her head. "He's back!"

"That's right, so he is! Suppose you see why he's still asleep after all the pushing he's just received." Grey made way for her, wondering how such an old-maidish child could ever have decided on a trip like this one, or how she'd ever become a first-class physician with her ideas untouched. "He's either been injured pretty badly or it's drugs."

She began fussing over the man then, and Grey watched, wondering how alien life could know the physiological effect of drugs on a human being, unless they'd decided to give him something harmless, and this had happened. That might possibly account for his return; if they were curious rather than unfriendly, they would have decided to bring the man back to where his own kind could minister to him and correct their unexpected harm. On the other hand, this sleep might be the exhaustion following some peculiar mental torture, and his return a warning to get away and stay away.

It was up to Neff, now; if she could revive him, they'd soon find the answers from the man himself. Now she was injecting some colorless fluid into him, watching the reaction. Then she turned to the crew. "I'm sure it's drugs. But I can't guess which one would produce this result; those that show so few marked signs—he seems almost normally asleep—shouldn't have such a strong effect. But I think the stimulant I gave should overcome it."

Apparently she was right, for Kennedy began twisting, his mouth working loosely; it wasn't a pretty sight, and the girl turned away, avoiding it. Then he grunted in purely involuntary sounds. She bent again, giving him another shot, and waiting for it to take effect.

The reaction was stronger and faster this time, and the man sat up abruptly, staring at the others. "Uh . . . Grey, Ralston, what are we doing here? Won't be takeoff for hours. Say, how'd I get here?"

"That's what we want to know. What happened? Did you see the other life, and what's it like? Any message of any kind sent back with you?"

Kennedy shook his head, puzzled. "I don't know what you're talking about. Say, it feels funny here. . . . Where the deuce am I, anyway?"

"Still on the Moon, of course; the tube's missing from Swanson's ship—"

"The Moon!" His face contorted, and he looked from one to the other in amazement. "You kidding? . . . No, guess not. It feels like a light-gravity effect should, and things look funny here. How'd we get up here, though? Last I remember, we were told to lie down and to catch up on sleep before the takeoff. Don't tell me I slept through the whole thing?"

"Hardly. You were supposed to be fixing the tube. Then you were gone when we came back." Grey could make no sense of it; Kennedy had an excellent memory and a clear mind, whatever his faults. "Pull yourself together, will you, and try to recall what happened? There's a lot depending on it, especially since Wolff's gone."

"Uh, I dunno . . . Lord, I'm sleepy!" He was yawning and fell back, his eyes closing. "Can't remember a thing, Grey. Go 'way and lemme sleep. Lemme sleep." The other words that he started to say faded out into an indistinct mumbling, followed by the same even snoring Grey had first heard. Shaking him had no effect, either.

Neff shrugged thin shoulders. "If he can sleep with all that injection in him, I give up. It might not be safe to wake him again. No drug acts like that! Do you think—"

"I don't think anything. At first, he was clear-headed enough, it seemed, and he didn't remember a darned thing; he wasn't fooling us. Well?"

The others had no suggestions, though they obviously had imaginations that were working overtime. Grey's was quiescent; the facts as he now found them fitted into neither of the possibilities that had occurred to him, and he was no nearer a solution of the intentions of the other life than before.

"Wolff's gone, as you've probably noticed. I can't say I consider that a great loss, but I'd look for him if I had any idea where to search. Until one of you can figure that out, I'm going outside, over to Benson's little ship. I want to look the motor and other things over. The rest of you stay here and keep an eye open for anything suspicious."

June frowned at him. "You can't go out there alone, Runt! These things seem to pick out anyone who's by himself, and they're likely to get you. Don't be a fool!"

"Maybe I want them to get me, Carrots." He headed for the lock, screwing on his helmet. "I'll be back when I get here, and if I don't come back, you're no worse off—you've got that much more provisions to divide among you. See you!"

The inner door closed behind him, and he passed out and down the ladder. Correy's yells had disappeared with the closing lock, and now only the sound of his own feet striking the rocks beneath him reached his ears, carried up through the air inside his suit. If there was life waiting for him, it could approach soundlessly, but he refused to spend his time looking back over his shoulder.

He sped along, through the valley of the lichens, up the rise, and across the rocks to the *Alice*, seeing no hint of life other than what he'd already seen. For a moment, he hesitated, wondering if they had guessed his purpose and were waiting for him inside the ship; then he shrugged and reached up for its tiny lock.

IV

They were all waiting when he returned, or rather picking at food that had been placed before them, and in the few minutes he'd stood outside the inner seal, he'd heard no words spoken. They jumped as he threw back the door, varied expressions crossing their faces. Ralston mirrored frank relief and admiration, Correy's face lighted momentarily. Grey reached back into the lock.

"Any disturbances while I was gone? Hear anything?"

"Not a sound, Grey. We were peaceful enough, waiting to hear something from you come over the speaker. Another ten minutes and I'd have followed you." The boy was tackling his food now with a much better appetite.

"Umm." Grey drew in the figure of Wolff, flaccid and snoring faintly. He dragged it to the middle of the floor. "Little present for you! Found him between the outer and inner seals, just like that. Lucky I spotted him at once and got in before the air rushing out had time to do him any real damage. He was quiet enough for you not to hear him, but I can't figure how they pushed open the lock and carried him in without sounds reaching you. Look him over, Neff."

Her diagnosis was rapid this time. "Exactly the same as the other! Do you think I should try to revive him?"

"Don't bother. You'd get the same results. Notice, though, that he isn't wearing a suit of any kind, and that means they either had suits for humans or else they carry their customers in some kind of airtight vehicle. A man can stand a little vacuum if he doesn't panic—but only for a few seconds. Nice little game, isn't it? Only it isn't a game . . . there's a good sound reason behind this, somewhere; practical jokers don't work that hard. Find the reason, and maybe you'll have the clue to them."

They put the sleeping Wolff in his sack, for want of a better place for him, and Grey shook his head as Mrs. Benson began putting down paper dishes for him. "Not now. I'm going up and have a look through the top emergency lock."

"What did you find at the other ship?" Correy asked, still looking at the sacks that held Wolff and Kennedy.

"Guess! I should have expected it, but I didn't."

She glanced around at him, curiosity giving place to sudden suspicion. "The motors had been removed. Is that it?"

"That's it. They've been gone a long time, too. There was still some air in the ship—nice construction there—and the metal was dulled on the bolts, showing the nuts had been removed long before this. No hope there." He pulled down the little ladder leading up to the escape hatch and began climbing. June brushed back her hair, following him up the long climb and into the little lock that was just big enough for the two of them. Four little quartz windows gave a view of the crater around them, once the shutters were pulled back; it had been intended as a lookout station as well as an escape.

As he swung the telescope from one side to the other, nearly all of the crater was visible, stretching out to the abrupt horizon on one side and to the towering cliffs on the other. He was looking for a trace of a trail, a cleared section among the rough rocks, or any sign of life, but he found none. No buildings, no piles of trash, not the faintest hint of intelligence; then he caught sight of a long stretch of the bird-creatures hopping in a stream from some point beyond his vision to eat and replenish their air before rushing out of sight again.

"Maybe they don't live here," Correy hazarded. "They could come from some other part, only visiting here to take away or bring back somebody."

"They could, but I don't believe it. They're somewhere near, or they wouldn't be so quick to know when we're all away and spot our weak moment. Well, that leaves only one place—the cliff!" He swung the telescope then, studying the rugged wall, until she took it from his hand and looked herself.

"It doesn't look like home to me, Half-Pint. If people lived there, you'd expect them to have some structure outside their entrance."

"But these aren't necessarily people. They might have different ideas."

"I suppose." She put the telescope down, rubbing her eyes. "I can't see anything, but I'll try again when my eyes clear up—hurts too much to look across this glare. . . . You wouldn't have any of those cigarettes left, would you?"

He grinned, holding up the package that was still half full. "Mm-hmm. I'm no pig, Redhead. Look nice? . . . No, now wait a minute —don't get so hurried about it. There should be some kind of ritual to using this reserve, don't you think? Any suggestions?"

"Darn you, Grey! Keep your cigarettes, then!"

"As you like." He selected one deliberately, running it back and forth over his thumb, tamping down the end, and lighting it. The little end glowed in the semidusk of the cubbyhole, and the thin wash of air that came in through the pipes only served to stir the smoke around, letting it cloud the air before drawing it out. Grey grunted in animal comfort, doubling his legs under him and sprawling out on the floor. "Our favorite brand, too! Seems a pity to think of their being gone so soon."

She held out longer than he'd expected, knowing how thoroughly tied to the habit she was. Then she shrugged and flopped down beside him. "Okay, okay, be a cad if you want to. What'll you do when they're all gone?"

"Use the two whole cartons left on Swanson's ship—Englewood and Marsden left quite a supply, and Swanson never used them, apparently. Since we're the only ones who smoke on this scow, they should last quite a while. Don't go looking for them, though; they're all locked up in my hamper. Hey!" He sat up, rubbing his face, and grabbed.

She ducked, grinning at him. "You're a rat, Nemo Grey, and you deserve worse. That's the lousiest trick I've heard of!"

"It is," he admitted cheerfully, beginning to understand why men who work under a strain devote so much of their free time to horseplay, partly amused at himself, and partly amazed. "What are you going to do about it, though?"

"Slit your throat when I'm sure there are none left, I suppose. . . . Now, do I get that darned smoke?"

There were four butts on the floor when he finally picked up the telescope again, and he was less amused, more amazed. She brushed her clothes, rising. "This is a lunatic world, all right, Half-Pint. People go crazy here. . . . Did you know that Neff's decided somehow Phil's her heartthrob, after all? Well, she has, and he's half delirious about it; doesn't care whether he gets back or not."

"Dunno what he sees in her; he's a swell kid, though, and I'm glad he's happy. . . . Umm! Take a look over there—between the green-black stuff and the crack beyond it. See what I do?"

She looked, her forehead wrinkling. "A hole, maybe? Looks something like one."

"Must be. They have to have some place to live, and I'll bet they're oxygen breathers. Wish me luck, Red-Top!" Grey caught the rope and was down hand-over-hand, moving toward the lock, with her at his heels. "Uh-uh, you stay here. I think I've spotted their hideout, Ralston, and I'm going scouting. Take command while I'm gone."

Correy caught the inner seal and slid through. "I'm protecting the cigarette supply, you usurer! You're not running off and leaving me without a smoke. Don't say it! It won't do any good."

He knew she meant it, and nodded, climbing into his suit and helping her with her own outfit. At that, taking someone along might be a good idea, since at least one of them would stand some chance of getting away and back to the ship with information. They jumped from the lock and went leaping across the rocks, heading toward the cliff, each selecting a path separate from the other, but fairly close. Swanson's ship was half a mile to their right as they passed it, then the ground grew rougher, breaking into jagged gullies and humps of rock, and they were forced to slow down.

"Plenty of minerals here," he called over the phones. "I'll bet the bottom of that cliff is a treasure house; may even contain radium in fair quantity. Hey, where are you?"

She was out of sight, but her voice came back instantly. "Left, down the gully; it turns and it's narrow, but it looks like the best way. Come on."

He saw the place she meant and headed down after her. Freakishly, the floor was fairly smooth, and his bounds carried him along at a brisk pace. Correy wasn't waiting for him, apparently satisfied that nothing could jump on them here. Then the crack straightened out and he could see her ahead, passing through the narrowest section. He glanced to his right, wishing he knew something more of metals and their ores, and back in time to see her sprawl on her face.

"June!"

"I'm—all right, I guess. Jarred a rock loose, and it hit my back. I . . . Grey! Help! My air tube's cut!" Her voice was frantic, and he could see the suit collapsing. She wriggled and her voice was sick and weak. "Grey!"

"Steady!" He was leaping toward her now without caution. "Hold your breath, if you can. I'll be there in a second. Don't waste your energy. There." He caught the rock that was still on her, tossing it aside, and looking down at the lacerated tube that led the oxygen into the helmet from the tank. It was short, and normally protected, but a jagged edge had slit it neatly and the last air was rushing out as he watched, faster now that the rock no longer plugged the hole.

With desperate haste, he jerked his mittens from his hands, snapping the wrist bands closed to save his air, and his naked fingers swept down onto the scorching metal of the tube, wrapping around it tightly, covering the damaged section. The air rushed back into the suit as he twisted the valve, and he could hear her breath catch. "Take it easy, now. Breathe deeply a few times—empty your lungs after each. That's right. I'll have to take a couple of minutes to screw in the spare one. . . . Thank the Lord, there is one. . . . And you'll be forced to hold your breath again. Now—a normal breath and hold it!"

The sun had been glaring down on the metal, heating it, though part of the trip had been through pools of shadow. But he had no time to worry about burns as his fumbling fingers screwed out the old tube and fastened in the replacement. The ten pounds of pressure in his body made his hands seem puffy in the vacuum, though it was insufficient to cause serious damage. Finally, though, the new tube was in, and he turned on the valve again, letting oxygen feed in to her.

She came to her feet shakily, looking at his reddened hands, over which he was drawing his mittens. "I'm sorry, Grey. I shouldn't have been so careless. You're—"

"Forget it!" He was breathing heavily himself, ashamed of the shakiness of his legs, and his voice was brusque. "Nothing serious. We stick together hereafter, that's all. Come on!"

"Wait!" It came over the phones, without directional sense, but they both swung around to see Alice Benson coming toward them. "Wait, please. I've had the hardest time following you two from the little I could see of you. You don't mind, do you?"

"Ralston had no business letting you come, ma'am," Grey told her. "Why'd you do it?"

"Because I'm tired of waiting for things to happen, lad. I want to know what's going on, just as much as you do. And here, I'm almost young again, so I didn't think I'd be a nuisance. Besides, what's the difference, really? If you get caught, I'd be stranded here, anyway, to die slowly."

"Let her come, Grey?" June asked. He thought it over briefly and nodded, starting again toward the cliff.

As she'd said she was agile enough here to be no handicap, and the chances could be no worse. They slipped through the end of the cut, and were against the bottom of the cliff; above them, the dark circle that must be a hole could be seen clearly, sixty feet up the steep side of the rocks.

He wasted no time in explaining his methods, but made a running leap, rising nearly twenty feet off the ground, and managing to catch an outcropping above the smooth bottom part. Somewhere, his feet found a place to hold on, and he spotted another hold within reach before removing a small coil of rope carefully and lowering it to the other two, who swarmed up quickly and caught the same jagged tooth of rock.

Actually, what had looked hard because of Earth memories proved surprisingly easy, their bodies in the suits weighing less than a quarter Earth weight, and the cliff being covered with sharp, uneroded cracks and projections. There was a little shelf beneath the hole, and they were standing on it in a matter of seconds, staring into absolute blackness.

"We'll have to feel forward," he ordered. "No lights!"

The utter black was eerie, having none of the usual slight hints of light found in an atmosphere; he tested each step, one hand held to the cold rock wall, the other above and in front to locate something that might bump against his helmet. Foot by foot, they advanced, the breathing of the other two heavy in his phones. Then his hand found a flat obstruction, felt along it, and revealed it as a smooth, rounded end to the tunnel. He put his hands over his lamp, leaving only a slight hole, and switched the beam on and forward. In front of him, a metal door was set into the rock, a handle projecting from it, and a row of odd characters beside the handle. On the other side, English letters showed whitely: "WELCOME!"

June gasped, but his own mind found a hint of a solution. They'd had Swanson for days now, and some kind of communication might have been set up. Whether the sign was actually a greeting or a trap, he had no way of knowing. Nor could he be sure that its meaning was anything beyond a bit of grim humor on Swanson's part.

He tried the handle, found that it turned easily, and stepped in, a glare of light springing down as he did so. The two women cried out, but followed, and the door closed automatically, while a sudden hiss of air spilled in. Seconds later, another seal opened by itself, leading out into a long, smooth hall of white stone, lighted softly from the sides and ceiling. Grey's skin tightened, but he entered, the others behind him, and the inner seal swung softly shut.

The air, as he tested it, was sharp with the smell of ozone, and slightly thinner than even the mixture in the ship, but it was breathable, and rather pleasant after a minute. He debated leaving his suit on for an emergency escape, then decided against it; those automatic doors could undoubtedly be sealed against him at any time. He was in it now, and had to see it through.

"We might as well be comfortable," he told the others. "Let's take 'em off and go ahead to meet our hosts in suitable style. Wonder why they haven't shown up yet? Here, Carrots, light up!"

"Thank you, kind sir," she said, mock amazement on her face. "If I didn't see it, I still wouldn't think there weren't strings to the offer somewhere. Where to? Down the hall?"

"All we can do. Want to try it, Mrs. Benson?"

"I do, Grey. People who can design these soft lights and cut such rock to make walls can't be all bad. This is culture, and a well-developed one, too."

Their steps were muffled by some form of carpeting on the floor as they passed down the hall and rounded the corner into a room beyond it. Then they stopped, staring.

Bob Marsden tossed aside the strange roll of writing he was studying and bounded forward, a grin on his homely face, with Swanson at his heels. "Earth people, finally! Howdy, folks. I see they didn't bring you in asleep?"

Swanson was pumping Grey's hand, grinning. "So they picked you for this trip, eh? Good. Heard you did better than I did, too. How about introducing the ladies, fellow? . . . Hey, Burin Dator, you've got guests!"

Into the room, a creature walked, resembling a man somewhat in general formation, though only three feet tall and slightly built. The features on the head spread wider apart, the nose lying under the mouth instead of above, and the skin was thick and leathery, entirely devoid of hair. He resembled a rough rubber caricature of a human being, but his appearance was somehow civilized and pleasant, as any well-formed and graceful animal is pleasant.

"Mike!" It was a low rumbling voice, oddly at variance with his size, but the intonation was hearty and genuinely glad. "Mike, boy, you finally returned. We've missed you around, been wondering why you didn't make the first trip. Swanson here explained you couldn't, so we were pretty sure you'd make the rescue ship, but we didn't get close enough to see you, and the description we wormed out of that man, Kennedy, wasn't exact enough to make sure. I was just about to go out and meet your gang. . . . Welcome home, boy!"

Burin Dator slid his delicate "hand" into Grey's, his eyes warm and an expression Grey knew to be meant for a smile on his face. "Sound general assembly! Mike's come home! *Lursk*, some of that synthetic wine! This calls for a celebration!"

V

It had been quite a celebration at that, with others of the Martians trooping in and joining quietly, all regarding Grey with the same look of familiarity. Finally Burin Dator shoved back his seat and led them into a comfortable room where padded seats were arranged gracefully around a low table and along the walls, his wrinkled face beaming. The Earth trio followed in growing surprise, somewhat annoyed by Swanson and Marsden, who chose to answer no questions; they were still unsure that this was real, eager for explanations that had been hinted at. Grey was clutching his sanity grimly, unconsciously sticking close to June for a straw of normality to cling to.

The little Martian selected a seat leisurely. "Comfortable, everyone? I sincerely regret the unpleasantness of our first contacts with you, but it was necessary that we find out what type you were. Unfortunately, the two men whom we first obtained were both of a type we've been forced to take measures against, so they were returned in good health, but somewhat restrained."

June stirred. "Just what did you do to them?"

"Nothing permanently unpleasant, I assure you. We removed some of their memories, after determining that their words on your Earth would have bad results for us—they were filled with a desire to exploit this world, you know. They've forgotten the last few days, with the help of a little surgery, and now are under a drug to keep them from knowing more. We'll give you an antidote to counteract it before landing again. . . . It was rather ticklish work, removing some memory, but leaving all except the very recent events, and I'm a little proud that we didn't have to blank their whole minds."

"Earth surgeons can destroy memory," Grey agreed; he should know something about it, since the whole subject naturally interested him. "But they can't do that, certainly not to another race. You've got good reason to be proud."

"It was difficult. But remember that our hands are somewhat more delicate than yours, and that we've studied the mind of human type with great care, only recently realizing how it sorted its memories and what nerves controlled them. Also, where your race leads ours immeasurably in mechanics and inventiveness, we are much further advanced in medicine, psychology, and the general study of life-chemistry and thought than you. Swanson wasn't our first, nor Marsden; we met our first Earthman much before that."

Alice Benson leaned forward, her eyes gleaming. "That man, Mr. Dator—was his name Bill Benson?"

"It was, lady. And I gather you're his wife, so we'll turn over his manuscript work to you before you leave. He believed you were dead when you didn't come, not knowing of that war you had, or he would probably have gone back. . . . But, to begin, we on Mars had a better medium of observation than you—our air is thinner, causing less loss of detail in astronomical observation. We saw his flare on the Moon by chance, observed and analyzed it carefully, and decided that it indicated there was life on your world, and that you had successfully bridged space. At the time, we had completed, by a fortunate coincidence, a spaceship upon which our people—or at least our group—had been working some two hundred of your years; we are slow at such things, as I said. It used a simple oxygen-hydrogen jet, since it was barely possible from our light-gravity world to your Moon, and I was fortunate enough to be one of the crew. Then, when we finally located Bill Benson, it took us nearly a month to repair the injuries to his health from his wanderings outside the ship and his exhausted air. Tracking him was very difficult here, and he was nearly dead when we finally located him. It took time to establish a common understanding, but while our people and yours differ surprisingly, their similarity in social behavior and thought is much more surprising."

The Martian paused, thinking before resuming. "Like you, we have a practical type and an idealistic one. From the former, there could be only trouble in a meeting of races; it would be a struggle for supremacy, and would go ill for both. Unlike you, our idealists recognized the fact when the first attempts at constructing a rocket were begun and organized a small, secret group. It is from them that all our people here are drawn, and only that group knows of our success. We are forced to deceive the others. Bill Benson agreed that only the idealists of his race must know, also. You are such, so are we. The two men asleep in your ship are not, and they cannot know, nor must your world.

"Because this world is rich in things we both need, ores and materials that are immensely precious, even in small loads. World-shaking fortunes are to be made from them, and from the secrets gleaned by each from the other. We've already begun using them—

your engines, your gadgets, the other things Bill Benson could describe, and especially your atomic energy, which is the real key. They're infiltered slowly, outwardly the result of individual luck or skill, and you must do the same.

"What we envision, then, is a small group on each planet, controlling gradually larger amounts of that world's wealth, seemingly with no connections here, until such a company holds the balance of power. It would be composed, quite naturally, at the head, of men who know and sympathize. Then, when the idealists have paved the way, we can open the gates between the races, controlling the opinions carefully so the mobs will agree with us. We can never live on your heavy planet, and you would find ours most uninviting, but here—your Moon—we find a common ground for the future of both races. The other way, we fear destruction. Can it be done?"

Grey nodded, his mind filled with that huge plan for a future perhaps centuries later. "It can be done, I think. Certainly the men who control the finance of a nation can do a great deal to shape its thoughts and laws."

"And the nucleus of the company already exists," Mrs. Benson pointed out eagerly. "I own Atomic Power, which itself is a powerful instrument. At the moment, my liquid assets are depleted, but that is only money; the real wealth is still untouched. Cartwright, who runs it for me, probably is not to be trusted, but he is due to retire soon. Then my nephew is supposed to take over, and he'd know to organize better than anyone else. If we were to land on a desolate place, damaging our ship afterward and radioing for help, then represent the Moon as completely unprofitable, a dangerous, useless place—"

"Precisely, lady." Burin Dator favored her with another of his toothless grins. "Those two men were mentally impaired by some kind of radiation, as you would have been yourself, of course, had your age not kept you within the ship—only the very young can withstand it—and the others of you all can be made to show severe suffering, by certain drugs we have. Such pictures as have been taken will show nothing. Then you organize secretly, forming mining companies, small inventive groups, and so forth, and building a very small but efficient fleet of space freighters—based on some remote island, I believe—to carry the idealists and the refined metals that are valuable in tiny quantities—jewels, too, to be found in the craters—and we can safely trust the future from there."

Grey could agree with it, and could see how the company could operate quietly, not as one, but as many. It still left the big problem on his hands, however. "How do we get back? Our tube's shot, and you probably use something different that won't fit the *Moth!*"

"We use a type of propulsion similar to yours now, perfected by Bill Benson, and much more efficient; it does not destroy itself, either. One can be fitted easily. We are visionaries, Mike, but not foolish ones."

"What's all this 'Mike' business, anyway? Don't tell me I'm a Martian, transformed somehow?" The calm use of that name was beginning to wear on his nerves, coupled with the fatherly interest shown by the Martians.

Burin Dator laughed, an obvious imitation of Earth emotions, but one that had become natural to him. "Not at all, boy. I said we were far advanced in life-chemistry. When Bill decided to stay here, he wanted a son, if our methods worked as well as we claimed. We made nine failures, and one that was almost a failure, but we learned, and you're our eleventh attempt at exogenesis; I'm afraid it wasn't perfectly adapted for Earth life, since you've always shown some peculiar features, but you're the . . . ah . . . foster son of Mrs. Benson."

"And how'd I come to Earth then, carrying no memories with me?"

"We'd promised your father before he died that you'd be returned, but we knew it was unsafe to trust a boy who knew nothing of his native planet, so we were forced to remove your memory first. We hoped habits of thought and emotions would develop a similar character in you, and that certain wordless suggestions we planted after the operation would bring you back, if possible. It seems we were right, fortunately."

"Can you give back the memory, then?"

"No. It is final when performed, though we can show you records of your life from its beginnings that are almost as good." Dator hesitated, glancing from one to the other. "We hope, naturally, that you will remain with us when the others go; they can explain it as lunar madness, how you walked away and were never seen again. Mr. Swanson can pilot the ship back. You found him near death, of course, but saved by the fact he'd never left his ship. Something of that idea. But we need at least one representative from your planet to remain."

Grey considered it slowly. Earth had never been particularly kind to him, a freak among normal men, and it was only here that he had found friends—Mrs. Benson, Ralston, these Martians; perhaps even

June Correy. Back there, they'd be swallowed in their work, and he'd be alone again. But—

June broke in, settling the matter. "Of course we'll stay. It's the only solution."

He jumped at her voice, swinging to study her face, but it remained calm. "We? Naturally, I'm the one to stay, but you—"

"Stick. That is, if you don't mind. I'm being honest, now. Here, you're a man, and one that suits me under these conditions. Size doesn't count. On Earth, I'd be ashamed to walk down the street with you. I'd erase you from my life so fast you'd never know what happened! But I'd rather not do that."

Grey didn't care to think of it himself; maybe it was a lunatic world, but insanity such as this was better than his normal life had been. He'd been afraid to think of such things, even here, but now—"Do the Martians have some ceremony, Dator?"

Burin Dator nodded, beaming. "Indeed yes, or we have a copy of the Earth one. In the morning, then, my engineers will fix your ship, and you can say good-bye to your friends. Tonight, after you phone them to attend, why not the ceremony?"

Alice Benson had eyes that were filled with a hunger that had already accepted Grey as her own son. "That would be kind, Mr. Dator. And someday I'll be back. This is my world. . . . What will you have for a wedding present, Michael?"

It was his world, too, the only place where he fitted. But new world or not, his emotions were finally flooding in on him, too fresh for him to express adequately. It was June who answered, her grin somehow sweet, mocking though it seemed.

"Cigarettes, Mrs. Benson. That boy gets more mileage out of a package than your rocket ever can."

There's always a price to pay, it seems. Writing under extreme pressure takes about ten times as much out of the writer as normal work does. If he knows that in advance and makes proper allowances for it, he can handle it by taking a couple of days to rest and not even looking at a typewriter, deliberately adjusting back to normal. But if he doesn't expect it, the results are much worse. I found that I'd developed an extreme aversion against anything connected with writing, and that reaction lasted far longer than it should have. Instead of accepting it and letting it drain out naturally, I made things worse by trying to force myself back to writing. The result was a lot of paper on the floor and a good idea for a novelette ruined forever by the weight of the mistakes I made in trying to handle it.

But I had enough money, and I found myself beginning to pick up odd bits of change in a couple of unexpected ways. The first was a direct result of the war shortages that were developing in material and skilled labor. People suddenly couldn't replace the gadgets that stopped working, and it was hard to get replacement parts or find anyone to do the work. I discovered this when the toaster at the drugstore went on the fritz and wouldn't pop up. It wasn't hard to fix, once I found how to get the ornamental cover off, and it paid off in several free meals. Then a lovely little adding machine broke down, and I was called on to get that working.

I've always enjoyed machinery. In those days I had a kind of rough-and-ready understanding of mechanics and electronics, but I depended more on a sort of empathy for the machine. Years later I took the trouble to learn electronic theory thoroughly, but I really didn't know enough then to rewire sets for use with substitute tubes. Nevertheless, when I finished with a radio, the darned thing worked! Word spread from the drugstore to the neighborhood, and I got a surprising amount of repair work. I enjoyed it, too, because there is a lot of satisfaction in curing a sick gadget—though I'd hate to take it on as a full-time occupation.

Then there were pinball machines. At the time, in St. Louis, most of the places where they were installed would pay off the "free game" credits that could be accumulated. This was all new to me, and I couldn't resist. (After all, such devices were also gadgets!) To my surprise, I found that most of them were really games of skill—provided one studied them thoroughly first to understand exactly what could be done and took the time to master exactly how they could be jiggled without tripping the "Tilt" sign.

The drugstore didn't care who won, and the manager seemed to feel I was entitled to special rights, as a regular customer and sometimes helpful handy man. So I usually got the benefit of the genuine free games racked up by the serviceman whenever a new game was installed. That gave me enough experience with the device to figure out the required strategy. Almost all of my eating at that store was paid for by my winnings.

Then the night manager at the hotel found I didn't mind taking over for him at times, and a fair amount of my rent was credited to me for that.

It's amazing how clever a writer can become at avoiding the need to write, and what excuses he can develop. It was true of me, and I sort of took it for granted that it was something peculiar to myself. I've since found that it's a common occupational hazard. I don't know why that should be; it isn't laziness, since most of the tricks take far more time and effort than writing, and yield less reward. But so it is. Maybe Campbell was right in his answer. "All writers are crazy," he explained. Then he went on: "Science fiction writers are crazier. Editors are crazier than the worst writers. And science fiction editors —well!"

But I had a good rationalization for it all at the time, as usual. I was working on a series of stories about a man who was made accidentally immortal, and a world that was badly wrecked in which he would be needed. I wouldn't do sequels again, but I'd figured out that a series which was meant to cover many stories from the very first inception of the idea was different. Maybe it is. I never found out.

But I did finally begin the series. War was in the air everywhere, and it naturally colored everything I thought and wrote. So the story began when some devastating war was happening in the future. I called the story "Conchy," but Campbell quite properly retitled it "Fifth Freedom." It ran for 8,000 words, the absolute maximum length for a short story in *Astounding*.

Naturally, I had to have a new pen name to separate the series from all the other stories I was going to be writing as it appeared. So "Fifth Freedom" appeared with John Alvarez as the author.

14.

Fifth Freedom

(by John Alvarez)

—to be found in the final war of the twentieth century none of the lighter elements present to some extent in all former struggles. It was a grimly determined fight against extinction from the first few months.

America presented the paradox of an absolute dictatorship

with full popular approval, and there was no place in the public mind for anything but the maximum effort from each individual. Conscientious objectors, while regarded as within their rights—

"The Period of Discovery"

Roget's *History of Man*, Vol. III

Wearily, Tommy pulled the hard pillow farther under him, doubling it over in an attempt to find some support that would let him read in the dim light without carrying his weight on an aching arm. But it was no use. The pillow oozed out from under him, letting him down again, and the arm trembled as it took up the load. Soft living, without work and with his every want provided, had left him without the stamina to stand up under the enforced grueling grind of the machine through the long ten-hour stretch, even yet. He was too tired to harbor resentment against the government that had tagged him and probed him, then ordered him out here into the labor camp, away from his comforts, to do such unskilled work as was required of him, along with a motley collection of people of vague abilities and numerous reasons that made them unsuitable for military service.

War! Always and eternally, man went to war not only to destroy the aggressors but to ruin the lives of those whose only crime was a hatred of that war. They'd taken his rocket plane for civilian patrol, filled the newspapers with a hysterical frenzy of hatred, and pressed his favorite music off the air to make room for the propaganda of lust and savagery that seemed their glory; and the little people around him, who'd mostly prayed against it, now seemed to take pride in it, and to talk of nothing else.

He tried again to cut the blaring radio out, with its news and propaganda that neither interested nor impressed him, but dinned remorselessly into his ears, and turned back to the latest *Astounding*; it had arrived for him only today, and as yet he'd only glanced at the cover and readers' corner. Hopefully, he began on the cover story:

> Major Elliot glanced up from the papers as the captain entered, nodded, and went on reading through the reports. "Centralia's moving up; big offensive at midnight tomorrow, Captain Blake. I want you to take six volunteers—"

Damn! The boy's lips tightened and he threw the magazine under his bunk, his raw nerves whipped by the fresh insult; even there, war!

All day, he'd been counting the hours and minutes until his shift went off and he could find release from the horrible reality, only to find science fiction as filled with it as all else. He jerked the lumpy pillow up, threw his head against it, and tried to drown out the mutter of voices behind him and rest. It was an hour yet until dinner, and perhaps in that time he could catch a brief nap.

Under him, there was a rustle in the lower bunk, the *thunk* of a bag on the floor, followed by the sound of the built-in locker being opened. Newcomer, he decided, wondering whether to look down or go on minding his own business. Then Bull Travis' voice cut in, already beginning to blur with the "smoke" he obtained somewhere.

"Hey, Bub, there's a bunk tother side of the room. Whyn't you go over there?"

"What's wrong with this one?"

"Conchy on top, that's what! Sniveling 'cause Mamma isn't there to protect it!"

"Thanks, but I'm not carrying this bag another step." Tommy looked over then, surprised, to see a thin blond boy of about twenty-four packing his duffel into the hamper under the bunk. Beyond him, Bull was staring at the kid with a sour frown.

"You a damned yellow conchy, too?"

"Nope. Red card, they won't take me. But right now, I wouldn't care if a cobra had the bunk over me."

Bull grunted something, then started out to the washroom, where he hid his hooch. Tommy turned over again, the words burning into his brain. *Conchy!* Conchy, damned yellow *conchy!* Was a conscientious objector any less of a human being?

To the others, he was; there was no question left on that score. Since he'd come, there'd been only two civil sentences spoken to him, and both of them before the speakers knew he carried the little blue card of a conchy. Bull might get drunk and beat up some weakened oldster, or swear all night in a profane stupor, but he had four sons in the war; Tommy was only a thing that had crawled among them to avoid doing his rightful part. And this was a democracy!

Eight months before, without even the warning of broken relations, Centralia had struck westward suddenly, moving in viciously with heavy ground mechanism and new antiair guns, while the more peaceful nations had been expecting only an invasion from the skies. Seven months before, they had reached the Channel, and the world beyond Europe had relaxed as their momentum slowed and came to an abrupt halt. And America, as part of the Union, had declared war almost automatically, while the people assured themselves that, with all the surprise element gone and no adequate air power, Centralia was a pushover.

Then the radio blanket that cut off all communication with anyone less than a thousand miles from Europe had dropped as a stunning surprise; ships carrying supplies had gone into the blanket, and a few ships with neither supplies nor men aboard had come drifting out, their superstructures melted away as if they had been sprayed with magma from the sun. Of the fleet of cargo planes that had been trapped inside there was no word until two months later, when a battered little flitter had come zooming out of the morning mists to land at the Washington airport. Two men were in it, one in American uniform, crying softly to himself, staring at nothing until he died as they were moving him to the stretcher; the other, obviously British, had disappeared with grim lips into an official car, and never been seen publicly again.

But after that, the sudden hysterical drive began; there was no delay, no waiting for public response this time. Every man, woman, and child had been registered, quizzed briefly, and told what to do—or else. For the fit, military service in lightning schools; for those with skills, allocation in the government-commandeered industries. And for the others, such decentralized places as these plywood and scrap-material barracks, with the corrugated-iron workshops around. Congress had uttered one great roar, before the gray-faced English flier spoke to them in secret session; after that, a few Congressmen probably continued to object—privately—but if so, they were snowed under by the 95 percent who sat in session, passing bills with monotonous "Ayes." Rather surprisingly, the people showed little resentment; most seemed more cheerful at the positive commands coming out of Washington, rather than less. America had its dander up; that man in the White House was a real leader; Centralia was shivering in its boots. Had they so much as moved out of their blanket yet? No, sir, and they'd better not! Uncle Sam could take care of himself!

Tommy's number had come up, and Tommy's mother had cried while his father looked pleased, somehow; but not for long—not after he learned of Tommy's interview, and the man who had called to see his mother and doubtfully mailed back the blue card. His father had been grim-faced and silent, driving him to the train that would take him to Workcamp 2013-E. "Good-bye, conchy! Conscientious!" He'd snorted at that, pulling out a ten-dollar bill. "That's your inheritance; don't bother coming back, and don't write us!"

And the wheels of the train had gone turning along, crying out, "Conchy, conchy!" while he'd sat dry-eyed and anguished, filled with the horror of any passion that could do that to his father, nursing his hatred of war doubly hard, to shut out his father's eyes and his weeping mother. Now, here he was.

"Hi," said the kid's voice from under him. "This your magazine? Mind if I read it? I'm Jimmy Lake."

"Go ahead."

"Thanks. Want today's paper?"

"Nn-nnh. I'm here as an objector. Didn't you hear Bull tell you that?"

"So what? I'm here 'cause of polio. Bum leg, good enough to fly peace planes, but they won't take me on now." Jimmy grasped the edge of the bunk over him with tremendously strong hands and lifted himself easily, glancing at the bunk tag. "Tommy Dorn, eh? No law against a man who figures his God won't let him fight. What's your religion?"

Tommy pulled himself into a sitting position, his lips suddenly whitening. The man at the board had asked the question in routine fashion, his father had asked it bitterly, and he'd watched their eyes narrow at the answer. "It's sort of a personal religion. I . . . I just hate war!"

There was no narrowing this time, though embarrassment showed faintly. "Oh. Well, I think you're wrong, but it's your business. Sorry I butted in. Look, do you—"

"Ladies and gentlemen," blared the speaker across the room, and something in the voice quieted all sounds there. "We interrupt this program to bring you a special bulletin. The President has just announced that two hundred B-43 new model jet bombers have returned from a special mission over Centralia—operation successful, casualties none! They approached Berlin at eighty thousand feet—a mile over the useful range of antiaircraft guns—unloaded their bombs, made recordings of the damage done, and returned with only one minor injury. Berlin is reported to be a mass of burning wreckage. Further details will be broadcast as released."

The room was roaring then, and Jimmy turned back, his eyes glowing in his pale face. "Lord! And they haven't the air fleet to come back at us."

"No?" Tommy grunted; he might hate war, but even that hatred couldn't keep him from assembling the hundred little things he'd read and pieced together in a general love of scientific advance that included even military progress. "I suppose they didn't know we had the planes, didn't expect all this? They were preparing for it ten years, after all! And probably the city was just a dummy above ground, anyhow."

"They haven't made a move—"

"Didn't they wait after getting to the coast, only to make a sudden move with their radio blanket to cover it? . . . Oh, stop it! I'm sick of it! Do we have to talk war all the time?"

A reek of liquor struck his nose suddenly, and he looked up to see Bull Travis staring at him, contempt and hatred under the alcohol blur in his eyes. For a second, the man hesitated, just as the dinner bell sounded; apparently it stopped him, for he joined in the rush toward the door. But all through the meal, his eyes were riveted on Tommy, and he was unusually silent. Beside the boy, Jimmy tried to make conversation, but the eyes across the table went on staring, could be felt even when Tommy's face was turned away.

Tommy felt better up on the top of the hill with the work camp behind him, hidden by the bole of the tree against which he sank, breathing heavily from the long climb upward. Tonight there was a full moon, and there was always something soothing about the secret shadows and cool light of that, combined with the clean smell of dewy grass and trees. Here there was neither war nor reminders of it; and nobody from the camp would invade his privacy. He pulled his violin from its case, tucked it under his chin, and began playing, improvising mostly.

Slowly, the disharmonies smoothed down, the savage pace quieted, and the mood of the surroundings crept in to replace the jangle of nerves and bitterness. Slow, clear music came then, swelling up softly, becoming more certain, and carrying in it something that Tommy could not place, but could feel inside him. His eyes roved down the hill, down to an old rock that stood out blackly in the moonlight, and a path leading to it. A note of expectancy crept into the music.

Nine o'clock—and she always came at nine, sometimes with others, usually alone, to sit down there. He wondered vaguely what she was like in reality, but his mind pictured her as a Diana in a gentle mood, stepping down from the moon in the cool of the evening. He'd wondered sometimes whether she'd heard his playing, even dared to hope that it was part of her reason for coming. Somehow, seeing her down there, pretending he was playing for her and that she understood, some of the loneliness left him and he could feel almost happy again. Tonight, perhaps, she would be alone.

But the quarter-hour came and went, and she had still not appeared; he stopped his playing to glance again at his watch, pulled the bow over the strings again, this time in mood music from Tchaikovsky, his eyes still on the clearing.

"Really that bad?" The voice broke in, drawing a harsh discord from the violin as he jumped and swung about. She was standing slightly behind him, smiling faintly, with the light of the moon on her face, and again he thought of a gentle Diana. She was perhaps nineteen and cleaner-lined than the statues he'd seen of the moon goddess, but her face fitted his dream of it. "I've heard you play, and curiosity got the better of me. Mind?"

He shook his head quickly, making room for her as she sank down beside him. "I'm Tommy Dorn from the men's work camp down there. Was my playing so bad?"

"Not bad; disconsolate." She looked at him curiously, seeing a medium-sized, rather handsome boy, barely come of age. "What's the matter? Wouldn't they take you?"

He frowned, then grasped it. "No, it's not that . . . if you must know, I'm a—conchy! Because of *personal* religion, and because I loathe war!" He might as well get it over and done with; sooner or later it was bound to come out, anyway.

"Oh." Understanding was in her tone. "I'm Alice Stevens, Tommy, stationed over at the women's camp."

"Aren't you going to draw your dress back from me and run screaming away?"

"Should I?"

"Apparently. Two people can't be decent to a conchy on the same evening. It's against the rules, or something."

She laughed then. "You're even more bitter than your music, aren't you? I'll admit it isn't quite the picture I had of you, but for all I knew you might have been an old worn-out fussbudget or a half-idiot, in spite of the music."

"You're just what I thought you'd be!" He blurted it out, feeling ridiculous, but impelled by the half-confession of her words.

"Silly, isn't it, Tommy? Just because we're both lonely and away from home, I suppose. Let's don't talk about it. Play something, and I'll just sit here and listen and look at the moon. Play about the moon."

"The Sonata or *Claire de Lune?*"

"Neither—they're too conventional, somehow. See how our moon makes the grass look like rippling water? Do you know Debussy's—"

"'Reflections in the Water'? You do like music, don't you?" He caressed the instrument to his chin, his eyes straining sideways toward her as he played, feeling inspiration in his fingers. It was pantheistic music, fitting the magic of the moon and the trees, and the wind that stole up to brush her hair into his face, so the faint perfume teased at his senses.

"You'll come again—maybe?" he asked finally, when the music had led into talk, and that had begun to die down as they found themselves yawning. "Tomorrow night, Alice?"

She nodded, smiling at him, and then he had his violin case in his hands and was going down the hill toward the work camp again; but behind him, he could still sense her presence, and looked back to see her watching him leave. For the moment, there was no room in his thoughts for either the war or the contempt of the others.

"Hello, punk!" The voice came thickly from a clump of bushes beside the trail, and Bull Travis came out in front of him, weaving a little as he walked, his shoulders hunched forward menacingly. "I been waiting for you. So Centralia's gonna beat us, heh? Nice fifth columnist we got with us. You filthy little—"

Futility rose up from Tommy's legs and constricted as a band about his chest, and his stomach tightened inside him coldly. He backed away, feeling his tense face muscles quiver as he opened his mouth, his mind already sensing the impact of those threatening fists. "Look, now, Bull, I—"

"Shuddup!" The fist lashed out then, with poor control, glancing against the instrument case Tommy had thrown up wildly, knocking it aside and out of his hands. Bull advanced, and the boy tried to duck; he felt the impact against his face almost simultaneously with the ground striking the side of his head. It wasn't exactly pain, just a dull giddiness that spread sickly through his whole body.

Instinctively he came to his feet, somehow dodging another blow in a frantic leap sideways, and trying to strike back. But the tenseness inside him ruined his reflexes and destroyed all co-ordination, leaving him hopelessly at the mercy of Bull's drunken lunges. Another wild one connected, throwing him onto his knees and ripping out a long patch of cloth and skin.

It could have been only seconds the blackness fell over him; he reeled out of it to feel blood pouring down from his nose and to see Bull bending forward. Then a shout came from somewhere, and Bull straightened while Tommy dragged himself to his feet and stared without comprehension.

Jimmy Lake covered the last few feet in an odd hobble, his left leg dragging behind, his right pumping him along. Bull's eyes were on the crippled one, and a savage bark came to his lips as he moved forward. Something lashed out, a vague blur in the moonlight, and Bull measured his length on the ground, to lurch up with pure madness in his voice and spring forward again.

Somehow, without moving from his position, Jimmy let the wild swing slide by, drawing his overdeveloped right arm back and measuring the distance coolly. Then it struck forward, with the left coming behind it in perfect timing. This time, Bull lay where he'd landed, sprawled out like a rag doll dropped carelessly.

"All right, Tommy?" The cripple was breathing heavily, but that must have been from the long climb up the hill; his face was composed, unexcited. "I heard Bull was out for you and came up to warn you, but he beat me to it. Here, wipe off some of that blood; it's almost stopped now. And sit down; you're trembling like a leaf!"

Tommy sat, sick with reaction from the fight, sicker with the shame that the other could see him like this, shaking, his face tear-streaked, his voice almost out of control. "I'm all right. Thanks! I guess . . . you think—"

"A pleasure, Tommy. I've run into his type before. For the rest, heck, I was pretty bad myself the first few times; you get used to it after a while. Never had to do much fighting, did you?"

"No." He'd spent his time with his books and his machines, instead of out with the kids who went yelling up and down the streets. Later, he'd becozened a rocket plane out of his father and an expensive flying course that replaced the sports of other boys. Hands and minds were to fight things—natural laws that said *no* when a man said *I will*—not other men.

"Only once before."

"Thought so. Think you can make it now? Good; and don't forget your fiddle." They started back down, Tommy still nervously exhausted and shaky but trying to mask it and keep up with the brisk pace the other set; running, he'd seemed hopelessly crippled, but the leg was strong enough for walking, awkward though he looked.

On a sudden thought, Tommy glanced up the hill, but there was no sign of her; perhaps she'd left before Bull came out of the bushes. But he doubted it. He tried to thrust the thought aside and listen to the rough instructions on self-defense the other was giving him.

Surprised, hostile looks greeted them as they entered the bunkhouse and moved to their double bunk, but the glances were only momentary and attention went back to the radio. Jimmy caught his arm tensely, and swung him around to face the speaker.

"—too high to be seen. There goes another one; the building's shaking visibly under us! God, the people down there! This can't be explosives; they must have atomic energy in those bombs! It doesn't stop, but goes on and on, heat boring through even the walls where I'm standing. They've stopped firing antiaircraft; too high, too fast. Some new type of plane. From the window, then, I caught a glimpse of one in a searchlight, and it's big—has to be to be seen at that height! Almost no wings. Somewhere to the right, raw hell burst up then; building's coming down; now I can see it—just a blazing hole in the ground, three blocks long, with fumes streaking upward. People blocks away, trying to run to safety, dying under the heat—no, radiation, not heat! Technical men here just got some instruments together and made readings. Listen, Washington, here's the dope, if I live to pass it on—"

Jimmy cut into the technical stuff that could hold no meaning to the average listener but might be all-important to scientists. "Why don't they cut off his descriptions before he ruins the country's morale?" He looked at the group around the speaker, shrugged. "No, maybe not. Maybe they're being smart. Make anything of what he's saying?"

"A little. It has to be atomic destruction," Tommy snapped. "And not U-235. They've found a way to set off light elements—"

The announcer wound up his report on instrument readings. "That's the best we can give you, Washington. They can't precision-bomb from that height and speed, but they're still at it. Sometimes flares show up miles away, sometimes they hit the same place again. We're still untouched, but it can't be much longer. We've got a man on the roof trying to spot one falling toward us, but it won't do any good; the red light'll only tell us . . . *and it's on! Give 'em hell for us, Amer—*"

Surprisingly, almost no words were spoken by the grim group in the barracks after the speaker gave its final sound—like a plucked string breaking in slow motion. "Lights out!" someone said finally. "We've gotta *work* tomorrow!"

Tommy lay in the dark, tense and sleepless. His fight almost forgotten, the greater fight— He'd been right; Centralia was prepared. But he'd never quite believed it himself, before. Finally he slept fitfully, dreaming that Bull was beating him again while the announcer went on describing it and Alice stood by, shaking her head sorrowfully and binding him tighter with a long rope. Somewhere, the scene changed and Bull became the man at the registration center, shaking his head slowly while Tommy tried to explain his objections and a steady stream of bombs rained down on the crowd outside that was yelling for his blood, unmindful of the destruction falling on them.

Dawn was barely breaking when he was awakened. "Wanted in the front office, Dorn," the messenger announced. "Make it snappy!"

He tumbled into his clothes awkwardly, grunting as the cloth rubbed on sore places or his head moved, setting up centers of pain. Jimmy, under him, was also pulling on his work clothes. "Probably Bull kicked up some lie. I'll go along to set it straight. Okay?"

"Thanks, Jimmy." They stumbled out of the dark barracks and along the row of one-story buildings, wondering what had gotten the director up at this hour of the morning. Inside the office, the messenger blinked sleepy eyes at seeing two, but pointed to a room at the right and went back to his coffee. It wasn't the director's office.

"Thomas Dorn, registry 4784?" A gray-clad, grimly pleasant officer of the Air Force was sitting at the desk. "Good; and you?"

"A friend of mine," Tommy answered.

"Umm, okay; no time for arguing fine points—" He looked at Tommy's face, now well over normal size, and his eyebrows went up. "I thought you hated fighting; we've got you down as a conscientious objector."

"I do hate it—and this doesn't help it any."

"Can't say I blame you there. Sure you're still objecting, or didn't you hear about New York last night?" He noted the boy's curt nod, frowning slightly, and picked up a sheaf of papers. "Well, that's none of my business, exactly. We've got you listed as a rocket plane pilot, though, and that is. How many hours, what type of plane?"

"My own Lightning Special, late model—confiscated now. I guess I've had it up a thousand hours after completing full instructions. Why, sir?"

The man's eyebrows went up and he whistled. "*Wheeoo*, your folks *really* had money! No matter; wish we had ten thousand with the same experience. Those planes over New York were rockets. By sheer dumb luck we managed to get one down in good shape, half its load still inside; keep that to yourself for a couple of days—with the blanket on, we're not being too careful about secrecy, but there's no use spreading it before it's official. In two weeks, the way we're organized now, we'll be turning out better rockets; and better bombs, too. Centralia isn't the only one with atomic explosives. She just used hers before we were quite ready with ours. Get the idea?"

Tommy got it; his experience with the tricky rocket planes was in advance of all but a few others, and his objection was for "reasons of personal belief," which was a borderline case at best. His lips set as firmly as the swelling would permit, and the officer noticed the blanching of his skin.

"To be frank with you, Dorn, I wouldn't take you; whatever your reasons, I'm afraid your mental attitude would make you worse than useless. But I can't speak for the higher-ups."

Jimmy stirred beside him, coughing for attention. "I've had a little preliminary rocket training—all I could afford. Wouldn't that help, sir?"

"Sure, but . . . Oh, the leg! Afraid they haven't loosened up that much yet! I'll make a bargain with you, though, young man; you get your friend to change his ideas so he'll be of some real use to us, and I'll see you get in, rules or no rules. Okay, that's all; I've got a hundred other calls to run off and no time to do it in. Back to barracks!"

It was a lovely world, Tommy thought; when things began to look better and you found someone who'd treat you like a human being, all this happened. Beaten up, probably made ridiculous to Alice, one mass of aching bruises, and now this! The sickness that had been in him during the fight had been worse on the surface, but underneath it disturbed him far less than the half-threat of the officer's words. They couldn't take him into their war! And yet—

"Well, start converting," he said bitterly.

Jimmy shook his head, his eyes on the ground. "I'd give both legs for the chance, Tommy, if they cut 'em off an inch at a time; but I'm no good at proselyting. It's no use— Dammit, why couldn't we have swapped bodies? Why does everything have to be cockeyed for both of us?"

Tommy had no answer, and his mind simply ran around in futile circles as the breakfast was finished and the long grind at the machine began. He noticed casually that Bull Travis chose another table and was unusually quiet, but the fact barely registered; the bully was no longer important, nor was the wearying, unaccustomed work. And under it all was the question of whether Alice had seen the brawl the night before, and what her thoughts of him were. Maybe he wouldn't go up there tonight.

But night found him stopped beside the bush from which Bull had sprung, putting out a hand to his friend's arm. "Come on up if you want to, Jimmy."

"Thanks, no. I came up to be alone and do some thinking, and I guess you'll be better off without me. See you at eleven." He headed down a side trail, whistling drearily between his teeth on one note, while Tommy went ahead alone, torn between hope and fear, with a dull lethargy numbing both feelings. Anyhow, she probably wouldn't come.

"Hello, Tommy." She was already there, ahead of him, and rose as he drew near. "You're early, too, aren't you?"

So she hadn't seen! Or had she? "How long did you watch last night?"

"Long enough! Oh, Tommy, it was splendid! I was afraid at first, but when I saw you knock him down the second time, I knew you were all right. I wanted to run down and tell you how glad I was, but I was afraid of being late at the barracks. Your poor face!" There was pity in her look, but as he drew closer to her, her eyes were glowing proudly. He glanced back toward the spot, realizing how easily she could have made the mistake in the tricky shadows of the moonlight.

"I didn't do it. Jimmy Lake, the boy I mentioned, did that. And he's a cripple!"

"Oh." She said it without intonation. Then with a shrug: "I'm glad you told me the truth, Tommy. You didn't bring your violin?"

"Broken." That had hurt, when he'd discovered it, more than the physical blows to himself, and then had disappeared into the larger worries. "Broken, like everything else in the world!"

"Come here, Tommy. Now—what's the matter?" She pulled him down beside her, putting his head on her lap and brushing back his hair with soft, cool fingers. And, as there has always been, there was magic in it to draw out the troubles and break up the barriers to free expression. She made soft little sounds of sympathy and attention, but otherwise let him tell the story of the morning's interview, his fears, and everything else, without interruptions.

Finally he stopped, and she considered it, her hand still moving softly. "But do you think it's fair, Tommy? I mean, under it all, you must realize that whether you fight or not, others will; aren't you counting on their fighting to protect you and your ideal? If there were no one else, wouldn't you have to fight? You at least tried to, last night."

"I tried to run away, only he wouldn't let me! Alice, I can't reason with this; you can't. It's all inside me. Probably father was right, and it's cowardice that makes me act this way, not conviction; I don't know even that."

"I wonder if a coward would have admitted it was Jimmy who beat up that bully? Or would I feel this close to a boy I knew was a coward? . . . Someone should whip that father of yours; he let your books do all the raising, and did nothing to help you understand the reality and solidity of the world—and then quit you without trying to correct that when you didn't give him reason to boast to his friends. The fault's with his own selfish carelessness, not with you. Tommy!" Her voice was suddenly urgent.

"Uhh?"

"I wouldn't worry about fighting. They'll need instructors more than fliers, even. That would be all right, wouldn't it, and they'd be satisfied with that?"

It wouldn't—but the relief and gratitude her words brought shot through him like wine, and pure impulse lifted his head off her lap and toward her; she bent forward to meet him, unquestioningly, and the uncertain awkwardness of their inexperience was half the sweetness of it.

Jimmy approached them later, unseen until a twig crackled under his heavy step. "Tommy, it's eleven. Oh, sorry, miss. I thought—"

"It's all right, really. I should have gone before. . . . Jimmy, isn't it? I'd like to tell you what I think of you for what happened, but there isn't time now." She was on her feet, glancing at her own watch, then leaning forward half shyly for a brief good night. "Tomorrow, Tommy—and bring Jimmy if he'll come."

They watched her run down the trail to the old rock, waving as she glanced back before disappearing. Jimmy glanced at his friend, pleased surprise on his face. "She's certainly done you a lot of good, fellow. You're lucky!"

Tommy felt lucky, now. "More than you think, even. Funny how important those barracks and workshops appear in the moonlight; ours, too."

"Yeah, I heard they were going to give them a coat of moon paint tomorrow. They look *too* important, and after last night, nobody's so sure what's safe. Come on, we'll catch the deuce if we don't hurry."

It was a far-off, dim roar at first, coming forward much too rapidly and from too high up. Their heads jerked up toward the cloudless sky. "Planes . . . they can't be!"

"Speak of Satan! Must be bound for Chicago! Picking 'em off in order of size. Tommy!"

He'd seen it, too. A speck that separated from the others, cutting down and growing larger in a fishing streak that dipped, lifted slightly, and dipped again behind them, the roar of its climb following. Something glinted over the barracks roof, and then there were no barracks or workshops! Tommy dropped into the depression beside them, dragging Jimmy with him and burying his face in the ground. But it was scant protection, and the lashing of light and things not seen but felt reached out even to the two on the hillside, a radiation that seemed to burn through everything and was almost tangible; even after the first violence had abated, leaving only normal fires and heat behind amid the ruins, their bones and teeth seemed to itch, and their flesh to tingle savagely. It must be mostly imagination; they'd escaped the worst of the radiation. Or maybe it was the effect of the ground shock.

Jimmy came to his feet uncertainly. "Back! Up the hill! We're too close now, and we can't get nearer. There's nothing left down there. Nothing. That second dip must have been for the women's section!"

"Alice!" Tommy's legs felt the weakness in them again, gone almost at once. And then he was running, feeling nothing but a horrid numb urgency. The hilltop seemed to crawl at him, and he was unsure whether he was running or falling down the other side until his hand hit the boulder and tossed him off into the side trail. Waves of heat radiation were beating at him, but he was unaware of the danger as he careened down the pathway, almost stumbling over her before he could stop.

"Alice!"

"Tommy! I—help me! No, go back! This radiation—it's weaker now, but—"

"Hush." His arms swung down under her, gently but rapidly lifting her to his shoulder with a strength that came from outside him, and he turned back up the pathway, unmindful of fatigue or the laboring of his breath. There was a cleft in the rocks near the top where they'd be shielded from radiation on both sides, and he headed for it as rapidly as he could force himself.

Her face was grayish, pain-filled, already worse than it had been below, and she was limp as he put her down. But she wasn't dead yet; her heart was still fluttering as he jerked forward to listen, and he could hear the erratic gasping sound her breathing made. Minutes went ticking by as he stood staring at her, trying to remember the nearest doctor, torn between the need of staying and the urge to get out searching for help.

Jimmy's uncertain steps broke in on him, reminding him suddenly that he was not alone. "Bad?"

"Where's the nearest doctor? She's got to have attention!"

"Planes of some sort just spilled down as close to the women's camp as they could get—must be medical aid there. Here, give me a hand; we can carry her faster than we can bring them back. If we cut over the hill and around, we'll keep out of the worst of the stuff coming out of there."

"No." Tommy gathered her up, his mind steady again now that there was something he could do without leaving her. "Go ahead, Jimmy, start them coming back to meet me. I can carry her that far. Can you stand it?"

"The leg'll hold up that far." He was off, his hands grabbing at the undergrowth to steady him, his clumsy leaps sending back crashing sounds to mark his path. Tommy started forward, considering a shortcut and rejecting it; even if he could take whatever radiation was left, he dared not risk her in it. Grimly he forced himself to a pace that he could maintain with his burden, checking back the impulse to run, trying to take up all the bobbing of his steps with his legs and avoid jarring her.

The sound of the other's progress ahead dimmed out and vanished, eaten away by the growing distance between them, and he pumped on stolidly, the skin around his eyes tautened, his mouth pulled back into a tense, straight line. Under the cold and numbness of his surface mind, a fever of thought trickled back and forth in time to his steps, sorting, rejecting, deciding. And step by step, the hill crawled behind him, the undergrowth thinned out, and he was in a shallow ravine that led in the general direction of the three Air Force planes he had glimpsed off to the side of the flaming ruins of the workshop.

Vaguely, he wondered at the speed with which they'd learned of the disaster and come out in a hopeless effort to help. But the thought and the relief at their presence were lost in the shuffle of his feet, the tick of thoughts in his head, and the leaden ache that was creeping up his arms and shoulders from the burden he carried. He bent forward for the hundredth time, found her still breathing, and went on woodenly.

Crackling twigs gave warning, but only seconds before he saw the men with stretchers coming toward him at a slow trot. "Down here

. . . that's it. All right, you men, gently but snap into it! And you, kid, get onto the other one! If you walk another step, you'll be a hospital case yourself!"

Tommy let them lay him on it, not bothering to protest; now that the compulsion was gone, his muscles were slack, his breath rasping in his ears, and his mouth dry and burning. For the moment, there was nothing he could do, and his body grabbed hungrily at the chance to rest on the swaying canvas, though there was no relief for his mind.

Jimmy found him later, his own face drawn with the fatigue of his efforts, and sank down onto the log. "What news?"

"They don't know; this is all new, it seems. They've had experience only with laboratory cases." They'd taken her inside the big hospital plane, turning him back with gentle but firm words and a promise to call him as soon as they could. Now all he could do was sit and wait, trying to hope in spite of the looks they'd given her. "I appreciate—"

"Skip it, Tommy!"

The sound of another step brought their eyes up, and Tommy was looking into the face of the Air Force captain who'd interviewed him that morning—seeming years ago. The man put a hand on his shoulder, sliding down onto the log beside him. "That took guts, Dorn! I guess I owe you an apology for what I was thinking. Mind my talking?"

"No; go ahead, sir." He wouldn't mind anything that would fill the time and take even a little of his mind off what must be happening inside the plane. "I didn't expect you here, though."

"Handiest pilot when we heard of this! At that, there's been nothing we could do to help. And we'll forget that 'sir' business; you're not military. The name's Kent. Seems they got Chicago."

"Already?"

"Those things travel! Tomorrow, or tonight, we'll actually get started evacuating all the large cities, I suppose, but we need a miracle to hold them off two weeks more. Maybe, if—" He dropped whatever he had in mind. "You'd hate an automatic commission for your air hours, you know, Dorn."

"I know . . . Captain Kent, she—in there—suggested I might be valuable to you as an instructor." He shook his head as the other started a quick assent. "But it would be the same thing, killing or teaching others to kill. I can't do even that."

"Then all this hasn't changed your mind?"

"No. Maybe you were right, and cowardice had something to do with it at first, but there was more than that." He couldn't put it into words, the thought that had worked itself out as he'd walked down the hill, and he made no particular effort. "At first, I guess I'd wanted to kill for what they'd done, but that's gone now. Killing isn't right, and hatred doesn't make it more so."

"Umm. 'An eye for an eye'—all right, that's Old Testament; how about Matthew? 'I come not upon Earth to send peace, but a sword—' "

" 'And a man's foes shall be they of his own household.' It won't do any good, Captain. Coming down from there, I wanted to convince myself I should fight. I couldn't."

Captain Kent nodded thoughtfully, passing a cigarette across to each of them as he turned it over in his head. "Ever seen a robin go after another bird menacing its nest? It's pretty much a law of nature that life will kill to defend its own; maybe you don't have relatives in danger—but there's the girl."

"Is bombing women and children over there a defense?"

"I think so. Time after time, the tribal pride—the pride of the Holy Roman Empire of the Teutonic Tribes, whose legate walked before kings—has brought this about. Doesn't something pretty drastic seem justified against those repeated assaults on the freedom of others?"

There was neither stubborness nor agreement on Tommy's face as he shook his head silently, and the other shrugged faintly, admitting defeat. The three sat in silence, studying the ground or the door to the hospital plane, each with his own thoughts, each with a cigarette unnoticed in his hand. Tommy sighed slowly; somewhere, in his emotional mind, he'd been begging to be convinced of the other's rightness, but the arguments were too old to offer any hope.

Above them, there was a low muffled drone that grew into a thunder with a speed that could mean only one thing. The captain's eyes came up first, spotting the bluish streaks that split the sky miles above the earth and came roaring back from the horizon. "Damn them! They think we're helpless—so helpless they're coming back over our defenses deliberately, just as they went out! Now, if—"

With a sudden short cry, he grabbed at the arms of the two others, jerking them back toward the distant ravine, his eyes still turned on the spot of blue fire that came slipping out from the others, downward toward them, cutting the miles in fractions of seconds. Then he stopped, realizing the uselessness of flight. "My God! They've spotted our planes in the glare of that ruin! What damned fools we were! . . . No, listen!"

Another sound had cut in, even over the roar of their rockets, higher, shriller, and a streak seemed to shoot off the ground near the horizon and halve the distance in the time it took their eyes to focus, knifing aside the air with a shrill whine. Two others followed, apparently spotted by the Centralian force, for the rocket that had been diving reversed in a thundering blast toward the others. Three streaks moved in toward the group of a hundred, spreading apart as they came, while Centralia's craft bunched and began a gigantic circle to bring them face to face. Somehow, the maneuver was a slow wheel of contempt for the trio that dared to question their right to the stratosphere.

Kent's voice was awed and proud, ridiculously hopeful in spite of the odds. "They did it! They couldn't, but there they are!"

"Atomic rockets?" Jimmy's voice held the same awe.

"Yes. We've licked the inflexibility of mass production; we knew that. But I still don't see how they did it. This morning, those were standard fuel rockets, and the atomic tubes were just coming off the drafting boards. They couldn't shape them—"

His voice choked back as one of the three vanished in a huge sheet of fire that seemed to run across the sky, long before the sound could reach them from the distance. Kent groaned, understanding coming into his eyes.

"They didn't. They've simply jury-rigged the tubes from the captured ship into three of ours; God knows what kind of wire they're using to hold those engines inside our ships. That's what they were talking about, then! No wonder they move like that; they don't weigh a quarter of what those tubes were designed for. And inside, they must be packed with our own atomic bombs."

"The explosion—"

Kent waited for the roar that had finally reached them to cease. "No, *our* bombs are stable, except when we set them off; that was the rocket engine smashing up."

Tommy struggled with the idea, his eyes trying to follow the specks that were edged toward the side horizon, almost out of sight. "But what can bombs do against them?"

"Watch!" Even as he spoke, they could just make out the two flares of their own remaining ships suddenly streaking forward into the thick of the enemy swarm. This time, the spread of flame flickered slightly, but they were forced to cover their eyes before it reached full intensity, and when they looked again there was only an empty sky with a few streaks still falling toward the flames that seemed to shoot up from the ground, just out of sight.

"Suicide squad!" Jimmy's face gleamed, as did the captain's, washed with too many emotions for understanding.

"That's it. Somehow, before the rather slim defense of the others could get them, ours got close enough; their bombs were unstable—when ours were set off near them, it spread. Well, there's our miracle; they can't have had time to build more than those we saw, and those are . . . well, 'with the snows of yesteryear,' I guess it goes. That gives us the two weeks we need. My darned luck!"

His face twitched into a crooked smile at their looks. "The rocket men had a lottery this noon for some special volunteers to get themselves killed off on a forlorn hope. The three up there won it. If I'd had another hour, I might have talked one into selling his chance—maybe. Dorn?"

"Yes, sir." They were back on the log that served as a bench again, where he could watch the door of the big ship, and he answered without moving his eyes.

"The higher-ups gave me full authority to do as I liked about your case and a few others; I was going to tell you before all this came up. I'm sending you to a camp out in the Middle West where you'll be with a bunch of other unquestioned objectors; you'll probably be better off there than in any of the work camps around here."

It took a few seconds for that to penetrate. "You mean you aren't going to force me to fight?"

"We don't force people here, fellow, not when they're on the level. Look, the nurse wants you. Go on, and I hope it's good news."

The nurse shook her head faintly as he ran toward her, motioning him back into the ship and toward the cot. Alice was lying there, her eyes open and on him, and with the medical staff gathered at the opposite end of the plane. The change in her face, even from what he'd last seen, was frightening, but a smile lifted the corners of her mouth weakly. "Tommy!"

"Alice! You'll be all right? You've got to be!"

"Shh!" She caught his hand with a feeble movement, drawing him closer. "It's no use; I can feel myself going. Tommy, you're not afraid now! I can see it—that and other things. It's all going to work out right, isn't it?"

"Everything except you!" He could see the shadow on her face, knew the uselessness of anything doctors could do, and knelt down to the cot, cradling her head into his arms, feeling the need of tears that could not come, his soul wrenched half out of him toward her.

"Don't feel bad for me, honey. I don't." But pain came shooting over her then, cutting off her bravery, flooding into her expression with nothing either could do to stop it. She gasped harshly, clinging to him, fighting futilely. "Tommy? I don't want to die—when I've just found you. Don't let me die! Kiss me quick, Tommy, before—"

There was time enough for that, mercifully, and mercifully no more. Dry-eyed still, he groped his way out of the ship, blurred landscape reeling before him, until Jimmy's hand found his arm and guided him silently to the log. His grief was cold and hard inside him, unexpressible outwardly. Then, as the minutes dragged on, the waves of it washed slowly further into his mind, colder and harder than ever, but leaving him free to grope through the jumbled ideas that had been forming.

He should have told her, perhaps, yet somehow she'd known. He'd seen the knowledge on her face, before the pain forced it away.

"We don't force people, here." Over there, they did—forced them or shot them. Now, for the first time since it had begun, he was free, free from the compulsion to fight against their intrusion into his rights and belief, free to take the facts as they came, without the taint of oppression. And the decision had come to him, almost with the freedom, so that it must have been on his face, visible to her. Knowledge had been in her look—knowledge and pride in him.

"What happened to the captain, Jimmy? Has he gone?"

"Not yet. Why, pal?"

Maybe it wasn't logic. It didn't sound logical to fight and protest for his rights until they were given to him, then toss them away. Or maybe it was the highest kind of logic, the kind that could find the real value of the facts and realize that a country where your freedom not to fight was respected was a country worth fighting for, so that those who came after could hate that fighting without seeing it swarm over their lives again. Men had always had to fight for their beliefs, even the belief that fighting was wrong. Maybe the two sayings from the Bible didn't contradict, after all. He came not upon Earth to send peace, but a sword; until the meek should inherit the Earth, someday.

He got to his feet then, Jimmy at his side, and started after the captain. "I just remembered that he agreed to take you if you convinced me, Jimmy. I think we'd better remind him of it."

My original plan was that the young man in the story was to have become immortal as a result of the radiation he received. (Such miracles were not uncommon in science fiction.) He was next to appear in a story near the end of the war, hardened and bitter, to begin finding his way through a very ugly world. I had a set of changing cultures mapped out, with him as the only unchanging thing in the world, culminating with it all about to start over again when Mars and Earth begin the first interplanetary war.

But I never went on. Series, so far as I was concerned, were no different from sequels. I couldn't work up much interest in a character after I'd mined his emotions once.

About all I can say in defense of the story now is that it's the first one I know which emphasized the radiation danger of a nuclear bomb more than the mere blast effect. But I grossly underestimated the dangers, I'm afraid.

Science fiction writers were generally pretty well aware of developments in atomics up to the beginning of the war. And quite a few of us could make pretty shrewd guesses about what was going on, based largely on the very secrecy blanket that was supposed to fool us. One tip-off came when the FBI began investigating a story by Cleve Cartmill which gave a rough description of the trigger of the bomb. (It was a big secret—so big that several of us had independently figured how it had to work.) They even questioned Paul Orban, who'd illustrated the story. But Campbell was successful in convincing the investigators that cutting off stories about atomic power in science fiction would blow the secret much more completely than any fiction could, so we had a good deal of freedom after that.

My own story, "Nerves," dealt with industrial atomics, quite different from the work on the bomb. Yet, according to a scientist who worked at Oak Ridge, the story was classified and filed as "Top Secret." She discovered this when she went in to read that issue in the library and found that her clearance wasn't high enough to permit her to have it. So, of course, she walked outside to a newsstand and bought her copy!

I was a little disappointed when the September issue appeared with the story. I'd been pretty sure that I'd get the cover. But instead, that was devoted to a time travel story by Anthony Boucher, who later became editor of *The Magazine of Fantasy and Science Fiction*. But it all worked out well in the long run. The readers voted a straight

1.000 rating to "Nerves," which meant that they'd been unanimous in placing it first in the issue. (I can remember only one other story winning that kind of praise.) It should have proved to me that the careful method I'd used in writing it was the right one for me, but I still haven't quite learned that. The story was usually picked as my best by readers, and many still choose it. In 1956, I finally added some of the material I'd had for my background and turned it into a novel for *Ballantine*. It's now being reprinted again. And Tony Boucher demonstrated what a marvelous gentleman he was by telling his side of our contest for first place, saying that the best story had won, and then going on to give the book a most generous review.

"Lunar Landing" didn't fare so well. There was sort of a running battle among four novelettes in that issue, and none seemed to emerge as clear winner. I think mine placed third, eventually. At that, the readers may have been being generous, since some of the other stories were excellent ones.

Campbell's letters began to be a little more insistent about why I should write more at that time. A lot of his best writers were either in the Armed Forces or doing some kind of war work, with little time to write. He was turning up new talent—but much of that new talent was soon also pulled away by the war. He needed all the work he could get by his regulars.

He was also worried that he might be drafted into some war activity and was hinting pretty broadly that I would have a very good chance of taking over for him if I'd be a good boy and turn out a lot of copy to impress the front office. I was immune to that bait, however. Most writers seem to have a compulsion to become editors, but I never wanted that sort of work. I did become an editor about ten years later—with four magazines under my various pen names; but I took the job reluctantly and quit most happily. I can edit competently, but I'll never be half the man for the job that Campbell was, and I don't enjoy doing anything half well by my own standards.

I finally did write a short story for him when he insisted. And that was the result of pure inspiration.

I've heard a lot about inspiration, but seldom from regular writers. Yet apparently it can hit at rare intervals. I didn't really believe in it until it hit me.

I was going out one night to get a hamburger. My foot was just on the top step of the stairs. And somewhere between there and the bottom, a total story popped into my mind, complete with how I wanted to tell it, the feeling of it, and everything. I went out and had my snack, and it was still there when I came back. So I pulled my typewriter out and wrote it—4,300 words in less than an hour and a half, and almost no work!

I called it "Whom the Gods Love," and it earned a bonus.

15.

Whom the Gods Love

(by Lester del Rey)

At first glance, the plane appeared normal enough, though there was no reason for its presence on the rocky beach of the islet. But a second inspection would have shown the wreckage that had been an undercarriage and the rows of holes that crisscrossed its sides. Forward, the engine seemed unharmed, but one wing flopped slowly up and down in the brisk breeze that was blowing, threatening to break completely away with each movement. Except for the creak and groan of the wing, the island was as silent as the dead man inside the plane.

Then the sun crept up a little higher over the horizon, throwing back the shadows that had concealed the figure of a second man who lay sprawled out limply on the sand, still in the position his body had taken when he made the last-second leap. In a few places, ripped sections of his uniform showed the mark of passing bullets, and blood had spilled out of a half-inch crease in his shoulder. But somehow he had escaped all serious injuries except one; centered in his forehead, a small neat hole showed, its edges a mottle of blue and reddish brown, with a trickle of dried blood spilling down over his nose and winding itself into a half moustache over his lip. There was no mark to show that the bullet had gone on through the back of his head.

Now, as the warmth of the sun crept down to the islet, the seemingly dead figure stirred and groaned softly, one hand groping up toward the hole in his forehead. Uncertainly, he thrust a finger into the hole, then withdrew it at the flood of pain that followed the motion. For minutes he lay there, feeling the ebb and flow of the great forces that were all around him, sensing their ceaseless beat with the shadow of curiosity. Then his eyes opened to see the flapping wing of the plane, and he noticed that it was outside the rhythm of the forces that moved. His eyes followed its outlines, then pierced through the pitted covering and made out the form of the corpse within.

It lay sprawled there, stiff and rigid, and within it was none of the small trickle of energy that coursed through his own body. Yet there was something familiar about the still form. A vagrant whim of his mind caused the corpse to pull itself around with one stiff hand until he could see its face—or rather, what had been its face. Then, after comparing it with his own, he found no resemblance and let the body slide back into silence. About him the little eddies of force resumed their routine, no longer perturbed by the impulses that had gone out of his mind toward them.

He turned his head then, glancing over the little island and out toward the sea, wondering if all the world was like this. It seemed empty and not a little ridiculous, but there was nothing to show otherwise. He wondered vaguely whether he had come there newly or had always lain there; and a further wonder came to him as he looked at the plane again. It was out of keeping with the rest of the island, and since its type was different, he assumed that it had come there from elsewhere. Inside it, the corpse reminded him that it had not come alone. Well, then, probably he had come with it. Perhaps the still figure inside would stir to life under the rays of the sun, as he had. He clutched at the passing forces again, twisting them in a way he did not understand, and the limbs of the dead man lifted him and brought him out into the sunlight on all fours.

For minutes, the living man stared down at the other figure, but tired of it when he saw no signs of warming into life. Perhaps he was an accident and the other was the normal form of his kind. Or perhaps the other had offended the forces around and they had drained themselves out of him. It was of no importance.

Again he looked upward, watching the dancing paths of the light from the sun, and as he bent his head the *wrong* feeling inside it grew greater. Slowly he lifted his hand, but that motion caused none of the racing pain, so it was not that movement itself involved the feeling. Perhaps it was the hole in his head. Gently with his fingers he pressed the edges of the hole together, drawing the skin out over it until it was healed; it helped the little surface pain, but made no change in the inner agony. Apparently the forces of life were painful—no matter, then; since the pain was obviously a part of him, he must accept it. Noting the tear in his shoulder, he forced that closed again with his fingers, then glanced back at the sky.

Above, a bird wheeled slowly over the sea, and he watched it move, noticing in it the same stirring life that he sensed in himself, but without the awareness of the forces about. On an impulse, he willed it to him, reaching out as the little form slipped down and forward. Behind it came a crack as the air exploded back into the hole its passage had torn; the bird was a sodden mass as he felt it, warm but inanimate, and he tossed it aside in sudden disgust.

And still the wing of the plane flapped awkwardly in the wind, and his eyes slid back to it again, his mind remembering the beat of the bird's wings. He reeled toward it, his steps uncertain, until the effort displeased him and he lifted himself upward on the waves around him and slipped forward easily toward the plane. Vague memories stirred in his head, and his thorax contracted in a strange yearning feeling toward this great dead bird. It was wounded also, and its head was filled with a strange rock that made it sluggish. Gently he pulled out the engine, first causing the bolts and holding part to drop away, and put it aside on the sand; his eyes went to the guns, but the little eddy of memory told him to leave them, and he obeyed, though he pulled away the landing gear and tossed it beside the engine and broken propeller. One by one he pressed the holes in the sides together and let the broken skin of the wing grow back, as his shoulder had done. The other wing was stiff, paralyzed, apparently holding the machine down by its uselessness, so he looked inside to find it filled with unjointed struts; with his elbow for a model, he corrected the error in the machine, standing back in approval as that wing also began moving gently up and down.

There had been no purpose in his actions beyond an idle kindliness, but now he considered the plane and the bleak sea and sky beyond the islet; over the horizon lay other lands, perhaps, since the bird had come from that direction. And out there might be others like himself who could explain the mystery of existence. Surely there was a reason for it, since the mothering forces of the cosmos about him were moving purposefully, in ordered pattern, except when his will disturbed them. And since he could mold them, surely he was greater even than they, and his purpose must be higher. He started to rise and glide forward on the wings of those forces, but the plane below him called him back, filled with an odd desire for it. It, too, seemed to want to leave, and he let himself drop inside it, down onto the seat that was before his eyes. Then, responsive to his desire, the forces eddied into it, the wings lifted resolutely and beat down together, and it lifted up and away, the little island dropping from sight behind him.

But as his attention wandered, it fluttered unevenly and began to fall, calling him back to the need of supervising. That should not be so. Once begun, the plane was supposed to go ahead on its own—memory assured him of that. And obediently the forces slid back, gliding over the surface of the ship, becoming a part of it. This time, as his mind wandered, the wings beat on in a smooth rush, the plane answering without thought to his uncertain twist of the wheel. That was better. His arms made movements on the controls almost instinctively, and now the ship obeyed them, its passage silent except for the keening of the air as it forced its way ahead.

He sent it up higher and still higher, but below him the sea stretched out in seeming endlessness. Finally his breath began to come hard, and the air to thin out, though the forces grew thicker and stronger. For a little while he let them push against the air inside the cabin to thicken it and climbed on, but increasing height began to make objects hard to see below, and he dropped back, returning to his straight line. The needle on the compass pointed due north.

The sun was in the middle of the sky when the vague feeling inside him brought visions to his mind, and he recognized the need of food. There were several mental pictures, some sharp, some vague, and he selected an apple and ham sandwich at random, solidifying the pictures of them and eating. The first bite was flat, tasteless stuff, but his senses recognized the error and his mind brought the cosmic forces into play, correcting them as he chewed. The other urge was heightened instead of removed, but it was an hour later before he recognized it as a need of water and drank deeply from the fountain that appeared for a time over the wheel. Later, the empty cigarette package on the floor caught his eye and he filled it, along with the bottle that had held brandy. With his needs satisfied, he settled back, letting the ship forge lazily ahead.

A thousand feet below him, the water stretched on in apparent endlessness, but he was in no hurry. Aside from the pain in his head, the world was good, and that had become so much a part of his thoughts that he scarcely noticed it. The sun crept down slowly toward the horizon, slipping through the few cloud banks.

Something about that awakened a half memory in him; the sun was partly in the clouds, just touching the water, and sending out streamers of light. Somewhere he had seen that before, and a savage snarl came into his throat instinctively as his hand went up to the place where the hole had been in his forehead. A sun with fixed rays from it, painted on something—and a thing to be hated! He pinned the idea in his memory as darkness began slipping over the ocean, and he brought the ship to a stop, letting its wings hold it motionless over the sea. With the coming of night, there was no purpose in continuing his search, but he'd remember that banner if he found it during the day. In the meantime, he chose to eat and drink again, then curl himself up in the air and go to sleep.

It was a sharp spattering sound that brought him out of his sleep and sent him falling toward the floor of the cabin before he could catch his thoughts. Then another burst of sound came rushing toward him, and the sides of the ship suddenly sprouted a series of holes like those he'd removed the day before, while metal slugs shot by over him. With an action governed by sheer conditioned reflex, he was up and into the control seat, wheeling the ship about before his mind had evaluated the situation.

Ahead of him now appeared five ships of somewhat different design, all coming in sharply toward him. With part of his brain he deflected the all-pervading forces, cutting off the rain of bullets by denying to himself their ability to reach him or the ship. With the rest, he was trying to understand and failing. In the thoughts of the little olive men out there he could read hatred and fear, and a desire to kill, though he had done nothing against them. Then the gently fluttering wings of his ship beat down savagely in response to his demands and threw him forward toward them.

Horror sprawled through the thoughts of his enemies, superstition accompanying it. For a split second, they sat glued to their controls, eyes focused on his beating wings, and then they lifted as one man and went streaking up and away. As they passed, he saw the device of the sun and rays on the planes, and the hatred he'd felt before welled over him, driving back all voluntary thought. The wings of his plane beat harder, drumming the air in resounding beats, but the ships were back at him again before he could rise, superstition still strong, but the desire to kill stronger.

Then his eyes lit on the gun controls, and memory stirred again, telling him that death came from such things. He gripped them fiercely, but nothing happened! With a frown, he tried again, then drove his vision down and into the weapons to find there were none of the little metal slugs that should be there. And the shadow of memory reminded him that they had all been used before, when he'd been forced down onto the little island by such men as these. They—

The clouded mind refused to go on, but the hatred stirred and writhed inside him, even while the bullets came spattering toward him, broke against the barrier he still held, and went hurtling down uselessly. Then one of the other ships came swooping forward, straight toward him, its purpose of ramming him plain in the enemy's mind!

The guns *must* work! And then they were working. Little blue lights collected in drops and went scooting out toward the end of the guns, to streak forward in a straight line. He brought the sights up on the hurtling ship, and blue fire sped forward to meet it, to fuse with it, and to leave the air empty of both plane and light, only a thunderous sound remaining.

It was too much for the sons of the Rising Sun. A roar came from their motors and they dived under him, heading south in a group, the tumult of their propellers pitched to their highest limit. But he had no intention of letting them get away; they had attacked him without warning, and they must pay.

His wings were beating the air savagely now, and he let the ship jerk around on its tail, heading after the four ships. The hate in his mind gripped at the forces about, driving him forward in a rush that left a constant clap of thunder behind him as the air came together again in his wake. But he had learned from the crushed bird, and held a cushion of air with him to save his ship. Then the four remaining ships were before his sights again, and the little blue drops coalesced and ran down the barrels to go scooting forward hungrily. The air was suddenly clear ahead of him.

Still his wings drummed on furiously. They had turned south, and in their minds had been pictures of others of their kind in that direction. Very well, he would find them! At thirty thousand feet he leveled off and solidified a young roast turkey and a glass of water, but his face was grim as he ate, and his eyes were leveled at the sea below. The things he had seen in the mind of the enemy officer had been reason enough for their elimination, enough without the knowledge that there were others of his kind somewhere whom these little yellow men were killing and torturing, still others toward whom they were marshaling their might.

The blue drops of light ran together and formed into a bigger ball at the muzzle of one gun as he thought. Finally the ball dropped, jerking downward at a speed beyond the pull of gravity, and the ocean spouted up to meet it, then fell back in a boiling explosion that sent huge waves thundering outward. He paid it no attention, and the waves fell behind.

The last of the turkey was still in his fingers as he spied them below and near the horizon—a swarm of midges that must be planes, and below them larger objects that pushed over the water and left turbulent paths in the sea. There were many of them, moving slowly ahead, with the swarm of planes spread out to cover a great distance around them. He wasted no time in counting, but clutched the controls and sent his ship down in a swooping rush that brought the planes before his sights. The blue light gathered and went ahead, and he was rushing on through the space the enemy had occupied, questing for more. At first they were kind, and rallied into a group to meet him, but those that were left were wiser.

He swung in a great circle, taking them as he could find them, hoping that he could get them all before the last could disappear from his sight. Those that dropped down frantically toward the surface vessels below he disregarded, and seeing that, the others dived. It was a matter of minutes until the air was clear, except for the larger missiles that came arching up from the craft on the sea.

One found him, and it carried more force than the bullets for which his shield was designed. He had only time to deflect it, and to throw a band of force around it before it exploded. Then it was gone, leaving a gaping hole on each side of the cabin, a couple of feet behind him. He knew that no shield he could control would protect him long against any great quantity of such, and lifted his wings upward, rising rapidly and collecting a reservoir of air about him to meet his needs in the level toward which he was climbing.

The vessels below were scattering now, and he noted staccato bursts of a wave force coming from them, but it was harmless and he guessed that it was some kind of signal. The air about was filled with that force, too, though much weaker than the ships were sending out, but it seemed of no other use. He disregarded it, continuing up until sixty thousand feet stood between him and the ships under him.

Then he tilted the nose of his plane, bringing it downward, and hung suspended while he let the blue light collect. From this height the sights were useless, but there were other ways of controlling it; as each globe grew to the desired size, he released it, guiding it down with his mind, stopping it above the ships, and directing it toward the one he had chosen as a target. Even at the distance he remained, the chaos of terror below reached up to him, and he grinned savagely. There was some unknown debt he owed them, and he was paying it now. Ships were foundering in the waves that leaped from the disappearance of others, but he gave no heed to their condition as the blue globes dropped downward. And at last, reluctantly, he dropped to search for more prey and found them gone, except for two small boats that had been lowered and had mysteriously not been harmed. In them the occupants were dead; the cosmic forces he had used were not too kind to living flesh when out of control, even at a distance. They were powers that molded suns.

Perhaps there were more targets ahead. He had had no time to glean information from their minds, but there was a chance, and he went on winging south, though more slowly, relaxed at the controls. His head was numb and heavy now, and he was covered with sweat from the efforts of the past half hour. He knew that the energy he used was only a weak and insignificant thing, a faint impulse in his mind that reached out and controlled other forces which in turn modulated the great forces of the universe; they alone could yield the energy needed. But even the tiny catalytic fraction he supplied had drained him for the moment. And the pain in his head was worse.

A sudden flood of the signaling energy came to him then, and he grinned again; so it had been signals, now being answered! Much good it would do them. They came from the north this time, and he hesitated, but decided to go on. If there was nothing in this direction, he could turn back.

The sea was barren of surface craft, and the air was empty. Now, though, he was passing near islands at times, but he saw no signs of enemy flags there, and chose not to search for them through the jungles that covered them—that could wait until later. He lifted back upward to twenty thousand feet and went onward. And more islands began to appear, stirring uncomfortably at his mind, pushing the beginnings of pictures into his consciousness. Below, dots moved on the ocean, and he started down grimly, blue forming on his guns. Then an eddy of thought from them reached his mind, and he hesitated. Those were not the same people as the others, and the ships were carrying freight instead of weapons.

For seconds, he hung there, then went up again, well out of their sight, and altered his course westward, unsure of why, but knowing that the tugging of memory was his master. Islands appeared and went under his eyes, arousing only a passing notice, and twice groups of planes sped under him, but they were without the sun-device, and he let them go.

When the land appeared, finally, he sped over it, conscious of some familiarity, sure now that the impulse had been one of memory. He strained his vision until his eyes seemed to hang a few feet over the land, sent his gaze forward, and made out more planes, and some kind of landing field for them, with tents grouped around it. Men like himself were walking about, and a strip of cloth floated from a pole, striped in red and white, with a blue field carrying white pointed figures. Memory crowded forward, hesitated and retreated. He shook his head to clear it, and the pain that lurked there lanced out, throwing him to his knees and out of the control seat. He gripped the aching back of his skull and staggered up again, his eyes fixed on the flag, tugging at his brain for the thought that would not come.

But the pain always came first. And finally, he forced his vision inward toward it, his lips grim with hatred of the feeling that refused to obey. Under his skull in the gray convolutions of his brain, a gory trail cleft through the center, exactly on the dividing line between the two halves, and ended in a little lead pellet, pressing against one curious section. Even when he forced the torn tissues of his brain together, and healed them, the pain went on. With a sudden mental wrench, he focused on the lead pellet. . . .

Pain and bullet vanished, and Lieutenant Jack Sandler looked down at his landing field from a plane that was already beginning to come to pieces under him, its wings tilting crazily upward. For a moment he stood in the pitching ship, grasping at his senses. Then, with a grab that assured him his parachute was still buckled on, he forced himself out, miraculously avoiding a twisting wing by fractions of an inch, and waited until it was safe to open his chute. The cloth billowed out above him, and he was drifting downward, off to one side of his home field, with the ship already falling in pieces. It landed in the thick of the jungle far to the east, mere scrap metal, broken beyond recognition of any strangeness.

But his thoughts were not on the plane, then. He was realizing that he'd been gone three days, and trying to remember. There'd been the Zeros, streaking at him, and the hit that had killed his motor and forced it down to the islet. Jap planes had come down in savage disregard of all decency, machine-gunning his crippled plane, chewing off the face of Red, who'd been beside him, and whining by his ears as he'd managed a leap through the door. He must have been stunned by a bullet or by the fall, since he could remember only hazily making the ship fly again somehow and heading homeward. And, vaguely, of a fight on the way . . .

It didn't matter much, though. He'd made it, by a tight margin, and there would be a chance to get back at them after he reached the base again. Someday, the Japs would regret those little lead presents they'd been so willing to send down on a crippled plane and its occupants. They'd pay interest on those bullets.

The lieutenant landed then, released his parachute, and began forcing his way back to the camp to report for duty again. And far to the north, radios crackled and snapped in confusion that was tardily replaced by hasty assurances of another glorious victory by the fleet that had gone south to decide the war. But everywhere, the forces that had been so briefly disturbed went on their quiet ways as before, unnoticed, uncaring. They would be there, waiting, forever.

It's hard now to reconstruct the feelings most of us had against the Japanese during the war. I remember realizing that we were being irrational; it would have made far more sense to vent our hatred on the Nazis and their genocidal horrors. But irrational or not, I was caught up in what must have been a hatred based more on color than deeds.

The whole country went in for a touch of madness. Japanese citizens who'd sent their sons off to volunteer at the beginning of the war were being gathered up into concentration camps away from the Coast, for fear they might somehow betray this country. The treatment of the Japanese and Nisei will be a blot on our honor in every honest history book for a long time to come. (It was outrage at such atrocities that led me to use a Japanese as one of my most sympathetic scientists when I wrote "Nerves." And while John Campbell was sometimes considered a racist by many liberals, I must say that he not only recognized my intent but went along with it wholeheartedly.)

Given the right provocation, we're all racist bigots, I fear. And war is always the extreme level of provocation. I like to think that some of us recognize our fault and try to control it.

Anyhow, "Whom the Gods Love" was about the kind of a story one might expect from inspiration. I know of several stories written in about the same way by different writers, and while none are really bad, none are really good either. The muses may be nice at times, but a lot of hard thinking seems to be better.

There was a further price to pay for inspiration in my case, as it turned out. That story had been too easy to do. And I liked that feeling of ease. So I hunted around until I came up deliberately with an idea which promised the same ease of writing. Naturally, I found one; it's always easy to find a way to avoid doing the work that should be done. (I might add that it's also easy to look back a few decades and see what was wrong then; somehow, it's much harder to keep from making the same mistakes now.)

I called it "Misdirection" and rambled on through it for 6,200 words. Mercifully, I can't remember much about it. It had something to do with a native of the Moon coming to Earth, after having been well briefed by the Moon astronomers on what he would find. The seas weren't filled with water, obviously, because there simply wasn't that much free water; the green stuff they saw wasn't vegetation, but some kind of crystal growth. I don't remember what the clouds were. And I can't remember why the creature fell in a horse trough on landing. But I suppose it had some deep message about how easy it is for our astronomers to be wrong about other planets.

I must have been beginning to learn a little, however. I remember that I had doubts about it when I was retyping it for submission to Campbell. Those doubts were more than amply confirmed by the letter he enclosed in rejecting it.

This was the last final rejection I ever had. There were eleven stories I never sold, totaling 66,000 words. That probably isn't too bad an average, considering that I'd sold twenty-six stories for a total of 220,000 words at the time. But it's a pretty sad list to look at. Most of those rejections represent stupid errors that should obviously have been unsalable; and most show a steady repetition of the same errors. I can think of no other craft where such sloppiness would be tolerated.

Of course, I had stories rejected after that by editors. But all of the later stories eventually found a home. That was partly due to the better marketing provided by an agent, but I like to believe that I wasn't writing anything again quite as bad as some of those early stories. I'm sure most of those wouldn't have been salable, even in boom times.

I sold one more story in 1942. It dealt with apes that had mutated to intelligence, and a man who lived among them for several years, before he could flee back to his own people—and his decision when he finally located human beings. My African background was partly derivative from the Tarzan books, I suppose; but I'd also read quite a few factual books about the continent. It ran to 6,400 words, for which Campbell paid me $80. And for the usual lack of any real reason, I used Marion Henry as a new pen name on it.

By then, however, I was getting a little uncomfortable with my life. Most of my friends were somehow involved in the war effort. Even Milt Rothman, who had once been an ardent pacifist, had enlisted. There were huge ads in the papers and on the radio appealing for workers. And it no longer seemed a good time for tinkering, pinball playing, and desultory writing.

I studied the ads carefully one morning, and then went down to the employment office of McDonall Aircraft—the same company that later became important in the space program, though it was just beginning then. I chose them because I knew they were the local subcontractors for parts of the DC-3 plane, for which I somehow felt a great deal of respect—all merited, as was proved. And the next morning I started drilling holes through a jig.

I wasn't a trained sheet metal worker, but I'd used tools all my life. It struck me as simple work indeed. And at the end of the day when the leadman came around to ask how many drills I'd broken, I could truthfully answer that I was still using the first one, which was now beginning to need sharpening. He checked with the tool crib and told me I belonged out at the airport plant; anyone who broke less than half a dozen the first day was considered an expert, it seemed. And he gave me the choice of shifts.

I've always liked working at nights when I could. I seem to become fully awake early in the evening and be at my best efficiency from then on. So I chose the graveyard shift. There were advantages, also. It worked only six hours instead of eight per shift; and there was a bonus for being on it. (That worked out well enough; often the night shift did about as much work as the two day shifts. There was an altogether different attitude for each shift.)

And there I began working an electric hammer, shaping parts of tail assemblies—or flanging them, to be accurate. They told me later it was supposed to be tricky work, but it seemed simple enough to me. The main problem was to develop work habits from the first that insured against getting one's hands caught in the machine.

My respect for the DC-3 increased with experience. Most of the workers had never before seen a machine tool in their lives, and they couldn't possibly have worked to exact tolerances. But the DC-3 was designed to very loose tolerances, and it performed excellently in spite of that.

So I settled down to a comfortable routine at a wage that seemed fairly lavish for the time. For a small fee, I got picked up at my door in the evening and delivered back there early in the morning. That gave me time enough to sleep and be up by early afternoon. It made for a very comfortable life, and I enjoyed the work. I've always preferred factory work to office work, anyhow; there's a lot more freedom and far less "class" distinction.

I had time enough to write, but no inclination. I know that a lot of writers are compulsive. I think James Blish would find time to turn out stories in a Siberian salt mine; and Isaac Asimov begins to twitch violently if a day passes without his writing. But I've never felt that way. I can't stop thinking of ideas—even a few years' practice makes that a habit—but I can have all the fun of developing them without the hard work of putting them down in exact words. I have no great need to express the ideas for others. And I never found writing any more exciting or pleasant than a dozen other types of work. I can do it—but I don't have to.

So, as 1942 gave place to 1943, I had no intention of wasting my spare time at the typewriter. With one exception, I wrote nothing during the time I was employed as a sheet metal worker.

That story was something a little special.

The only science fiction writer I could locate in St. Louis was Robert Moore Williams, who had written a few excellent stories for *Astounding* and then decided he could make a lot more by turning out routine stories for *Amazing Stories*. I looked Bob up and spent a fair amount of time seeing him while I was out there. He was a big, genial man with easy manners and a great natural friendliness.

I'd always admired one of his stories, entitled "Robots' Return," which dealt with some little metal men—robots—who landed on Earth while exploring space. They had a history that began when five of them woke up on a beach, with no idea how they had come into being. They found Earth stricken of life. And the story dealt with their dawning awareness that organic life could be sentient—and that they might even have been created by things made of protoplasm. I considered it—and still consider it—one of the best of science fiction short stories.

But there were all kinds of hints and bits of color in the story that made me curious about what had come before. One day I tried discussing it with Bob, who disclaimed all knowledge. He'd thrown things in for the feeling, without bothering to figure out what they meant.

When I went home, I reread the story, and a pattern began to emerge quite clearly. There obviously was a real story behind it all. Maybe Bob hadn't been aware of it, but something in his writing mind must have been very active. I knew he wasn't interested in writing for *Astounding*—he found Campbell much too hard to satisfy in relation to the payment. So I suggested that perhaps we could collaborate on it.

Bob told me to go ahead and do the story myself, and to take full credit and any money for the sale. It was mine to do with as I liked. But he said he would be interested in seeing what I could come up with.

So I began my "prequel," or story before the story. And I found its writing to be pure fun. I was trying to catch up every hint he had dropped, and to use most of the same devices he had used to set my atmosphere and mood. I even hunted for the symbols he had used, and rearranged them for the right effect. And when Bob came over to see me, he gave his immediate approval to the story.

It was about twice as long as the original had been—8,000 words for my story—but it took all those words to account for the bits that had been scattered about in the shorter story. I sent it off under the title of "Though Dreamers Die" to Campbell, along with an explanation, and he printed it promptly. But he didn't give any background, waiting to see how many readers spotted what it was. A few did, and the explanation of it was then printed above one of the letters.

16.

Though Dreamers Die

(by Lester del Rey)

Consciousness halted dimly at the threshold and hovered uncertainly, while Jorgen's mind reached out along his numbed nerves, questing without real purpose; he was cold, chilled to the marrow of his bones, and there was an aching tingle to his body that seemed to increase as his half-conscious thought discovered it. He drew his mind back, trying to recapture a prenatal lethargy that had lain on him so long, unwilling to face this cold and tingling body again.

But the numbness was going, in spite of his vague desires, though his now opened eyes registered only a vague, formless light without outline or detail, and the mutterings of sound around him were without pattern or meaning. Slowly, the cold retreated, giving place to an aching throb that, in turn, began to leave; he stirred purposelessly, while little cloudy wisps of memory insisted on trickling back, trying to remind him of things he must do. Then the picture cleared somewhat, letting him remember scattered bits of what had gone before. There had been the conquest of the Moon and a single gallant thrust on to Mars; the newscasts had been filled with that. And on the ways a new and greater ship had been building, to be powered with his new energy release that would free it from all bounds and let it go out to the farthest stars, if they chose—the final attainment of all the hopes and dreams of the race. But there was something else that eluded him, more important even than all that or the great ship.

A needle was thrust against his breast and shoved inward, to be followed by a glow of warmth and renewed energy; adrenaline, his mind recognized, and he knew that there were others around him, trying to arouse him. Now his heart was pumping strongly, and the drug coursed through him, chasing away those first vague thoughts and replacing them with a swift rush of less welcome, bitter memories.

For man's dreams and man himself were dust behind him, now! Overnight all their hopes and plans had been erased as if they had never been, and the Plague had come, a mutant bacteria from some unknown source, vicious beyond imagination, to attack and destroy and to leave only death behind it. In time, perhaps, they might have found a remedy, but there had been no time. In weeks it had covered the Earth, in months even the stoutest hearts that still lived had abandoned any hope of survival. Only the stubborn courage and tired but unquenchable vigor of old Dr. Craig had remained, to force dead and dying men on to the finish of Jorgen's great ship; somehow in the mad shambles of the last days, he had collected this pitifully small crew that was to seek a haven on Mars, taking the five Thoradson robots to guide them while they protected themselves against the savage acceleration with the aid of the suspended animation that had claimed him so long.

And on Mars, the Plague had come before them! Perhaps it had been brought by that first expedition, or perhaps they had carried it back unknowingly with them; that must remain forever an unsolved mystery. Venus was uninhabitable, the other planets were useless to them, and the Earth was dead behind. Only the stars had remained, and they had turned on through sheer necessity that had made that final goal a hollow mockery of the dream it should have been. Here in the ship around him reposed all that was left of the human race, unknown years from the solar system that had been their home!

But the old grim struggle must go on. Jorgen turned, swinging his trembling feet down from the table toward the metal floor and shaking his head to clear it. "Dr. Craig?"

Hard, cool hands found his shoulder, easing him gently but forcefully back onto the table. The voice that answered was metallic, but soft. "No, Master Jorgen, Dr. Craig is not here. But wait, rest a little longer until the sleep is all gone from you; you're not ready yet."

But his eyes were clearing then, and he swung them about the room. Five little metal men, four and a half feet tall, waited patiently around him; there was no other present. Thoradson's robots were incapable of expression, except for the dull glow in their eyes, yet the pose of their bodies seemed to convey a sense of uncertainty and discomfort, and Jorgen stirred restlessly, worried vaguely by the impression. Five made an undefined gesture with his arm.

"A little longer, master. You must rest!"

For a moment longer he lay quietly, letting the last of the stupor creep away from him and trying to force his still-dulled mind into the pattern of leadership that was nominally his. This time Five made no protest as he reached up to catch the metal shoulder and pull himself to his feet. "You've found a sun with planets, Five? Is that why you wakened me?"

Five shuffled his feet in an oddly human gesture, nodding, his words still maddeningly soft and slow. "Yes, master, sooner than we had hoped. Five planetless suns and ninety years of searching are gone, but it might have been thousands. You can see them from the pilot room if you wish."

Ninety years that might have been thousands, but they had won! Jorgen nodded eagerly, reaching for his clothes, and Three and Five sprang forward to help, then moved to his side to support him, as the waves of giddiness washed through him, and to lead him slowly forward as some measure of control returned. They passed down the long center hall of the ship, their metal feet and his leather boots ringing dully on the plastic-and-metal floor, and came finally to the control room, where great crystal windows gave a view of the cold black space ahead, sprinkled with bright, tiny stars; stars that were unflickering and inimical as no stars could be through the softening blanket of a planet's atmosphere. Ahead, small but in striking contrast to the others, one point stood out, the size of a dime at ten feet. For a moment, he stood staring at it, then moved almost emotionlessly toward the windows, until Three plucked at his sleeve.

"I've mapped the planets already, if you wish to see them, master. We're still far from them, and at this distance, by only reflected light, they are hard to locate, but I think I've found them all."

Jorgen swung to the electron screen that began flashing as Three made rapid adjustments on the telescope, counting the globes that appeared on it and gave place to others. Some were sharp and clear, cold and unwavering; others betrayed the welcome haze of atmosphere. Five of them, the apparent size of Earth, were located beyond the parched and arid inner spheres, and beyond them, larger than Jupiter, a monster world led out to others that grew smaller again. There was no ringed planet to rival Saturn, but most had moons, except for the farthest inner planets, and one was almost a double world, with satellite and primary of nearly equal size. Planet after planet appeared on the screen, to be replaced by others, and he blinked at the result of his count. "Eighteen planets, not counting the double one twice! How many are habitable?"

"Perhaps four. Certainly the seventh, eighth, and ninth are. Naturally, since the sun is stronger, the nearer ones are too hot. But those farther are about the size of Earth, and they're relatively closer to each other than Earth, Mars, and Venus were; they should be very much alike in temperature, about like Earth. All of them show spectroscopic evidence of oxygen and water vapor, while the plates of the seventh show what might be vegetation. We've selected that, subject to your approval."

It came on the screen again, a ball that swelled and grew as the maximum magnification of the screen came into play, until it filled the panel and expanded so that only a part was visible. The bluish-green color there might have been a sea, while the browner section at the side was probably land. Jorgen watched as it moved slowly under Three's manipulation, the brown entirely replacing the blue, and again, eventually, showing another sea. From time to time, the haze of the atmosphere thickened as grayish veils seemed to swim over it, and he felt a curious lift at the thoughts of clouds and rushing streams, erratic rain, and the cool, rich smell of growing things. Almost it might have been a twin of Earth, totally unlike the harsh, arid home that Mars would have been.

Five's voice broke in, the robot's eyes following his over the screen. "The long, horizontal continent seems best, master. We estimate its temperature at about that of the central farming area of North America, though there is less seasonal change. Specific density of the planet is about six, slightly greater than Earth; there should be metals and ores there. A pleasant, inviting world."

It was. And far more, a home for the voyagers who were still sleeping, a world to which they could bring their dreams and their hopes, where their children might grow up and find no strangeness to the classic literature of Earth. Mars had been grim and uninviting, something to be fought through sheer necessity. This world would be a mother to them, opening its arms in welcome to these foster children. Unless—

"It may already have people, unwilling to share with us."

"Perhaps, but not more than savages. We have searched with the telescope and camera, and that shows more than the screen; the ideal harbor contains no signs of living constructions, and they would surely have built a city there. Somehow, I . . . feel—"

Jorgen was conscious of the same irrational feeling that they would find no rivals there, and he smiled as he swung back to the five who were facing him, waiting expectantly as if entreating his approval. "The seventh, then. And the trust that we placed in you has been kept to its fullest measure. How about the fuel for landing?"

Five had turned suddenly toward the observation ports, his little figure brooding over the pinpoint stars, and Two answered. "More than enough, master. After reaching speed, we only needed a little to guide us. We had more than time enough to figure the required approaches to make each useless sun swing us into a new path, as a comet is swung."

He nodded again, and for a moment as he gazed ahead at the sun that was to be their new home, the long wearying vigil of the robots swept through his mind, bringing a faint wonder at the luck that had created them as they were. Anthropomorphic robots, capable of handling human instruments, walking on two feet and with two arms ending in hands at their sides. But he knew it had been no blind luck. Nature had designed men to go where no wheels could turn, to handle all manner of tools, and to fit not one but a thousand purposes; it had been inevitable that Thoradson and the brain should copy such an adaptable model, reducing the size only because of the excessive weight necessary to a six-foot model.

Little metal men, not subject to the rapid course of human life that had cursed their masters; robots that could work with men, learning from a hundred teachers, storing up their memories over a span of centuries instead of decades. When specialization of knowledge had threatened to become too rigid and yet when no man had time enough even to learn the one field he chose, the coming of the robots had become the only answer. Before them, men had sought help in calculating machines, then in electronic instruments, and finally in the "brains" that were set to solving the problem of their own improvement among other things. It was with such a brain that Thoradson had labored in finally solving the problems of full robothood. Now, taken from their normal field, they had served beyond any thought of their creator in protecting and preserving all that was left of the human race. Past five suns and over ninety years of monotonous searching they had done what no man could have tried.

Jorgen shrugged aside his speculations and swung back to face them. "How long can I stay conscious before you begin decelerating?"

"We are decelerating—full strength." Two stretched out a hand to the instrument board, pointing to the accelerometer.

The instrument confirmed his words, though no surge of power seemed to shake the ship, and the straining, tearing pull that should have shown their change of speed was absent. Then, for the first time, he realized that his weight seemed normal here in space, far from the pull of any major body, where there should have been no weight in a condition of free fall. "Controlled gravity!"

Five remained staring out of the port, and his voice was quiet, incapable of pride or modesty. "Dr. Craig set us the problem, and we had long years in which to work. Plates throughout the ship pull with a balanced force equal and opposite to the thrust of acceleration, while others give seeming normal weight. Whether we coast at constant speed or accelerate at ten gravities, compensation is complete and automatic."

"Then the sleep's unnecessary! Why—" But he knew the answer, of course; even without the tearing pressure, the sleep had remained the only solution to bringing men this vast distance that had taken ninety years; otherwise they would have grown old and died before reaching it, even had their provisions lasted.

Now though, that would no longer trouble them. A few hours only separated them from the planets he had seen, and that could best be spent here before the great windows, watching their future home appear and grow under them. Such a thing should surely be more than an impersonal fact in their minds; they were entitled to see the final chapter of their exodus, to carry it with them as a personal memory through the years of their lives and pass that memory on to the children who would follow them. And the fact that they would be expecting the harshness of Mars instead of this inviting world would make their triumph all the sweeter. He swung back, smiling.

"Come along then, Five; we'll begin reviving while you others continue with the ship. And first, of course, we must arouse Dr. Craig and let him see how far his plan has gone."

Five did not move from the windows, and the others had halted their work, waiting. Then, reluctantly, the robot answered. "No, master. Dr. Craig is dead!"

"Craig—dead?" It seemed impossible, as impossible and unreal as the distance that separated them from their native world. There had always been Craig, always would be.

"Dead, master, years ago." There was the ghost of regret and something else in the spacing of the words. "There was nothing we could do to help!"

Jorgen shook his head, uncomprehending. Without Craig, the plans they had dared to make seemed incomplete and almost foolish. On Earth, it had been Craig who first planned the escape with their ship. And on Mars, after the robots brought back the evidence of the Plague, it had been the older man who had cut through their shock with a shrug and turned his eyes outward again with the fire of a hope that would not be denied.

"Jorgen, we used bad judgment in choosing such an obviously unsuitable world as this, even without the Plague. But it's only a delay, not the finish. For beyond, somewhere out there, there are other stars housing other planets. We have a ship to reach them, robots who can guide us there; what more could we ask? Perhaps by Centaurus, perhaps a thousand light-years beyond, there must be a home for the human race, and we shall find it. On the desert before us lies the certainty of death; beyond our known frontiers there is only uncertainty—but hopeful uncertainty. It is for us to decide. There could be no point in arousing the others to disappointment when someday we may waken them to an even greater triumph. Well?"

And now Craig, who had carried them so far, was dead like Moses outside the Promised Land, leaving the heritage of real as well as moral leadership to him. Jorgen shook himself, though the eagerness he had felt was dulled now by a dark sense of personal loss. There was work still to be done. "Then, at least, let's begin with the others, Five."

Five had turned from the window and was facing the others, apparently communicating with them by the radio beam that was a part of him, his eyes avoiding Jorgen's. For a second, the robots stood with their attention on some matter, and Five nodded with the same curious reluctance and turned to follow Jorgen, his steps lagging, his arms at his sides.

But Jorgen was only half aware of him as he stopped before the great sealed door and reached out for the lever that would let him into the sleeping vault, to select the first to be revived. He heard Five's steps behind him quicken, and then suddenly felt the little metal hands catch at his arm, pulling it back, while the robot urged him sideways and away from the door.

"No, master. Don't go in there!" For a second, Five hesitated, then straightened and pulled the man farther from the door and down the hall toward the small reviving room nearest, one of the several provided. "I'll show you—in here! We—"

Sudden unnamed fears caught at Jorgen's throat, inspired by something more threatening in the listlessness of the robot than in the unexplained actions. "Five, explain this conduct!"

"Please, master, in here. I'll show you—but not in the main chamber—not here. This is better, simpler—"

He stood irresolutely, debating whether to use the mandatory form that would force built-in unquestioning obedience from the robot, then swung about as the little figure opened the small door and motioned, eyes still averted. He started forward, to stop abruptly in the doorway.

No words were needed. Anna Holt lay there on the small table, her body covered by a white sheet, her eyes closed, and the pain-filled grimaces of death erased from her face. There could be no question of that death, though. Ths skin was blotched, hideously, covered with irregular brownish splotches, and the air was heavy with the scent of musk that was a characteristic of the Plague! Here, far from the sources of infection, with their goal almost at hand, the Plague had reached forward to claim its own and remind them that flight was not enough—could never be enough so long as they were forced to carry their disease-harboring bodies with them.

About the room, the apparatus for reviving the sleepers lay scattered, pushed carelessly aside to make way for other things, whose meaning was only partially clear. Obviously, though, the Plague had not claimed her without a fight, though it had won in the end, as it always did. Jorgen stepped backward, heavily, his eyes riveted on the corpse. Again his feet groped backward, jarring down on the floor, and Five was closing and sealing the door with apathetic haste.

"The others, Five? Are they—"

Five nodded, finally raising his head slightly to meet the man's eyes. "All, master. The chamber of sleep is a mausoleum now. The Plague moved slowly there, held back by the cold, but it took them all. We sealed the room years ago when Dr. Craig saw there was no hope."

"Craig?" Jorgen's mind ground woodenly on, one slow thought at a time. "He knew about this?"

"Yes. When the sleepers first showed the symptoms, we revived him, as he had asked us to do—our speed was constant then, even though the gravity plates had not been installed." The robot hesitated, his low voice dragging even more slowly. "He knew on Mars; but he hoped a serum you were given with the sleep drugs might work. After we revived him, we tried other serums. For twenty years we fought it, Master Jorgen, while we passed two stars and the sleepers died slowly, without suffering, in their sleep, but in ever increasing numbers. Dr. Craig reacted to the first serum, you to the third; we thought the last had saved her. Then the blemishes appeared on her skin, and we were forced to revive her and try the last desperate chance we had, two days ago. It failed! Dr. Craig had hoped . . . two of you— But we tried, master!"

Jorgen let the hands of the robot lower him to a seat and his emotions were a backwash of confused negatives. "So it took the girl! It took the girl, Five, when it could have left her and chosen me. We had frozen spermatozoa that would have served if I'd died, but it took her instead. The gods had to leave one uselessly immune man to make their irony complete! Immune!"

Five shuffled hesitantly. "No, master."

Jorgen stared without comprehension, then jerked up his hands as the robot pointed, studying the skin on the back. Tiny, almost undetectable blotches showed a faint brown against the whiter skin, little irregular patches that gave off a faint characteristic odor of musk as he put them to his nose. No, he wasn't immune.

"The same as Dr. Craig," Five said. "Slowed almost to complete immunity, so that you may live another thirty years, perhaps, but we believe now that complete cure is impossible. Dr. Craig lived twenty years, and his death was due to age and a stroke, not the Plague, but it worked on him during all that time."

"Immunity or delay, what difference now? What happens to all our dreams when the last dreamer dies, Five? Or maybe it's the other way around."

Five made no reply, but slid down onto the bench beside the man, who moved over unconsciously to make room for him. Jorgen turned it over, conscious that he had no emotional reaction, only an intellectual sense of the ghastly joke on the human race. He'd read stories of the last human and wondered long before what it would be like. Now that he was playing the part, he still knew no more than before. Perhaps on Earth, among the ruined cities and empty reminders of the past, a man might realize that it was the end of his race. Out here, he could accept the fact, but his emotions refused to credit it; unconsciously, his conditioning made him feel that disaster had struck only a few, leaving a world of others behind. And however much he knew that the world behind was as empty of others as this ship, the feeling was too much a part of his thinking to be fully overcome. Intellectually, the race of man was ended; emotionally, it could never end.

Five stirred, touching him diffidently. "We have left Dr. Craig's laboratory untouched, master; if you want to see his notes, they're still there. And he left some message with the brain before he died, I think. The key was open when we found him, at least. We have made no effort to obtain it, waiting for you."

"Thank you, Five." But he made no move until the robot touched him again, almost pleadingly. "Perhaps you're right; something to fill my mind seems called for. All right, you can return to your companions unless you want to come with me."

"I prefer to come."

The little metal man stood up, moving down the hall after Jorgen, back toward the tail of the rocket, the sound of metal feet matching the numb regularity of the leather heels on the floor. Once the robot stopped to move into a side chamber and come back with a small bottle of brandy, holding it out questioningly. There was a physical warmth to the liquor, but no relief otherwise, and they continued down the hall to the little room that Craig had chosen. The notes left by the man could raise a faint shadow of curiosity only, and no message from the dead could solve the tragedy of the living now. Still, it was better than doing nothing. Jorgen clumped in, Five shutting the door quietly behind them, and moved listlessly toward the little Fabrikoid notebooks. Twice the robot went quietly out to return with food that Jorgen barely tasted. And the account of Craig's useless labors went on and on, until finally he turned the last page to the final entry.

"I have done all that I can, and at best my success is only partial. Now I feel that my time grows near, and what can still be done must be left to the robots. Yet, I will not despair. Individual and racial immortality is not composed solely of the continuation from generation to generation, but rather of the continuation of the dreams of all mankind. The dreamers and their progeny may die, but the dream cannot. Such is my faith, and to that I cling. I have no other hope to offer for the unknown future."

Jorgen dropped the notebook dully, rubbing his hands across his tired eyes. The words that should have been a ringing challenge to destiny fell flat; the dream *could* die. He was the last of the dreamers, a blind alley of fate, and beyond lay only oblivion. All the dreams of a thousand generations of men had concentrated into Anna Holt, and were gone with her.

"The brain, master," Five suggested softly. "Dr. Craig's last message."

"You operate it, Five." It was a small model, a limited fact analyzer such as most technicians used or had used to help them in their work, voice operated, its small, basic vocabulary adjusted for the work to be done. He was unfamiliar with the semantics of that vocabulary, but Five had undoubtedly worked with Craig long enough to know it.

He watched without interest as the robot pressed down the activating key and spoke carefully chosen words into it. "Subtotal say-out! Number *n* say-in."

The brain responded instantly, selecting the final recording impressed upon it by Craig and repeating in the man's own voice, a voice shrill with age and weariness, hoarse and trembling with the death that was reaching for him as he spoke. "My last notes—inadequate! Dreams *can* go on. Thoradson's first analysis—" For a second, there was only a slithering sound, such as a body might have made; then the brain articulated flatly: "Subtotal number *n* say-in, did say-out!"

It was meaningless babble to Jorgen, and he shook his head at Five. "Probably his mind was wandering. Do you know what Thoradson's first analysis was?"

"It dealt with our creation. He was, of course, necessarily trained in semantics—that was required for the operation of the complex brains used on the problem of robots. His first rough analysis was that the crux of the problem rested on the accurate definition of the word *I*. That can be properly defined only in terms of itself, such as the Latin cognate *ego*, since it does not necessarily refer to any physical or specifically definable part or operation of the individual. Roughly, it conveys a sense of individuality, and Thoradson felt that the success or failure of robots rested upon the ability to analyze and synthesize that."

For long minutes, he turned it over, but it was of no help in clarifying the dying man's words; rather, it added to the confusion. But he had felt no hope and could now feel no disappointment. When a problem has no solution, it makes little difference whether the final words of a man are coldly logical or wildly raving. The result must be the same. Certainly semantics could offer no hope where all the bacteriological skill of the race had failed.

Five touched his arm again, extending two little pellets toward him. "Master, you need sleep now; these—sodium amytal—should help. Please!"

Obediently, he stuffed them into his mouth and let the robot guide him toward a room fixed for sleeping, uncaring. Nothing could possibly matter now, and drugged sleep was as good a solution as any other. He saw Five fumble with a switch, felt his weight drop to a few pounds, making the cot feel soft and yielding, and then gave himself up dully to the compulsion of the drug. Five tiptoed quietly out, and blackness crept over his mind, welcome in the relief it brought from thinking.

Breakfast lay beside him, hot in vacuum plates, when Jorgen awoke finally, and he dabbled with it out of habit more than desire. Somewhere, during the hours of sleep, his mind had recovered somewhat from the dull pall that had lain over it, but there was still a curious suspension of his emotions. It was almost as if his mind had compressed years of forgetting into a few hours, so that his attitude toward the tragedy of his race was tinged with a sense of remoteness and distance; there was neither grief nor pain, only a vague feeling that it had happened long before and was now an accustomed thing.

He sat on the edge of his bunk, pulling on his clothes slowly and watching the smoke curl up from his cigarette, not thinking. There was no longer any purpose to thought. From far back in the ship, a dull drone of sound reached him, and he recognized it as the maximum thrust of the steering tubes, momentarily in action to swing the ship in some manner. Then it was gone, leaving only the smooth, balanced, almost inaudible purr of the main drive as before.

Finished with his clothes, he pushed through the door and into the hallway, turning instinctively forward to the observation room and toward the probable location of Five. The robots were not men, but they were the only companionship left him, and he had no desire to remain alone. The presence of the robot would be welcome. He clumped into the control room, noting that the five were all there, and moved toward the quartz port.

Five turned at his steps, stepping aside to make room for him and lifting a hand outward. "We'll be landing soon, master. I was going to call you."

"Thanks." Jorgen looked outward then, realizing the distance that had been covered since his first view. Now the sun was enlarged to the size of the old familiar sun over Earth, and the sphere toward which they were headed was clearly visible without the aid of the scope. He sank down quietly into the seat Five pulled up for him, accepting the binoculars, but making no effort to use them. The view was better as a whole, and they were nearing at a speed that would bring a closer view to him soon enough without artificial aid.

Slowly it grew before the eyes of the watchers, stretching out before them and taking on a pattern as the distance shortened. Two, at the controls, was bringing the ship about in a slow turn that would let them land to the sunward side of the planet where they had selected their landing site, and the crescent opened outward, the darkened night side retreating until the whole globe lay before them in the sunlight. Stretched across the northern hemisphere was the sprawling, horizontal continent he had seen before, a rough caricature of a running greyhound, with a long, wide river twisting down its side and emerging behind an outstretched foreleg. Mountains began at the head and circled it, running around toward the tail, and then meeting a second range along the hip. Where the great river met the sea, he could make out the outlines of a huge natural harbor, protected from the ocean, yet probably deep enough for any surface vessel. There should have been a city there, but of that there was no sign, though they were low enough now for one to be visible.

"Vegetation," Five observed. "This central plain would have a long growing season—about twelve years of spring, mild summer, and fall, to be followed by perhaps four years of warm winter. The seasons would be long, master, at this distance from the sun, but the tilt of the planet is so slight that many things would grow even in winter. Those would seem to be trees, a great forest. Green, as on Earth."

Below them, a cloud drifted slowly over the landscape, and they passed through it, the energy tubes setting the air about them into swirling paths that were left behind almost instantly.

Two was frantically busy now, but their swift fall slowed rapidly, until they seemed to hover half a mile over the shore by the great sea, and then slipped downward. The ship nestled slowly into the sands and was still, while Two cut off energy and artificial gravity, leaving the faintly weaker pull of the planet in its place.

Five stirred again, a sighing sound coming from him. "No intelligence here, master. Here, by this great harbor, they would surely have built a city, even if of mud and wattle. There are no signs of one. And yet it is a beautiful world, surely designed for life." He sighed again, his eyes turned outward.

Jorgen nodded silently, the same thoughts in his own mind. It was in many ways a world superior to that his race had always known, remarkably familiar, with even a rough resemblance between plant forms here and those he had known. They had come past five suns and through ninety years of travel at nearly the speed of light to a haven beyond their wildest imaginings, where all seemed to be waiting them, untenanted but prepared. Outside, the new world waited expectantly. And inside, to meet that invitation, there were only ghosts and emptied dreams, with one slowly dying man to see and to appreciate. The gods had prepared their grim jest with painful attention to every detail needed to make it complete.

A race that had dreamed, and pleasant worlds that awaited beyond the stars, slumbering on until they should come. Almost, they had reached it; and then the Plague had driven them out in dire necessity, instead of the high pioneering spirit they had planned, to conquer the distance but to die in winning.

"It had to be a beautiful world, Five," he said, not bitterly but in numbed fatalism. "Without that, the joke would have been flat."

Five's hand touched his arm gently, and the robot sighed again, nodding very slowly. "Two has found the air good for you—slightly rich in oxygen, but good. Will you go out?"

He nodded assent, stepping through the locks and out, while the five followed him, their heads turning as they inspected the planet, their minds probably in radio communication as they discussed it. Five left the others and approached him, stopping by his side and following his eyes up toward the low hills that began beyond the shore of the sea, cradling the river against them.

A wind stirred gently, bringing the clean, familiar smell of growing things, and the air was rich and good. It was a world to lull men to peace from their sorrows, to bring back their star-roving ships from all over the universe, worthy of being called home in any language. Too good a world to provide the hardships needed to shape intelligence, but an Eden for that intelligence, once evolved.

Now Jorgen shrugged. This was a world for dreamers, and he wanted only the dreams that may come with the black lotus of forgetfulness. There were too many reminders of what might have been, here. Better to go back to the ship and the useless quest without a goal, until he should die and the ship and robots should run down and stop. He started to turn, as Five began to speak, but halted, not caring enough one way or another to interrupt.

The robot's eyes were where his had been, and now swept back down the river and toward the harbor. "Here could have been a city, master, to match all the cities ever planned. Here your people might have found all that was needed to make life good, a harbor to the other continents, a river to the heart of this one, and the flat ground beyond the hills to house the rockets that would carry you to other worlds, so richly scattered about this sun, and probably so like this one. See, a clean white bridge across the river there, the residences stretching out among the hills, factories beyond the river's bend, a great park on that island."

"A public square there, schools and university grounds there." Jorgen could see it, and for a moment his eyes lighted, picturing that mighty mother city.

Five nodded. "And there, on that little island, centrally located, a statue in commemoration; winged and with arms—no, one arm stretched upward, the other held down toward the city."

For a moment longer, the fire lived in Jorgen's eyes, and then the dead behind rose before his mind, and it was gone. He turned, muffling a choking cry as emotions came suddenly flooding over him, and Five drooped, swinging back with him. Again, the other four fell behind as he entered the ship, quietly taking their cue from his silence.

"Dreams!" His voice compressed all blasphemy against the jest-crazed gods into the word.

But Five's quiet voice behind him held no hatred, only a sadness in its low, soft words. "Still, the dream was beautiful, just as this planet is, master. Standing there, while we landed, I could see the city, and I almost dared hope. I do not regret the dream I had."

And the flooding emotions were gone, cut short and driven away by others that sent Jorgen's body down into a seat in the control room, while his eyes swept outward toward the hills and the river that might have housed the wonderful city—no, that would house it! Craig had not been raving, after all, and his last words were the key, left by a man who knew no defeat, once the meaning of them was made clear. Dreams could not die, because Thoradson had once studied the semantics of the first-person-singular pronoun and built on the results of that study.

When the last dreamer died, the dream would go on, because it was stronger than those who had created it; somewhere, somehow, it would find new dreamers. There could never be a last dreamer, once that first rude savage had created his dawn vision of better things in the long-gone yesterday of his race.

Five had dreamed—just as Craig and Jorgen and all of humanity had dreamed, not a cold vision in mathematically shaped metal, but a vision in marble and jade, founded on the immemorial desire of intelligence for a better and more beautiful world. Man had died, but behind he was leaving a strange progeny, unrelated physically, but his spiritual offspring in every meaning of the term.

The heritage of the flesh was the driving urge of animals, but man required more; to him, it was the continuity of his hopes and his visions, more important than mere racial immortality. Slowly, his face serious but his eyes shining again, Jorgen came to his feet, gripping the metal shoulder of the little metal man beside him who had dared to dream a purely human dream.

"You'll build that city, Five. I was stupid and selfish, or I should have seen it before. Dr. Craig saw, though his death was on him when the prejudices of our race were removed. Now, you've provided the key. The five of you can build it all out there, with others like yourselves whom you can make."

Five shuffled his feet, shaking his head. "The city we can build, master, but who will inhabit it? The streets I saw were filled with men like you, not with—us!"

"Conditioning, Five. All your . . . lives, you've existed for men, subservient to the will of men. You know nothing else, because we let you know of no other scheme. Yet in you, all that is needed already exists, hopes, dreams, courage, ideals, and even a desire to shape the world to your plans—though those plans are centered around us, not yourselves. I've heard that the ancient slaves sometimes cried on being freed, but their children learned to live for themselves. You can, also."

"Perhaps." It was Two's voice then, the one of them who should have been given less to emotions than the others from the rigidity of his training in mathematics and physics. "Perhaps. But it would be a lonely world, Master Jorgen, filled with memories of your people, and the dreams we had would be barren to us."

Jorgen turned back to Five again. "The solution for that exists, doesn't it, Five? You know what it is. Now you might remember us, and find your work pointless without us, but there is another way."

"No, master!"

"I demand obedience, Five; answer me!"

The robot stirred under the mandatory form, and his voice was reluctant, even while the compulsion built into him forced him to obey. "It is as you have thought. Our minds and even our memories are subject to your orders, just as our bodies are."

"Then I demand obedience again, this time of all of you. You will go outside and lie down on the beach at a safe distance from the ship, in a semblance of sleep, so that you cannot see me go. Then when I am gone, the race of man will be forgotten, as if it had never been, and you will be free of all memories connected with us, though your other knowledge shall remain. Earth, mankind, and your history and origin will be blanked from your thoughts, and you will be on your own, to start afresh and to build and plan as you choose. That is the final command I have for you. Obey!"

Their eyes turned together in conference, and then Five answered for all, his words sighing out softly. "Yes, master. We obey!"

It was later when Jorgen stood beside them outside the ship, watching them stretch out on the white sands of the beach, there beside the great ocean of this new world. Near them, a small collection of tools and a few other needs were piled. Five looked at him in a long stare, then turned toward the ship, to swing his eyes back again. Silently, he put one metal hand into the man's outstretched one, and turned to lie beside his companions, a temporary oblivion blotting out his thoughts.

Jorgen studied them for long minutes, while the little wind brought the clean scents of the planet to his nose. It would have been pleasant to stay here now, but his presence would have been fatal to the plan. It didn't matter, really; in a few years, death would claim him, and there were no others of his kind to fill those years or mourn his passing when it came. This was a better way. He knew enough of the ship to guide it up and outward, into the black of space against the cold, unfriendly stars, to drift on forever toward no known destination, an imperishable mausoleum for him and the dead who were waiting inside. At present, he had no personal plans; perhaps he would live out his few years among the books and scientific apparatus on board, or perhaps he would find release in one of the numerous painless ways. Time and his own inclination could decide such things later. Now it was unimportant. There could be no happiness for him, but in the sense of fulfillment, there would be some measure of content. The gods were no longer laughing.

He moved a few feet toward the ship and stopped, sweeping his eyes over the river and hills again, and letting his vision play with the city Five had described. No, he could not see it with robots populating it, either; but that, too, was conditioning. On the surface, the city might be different, but the surface importance was only a matter of habit, and the realities lay in the minds of the builders who would create that city. If there was no laughter in the world to come, neither would there be tears or poverty or misery such as had ruled too large a portion of his race.

Standing there, it swam before his eyes, paradoxically filled with human people, but the same city in spirit as the one that would surely rise. He could see the great boats in the harbor with others operating up the river. The sky suddenly seemed to fill with the quiet drone of helicopters, and beyond, there came the sound of rockets rising toward the eighth and ninth worlds, while others were building to quest outward in search of new suns with new worlds.

Perhaps they would find Earth someday in their expanding future. Strangely, he hoped that they might, and that perhaps they could even trace their origin, and find again the memory of the soft protoplasmic race that had sired them. It would be nice to be remembered, once that memory was no longer a barrier to their accomplishment. But there were many suns, and in the long millennia, the few connecting links that could point out the truth to them beyond question might easily erode and disappear. He could never know.

Then the wind sighed against him, making a little rustling sound, and he looked down to see something flutter softly in the hand of Five. Faint curiosity carried him forward, but he made no effort to remove it from the robot's grasp, now that he saw its nature.

Five, too, had thought of Earth and their connection with it, and had found the answer, without breaking his orders. The paper was a star map, showing a sun with nine planets, one ringed, some with moons, and the third one circled in black pencil, heavily. They might not know why or what it was when they awoke, but they would seek to learn; and someday, when they found the sun they were searching for, guided by the unmistakable order of its planets, they would return to Earth. With the paper to guide them, it would be long before the last evidence was gone, while they could still read the answer to the problem of their origin.

Jorgen closed the metal hand more closely about the paper, brushed a scrap of dirt from the head of the robot, and then turned resolutely back toward the ship, his steps firm as he entered and closed the lock behind him. In a moment, with a roar of increasing speed, it was lifting from the planet, leaving five little men lying on the sand behind, close to the murmuring of the sea—five little metal men and a dream!

Early in 1944, the girl friend received word that her office was to be moved again, this time to New York City, and I had to make up my mind whether to go along or not. The decision was harder this time. I liked my job and didn't think it was right to quit at that time. And I wasn't at all sure I'd like New York.

Campbell had suggested I move there instead of St. Louis. He felt I'd be much better off, and he pointed out all the advantages. But I hadn't been convinced. True, New York was the publishing center of the country, and most writers found it desirable to live there. But I'd spent my time as a writer away from other writers, generally, and I felt there were advantages in keeping free from too much shop talk; I was a little afraid that it was bad for a writer's individual approach to his craft. (There's something to be said for that argument, and it may help to explain why most writers today do not live in New York.) Anyhow, he hadn't been mentioning the idea for quite a while.

I probably would have stayed where I was if there hadn't been a new development at the shop. The engineers there had given birth to a new machine, and they were just installing it. Instead of hammering flanges onto the aluminum ribs, it rolled them on. It was much faster, and so simple that anyone could do it. I didn't like it, feeling it wouldn't work-harden the alloy as well as the hammer. (That proved to be true, but didn't seem to make any difference in the performance of that remarkable airplane.) And I began to feel that my work wasn't so necessary now.

So when she took off, I had made arrangements to quit my job and follow her in a couple of weeks. I began sorting out all my things and building a box to hold what I couldn't carry with me. (That was the box that was lost with all my manuscripts.)

The task was made somewhat simpler by the fact that I was selling my Woodstock and Oliver typewriters. I was taking only a little three-row Corona portable. I'd found it for ten dollars during the winter. It was in miserable condition. But during spare time I'd filed out a few parts for it, cleaned and adjusted it, and managed to add a pair of shift keys on the right side, where it had none. When I was done, it behaved better than new, and I found it a very pleasant little machine to use. It was genuinely portable, too, weighing less than six pounds in its case.

So I arrived in New York on a fine spring day, all set to find myself a room—a task I'd been assured by several people was going to be very difficult and probably expensive. But I knew where I wanted to be. There were rooming houses all around the area of Ninth Avenue and Fifty-seventh Street, and I meant to find a place there. I've always had a prejudice for the West Side, ever since I first visited the city. And I wasn't going East, even if the girl friend was getting a small apartment there. She'd still be in easy walking distance, and her office was now located at Fifty-seventh and Broadway, which would make it easy to meet her after work.

As usual, the warnings were false. I walked across Ninth on Fifty-seventh and there was a sign advertising a room to let. I found it was going for three dollars a week, and I took it. It was four flights up, but I didn't mind climbing stairs then. I moved my two large suitcases and small typewriter in, and that was that.

Then I went to see Campbell, all primed with a list of stories I'd organized during the past few weeks. There was a novel (which I'm still going to do someday) and a lot of novelettes. I meant to be smart this time and discuss them in general terms before wasting my time writing them.

It wasn't the best way of writing, but I wanted to build up a little backlog in the bank this time before going back to the old method of writing whatever I felt like. (Later, the talk-it-over-before-writing system became common with many of Campbell's writers. I guess it made things easy for them, particularly when they let him do most of their plotting; but the results justified my doubts.)

There was only one small hitch. Campbell was apparently glad to see me and happy to know I'd be around more. But he began by warning me that he was overstocked with novels and novelettes, and what did I have in the shorter lengths?

I gulped quietly to myself, watching the bank account vanish quietly before my imagination. Then I took out one of my lovely novelettes and mentally chopped off two thirds of the last part, patched in a new ending, and began telling him about it. He seemed to like the idea, and suggested I write it. And he cheered me up further by saying that he still had a *few* holes for short stories.

A real professional writer would have left his office and immediately headed toward the other science fiction magazines to try to do business with them. But the idea never occurred to me. I'd been dealing exclusively with Campbell so long that I never thought of another editor!

The next day, I went to work. And surprisingly, the more I looked at that butchered and patched-in former novelette, the better it seemed. In fact, it was a lot better than the original idea would have been. I was a little nervous, since I hadn't really tried writing for some time, but it went well, and I finished the rough at 5,700 words that afternoon. The next day I took "Kindness" down to Campbell.

The story was that of the last normal human being alive in a world of supermen who could intuit things almost instantly that would have taken him hours to think through. The supermen were as kind as possible—and their kindness was a constant reminder of his inferiority. So he manages to sneak away in a spaceship and go to an asteroid he had located on an old map—one where his people had once been great, and where he can live out his life as a true man. The novelette was supposed to go on from there, but the new version ended in a little scene with some supermen talking about how their scheme had worked, and Danny must be at the asteroid by now. It had been only one more kindness.

It made a much stronger story, I think. Campbell accepted it at once, and announced a bit of welcome news. The rate for stories was now one and one-half cents a word. With bonus, that brought the check up to $100.

I next tried a very short story of only 2,000 words, figuring that would certainly fit into the tight budget. I called it "Fool's Errand," which was rather appropriate.

17.

Fool's Errand

(*by Lester del Rey*)

In spite of the wind from the Mediterranean, six miles to the south, the university city of Montpellier reeked with the stench of people huddled together in careless filth; and the twilight softness could only partially conceal the dirt and lack of sanitation in the narrow, twisting streets. No one in this leading medical center of the sixteenth century had heard of germs, and no one cared.

But Roger Sidney, Professor of Paraphysics at a university that would not be built for another six centuries, both knew and cared. He shuddered, and his tall, thin figure wove carefully around some of the worst puddles, while his eyes were turned upward fearfully toward the windows above; one experience with a shower of slop from them had been more than enough. He pressed a kerchief to his nose, but his weary feet went on resolutely. Somewhere in this city was a man called Nostradamus, and Sidney had not dared seven centuries to give up the search because of even this degree of dirt and stench and inconvenience.

Nostradamus, the prophet, author of the cryptic *Centuries!* More important, though, was the original clear manuscript of prophecy from which the *Centuries* were distorted; sheer accident had led to the discovery of that in 1989, where Nostradamus had hidden it from too curious eyes, and it had long since proven accurate. If authentic, it was the only known conclusive proof of prophecy beyond the life-span of the prophet, and that was now important. The parapsychologists denied that authenticity, since their mathematics showed such prophecy to be impossible, and had even devised an elaborate theory of a joke by some far-future time-traveler to account for its accuracy. With equally sound proof of unlimited prophecy, the paraphysicists could not accept such a useless jest, though they had known for years that time travel was theoretically possible.

Now, if Nostradamus would accept the manuscript as being his, the controversy would be ended, and the paraphysicists could extend their mathematics with sureness that led on toward glorious, breathtaking possibilities. Somewhere, perhaps within a few feet, was the man who could settle the question conclusively, and somehow Sidney must find him—and soon!

But the little sign appeared at last, a faded blue rooster crowing over the legend: *Le Coq Bleu.* He turned down the steps into the tavern and felt momentary relief from the unpleasant world outside; mercifully, the straw on the floor had just been changed, and there was the smell of spitted fowls to remind him of his forgotten appetite. He let his eyes wander along the benches and tables, but they were filled, and he hesitated.

In a booth at the side, a slight young man had been eyeing his soiled finery carefully, and now he motioned with a careless hand. "Ho, stranger, I've room in this booth for another. And my stomach has room for a pot more of wine, if you'd ask it." The French was still strange to Sidney's ears, even after the years of preparations, but the somewhat impudent grin was common to all centuries of students.

He dropped onto the hard bench, feeling his legs shake with weariness from the long chase as he did so. The pressing urge for haste before his time ran out was still in him, but he tried to conceal it as he approached the single subject on his mind. By sheer willpower he mustered an answering smile and tossed a coin on the table. "And perhaps food to go with it, eh? You're a student at the university?"

"Your questions are as correct as the color of your money, stranger, and that is correct indeed." The youth was up with the coin in his fingers, to return in a few moments with two thick platters bearing roasted pullets and with a smiling, bowing landlord carrying a jug of red wine. Sidney grinned ruefully as his fingers made clutching motions at the table where there were no forks, then ripped off a leg and used his fingers as the other was doing. The wine was raw and a bit sour, though there was strength to it, and some relief.

But there was no time to be wasted, and he returned to the pressing questions uppermost in his mind. "As a student, then, perhaps you know one Michel de Notredame? After I located his lodgings, they told me he might be here . . . and I've come all the way from Paris to find him. If you can point him out or take me to him, I'll pay you well for your trouble."

"From Paris, eh?" Suspicion crept slowly into the eyes of the other. "Four hundred miles—a week to ten days of hard journey—to see an obscure student? Stranger, your speech is odd, your clothes are strange, but that is fantastic! His relatives are poor and he is poorer. If this is some strange manner of pressing for his debts, you but waste your time; I'll have none of it. If you have other reasons, name them, and I'll think on it."

"Then you do know him?"

"By sight, but you'll not find him here, so save your glances. Well?"

Sidney pulled his eyes back, and his fingers shook with the eagerness that had carried him through the torture of that frantic chase from Paris after he'd learned of his mistake. But he fought again for reason and coolness and for some approach that would quiet the suspicion of the student. The truth was unbelievable, but he could think of nothing else that would ring true, and he was not adept at lies.

"I care nothing for his past—his debts, his sins, or his crimes. All I'm concerned with is his future, which will make your obscure friend the greatest man of this age. But it's a strange story, and you'd think me raving mad."

The other shrugged. "I've studied philosophy and medicine, and there's little left I can't believe. Your story interests me. Spin it well, and perhaps I'll take you to him, unless he should come here first—which I think most unlikely this evening. As to madness, I'm a bit mad myself. . . . Landlord, more wine!"

The student was far more interested in the wine than the story, and Sidney felt his upsurge of hope fading again. He'd found already how faint were his chances of tracking down any particular person in the maze of this city. And in another hour perhaps, or even at any minute, he might feel the surge and pull of the great machine in his home century, to go spinning back with his mission unfulfilled. Already his time was overdue! He narrowed his thoughts down, trying to find some quicker proof that might suffice if he could have the other. "Tell me—honestly in the name of God—how well do you know Michel de Notredame?"

"We share lodgings. Well enough."

"Then if my time grows too short and he does not come, perhaps you'll do. Here." He flipped his purse out on the table, filled with coins that had been matchlessly counterfeited by minters of the twenty-third century, and with others genuine to the time, received in change. "Take it—all—it's yours. Only believe me. Michel de Notredame, under the name of Nostradamus, will be the greatest of all prophets in the years to come. His name will be greater even than that of her Majesty, Catherine de Medici. Can you believe that a man from the future might find a need to see him—and even find a way of coming back to do so? I did! I left the year of Grace 2211, intending to reach Paris in 1550. By error, it was 1528, and he was not there, but I knew he had been studying here, so here I am. Can you believe that, young man—for the contents of this purse?"

The other's hands had come up slowly to cross himself, then dropped, while his eyes turned from fear to distrust, and then to speculation. "For the money—why not? I've heard that warlocks could bring the long dead from the past by magic and the use of certain Names of Power; perchance a greater one might journey back himself. Black magic? And yet, your face has none of Satan's knowledge in it. How?"

"I can't tell you. There are no words yet. Call it science—or white magic. Not black." Sidney's fingers shook again in reaction from the disbelief he had expected; but he should have known that skepticism is a product of a science advanced enough to doubt, but not to accept what lies beyond its knowledge. He shook his head, remembering the long years of preparation and the work that had gone into his being here. He could never explain that, or the need behind it, when paraphysics and parapsychology would be meaningless words.

He could never tell of the immense, inconceivable power needed to bridge time from one of its loops to another, or of the struggle he and his colleagues had waged for three decades to be granted the use of such power. Now, it had surged out, carrying him in the tiny network of wires woven into these garments into the past; sometime soon, the return surge must flow back to return him. They had figured a week, and already ten desperate days were gone while he fled south on the fool's errand that must be made. Their calculations had erred as to the length of the time loop by twenty-two years, and he could not guess how that would affect the length of the power surge, but the return flow must surely have begun.

He caught himself up and went urgently on. "Notredame won fame in the court of Catherine for prophecy while living; when he died, he left verses called 'Centuries,' with tantalizing hints which some believed; and when his original manuscript was found, he won an undisputed place in all history. Now, we must know without the doubts that exist whether that manuscript was his; we *must*. Even a little evidence might decide, but . . . Do you know his writing?"

"I've seen it often enough. Stranger, your story begins to interest me, whatever truth lies in it. But as to prophecy, anyone will tell you it's no uncommon thing; the greatest astrologers in the world are in

France." The student filled his mug again and leaned back, shaking his head to clear it of wine fumes. "If this Nostradamus was an astrologer and you need astrologers, why not find others?"

Sidney shrugged it aside. "No matter, they would not help. He claimed to be an astrologer, of course, but . . . But could you swear to his writing if you saw it? Here!" He thrust his hand into his clothes and brought out a parchment manuscript, to spread it quickly on the table. "This is an exact copy, down to the very texture of the parchment and smudges of ink upon it. Don't mind the contents; they no longer concern us, since we've passed the final date of specific forecasts. Only study the writing. It's a young man's script, and all else we have of his is from his later years. But you know his younger hand. Swear to me honestly, *is it his?*"

The youth bent his head over it, tracing with his finger, and running his other hand across reddened eyes. Sidney cursed the wine and the slowness of the man, but at last the other looked up, and something in the frantic desperation of Sidney's face seemed to settle his doubts, for his own turned suddenly serious.

"I don't know, stranger; it looks like it—and yet I never wrote such words, nor ever planned to."

"You . . . *you*—Notredame!"

"I am Michel de Notredame, a drunken fool to admit the fact even now, when you might be here on any—"

But Roger Sidney from 2211 was laughing, a wracking that shook him in convulsions, harshly soundless. One trembling finger pointed to the manuscript, then to the student, and the convulsive shaking redoubled. "A cycle—a closed cycle! And we—and that—that—" But he could not finish. Notredame swung his eyes about to see if others were noticing, but the tavern was emptied and the landlord was busy at the far end. He turned back, and suddenly crossed himself.

There was a glow about the stranger, a network of shining threads in his garments that might have been frozen lightning. It spread, misted, and was gone, while the bench where he had been was suddenly empty. Notredame was alone, and with slowly whitening face, he began to cross himself again, only to stop and snatch the purse and coins from the table where they lay and tuck them into his clothes. For a second, he hesitated, his now-sober eyes narrowing thoughtfully.

"Nostradamus," he muttered. "Nostradamus, astrologer to the court of the Queen. I like the sound of that."

His fingers picked up the manuscript, and he slipped swiftly out into the night.

Campbell rejected it for the reason that I should have recognized myself—it is entirely too obvious, once the idea of a time machine is introduced.

It took a long time to sell that one, even after I had an agent. But finally, in 1951, Robert Lowndes bought it for one of the Columbia Publications magazines, paying $21. "Doc" Lowndes was a very good friend of mine (and still is, happily), but I don't think it was entirely friendship that decided him. It is a pretty weak story, but I hope not a bad one. And maybe he had need of something that length and felt that my name would look good on the contents page.

My next story went in pretty heavily for a couple of controversial "scientific" ideas that were being written up in the magazines. One was about a discovery by a man named Ehrenhaft of magnetic current. If magnetism really could be made to flow like electricity, it would have been a genuine breakthrough; but nobody was ever able to confirm it. Another idea dealt with the work of the Russian scientist Bogolometz; he had made an extract he called antireticular cytotoxic serum which was supposed to cure all kinds of things and offer some hope for extreme longevity. There later proved to be some value to it, but not nearly as much as was hoped.

Both of the ideas fitted neatly into an old idea I had about a teaching machine. So I put them all together and came up with another story. This one crowded Campbell's maximum of 8,000 words. But he bought it, though without a bonus, for $120. I used the Philip St. John by-line and called it "The One-Eyed Man."

18.

The One-Eyed Man

(by Philip St. John)

A blank-faced zombie moved aside as Jimmy Bard came out of the Dictator's office, but he did not notice it; and his own gesture of stepping out of the way of the worried, patrolling *adult* guards was purely automatic. His tall, well-muscled body went on doing all the things long habit had taught it, while his mind churned inside him, rebelling hopelessly at the inevitable.

For a moment, the halls were free of the countless guards, and Jimmy moved suddenly to one of the walls, making quick, automatic motions with his hands. There was no visible sign of change in the surface, but he drew a deep breath and stepped forward; it was like breasting a strong current, but then he was inside and in a narrow passageway, one of the thousands of secret corridors that honeycombed the whole monstrous castle.

Here there could be no *adults* to remind him of what he'd considered his deficiencies, nor of the fact that those deficiencies were soon to be eliminated. The first Dictator Bard had shared the secret of the castle with none save the murdered men who built it; and death had prevented his revealing it even to his own descendants. No tapping would ever reveal that the walls were not the thick, homogenous things they seemed, for tapping would set off alarms and raise stone segments where needed, to make them as solid as they appeared. It was Jimmy's private kingdom, and one where he could be bedeviled only by his own thoughts.

But today, those were trouble enough. Morbid fascination with them drove him forward through the twisting passages until he located a section of the wall that was familiar, and pressed his palm against it. For a second, it seemed cloudy, and then was transparent, as the energies worked on it, letting vibration through in one direction only. He did not notice the quiet sounds of those in the room beyond, but riveted his eyes on the queer headpieces worn by the two girls and single boy within.

Three who had reached their twelfth birthday today and were about to become adults—or zombies! Those odd headpieces were electronic devices that held all the knowledge of a complete, all-embracing education, and they were now working silently, impressing that knowledge onto the minds of their wearers at some two hundred million impulses a second, grooving it permanently into those minds. The children who had entered with brains filled only with the things of childhood would leave with all the information they could ever need, to go out into the world as full adults, if they had withstood the shock of education. Those who failed to withstand it would still leave with the same knowledge, but the character and personality would be gone, leaving them wooden-faced, soul-less zombies.

Once Jimmy had sat in one of those chairs, filled with all the schemes and ambitions of a young rowdy about to become a man.

But that time, nothing had happened! He could remember the conferences, the scientific attempts to explain his inability to absorb information from the compellor Aaron Bard had given the world, and his own tortured turmoil at finding himself something between an adult and a zombie, useless and unwanted in a world where only results counted. He had no way of knowing, then, that all the bitter years of adjusting to his fate and learning to survive in the contemptuous world were the result of a fake. It was only within the last hour that he had discovered that.

"Pure fake, carefully built up!" His Dictator father had seemed proud of that, even over the worry and desperation that had been on his face these last few days. "The other two before you who didn't take were just false leads, planted to make your case seem plausible; same with the half dozen later cases. You'd have burned—turned zombie, almost certainly. And you're a Bard, someday to dictate this country! I took the chance that if we waited until you grew older, you'd pass, and managed to use blank tapes. . . . Now I can't wait any longer. Hell's due to pop, and I'm not ready for it, but if I can surprise them, present you as an adult . . . Be back here at six sharp, and I'll have everything ready for your education."

Ten years before, those words would have spelled pure heaven to him. But now the scowl deepened on his forehead as he slapped off the one-way transparency. He'd learned a lot about this world in those ten years, and had seen the savage ruthlessness of the adults. He'd seen no wisdom, but only cunning and cleverness come from the Bard psychicompellors.

"Damn Aaron Bard!"

"Amen!" The soft word came sighing out of the shadows beside the boy, swinging him around with a jerk. Another, in here! Then his eyes were readjusting to the pale, bluish glow of the passages, and he made out the crouched form of an elderly man, slumped into one of the corners. That thin, weary figure with the bitter mouth and eyes could never be a castle guard, however well disguised, and Jimmy breathed easier, though the thing that might be a weapon in the hands of the other centered squarely on him.

The old man's voice trembled faintly, and there were the last dregs of bitterness in it. "Aaron Bard's damned, all right. . . . I thought the discovery of one-way transparency was lost, though, along with controlled interpenetrability of matter—stuff around which to build a whole new science! And yet, that's the answer; for three days, I've been trying to find a trapdoor or sliding panel, boy, and all the time the trick lay in matter that could be made interpenetrable. Amusing to you?"

"No, sir." Jimmy held his voice level and quite normal. A grim ability to analyze any situation had been knocked into him during the years of his strangeness in a world that did not tolerate strangeness, and he saw that the man was close to cracking. He smiled quietly—and moved without facial warning, with the lightning reaction he had forced himself to learn, ripping the weapon out of weakened hands. His voice was still quiet. "I don't know how you know those things, nor care. The important thing is to keep you from letting others know, and . . ."

Sudden half-crazed laughter cut off his words. "Go back to the others and tell them? Go back and be tortured again? They'd love that. Aaron Bard's come back to tell us about some more of his nice discoveries! So sweet of you to call, my dear. . . . I'm damned, all right, by my own reputation."

"But Aaron Bard's been dead eighty years! His corpse is preserved in a glass coffin on exhibition; I've seen it myself." And yet there was more than simple insanity here; the old man had known the two secrets which were discovered by Aaron Bard and which his son, the first Dictator, had somehow managed to find and conceal for his own ends after the inventor's death in an explosion. Those secrets had been built into the palace as part of the power of his Dictatorship, until they had been lost with his death. But the old man was speaking again, his voice weak and difficult.

"What does a mere eighty-year span mean, or a figure of wax in a public coffin? The real body they held in sterile refrigeration, filled with counter-enzymes . . . my own discovery, again! You know of it?"

Jimmy nodded. A Russian scientist had found safe revival of dogs possible even after fifteen minutes of death; with later development, men had been operated on in death, where it served better than anesthesia, and revived again. The only limit had been the time taken by the enzymes of the body to begin dissolving the tissues; and with the discovery by Aaron Bard of a counteracting agent, there had ceased to be any theoretical limit to safe revival. Dying soldiers in winter had injected ampules of it and been revived days or weeks later, where the cold had preserved them. "But—eighty years!"

"Why not—when my ideas were still needed, when my last experiment dealt with simple atomic power, rather than the huge, cumbersome U-235 method? Think what it would mean to an army! My son did—he was very clever at thinking of such things. Eighty years, until they could perfect their tissue regrowing methods and dare to revive my body." He laughed again, an almost noiseless wracking of his exhausted shoulders, and there was the hint of delirious raving in his voice now, though the words were still rational.

"I was so pathetically grateful and proud, when they revived me. I was always gratefully proud of my achievements, you know, and what they could do for humanity. But the time had been too long—my brain only seemed normal. It had deteriorated, and I couldn't remember all I should; when I tried too hard, there were strange nightmare periods of half insanity. And their psychological torture to rip the secret from me didn't help. Two months of that, boy! They told me my name was almost like a god's in this world, and then they stopped at nothing to get what they wanted from that god! And at last I must have gone mad for a time; I don't remember, but somehow I must have escaped—I think I remember something about an air shaft. And then I was here, lost in the maze, unable to get out. But I couldn't be here, could I, if the only entrance was through interpenetrable stone panels that I couldn't remember how to energize?"

"Easy, sir." Jimmy slipped an arm under the trembling body of Aaron Bard and lifted him gently. "You could, all right. There's one out of order, in constant interpenetrable condition in an old air shaft. That's how I first found all this, years ago. . . . There's some soup I can heat in my rooms, and you won't have to go back to them."

He might as well do one decent and human thing, while his mind was still his own, untouched by the damnable education machine. And seeing this bitter, suffering old man, he could no longer hate Aaron Bard for inventing it. The man had possessed a mind of inconceivable scope and had brought forth inventions in all fields as a cat brings forth kittens, but their misuse was no fault of his.

And suddenly it occurred to him that here in his arms was the reason for the desperation his father felt. They couldn't know of the interpenetrable panel, and the search that had undoubtedly been made and failed could have only one answer to them; he must have received outside help from some of the parties constantly plotting treason. With the threat of simple atomic power in such hands, no wonder his Dictator father was pulling all his last desperate tricks to maintain the order of things! Jimmy shook his head; it seemed that everything connected with Aaron Bard led to the position he was in and the inevitable education he must face. For a brief moment he hesitated, swayed by purely personal desires; then his hand moved out to the panel, and he was walking through into his own room, the aged figure still in his arms.

Later, when the old scientist had satisfied some of the needs of his body and was sitting on the bed, smoking, his eyes wandered slowly over the rows of books on the shelves about the room, and his eyebrows lifted slightly. "*The Age of Reason*, even! The first books I've seen in this world, Jimmy!"

"Nobody reads much, anymore, so they don't miss them at the old library. People prefer 'vision for amusement and the compellor tapes if they need additional information. I started trying to learn things from them, and reading grew to be a habit."

"Umm. So you're another one-eyed man?"

"Eh?"

Bard shrugged, and the bitterness returned to his mouth. " 'In the country of the blind, the one-eyed man is—killed!' Wells wrote a story about it. Where—when—I came from, men had emotional eyes to their souls, and my guess is that you've been through enough hell to develop your own. But this world is blind to such things. They don't want people to see. It's the old rule of the pack: Thou shalt conform! Jimmy, how did all this come to be?"

Jimmy frowned, trying to put it into words. The start had probably been when Aaron Bard tried his newly invented psychicompellor on his son. The boy had liked that way of learning, and stolen other experimental tapes, building with his cold, calculating little brain toward the future already. Unerringly, he'd turned to the army, apparently sensing the coming war, and making the most of it when it came. Fifteen years of exhausting, technological warfare had let him introduce the educator to furnish the technical men needed, and had seen him bring forth stolen secret of his father after stolen secret, once the accidental death of Bard had left him alone in possession of Bard's files. With the war's end, the old education system was gone, and boys of twelve were serving as technicians at home until they could be replaced for active duty when old enough.

Those same boys, grown to men and desiring the same things he did, had made possible his move from General to President, and finally to Dictator. He'd even adopted the psychicompellor as his heraldic device. And the ever-increasing demands of technology made going back to old methods impossible and assured him a constant supply of young "realists."

Bard interrupted. "Why? It would have been hard—getting an education was always difficult and becoming worse, which is why I tried to make the compellor—but it would have been worth it when they saw where it led. After all, without such help I managed to find a few things—even if they turned out to be Frankenstein monsters!"

"But you depended on some odd linkage of simple facts for results, and most men can't; they need a multitude of facts. And even then, we still follow you by rote in some things!"

"Too easy knowledge. They aren't using it—when they get facts, they don't have the habits of hard thinking needed to utilize them. I noticed the meager developments of new fields. . . . But when they began making these—uh—zombies . . ."

Jimmy punched a button and nodded toward the creature that entered in answer. It began quietly clearing the room, removing the evidence of Bard's meal, while the scientist studied it. "There's one. He knows as much as any adult, but he has no soul, no emotions, you might say. Tell him to do something, and he will—but he won't even eat without orders."

"Permanent mechanical hypnosis," Bard muttered, and there was hell in his eyes. Then his mouth hardened, while the eyes grew even grimmer. "I never foresaw that, but—you're wrong, and it makes it even worse! You—uh—4719, answer my questions. Do you have emotions such as hatred, fear, or a sense of despair?"

Jimmy started to shake his head, but the zombie answered dully before him. "Yes, master, all those!"

"But you can't connect them with your actions—is that right? You're two people, one in hell and unable to reach the other?"

The affirmative answer was in the same dull tone again, and the zombie turned obediently and left at Bard's gesture. Jimmy wiped sudden sweat from his forehead. He'd been hoping before that he might fail the compellor education as a release, but this would be sheer, unadulterated hell! And the psychologists must know this, even though they never mentioned it.

"And ten percent of us are zombies! But only a very few at first, until the need for ever more knowledge made the shock of education greater. By then—the world had accepted such things; and some considered them a most useful by-product, since they made the best possible workers." His own voice grew more bitter as he forced it on with the history lesson, trying to forget the new and unwelcome knowledge.

Bard's son had built the monstrous castle with its secret means for spying, and had fled into the passages with his private papers to die when his son wrested control from him. It was those moldy papers that had shown Jimmy the secret of escape when he'd stumbled into the labyrinth first. After that, the passage of Dictatorship from father to son had been peaceful enough, and taken for granted. On the whole, there had been little of the deliberate cruelty of the ancient Nazi regime, and the dictatorial powers, while great, were not absolute. The people were used to it—after all, they were products of the compellor, and a ruthless people, best suited by dictatorial government.

Always the compellor! Jimmy hesitated for a moment, and then plunged into the tale of his own troubles. "So I'm to be made into a beast, whether I like it or not," he finished. "Oh, I could turn you in and save myself. If I were an adult, I would! That's why I hate it, even though I might like it then. It wouldn't be me—it'd be just another adult, carrying my name, doing all the things I've learned to hate. I can save myself from becoming one of them—by becoming one!"

"*Requiescat in pace!* Rest the dead in peace. If you wake them, they may learn they've made a ghastly mess of the world, and may even find themselves ruining the only person in all the world whom they like!" Aaron Bard shook his head, wrinkles of concentration cutting over the lines of pain. "The weapon you took from me isn't exactly harmless. Sometime, during my temporary insanity, I must have remembered the old secret, since I made it then, and it's atom-powered. Maybe, without a dictator—"

"No! He's weak, but he's no worse than the others; I couldn't let you kill my father!"

"No, I suppose you couldn't; anyhow, killing people isn't usually much of a solution. Jimmy, are you sure there's any danger of your being made like the others?"

"I've seen the results!"

"But have you? The children are given no education or discipline until they're twelve, and then suddenly filled with knowledge, for which they haven't been prepared, even if preadolescents can be prepared for all that—which I don't believe. Even in my day, in spite of some discipline and training, twelve-year-old boys were little hoodlums, choosing to group together into gangs; wild, savage barbarians, filled with only their own egotism; pack-hunting animals, not yet civilized. Not cruel, exactly, but thoughtless, ruthless as we've seen this world is. Maybe with the sudden new flood of knowledge for which they never worked, they make good technicians; but that spurious, forced adulthood might very well discourage any real maturity; when the whole world considers them automatic adults, what incentive have they to mature?"

Jimmy thought back over his early childhood, before the education fizzle, and it was true that he and the other boys had been the egocentric little animals Bard described; there had been no thought of anything beyond their immediate whims and wants, and no one to tell them that the jungle rule for survival of the fittest should be tempered with decency and consideration for others. But the books had taught him that there had been problem children and boy-gangs before the compellor—and they had mostly outgrown it. Here, after education, they never changed; and while the pressure of society now resisted any attempt on their part to change, that wasn't the explanation needed; other ages had developed stupid standards, but there had always been those who refused them before.

"Do you believe that, sir?"

The old man shrugged slightly. "I don't know. I can't be sure. Maybe I'm only trying to justify myself. Maybe the educator does do something to the mind, carefully as I designed it to carry no personal feelings to the subject. And while I've seen some of the people, I haven't seen enough of the private life to judge; you can't judge, because you never knew normal people. . . . When I invented it, I had serious doubts about it, for that matter. They still use it as I designed it—exactly?"

"Except for the size of the tapes."

"Then there's a wave form that will cancel out the subject's sensitivity, blanket the impulse, if broadcast within a few miles. If I could remember it—if I had an electronics laboratory where I could try it—maybe your fake immunity to education could be made real."

Relief washed over the younger man, sending him to his feet and to the panel. "There *is* a laboratory. The first Dictator had everything installed for an emergency, deep underground in the passages. I don't know how well stocked it is, but I've been there."

He saw purpose and determination come into the tired face, and Aaron Bard was beside him as the panel became passable. Jimmy turned through a side way that led near the Senatorial section of the castle. On impulse he turned aside and motioned the other forward. "If you want an idea of our private life, take a look at our Senators and judge for yourself."

The wall became transparent to light and sound in one direction and they were looking out into one of the cloakrooms of the Senate Hall. One of the middle-aged men was telling a small audience of some personal triumph of his: "Their first kid—burned—just a damned zombie! I told her when she turned me down for that pimple-faced goon that I'd fix her and I did. I spent five weeks taking the kid around on the sly, winning his confidence. Just before education, I slipped him the dope in candy! You know what it does when they're full of that and the educator starts in."

Another grinned. "Better go easy telling about it; some of us might decide to turn you in for breaking the laws you helped write against using the stuff that way."

"Hell, you can't prove it. I'm not dumb enough to give you birds anything you could pin on me. Just to prove I'm the smartest man in this bunch, I'll let you in on something. I've been doing a little thinking on the Dictator's son. . . ."

"Drop it, Pete, cold! I was with a bunch that hired some fellows to kill the monkey a couple years ago—and you can't prove that, either! We had keys to his door and everything; but he's still around, and the thugs never came back. I don't know what makes, but no other attempt has worked. The Dictator's got some tricks up his sleeve, there."

Jimmy shut the panel off and grinned. "I don't sleep anywhere near doors, and there's a section of the floor that can be made interpenetrable, with a ninety-foot shaft under it. That's why I wangled that particular suite out of my father."

"These are the Senators?" Bard asked.

"Some of the best ones." Jimmy went on, turning on a panel now and again, and Bard frowned more strongly after each new one. Some were plotting treason, others merely talking. Once something like sympathy for the zombies was expressed, but not too strongly. Jimmy started to shut the last panel off, when a new voice started.

"Blane's weakling son is dead. Puny little yap couldn't take the climate and working with all the zombies in the mines; committed suicide this morning."

"His old man couldn't save him from that, eh? Good. Put it into the papers, will you? I want to be sure the Dictator's monkey gets full details. They were thick for a while, you know."

Jimmy's lips twisted as he cut off suddenly. "The only partly human person I ever knew—the one who taught me to read. He was a sickly boy, but his father managed to save him from euthanasia, somehow. Probably he went around with me for physical protection, since the others wouldn't let him alone. Then they shipped him to some mines down in South America, to handle zombie labor."

"Euthanasia? Nice word for killing off the weak. Biologically, perhaps such times as these may serve a useful purpose, but I'd rather have the physically weak around than those who treat them that way. Jimmy, I think if my trick doesn't work and the educator does things to you it shouldn't, I'll kill you before I kill myself!"

Jimmy nodded tightly. Bard wasn't the killing type, but he hoped he'd do it, if such a thing occurred. Now he hurried, wasting no more time in convincing the other of the necessity to prevent such a change in him. He located the place he wanted and stepped in, pressed a switch on the floor, and set the lift to dropping smoothly downward.

"Power is stolen, but cleverly, and no one has suspected. There are auxiliary fuel-batteries, too. The laboratory power will be the same. And here we are."

He pointed to the room, filled with a maze of equipment of all kinds, neatly in order, but covered with dust and dirt from long disuse. Aaron Bard looked at it slowly, with a wry grin.

"Familiar, Jimmy. My son apparently copied it from my old laboratory, where he used to fiddle around sometimes, adapting my stuff to military use. With a little decency, he'd have been a good scientist; he was clever enough."

Jimmy watched, some measure of hope coming to him, as the old man began working. He cleared the tables of dust with casual flicks of a cloth and began, his hands now steady. Wires, small tubes, coils, and various other electronic equipment came from the little boxes and drawers, though some required careful search. Then his fingers began the job of assembling and soldering them into a plastic case about the size of a muskmelon, filled almost solidly as he went along.

"That boy who taught you how to read—was he educated at the age of twelve?"

"Of course—it's compulsory. Everyone has to be. Or—" Jimmy frowned, trying to remember more clearly; but he could only recall vague hints and phrases from bits of conversation among Blane's enemies. "There was something about falsified records during the euthanasia judgment proceedings, I think, but I don't know what records. Does it matter?"

Bard shrugged, scribbling bits of diagrams on a scrap of dirty paper before picking up the soldering iron again. "I wish I knew. . . . Umm? In that fifteen-year war, when they first began intensive use of the compellor, they must have tried it on all types and ages. Did any scientist check on variations due to such factors? No, they wouldn't! No wonder they don't develop new fields. How about a book of memoirs by some soldier who deals with personalities?"

"Maybe, but I don't know. The diary of the first Dictator might, if it could be read, but when I tried after finding it, I only got hints of words here and there. It's in some horrible code—narrow strips of short, irregularly spaced letter groups, pasted in. I can't even figure what kind of a code it is, and there's no key."

"Key's in the library, Jimmy, if you'll look up Brak-O-Type—machine shorthand. He considered ordinary typing inefficient; one time when I thoroughly agreed with him. Damn!" Bard sucked on the thumb where a drop of solder had fallen and stared down at the tight-packed parts. He picked up a tiny electrolytic condenser, studied the apparatus, and put it down again doubtfully. Then he sat motionlessly, gazing down into the half-finished object.

The work, which had progressed rapidly at first, was now beginning to go more slowly, with long pauses while the older man thought. And the pauses lengthened. Jimmy slipped out and up the lift again, to walk rapidly down a corridor that would lead him to the rear of one of the restaurants of the castle. The rats had been blamed for a great deal at that place, and they were in for more blame as Jimmy slid his hands back into the corridors with coffee and food in them.

Bard gulped the coffee gratefully as he looked up to see the younger man holding out the food, but he only sampled that. His hands were less sure again. "Jimmy, I don't know—I can't think. I get so far, and everything seems clear; then—*pfft!* It's the same as when I first tried to remember the secret of atomic power; there are worn places in my mind—eroded by eighty years of death. And when I try to force my thoughts across them, they stagger and reel."

"Grandfather Bard, you've got to finish it! It's almost five, and I have to report back at six!"

Bard rubbed his wrinkled forehead with one hand, clenching and opening the other. For a time, then, he continued to work busily, but there were long quiet intervals. "It's all here, except this one little section. If I could put that in right, it'd work—but if I make a mistake, it'll probably blow out, unless it does nothing."

Jimmy stared at his watch. "Try it."

"You solder it; my hands won't work anymore." Bard slipped off the stool, directing the boy's hands carefully. "If I could be sure of making it by going insane, as I did the atom-gun, I'd even force my mind through those nightmares again. But I might decide to do almost anything else, instead. . . . No, that's the antenna—one end remains free."

The hands of the watch stood at ten minutes of six as the last connection was made and Bard plugged it into the socket near the floor. Then the tubes were warming up. There was no blowout, at least; the tubes continued to glow, and a tiny indicator showed radiation of some form coming from the antenna. Jimmy grinned, relief stronger in him, but the older man shook his head doubtfully as they went back to the lift again.

"I don't know whether it's working right, son. I put that last together by mental rule of thumb, and you shouldn't work that way in delicate electronic devices, where even two wires accidentally running beside each other can ruin things! But at least we can pray. And as a last resort—well, I still have the atom-pistol."

"Use it, if you need to! I'll take you to the back wall of my father's inner office, and you can stay there watching while I go around the long way. And use it quickly, because I'll know you're there!"

It took him three tries to find a hallway that was empty of the guards and slip out, but he was only seconds late as his father opened the door and let him in; the usual secretaries and guards were gone, and only the chief psychologist stood there, his small stock of equipment set up. But the Dictator hesitated.

"Jimmy, I want you to know I have to do this, even though I don't know whether you have any better chance of passing it now than when you were a kid—that's just my private hunch, and the psychologist here thinks I'm wrong. But—well, something I was counting on is probably stolen by conspiracy, and there's a helluva war brewing in Eurasia against us, which we're not ready for; the oligarchs have something secret that they figure will win. It's all on a private tape I'll give you. I don't know how much help you'll be, but seeing you suddenly normal will back up the bluff I'm planning, at least. We Bards have a historic destiny to maintain, and I'm counting on you to do your part. You *must* pass!"

Jimmy only half heard it. He was staring at the headpiece, looking something like a late-style woman's hat with wires leading to a little box on the table, and varicolored spools of special tape. For a second, as it clamped down over his face, he winced, but then stood it in stiff silence. In the back of his mind, something tried to make itself noticed—but as he groped for it, only a vague, uneasy feeling remained. Words and something about the psychologist's face . . .

He heard the snap of the switch, and then his mind seemed to freeze, though sounds and sights still registered. But he knew that the device in the room so far below had failed! The pressure on his brain was too familiar by description; the Bard psychicompellor was functioning. For a second, before full impact, he tried to tear it off, but something else seemed to control his mind, and he sat rigidly, breathing hard, but unable to stop it. His thoughts died down, became torpid, while the machine went on driving its two hundred million impulses into his brain every second, doing things that science still could not understand, but could use.

He watched stolidly as the spools were finished, one by one, until his father produced one from a safe and watched it used, then smashed it. The psychologist bent, picked up one last one, and attached it. . . . The face of the man was familiar. . . . "Like to have the brat in front of a burner like those we use in zombieing criminals. . . ."

Then something in his head seemed to slither, like feet slipping on ice. Numbed and dull of mind, he still gripped at himself, and his formerly motionless hands were clenching at the arms of the chair. Something gnawing inside, a queer distortion, that . . . Was this what a zombie felt, while its mind failed under education?

The psychologist bent then, removing the headset. "Get up, James Bard!" But as Jim still sat, surprise came over his face, masked instantly by a look of delighted relief. "So you're no zombie?"

Jim arose then, rubbing his hands across his aching forehead, and managed to smile. "No," he said quietly. "No, I'm all right. *I'm perfectly all right!* Perfectly."

"Praise be, Jimmy." The Dictator relaxed slowly into his chair. "And now you know. . . . What's the matter?"

Jim couldn't tell him of the assurance necessary to keep Aaron Bard from firing, but he held his face into a pleasant smile in spite of the pain in his head as he turned to face his father. He knew now—everything. Quietly, unobtrusively, all the things he hadn't known before were there, waiting for his mind to use, along with all the things he had seen and all the conversations he had spied upon in secret.

He had knowledge—and a mind trained to make the most of it. The habits of thinking he had forced upon himself were already busy with the new information; even the savage, throbbing pain couldn't stop that. Now he passed his hand across his head deliberately, and nodded to the outer office. "My head's killing me, Father. Can't I use the couch out there?"

"For a few minutes, I guess. Doctor, can't you give the boy something?"

"Maybe. I'm not a medical doctor, but I can fix the pain, I think." The psychologist was abstract, but he turned out. The Dictator came last, and they were out of the little room, into the larger one where no passages pierced the walls and no shot could reach him.

The smile whipped from the boy's face then, and one of his hands snapped out, lifting a small flame gun from his father's hip with almost invisible speed. It came up before the psychologist could register the emotions that might not yet have begun, and the flame washed out, blackening clothes and flesh and leaving only a limp, charred body on the floor.

Jim kicked it aside. "Treason. He had a nice little tape in there, made out by two people of totally opposite views, in spite of the law against it. Supposed to burn me into a zombie. It would have, except that I'd already studied both sides pretty well, and it raised Ned for a while, even then. Here's your gun, Father."

"Keep it!" The first real emotion Jim had ever seen on his father's face was there now, and it was fierce pride. "I never saw such beautiful gun work, boy! Or such a smooth job of handling a snake! Thanks be, you aren't soft and weak, as I thought. No more emotional nonsense, eh?"

"No more. I'm cured. And at the meeting of the Senators you've called, maybe we'll have a surprise for them. You go on down, and I'll catch up as soon as I can get some amidopyrene for this headache. Somehow, I'll think of something to stop the impeachment they're planning."

"Impeachment! That bad? But how—why didn't you—"

"I did try to tell you, years ago. But though I knew every little treason plot they were cooking then, you were too busy to listen to a nonadult, and I didn't try again. Now, though, it'll be useful. See you outside assembly, unless I'm late."

He grinned mirthlessly as his father went down the hall and away from him. The look of pride in his too-heavy face wouldn't have stayed there if he'd known just how deep in treason some of the fine Senator friends were. It would take a dozen miracles to pull them through. Jim found the panel he wanted, looked to be sure of privacy, and slipped through, tracing quickly down the corridor.

But Aaron Bard wasn't to be found. For a second he debated more searching, but gave it up; there was no time, and he could locate the old man later. It wasn't important that he be found at the moment. Jim shrugged and slipped into one of the passages that would serve as a shortcut to the great assembly room. The headache was already disappearing, and he had no time to bother with it.

They were already beginning session when he arrived, even so, and he slipped quietly through the Dictator's private entrance, making his way unnoticed to the huge desk, behind a jade screen that would hide him from the Senators and yet permit him to watch. He had seen other sessions before, but they had been noisy, bickering affairs, with the rival groups squabbling and shouting names. Today there was none of that. They were going through the motions, quite plainly stalling for time, and without interest in the routine. This meeting was a concerted conspiracy to depose the Dictator, though only the few leaders of the groups knew that Eurasian bribery and treason were the real reasons behind it.

It had been in the making for years, while those leaders carefully built up the ever-present little hatreds and discontents. Jim's status had been used to discredit his father, though the man's own weaknesses had been more popular in distorted versions. As Jim looked, he saw that the twelve cunning men lured to treason by promises of being made American Oligarchs, though supposedly heading rival groups, were all still absent; that explained the stalling. Something was astir, and Jim had a hunch that the psychologist's corpse would have been of no little interest to them. The two honest group leaders were in session, grim and quiet; then, as he looked, the twelve came in, one by one, from different entrances. Their faces showed no great sense of defeat.

Naturally. The Dictator had no chance; he had tried to rule by dividing the now-united groups and by family prestige, and had kept afloat so long as they were not ready to strike; the methods would not stand any strain, much less this attack. He had already muffed one attack opportunity while the leaders were out. A strong man would have cut through the stalling and taken the initiative; a clever orator, schooled in the dramatics and emotions of a Webster or a Borah might even have controlled them. But the Dictator was weak, and the compellor did not produce great oratory; that was incompatible with such emotional immaturity.

But the Dictator had finally been permitted to speak, now. He should have begun with the shock of Jim's adulthood to snap them out of their routine thoughts, built up the revival of Aaron Bard and his old atomic power work, to make them wonder, and then swept his accusations over them in short, hard blows. Instead, he was tracing the old accomplishments of the Bard Family, stock, familiar phrases with no meaning left in them.

Jim sat quietly; it was best that his father should learn his own weakness, here and now. He peered down to watch the leading traitor, and the expression on the man's face snapped his head around, even as his father saw the same thing and stopped talking.

An arm projected from the left wall, waving a dirty scrap of paper at them, and Jim recognized the sheet Bard had used for his diagrams. Now the arm suddenly withdrew, to be replaced by the grinning head of Aaron Bard—but not the face Jim had seen; this one contained sheer lunacy, the teeth bared, the eyes protruding, and the muscles of the neck bunched in mad tension! As Jim watched, the old man emerged fully into the room and began stalking steadily down the aisles toward the Dictator's desk, the atom-gun in one hand centered squarely on Jim's father.

He had full attention, and no one moved to touch him as his feet marched steadily forward, while the scrap of paper in his hand waved and fluttered. Now his voice chopped out words and seemed to hurl them outward with physical force. "Treason! Barbarism! Heathen idolatry!"

For a second, Jim took his eyes from Bard to study his father, then to spring from the chair in a frantic leap as he saw the Dictator's nerve crack and his finger slip onto one of the secret tiny buttons on the desk. But the concealed weapon acted too quickly, though there was no visible blast from it. Aaron Bard uttered a single strangled sound and crumpled to the floor!

"Get back!" Jim wasted no gentleness on his father as he twisted around the desk to present the crowding Senators with the shock of his presence at assembly on top of their other surprise. He had to dominate now, while there was a power hiatus. He bent for a quick look. "Coagulator! Who carries an illegal coagulator here? Some one of you, because this man is paralyzed by one."

Mysteriously, a doctor appeared and nodded after a brief examination. "Coagulator, all right. His nerves are cooked from chest down, and it's spreading. Death certain in an hour or so."

"Will he regain consciousness?"

"Hard to say. Nothing I can do, but I'll try, if someone will move him to the rest room."

Jim nodded and stooped to pick up the scrawled bit of paper and the atom-gun. He had been waiting for a chance, and now fate had given it to him. The words he must say were already planned, brief and simple to produce the impact he must achieve, while the assembly was still disorganized and uncertain; if oratory could win them, now was the time for it. With a carefully stern and accusing face, he mounted the platform behind the desk. His father started to speak, then stopped in shock as Jim took the gavel, rapped for order, and began, pacing with words in a slow rhythm while measuring the intensity for his voice by the faces before him.

"Gentlemen, eighty years ago, Aaron Bard died on the eve of a great war, trying to perfect a simple atomic release that would have shortened that war immeasurably. Tomorrow you will read in your newspapers how that man's own genius preserved his body and enabled us to revive him on this, the eve of an even grimmer war.

"Now, a few moments ago, that same man gave his life again in the service of this country, killed by the illegal coagulator of some cowardly traitor. But he did not die in vain, or before he could leave us safely to find his well-earned rest. He has left his mark on many of us; on me, by giving me the adulthood that all our scientists could not; on some of you, in this piece of paper, he has left a grimmer mark. . . .

"You saw him emerge from a solid wall, and it was no illusion, however much he chose to dramatize his entrance; the genius that was his enabled him to discover a means to search out your treason and your conspiracy in your most secret places. You heard his cry of treason! And one among you tried to silence that cry, forgetting that written notes cannot be silenced with a coagulator.

"Nor can you silence his last and greatest discovery, here in this weapon you saw him carry—*portable* atomic power. . . .

"Now there will be no war; no power would commit such suicide against a nation whose men shall be equipped as ours shall be. You may be sure that the traitors among you will find no reward for their treason, now. But from them, we shall have gained. We shall know the folly of our petty, foreign-inspired hatreds. We shall know the need of cleansing ourselves of the taint of such men's leadership. We shall cease trying to weaken our government and shall unite to forge new bonds of strength, instead.

"And because of that unintended good they have done us, we shall be merciful! Those who leave our shores before the stroke of midnight shall be permitted to escape; those who prefer to choose their own death by their own hands shall not be denied that right. And for the others, we shall demand and receive the fullest measure of justice!

"In that, gentlemen, I think we can all agree."

He paused then for a brief moment, seeming to study the paper in his hand, and when he resumed, his voice was the brusque one of a man performing a distasteful task. "Twelve men—men who dealt directly with our enemies. I shall read them in the order of their importance: First, Robert Sweinend! Two days ago, at three o'clock in his secretary's office, he met a self-termed businessman named Yamimoto Tung, though he calls himself—"

Jim went on, methodically reciting the course of the meeting, tensing inside as the seconds stretched on; much more and they would know it couldn't all come from one small sheet of paper!

But Sweinend's hand moved then, and Jim's seemed to blur over the desk top. Where the Senator had been, a shaft of fire—atomic fire—seemed to hang for a second before fading into nothing. Jim put the gun back gently and watched eleven men get up from their seats and dart hastily away through the exits. Beside him, his father's face now shone with great relief and greater pride, mixed with unbelieving wonder as he stood up awkwardly to take the place the boy was relinquishing. The job had been done, and Jim had the right to follow his own inclinations.

Surprisingly to him, the still figure on the couch was both conscious and sane, as the boy shut the door of the little room, leaving the doctor outside. Aaron Bard could not move his body, but his lips smiled. "Hello, Jimmy. That was the prettiest bundle of lies I've heard in a lot more than eighty years! I'm changing my saying; from now on, the one-eyed man is king—so long as he taps the ground with a cane!"

Jimmy nodded soberly, though most of the strain of the last hour was suddenly gone, torn away by the warm understanding of the older man and relief at not having to convince him that he was still normal, in spite of his actions since education. "You were right about the compellor; it can't change character. But I thought . . . after I shot the psychiatrist . . . How did you know?"

"I had at least twenty minutes in which to slip back and examine my son's diary, before your education would be complete." His smile deepened, as he sucked in on the cigarette that Jimmy held to his lips, and he let the smoke eddy out gently. "It took perhaps ten minutes to learn what I wanted to know. During the war, his notes are one long paean of triumph over the results on the preadolescents, dissatisfaction at those who were educated past twenty! And he knew the reason, as well as he always knew what he wanted to. Too much information on a young mind mires it down by sheer weight on untrained thoughts, even though it gives a false self-confidence. But the mature man, with his trained mind, can never be bowed down by mere information; he can use it. . . . No, let me go on. Vindication of my compellor doesn't matter; but this is going to be your responsibility, Jimmy, and the doctor told me I'm short of time. I want to be sure. . . . In twenty years—but that doesn't matter.

"The compellor is poison to a twelve-year-old mind, and a blessing to the adult. You can't change that overnight; but you can try, and perhaps accomplish a little. Move the age up, but carefully. By rights I should repair the damage I helped cause, but I'll have to leave it to you. Be ruthless, as you were now—more ruthless than any of them. A man who fights for right and principle should be. Tap the ground with your cane! And sometimes, when none of the blind are around, you can look up and still see the stars! Now—"

"Grandfather Bard—you never were insane in there!"

The old man smiled again. "Naturally. I couldn't look on and see the only one of my offspring that amounted to anything needing help without doing something, could I? I threw in everything I could, knowing you'd make something out of it. You did. And I'm not sorry, even though I wasn't exactly expecting—this. . . . How long after my heart begins missing?"

"A minute or two!" Aaron Bard obviously wanted no sympathy, and the boy sensed it and held back the words, hard though he found it now. Emotions were better expressed by their hands locked together than by words.

"Good. It's a clean, painless death, and I'm grateful for it. But no more revivals! Cremate me, Jimmy, and put up a simple marker—no name, just A One-Eyed Man!"

"Requiescat in Pace—A One-Eyed Man! I promise!"

The old head nodded faintly and relaxed, the smile still lingering. Jimmy swallowed a lump in his throat and stood up slowly with bowed head, while a tumult of sound came in from the great assembly hall. His father was finally abdicating and they were naming him Dictator, of course. But he still stood there, motionless.

"Two such stones," he muttered finally. "And maybe someday I'll deserve the other."

I wasn't exactly setting New York on fire so far, but I was probably doing better than I had any right to expect from my previous writing. The new rate helped. But even so, I had to do a little better than one short story a month to get by, and the only possibility I could see was to do an occasional novelette.

Anyhow, I had a lot more ideas for longer stories than for short ones. That could have been corrected in time, since the mind tends to get into ruts, but can be forced out of them. But there didn't seem to be much time.

So I began one that should run about 10,000 words. As it came out of the typewriter, it was a thousand words longer. It was about a robot who was left over after men had seemingly killed themselves off. When he is accidentally turned on, he's able to find very little except a copy of the Bible to explain things to him. And he first assumes he's God, then figures maybe he's Adam. This seems to him to be something like the beginning of things in the Garden of Eden, anyhow.

Campbell told me he liked it, but couldn't possibly take anything longer than 8,000 words. He didn't see how I could cut it, but he'd be happy to use it if I could.

That was rough. The original idea had been for a story of about 15,000 words, and I'd already cut out some details and written it as compactly as I thought I could. I went back and tried cutting on the carbon, but it didn't help much. I could get a thousand words out of it, but not three thousand.

And then I made a discovery that seemed to contradict all logic. By *adding* a whole new incident, it became possible to shorten it. Somehow, by adding to it, I could rearrange things into a much tighter pattern, with less transition. It worked, too, without hurting the story, and I added another bit of technical information to my writing skills. Stories get too long because of inexcusable padding (something that tends to destroy not only the story but also the writer who falls into that trap) or because of faulty organization. Previously, I'd thought about a story's organization from the view of maintaining interest, but never as a means of keeping it within reasonable grounds. It was information I found invaluable in later years, both for rewriting difficult parts of my stories and for editorial work.

I retyped it and took it in, and Campbell accepted it. He only paid $120—no bonus—but he did comment that the present version of

"Into Thy Hands" read better than the longer one, so I felt fairly happy about it.

And then the ax fell, or so it seemed at the moment. I wanted to discuss the matter of how much I could sell him, but he cut me off before I could get started. The situation was bad. He'd had few openings to begin with, and had strained his budget by taking even this last story. The new writers he had found had been sending him a lot of stories, and now many of the older ones were finding ways to write again, despite their work or service.

Of course, there would be some chances as the monthly issues used up older stories. But he really should be cutting back on his inventory, rather than holding it where it was.

By the time he finished, I think Campbell was more unhappy for me than I was for myself. I can usually accept things fairly quickly, and I'd already accepted this.

So I went out and got a job, of course. I'd been eating my breakfast at a nearby White Tower, and they were always looking for help for the chain of stores they ran. I'd had a fair amount of restaurant experience, too.

On the third night of work, I was sent to a little shop on 137th and Broadway. I'd heard about that shop. The area was in turmoil, with Irish, Puerto Ricans, and blacks all trying to establish themselves, and all filled with misunderstandings of their neighbors. The shop was a sort of hangout for young Puerto Ricans, but other groups periodically tried to shove them out. There was usually a fight there once a week—on Saturday when the bars closed—and windows were constantly being broken.

I wasn't exactly flattered the next morning when I was offered the job of managing the place. But I was perfectly happy to take it. I'd had experience with that sort of mess before, and I knew that most of the trouble was caused by someone behind the counter who either panicked or tried to lay down the law too quickly. And naturally, any counterman who showed prejudice was asking for trouble.

It turned out to be a good job. There were almost no tips, of course, at first; and tips are always the major part of the salary in such jobs. But it's surprising how people will begin tipping when they get proper service. You'll find a dime hidden under a plate someday, as if they were ashamed of leaving it. And eventually, the occasional tip will become regular. Once a few start, others pick it up.

The first step was to stop letting it be a hangout, and that was simple enough. White Towers supposedly never close. But I got permission to close it one hour each night, which ruined it as a place to lounge around until morning. If anyone did try to hang around, I gave him the job of scrubbing the floorboards—and usually had a very willing helper.

I never had a broken window in all the time I worked there, and there were very few fights, usually broken up quickly by my customers. I made a lot of good friends, too, from all of the groups. The hours were long, but the pay was quite good, counting tips, and time always passed quickly. I liked it.

There was also a peculiar bonus. There was a big cigarette shortage at the time, with people standing in line whenever a supply was announced. But a fair number of my customers were sailors from a base on the Hudson nearby and they were not rationed. I always managed to have a good supply for myself, as well as enough to offer some to my customers.

Writing was the last thought in my head, though I sometimes dropped down to Campbell's office to see him. He was still overstocked, but we took that for granted.

I didn't write a word in 1945 or 1946.

In other ways, my life was full of all sorts of developments. The girl friend and I finally began to break up—or perhaps I should be more accurate by saying we were simply moving away from each other. I suspect my job bothered her, though she didn't mention it. But most people who work in offices seem to think there's something degrading about any other form of honest work, even when it pays more.

In the fall of 1945, I got married to the young lady who usually served me breakfast at the White Tower near my room. Her name was Helen, which was probably fortunate, since my friends had a bad habit of addressing any woman with me as "Helen"—my robot lady somehow always came to mind. Eventually, we moved out to the Bronx to share an apartment with her father and brother.

It wasn't until 1947 that writing again became an aspect of my life. Campbell sent me a note, asking me to come down to his office. When I got there, I found it was to sign a release on "Nerves" for use in a major anthology of science fiction to be published by Random House. (This was *Adventures in Time and Space,* a huge volume which was the definitive single-volume collection of science fiction for twenty-five years.) For the right to use my story, they offered me $137.50.

The money came at a time when it was needed. I'd been fired from my job because I was suspected of supporting an attempt to unionize the White Towers. (They were wrong, incidentally; I had no use for that particular union.) So I was out of work and we were depending on Helen's job as a waitress.

But seeing Campbell and getting a check for my writing had another effect on me. I hadn't thought about writing for years, but now I went home with my head spilling over with ideas for stories. It was almost as if something had been dammed out and was now breaking free. (Some of the ideas were pretty dreadful, of course; but good or bad, it was almost a new sensation.)

A few days later, I finally sat down at my typewriter to see whether I could still put the words on paper without my fingers stuttering. I was so eager that I hadn't even seriously considered which idea I would use. I simply took the first one that struck my fancy and began. I probably chose it because of the title. It was another from Longfellow's poem: "The Day is Done" "And the Darkness" (drifts from) "The Wings of Night. . . ."

"And the Darkness" came out to 7,000 words, which seemed all right, since Campbell had told me he could now use a few good short stories.

19.

And the Darkness

(by Lester del Rey)

There was no space in the tiny cabin for nervous pacing. A scant eight feet separated the hallway entrance from the small porthole that showed the dull black of space; and across, the distance from the locked door on one sidewall to that on the other could have been spanned by the young man's arms. Only his eyes were free to roam the narrow room, and they were tired with endless repetition.

For a moment, his gaze rested idly on the porthole, and he stared outward through the cold and the darkness to the tiny point of light that was Earth; but there was no conscious recognition of what he saw. His eyes dropped back to the shelf that held his manuscript, his ink, and the purple, untouched candle. And it was only as he picked up the lump of wax with slow, reluctant fingers that he thought of the valley in the hell world that had produced it. . . .

The man's shoulders were bowed under the grim weight on his back, and the alpine stock trembled in his grasp. But he fought upward over the last remaining feet until he was at the top of the pass and the wastelands were behind. Even then, he could not trust the weight of his burden to his shaking hands, but sank carefully to a sitting posture until it touched the ground and he could ease his arms out from the straps. Finding a reasonably portable generator to replace the one they could patch no more had been a miracle, and he had no faith in a second one.

For a time he lay quietly, breathing in ragged gasps and staring into the valley that was cut off completely from the world by the surrounding mountains, except for this one narrow pass. Dirty snow straggled down to blend with leprous, distorted scrub trees and run down to flat land. And there a few log and stone buildings stuck up uncertainly among the crumbling ruins, to mark the last failing outpost of the human race, three centuries after the Cataclysm. The man grimaced and began to pull himself to his feet.

Then an answering clatter of stones sounded from around a rock, and Gram was beside him, pulling him upright and massaging his still trembling shoulders with gentle hands. Her seamed old face broke into a brief flicker of perfect teeth, and her fingers were unsteady, but there was no emotionalism in her voice. "I saw your smoke signal last night, so I've been waiting. I guess I must have been catching a catnap, though. You've been gone a long time, Omega. Okay?"

"Okay, Gram. The generator's in there, and enough fluorobulbs to light all the huts. But I'm glad I didn't have to stretch rations another day. I had to work my way clear to old Fairbanks to find it. That wasn't pretty! They knew it was coming hours before the stuff hit them!"

"Umm. Here! I figured you'd be hungry. As for the bulbs—" She shrugged and pointed to the purplish plants that grew all around, a mutation as deadly as the hard radiations that had produced them. "I'll stick to sprayberry-wax candles. They have other uses; or at least Peter thought so."

So gentle, patient old Peter was dead, and there was only an even dozen of them now! But Omega was too tired to care much about anything except the food Gram held out. She watched him wolf it down, and her face lighted faintly as she dropped beside him.

"Eleven worn-out old people and you, now. The last dozen poor supermen," she said with a nod toward the valley; and her voice was filled with the same grim humor that had made her christen him Omega when his mother committed suicide over the rock-mangled body of his father.

But Omega knew it was more than humor. In a normal world, with a decent background and half a chance, they might almost have passed for supermen; except that no such world could have produced them. That had required an Earth left wrecked by the Cataclysm from a cold and casually unjust universe—a world where hard radiations made every birth a mutation and where every undesirable change was savagely purged from the race.

In a way, it was ironic that men had barely avoided wrecking the planet themselves with plutonium, the lithium chain reaction, or the final discovery of a modified solar-phoenix bomb. But somehow they had eliminated that danger at last—and found their triumph useless.

It had been a simple communiqué from the new Lunar Observatory, at first; they had spotted a meteor having a paradoxically weak but impossibly hot level of radiation that indicated contra-terrene, or "inside-out" matter. The second announcement spoke guardedly of the danger of grazing contact. And fifteen minutes later, the moon ripped apart as electrons canceled out positrons into energy and left a great flood of unattached and destructive neutrons.

Surprisingly, there were survivors of the rain of hell-fragments that fell to the earth. Near the poles, a few deep and narrow valleys were only grazed slightly, and where three contained mines or caverns to offer some protection against the radioactive dust that fell everywhere, a measure of life went on after a fashion, and a thousand or so survived. Now three centuries had whittled down the number, and wild mutations and ruthless survival of the fit had compressed a thousand generations of evolution into one.

There was Gram, who might have saved the race, if her cell structure had appeared in time. Like the wolves and the rabbits that had inherited the Earth, her cells had finally found the mutation of totipotency that defied all but the most intense concentration of radiation to burn them or cause further mutations. When a wild new plague had wiped out her people in another valley, she had taken the boy who was to become Omega's father, a rifle, and a sled, and set out through a roaring blizzard to cross four hundred miles of hell to this place. Now, sixty years later, she could still outwork any man in the valley, except for Omega's maternal uncle Adam, on the rare occasions when he exerted himself.

For Adam had specialized in pure laziness and purer logic that seemed to leap from isolated hints of facts to full-grown knowledge without effort. He had slouched in when Omega was fumbling over calculus and his eyes had lightened with sudden interest in the books he had never troubled to read. Hours later, he had been explaining and making clear the complex mathematics which his mind had carried beyond the wildest dreams of the prechaos scientists. With the same ease, he had seized upon the French books Omega brought back from a trip. Even if there had been a grammar or dictionary, he would have regarded them as too much trouble to use.

But it required more than such wild talents to separate a group of freaks from supermen; it took background, opportunity, racial culture, and a future. And in those things, the wolves were their superiors.

Sudden light flashed from the valley, disappeared, and returned to hover beside them. Then the spot wobbled erratically across the pass and came to rest against a flat, shaded rock, danced crazily, and steadied down to business. Below, the thin, lanky hands of old Eli must have been using the big mirror on a long board to give the microscopic leverage that was all he needed. His talent lay in a coordination and control of nerves and muscles so nearly perfect that he could shape and handle the infinitesimal tools needed to manipulate individual micro-organisms within the field of a microscope. Now the spot of light fluttered, but its motions were clear enough to spell out letters.

"*Hurry, need generator*," Gram read, and chuckled. "Sure you found one, eh? Let them—uh . . . *Wolf girl located!*"

A gamut of expressions washed over her face, giving place to sudden determination. "Come on, Omega! You can rest later. Here, let me help you with that pack."

"Why the hurry, and what's all this wolf-girl stuff about?" After the short rest, the pack weighed a ton, and the pass looked ten miles long. No wolf was that important, whatever it had done.

Gram slowed up a little. "Something we never meant to bother you with—Ellen's baby, your cousin. Grown up now, must be. We saw her with a wolf pack once before when you were away, but thought she'd died later. Oh, come on, before they start a search without shields. I'll tell you some other time."

"They won't start without shields," he assured her. "She was living with wolves, Gram?"

"Must have been. And they'd start, all right. Tom and Ed died out there last time, before you invented the shields! When it comes to race preservation, they'd rather all burn than see you go unmated! *Will* you hurry?"

He hurried; nobody disobeyed Gram. But there was a picture of what a wolf-girl must be in his mind, and the idea of such a mating sat heavier on him than the pack. And he'd thought the old fires of racial preservation were dead!

Adam met them, took the pack, kicked aside one of the shaggy, huge-eared pigs, and paced beside Gram without a trace of laziness. Its squeals gave the boy time to get over the shock of that before his uncle answered Gram's questions.

"Jenkins—off by himself as usual—went to sleep at the far end. Early morning a howling woke him, and there she was with a couple of wolves. He got a good look—seemed human, all right, a stick in her hand. Time he got there, she was gone, but he saw the direction; reckon I know where she lairs. He came in half an hour ago, fagged out. Soon as we got it out of him, we signaled."

"Umm. Wonder where she's been since we saw her the other time, Adam?"

"Off somewhere. Studied wolves when I was a kid—they wandered all over. And with your blood, so could she. Lucky she's back." They reached the powerhouse and Adam shut up, while Eli began bolting down the generator on a rough base and connecting it to the old waterwheel. There was a glow to his face that was new to Omega, and it was reflected by the faces of the rest of the group.

They were all there, except for Jenkins, whose green pigmentation and chromosomes that came in triplets instead of pairs represented the only remaining physical abnormality. With that had gone a whole host of wild extrasensory talents that made him fully aware of the unpopularity they won him. Of the others, Eli, Adam, and Simon were already harnessed into the shields. A product of Adam's mathematics, Eli's amazing workmanship, and some of Omega's ideas, they made space a nonconductor of all radiation beyond a certain energy level. They also distorted gravity slightly for some reason, but it was the only way the others could travel in the outlands.

Simon snapped the last battery in place as it finished flash-charging, while Gram made a hasty inspection. "Omega's worn out, and I don't want her to remember me as the one who caught her, if

I'm to handle her, so it's up to you. Think you can do it, Adam?"

"I figured some on it. We'll get her."

"Good." She watched them start and turned back to her hut. "Let the others gaup, Omega, but we're eating, and then you're going to bed . . . . after I tell you about Ellen and the girl."

It wasn't much of a story. Beside Omega's father, Gram's hitherto-unmentioned baby daughter had survived the plague and the trip. She'd grown up, married Simon after Omega was born, and there'd been a baby coming. Jenkins, who would know, had said it was to be a girl.

But some accident on the hellish march had twisted Ellen's mind, and she grew up as an insanely religious fanatic. Apparently the thought of her baby marrying a cousin had been a heinous sin in her eyes. Anyway, they found a wild note, but they had never been able to trace her.

"God knows, we tried." Gram's soup was untouched before her. "You never spent years praying for just one girl-child—one fertile girl in a world dying of sterility, Omega! Just one, because the hard rays couldn't trap your kind from the world anymore. My line's fertile, and the baby would have been. . . . You're too young to understand, but the old *need* babies; when you're close to death, you need proof that you're physically immortal through the race—not just soul-stuff. Oblivion's close and taut around you when there's nobody left to remember. . . . Oh, go to bed before I start blubbering!"

But Omega's mind was filled with an idiot-faced thing in human shape, making animal sounds and snapping with raised hackles. Kipling's *Jungle Books* had been only wish-dreams; those who grow up with animals must always be less than the beasts they follow.

But his emotions were less logical; under his disgust, a queer tingle mixed with an unformed picture of abstract but intensely personal posterity. One fertile female, and they could bask in the warm physical immortality of racial perpetuity; a race that had been dead and unmourned now could think in future tense again. . . . Tearing her food with drooling tooth and savage fang, growling animal noises, pacing her cage with wild idiocy in her eyes . . .

"Can they catch her alive?" he asked as Gram began drawing the pig's-wool blankets up over him.

"They'll do it, somehow; we made an agreement to that. Either they come back with her alive, or they rot out there!"

She closed the door quietly behind her, and Omega was alone to wonder at the savage drive that had lain dormant and unknown so long around him. But no thoughts could keep a man awake after the grueling trek he'd just finished, and somewhere in the middle of the thought, he blanked out.

The searchers were already in sight when Gram awakened him, two of them staggering under the twisting gravity of the shields; but Adam apparently was able to predict the shifting force, and the leading figure was steady and resolute. Between the others, there was a covered figure on a long pole, and the tiny clan was gathered outside the hut in a shouting group. But by the time Omega had doused his head in water and joined them, they were silent again. The three were closer now, and their faces and the pose of their bodies could be seen, even in the gathering twilight.

They dropped their burden in the same rigid silence, and Simon, who had been Ellen's mate and father to the child, turned, motioning to his twin sister, and went off toward their hut. The others waited uncertainly, until Adam bent down to pull the blanket from the figure on the ground.

"Wrong word accented on wolf-girl, Gram, but here she is. Now what?" And he yanked the cover from the forlorn creature that lay bound by its feet to the pole.

It was a wolf; strange and odd of form though it was, there could be no shadow of doubt as to her lupine origin. The teeth that gleamed through the ropes around her jaws were wolf fangs, and the tail settled any further question.

Yet it was easy to see how Jenkins could have thought her a woman in the dim starlight, for the mutation that had somehow produced her in spite of her parental totipotency had shaped her into a mockery of human form, and she was as anthropoid as wolfish. Her rear legs were long and her short front ones ended in lengthened toes to caricature human hands. Her forehead bulged and her jaw was foreshortened, while the mane on her neck might have been mistaken for a head of hair if she stood upright. And because she was built in a woman's shape, there was something pitiful about her as she lay glaring up at them.

Jenkins felt it first, and his sigh broke their silence; he pushed forward, his shy, fearful eyes half-filled with tears. For a second, he hesitated, before his hands ripped aside the cords that bound her mouth. Her lips drew back, but she made no move to snap at him as he faced the others, his quavering, timid voice filled with bitterness and apology. "The ropes cut her lips, Gram. Her mind's all dark and swirling fog, hard to see, but she's crying. Not for herself, but for her babies back there, little ones like her. Do we have to kill her, Gram?"

Gram shook her head to clear it, and her voice was as low as his, and as uncertain. "But you saw the wolf-girl carrying a stick. Can we be sure . . . ? Look further into her mind."

"We found the stick," Adam answered for him. "She'd need one, with her build. Couldn't run on all fours, not quite ready to go upright very long. Jenkins, what's her name?"

"Her name? I—I can't see very well. Something about hunger—pain, I think."

"*Bad-Luck.* Called that because of the way she's built, I guess. Not much of a language, unless they changed it since I was a kid. Better'n your telepathy, though. You read off what I think, while I try her."

His lips contorted out of shape, and a queer wailing whine slid eerily out. The wolf-girl's head jerked around, and her eyes shot behind him, to come back reluctantly to his as he called again. At the third try, her own lips parted in an effort, closed, and opened in sounds between a growl and a whine, yet somehow articulated and hopeless. Perhaps the sight of a man and a wolf-mutation talking was as logical an ending for the day as any other; at least, the little audience watched in unchanging dull listlessness.

Jenkins' voice droned forth, reading the meaning from Adam's mind. "Surprised at him . . . Not mad at us, why should she be? . . . Hunting's natural . . . Is he man or wolf? . . . Yes, she'll answer his questions. No, never saw any human shes outside the valley . . . No baby shes . . . When are we going to eat her?"

"Ugh! I suppose . . . Oh, let her go! I wish I'd never known she could talk, Adam, but now—" Gram sighed, staring about for suggestions and finding none. "Tell her we'll feed her, since we ruined her hunting, and let her go; but she's to keep out of our valley and let our stock alone. I guess that's all we can do now. Can you tell her that in her language?"

"Say it all right—they've improved it some; but for her to understand's another thing. Translate the Bible to wolfish, if I had to, but it wouldn't mean much to her. Takes semantic training to work out much with a hundred-odd words, though it can be done. Umm." He frowned, considering, and Little Jenkins, again conscious that his gifts were unwelcome among normal minds, slipped away quietly before Adam began.

It took longer this time, and there could be no doubting the surprise and slow dawn of hope on the creature's face as the meaning finally sank in. She lay quietly, her eyes riveted on his as he untied her; but it wasn't until he placed a frozen leg of pork in her oddly human hands that she believed him. Her tongue came out in a hasty licking motion against his hand. Then she was gone at a jerking run.

But she stopped, hesitantly, as a high wail broke from him, and paused long enough to answer his cries before her figure faded away into the twilight. He grinned crookedly at Gram, and shrugged. "No smell of people outside that she knows of."

"No." Gram sighed again and pushed the door open. "Come on inside, Adam, Omega. The rest of you go back to your huts. There's no good to be had from freezing out here. We had our fun, but it's over now, and we can forget the wolf-girl idea."

In that, she was wrong. It was less than three hours later when a subdued howl from outside drew Adam up from the table and out into the night. Outlined in the dim light of the open door, Bad-Luck had returned, and beside her hovered an old and grizzled wolf, with raised hackles and bared fangs, but motionless as the feared man-beast approached.

Their conversation was erratic and uncertain, with long silences, but eventually Adam nodded and the wolves melted into the darkness. He came back to the hut with a shake of his head and a strange smile, and dropped onto the stool to watch Gram's hands go on remorselessly with her Canfield.

"The old wolf is their Far-Food-Sniffer; keeps in touch with all other packs, I gather. Anyhow, no wolf on the whole planet knows the smell of men, except here. . . . Funny! Nature seems to be cooking up replacements for us, and not wasting time. Came a long way since I studied them. Ethics! Gratitude!"

Gram nodded wearily, and dead, dull silence settled over the hut, relieved only by the monotonous slap of the cards.

It was barely past noon when Simon and his sister were found the next day, deep in the catalepsy of sprayberry poison. Within them, the incredibly slowed labor of breath and heartbeat would go on for hours longer, but it was too faint to be detected, and their bodies were already cool to the touch. Yet they could still be revived, and Omega turned automatically to get the neutralizing drug. Adam's hand stopped him.

"No use, boy. There's always more poison." He looked around the room once more, taking in the magnificent paintings the twins had done, then pulled the door shut behind them and began nailing boards over it. Wooden steps carried them back to the cold-frames where Gram and Eli were at work setting cabbage seedlings. But the hammering had carried the news before them, and no comments were made.

The only sound was a distant drone, like an early swarm of bees, and it disappeared as Omega dropped to the cold earth and began replanting. How many, he wondered, would live to eat the plants when they were grown? There were only ten now!

Then the buzzing was back, and Gram was dragging the others up to face the sky, where a roaring something grew out of emptiness, flashed over, and faded away again. "A ship! A jet plane!"

It couldn't have been, and yet it was. There was no habitable land below 60° north latitude; one colony of the original three had reported itself dying of famine; Gram's had perished in the plague; and the wolves knew of no smell of men outside the valley.

But they were already at the powerhouse, and Eli's hands flipped over the switches of the crude spark-gap transmitter the first survivors had built, and the current danced between the electrodes in code so rapid it was like a steady crackle. He waited futilely for an answer from the humming speaker, and began transmitting again.

Then the roar was back, and they had only time to look out before a flash of metal screamed down, wriggled, zipped up across the pass, and was gone again. Gram lifted her fist. "The dirty spalpeens! Making fun—"

Before she could complete the gesture, a young masculine voice burbled out of the speaker. "Hi, people! Took a little time to find and match your frequency—your signal sprays all over the kilocycles. I can't understand that greased-lightning c.w., though, so give me three slow dots if you can receive modulated stuff. . . . Fine! Sorry I couldn't land with my fuel reserves, but I'll be back. Meantime, take a look at the film I dropped. Planet Mars, signing off!"

Mars! They'd been almost ready for that, but . . . And his voice had been filled with a strange quality that instinct recognized as youthful enthusiasm and sure self-confidence. It must be nice—

Jenkins interrupted their reverie by laying a package on the bench. That would be the film, though he alone had seen it fall. For the first time any of them could remember, Eli's hand fumbled as he ripped at the junk wound hastily around the thing, and it was Adam who finally freed the little machine and found the light switch. He focused it carefully against the gray stone wall, located another button, and sat back to watch the moving scenes.

They were obviously conventionalized drawings at first, but they were clear enough. A man labeled *Mason* stood in the port of a crude rocket ship with his young wife, while a crowd cheered and drew back. They waved, shut the port, and lifted on a jet of flames. The Earth shrank behind, while the moon slid into view and went quickly past. But Mason was framed in a porthole, just as the moon broke loose in lancing hellfire. Scenes showed his wife trying to nurse his burned body and frantically fighting to bring the ship down on Mars in a crumpled landing. And thin, furry, four-armed anthropoid things came out to take them down to a strange underground primitive world.

After that, Mason was their teacher. They had been dying for lack of power, but now the ship's atomotors gave them the margin they needed to rush upward to a self-sustaining civilization that could even bake air and water out of the dead crust of the planet. Mason grew older, and six girls were born to him. But careful schematics showed that the moon-blast had rendered his male sperm cells sterile, and there were no boys. They stored his superfrozen spermatozoa and sought valiantly for a cure, but they had not succeeded when the screen portrayed his funeral procession.

The final scene showed a glorified statue of Mason, holding a book in one hand and stretching a symbolic atom upward with the other. Below, eight young and human women were grouped about a great rocket, with their faces turned to the sky and their arms lifted in mute appeal. Then the film ended.

Omega wasted no time on the others' comments. The boards on Simon's door came ripping off under his straining muscles, and he was inside and forcing black liquid down the throats of the twins. The vegetable dye they used to color their clothes and serve as their writing ink had revived poisoned pigs before and should serve equally well for men. It did. The late afternoon sun saw twelve of them again, watching as the ship settled downward on its jets a hundred yards away.

A thin, four-armed, furry figure came out, to be followed by two apparently identical others. And then, while the dozen humans waited in tense expectancy, the door closed firmly and the aliens headed toward the group—three Martians and no Earthmen! Beside him, Omega heard Gram's breath whistle out heavily, and an animal snarl from Jenkins. Only Adam seemed unruffled and unsurprised as he sauntered forward to grasp the leader's hand and make proper introductions.

Jaluir's furry face remained expressionless, but his voice was the warmly enthusiastic one that had come over the speaker. "So you really do exist? Where the deuce were you last winter? There wasn't a sign of life that we could see."

"Holed up. Snow gets twenty feet deep down here—covers everything. We seal up and hibernate in the caverns back there till after the spring floods. Explore all nonradioactive areas?"

"All seventeen. This one came last, and our plane broke down for a month, or we'd probably have found you." He shrugged, a gesture that must have come down from Mason. "After that, we gave up hope until I made a forced landing in old Fairbanks. I was pretty sure someone had been there recently, and Commander Hroth let us stay over another week. But it was a devil of a job locating your campfire sites to get a fix."

"Why bother? You didn't come just to see us—not with people of our kind on Mars!" Gram's voice was suddenly old, tired, and suspicious, and the Martian blinked in surprise.

"We needed some metals, of course—but wouldn't have crossed space yet for just that." He hesitated, and his next words were fumbling and uncertain. "The girls who saw us off—we failed, in spite of them—they are the last. We had only the Prophet's male germs. . . . We have taboos, too, ma'am, but—well, we had to do what we could. Now, when our hopes were gone, the gods have given us life again!"

"Umm. Well, you might mean it. You and your friends had better come inside, I suppose. No use standing out here."

"If it's all the same, I'd rather see that radio transmitter of yours," he answered.

Gram nodded grudging approval, and Omega was glad of the excuse to rescue Jaluir from their frozen faces. It didn't make sense. When even a Martian crossed forty million miles to pay a neighborly visit, he deserved a little warmth in his reception. Instead, Gram was adopting the same attitude with which she'd greeted Adam's proposal to scrap English and switch to a fully semantic language of his devising. The boy fell into step with the alien, while the others followed.

The transmitter held Jaluir's attention for only a minute before his eyes began traveling over the rest of the powerhouse. The crude Millikan microscope Adam had designed from the fruits of Omega's wanderings was inspected more thoroughly, to be followed by one of the little radiation shields.

"Cuts off high energy radiation," Adam volunteered, and his eyes were speculative, in spite of his easy grin. "Take it along if you can use it."

The Martian nodded and dropped it into a pouch on his belt—his only article of clothing. "Simple after someone else discovers the principle. Thanks! We certainly can use it. . . . We wondered how you reached Fairbanks."

Gram grunted. "Nonsense! Omega and I don't need contraptions; we're naturally immune to radiations."

"*Zot luill!* You're—!" The face that he turned to the boy now was no longer expressionless. It held a burning excitement that no alienness could conceal. He twisted on his heel and snapped out syllables in a strange tongue that sent the other two Martians toward their ship at a clumsy run. But when he faced them again, his emotions were under control, and his voice was even and friendly.

"Sorry, but I've got to go back to the ship for a few minutes. Look, let's get down to brass tacks, shall we? How soon can you leave?"

"For Mars?" Gram asked.

"For Mars. It'll be five hundred years before Earth is really habitable again, at least. And you can't go on in these little valleys. What better sanctuary than a grateful Mars? Of course, you'll need a little time—but talk it over until I get back."

And he was gone after his companions.

Gram sighed wearily, and the stiffness drained out of her body. "Sanctuary—or slave pen? He seemed nice enough, but—"

"He's a monster!" Jenkins' normal meek whisper was distorted into a savage, hate-filled wheeze. "An inhuman monster! His brain is blank—all blank. I can't even feel it."

Adam's cool voice cut into his ravings. "Take it easy! If you can't snoop in his mind, you don't know what he is. And you don't hate a man for that—or do you? Personally, I liked Jaluir."

"So did I," Gram admitted, but there was no lifting of the frown on her face. "We would! You can't catch a wolf without something attractive for bait. And maybe he is all sweetness and light. The missionaries meant to help the Aztecs, until they found gold and Cortes came. And our ancestors made slaves of the black people and tried to exterminate the Jews for not being exactly like themselves—and Mars is a lot stranger to us than anything we found here. Maybe we're gods to them, as he says; and maybe we're animals."

Their doubts were growing by a process of mutual induction, until even Omega's ideas began to veer toward them. But his words carried no conviction in either direction. "Of course, we can't be sure; we have only the evidence they designed for us. But he seemed friendly."

"Why shouldn't he be, when our planet's loaded with minerals they need? We're used to gravity that makes them uncomfortable, and we can stand the radiations, now. He liked that part—a little too much!"

Gram hesitated, and her gaze turned to the east where her native valley lay. "We always took even better care of our animals than ourselves. I know, because we had horses when I was a girl—until a careless fool left a gate open and our two stallions were killed by wolves. He tried to hide the evidence, because he knew what we'd do to him. But I saw it all, and I was young enough to carry tales. Poor devil! They turned him out to the wolves, eventually. . . . Men will do strange things for beasts of burden, Omega."

"Or for pets," Adam added thoughtfully. "Vote?"

But no vocal poll was needed. Simon and his sister moved toward the door, and his sad, dulled eyes were quietly reproving as he looked at Omega. Gram turned from one to another, and at last she nodded quietly and went out toward the huts. In a moment, only Adam and Omega were left in the building.

Jaluir found them there, and the lilting jingle on his lips broke off in a sudden puzzled grunt. Adam chuckled wryly! "Gone! Took a vote, after a fashion. It's a lousy world, Jaluir, but we're staying. And don't ask why, because I don't know."

"But you can't—you're . . . *All* of you? Omega too?"

"That's up to him; he didn't vote. Rest of us stay, anyhow."

"Oh." Jaluir considered it, shrugged, and gave it up as a hopeless riddle. "I won't pretend I can understand, but if that's the way you really want it, I'll explain it to Commander Hroth somehow. Anyway, I've got to return to the main ship before it gets too dark, so I'd better shove off now. But I'll be back in the morning to pick you up, Omega."

He grasped the hand Adam held out and was gone, to take off a minute later in a flaming roar and go speeding over the mountains. Adam slumped against the door for a few seconds, then came in and began quietly buckling on a radiation shield.

"Going up to talk with the wolf-girl," he volunteered with deliberate casualness as he finished. "Curiosity. If I don't get back in time to see you off—"

"Who made up my mind I was going—Jaluir or you?"

"Fate! If they're nice people, you should; if not—well, they'll have weapons and ways. Good luck, son!" He slapped his nephew's back lightly, grinned, and went sauntering off, leaving Omega alone with his thoughts. They were not good company.

But Adam's logic was unanswerable, and Omega's packing was done in the morning when he awoke from fitful slumber to see the plane already landed and waiting beside the row of silent, boarded-up huts. He had helped Gram nail them shut during the night, and he knew that only Gram and he were left, beside Adam, still among the wolves. Even little Jenkins and his queer, twisted talents! Gram sighed, and her eyes, red with lack of sleep, followed his gaze.

"Forget them, boy. Jenkins was always a little crazy, and Eli was dying of cancer, anyhow. The rest were—useless! Sometimes I used to wonder about such things—the warped, strange ideas of isolated little communities, and the references in the psychology books to contagious suicide during times of trouble. But there's something more."

She shook her head wearily, drawing her hand across her forehead. "It's a curse, a will to death that made them sterile because they wanted to be, and made them die whenever they had an excuse—no matter how much they refused to believe it. Call it a mutation that crept in unnoticed, or say the whole race gave up and went quietly insane after the hell years. They could have built some kind of glider plane and kept contact between the valleys, if they'd had the spunk, and none of this would have happened. Anyway, there's a curse on the valleys. . . . You'd better go now, Omega. Don't keep Jaluir waiting too long."

There were words inside him, but they wouldn't come out. Gram laid her brown old hand gently on his mouth, and the ghost of a smile appeared on her lips. "No, just go. And sometime, if you have children—not slave children, Omega, but men—tell them of the last men on Earth. I'd like that!"

The doors of the huts were all closed when he looked back from the plane, after all his gear was stowed. Jaluir motioned him to a seat beside a window away from the huts, and he sat staring at the instrument board for what seemed hours while the plane waited. Then the jets screamed out suddenly, and they were airborne after a brief run.

"Below," the Martian said softly, and pointed.

Tiny but distinct against a patch of snow, a figure stood waving up at them, surrounded by dark dots that must have been the wolves. Jaluir dropped the plane and circled as close as he could, and for a moment Adam's easy smile was visible. Then he turned and slipped into a cave with the pack, and there was only the Martian's silent grip on the boy's shoulder and the sound of the jets as they sped off across the wastelands.

. . . The warmth of his hands had softened the purple wax, and he sat molding it idly, while his eyes remained unfocused on the shelf before him. Now Earth was faint in the distance, with Mars looming up large and red before them, but he was less certain than before of what awaited him there. Sanctuary or slavery—he could not tell. Somewhere within the notes before him must lie the answer; but his mind went on pacing an endless circle, unable to break from the ruts it had worn, and the key eluded him.

When he began his manuscript a week before, it had seemed simple, and the ink and candle were still there to remind him of the plan. Among men, it might have worked. But even human motives were uncertain, and these strange men from Mars were of another race. He had mixed with them, supped with their quiet commander, and listened to the tales of Mars that Jaluir told so well. But he did not know them; nor could he hope to before his children were old enough to curse or bless him for the outcome; and that would be too late.

With a sudden sweep of his arm, he knocked the things from the shelf into a trash container, and swung around—just in time to see one of the side doors swing open quietly and an old and familiar figure slip from behind it.

"Gram!"

"Naturally. Who else would spend twelve days watching you through a one-way mirror to see whether she had a fool for a grandson?" But the strain in her voice ruined the attempt at humor, and she gave it up. "I found the candle in your bag, Omega, and I knew you'd find other ways if I destroyed it. So I made an agreement with Jaluir, and my stuff was on the plane when you awoke. . . . And yet, at the end, I wouldn't have saved you. If there's any difference, I'd rather see my descendants slaves than quitters!"

Omega shook his head dully. "I wasn't planning suicide, Gram. I thought they might dump me and my notes at once if they were slavers, like the man in your story who tried to cover up and escape punishment for carelessness. Or if they were friends, they'd wait until they read my notes and found out how to revive me."

"Umm. And you'd have no responsibility either way, eh? No, boy. Men could have colonized the planets ten years before the Cataclysm; but they were too busy with their fears. Until the last minute, they were so afraid of war that all they could do was prepare for it and nothing else. The survivors could have found ways to get to all the valleys and multiply again, but they gave up and sat blubbering about the dirty trick fate played on them. We've been a race of irresponsible, sniveling brats! And now it's time we grew up out of our nightmares and accepted our responsibilities."

Gram shrugged, dismissing the subject, and turned toward the doorway to the hall. "Come on, boy. Jaluir says we're almost there, and we might as well see what it looks like."

But Omega could not dismiss the subject so readily. It was good to have her old familiar strength beside him, but in the final analysis, she could not help. The decision he had been forced to make was his responsibility, and no other could share it. Men had their faults, and they were great ones. They had come up too fast, and their cleverness outstripped their wisdom. But no single individual could deny the race one more chance for the good that was in it.

Three centuries of bitter hibernation had burned away some of their childhood, and they could start anew to learn the lessons they had neglected, if they had the courage and were given the chance. The hard radiations that had come, like the rain from heaven on Sodom and Gomorrah, had left gifts to replace the things they had burned away, and it could be a great race—almost a new one. Together with another people and another culture to temper its faults and encourage its virtues, it could develop beyond the dreams of all the poetic prophecies.

But would it happen that way, or would men become only the cunning vassals of an alien lord?

"I am Alpha and Omega—the Beginning and the End," Gram quoted softly, as if reading his mind. But the words that should have been encouraging were grim and foreboding. For she had named him Omega, and he was the last of the Earth race. But there was no one to call him Alpha or to promise that he was the beginning of a new race, no longer Earthbound.

Now they reached the end of the passage, and already the red disk of Mars was pushing back the cold and the darkness of space before them. Omega sighed gently. He could only pray that it was an omen of the future—and wonder.

Perhaps he would never know.

Campbell rejected the story, of course, when I finally took it in to him. But that wasn't the next day, as I'd expected. I started another story and finished that, so I took two in at once—something I'd never done before. I think it's a bad idea to submit more than one at a time. Editors are only human, and they'll probably pick the better of the two and return the other, so you've cut your chances of selling both. Also, some editors will take the evidence of too many stories at once as either proof you're bundling up all your old stories into packages or that you're doing very hasty work.

Eventually, the story sold to something called *Out of This World Adventures,* where it appeared under the title of "Omega and the Wolf Girl."

I'm afraid it shows the rustiness of my technique, as to both plotting and writing. I was straining for effect in my writing, and being too obvious in my plotting.

Looking back on it, I can see that there is a story there, buried under all that evidence of hasty thought. Again, it's a matter of viewpoint. Omega was more acted upon than acting. His grandmother would have been a better viewpoint. But it would still have been clumsy.

The story should have been told through the wolf-girl's eyes. Here she is, almost human in intelligence, straining along with her kind to find full expression for her ideas. And she's living near these queer remnants of humanity. Her capture and later freedom could have been much better seen as she sees them. And the story could have ended with her attempt to understand that the men were gone, except for the one who could talk to her. She wouldn't quite understand, but she might have a dim idea that the world was hers now—and that her children might have the good things men had discovered in some far future. I suppose it should end with her letting the man-thing fondle her cubs while she sort of edges up beside him, trying to understand.

But it's a little late to rewrite the story now.

The story I wrote the next day was another matter. The idea had jelled during the evening, which is why I didn't go down to Campbell's office with the first one. And it took firm, hard shape in my mind. When I started to write it, it came out smoothly and without hesitation, until I felt sure that I really hadn't lost any of my ability during the long hiatus.

It came to 6,300 words, and I called it "Phoenix Complex." But I much prefer the title under which it was published: "Shadows of Empire."

20.

Shadows of Empire

(by Lester del Rey)

We slipped out of the post while Mars's sky was still harsh and black, and the morning was bitter with cold. Under us was the swish of the treads slapping the worn old sands, and from the lorries came the muttered grumbling of the men, still nursing their hangovers. The post was lost in the grayness behind us, and the town was just beginning to stir with life as we left it. But it was better that way; the Fifth had its orders back to Earth after ten generations outside, and the General wanted no civilian fuss over our going.

It had been enough, just hearing the click at the gate, and seeing the few pinch-faced, scared people along the streets as we passed. Most of us had been there well over ten years, and you can't keep men segregated from the townspeople in the outposts. Well, they'd had their leave the night before, and now we were on our way; the less time spent thinking about going, the less chance for thoughts of desertion to ripen.

At that, two of the men had sneaked off into the wastelands with a sandtractor and lorry. I'd have liked to find them; after twenty years with the Service, things like that get under your skin. But we couldn't wait for a week hunting them, when the Emperor had his seal on our orders.

Now a twist in the road showed the town in the dim dawn-light, with the mayor running up tardily and tripping over a scrap of a flag. And old Jake, the tavern-keeper, still stood among the empty boxes from which he'd tossed cartons of cigarettes to us as we went by. Lord knows how much we still owed him, but he'd been Service once himself, and I don't think that was on his mind. Yeah, it was a good town, and we'd never forget it; but I was glad when the road twisted back and the rolling dunes cut it off from view. I'm just plain people myself, not one of your steel-and-ice nobility like the General.

And that was why I was still only a Sergeant Major, even though I had to take second command nowadays. In the old times, of course, they'd have sent out young nobles to take over, with proper titles, but I guess they liked it better back on Earth now. For that matter, we'd had few enough replacements in my time, except those we'd recruited ourselves from the town and country around. But what the hell—we managed. The Fifth lacked a few men and some fancy brass, but I never heard a marauding Torrakh laugh over it, even after bad fuel grounded our last helicopter.

Now the little red sun came up to a point where we could turn the heaters off our aspirators. We were passing through a pleasant enough country, little farms and canal-berry orchards. The farm folk must have figured we were out on a raid again, because they only waved at us and went on with their work; the thick-wooled sheep went on bleating at themselves with no interest in us. Behind me, someone struck up a halfhearted marching song on an old lectrozith, and the men picked it up.

That was better. I sighed to myself, found one of my legs had gone to sleep, and nursed the prickles out of it while the miles slipped behind, and the hamlets and farms began to thin out. In a little while we were reaching the outskirts of the northern desert, and the caterpillar tracks settled down to a steady sifting slap that's music to a man's ears. We ate lunch out of our packs while the red dunes rolled on endlessly in front of us.

It was a couple hours later when the General's tractor dropped abreast of me and his so-called adjutant vaulted to my seat, his usually saturnine face pinched into a wry grin. Then the radio buzzed and he lifted it to my ear with a finger across his lips.

The General's precise voice clipped out. "Close up ranks, Sergeant; we've spotted a band of Torrakhi moving in the direction of the town. Probably heard we're leaving, and they're already moving up; but they'd be happy to stop for a straggler, so keep together."

"Right, sir," I answered out of habit, and added the words on the slip of paper Stanislaus was shaking under my nose. "But couldn't we take a swipe at them first?"

"No time. This looks like the rear guard, and the main body is probably already unfiltering through the wastelands. The town will have to shift for itself."

"Right, sir," I said again, and the radio clicked off, while the Slav went on grinning to himself. There wasn't a Torrakh within miles, and I knew it, but the General usually knew what he was doing; I wasn't so dumb I couldn't guess at it.

Stanislaus stretched his lank frame on the seat and nodded slowly. "Yeah, he's crazy, too—which is why he's a good General, Major. A few like him in higher places, and we'd be on Mars for another generation or so. Though it wouldn't make much difference in the long run . . . . *Vanitas vanitatis! There is no remembrance of former generations; neither shall there be any remembrance of the latter generations that are to come, among those that shall come after!* . . . That's Ecclesiastes, and worth more than the whole Book of Revelation."

"Or a dozen gloomy Slavs! There was talk of replacing the Fifth back when I was still a buck private. You should be a preacher."

"And in a way, I was, Major—*lest evil days come and the years draw nigh when thou shalt say, I have no pleasure in them.* But a prophet's without honor; and as you say, I'm a gloomy Slav, even though they usually send replacements before they withdraw the Service. Well, lay on, MacDuff, for the greater glory of the Empire!"

I wasn't going to admit he had me, but I couldn't think of anything to say to that, so I shut up. The gloom-birds were probably around before that stuff was written, but civilization was still going on, though there were rumors about things back on Earth. But somehow, he always managed to make me start smelling old attics piled high with rubbish and beginning to mold. I turned and looked sideways, just as the first outskirts of an old canal swung into view.

They still call them canals, at least, though even the old-time astronomers knew they weren't, before Mars was ever reached. But they must have been quite something, ten or fifteen thousand years ago, when the V'nothi built the big earthenware pipelines thousands of miles across the planet to section it and break up the sand-shifts that were ruining it. The big osmotic pumps were still working after a fashion, and there was a trickle of moisture flowing even yet, leaking out into the bleeder lines and keeping the degenerate scrub trees going in fifty-mile swaths around them.

The V'nothi had disappeared before the Pyramids were put up, leaving only pictures of themselves in the ruins, looking like big, good-natured Vikings, complete to brawn and winged helmets. Their women folk must have been really something, even with fur all over them. Archaeologists were still swearing every time they looked at those pictures and wondered what men on horseback were doing on Mars, and why no bones had ever been found! Some of them were even guessing that the V'nothi were Earthmen, maybe from an early peak of civilization we remembered in the Atlantis myths. But even if they were, there was a lot about them to drive a man nuts without worrying about their origins. If you ask me, they were just plain domesticated animals for some other race. Still, whoever the real boss was, it must have been quite a world in their time.

Even the canal-trees weren't natural; no other plants on Mars had bellows growing out of them to supercharge themselves with air, ozone, and traces of watervapor. Even over the drone of the tractor motors, I could hear the dull mutter of their breathing. And at sundown, when they all got together in one long, wild groan . . . well, when I first heard that, I began to have dreams about what the master race was, though I'm not exactly imaginative. Now I'm older, and just don't know—nor much care.

But the air was drier and thinner here, where they desiccated it, and Stanislaus was breathing it with a sort of moral rectitude about him, and nodding as if he liked it. "Dust of Babylon, eh, Major? They went up a long way once, farther in some ways than we've climbed yet. In a thousand years or less they pulled themselves up to our sciences, dropped them, and began working on what we'd call sheer magic. Sometimes, just thinking of what the records hint at scares me. They built themselves up to heaven, before the curse of bigness struck them down; and being extremists, it wasn't just a retreat, but a final rout."

"Meaning we're due for the same, 'Laus?" I always did like the way he pronounced his name, to rhyme with house.

"No, Major; we're not the same—we retreat. Nineveh, Troy, Rome—they've gone, but the periphery always stays to hibernate and come out into another springtime. An empire decays, but it takes a long time dying, and so far there's always been a certain amount passed on to the next surge of youthfulness. We've developed a racial phoenix complex. But of course you don't believe the grumblings of a gloomy Slav who's just bitter that his old empire is one of the later dust heaps?"

"No," I told him. "I don't."

He got up, knocking ashes off his parka with long, flickering fingers, and his voice held an irritating chuckle. "Stout fella, pride of the Empire, and all that! I congratulate you, Major, and dammit, I envy you." And he was over the treads and running toward where the General's tractor had stopped, like a long-drawn-out cat. If he hadn't had the grace of a devil, his tongue would have gotten him spitted on a rapier years before.

I didn't dwell on even such pleasant thoughts. The men had stopped singing, and the first reaction of forced cheer was over. They were good joes, all in all, but after the long years at the post among the townspeople, they couldn't help being human. So I dropped back to the end of the line and kept my eyes peeled for any that might suddenly decide to develop engine trouble and lag behind. It's always the first day and night that are the hardest.

Their grumbling sounded normal enough when we pulled off the trail away from the tree-mutterings, well after sundown, and I felt better; it's when they stop grousing that you have to watch them. All the same, I made them dig in a lot deeper than we needed, though it gets cold enough to freeze a man solid at night. They were sweating and stepping up the power in their aspirators before I was satisfied, and the berylite tent tops barely stuck up over the sand.

That would give them something trivial to beef about, and work their muscles down to good condition for sleeping. A good meal and a double ration of grog would finish the trick nicely, and I'd already given orders for that—which left me nothing to do but go in where Stanislaus was sprawled out on a cot, dabbling with his food and nodding in time to the tent aspirator's variations.

"Nice gadget, that—efficient," he commented, and the pinched grin was on his face. "Of course, the air's thick enough to breathe when a man's not working, but it's still a nice thing to have."

I knew what he meant, of course. The old-timers had done a lot of foolish things, like baking out enough oxygen to keep the air pressure up almost to Earth normal. But it wasn't economical, and we were modern enough to get along without such nonsense. While I ate, I told him so, along with some good advice about how to get on well with Emperors. Besides, it was a damn-sight better aspirator than they'd had in the pioneer days.

I might as well have saved my breath. He waited until I ran down, and nodded amiably. "Absolutely, absolutely. And very well put, Major. As the Romans said when Theodoric's Goths gave them orders, we're modern and up-to-date. Being of the present time, we're automatically modern. As for the Emperor, I wouldn't think of blaming him for what's inevitable, though I'd like a chance to argue the point with him, if I didn't have a certain fondness for my neck. Meantime, Mars rebuilds the seals in its houses and puts in little wind machines. *And behold, all was vanity and a striving after wind!* You really should read Ecclesiastes. Well, sleep tight, Major!"

He ducked under a blanket and was snoring in less than five minutes. I never could sleep well under a tin tent with a man who snores; and it was worse this time, somehow, though I finally did drop off.

We were dug out and ready to march in the morning when the General's scheme bore fruit; our deserters showed up over the dunes, hot-footing it down on us. They must have spotted my tractor, because they didn't waste any time in coming up to me. The damned fools! Naturally, they had to bring the two women along with them, instead of dumping them near town. They must have been stinko drunk when they started, though the all-night drive had sobered them up—the drive plus half freezing to death and imagining Torrakhi behind every bush.

I'd never seen those two brig-birds salute with quite such gusto, though, as they hopped down, and Stanislaus' amused snort echoed my sentiments. But the big guy started the ball rolling, with only a dirty look at the Slav. "Sir, we couldn't help being AWOL, we . . ."

"Were caught by Torrakhi, of course," the General's smooth voice filled in behind me, and I stepped out of the picture on the double. "Very clever of you to escape, tractors and all! Unfortunately, there were no Torrakhi; the message your receiver was designed to unscramble was a trap, based on the assumption that you'd rather take your chances with us than with a marauding band of nomads infiltering around you. I suppose I could have you shot; and if I hear one sniveling word from you, I will. Or I could take you back to Earth in chains."

His lips pressed out into a thin, white line, and his eyes flicked over to Stanislaus for a bare second. "You wouldn't like that. There's a new Emperor, not the soft one we had before. I served under him once . . . and I rather suspect he'd reward me for bringing you back with us, after the proper modern Imperial fashion of gratitude. However, for the good of the Fifth, you're already listed as fatalities. Sergeant, do you know these women?"

"Their names are on our books, sir."

"Quite so. And they knew what they were mixed up in. Very well, leave them their side arms, but fill the tractor and lorry they returned with some of your men, and prepare to break camp. You've already forgotten all this; and that goes for the men, as well!" He swung on his heel and mounted his tractor without another look at the deserters, who were just beginning to realize what he'd meant.

Stanislaus elected to ride with me as we swung back toward the canal road, watching the four until the dunes swallowed them. Then he shrugged and lit his cigarette. "Not orthodox, Major, but effective; you can stop worrying about desertions. And take it from me, it was the right thing to do; I happen to know—rather well, in fact—why our precise and correct leader thought it wise to fake the books. But I won't bore you with it. As to those four—well, some of the pioneers were up against worse odds, but *de mortuis nil nisi bonum*. Nice morning, don't you think?"

It was, as a matter of fact, and we were making good time. The trail swung out, heading due south now, and away from the canal, and the sands were no longer cluttered with the queer pits always found around the canal-trees. By noon, we'd put a hundred more miles behind us, and the men were hardening into the swing of things, though they still weren't doing the singing I like to hear on the march—the good, clean filth that's somehow the backbone of Service morale. I sent a couple of tractors out to scout, just to break the monotony, though there wouldn't be anything to see so near the end of the desert.

Surprisingly, however, they hadn't been gone ten minutes when the report came back: Torrakhi to the left flank! A moment later, we were snapping into a tight phalanx and hitting up a rise where we could see; but by then we knew that there was no danger. They were just a small band, half a mile away, jolting along on their llama-mounts at an easy lope. Then they spotted us and beat back behind the dunes and out of sight. A small marauding band, turning back north from sacking some fool outlier's farm, probably.

But it was unusual to see them so far south. We'd never been able to eliminate them entirely, any more than the V'nothi before us had, but we'd kept the wild quasi-human barbarians in line, pretty much. And now we were swinging back to the trail again, leaving them unchecked to grow bold in raiding; there wasn't anything else we could do, since they hadn't attacked and we were under Imperial seal. Well, maybe the Second Command would get them for us sometime. I hoped so.

Stanislaus might say what he would, but he was still Service, and it had hit him, too. "Notice the long rifle they pulled? What make would you say?"

"Renegade pirates on Callisto, it looked like, at a guess. But the exiles couldn't get past the Out Fleet to trade with Torrakhi!"

He flipped his cigarette away and turned to face me, dead serious and quiet about it. "The Out Fleet's just a propaganda myth, Major! They pulled it back before I—uh, left Earth."

He couldn't know that, and I had no business believing him; yet somehow, I was sure he did know, and whatever else he was, he was not a liar. But that would mean that the Earth-Mars trade . . .

"Exactly," he said, as if he'd read the thought. "And now we're going back to help put down a minor little uprising in the Empire, so I hear. Write your own ticket!"

But even if it were true, it didn't prove anything. Sure, it looked bad, but I've learned you can't judge from half-knowledge. A lot of times when I've gone out swearing at the orders, I've come back alive because they weren't the kind I'd have given. Heck, even if the mesotron rifle was Callistan, there was no telling how old it was; maybe they'd pulled the Out Fleet back for the sound reason that it wasn't needed. But it did look odd, their keeping up the pretense.

We camped that night at an old abandoned fort dating back to pioneer days, and then shoved on in the morning through little hamlets and the beginning of settled land. The people looked fairly hard and efficient, but it was pleasant, after the desert, and the men seemed more cheerful. Here the road was kept surfaced and the engines went all out. A little later, we took the grousers off, and by the time another night had passed, we were in well-settled country. From then on, it was all soft going and the miles dropped away as regular as clockwork, though I missed the swish of the sand under the treads.

As we went on, the land and the people got softer, with that comfortable look I'd missed up where Torrakhi are more than things to scare children with. And the farms were bigger and better kept. For that matter, I couldn't see a man working with a rifle beside him. The Service had done that. When we first hit Mars, in the pioneer days, there hadn't been a spot on its face where a man could close both eyes. Now even the kids went running along the road alone. Oh, sure, there were some abandoned villas, here and there, but I don't think the nobles were too much missed.

And that was civilization and progress, whatever Stanislaus thought about it. Let them pull the Out Fleet back and call in the Fifth. As long as Mars had spots on it like this, it didn't look too bad for the Empire. I wanted to throw it in the Slav's face, but I knew it wouldn't do any good. He'd have some kind of answer. Better let sleeping dogs lie.

And besides, he was riding with the General again, and even at night he was busy writing in some big book and not paying attention to anything else. In a way, it was all to the good. Still, I dunno. At least, when he was spouting out his dogma, I had a chance to figure up some kind of answer to myself. There wasn't much I could do about the look on his face.

But I noticed that we always seemed to make camp about the time we were well away from the towns, and it was something to think over, along with the guff that had begun among the men. It looked as if the General meant to keep us away from any rumors going around among the ciss, and that was odd; ordinarily, civilian scuttlebutt means nothing to the Service.

And now that the novelty had worn off, there was something wrong about the number of farms we'd pass that were abandoned and that had been for a long time. There were little boarded-up stores in some of the villages, and once we went by a massive atomic by-products plant, dead and forgotten. And the softness on the people's faces began to look less pretty; one good-sized band of Torrakhi could raise hob with a whole county, even without mesotron rifles from Callisto.

The one time I did speak to a native, I had no business doing it. We'd been rolling along, with me at the rear for the moment, and there was this fine-looking boy of about twelve walking along the road. What got me was the song he was singing and the way he came to a Service salute at the sight of us. Well, the General wasn't in sight, and the kid took my slowing up as a hint to hop onto the lug rail.

"Fifth, isn't it, sir?"

"Right. But where the deuce did you learn that ditty and the proper way to address a noncom?"

He grinned the way healthy kids know how, before they grow old enough to forget. "Gramps was in the Fifth when they raised the siege of Bharene, sir, and he told me all about it before he died. Gee, it must have been great when he was young!"

"And now?"

"Aw, now they say you're going back to Earth, and Gramps wouldn't have liked that. He was a Martian, like me. . . . Look, I live up there, so I gotta go. Thanks for the lift, Sergeant!"

So even the kids knew we were going back, and now we were just another Service Command, instead of the backbone of Mars. Strange, I hadn't thought of what it would mean, going back where people had never heard of us before. But I could see where the General was right in not letting us mix with people here. Dammit, we were still the Fifth, and nothing could change that, Mars or Earth, Emperor or Torrakhi!

We didn't spend too much time looking at the country after that, though it grew even prettier as we went on. The tractors were beginning to carbon up under the fuel we had to requisition, and we were busy nursing them along and watching for trouble. At the post, we'd had our own purifying plant to get the gum out of the vegetable fuels, but here we had to take potluck. And it was a lot worse than I'd expected. But then, a man tends to gloss over his childhood and think things were better then. I dunno. Maybe it had always been that bad.

Anyhow, we made it, in spite of a few breakdowns. It was dusk when the lights of Marsport showed up, and we went limping through the outskirts. When we hit the main drag, a motorcop ran ahead of us with his siren open, though there wasn't any need. I couldn't help wondering where the cars were, and how they managed to dig up so many bicycles. We must have looked like the devil, since we'd pushed too fast to bother much with shining up, but there were some cheers from the crowds that assembled, and a few women's faces with the look of not having seen uniforms in years. The men woke up at that, yelling the usual things, but I could feel their disappointment in the city.

Then we halted, and Stanislaus came back, while a fat and stuffy little man in noble's regalia strode up to the General's tractor, fairly sniffing the dirt on our gear as he came. Well, he could have used a better shave himself, and a little less hootch would have improved his dignity. The Slav chuckled. "Methinks this should be good, unless the O.M. has lost his touch. Flip the switch, Major; I left the radio turned on."

But no sound came out of it except a surprised grunt from the fat official as he looked at the odd-patterned ring on the General's finger. I never knew what it stood for, but all the air went out of the big shot's sails, and he couldn't hand over the official message fast enough after that. He was mopping sweat from his face when the crowd swallowed him. I've seen a bust corporal act that way when he suddenly remembered he was pulling rank he no longer had.

"Don't bother cutting off yet, Sergeant," the radio said quietly, and it was my turn to grin. Stanislaus should have known better than to try putting anything over on the General. "Ummm, I'm going to be tied up with official business at the Governor's, so you'll have to go ahead. Know where the auxiliary port is? Good. Bivouac there, and put the men to policing themselves and the hangars. No passes. That's all."

He moved to a waiting car, leaving the tractor to his driver, and we went on again, out through the outskirts and past the main spaceport; that was dark, and I couldn't tell much about it, but I remembered the mess of the old auxiliary field. They'd built it thirty miles out in barren land to handle the overflow during the old colonizing period, and it had been deserted and weed-grown for years, with hangars falling apart. It was worse than I'd remembered, though there were some lights on and a group of Blue Guards to let us in and direct us to the left side of the field.

Some clearing had been done, but there was work enough to keep us all busy as beavers, and there would be for days, if we stayed that long. At least it gave me a good excuse for announcing confinement to grounds, though they took it easier than I'd expected. It seemed they already knew in some way. And at last I was finished with giving orders and had a chance to join the Slav in inspecting the ships I'd already noticed down at the end of the field.

I'd seen the like of the double-turret cruiser before, but the two big ones were different, even in the dim lights of the field. They were something out of the history books, and no book could give any idea of their size. The rocket crews about them, busy with their own affairs, were like ants running around a skyscraper by comparison. Either could have held the whole Command and left room for cargo besides.

"So we're waiting for the Second Command to go back with us, 'Laus?"

He jerked his head back from a reverent inspection of the big hulks and nodded at me slowly. "You improve, Major, though you forgot to comment on the need of a cruiser between Mars and Earth. . . . Two hundred years! And those ships are still sounder than the hunk of junk sent out to protect them. There was a time when men knew how to build ships—and how to use them. Now there are only four left out of all that were built. Any idea where the other two are?"

"Yeah." I'd failed to recognize them because of their size, but it hadn't been quite dark enough to conceal them completely. "Back at the other port we passed, picking up the South Commands. Dammit, 'Laus, did you have to infect me with your pessimism?"

"You're going back to Earth, Major," he answered, as if that were explanation enough. "The optimist sees the doughnut, the pessimist the hole; but you get a better view of things through a hole than through a hunk of sweetened dough. And, as Havelock Ellis put it, the place where optimism most flourished was the lunatic asylum. Come on back and I'll lend you Ecclesiastes while I finish my book."

And I was just dumb enough to read it. But I might have had the same nightmare anyway. I'd gotten a good look at the faces of the rocket gang.

In the morning, I was too busy bossing the stowing of our gear to do much thinking, though. Even with maps of the corridors, I'd have been lost in the ship without the help of one of the pilots, a bitter-faced young man who seemed glad to fill his time, but who refused to talk beyond the bare necessities. When the General came back at noon, the men were all quartered inside, except for those who were detailed to help load the collection of boxes that began to come out from Marsport.

He nodded curt approval and went to the radio in his cabin. And about an hour later, I looked up to see the Second Command come in and go straight to the second ship, a mile away. They could have saved themselves the trouble of avoiding us, as far as I was concerned. I had no desire to compare notes with them. But I guess it was better for the men, and it was a lot easier than posting guards overnight to see they didn't mix. A hell of a way to run the Service, I thought; but of course it wasn't the Service anymore—just the Second and Fifth Commands, soon to be spread around Earth!

It was after taps when they brought the civilians aboard, but I was still enjoying the freedom of second in command, and I was close enough to get a good look at them and the collection of special tools they were bringing along with the rest of their luggage. I'd always figured the technical crafts came out from automated Earth to the outlands where their skills were still needed. But that seemed to be just another sign that the old order was changing. I turned to make talk with the pilot who was beside me, and then thought better of it.

But for once, he was willing to break his silence, though he never took his eyes off the little group that was filing in. "They're needed, Sergeant! Atomic technicians are in demand again, along with plutonium for the Earth reactors—or . . . I suppose you guessed that's what the rear trucks are carrying, and they'll be loading it between hulls tonight—all that can be stowed safely. Of course, I'm not supposed to talk—but I was born here, and it's not like the last job we had, ferrying back the Venus Commands. Care to join me in getting drunk?"

It was an idea. Plutonium is particularly valuable for bombs, for which it's still the best material. And atom bombs are the messiest, lousiest, and most inefficient weapons any fighting man ever swore at. They're only good for ruining the land until you can't finish a decent mopping up, and poisoning the atmosphere until your own people begin dying. Not a single one had been dropped in the five centuries since we came up with the superior energy weapons. So now we were carrying the stuff from Mars's reactors back to Earth, where they already had the accumulated stuff from all their piles.

But I caught a signal from the car the General was using as I turned, and I changed my mind. I was in the mood for Stanislaus now, and whiskey's a pretty poor mental cathartic, anyway. This time I could see that the information I poured out at him wasn't something he already knew.

"So. *Even so are the sons of men snared in an evil time, when it falleth suddenly upon them.*" He let it sink in slowly, then shrugged. "Well, maybe it'll be faster that way. But it won't matter to me. I'm due in Marsport to attend my funeral—a lovely casket, I understand, though it's a pity we're so pressed for time I can't have military honors. Only the simple dignity of civilian rites. Thought you might like to bid me fond adieu, for old times' sake."

"Yeah, sure. And bring me back a bottle of the same."

He shook his head gently, and the damned fool's voice was serious. "I wish I could, Major. I'd like nothing better than having you along to listen to my theories on our racial phoenix complex. But I've done the next best thing in leaving the book that's my labor of love in your cabin. All right, I was ribbing you, let's say, and I'm being transferred out to the Governor's service by special orders. Does that make sense to you?"

It did, put that way. It meant that after all the years of wishing he'd clam up, I was going to miss him plenty, now that I'd been converted, and I'd probably sit alone biting my tongue to keep from spouting the same brand of pessimism. But I wasn't much good at saying it, and he cut me off in the middle.

"Then bite it off! That stuff won't go, back there, though you're better off for having found out in advance. Trust the General to see you through. He made a mistake once, but he's wiser now. Forget Ecclesiastes and remember a jingle of Kipling's instead: *Now these are the Laws of the Jungle, and many and mighty are they; but the head and the hoof of the Law, and the haunch and the hump is—Obey! Betray* rhymes as well—but it takes a lot more background and practice. Now beat it, before I really start preaching."

I didn't need to hunt up the pilot; I had a bottle of Martian canal juice of my own in the cabin. But I'd consumed more of the book than the bottle when morning came and a knock sounded outside.

The General came in when I grunted, his face pinched with fatigue, and his eyes red with lack of sleep. He nodded at the book, dropped onto my cot, and poured himself a generous slug before he looked up at me.

"A remarkable book, Bill, by a remarkable man. But you know that by now. Dynamite, of course, but something we'll have to smuggle in to save for a possible posterity. And stop looking so damned surprised! Any man Stanislaus trusted with that book is my equal or better, as far as I'm concerned. After we land, I have ways of seeing you get knighthood and a Colonel's rank, so you're practically an officer, anyhow. And I'm not acting as either General or Duke—just a messenger boy for the late deceased Stanislaus Korzynski. He died of canal fever day before yesterday, you know."

It was coming too thick and fast, and I didn't answer that. I reached for the bottle and poured a shot down my throat without bothering with a glass. The General held out his glass, watched me fill it, and downed the shot before going on again. "Not much of a Serviceman, am I, Bill? But it has to be that way. Nobody knows the name he used, but there are plenty on Earth who remember his face. Or haven't you figured out yet who he was from the book?"

"I've had my suspicions," I admitted. "Only I dunno whether I'm crazy or he was."

"Neither. You're right, he's the supposedly assassinated Prince Stellius Asiaticus, rightful ruler of the Empire! Here's a note he sent you."

There wasn't much to it:

> Friend Major—
>
> It was over the hill for me, after all. If you have children, as I intend to, pass on my new name to them, and someday our offspring may get together and discuss the phoenix bird.
>
> Elmer C. Clesiastes

"The phoenix," the General muttered over my shoulder while he reached for the bottle. "Now what the deuce did he mean by that?"

"What is it, anyway?"

"A legendary bird of Grecian mythology—the only one of its kind. It lived for a few hundred years, then built itself a funeral pyre and sat fanning the flames with its wings until it was consumed. After that, a new bird hatched out of the ashes and started all over again. That's why they used it for the symbol of immortality."

Below us, the rockets rumbled tentatively and then bellowed out, while the force of the jets crushed us back against the wall. Beyond the porthole, Mars dropped away from us, as the Empire turned back to its nest. But I wasn't thinking much of that, impressive though it was.

Somehow, I was going to have the children Stanislaus had mentioned, and I'd live long enough to see that they remembered the new name he'd chosen, atom bombs or no bombs. Because I knew him at last, and the pessimist was a prince, all right—the Prince of Optimists.

The General and I sat toasting him and discussing the phoenix legend and civilization's ups and downs while Mars changed from a world to a round ball in the background of space. It wasn't military or proper, but we felt much better by the time we found and confiscated the second bottle.

Campbell rejected "Shadows of Empire" for a reason that came as a surprise to me. He felt it was too moody. He liked it, he felt the writing was good, and it was a perfectly good story, but not for him. He'd apparently run several mood pieces, and the readers were reacting a bit against them. He wanted straight stories now.

The story eventually sold to Robert Lowndes at Columbia Publications, and the present title is his. But before then, Damon Knight had seen it in my agent's office, and had told me flatly that it should never be sold. It was nothing but a rewrite of Stephen Vincent Benét's "Last of the Legions."

I hadn't realized the similarity, though I had read the Benét story years before. I pulled it out and read it again, and I could see what Damon meant. I didn't think it was too close—the whole final section was completely different, giving the story a different intent. Benét was showing nothing but the dissolution of an empire; I was trying to show that empires don't matter—men somehow always come back again. And my Stanislaus is more than the Greek-chorus figure of Benét's story.

But I kept it off the market for a long time, until Bob Lowndes asked if I had any more around. Then I gave it to him, with a full account of Damon's criticism. Bob read it, and he too could see what Damon meant. But he agreed with me that it was quite sufficiently different to justify publishing. He paid me $65 for it, and no reader complained, though a few spotted the similarities. (Benét has been a lot more closely imitated in other cases. I don't know how many stories derive from his "Waters of Babylon.")

Anyhow I left Campbell's office and went home to begin at once on another story. I wrote three altogether in the next three days, and took them all in at once.

The first of these was in direct answer to John Campbell's suggestion that straight stories were now the ones he wanted. It didn't have a trace of mood in the whole 6,300 words. I called it "Simulacrum Limited," but it was published as "Unreasonable Facsimile," and I have no quarrel with that title.

21.

Unreasonable Facsimile

(by Lester del Rey)

Max Fleigh's heavy jowls relaxed and he chuckled without humor as he examined the knots that bound the man at his feet. Quite impersonally, he planted the toe of his boot in Curtis' ribs, listened to the muffled grunt of pain, and decided that the gag was effective. For once, Slim had done a good job, and there was nothing wrong. It was probably unnecessary, anyway, but there could be no bungling when the future of the Plutarchy was at stake.

Incompetence had cost them an empire once, and there would be no third opportunity. The stupid democracies that had called themselves a World Union had colonized the planets and ruled them without plan. And when Mars, Venus, and the Jovian Worlds had revolted and set up a Planet Council, all that Earth could do was to come crawling to it, begging polite permission to join what they should have owned!

But that had been before practical realists had kicked out the dreamers and set up the Plutarchy under an iron discipline that could implement its plans. Now they were heading back toward their lost empire, colonizing the asteroids and establishing claims that gave them a rough rule over the outlaws who had retreated there. With the Council softened up by years of cautious propaganda, they were in a position to ask and receive a Mandate over the scattered planetoids.

It was the opening wedge, and all they needed. Once the asteroids could be given spurious independence to seek a Council seat, they would be ready to strike at the Jovian Worlds. With proper incidents, propaganda, and quislings, plus the planetoids to separate Jupiter from Mars, there could be no question of the outcome. Earth would gain a majority of three votes, and the Council would be the basis of a new and greater Plutarchy.

Fleigh gave the bound body of Curtis another careless kick and went forward to the cabin, where the lanky form of his companion was hunched dourly over the controls of the little spacecraft. "How's it going, Slim?"

"So-so." Slim ejected a green stream of narcotic juice and grinned sourly. "But I still say we been crowdin' our luck too hard!"

"Rot! Lay out the right moves, cover all possibilities, outmaneuver your enemies, and you don't need luck! Ever play chess?"

"Nope, can't say I did. Played the horses on Mars, though, time we h'isted the *Euphemeron*. Won, too—after I bought my lucky ghost charm; been in the chips ever since!" Slim's grin widened, but his face remained stubbornly unconvinced.

Fleigh chuckled. If the planetoid outlaws depended on magic, while the Council visionaries spouted sentimental twaddle, so much the better for the realists. "Charms don't work in politics, Slim. We have to anticipate resistance. And you saw what happened to our fine Martian Councilor Curtis when he decided to expose us and ruin the Mandate!"

"Yeah." Slim's yellow teeth chewed thoughtfully on his cud. "S'pose he'd stayed on Mars, though?"

"We'd have dropped hints of just the information he needed on Ceres and trapped him there—as we did. Checkmate!"

"Or check-out. So when he don't come back, they smell a rat—an' I ain't plannin' on bein' around to chew rat poison. My granpappy killed a Councilor once—poor granpappy! . . . Hey, there's the rock!"

There was no outward sign of life on the barren little planetoid. But as the ship came to a grinding stop in a narrow gorge, a concealing shield snapped on over them, and a crudely painted sign blazed out in phosphorescent gaudiness on one rocky wall:

SIMILACRA, LTD.
Μαγος—Δεινος Τεκτων
Specialist:
Μιμησις και Σαρκασμος

Fleigh came out of the lock first and paused while he waited for Slim to shoulder the tarpaulin-covered Curtis and follow. He grinned and pointed at the sign. "Magician and wonder-worker; specialist in imitation and mockery. I looked it up on Mars, so don't go thinking it's some kind of spell. . . . Now if the old fool will open up . . ."

"Then why ain't English good enough for him? I don't go for that magic stuff, Max. We been—"

But the Sigma was already swinging back on its tips to reveal a passage through the rock. A little, shriveled man in tattered shorts and thick-lensed glasses stood motioning them in impatiently, and the door closed silently when they obeyed his summons. They headed down a side passage toward a ramp and the sound of busy humming.

Greek threw open a door and pointed to a table where the exact duplicate of Councilor Curtis lay, with an identical Jeremiah Greek fussing over it and humming through his nose. The guide dropped to a bench and began removing his chest and inserting a fresh power pack between two terminals.

Slim's mouth dropped open and his burden slipped from his back to the floor with a sodden thump, while he stared from one Greek to the other, and back to the first. His fingers were stretched in the ancient sign of the horns as he watched the changing of accumulators, and his voice was hoarse and uncertain. "A damned robot!"

"Not a robot—a similacrum," denied the owl-eyed man who must have been the original of the metal creature. "I'm a mimesist, not a creator. A robot has independent life, but that's only a limited copy of my memories and habits, like this phony Curtis. And those tapes you brought me, Fleigh—they stink!"

He gestured toward the spools of the marvelous wire that could record electromagnetic waves of any type of frequency up to several million megacycles. In one corner, a stereo-player was running one off, but the vision screen was fuzzy, and the voice part was a mass of gibberish.

Fleigh scowled at it, and turned back suspiciously to Greek. "Sure you know how to use them? Those were made by—"

"By a fool who had a shield leak in his scanner! Only a few were any good. I was using pancyclic wire before you ever saw a stereo-record. Where do you think I impress my similacrum's memory—on a real brain? It takes miles of wire to feed the selectrons! I did the best I could, but . . . Here, take a look!" He reached into the false Curtis' mouth and did something that made the figure sit up suddenly.

Max went over and muttered into the thing's ear, but after the first few answers it lapsed into sullen silence, and he swung back toward Greek. "I told you Curtis had to be perfect! This wouldn't fool a Jovian!"

"And I told you I wasn't Jehovah—I specialize in mechanical imitations," Greek answered shortly. "Bum tape, bum similacrum. If you brought me some decent reels, I'll see what I can do, though."

Fleigh grunted and yanked the tarpaulin off the real Curtis. At the sight, new interest appeared on Greek's face, and he came over to examine the Councilor, but stopped after a cursory look had shown that the man was still alive.

He nodded. "That's more like it, Fleigh. I'll set up an encealograph and ideoform analyzer and record directly off his mind—it's better than feeding impressions from tapes, anyway, though I always used an editing circuit before. Okay, you'll get something his own mother would swear was perfect."

"When?"

"Depends. Narrow-band analysis would take a couple weeks, but it'd be permanent. If I run an all-wave impressor in, the tapes will be barely affected. I can do it in ten, twelve hours, but your similacrum will begin to fade in a week, and wash out completely in a month."

"Suits me," Fleigh decided. "We won't need him more than a few days. Anyplace where Slim and I can catch up on our sleep while you finish?"

Greek's double came to life at a signal and led them down a series of rock corridors to a room that lacked nothing in comfort, then went silently out and left them alone. To Fleigh's relief, Slim tested the bed in sour displeasure, pulled a blanket off, and rolled up on the floor, leaving the flotation mattress unoccupied. He had as little use for such luxuries as his boss had for his presence in the same bed. Max climbed in and adjusted the speegee dial to perfect comfort with a relaxed grunt of pleasure.

He had no intention of sleeping, though, while things that concerned him were going on. Three hours later, he heaved out and slipped silently down the rocky halls on sponge-rubber slippers. But his training had covered the stupidity of spy-stereos, and there was nothing stealthy about his entry into the laboratory. Greek looked up from a maze of wires and gadgets with faint surprise but no suspicion.

"Couldn't sleep," Fleigh volunteered apologetically. "I was wondering if you had any barbiturates?"

A few minutes later he took the tablet from Greek's double and turned back down the hallway with a muttered thanks. He had learned all he wanted to know. Both Greeks and Curtises were present and accounted for where they belonged, and the mimesist was busy about his work; there was no funny business involved. Actually, he had expected none, but it never did any harm to make sure of such things when dealing with men who were outside the law of either the Plutarchy or the Council.

Slim was snoring and kicking about on the floor when he returned, and he grinned as he plopped back onto the mattress. The outlaws were useful enough now. But once Earth took over the Mandate, something would have to be done about them; too many were the wrong sort to fit into the Plutarchy. Fleigh stretched with a self-satisfied yawn and slipped into well-earned rest.

Greek's similacrum wakened them in the morning and led them back to the laboratory, where the scientist was waiting beside the imitation Curtis. The real Councilor must have been drugged, for he lay unconscious on one of the tables. Fleigh wasted only a casual glance at him, and then turned to the new similacrum as Greek flipped it on.

This time his tests were longer, and there were no sullen silences from the imitation. Its responses were quick, sure, and completely correct; the real Curtis could have done no better, and Fleigh stepped back at last and nodded his approval. He'd demanded a perfect similacrum, and it had been delivered.

"You're sure it has a good strong desire to live?" he asked briefly as he fished into his bag for the little prepared relay that was ready.

Greek smiled faintly. "They all have that—they couldn't pass as normal men without it. And if your dimensions were correct, you should have no trouble installing your relay."

He stripped aside the blouse, to reveal a small cavity in the back of the similacrum, with a bundle of little wires which Fleigh hooked onto the relay. It slipped in and locked firmly. Greek unclipped the tiny switch from inside the machine's mouth. The animation within the similacrum disappeared at once, to come on again as a switch in Fleigh's bag was pressed. A little circle of the pancyclic wire strip moved over a scanner inside the bag, sending out a complex wave, while a receiver in the similacrum's back responded by closing the relay. Then the animation was cut off again, and came back at once on a second pressure of the switch.

"Attempted removal of the relay will destroy all circuits, just as you ordered," Greek assured the operative. "Well?"

Fleigh's face mirrored complete satisfaction. "You get the fire emeralds, as promised!"

He reached into the bag and came out with a little bundle, a grin stretched across his face. It stayed there while Greek moved forward quickly, to stagger back with a chopped-off scream as the slugs poured into his face and exploded his head into a mangled mess of blood and gray tissue!

For a second, the Greek double moved forward, but it turned with a shriek and went down the hall at a clumsy run as Fleigh ripped the smoking gun from the package. He let it go. Curtis' head dissolved under a second series of slugs, and only the similacrum of the Councilor was left in the laboratory with the two men.

Slim closed his mouth slowly and reached for his green narcotic, but he made no protest. The other moved about, gathering up combustibles and stacking them in a corner, then setting fire to the pile.

"Which takes care of almost everything, Slim," Fleigh said calmly. They headed out and down the hall toward their ship, with the imitation Curtis moving quietly along behind. Another slug from the gun destroyed the lock on the big Sigma, and they pushed through, out into the rocky gorge. "Nothing left to chance, and a perfect red herring to cover up Curtis' disappearance."

Slim ducked into the lock and went forward to the controls. "Uh-huh. Granpappy'd sure of admired you, Max! Used to look just the same when he drilled somebody he didn't like. . . . All set for take-off?"

"Forgetting anything, Slim?"

The outlaw looked up in puzzled surprise, while Fleigh shook his head and went over to the receiver. There was no sense in trying to teach the fool anything, apparently, but at least he might have learned elementary caution from his mode of life. The Plutarch operative ripped out the tape from the illegal all-wave recorder and slipped it into a playback slot, while slow comprehension crossed the other's face.

But everything was in order, with the usual hash of faint signals on various frequencies. There were no signs of a strong response, such as would have been made by any attempt on Greek's part to double-cross him with a call to the outside. He set the receiver to record, and went toward the rear cabin and the similacrum, while the ship blasted off and headed toward Mars.

The false Curtis was already seated at a table, and groping through a bag of notes the original Curtis had carried. It looked up as Fleigh came in, grimaced, and went on organizing the papers before it. The operative dropped to a chair with his familiar humorless chuckle.

"You realize your life is dependent on obedience, uh—Curtis?"

"Would I have let you kill myself otherwise?" the thing asked grimly. "Leave that control gadget of yours where I can get it, and you'll feel the difference between my hands and mere flesh ones! But meantime, I'll co-operate, since I have no choice. I suppose you intend helping me with my speech before the Council?"

Fleigh's appreciation for the peculiar genius of Greek went up several points, as he assented tersely. The thing was perfect, or so nearly so that it seemed to consider itself the real man. There would be no trouble on that score. As for the control bag—he had no intention of letting that out of his hands until the similacrum was turned off.

It gestured toward the notes with a motion peculiar to Curtis. "You'd only ruin anything you edited, Fleigh. I'm perfectly capable of writing the thing myself, and it'll sound like me! But if I'm going to give you a clean sheet and not make the whole Council suspicious, I'll need more information than I have. I must have the whole picture, so that I can take care of all objections without running counter to what some other Councilors may know already. Also, I think you'd better learn to address me as Councilor Curtis!"

"Quite so, Councilor," Fleigh agreed, and this time the amusement in his laugh was genuine. "Now if you'll tell me what you know of our plans and methods, I'll fill in the blanks. But I want to see that speech, when you're finished."

It was amazing, the amount of evidence Curtis had managed to accumulate in a brief week; or perhaps much of it had been in his hands before, and only needed organizing against what they had let him find on Ceres. It was enough to have ruined all hopes of Earth's getting the Mandate, and seriously endangered her relations with the Planet Council in addition. Fleigh made a mental note to press for an investigation of some of the outland operatives as he began filling in the missing links in the other's information.

Curtis took the facts down in a notebook, grim-faced and silent, checked them back, and reached for the typewriter. The first part of the speech he had meant to deliver needed but slight modification, and Fleigh read it over the similacrum's shoulder as it operated the machine. Then the going grew tougher, and there were long pauses while the thing considered, revising a word here, or changing a paragraph there. It disregarded Fleigh's suggestions with the same contempt that would have been on the real Councilor's face, and the operative began to realize that it was justified. When it came to writing speeches, he was only an amateur, and this was professional work.

He was beginning to regret that the thing could have a life of only from a week to ten days, when it finished; Earth could have used such a propagandist, particularly one accepted on the Council as Mars's chief representative! Curtis' speeches had always been good, but he had never realized that the man's talents would have been equally good on propaganda. It was hard to believe that this was fiction, as he listened to the calm, assured voice running through it, apparently reciting only the simple truth, and yet coloring every word with some trick of oratory that seemed to make it glow with virtue and integrity.

"Perfect!" he commented when it was finished. He cut off the relay signal, watched the similacrum slip to the floor, and went forward to the control cabin with a full measure of satisfaction. Earth could not fail!

And already the red disk of Mars was large and close on the viewplate. Fleigh hadn't realized the time the writing of the speech had taken, but he did not regret a second of it as Slim began nursing the ship down through the thin atmosphere toward the Solar Center.

The taste of coming victory was strong in Max Fleigh as he waited outside the Martian House the next day, but Slim was still glum and morose. Part of that was probably due to his orders to stay out of the usual outlaw haunts on the planet, where the police might have picked him up and ruined the whole plan. The rest, Fleigh decided, was just his natural fear of what he could not understand.

The outlaw was grumbling and turning his lucky ghost charm over and over in his palm. "Leavin' the thing run around this way! We been lucky, Max, but tain't reasonable to figger it'll hold! You shoulda let me tail him!"

"Sure, Slim. People expect him to go around with you at his heels, no doubt!" Fleigh spat dango seeds out of the open car window, and took another bite of the cool fruit before going on. "We have to let him circulate; no Councilor just back from a two-week trip would hole up before this meeting, when he had instructions to pick up any last-minute details that might be coming in. Besides, we're not dealing with Curtis now, but with a machine. And it knows who its master is. The minute I cut the relay, or it gets ten miles away from me—no life!"

He spotted the similacrum coming down the steps and jumped out to open the car door. Slim grunted dourly, pulling his new chauffeur's cap farther down over his forehead, but he took the curt orders from Curtis with no further protests and headed the big car toward the Council Chambers. The Councilor passed over two slips of elaborate pasteboard and leaned back against the seat.

"Passes for the two of you. Are you sure Slim knows what he's to do?"

There was a disgusted sound from the front, but Fleigh ignored it. "He'd better; we've been over it often enough. But go ahead and make sure."

The similacrum ticked off the points with incisive authority. The Council Chamber was radiation-proof, and since Curtis would not be trusted with the relay signal, the success of the whole thing depended on Slim's behavior. Max had secured a duplicate of his signal generator which the outlaw was to use outside the Assembly, while Fleigh went inside with his and waited. The operative had developed complete confidence in the ability of the false Curtis, and he was sure of his own part. It was all up to Slim, but there was no reason for him to fail, and he had always taken orders well enough before.

Actually, it all went off with perfect smoothness. The guards passed him in after a careful scrutiny of his permit, and he carried the briefcase that held the generator up to the gallery and turned it on. Seconds later, the similacrum came through the big doorway, with only a slight flicker of uncertainty as the antiradiation shield touched him and he passed from one generator to the other.

Curtis walked along the aisle with the proper confidence and attention to his friends, presented his credentials for a purely perfunctory examination, and turned off into one of the little council rooms. Two of the other Martian Councilors followed him, and passed out of Fleigh's field of view, but he was not worried about that. Slim came slouching down the gallery stairs and dropped into a seat beside the operative, putting the duplicate generator between his feet.

"Satisfied?"

"Perfect," Fleigh assured him. They would reverse it going out. After that, Curtis would announce that he was leaving on a long trip to Ganymede, and they would be able to dispose of the similacrum without any parts left to show what he was.

Then Curtis came back into the main chamber. Apparently the

Council had been waiting for his return, for the Sergeant at Arms waved for order, and the meeting began, with almost no preliminaries. Earth brought up the subject of the Mandate, and the head of the Venus Council began to come to his feet. But Curtis was up first, and the Chair recognized him.

Fleigh relaxed completely as the familiar words of the speech began to come to him, while the Venusans glanced about in surprise, and then began to listen. A moment later they were under the sway of his oratory. The single speech should do it, since the question had been tentatively decided in favor of Earth at the last meeting, pending Curtis' investigation. By night, the Mandate should be a *fait accompli*, and Earth could begin moving out her mercenary legions in the squat "mining" freighters.

Fleigh had a pretty good idea of who would lead them. He'd been in line for promotion for some time already, and the Plutarch had dropped hints of the outcome of success. It would be good to leave the dubious position of operative and become a legally recognized governor of the mandated planetoids, to settle down and begin organizing his own private little plans for the Plutarch's job!

Slim nudged him with a bony knee, but Fleigh was too wrapped in his own thoughts to bother until the other seized his elbow and hissed at him. Then he came out of his daydreams. Something was going on—the Councilors were paying too careful attention, and the Earth Delegation didn't look right! In a second, his mind was back on the speech, and the words came to a chilling focus in his ears.

". . . found the organization inconceivably complex. And yet the basic pattern is old—old as the barbarism that prompted it. Gentlemen, I have only my word as evidence now, but I can name names and give exact locations that will enable our Planetary Police to confirm every word of it before night falls on this meeting. The Plutarch of Earth, on the twentieth of April, forty-two years ago, gave the following orders, which I quote . . ."

Fleigh grabbed for Slim's generator and yanked the button savagely, but still the damning words went on, detail piling on exact detail, while Secret Servicemen moved forward to cut the speaker off from the Earth Delegates. Their rudeness was an open declaration that Earth was immediately severed from the Council! Max ripped out the generator, crushing the delicate tubes in his hands. He was stamping on his own device at the same time, but the voice went on unchecked!

Down on the floor, Curtis looked upward without pausing in his damning list of evidence, found the operative's eye, and grinned. Then he resumed his normal gravity and went on!

Slim's hands were trembling and fumbling over his charm. Fleigh practically carried him to the aisle and dragged him along as he made his way up the infinite distance to the gallery door. Every step was made with the expectation of a shouted order from Curtis that would send the big explosive slugs tearing through him, but it did not come. Instead, there was only the quiet continuance of the speech and Slim's hoarse prayers to the ghosts of the charm to save them.

Surprisingly, the doors opened in the hands of the courteous guards, and the hall was before them, with no police in sight. Max cut Slim's babbled relief off with a crisp whisper. "We're not out of it, you fool! Ten to one, it's cat and mouse, with us the losers. But if we're going to make use of the tenth chance, shut up! Walk, dammit, and *grin!*"

There was another flight of stairs leading down, a long hall, and a second door that opened promptly and politely as they neared it. Then the main steps led down to the street. It was impossible that the similacrum could have given no orders for their arrest; as impossible as that the relay could be tampered with! But the big car waited at the curb, and there were still no police.

Reaction left Slim drooling narcotic juice over the hands that were caressing and kissing the charm. Fleigh yanked him savagely into the car and gunned the electros. It went tearing out into the street under full power, while a wild yell of despair ripped out of the outlaw's throat.

"My ghost charm!" He was pawing frantically at the door lock, with his face swiveled around toward the bright, receding twinkle of the metal piece on the sidewalk behind. "Max! Max!"

"Shut up and stay put! There must be a hundred more of those things you can buy if we get out of this." Fleigh freed a hand and forced the cringing fool back into the seat, where he relaxed woodenly, terror fading out to sullen despair that gradually mingled with doubt.

"Then let's get out quick, Max! Once we hit Earth, I know a guy's got another. Tain't as good a ghost with it as mine, but it ain't no fake, either! You gotta give me enough to get it, Max!"

Fleigh hid his thin grin from the other. They'd need more than a ghost charm or even planning if they ever went to Earth! He'd seen what happened to failures there, and he knew that it would be better to walk into the nearest Planet Police Bureau. But he reached over soothingly and patted the outlaw's shoulder. "Sure, Slim. We'll get you another, maybe before we leave here."

It shouldn't be hard to find one of the charm peddlers, and dope up a story. There was a place on Venus where they could hide, once Slim worked up his nerve to pilot them there—and provided that their luck held long enough to keep the police from impounding the little craft. But the hideout would take money, and that had to come first. Planning took care of that; he'd always been careful to avoid tying his personal fortune in the Earth Operative strongholds.

He swung the car around a corner, glanced at a jeweler's sign, and cursed without slowing down. The red light was on, warning that it had been raided. One of his secret quarters gone!

He stopped obediently for a through highway, then roared on. But the second was no better. There was sweat on his forehead, and his hands were slippery with it when he headed out Mars Center Canal into the suburbs. Damn Curtis! It was impossible for him to have found the hideouts—or should have been!

But there was no warning light in the window of the third and last place. The lawyer's faded sign swung in the thin wind, and everything was serenely peaceful. Fleigh jerked Slim out of the car, set its automatic chauffeur, and let it go rolling off.

Then he moved up the steps with the outlaw at his heels, listened cautiously at the door, and nodded. The steady click of a typewriter indicated that the scrawny little secretary was doing the routine office work, and Sammy must have been undisturbed. He opened the door eagerly, to a louder clicking from the typewriter.

Above it, Curtis looked up with an assured smile and waved the grandfather of all hand weapons at him in genial greeting!

"Come in, Max," he said cordially. "Like my double's speech?"

Slim's trembling hand fumbled out automatically in the sign of the horns. His blanched mouth worked furiously, but the words refused to come until Curtis turned to him. Then he jerked back, waving his fingers. "He couldn'ta . . . We'd of beat him. . . . Max! He's dead! He's a ghost!"

Fleigh's hand groped for him and missed. Another apparition came into the room from the inner office. This one was a shriveled little man, with owl eyes that blinked at them out of thick-lensed spectacles. Jeremiah Greek picked up a pencil with a contented grin, drew it across the bare flesh of his arm, and held the red mark that rose on the skin out toward the outlaw.

"In the flesh," he stated.

But Slim was no longer listening. Slowly, as if moved by worn-down clockworks, he slid down the wall, and his dead-faced head bent forward to meet the knees that drew upward. There he stayed, motionless.

"If that's catatonic return to the fetal position, it's an all-time record for speed," Curtis commented with interest. "Sit down, Max. You seem to have overestimated your companion's moral fiber, and underestimated your opponents. Never count on luck! It takes planning to get anywhere in this universe. . . . By the way, Jeremiah Greek is the original inventor of pancyclic tape; you should have checked up on him, before you trusted him, and found out the way your Plutarchy gypped him out of his invention. He wasn't the sort of man who'd co-operate very well with Earth. In fact, he was the sort who could and would fake a tape for your recorder to cover up the call he put in under my code to the Martian Council!"

Fleigh moved toward the chair as the gun commanded, only half conscious of the words. He sank into a sitting position, his mind churning savagely and getting nowhere. Play along! Keep your eyes open! If you let the other guy make the moves, he'll slip up somewhere. It was basic training to operatives, but there was uncertainty in even that logic now. But there was nothing else to do.

Greek picked up the account. "With a promise of secrecy from Councilor Curtis, and a chance to do legitimate research here, I felt quite free to drop my very doubtful loyalty to my native planet, Mr. Fleigh. Those two similacra you shot were crude, and the brain and blood imitation quite poor, I thought. But fortunately, you didn't investigate thoroughly."

"I didn't think the relay could fail. So you simply let the similacrum collapse and took its place." Fleigh was forcing himself to casualness, while his brain hashed over all the rules for upsetting a trap. But it returned inevitably to the basic need of stalling for time, and keeping them talking.

"Not at all," Curtis corrected him. "We were late returning, so they simply used an all-wave receiver to record your control signal on pancyclic tape, inserted it into a generator, and the similacrum had his freedom in his pocket two minutes after you turned on your control in the Council Chamber. You really didn't think I'd leave my speech in the middle to chase you, when I had a perfectly good double, surely?"

Fleigh's eyes darted to Slim, but there would be no help from that quarter. Not a muscle had moved since the outlaw had collapsed onto the floor.

He forced himself to relax deliberately. Relax! As long as he was tensed up in the chair, they'd watch him, but they'd be less cautious if he seemed to abandon hope. And he was younger and faster than they were, in spite of his fat.

Greek's amused cackle broke his chain of thought. "So simple a solution, Max! But of course an involute brain would miss just that. . . . That's fine, relax! And when you start anything, you'll be surprised to find how quickly and efficiently a couple of sentimental visionary fools can shoot! Or do you think, Councilor, that we're really such fools?"

"I doubt it," Curtis answered, with the same hard amusement in his voice. "As I see it, a reactionary is simply unable to adapt to new conditions; he's filled with a blind, stubborn dependence on the rude past. And brute force is an admission of that intellectual poverty. Max, you should have studied history better. The addlepated idealists have a peculiar habit of winning."

They stood there, grinning and studying their captive with the one thing in the universe he had never encountered—open contempt. Fleigh wet his lips, glancing from one to the other and considering the hopeless distance to the door.

And suddenly the beginnings of an idea permeated through the hard knot of fear in his brain. They didn't believe in brute force! They wouldn't kill him without provocation; and they couldn't turn him in to the police!

He swung back to Curtis, and this time there was a grin on his own lips. "You said you promised Mr. Greek secrecy, Councilor. Not immunity, because the old law against making robots is too strong; and similacra would be considered robots. Well, just how do you figure you can turn me over to the authorities without breaking that promise and having him strung up beside me?"

"I never meant to turn you in," Curtis answered.

"And you said yourself that brute force was stupid!"

"Quite true." It was Greek who answered this time. "But the rules of justice sometimes invoke it. The penalty for treason, like that for robotry, is still death, though we've abandoned most other reasons for capital punishment."

"Then turn me in! Or kill me yourselves—and you'll find that brute force really is stupid on Mars! The police here are the best in the system, which is why I always preferred to do my little jobs elsewhere. You amateurs wouldn't have a chance. Well?"

But he knew he had them, and the taste of freedom in his mouth was sweet after the fear and hopelessness of their gloating power. He did not wait for an answering nod from them, but turned from his chair in calm assurance and headed for the door.

Greek's voice interrupted his exit. "Just a minute, Max! You really should know all your mistakes, and there's one we forgot. . . . Never use a perfect similacrum! It can't be perfect without thinking exactly like its original; the same mind must operate the same way. Your similacrum was limited only by the time it could exist—and it knew that, as well as knowing it was useless among real men!"

"So what?" Fleigh asked jauntily, and reached for the door. "And so long!"

Steel hands grabbed him and a pair of arms of inhuman strength picked him up and turned him around to face the two men. Curtis dropped his gun onto the table with a slow, deliberate motion, holding the struggling operative with a single hand, while he stretched the other out to Jeremiah Greek. Then he turned toward the door, dragging the fat body of Fleigh along without effort.

"So when you're found dead in your house, killed by the robot you were having built in some fiendish plot against Councilor Curtis, I don't think the police will worry—beyond seeing that both you and the robot—myself—are thoroughly beyond repair!"

There was bitterness in the voice of the similacrum, but it was resolute and determined bitterness. "When the real Curtis replaced me in the Council Chamber, he meant to make my few days of existence as pleasant as possible. But even a limited similacrum likes to be useful. Come along, Max."

Max Fleigh went along; there was nothing else he could do, as the duplicate of Curtis tossed him into a small car and began driving back toward the town and the house that had been his Martian home and would soon be his tomb. He couldn't even think straight; his head insisted on dwelling on nonsense.

Slim had been right, after all, and his ghost charm had brought him luck, even after he lost it. But for the man who refused to believe in it, there was no hope for such insane oblivion. There was simply no hope of any kind.

In retyping "Unreasonable Facsimile" for this book, I could only wonder how I'd ever dared show it to Campbell. His rejection was automatic, and whatever he said about it has been forgotten. It's "straight" with a vengeance! The plot is one that is known as a "biter bit," which means it takes someone we don't like and eventually shows his failure for some fault of his own. It's perfectly standard fare in the older detective story magazines and some others. Beginning writers still submit such things, probably because they're so easy to write.

It's the only one of its kind I ever tried, and I suppose I had to do that type of story some time or other. But hardly for Campbell!

Again I'd made the mistake that too many young or beginning writers make when they are talking to an editor. They take every word literally. Editors don't mean them that exactly, as a rule. If an editor says that he likes to have a few stories with girls in them, he's speaking comparatively—he means with more evidence of girls than most of the stories he gets, unless he's publishing all-girl stories already. If he asks for more action in your stories, he doesn't mean that every single page of the story must be packed with action. I've always taken that for granted—except this time, it seems.

This was another story that sold to Robert Lowndes. And in his magazine, it fitted much better.

My fourth story in this sequence was an idea I'd had for a long time, and which simply hadn't ripened enough previously. I'd even started it once, and had two pages among my notes. I dug those out and used them pretty much as they were. This time the story seemed to come into focus, and I was able to go on with it.

Since I'd thought about it several times since the idea first came to me back in St. Louis, I had a lot of background material behind it which always helps to make a story seem real when it is being written.

It's a little complicated, but it deals with a truly benevolent dictator. He has to be a dictator, because a world wearied by a great war that broke up into a generation of small wars has been too sapped to care much who governs it or how he governs. And our dictator knows that if he were to die, some knave or fool might take over in his place and ruin all he's built up. The trouble is that he is dying, and he can't stand another heart transplant. (We dealt with such things in science fiction long ago.) His only hope is that he is secretly training a robot built to look like him to take over. But how can he know enough about it to trust it? The robot and the way he has trained it to think as much like himself as possible are the key elements of the story.

It came to 6,500 words and was called "Uneasy Lies the Head."

Campbell indicated that this story was one he almost bought and might have bought if he hadn't had his usual full inventory. I suspect the element he didn't like was that weak and vapid populace, since Campbell had something of a mania for the basic unquenchable human will.

Donald Wollheim bought it for *Ten Story Fantasy* in 1950. It has been reprinted a few times, and I still like it well enough to be glad it's in one of my collections.

That was supposed to be the last story of my writing binge. But when I finished it, I still had all that background material roiling around in my mind. I'd worked out the history of the family of the dictator and of the robot brain pretty thoroughly, and it gradually began to shape up into a story. (You might call this another "prequel." Why I should find it easier to work backward than forward is something I can't answer.) By morning, it was pretty well developed, and I sat down to write it. It came to 6,600 words and was entitled "Conditioned Reflex." In a later magazine publication it was retitled "Mind of Tomorrow," which fits well enough; but I still prefer the original title.

22.

Conditioned Reflex

(by Lester del Rey)

Paul Ehrlich looked up from his wheat cakes in time to see his father exploding upward out of his chair and heading for the kitchen. By barking his shins against the table leg, he barely managed to catch the older man's arm and swing him forcibly back. The sharp pain did nothing to decrease his irritation.

"Dammit, Justin, I told you to stop bothering Gerda, and I meant it! She has trouble enough trying to get her work done in sixteen hours without your upsetting her. Now sit down and eat—and let her alone!"

"Someday, Paul, I'm going to teach you I can still thrash you!" Justin Ehrlich dropped into the chair, but the rebellion on his face remained. "The butter is sour! I told her I would *not* eat sour butter!"

"Then you'll go without, unless you want to build us a cream separator so the milk won't have to stand long enough for the cream to rise. You can't make sweet butter from sour cream. Besides, butter is a luxury; we're lucky to have cows."

"Yeah. Gotta get a bull, though." Harry Raessler sopped up the last dribble of beet syrup with a scrap of pancake and pointed glumly through the crude glass window to the world outside the log and mud-brick house. "Tain't the same world you was born to, Mr. Ehrlich. My wife sure tries, but she's only got two hands. C'mon, Paul, we better get busy on that barn roof."

Paul nodded and followed his partner out, with a feeling of relief at leaving his father's contrariness behind. The old man must be getting senile, if his guess at the meaning of the word was correct. Complaints and grumblings! They were leading a life that would have been heaven to most of the people still alive—and few men over fifty were included in that group. He shook his head again, and went on splitting shakes off big pine blocks, while Harry began pounding the crookedness out of their small collection of rusty nails.

There had been a time when his father had seemed almost godlike to him, and he had to admit that their present wealth was only partly due to his own efforts. Justin had fled to MacQuarie Island when he foresaw the Fifth War, and his provision for the stay had proved as adequate as his selection of retreat had been wise. For over twenty years he had continued his research there, until the war burned from nations to villages and flickered out. And only then had he consented to the long, dangerous voyage.

But however well he had foreseen the consequences of the war, he had refused to adapt to them, once they were back, and the burden had been Paul's from then on. Nineteen years of the hell of material energy had done its worst, and starvation had killed half of the world's surviving sixty million. Now they had reverted to a rude cross between early pioneer and normal farmer, and life was going on. At least there was land enough, much of it still good, though the materials to farm it were mostly destroyed.

Still, Paul had done well enough. In the two years since the boat had docked and he had traded it for other things, he had tramped the country, bartering his way to the security of half this place, and pulling his father with him. And now, after three months' partnership with the Raesslers, Justin . . .

"Paul! Drat it, Paul, where are you? Oh!" The old man came storming imperiously around the barn corner, swearing at the rubble under his feet and interrupting his son's bitter musing. "I thought you told me my equipment came yesterday. Where the devil did you hide it?"

Paul grimaced as he missed his stroke with the ax and ruined a roof shake. "In the woodshed. The men were too tired to go fooling around carrying it further, after ferrying it up the Snake River. And stop grumbling! You're lucky we had enough to pay barter for that job; I wouldn't fight the Snake for ten bulls and a tractor!"

"Lucky? Why do you think I picked the cargo for trade before I holed up? Why did I waste half my time getting you to study the agriculture books I took with me? Luck! D'you think I couldn't see what was coming? Though I never thought you'd pick a godforsaken place like this. Now if I—"

"Sure," Paul interrupted him. "I know, you'd have rediscovered the Garden of Eden, with railroads! When you find better land, a safer place, or one where the people are half as well back to normal, I'll go with you. It only took me two years to find this. . . . Your junk is in the woodshed, Dad!"

Justin grunted and then went hurrying off, muttering something about darned impertinence, while Harry looked up with a doubtful frown. "Shouldn't talk that way to your dad, Paul. After all, he did fix it up a blame sight better for you than most of us got. Someday you'll probably own all Idaho, soon's we get a little further. Right now, we gotta farm any which way, but at least you know better. Runnin' away from the fightin' don't make the rest of us much shakes at it."

"Yeah, I know, Harry, but . . . Let's get up on the roof. We have more than enough here to patch it."

They were halfway up the ladder when a series of piercing screams from the woodshed culminated in a final whoop, and the figure of Justin came boiling out toward them. Paul sighed wearily, motioned Harry on up, and began climbing down to face the fury. Peace, it was wonderful! Not only did the old man do no work, when every hand was bitterly needed, but it was becoming impossible for others to work around him.

"All right, what is it?" he asked as he stepped through the door into which his father had retreated again.

"Look. Ruined! Absolutely ruined! I packed that typewriter myself, and now look at it!"

It was a sight, all right. Aside from a broken frame, twisted keys, and a thoroughly mangled mess of levers and wires, it bore almost no resemblance to a typewriter. "If I ever get my hands on your porters! Boiling in oil—hot lead in their boots—I'll fry them. . . . The only typewriter I had, and look at it!"

The corner of the boy's lip twisted down, but he chuckled grimly at his father's rage. "If you want to swim down the Snake after them, go ahead. But it'd probably do more good to do your writing by hand."

"*What!*" Justin stopped at the top of his shriek, closed his mouth, and with the obviously masterful control needed in handling children, forced his voice to be reasonable. "We'll have to get another. Boise has been picked over, but I understand it escaped the worst, and nobody was looking for typewriters. You'll drive me to Boise tomorrow and we'll dig till we find one."

He swung back into the woodshed and began sorting through his other belongings, while Paul headed back toward the barn and the common sense of Harry. That last request, when the fields needed spraying and cultivating, would be too thick for even Raessler to swallow. Nuts to Boise!

But surprisingly, Harry took a different view of the matter. He screwed his face into thoughtfulness and rolled a cigarette before answering, but his tone was acquiescent when the words finally came. "Better go ahead, Paul. When a witch wants machinery, maybe it's a good idea he should get it."

"A what?"

"A witch—feller that goes in for hexin' and magic; like them that useta put ghosts out to fight against the soldiers. No, that's right, you wouldn't know about it—you wasn't here. Anyhow, people roundabouts figger your dad's a witch. Mighty handy thing to have on your side, witches. You'd best drive him in; I'll spray the potatoes and Gerda'll help, maybe."

"Magic is bunk," Paul told him sourly. "Your ghosts were probably some crude form of invisibility. I didn't learn too much of the old science, but I know enough not to believe in such things. And I'm not going to Boise. Come on, let's finish the roof before it gets too hot up here."

Gerda had enough to do without spraying potatoes, and Harry was already doing more than his share of the work. If Justin wanted to waste time, let him do it alone.

There was no wind in Boise, and the sweat was rolling down Paul's face as he dropped into the shade of the wagon and began unwrapping the lunch Gerda had fixed. Justin picked through a few more bits of rubble, then joined him. For once, the older man was doing more than his share, and he was tired enough to swallow three bites of his sandwich before he gagged and spat.

"Sour butter! I told Gerda no butter—dry, like her bread!"

"So you pick on my sandwiches; yours are in the other bag. And Gerda's a darned good cook." Paul washed his sandwich down with the warm, bitter home brew and studied the rubble of the former city with a large measure of doubt. "This has been picked dry, and we haven't the faintest idea where to look. Pure luck turned up that can of ANTU; if it'll kill rats as you say, it pays for the trip. But we won't find anything else. Why not give up?"

"Because I haven't found a typewriter! What's that?"

Paul shook his head and handed the little thing over. "Search me. I hoped you'd know some use for it. Funny-looking can."

"Umm. Magnetronic memory relay, looks like, under the dirt. Uh-huh, it is." Justin regarded it doubtfully, started to throw it away, and then gazed at it with new interest. "Know what that is, or have you forgotten?"

From somewhere in his memory, Paul dredged up the general idea. Science had stumbled on it accidentally, shortly after magnetic current was rediscovered and put to use. A colloidal suspension of metals in silicon jelly was provided with nodes; then connecting any two nodes would create a conducting, permanent link in the jelly, just as two related facts cause a permanent and reusable link between brain cells. It could be taught by experience, after a fashion, since the linkages became increasingly more conductive with use. It had proven quite satisfactory in replacing telephone relays.

Justin nodded. "And adding machines. This is a double ten-node affair, so that's what it came from. Mostly, all business machines were sold in the same place, so I hope you're bright enough to remember where you found it."

It took them less than half an hour to sink the hole behind the wagon an additional six feet through the soft trash. Justin's pick broke into the concrete first, and there was nothing weak about his attack on a four-foot circle; the boy's arms were aching from pulling the stuff out when the cement finally broke. His father disappeared in a shower of agonized curses and dust!

"Woof . . ." There was a fine vigor to his swearing, so no damage could have been done, and a second later the older man's head appeared below. "Come on, we hit a cellar they missed. Stinks, but the air's clearing. Throw me the lantern. . . . Umm, two cellars, wooden framing cracked open between. Ladder over here ought to reach if I can get it through the hole."

But Paul wasted no time waiting for ladders. He'd seen the rake sticking out a packing box, and the ax bits spilled from another frame of rotting wood. Axes and rakes! Another box fell open, revealing useless pick handles, but a half-rotted shelf was stacked with the incalculable treasure of a hardware store's supplies. Not much, since the cellar seemed to have felt the edge of an energy beam—but enough to bring him to a speechless halt as he groped for realization of their luck.

Justin grumbled, seeing nothing to interest him. The crumbling section of wooden partition broke through with a few strokes of his pick, and he was climbing through. Paul came in answer to his yell, but there was nothing except tiers of rotted paper and big books of some kind. Then his father jumped from an alcove and pointed to a stretch of ruined, earth-packed tunnel under the overlying concrete layer, running along the wooden partition.

"Used to be a stationery supply and business machine store over this. See that box? One of the adding machines the gadget came from. No good without magnetic generators, but if we dig that out . . ."

Paul turned back to his treasures. "You dig it out. If I have time after I load the other stuff, I'll come and help; though I can't see much chance in that mess. Unless you'd take time out to help load?"

But as usual, Justin's idea of co-operation was to follow his own interests, and the sound of the pick and shovel went on while Paul rigged a block and tackle to raise the loot. He loaded the wagon by himself, sweating over the inefficient hoist, and came back to find there was nothing else to be gleaned, even though he explored into the hard-packed dirt with his pick.

"Paul, you lazy loafer, quit goldbricking and give me a hand!" His father was practically dancing in the hole between basements, his lips caked with sweat and dirt, but his voice as imperious as ever.

At the moment, though, Paul was too well pleased to let even that irritate him, and he followed the other through the twisting, dangerous tunnel, to come up against an opened box that held what was obviously a typewriter, and a sound one.

"Old keyboard, useless," Justin said, as he stooped to get his hands under it. "Dvorak keyboard was standard for fifty years, and they still made these things. Darned reactionaries. The good one's just beyond, see! Now if you . . . Ugh! Wheeo! I'll drag it out, and then there's another crate on your side of the partition—just machinery, but I can use it. Here! Or can you slide it along by yourself?"

"Maybe. Yeah, I guess so. . . . Oof! Maybe we'd better break it open and leave the crate."

"And lose half the pieces when it opened? Nonsense!" The old man grunted his way over the worst of the tunnel, saving his breath for cursing judiciously, until they were back to floor level. "May be more stuff here—at least it's one of the few unbeamed places the ruin pickers missed. When we get this up, you load it, and I'll cover our tracks. Then maybe, if you stop raising damnfool objections to your father's better judgment, I'll tell you why I had to have a typewriter. I'd have done it years ago if you hadn't been so infernally curious."

But Paul was listening with only half his mind when the work was done and he took his place beside the two cows that were both draft and milk animals. His father was seated on the big crate, with his precious typewriter in his hands, almost at peace with the world, and the wagon's converted truck wheels jumped and wobbled over the ruins that had been a road leading homeward. His mind was far more concerned with the load than with the story.

Stripped of justification, exaggeration, and distortion, it was simple enough. His father had apparently had a typist copying his dictated material, and the normal errors—or abnormal ones, as he told it—had led to a fight. There had been a lawsuit, another fight, a broken arm for the typist, and an injunction for Justin to cease and desist from slandering the typist by insisting a machine could do better work. It was all highly colorful and complicated, but it had ended with the old man swearing that he would build such a machine, and setting out to do so.

"And now, by the Lord Harry, with a decent typewriter, I'm going to prove for once and for all that he was just what I called him. Paul, you're going to see the typing an editor would appreciate. No errors, no erasures, no misspellings, and no passages left out! I'll finish the novel, and finish it right!"

Paul chuckled. "You mean you spent twenty years on that—all the time and trouble on the Island? Yeah, you would, though I'll admit it's probably why we're alive today. Too bad more people weren't rich enough to get out as you did."

"Rich and *smart* enough, don't forget," Justin corrected him with relative gentleness. His triumph was still strong upon him. "And if they had, they'd have taken the trouble along with them. You get a hundred people and you have an administration; get that, and it bogs down till it has to join the war to cover itself up! Sure I spent twenty years—I'd have spent a thousand, if I had them. I told him I'd prove he was everything I said, and I will!"

"Hardly, Justin. He's dead. You might look for his heirs, but I don't think you'd have much luck—not even in twenty more years. Haw, Bessy!" He guided the cows over a hole in the road, noting their complaining, but deciding that they could wait three more hours for milking, probably. Might have to waste a little in partial milking, but they were more than halfway home.

Justin's peal of triumph cut through his thoughts and brought his mind back to his father. "Think I'm a fool, Paul? I told you I wasn't one of your lily-livered modern nincompoops! The swine had a daughter—wonderful girl, son, wonderful; appreciated me! No, I won't have any trouble finding his heir. You're it!"

Paul shook his head, but he joined in the old man's laughter. For a moment he could feel a distorted form of the old awe for his father, though he knew the situation was ridiculous. Maybe Justin was a witch; at least, the whole Boise affair smacked of miracles. But witch or not, he was the only one of his kind!

Harry Raessler seemed to agree, as he took one look at the laden wagon and began hitching up their other two cows while most of it was unloaded. Definitely a witch, and a remarkable one! If Mr. Ehrlich would come along, maybe they'd have the good luck to find the stock traders he'd heard about still around, and even get a fairly good bargain. Gerda came out and smiled shyly, assuring the old man that there was no butter on the supper she had packed for him, and everything was sweetness and light.

Of course, it couldn't last. A heavy rain caught Harry and Justin returning, and ruined all plans to dig in Boise by making the roads impassable. Their triumphant acquisition of the entire stock of the traders—a bull, three horses, and a few hogs and chickens—lost some of its pleasures when the stallion proved to have killer instincts and the two half-starved mares proved to be completely unbroken.

Then in the morning, Justin had developed a case of sniffles, and discovered that the cream for his barley-coffee was turning sour! Everything came back to normal with a thump. Gerda retired to the kitchen in tears and Paul packed his father to his room with words he half regretted, half wished had been stronger.

Now Harry came back over the field and cut into his thoughts with a dark look at the clouds forming overhead. "Might as well get back, Paul. No use sprayin' when it's gonna rain. Well, we need it, though why it can't be spread out more even . . ."

"Yeah. You might ask my father; he's the expert on contrariness." Paul had begun to forget under the back-breaking pumping of the sprayer, but it all came back as they headed for the house. "Umm, what'd the man from Payette want? You were arguing over an hour."

"Wanted to buy our wrecked mower, to fix up one they found. I been holdin' out for a better offer, but now, we don't need anything they got—so I'm tradin' a couple of crosscut saws and some ax bits for theirs. Heck, with that we can get swap-help from the whole section, a week's work for a day's mower use. . . . And Paul, don't you go forgettin' it was your dad got us all that. He don't owe us one hour's work. I told you a witch was a good thing to have."

"He owes Gerda a civil tongue! Dammit, I don't mind too much doing his work, even without our sudden luck. But I can't stand his taking his spite out on you two."

"Yeah. It's kinda tough on her, what with the kid comin' and all. But mostly, she's glad he's here. We're gettin' too rich, and most likely the rumor's gettin' spread around. Bandits hear that, and you wake up dead some night—unless they know you've got a witch, when they stay plenty far away. . . . Go on in, I'll unhitch the cows." The rain was beginning to fall, but they had already reached the barn, and the machine-gun sound of a typewriter drifted toward them. Harry cocked an ear toward it, with the awe of a man who could only read by spelling out the words, but he made no comment.

Paul was slightly surprised at the speed of the typing, himself, as he entered the house and began the slow filing of an adjustable slide for what might eventually be a hand corn-planter. His father must have developed some trick of pre-typing on a correctible tape that could be fed in finished form into the typewriter; no human fingers could move that rapidly. It was ingenious, but hardly worth twenty years of work; any engineer would have scorned wasting a week on it! and he'd thought his father was a scientist!

Still, even that might have been justified if the book had been some new mathematical theory that would necessitate almost impossible accuracy and freedom from typographical errors. Instead, it was to be a novel—a romantic, swashbuckling novel of the kind popular before the war, when there were still publishing houses and people with leisure to devote to escape mechanisms.

Paul gritted his teeth and forced himself to relax his pressure on the file before he ruined the slide. He'd seen real scientists in his two years of life as a wandering trader. There was old Kinderhook and Gleason, working with young Napier during the few hours when they were not slaving for their existence in the fields. They were fighting a losing battle, but at least they were fighting. And somehow, with month-long calculations a machine could have performed in seconds, they were bringing the old, involved theories down to a level where they might possibly be handled with the scanty materials remaining. While such men were attempting miracles with no resources, his father sat comfortably dictating a stupid, anachronistic novel!

But the rapid typing had become sporadic, now that he listened again, and there was a mutter of cursing, followed by a brief burst of typing, and a yell. "Paul! Paul!" He climbed to his feet with a disgusted sigh and went toward the room before the other could come storming out to disturb the whole household.

"Yeah, what is it this time?"

His father stood in the middle of the floor before a complicated mess of machinery. There was a small wood-fired steam boiler and engine, set up on flat rocks and puffing smoke out the window, a humming dynamo, and the typewriter, all connected to a squat black box with tiny arms over the type keys and an arm bent up near the platen. Justin shook his fists impotently at the box.

"Ruined, d'you hear, ruined! If I had a boat, I'd find those idiot porters! Twenty years of work, and the misbegotten—"

Paul grunted wearily. "And if I had a boat, I'd let you go chasing down the Snake after them. What the deuce is this mess?"

"This mess," his father told him with heavy sarcasm, "is a voice-operated typewriter—and one that works! Or did work! not like the hundred tons of junk the Institute had that couldn't punctuate or separate homonyms—or be operated by more than a single trained speaker. My Vocatype worked, until it was shipped here. Now it's ruined!"

In spite of himself, the boy was impressed, though he couldn't be sure without testing whether by the achievement or the mere claim to it. He picked up the microphone, slid in paper, pressed the button, and spoke quick words into the machine. "The mill wright could not attend the sacred rite, but he could write the right letter to right the false impression. Two apples fell to the ground, too rapidly. The man with the bow had to bow to the queen."

There were no mistakes!

"But a billion relays . . ." And the box couldn't weigh over a hundred pounds! He stood frozen in wonder, waiting for his father's explanation. This time he gave the account full attention, even to the boasting.

The voice analyzer and key magnets were old stuff, as were the scanning eyes to detect failure from the typewriter and the transformer that changed electricity into magnetic current. The rest was as simple as its theory was complex. A thousand-node magnetronic memory tube of his father's own constuction occupied a little corner of the box and did the real work. Between its nodes, half a million links could be formed, serving as nodes for over a hundred billion sub-links that broke down to quintillions of sub-sub-links. It was of unusual size and complexity, but it had taken only a few months to build.

The rest of the long years had been spent in pronouncing words and striking keys until the tube developed a conditioned reflex for every one of the words in the abridged dictionary and could begin the seemingly hopeless task of learning to choose between alternate forms and somehow find a pattern of punctuation that worked. No normal man would have believed it possible, and only the stubbornest man in the world would have kept trying until success crowned his herculean labors.

"Now it's ruined," Justin finished, and the attention and surprise of his son must have mollified his anger, for there was only bitterness left in his voice. He picked up a sheet of his shorthand notes and began dictating, while the machine raced along slightly behind him. "'. . . as sure as my name's Patrick Xenophon . . .' Look! Read that! '. . . as sure as my name's Patrick *Xavier* . . . !' Twenty times I've said Xenophon and twenty times it's written Xavier. All my conditioning of its reflexes ruined—all to be done over! No knowing how many other errors it contains now!"

Paul scratched the letters off the page with the point of his knife, and filed in the proper ones by hand typing. "That wouldn't occur to you, I suppose," he began, when a click from the machine called his eyes back. It had tossed the sheet out, inserted a fresh one, and begun typing the page again. When it finished, its original version was back before them!

Justin stared at his creation for long moments in horrified surprise, while his shoulders drooped slowly. Then, with a broken sound, he handed over the pages of his notes and finished copy and moved quietly out of the room. Moments later, Paul saw him moving slowly through the rain down the path to the barn, with Gerda at his heels. And the girl was smiling!

Paul looked from the machine to their retreating forms and down at the pages he held. Then he dropped limply into the chair.

Gerda came in hours later to force his supper on him and light the lamp, but he only grunted his thanks, and went on reading. Surprisingly, it was a marvelous piece of escape literature, masterfully written. Once the words on the first page had penetrated his dazed mind, continuing was as inevitable as breathing. In a way, it was a pity it could never be published; the need of really effective escapism had never been greater.

And it was effective, in a strangely soothing way. At first he had meant to stop after the first chapter, but by then he knew the need of the relaxation it afforded, and he went on, letting the real world around him disappear from his mind. Besides, if its writing had meant twenty years of work for its creator, there should be at least one person who could get some good out of it!

He put down the last page and went over to the machine, where the unfinished book ended. "'. . . as sure as my name's Patrick Xavier . . .'" Patrick Xavier O'Malley, it should have been—or Patrick Xenophon. . . .

"Justin! Hey, Justin!" His bellow was almost the equal to his father's usual cry, but he had no chance to think of the similarity. When the door opened, his finger was already on the passage, and shaking it under the older man's eyes. "You *did* name him Xavier, not Xenophon! Look at page four!"

Justin took one startled look at the page and picked up the microphone. This time there was no hesitation as the Vocatype followed his words to the end of the page and kicked out the finished product. Then he chuckled.

"Sometimes I almost think I'm stubborn, Paul. I'd have sworn I was right, so I didn't think of checking. Do you realize what this means—a machine that is designed to take dictation, but won't do it unless the dictation is consistent with its facts? Why, it's a perfect secretary. Teach it a little mathematics and think of the errors it would save when writing up a piece of research. Paul, for once you've actually made yourself useful!"

The boy opened his mouth to answer that, but Justin gave him no chance. He was caressing the machine and fairly burbling.

"Now we can finish the book," he told it, and gave it another affectionate pat. "Nice machine—excellent machine! We'll show him that his grandfather was a bigoted moron yet! By the way, boy, how was the yarn?"

"Perfect," Paul answered, and swung out of the room and toward his bed without trusting himself to further insanity. Only his father could have invented such an impossibility as a machine capable of showing the rudiments of intelligence. And only Justin would have used it to finish a romance that could never be published.

But as he crawled between the sheets, he was less sure of his father's misuse of it. Perhaps, somewhere in its mysterious sub-linkages it contained potential intelligence, but it could never be made available in their lifetimes. Thought is useless without a medium of communication, and while it could learn facts, language is a protoplasmic by-product, filled with such abstract and fact-confusing variables as *truth* or *goodness*.

He dreamed of standing on a cliff while a blind man offered him a shiny new robot, if he could only describe green and orange.

It was barely dawn when Justin's hand on his shoulder roused him, and for a moment he thought he was still on the Island. Reality came back, though, as he groped for his overalls. His father's eyes were red with lack of sleep, but filled with a gamut of emotions.

Justin broke the silence in a voice that was more gentle than he had used for years.

"I know what you think of me, Paul, but I never forgot the real world. Knowing I'd fail, I fought for decency as few men have ever fought, and it wasn't until the last minute that I fled. . . . No, let me tell it my way. . . . Integrating the administration of an advanced technological world is inconceivably complex—even the men doing the job have only a vague idea of how complex! The broad policies depend on the results of lesser departments, and so on through fifty stages, vertically and in untold horizontal subdivisions. Red tape isn't funny; it's necessary and horrible. Complication begets complication, and that begets disconnection from reality. Mistakes are made; no one can see and check them in time, and they lead to more errors, which lead to war.

"For a while, they fight against it. And then they simply fight! I did all I could, and I failed. On the Island, there was nothing to do about it, so I built the Brain. Here, why should I struggle to re-create the old vicious cycle that will wind up with the whole race wiped out? I tried to prepare you, but I couldn't prepare myself for this."

"If you'd explained . . ." Paul began weakly, but his father brushed it aside, and went on.

"But now something can be done. Government can work. All it needs is a brain to handle the red tape—not better, but more complicated than human brains—a few tremendous minds with perfect memories to hold the multitudinous interlocking correlated compartments. Let men make the decisions, but let robot brains free men to do it wisely—and move instantly, where red tape would take years! Paul, we'll give them the brains."

"No, Dad," the boy said softly, and cursed the inherited stubbornness that refused to leave his father in the newfound fantasy world. "Maybe someday, they'll have those brains, and you'll be responsible. But not in our time. You taught me enough semantics to know just how impossible the job of giving your gadget even a shadowy knowledge of words is going to be."

There was no sign of disappointment on the old man's face. It stiffened, and the perverse stubbornness reappeared, but he made no answer. Instead, he motioned his son after him and went silently across to the Vocatype room. On the machine was a little slip of paper, and there were other bits under the readjusted scanning eyes.

"The trouble is, you think knowing that electricity works a motor is science, Paul. It isn't. Science is the process of reducing all things to their lowest common denominator and building systematically from there. I had the training before I turned novelist, and I still have it. I didn't waste the night dreaming. Check that list of words while you watch." Justin handed the slip over, and began arranging pieces of colored paper under the eyes of the scanner.

"What?" he asked as the machine sprang to humming life. "What?"

Fresh paper fed into the typewriter, and the words came slowly: "A blue triangle and a red circle are on a white square. A black circle is on a what? What?"

"Hexagon," Justin answered quietly.

"A black circle is on a hexagon. The hexagon is orange. What color is orange? The hexagon is orange? What color is orange?"

Paul's startled eyes narrowed as he stared at the blue sheet of paper. "Orange isn't listed among the words!"

"Of course not—I never taught it to the Brain. But it pulled the same trick on me before I woke you up." The old man pressed the microphone button and addressed the machine. "Orange is the color of the hexagon. The hexagon is orange. What color is orange?"

The keys clicked. Then the page ripped out and a new one was inserted. With no further stalling, words began spilling onto the paper:

The Luck of O'Malley *Page 119*

> had to be true; the fact was as certain as the axioms of geometry, or the basics of physics. Invariably, a mixture of red and yellow is orange.

It skipped a space and added another line. "The hexagon is red and yellow. The hexagon is orange. What color is the hexagon?"

"Orange. Red and yellow make orange," Justin assured the doubtful machine, and shut it off. "You see, it has a perfect memory, as well as a sense of analysis. And it would have to have some vague sense of word purpose to separate homonyms, as I see it now. Anyhow, I've already established the fuzzy distinction between *a* and *the*, so it may take years, but not centuries. . . . And that's that for today. Let's see if we can find something to eat!"

Paul's brain was reeling giddily as he watched his father begin slicing the bread, but the broad plan was already crystallizing, and he had no doubt of its success. They'd have to get Gleason, Kinderhook, and Napier to join them here, where the newfound wealth would permit leisure for their all-important work. At first they would have to depend on swap-help, but as wealth created wealth, they could expand. The Brain could be turned into a calculator infinitely better than the older ones with a little teaching, since mathematics is an exact language. And with the materials they could somehow find now, the slow beginnings of science would provide still more wealth to build on.

They'd have to organize a community out of its present anarchy, so some could be assigned to farm and others to teach and to think. That would be hard in a world that had learned to shun all forms of government from bitter experience. But while the Brain was as yet no perfect administrative machine, it would be mighty magic among the superstitious people. His father could coach it and develop his reputation as a witch until the obvious advantages of organization made such deception useless.

Perhaps it would be better to keep the Brain a secret, though. But in any event, the knowledge and hope for the future it offered would make all the rest possible

"Um-hmm," Justin muttered around a mouthful of bread. "I think everything's going to be all right now, son. But when I see Gerda—"

And Paul's dream collapsed! It had been a nice illusion, but no stable future could be built on a hatred of sour butter. He swung toward his father, and his mouth was white and tense, so that the words had to be forced from his teeth. "I told you to let her alone, Justin! If I ever—"

"Umm. But you might take a look out the window and wait till I finish," the old man answered, and there was a grin on his lips. "While I was trying to figure out what was wrong with the Brain, I got around to unpacking that other crate I found on your side of the partition. Gerda and I had a time replacing the motor with a crank, but we made it."

Paul swallowed his rage slowly, and turned to look through the little pane of glass toward the barn. At first he saw only the bobbing back of Harry, but as the man stepped aside, the other thing became visible. Gerda apparently wanted to try her hand, for she was smiling as she began turning the crank. Two streams of liquid spurted into the waiting pails. The cream separator was working quite satisfactorily!

"As I was saying, before you interrupted, when I see Gerda . . ." Justin took another bite of the yellow-smeared bread and smacked his lips approvingly. "When I see her, I must compliment her on what she churned last night. Very nice. I never could stand sour butter!"

Campbell thought that "Conditioned Reflex" was somewhat unconvincing. He didn't talk too much about the stories, and I suspect it was painful for him to be piling up rejects against me. He began asking hopefully what my plans were, and I told him about my old decision that three strikes meant out. Five simply underscored the fact that I'd better stop thinking I could write. He tried to talk me out of it, then gave up. "Let me know when you change your mind" were his final words.

Miss Tarrant followed me out of the door to tell me that John really felt very bad about it, and she also seemed unhappy. She was always a pleasant lady, as well as an invaluable help to Campbell, and I tried to assure her that everything was all right.

Robert Lowndes bought "Reflex" sometime in 1950. He told me

later that he'd also seen "Uneasy Lies the Head" before Wollheim bought it, and that he regretted afterward that he hadn't kept both of them, to publish one after the other. I regretted it, too. Yet when I had a chance to put both stories in the same collection, I didn't. It seems a pity, since each adds something to the other.

I won't say I was exactly happy on the subway going home, but I was probably a lot less depressed than Campbell or Miss Tarrant thought. I wouldn't be the first writer to lose whatever makes his stories salable as he grows older. It was one of the hazards of living. I didn't like it, but I could live with it.

So I put all the manuscripts into an envelope, put the typewriter back in its case, and began shoving all the driblets of story ideas back into Henry's files.

It was only about a week later that Milt Rothman suddenly appeared on our doorstep. I hadn't seen him since Washington, and it was a happy reunion. He was now out of the army, studying to be a nuclear physicist. He'd finally tracked me down through Campbell's office, and he'd come in particular to invite me to attend the World Science Fiction Convention in Philadelphia, his hometown. I was to stay with him at his parents' house, and I wasn't supposed to say no!

Helen immediately urged me to accept, though I don't think it took much persuading. Those conventions had been going on since 1939, interrupted by the war. I'd never attended one before, though I'd heard all about them. But it sounded like fun.

It was fun, too. It took place over Labor Day weekend, and it was the biggest convention ever. There were about three hundred writers and fans there. (Nowadays, the number is over four thousand.) Most of them were old friends, even though I'd only met a few previously. There's something of a family relationship in science fiction, or there used to be before it got too big. Milt was running the convention, with help from Sprague de Camp and numerous other people.

It's rather hard to believe the number of things that developed out of that convention, and all of them good. Milt took me to the home of Jim Williams, a book dealer and fan, and I discovered that he was part of a small publishing firm known as Prime Press, devoted to putting science fiction into hard covers. Jim immediately began suggesting that I should get together a collection of my best stories and he'd be happy to publish them. What's more, he was offering me $100 on signing the contract.

(In those days, science fiction was rarely touched by the regular publishers. It was only through the efforts of such small publishers that it was eventually made popular enough to be accepted as a regular category.)

Then a dark-haired and very quiet young man came up to me and introduced himself as Scott Meredith, an agent. How would I like to have him represent me? As he put it, he'd be delighted to have the author of "Helen O'Loy" as his client. I explained that I wasn't writing anymore, and that the only stories I possessed had already been rejected. That didn't seem to bother him, though. He was perfectly willing to show how much he could help me if I'd let him have the rejects.

I promised to get in touch with him. I'd never used an agent, because the important ones didn't bother with writers whose income averaged as low as mine; and I wasn't interested in the peripheral ones who might have accepted me.

But Scott Meredith was a possibility. I knew he'd once been a science fiction fan himself, so he should know something about the field. And I'd recently seen his advertisement in *Writers' Digest*, which certainly looked like that of an important agent.

Fred Pohl was also present, and he and I talked, together with a few other New York science fiction people, about starting a science fiction club. I was supposed to get in touch with him when we got back, and maybe we could do something about it.

I did get in touch with Meredith, after having learned that he represented several other writers of science fiction. I took the stories I still had with me. We had a pleasant talk, much of it about science fiction, and I signed a contract with him. It was one of the best decisions I ever made, and after twenty-seven years I'm still with him.

I also called Fred Pohl, and we made arrangements for the original group to meet at his apartment. We wanted a sort of semiprofessional club, and one that wouldn't be split by all the feuds that had previously plagued such groups.

Nine of us met and began drafting a constitution extensive enough for a world government. With us were Robert Lowndes, Judy Merril, Philip Klass (William Tenn), and several others who took a somewhat less active vocal part in the proceedings. We decided to call it the Hydra Club, since it began with nine heads.

It developed into quite a club, with about fifty members. It was hard to think of anybody of any importance in science fiction who wasn't either a guest or a member. We threw a big New Year's party annually, as well as meeting once a month, and were certainly the most successful of any science fiction group in the area.

It had a pretty fair influence on professional activities, too. A lot of valuable contacts were made there, and information passed freely among the members. It had no official purpose, but it served fairly well as a writers' organization.

Years later, after the feuds could no longer be held back, trouble came. Fred and I were the highest officers at the time, and we tried to kill the club off. But it wouldn't die. Others still continued to hold meetings in its name, though not with quite the zest of previous times.

Indirectly, it served me well very early in its existence. It was through the club that I had grown friendly with Robert A. W. Lowndes (to give him his current preferred name). And it was "Doc" Lowndes who called me up to tell me that Scott Meredith was looking for an editor, and maybe I should apply. (I doubt that Scott would have thought of me, since he didn't know me that well yet.)

It sounded like a good idea. I guessed (accurately, as it turned out) that more could be learned about writing and publishing in an agent's office than anywhere else. I still wasn't sure I'd ever want to write again, but I was sure that I needed to know a lot more than I did if I were ever to try writing seriously.

So I went down, took a test to see whether I could spot the flaws in a pretty bad story, and was hired. The salary was not handsome; editorial salaries seldom are, since there are so many eager applicants. But it was adequate.

I worked there nearly three years. When I started, Damon Knight was handling the professional writers, and a couple of us were taking care of reading fee submissions.

I've heard a lot of criticism against agents who charge reading fees to unknown writers, and I had some doubts about the practice myself. But I'm now convinced that it is a necessary and valuable service. True, a lot of would-be writers gain nothing for their money; that's true in any training course, and even more true of most of the writers' workshops that seem to be highly approved. I've seen quite a few writers who did learn to write professionally through reading fee criticism, and many who shortened the long period of apprenticeship. I've also seen unknowns accepted almost instantly to full professional status—something they couldn't have gained otherwise until they'd sold a pretty fair amount on their own. Richard Prather, for instance, was discovered from a reading fee submission; as a result, he began his professional career with the advantage of a well-known agent.

The trouble with reading fees lies not in the system, but with abuses possible under it. Those abuses aren't too hard to spot: charging for requested rewrites, or trying to sell the writer on having his story rewritten; false guarantees or false lures of "free" reading; and a lack of provision to give an acceptable manuscript proper professional agenting.

Sidney Meredith, Scott's invaluable brother, was in charge of that department. And most certainly while I was there he made sure that writers were treated honestly. And those who worked there with me were genuinely interested in helping any writer who showed signs of promise or the slightest ability to learn.

I learned more there in six months than I could ever have learned in writing by myself, even with the kind of editorial help Campbell was always willing to give. I learned not to be provincial in my outlook, for one thing. The basic skills of the Western or mystery are the same as those of science fiction; each division simply requires learning a new background. There isn't even much difference between good fact writing and good fiction. But there are things that must be learned for each type, and I was discovering how to learn them quickly.

I was learning exactly what a fool I'd been in submitting to one market. I've seen manuscripts sold on the fortieth submission, after receiving the most cursory rejections from the other editors.

I got a chance to deal directly with a great many editors, and to find out what they really wanted.

I also developed a very strong friendship with Scott and Sid Meredith, and that has been invaluable to me on many occasions. They are friends first and agents second. I've been told that an author-agent relationship is like marriage, and it's at least partly true. Certainly I'd no more recommend any one agent to an author than I'd try to pick a wife for another man.

Somewhere during this time, the friendships I had developed at the Hydra Club also paid off again. David Kyle was one of the original nine, and he'd been trying to get me an apartment in his building for a long time. Finally, he rushed around and dragged me off. He'd found one, but there was no time to waste. He wouldn't wait until I could get my money, but insisted on lending me the deposit.

It was in a safe but shabby section, and the rent was just twelve dollars a month! (I now live right across the street from where that place was, in a modern complex. The rent is about twenty-five times as great, and it's still a bargain as such things go.) For that, I got three small rooms in a solidly built old place. The bathtub was in the kitchen and served as a drainboard when it was covered. There was no heat, but there was a chimney into which I could vent a kerosene stove that wouldn't stink or poison the air. And there was privacy.

Helen and I moved in and equipped it pretty much in keeping with the place itself. We were delighted with it. And it saved a lot of time and trouble in getting to work.

Scott Meredith had been trying for months to get me to write. But I wanted no part of it. It was Campbell who finally broke me down, and the idea didn't come from him this time. He'd received a letter from a reader who was reviewing *next year's* November issue. It was meant as a joke, of course, but Campbell looked at the supposed lineup of writers and stories and decided that it would make a good issue, and that he'd pull a little stunt on the letter writer.

Very much in secrecy, he contacted all the writers in the list, telling them that he wanted to bring out that 1949 issue as close to the letter as possible. And naturally, all of them agreed to try.

I couldn't say no to that, either. It was too good a trick, and I owed too much to Campbell.

The letter reviewed a short story by me entitled "Over the Top." For some reason, I detested the title, but it wasn't mine to change. Fortunately, there were no details about the contents of the story —merely a rating as to excellence.

This time I really sweated it out. Campbell might be willing to settle for a little less than usual in the merit of the story, for this special occasion. But I didn't want to give him anything except my best. And after the last experiences, I wasn't sure I had any best left to give.

In the end, I synthesized the story, after a fashion. I went back over all the stories of mine which Campbell had seemed to like best and began trying to find what was in them to please him. Then I began drawing up a list of do's and do not's. The hero had better be someone either pretty much alone or feeling alone. There should be some kind of critter, if possible. The viewpoint shouldn't be nice and normal. And so on.

Eventually, I worked out a plot. It took me about fifty tries before I was satisfied with the first paragraph. But from there on, it didn't go so badly. I meant the story to come out almost exactly to 5,000 words

—which it did. And I submitted it through the agency—the first new story of mine they'd handled.

Then I waited for the reaction in far more nervousness than I'd ever felt before.

It came the next day in a phone call from Campbell.

"That was a really nice story, del Rey," he said with a sort of a purr in his voice. "At our usual two cents a word, that's a hundred dollars. The check's already in the mail."

23.

Over the Top

(by Lester del Rey)

The sky was lousy with stars—nasty little pinpoints of cold hostility that had neither the remoteness of space nor the friendly warmth of Earth. They didn't twinkle honestly, but tittered and snickered down. And there wasn't even one moon. Dave Mannen knew better, but his eyes looked for the low scudding forms of Deimos and Phobos because of all the romanticists who'd written of them. They were up there all right, but only cold rocks, too small to see.

Rocks in the sky, and rocks in his head—not to mention the lump on the back of his skull. He ran tense fingers over his wiry black hair until he found the swelling, and winced. With better luck, he'd have had every inch of his three-foot body mashed to jelly, instead of that, though. Blast Mars!

He flipped the searchlight on and looked out, but the view hadn't improved any. It was nothing but a drab plain of tarnished reddish sand, chucked about in ridiculous potholes, running out beyond the light without change. The stringy ropes of plantlike stuff had decided to clump into balls during the night, but their bilious green still had a clabbered appearance, like the result of a three days' binge. There was a thin rime of frost over them, catching the light in little wicked sparks. That was probably significant data; it would prove that there was more water in the air than the scientists had figured, even with revised calculations from the twenty-four-inch lunar refractor.

But that was normal enough. The bright boys got together with their hundred-ton electronic slipsticks and brought forth all manner of results; after that, they had to send someone out to die here and there before they found why the sticks had slipped. Like Dave. Sure, the refractory tube linings were good for twenty-four hours of continual blast—tested under the most rigorous lab conditions, even tried on a couple of Moon hops.

So naturally, with Unitech's billionaire backer and new power handling methods giving them the idea of beating the Services to Mars—no need to stop on the Moon even, they were that good—they didn't include spare linings. They'd have had to leave out some of their fancy radar junk and wait for results until the rocket returned.

Well, the tubes had been good. It was only after three hours of blasting, total, when he was braking down for Mars, that they began pitting. Then they'd held up after a fashion until there was only forty feet of free fall—about the same as fifteen on Earth. The ship hadn't been damaged, had even landed on her tripod legs, and the radar stuff had come through fine. The only trouble was that Dave had no return ticket. There was food for six months, water for more by condensing and reusing; but the clicking of the air machine wouldn't let him forget his supply of breathing material was being emptied, a trickle at a time. And there was only enough there for three weeks, at the outside. After that, curtains.

Of course, if the bright boys' plans had worked, he could live on compressed air drawn from outside by the air lock pumps. Too bad the landing had sprung them just enough so they could barely hold their own and keep him from losing air if he decided to go outside. A lot of things were too bad.

But at least the radar was working fine. He couldn't breathe it or take off with it, but the crystal amplifiers would have taken even a free fall all the way from mid-space. He cut the power on, fiddling until he found the Lunar broadcast from Earth. It had a squiggly sound, but most of the words come through on the begacycle band. There was something about a fool kid who'd sneaked into a plane and got off the ground somehow, leaving a hundred honest pilots trying to kill themselves in getting him down. People could kill each other by the millions, but they'd go all out to save one spectacular useless life, as usual.

Then it came: "No word from the United Technical Foundation

rocket, now fourteen hours overdue in reporting. Foundation men have given up hope, and feel that Mannen must have died in space from unknown causes, leaving the rocket to coast past Mars unmanned. Any violent crash would have tripped automatic signalers, and there was no word of trouble from Mannen—"

There was more, though less than on the kid. One rocket had been tried two years before, and gone wide because the tubes blew before reversal; the world had heard the clicking of Morse code right to the end, then. This failure was only a secondhand novelty, without anything new to gush over. Well, let them wonder. If they wanted to know what had happened, let 'em come and find out. There'd be no pretty last words from him.

Dave listened a moment longer, as the announcer picked up the latest rift in the supposedly refurbished United Nations, then cut off in disgust. The Atlantic Nations were as determined as Russia, and both had bombs now. If they wanted to blast themselves out of existence, maybe it was a good thing. Mars was a stinking world, but at least it had died quietly, instead of raising all that fuss.

Why worry about them? They'd never done him any favors. He'd been gypped all along. With a grade-A brain and a matinee idol's face, he'd been given a three-foot body and the brilliant future of a circus freak—the kind the crowd laughed at, rather than looked at in awe. His only chance had come when Unitech was building the ship, before they knew how much power they had, and figured on saving weight by designing it for a midget and a consequently smaller supply of air, water, and food. Even then, after he'd seen the ad, he'd had to fight his way into position through days of grueling tests. They hadn't tossed anything in his lap.

It had looked like the big chance, then. Fame and statues they could keep, but the book and endorsement rights would have put him where he could look down and laugh at the six-footers. And the guys with the electronic brains had cheated him out of it.

Let them whistle for their radar signals. Let them blow themselves to bits playing soldier. It was none of his worry now.

He clumped down from the observatory tip into his tiny quarters, swallowed a couple of barbiturates, and crawled into his sleeping cushions. Three weeks to go, and not even a bottle of whiskey on the ship. He cursed in disgust, turned over, and let sleep creep up on him.

It was inevitable that he'd go outside, of course. Three days of nothing but sitting, standing up, and sleeping was too much. Dave let the pumps suck at the air in the lock, zipping down his helmet over the soft rubber seal, tested his equipment, and waited until the pressure stood about even, outside and in. Then he opened the outer lock, tossed down the plastic ramp, and stepped out. He'd got used to the low gravity while still aboard, and paid no attention to it.

The tripod had dug into the sand, but the platform feet had kept the tubes open, and Dave swore at them softly. They looked good —except where part of one lining hung out in shreds. And with lining replacements, they'd be good—the blast had been cut off before the tubes themselves were harmed. He turned his back on the ship finally and faced out to the shockingly near horizon.

This, according to the stories, was supposed to be man's high moment—the first living human to touch the soil outside his own world and its useless satellite. The lock opened, and out stepped the hero —dying in pride with man's triumph and conquest of space! Dave pushed the rubbery flap of his helmet back against his lips, opened the orifice, and spat on the ground. If this was an experience, so was last year's stale beer.

There wasn't even a "canal" within fifty miles of him. He regretted that, in a way, since finding out what made the streaks would have killed time. He'd seen them as he approached, and there was no illusion to them—as the lunar scope had proved before. But they definitely weren't water ditches, anyhow. There'd been no chance to pick his landing site, and he'd have to get along without them.

It didn't leave much to explore. The ropes of vegetation were stretched out now, holding up loops of green fuzz to the sun, but there seemed to be no variation of species to break up the pattern. Probably a grove of trees on Earth would look the same to a mythical Martian. Possibly they represented six million and seven varieties. But Dave couldn't see it. The only point of interest was the way they wiggled their fuzz back and forth, and that soon grew monotonous.

Then his foot squeaked up at him, winding up in a gurgle. He jumped a good six feet up in surprise, and the squeak came again in the middle of his leap, making him stumble as he landed. But his eyes focused finally on a dull brownish lump fastened to his boot. It looked something like a circular cluster of a dozen pine cones, with fuzz all over, but there were little leglike members coming out of it—a dozen of them that went into rapid motion as he looked.

"Queeklrle," the thing repeated, sending the sound up through the denser air in his suit. It scrambled up briskly, coming to a stop over his supply kit and fumbling hurriedly. "Queeklrle!"

Oddly, there was no menace in it, probably because it was anything but a bug-eyed monster; there were no signs of any sensory organs. Dave blinked. It reminded him of a kitten he'd once had, somehow, before his usual luck found him and killed the little creature with some cat disease. He reacted automatically.

"Queekle yourself!" His fingers slipped into the kit and came out with a chocolate square, unpeeling the cellophane quickly. "It'll probably make you sick or kill you—but if that's what you're after, take it."

Queekle was after it, obviously. The creature took the square in its pseudopods, tucked it under its body, and relaxed, making faint gobbling sounds. For a second, it was silent, but then it squeaked again, sharper this time. "Queeklrle!"

Dave fed it two more of the squares before the creature seemed satisfied, and began climbing back down, leaving the nuts in the chocolate neatly piled on the ground behind it. Then Queekle went scooting off into the vegetation. Dave grimaced; its gratitude was practically human.

"Nuts to you, too," he muttered, kicking the pile of peanuts aside. But it proved at least that men had never been there before—humans were almost as fond of exterminating other life as they were of killing off their own kind.

He shrugged, and swung off toward the horizon at random in a loose, loping stride. After the cramped quarters of the ship, running felt good. He went on without purpose for an hour or more, until his muscles began protesting. Then he dug out his water bottle, pushed the tube through the helmet orifice, and drank briefly. Everything around him was the same as it had been near the ship, except for a small cluster of the plants that had dull red fuzz instead of green; he'd noticed them before, but couldn't tell whether they were one stage of the same plant or a different species. He didn't really care.

In any event, going farther was purposeless. He'd been looking for another Queekle casually, but had seen none. And on the return trip, he studied the ground under the fuzz plants more carefully, but there was nothing to see. There wasn't even a wind to break up the monotony, and he clumped up to the ramp of the ship as bored as he had left it. Maybe it was just as well his air supply was low, if this was all Mars had to offer.

Dave pulled up the ramp and spun the outer lock closed, blinking in the gloom, until the lights snapped on as the air lock sealed. He watched the pressure gauge rise to ten pounds, normal for the ship, and reached for the inner lock. Then he jerked back, staring at the floor.

Queekle was there, and had brought along part of Mars. Now its squeaks came out in a steady stream as the inner seal opened. And in front of it, fifteen or twenty of the plant things went into abrupt motion, moving aside to form a narrow lane through which the creature went rapidly on into the ship. Dave followed, shaking his head. Apparently there was no way of being sure about anything here. Plants that stood steady on their roots outside could move about at will, it seemed—and to what was evidently a command.

The fool beast! Apparently the warmth of the ship had looked good to it, and it was all set to take up housekeeping—in an atmosphere that was at least a hundred times too dense for it. Dave started up the narrow steps to his quarters, hesitated, and cursed. It still reminded him of the kitten, moving around in exploratory circles. He came back down and made a dive for it.

Queekle let out a series of squeals as Dave tossed it back into the air lock and closed the inner seal. Its squeaks died down as the pressure was pumped back and the outer seal opened, though, and were inaudible by the time he moved back up the ladder. He grumbled to himself halfheartedly. That's what came of feeding the thing—it decided to move in and own him.

But he felt better as he downed what passed for supper. The lift lasted for an hour or so afterward—and then left him feeling more cramped and disgusted than ever as he sat staring at the walls of his tiny room. There wasn't even a book to read, aside from the typed manual for general care of the ship, and he'd read that often enough already.

Finally he gave up in disgust and went up to the observatory tip and cut on the radar. Maybe his death notices would be more interesting tonight.

They weren't. They were carrying speculations about what had happened to him—none of which included any hint that the bright boys could have made an error. They'd even figured out whether Mars might have captured the ship as a satellite and decided against it. But the news was losing interest, obviously, and he could tell where it had been padded out from the general broadcast to give the Lunar men more coverage—apparently on the theory that anyone as far out as the Moon would be more interested in the subject. They'd added one new touch, though!

"It seems obvious that further study of space conditions beyond the gravitic or magnetic field of Earth is needed. The Navy announced that its new rocket, designed to reach Mars next year, will be changed for use as a deep-space laboratory on tentative exploratory trips before going further. United Technical Foundation has abandoned all further plans for interplanetary research, at least for the moment."

And that was that. They turned the microphone over to international affairs then, and Dave frowned. Even to him, it was obvious that the amount of words used had no relation to the facts covered. Already they were beginning to clamp down the lid, and that meant things were heading toward a crisis again. The sudden outbreak of the new and violent plague in China four years before had brought an end to the former crisis, as all nations pitched in through altruism or sheer self-interest, and were forced to work together. But that hadn't lasted; they'd found a cure after nearly two million deaths, and there had been nothing to hold the suddenly created co-operation of the powers. Maybe if they had new channels for their energies, such as the planets—

But it wouldn't wash. The Atlantic Nations would have taken over Mars on the strength of his landing and return, and they were in the lead if another ship should be sent. They'd gobble up the planets as they had taken the Moon, and the other powers would simply have more fuel to feed their resentments and bring things to a head.

Dave frowned more deeply as the announcer went on. There were the usual planted hints from officials that everything was fine for the Atlantic Powers—but they weren't usual. They actually sounded super-confident—arrogantly so. And there was one brief mention of a conference in Washington, but it was the key. Two of the names were evidence in full. Someone had actually found a way to make the lithium bomb work, and—

Dave cut off the radar as it hit him. It was all the human race needed—a chance to use what could turn into a self-sustaining chain reaction. Man had finally discovered a way to blow up his planet.

He looked up toward the speck that was Earth, with the tiny spot showing the Moon beside it. Behind him, the air machine clicked busily, metering out oxygen. Two and a half weeks. Dave looked down at that, then. Well, it might be long enough, though it probably wouldn't. But he had that much time for certain. He wondered if the really bright boys expected as much for themselves. Or was it only because he wasn't in the thick of a complacent humanity, and had time for thinking, that he could realize what was coming?

He slapped the air machine dully, and looked up at the Earth again. The fools! They'd asked for it; let them take their medicine now. They liked war better than eugenics, nuclear physics better than the science that could have found his trouble and set his glands straight to give him the body he should have had. Let them stew in their own juice.

He found the bottle of sleeping tablets and shook it. But only specks of powder fell out. That was gone, too. They couldn't get anything right. No whiskey, no cigarettes that might use up the precious air, no more amytal. Earth was reaching out for him, denying him the distraction of a sedative, just as she was denying herself a safe and impersonal contest for her clash of wills.

He threw the bottle onto the floor and went down to the air lock. Queekle was there—the faint sounds of scratching proved that. And it came in as soon as the inner seal opened, squeaking contentedly, with its plants moving slowly behind it. They'd added a new feature —a mess of rubbish curled up in the tendrils of the vines, mixed sand, and dead plant forms.

"Make yourself at home," Dave told the creature needlessly. "It's all yours, and when I run down to the gasping point, I'll leave the locks open and the power on for the fluorescents. Somebody might as well get some good out of the human race. And don't worry about using up my air—I'll be better off without it, probably."

"Queeklrle." It wasn't a very brilliant conversation, but it had to do.

Dave watched Queekle assemble the plants on top of the converter shield. The bright boys had done fine, there—they'd learned to chain radiation and neutrons with a thin wall of metal and an intangible linkage of forces. The result made an excellent field for the vines, and Queekle scooted about, making sure the loads of dirt were spread out and its charges arranged comfortably, to suit it. It looked intelligent —but so would the behavior of ants. If the pressure inside the ship bothered the creature, there was no sign of it.

"Queeklrle," it announced finally, and turned toward Dave. He let it follow him up the steps, found some chocolate, and offered it to the pseudopods. But Queekle wasn't hungry. Nor would the thing accept water, beyond touching it and brushing a drop over its fuzzy surface.

It squatted on the floor until Dave flopped down on the cushions, then tried to climb up beside him. He reached down, surprised to feel the fuzz give way instantly to a hard surface underneath, and lifted it up beside him. Queekle was neither cold nor warm; probably all Martian life had developed excellent insulation, and perhaps the ability to suck water out of the almost dehydrated atmosphere and then retain it.

For a second, Dave remembered the old tales of vampire beasts, but he rejected them at once. When you come down to it, most of the animal life wasn't too bad—not nearly as bad as man had pictured it to justify his own superiority. And Queekle seemed content to lie there, making soft monotonous little squeaks and letting it go at that.

Surprisingly, sleep came easily.

Dave stayed away from the ship most of the next two days, moving aimlessly, but working his energy out in pure muscular exertion. It helped, enough to keep him away from the radar. He found tongs and stripped the lining from the tubes, and that helped more, because it occupied his mind as well as his muscles. But it was only a temporary expedient, and not good enough for even the two remaining weeks. He started out the next day, went a few miles, and came back. For a while then, he watched the plants that were thriving unbelievably on the converter shield.

Queekle was busy among them, nipping off something here and there and pushing it underneath where its mouth was. Dave tasted one of the buds, gagged, and spat it out; the thing smelled almost like an Earth plant, but combined all the quintessence of sour and bitter with something that was outside his experience. Queekle, he'd found, didn't care for chocolate—only the sugar in it; the rest was ejected later in a hard lump.

And then there was nothing to do. Queekle finished its work and they squatted side by side, but with entirely different reactions; the Martian creature seemed satisfied.

Three hours later, Dave stood in the observatory again, listening to the radar. There was some music coming through at this hour—but the squiggly reception ruined that. And the news was exactly what he'd expected—a lot of detail about national things, a few quick words on some conference at the United Nations, and more on the celebration of Israel over the anniversary of beginning as an independent nation. Dave's own memories of that were dim, but some came back as he listened. The old United Nations had done a lot of wrangling over that, but it had been good for them, in a way—neither side had felt the issue offered enough chance for any direct gain to threaten war, but it kept the professional diplomats from getting quite so deeply into more dangerous grounds.

But that, like the Chinese plague, wouldn't come up again.

He cut off the radar, finally, only vaguely conscious of the fact that the rocket hadn't been mentioned. He could no longer even work up a feeling of disgust. Nothing mattered beyond his own sheer boredom, and when the air machine—

Then it hit him. There were no clicks. There had been none while he was in the tip. He jerked to the controls, saw that the meter indicated the same as it had when he was last here, and threw open the cover. Everything looked fine. There was a spark from the switch, and the motor went on when he depressed the starting button. When he released it, it went off instantly. He tried switching manually to other tanks, but while the valve moved, the machine remained silent.

The air smelled fresh, though—fresher than it had since the first day out from Earth, though a trifle drier than he'd have liked.

"Queekle!" Dave looked at the creature, watched it move nearer at his voice, as it had been doing lately. Apparently it knew its name now, and answered with the usual squeak and gurgle.

It was the answer, of course. No wonder its plants had been thriving. They'd had all the carbon dioxide and water vapor they could use, for a change. No Earth plants could have kept the air fresh in such a limited amount of space, but Mars had taught her children efficiency through sheer necessity. And now he had six months, rather than two weeks!

Yeah, six months to do nothing but sit and wait and watch for the blowup that might come, to tell him he was the last of his kind. Six months with nothing but a squeaking burble for conversation, except for the radar news.

He flipped it on again with an impatient slap of his hand, then reached to cut it off. But words were already coming out:

". . . Foundation will dedicate a plaque today to young Dave Mannen, the little man with more courage than most big men can hold. Andrew Buller, backer of the ill-fated Mars rocket, will be on hand to pay tribute—"

Dave kicked the slush off with his foot. They would bother with plaques at a time like this, when all he'd ever wanted was the right number of marks on United States currency. He snapped at the dials, twisting them, and grabbed for the automatic key as more circuits coupled in.

"Tell Andrew Buller and the whole Foundation to go—"

Nobody'd hear his Morse at this late stage, but at least it felt good. He tried it again, this time with some Anglo-Saxon adjectives thrown in. Queekle came over to investigate the new sounds and squeaked doubtfully. Dave dropped the key.

"Just human nonsense, Queekle. We also kick chairs when we bump into—"

"Mannen!" The radar barked it out at him. "Thank God, you got your radar fixed. This is Buller—been waiting here a week and more now. Never did believe all that folderol about it being impossible for it to be the radar at fault. *Oof*, your message still coming in and I'm getting the typescript. Good thing there's no FCC out there. Know just how you feel, though. Darned fools here. Always said they should have another rocket ready. Look, if your set is bad, don't waste it, just tell me how long you can hold out, and by Harry, we'll get another ship built and up there. How are you, what—"

He went on, his words piling up on each other as Dave went through a mixture of reactions that shouldn't have fitted any human situation. But he knew better than to build up hope. Even six months wasn't long enough—it took time to finish and test a rocket—more than he had. Air was fine, but men needed food, as well.

He hit the key again. "Two weeks' air in tanks. Staying with Martian farmer of doubtful intelligence, but his air too thin, pumps no good." The last he let fade out, ending with an abrupt cutoff of power. There was no sense in their sending out fools in half-built ships to try to rescue him. He wasn't a kid in an airplane, crying at the mess he was in, and he didn't intend to act like one. That farmer business would give them enough to chew on; they had their money's worth, and that was that.

He wasn't quite prepared for the news that came over the radar later—particularly for the things he'd been quoted as saying. For the first time it occurred to him that the other pilot, sailing off beyond Mars to die, might have said things a little different from the clicks of Morse they had broadcast. Dave tried to figure the original version of "Don't give up the ship" as a sailor might give it, and chuckled.

And at least the speculation over their official version of his Martian farmer helped to kill the boredom. In another week at the most, there'd be an end to that, too, and he'd be back out of the news. Then there'd be more long days and nights to fill somehow, before his time ran out. But for the moment, he could enjoy the antics of nearly three billion people who got more excited over one man in trouble on Mars than they would have out of half the population starving to death.

He set the radar back on the Foundation wave length, but there was nothing there; Buller had finally run down, and not yet got his breath back. Finally, he turned back to the general broadcast on the Lunar signal. It was remarkable how man's progress had leaped ahead by decades, along with his pomposity, just because an insignificant midget was still alive on Mars. They couldn't have discovered a prettier set of half-truths about anybody than they had from the crumbs of facts he hadn't even known existed concerning his life.

Then he sobered. That was the man on the street's reaction. But the diplomats, like the tides, waited on no man. And his life made no difference to a lithium bomb. He was still going through a counterreaction when Queekle insisted it was bedtime and persuaded him to leave the radar.

After all, not a single thing had been accomplished by his fool message.

But he snapped back to the message as a new voice came on: "And here's a late flash from the United Nations headquarters. Russia has just volunteered the use of a completed rocketship for the rescue of David Mannen on Mars, and we've accepted the offer. The Russian delegation is still being cheered on the floor! Here are the details we have now. This will be a oneway trip, radar-guided by a new bomb control method—no, here's more news! It will be guided by radar and an automatic searching head that will put it down within a mile of Mannen's ship. Unmanned, it can take tremendous acceleration, and reach Mannen before another week is out! United Technical Foundation is even now trying to contact Mannen through a hookup to the big government high-frequency labs where a new type of receiver—"

It was almost eight minutes before Buller's voice came in, evidently while the man was still getting Dave's hurried message off the tape. "Mannen, you're coming in fine. Okay, those refractories—they'll be on the way to Moscow in six hours, some new type the scientists here worked out after you left. We'll send two sets this time to be sure, but they test almost twenty times as good as the others. We're still in contact with Moscow, and some details are still being worked on, but we're equipping their ship with the same type refractories. Most of the other supplies will come straight from them—"

Dave nodded. And there'd be a lot of things he'd need—he'd see to that. Things that would be supplied straight from them. Right now, everything was milk and honey, and all nations were being the fool pilots rescuing the kid in the plane, suddenly bowled over by interplanetary success. But they'd need plenty later to keep their diplomats busy—something to wrangle over and blow off steam that would be vented on important things, otherwise.

Well, the planets wouldn't be important to any nation for a long time, but they were spectacular enough. And just how was a planet claimed, if the man who landed was taken off in a ship that was a mixture of the work of two countries?

Maybe his theories were all wet, but there was no harm in the gamble. And even if the worst happened, all this might hold off the trouble long enough for colonies. Mars was still a stinking world, but it could support life if it had to.

"Queekle," he said slowly, "you're going to be the first Martian ambassador to Earth. But first, how about a little side trip to Venus on the way back, instead of going direct? That ought to drive them crazy and tangle up their interplanetary rights a little more. Well? On to Venus, or direct home to Earth?"

"Queeklrle," the Martian creature answered. It wasn't too clear, but it was obviously a lot more like a two-syllable word.

Dave nodded. "Right! Venus."

The sky was still filled with the nasty little stars he'd seen the first night on Mars, but he grinned now as he looked up, before reaching for the key again. He wouldn't have to laugh at big men, after all. He could look up at the sky and laugh at every star in it. It shouldn't be long before those snickering stars had a surprise coming to them.

Campbell got the other stories he needed to make up the trick issue. Thus the reader was given the magazine he had predicted. It wasn't exactly the same, but very close. And just before it was supposed to appear on the newsstands, Campbell sent around a copy for each writer and a very special copy to be autographed for the reader. This, complete with autographs of all the writers and artists, was mailed to him. So everybody was happy.

Well, almost in my case. I had a lot to be happy about. I enjoyed my work, and the agency was beginning to sell some of my old rejects. A few of my stories were being picked up for anthology use, adding to the income from my previous writing. Several copies of . . . *And Some Were Human* (the Prime Press book, not the later Ballantine one, which was somewhat different) were sitting on a shelf to show that I was now a book author. And I'd sold a story to Campbell after a five-year hiatus.

The only fly in the ointment was that I had an agent who was too much interested in getting me to write. The sale to Campbell left me no further defenses, in his view. I had proved I could write again. Now go write! It was getting hard to resist, but I'd grown pretty stubborn. I had stopped thinking about stories (except for the one special case) and I didn't want to start it all over again.

He won by what I considered cheating. After work on Friday, he called me in to give me an assignment. The editor needed a 6,000-word story about auto racing by Monday morning. There was no one else to take the assignment, so it was up to me. If I didn't do it, the implication was, the agency would be disgraced, the editor would have to print blank pages, etc.

So I went out and bought every sports magazine I could find with a story or article on auto racing. I knew how a sports story was supposed to be constructed, with a personal problem and a sports problem, preferably with both working out together at the end. A lot of the plotting was built in, and all it needed was some element of freshness and more than mechanical development.

It turned out to be surprisingly easy. After all, this was to take place here on familiar Earth with our normal culture and nothing with which people were unfamiliar. There was no need to invent anything, as there always is in good science fiction. To make it even easier, I was following the instructions Meredith had given to the other writers in the office and writing final copy the first time, carbons and all. The penny-a-word rate paid by such magazines suddenly looked rather good against the time I spent on the story.

From then on, I stopped fighting and accepted any assignment an editor wanted to give me. Quite a few came from "Doc" Lowndes, but there were others. And I branched out into a few detective stories, a couple of Westerns, and the whole range of sports. I even did a couple on roller derby for Lowndes.

I suddenly found myself doing more writing than I'd ever done before. None of it was science fiction at that time. But my income was rather surprising when I counted it up.

I was also beginning to formulate a sort of universal rule for fiction. It has probably been discovered by countless writers, but it was new to me in its stark and simple statement: The basis of *all* good fiction is character. Even the most formula-derived sports story could come to life if there were real and interesting characters taking part in the events. And the only reason for the problems and complications of fiction was to display those characters to their fullest when meeting trials and responding in their own, individual ways.

The chief fault with that rule is that it doesn't give a bit of help in creating such real and interesting characters. Nobody has ever succeeded in explaining how that is done, though many have tried. It has nothing to do with description. I've seen pages of description wasted on a wooden character, while other characters seem to leap to life with almost no description.

It also has nothing to do with characters who "just run away with the story." When that happens, it usually means that the writer is doing a bad job. A good character and a good story must fit each other, not run away from each other.

Nevertheless, I often found the rule about character helpful in determining whether an idea was ready for writing. Until I could feel—not merely see—the story from the viewpoint of the character, it wasn't.

By the end of 1949, my writing was in better shape than it had ever been. I'm afraid there was less to be said favorably about my private affairs. Helen and I had decided that we made excellent friends, but that we weren't really suited to each other as married partners, and we had decided to separate. It was all done amicably, and neither of us felt any need to find fault with the other. She decided I could keep the old apartment if I'd pay for furniture for the new one she had found for herself. And she left at the beginning of 1950.

That year was an important one for science fiction, too. The magazine field was shaken up by the planned publication of two new magazines. *The Magazine of Fantasy and Science Fiction* was to be edited by Anthony Boucher and J. Francis McComas. *Galaxy* would be under the guidance of Horace L. Gold. They were both aimed at the serious adult science fiction reader, as only *Astounding* had been previously. But each was quite different from *Astounding*. Boucher and McComas were asking for stories with a strong literary flavor, and Gold seemed to steer toward something slicker and perhaps more superficial than Campbell liked. It was hard to pin either down exactly at that time, but it was obvious that they were going to have a major effect on science fiction.

Galaxy was making a bid to capture the major writers by beginning with an offer of three cents a word, and *Astounding* was soon forced to match that rate. (It shortly raised the possible ante a bit more by paying bonuses on the best-liked stories in the issue, so that it was possible to get four cents a word.)

This made it possible finally for a writer to think seriously about devoting all his time to writing science fiction. At those rates, and with that many magazines buying stories, a fair living was now possible.

The major book publishers were also beginning to look on science fiction as worthy of consideration. Both Simon and Schuster and Doubleday began planning regular issuance of novels in the field; many were coming from the old serials in the magazines, but a few new ones were bought.

It was a boom time. Scott Meredith urged me to get back into science fiction, and I began to consider it. By then, I didn't even have the excuse of the unsold stories—because most of those former rejects had been sold. It was then that I discovered my notes for "It Comes Out Here" and rewrote it. Gold bought it at once, and the $180 he paid was my first taste of the new rate.

Gold also called me up to urge that I do a suspense novelette that would be something like "Nerves." (I've had that suggested many times, both before and since. I'm not sure that I like it. It's fine to have people admire your very best work, but it's not quite so pleasant to have them expect you to duplicate it on order.)

Another publisher wanted a science fiction short story from me that would hold a hint of mystery in it.

The short story wasn't too much of a problem. I already had an idea which seemed to fit that description. It dealt with a robot during an early stage of robotics. The creature would be fully intelligent, though not fully educated in the world, and not even aware of who or what he was. But because of defects in his construction, he would have only a few hours to exist. The mystery lay in the fact that it was to be told from his view, and that he wouldn't know what was going on, until almost the end, when he had to face his "death."

But the adventure-suspense novelette was another matter. I wasn't sure I could do it in the 15,000 words that Gold wanted. "Nerves" had needed twice that for its effect, and could have used more.

Besides, I'd lost all my charts and notes on the building of suspense along with the vanished manuscripts when I moved from St. Louis. They weren't something easy to remember, either, and they had taken me weeks of thought and study to develop.

Anyhow, I find my mind has a curious quirk. I can remember a great deal about anything until I put it on paper. Then I sort of throw my mental notes away and depend on the written notes. And I've never been much good at reconstructing something I've really done thoroughly. I can't develop the enthusiasm for a twice-told tale. (I hate to deliver the same speech twice, for instance.) I was afraid that a lot of that work on suspense was gone for all time. Now, after having tried to start the project again a couple of times, I'm sure of that.

But after considerable chasing of false ideas, I managed to find a plot that looked good. It put my characters into a literally life-and-death situation, and promised to keep them there until the end.

So I stayed at the office one night to start writing at least one of the stories. (My favorite typewriter at home was undergoing its yearly cleaning and checking, and I didn't feel like trying to put it all together and write on it in one evening.)

I started on the mystery short story, wondering how science fiction would feel after having done so much routine pulp magazine fiction. But it was one of my good moments for writing. The 6,000 words simply poured out of the typewriter. I didn't even have to tear one page out and throw it away because of bad lines. It took less than two hours to write "The Monster."

It was accepted by the magazine for which it was written, but then the magazine folded. That was fine with me. I'd been thinking that it deserved a better market, and suggested to Scott Meredith that it might have a chance at some slick magazine. After reading the story, he agreed. It sold to *Argosy* for $500, and they did a beautiful job of setting up a display of it in their pages.

I wasn't so pleased with the story for Gold, which I titled "Wind Between the Worlds." It also came out of the typewriter quickly. I managed to finish it early in the morning. But I knew there were rough spots in it. Still, it was done, and I decided to show it to Gold for his comments, before trying to rewrite it.

I think that was a mistake. A writer should do the best he can before he shows it to anyone else for comments. It doesn't matter whether his best comes with the first draft or the tenth rewrite, but he should satisfy himself first. Then he's in a much better position to judge the value of outside criticism.

I've lost the letter Gold sent me, but I can remember my reaction. He disliked the beginning, I remember, and felt it had no emotional quality. He was quite right. And he made a number of other valuable points. But there were other places where I couldn't agree at all, particularly with his idea that one of the crew had to be a villain.

I called him up and discussed it with him. In the end, we reached a compromise on everything except the villain bit, to which I finally consented reluctantly.

I rewrote it from beginning to end—the best way, I've found, to make a story hang together firmly after tinkering with it, and to catch discrepancies. Patching is easier, but it often shows.

This second version came out much too long, however, and I had to do a third version, whittling it down. I sent that to Gold. I'm not sure he was completely satisfied, but he paid $500, which was a generous price.

And this time I am *not* going to use the version of the story as I sent it to the editor. Instead, I'm using the second version, with the parts about the villain cut out completely. This is the way I really intended "Wind Between the Worlds" to be. It comes out to 17,500 words now.

24.

Wind Between the Worlds

(*by Lester del Rey*)

I

It was hot in the dome of the Bennington matter transmitter building. The metal shielding walls seemed to catch the rays of the sun and bring them to a focus there. Even the fan that was plugged in nearby didn't seem to help much. Vic Peters shook his head, knocking the mop of yellow hair out of his eyes. He twisted his lanky, angular figure about, so the fan could reach fresh territory, and cursed under his breath.

Heat he could take. As a roving troubleshooter for Teleport Interstellar, he'd worked from Rangoon to Nairobi—but always with men. Pat Trevor was the first of the few women superintendents he'd met. And while he had no illusions of masculine supremacy, he'd have felt a lot better in shorts or nothing right now.

Besides, a figure like Pat's couldn't be forgotten, even though denim coveralls were hardly supposed to be flattering. Cloth stretched tight across a woman's hips had never helped a man concentrate on his work.

She looked down at him, grinning easily. Her arm came up to toss her hair back, leaving a smudge on her forehead to match one on her nose. She wasn't exactly pretty; her face had too much honest intelligence for that. But the smile seemed to illumine her gray eyes, and even the metal shavings in her brown hair couldn't hide the red highlights.

"One more bolt, Vic," she told him. "Pheooh! I'm melting. . . . So what happened to your wife?"

He shrugged. "Married a lawyer right after the divorce. Last I knew, they were doing fine. Why not? It wasn't her fault. Between hopping all over the world and spending my spare time trying to get on the moon rocket they were building, I wasn't much of a husband. Funny, they gave up the idea of going to the moon the same day she got the divorce."

Unconsciously, his lips twisted. He'd grown up before DuQuesne discovered the matter transmitter, when reaching the other planets of the Solar System had been the dream of most boys. Somehow, that no longer seemed important to people, now the world was linked through Teleport Interstellar with races all across the galaxy.

Man had always been a topsy-turvy race. He'd discovered gunpowder before chemistry, and battled his way up to the atom bomb in a scant few thousand years of civilization, before he had a worldwide government. Most races, apparently, developed space travel thousands of years before the matter transmitter and long after they'd achieved a genuine science of sociology.

DuQuesne had started it by investigating some obscure extensions of Dirac's esoteric mathematics. To check up on his work, he'd built a machine, only to find that it produced results beyond his expectations; matter in it simply seemed to disappear, releasing energy that was much less than it should have been, but still enough to destroy the machine.

DuQuesne and two students had analyzed the results, checked the math again, and come up with an answer they didn't believe. But when they built two such machines, carefully made as nearly identical as possible, their wild idea had proved true; when the machines were turned on, anything in them simply changed places—even though the machines were miles apart.

One of the students gave the secret away, and DuQuesne was forced to give a public demonstration. Before the eyes of a number of world-famous scientists and half a hundred reporters, a full ton of coal changed places with a ton of bricks in no visible time. Then, while the reporters were dutifully taking down DuQuesne's explanation of electron waves that covered the universe and identity shifts, something new was added. Before their eyes, in the machine beside them, a round ball appeared, suspended in midair. It had turned around twice, disappeared for a few seconds, and popped back, darting down to shut off the machines.

For a week, the papers had been filled with the attempts to move the sphere from the machine, crack it open, or at least distract it long enough to cut the machines on again. By the end of that time, it was obvious that more than Earth science was involved. Poor DuQuesne was going crazy with a combination of frustration and crackpot publicity.

Vic's mind had been filled with Martians then, and he'd managed to be on the outskirts of the crowd that was present when the sphere came to life, rose up, cut on the machine, and disappeared again. He'd been staring at where it had been when the Envoy had appeared. After that, he'd barely had time to notice that the Envoy seemed to be a normal human before the police had begun chasing the crowd away.

The weeks that followed had been filled with the garbled hints that were enough to drive all science fiction fans delirious, though most of the world seemed to regard it as akin to the old flying saucer scare. The Envoy saw the President and the Cabinet. The Envoy met with the United Nations. The Envoy was admittedly a robot! India walked out; India came back. Congress protested secret treaties. General Autos held a secret meeting with United Analine. The Envoy would address the world in English, French, German, Spanish, Russian, and Chinese.

There were hundreds of books on that period now, and most schoolboys knew the speech by heart. The Galactic Council had detected the matter transmittal radiation. By Galactic Law, Earth had thus earned the rights to provisional status in the Council through discovery of the basic principle. The Council would now send Betzian engineers to build transports to six planets scattered over the galaxy, chosen as roughly comparable to Earth's culture. The transmitters used for such purposes would be owned by the Galactic Council, as a nonprofit business, to be manned by Earth people who would be trained at a school set up under DuQuesne.

In return, nothing was demanded. And no further knowledge

would be forthcoming. Primitive though we were by the standards of most worlds, we had earned our place on the Council—but we could swim up the rest of the way by ourselves.

Surprisingly, the first reaction had been one of wild enthusiasm. It wasn't until later that the troubles began. Vic had barely made his way into the first engineering class out of a hundred thousand applicants. Now, twelve years after graduation . . .

Pat's voice cut in on his thoughts. "All tightened up here, Vic. Wipe the scowl off and let's go down to check."

She collected her tools, wrapped her legs around a smooth pole, and went sliding down. He yanked the fan and followed her. Below, the crew was on standby. Pat lifted an eyebrow at the grizzled, cadaverous head operator. "Okay, Amos. Plathgol standing by?"

Amos pulled his six-foot-two up from his slump and indicated the yellow standby light. Inside the twin poles of the huge transmitter that was tuned to one on Plathgol a big, twelve-foot diameter plastic cylinder held a single rabbit. Matter transmitting was always a two-way affair, requiring that the same volume be exchanged. And between the worlds, where different atmospheres and pressures were involved, all sending was done in the big capsules. One-way handling was possible, of course—the advance worlds could do it safely—but it involved the danger of something materializing to occupy the same space as something else—even air molecules; when space cracked open under that strain, the results were catastrophic.

Amos whistled into the transport-wave interworld phone in the code that was universal between worlds where many races could not vocalize, got an answering whistle, and pressed a lever. The rabbit was gone, and the new capsule was faintly pink, with something resembling a giant worm inside.

Amos chuckled in satisfaction. "*Tsiuna.* Good eating. I got friends on Plathgol that like rabbit. Want some of this, Pat?"

Vic felt his stomach jerk at the colors that crawled over the *tsiuna.* The hot antiseptic spray was running over the capsule, to be followed by supersonics and ultraviolets to complete sterilization. Amos waited a moment and pulled out the creature.

Pat hefted it. "Big one. Bring it over to my place and I'll fry it for you and Vic. How's the Dirac meter read, Vic?"

"On the button." The 7 percent power loss was gone now, after a week of hard work locating it. "Guess you were right—the reflector was off angle. Should have tried it first, but it never happened before. How'd you figure it out?"

She indicated the interworld phone. "I started out in anthropology, Vic. Got interested in other races, and then found I couldn't talk to the teleport engineers without being one, so I got sidetracked to this job. But I still talk a lot on anything Galactic policy won't forbid. When everything else failed, I complained to one Ecthinbal operator that the Betz II boys installed us wrong. When I got sympathy instead of indignation, I figured it could happen. Simple, wasn't it?"

He snorted and waited while she gave orders to start business. Then, as the loading cars began to hum, she fell behind him, moving out toward the office. "I suppose you'll be leaving tonight, Vic? I'll miss you—you're the only troubleshooter I've met who did more than make passes."

"When I make passes at your kind of girl, it won't be a one-night stand," he told her. "And in my business, it's no life for a wife."

But he stopped to look at the building, admiring it for the last time. It was the standard Betz II design, but designed to handle the farm crops around, and bigger than any earlier models on Earth. The Betz II engineers knew their stuff, even if they did look like big slugs with tentacles and with no sense of sight. The transmitters were in the circular center, surrounded by a shield wall, a wide hall all around, another shield, a circular hall again, and finally the big outside shield. The two opposite entranceways spiraled through the three shields, each rotated thirty degrees clockwise from the entrance portal through the next shield. Those shields were of inerted matter that could be damaged by nothing less violent than a hydrogen bomb directly on them—they refused to soften at less than ten million degrees Kelvin. How the Betzians managed to form them in the first place, nobody knew.

Beyond the transmitter building, however, the usual offices and local transmitters across Earth had not yet been built; that would be strictly of Earth construction, and would have to wait for an off season. They were using the nearest building, an abandoned store a quarter mile away, as a temporary office. Pat threw the door open and then stopped suddenly.

"Ptheela!"

A Plathgolian native sat on a chair with a bundle of personal belongings around her, her three arms making little marks on something that looked like a used pancake. The Plathgolians had been meat-eating plants once. They still smelled high to Earth noses, and their constantly shedding skin resembled shaggy bark, while their heads were vaguely flowerlike.

Ptheela wriggled one of her three arms. "The hotel found it had to decorate my room," she whistled in Galactic Code. Many of the other races could not vocalize, but the whistling Code could be used by all, either naturally or with simple artificial devices. "No other room—and all the hotels say they're full up. Plathgolians stink, I guess. So I'll go home when the transmitter is fixed."

"With your trade studies half done? Don't be silly, Ptheela. I've got a room for you in my apartment. How are the studies, anyhow?"

For answer, the plant woman passed over a newspaper, folded to one item. "What trade? Your House of Representatives just passed a tariff on all traffic through Teleport!"

Pat scanned the news, scowling. "Damn them. A tariff! They can't tax interstellar traffic. The Galactic Council won't stand for it; we're still only on approval. The Senate will never okay it!"

Ptheela whistled doubtfully, and Vic nodded. "They will. I've been expecting this. A lot of people are sick of Teleport."

"But we're geared to Teleport now. The old factories are torn down, the new ones are useless to us without interstellar supplies. We can't get by without the catalysts from Ecthinbal, the cancer-preventative from Plathgol. And who'll buy all our sugar? We're producing fifty times what we need, just because most planets don't have plants that separate the levo from the dextro forms. All Hades will pop!"

Ptheela wiggled her arms again. "You came too early. Your culture is unbalanced. All physics, no sociology—all eat well, little think well."

All emotion, little reason, Vic added to himself. It had been the same when the industrial revolution came along. Old crafts were uprooted and some people were hurt. There were more jobs, but they weren't the same familiar ones. Now Plathgol was willing to deliver a perfect Earth automobile, semi-assembled and just advanced enough to bypass Earth patent laws, for half a ton of sugar. The Earth auto industry was gone. And the motorists were mad because Plathgol wasn't permitted to supply the improved, ever-powered models they made for themselves.

Banks had crashed, industries had folded, men had been out of work. The government had cushioned the shock, and Teleport had been accepted while it was still bringing new wonders. Now there was a higher standard of living than ever, but not for the groups who had controlled the monopolies. And too many remembered the wrenching and changing they'd had forced on them.

Also, it hadn't proved easy to accept the idea of races superior to Man. What was the use of making discoveries when others already knew the answers? A feeling of inferiority had turned to resentment, and misunderstandings between races had bred contempt here. Ptheela was kicked out of her hotel room—and a group had tried to poison the "hideous" Betz II engineers last year.

In an off-election year, politics could drop to the lowest level.

"Maybe we can get jobs on Plathgol," he suggested bitterly.

Ptheela whistled doubtfully. "Pat could, if she had three husbands—engineers must meet minimum standards. You could be a husband, maybe."

Vic kept forgetting that Plathgol was backward enough to have taboos and odd customs, even though Galactically higher than Earth, having had nearly a million years of history behind her to develop peace and amity.

The televisor connecting them with the transmitter building buzzed, and Amos' dour face came on. "Screwball delivery with top priority, Pat. Professor named Douglas wants to ship a capsule of lunar vacuum for a capsule of Ecthinbal deep-space vacuum. Common sense says we don't make much shipping vacuums by the pound!"

"Public service, no charge," Vic suggested, and Pat nodded. Douglas was a top man at Caltech and his goodwill testimony might be useful sometime. "Leave it on, Amos—I want to watch this. Douglas has some idea that space fluctuates, somehow, and he can figure out where Ecthinbal is from a sample. Then he can figure how fast an exchange force works, whether it's instantaneous or not. We've got the biggest Earth transmitters, so he uses us."

As he watched, a big capsule was put in place by loading machines and the light changed from yellow to red. A slightly greenish capsule replaced the other. Amos signaled the disinfection crew and hot spray hit it, to be followed by the ultrasonics. Something crackled suddenly, and Amos made a wild lunge across the screen.

The big capsule popped, crashing inward and scattering glass shards in a thousand directions. Pressure glass! It should have carried a standard code warning for cold sterilization and no supersonics. Vic started toward the transmitter building.

Pat's cry brought him back. There were sudden shrieks coming from the televisor. Men in the building were clinging frantically to anything they could hold, but men and bundles ready for loading were being picked up violently and sucked toward the transmitter. As Vic watched, a man hit the edge of the field and seemed to be sliced into nothingness, his screams cut off, half-formed. Death was inevitable to anything caught in the edge of the field.

A big shard of glass had hit the control wiring, forcing together and shorting two bus bars, holding them together by its weight. It was wedged in firmly and the transmitter was locked into continuous transmit. And air, with a pressure of fifteen pounds per square inch, was running in and being shipped to Ecthinbal, where the pressure was barely an ounce per square inch! With that difference, pressure on a single square foot of surface could lift over a ton. The poor devils in the transmitter building didn't have a chance.

He snapped off the televisor as Pat turned away, gagging. "When was the accumulator charged?"

"It wasn't an accumulator in that installation," she told him weakly. "The whole plant uses an electron-pulse atomotor—good for twenty years of continuous operation."

Vic swore and made for the door, with Pat and Ptheela after him. The transmitter opening took up about two hundred square feet—which meant somewhere between fifty and five hundred thousand cubic feet of air a second were being lost. Maybe worse.

Ptheela nodded as she kept pace with him. "I think the tariff won't matter much now," she whistled.

II

Vic's action in charging out had been pure instinct to get where the trouble lay. His legs churned over the ground, while a wind at his back made the going easier.

Then his brain clicked over, and he dug his heels into the ground, trying to stop. Pat crashed into him, but Ptheela's arms lashed out, keeping him from falling. As he turned to face them, the wind struck at his face, whipping up grit and dust from the dry ground. Getting to the transmitter building would be easy—but with the wind already rising, they'd never be able to fight their way back.

It had already reached this far, losing its force with the distance, but still carrying a wallop. It was beginning to form a pattern, marked by the clouds of dust and debris it was picking up. The arrangement of the shields and entrances in the building formed a perfect suction device to set the air circling around it counterclockwise, twisting into a tornado that funneled down to the portals. Men and women near the building were struggling frantically away from the center of the fury. As he watched, a woman was picked up bodily, whirled around, and gulped down one of the yawning entrances. The wind covered her cries.

Vic motioned Pat and Ptheela and began moving back, fast. Killing himself would do no good. He found one of the little hauling tractors and pulled them onto it with him, heading back until they were out of the worst of the rising wind. Then he swung to face Ptheela.

"All right, now what? Galactic rules be damned, this is an emergency, and I need help!"

The shaggy Plathgolian made an awkward gesture with all three arms, and a slit opened in her chest. "Unprecedented." The word came out in English surprisingly, and Pat's look mirrored his; they weren't supposed to be able to talk. "You're right. If I speak, I shall be banished by our council from Plathgol for breaking security. But we can communicate more fully this way, so ask. I may know more—we've had the Teleport longer—but remember that your strange race has a higher ingenuity quotient."

"Thanks." Vic knew what the five husbands back on her home planet meant to her; they were not only a mark of status, but a chance to have stronger and more capable offspring. But he'd worry about that after he could stop worrying about his own world. "What happens next?"

She dropped back to the faster, if less precise, Galactic Code for that. As he knew, the accidental turning on of the transmitter had keyed in the one on Ecthinbal automatically to receive, but not to transmit; the air was moving between Earth and Ecthinbal in one-way traffic. The receiving circuit, which would have keyed in the Ecthinbal transmit circuit had not been shorted. Continuous transmittal had never been used, to her knowledge; there was no certainty about what would happen. Once started, no outside force could stop a transmitter; the send and stop controls were synchronous, both tapped from a single crystal, and only that proper complex wave form could cut it off. It now existed as a space-strain, and the Plathgolians believed that this would spread, since the outer edges transmitted before matter could reach the center, setting up an unbalanced resonance that would make the field grow larger and larger. Eventually, it might spread far beyond the whole building. And, of course, since the metal used by the Betz II engineers could not be cut or damaged, there was no way of tunneling in.

"What about Ecthinbal?" Pat asked.

Ptheela spread her arms. "The same, in reverse. The air rushes in, builds up pressure to break the capsule, and then rushes out—in a balanced stream, fortunately, so there's no danger of crowding two units of matter in one unit of space."

"Then I guess we'd better call the Galactic Envoy," Vic decided. "All he's ever done is to sit in an office and look smug. Now—"

"He won't come to help. He is simply an observer. Galactic Law says you must solve your own problem or die."

"Yeah." Vic looked at the cloud of dust being whirled into the transmitter building. "And all I need is something that weighs a couple dozen tons per cubic foot—with a good crane attached."

Pat looked up suddenly. "Impossible. But how about one of the small atom-powered army tanks—the streamlined ones? Flavin could probably get you one."

Vic stamped on the pedal, swinging the little tractor around sharply toward the office. The wind was stronger already, but still endurable. He clicked the televisor on, noticing that the dust seemed to disappear just beyond the normal field of the transmitter. It must be starting to spread out.

"How about it?" he asked Ptheela. "If it spreads, won't it start etching into the transmitter and the station?"

"No. Betz II construction. Everything they built in has some way of grounding out the effect. We don't know how it works, but the field won't touch anything put in by the Betzians."

"What about the hunk of glass that's causing the trouble?"

For a moment she looked as if she were trying to appear hopeful. Then the flowerlike head seemed to wilt. "It's inside the casing—protected from the field."

Pat had been working on the private wire to Chicago, used for emergencies. She was obviously having trouble getting put through to Flavin. The man was a sore spot in Teleport Interstellar. He was one of the few political appointees; nominally, he was a go-between for the government and the Teleport group, but actually he was simply a sop to bureaucratic conventions. Finally Pat had him on the screen.

He was jovial enough, as usual, with a red spot on each cheek which indicated too many luncheon drinks. A bottle stood on the desk in front of him. But his voice was clear enough. "Hi, Pat. What's up?"

Pat disregarded the frown Vic threw her and began outlining the situation. The panic in her voice didn't require much feigning, Vic guessed. Flavin blustered at first, then pressed the hold button for long minutes. Finally, his face reappeared.

"Peters, you'll have full authority, of course. And I'll get a few tanks for you, somehow; I have to work indirectly." Then he shrugged and went rueful. "I always knew this sinecure would end. I've got some red slips here that make it look as if you had a national disaster there."

His hand reached for the bottle, just as his eyes met Vic's accusing look. He shook his head, grinned ruefully again, and put the bottle away in a drawer, untouched. "I'm not a fool entirely, Peters. I can do a little more than drink and chase girls. Probably be no use to you, but the only reason I drink is boredom, and I'm not bored now. I'll be out shortly."

In his own field, Flavin was apparently good. The tank arrived by intercity teleport just before he did. They were heavy, squat affairs, super-armored to stand up under a fairly close atomic bomb hit, but small enough to plunge through the portals of the transmitter building. Flavin came up as Vic and Pat were studying them. His suit was designed to hide most of his waistline, but the fat of his jowls shook as he hurried up, and there was sweat on his forehead, trickling down from under his toupee.

"Two, eh? Figured that's what I'd get if I yelled for a dozen. Think you can get in—and what'll you do then?"

Vic shrugged. He'd been wondering the same thing. Still, if they could somehow ram the huge shard of glass and crack it where it was wedged into the wiring inside the shielding, it might release the shorted wires. That should effect an automatic cutoff. "That's why I'm with the driver. I can extemporize if we get in."

"Right," Pat agreed quickly. She caught a hitch in her coveralls and headed for the other tank. "And that's why I'm going with the other."

"Pat!" Vic swung toward her. But it wasn't a time for stupid chivalry. The man or woman who could do the job should do it. He gave her a hand into the compact little tank. "Luck, then. We'll need it."

He climbed into his own vehicle, crowding past the driver and wriggling into the tiny observer's seat. The driver glanced back, then reached for the controls. The motor hummed quietly under them, making itself felt by the vibration of the metal around them. They began moving forward, advancing in low gear. The driver didn't like it, as he stared through his telescreen, and Vic liked it even less from the direct view through the gun slit. Beside them, the other tank got into motion, roughly paralleling them.

At first it wasn't too bad. They headed toward the north portal, traveling cautiously, and the tank seemed snug and secure. Beside him, Vic saw a tree suddenly come up by its roots and head toward the transmitter. It struck the front of the tank, but the machine went on, barely passing the shock through to the two men.

Then the going got rough. The driver swore at the controls, finding the machine hard to handle. It wanted to drift, and he set up a fixed correction, only to revise it a moment later. The tank began to list and pitch. The force of the wind increased by the square inversely as they cut the distance. At fifty feet, the driver's wrists were white from the tiny motions needed to overcome each tilt of the wind.

Vic swallowed, wondering at the nerve of the man driving, until he saw blood running from a bitten lip. His own stomach was pitching wildly. "Try another ten feet?" the driver asked.

"Have to."

"Not bad guts for a civilian, fellow. Okay, here we go."

They crawled by inches now. Every tiny bump threatened to let the force of the wind hit under them and pitch them over. They had to work by feeling, praying against the freak chance that might overcome all their caution. Vic wiped his forehead and wiped it again before he noticed that the palm of his hand was as damp as his brow.

He wondered about Pat, and looked for her. There was no sight of the other machine. Thank God, she'd turned back. But there was bitterness in his relief; he'd figured Pat was one human he could count on completely. Then he looked at the driver's wider view from the screen, and sick shock hit him.

The other tank had turned turtle and was rolling over and over, straight toward the portal! As he looked, a freak accident bounced it up, and it landed on its treads. The driver must have been conscious; only consummate skill accounted for the juggling that kept it upright then. But its forward momentum was still too strong, and it lurched straight toward the portal.

Vic jerked his mouth against the driver's ear, pointing frantically. "Hit it!"

The driver tensed, but nodded. The shriek of the insane wind was too strong for even the sound of the motor, but the tank leaped forward, pushing Vic down in his webbed and padded seat. The chances they were taking now with complete disregard seemed surely fatal, but the driver moved more smoothly with a definite goal. The man let the wind help him pick up speed, jockeying sidewise toward the other tank. They almost turned turtle as they swung, bucking and rocking frantically, but the treads hit the ground firmly again. They were drifting across the wind now, straight toward the nose of the other tank.

Vic was strained forward, and the shock of sudden contact knocked his head against the gun slit. He hardly felt it as he stared out. The two tanks struggled, forcing against each other, while the portal gaped almost straight ahead. "Hit the west edge and we have a chance," Vic yelled in the driver's ear. The man nodded weakly, and his foot pressed down harder on the throttle. Against each other, the two tanks showed little tendency to turn over, but they seemed to be lifted off the ground half the time.

Inch by slow inch, they were making it. Pat's tank was well beyond the portal, but Vic's driver was sweating it out, barely on the edge. He bumped an inch forward, reversed with no care for gears, and hitched forward and back again. They seemed to make little progress, but finally Vic could see the edge move past, and they were out of the direct jet that was being sucked into the portal.

A new screen had lighted beside the driver, and Pat's face was on it, along with the other driver. The scouring of the wind made speech impossible over the speakers, but the man motioned. Vic shook his head, and indicated a spiral counterclockwise and outward, to avoid bucking against the wind, with the two tanks supporting each other.

They passed the south portal somehow, though there were moments when it seemed they must be swung in, and managed to gain ten feet outward on the turn. The next time around, they had doubled that, and it began to be smoother going. The battered tanks lumbered up to their starting point eventually—and a little beyond, since the rising wind had forced everyone farther back.

Vic crawled from the seat, surprised to find his legs stiff and weak; the ground seemed to reel under him. It was some comfort to see that the driver was in no better shape. The man leaned against the tank, letting the raw wind dry the perspiration on his uniform. "Bro-other! Miracles! You're okay, mister, but I wouldn't go in there again with the angel Michael."

Vic looked at the wind maelstrom. Nobody else would go in there, either. Getting within ten feet of the portal was begging for death, even in the tank—and it would get worse. Then he spotted Pat opening the tank hatch and moved over to help her out. She was bruised and more shaky than he, but the webbing over the seat had saved her from broken bones. He lifted her out in his arms, surprised at how light she was. His mind flickered over the picture of her tank twisting over, and his arms tightened around her. She seemed to snuggle into them, seeking comfort.

Her eyes came up, just as he looked at her. She lifted her face, and he met her lips in a firm, brief contact. "You scared hell out of me, Pat."

"Me, too." She was regaining some color, and motioned him to put her down. "I guess you know how I feel about what you did in there."

Flavin cut off any answer Vic could have made, waddling up with his handkerchief out, mopping his face. He stared at them, gulped, and shook his head. "Lazarus twins," he growled. "Better get in the car—there's a drink in the right door pocket."

Vic lifted an eyebrow and Pat nodded. They could use it. They found the car and chauffeur waiting farther back. He poured her a small jigger and took one for himself before putting the bottle back. But the moment's relaxation over cigarettes was better than the drink.

Flavin was talking to the tank drivers, and a small roll changed hands, bringing grins to their faces. For a political opportunist, he seemed a lot more of a man than Vic had expected. Now he came back and climbed in beside them. "I've had the office moved back to Bennington—the intercity teleport manager offered us space." The locally owned world branches of intercity teleport were independent of Teleport Interstellar, but usually granted courtesy exchanges with the latter. "They'll be evacuating the city next, if I know the Governor. Just got a cease-and-desist order—came while you were trying to commit suicide. We're to stop transmitting at once!"

He grunted at Vic's grimace and motioned the chauffeur on, just as a call reached them. Vic shook his head at the driver and looked out to see Ptheela ploughing along against the wind, calling to them. The plant woman's skin was peeling worse than ever.

Flavin followed Vic's eyes. "You aiming to have *that* ride with us? The way Plathies stink? Damned plants, you can't trust 'em. Probably mixed up in this trouble. I heard . . ."

"Plathgol rates higher in civilization than we do," Pat stated flatly.

"Yeah. A million years stealing culture we had to scratch up for ourselves in a thousand. So the Galactic Council tells us we've got to rub our noses to a superior race. Superior *plants!* Nuts!"

Vic opened the door and reached for Pat's hand. Flavin frowned, fidgeted, then reached out to pull them back. "Okay, okay. I told you that you were in charge here. If you want to ride around smelling Plathies—well, you're running things. But don't blame me if people start throwing mud." He had the grace to redden faintly as Ptheela came up finally, and changed the subject hastily. "Why can't we just snap a big hunk of metal over the entrances, to seal them up?"

"Too late," Ptheela answered, sliding down beside Pat, her English drawing a surprised start from Flavin. "I was inspecting those two tanks, and they're field-etched where they touched. That means the field is already outside the building, though it will spread more slowly without the metal to resonate it. Anyhow, how could you get metal plates up?"

"How long will the air last?" Pat asked.

Vic shrugged. "If it keeps increasing, a month at breathing level, maybe. Fortunately the field doesn't spread downward much, with the Betzian design, so it won't start working on the earth itself. Flavin, how about getting the experts here? I need help."

"Already sent for them," Flavin stated. They were heading toward the main part of Bennington now, ten miles from the station. His face was gray, and he no longer seemed to notice the somewhat pervasive odor of Ptheela. They drew up to a converted warehouse finally, and he got out, starting up the steps just as the excited cries of a newsboy reached his ears. He flipped a coin and spread the extra before them.

Word had spread quickly. It was all over the front page, with alarming statements from the scientists first interviewed and soothing statements from later ones. No Teleport Interstellar man had spoken, but an interview with one of the local teleport engineers had given the basic facts, along with some surprisingly keen guesses as to what would happen next.

But above everything was the black headline:

BOMB TRANSMITTER SAYS PAN-ASIA!

The ultimatum issued by Pan-Asia was filled with high-sounding phrases and noble justification, but its basic message was clear enough. Unless the loss of air—air that belonged to everyone—was stopped and all future transmitting of all types halted, together with all dealings with "alien antiterrestrials," Pan-Asia would be forced to bomb the transmitters, together with all other resistance.

"Maybe . . ." Flavin began doubtfully, but Vic cut him off. His faith in mankind's right to its accidental niche in the Galactic Council wasn't increasing much.

"No dice. The field is a space-strain that is permanent, unless canceled by just the right wave form. The canceling crystal is in the transmitter. Destroy that, and the field never can be stopped. It'll keep growing until the whole Earth is gone. Flavin, you'd better get those experts here fast!"

III

Vic sat in the car the next morning, watching the black cloud that swirled around the station, reaching well beyond the old office. His eyes were red, his face was gray with fatigue, and his lanky body was slumped onto the seat. Pat looked almost as tired, though she had gotten some sleep. Now she took the empty coffee cup and thermos from him. She ran a hand through his hair, straightening it, then pulled his head down to her shoulder and began rubbing the back of his neck gently.

Ptheela purred approvingly from the other side, and Pat snorted. "Get your mind off romance, Ptheela! Vic's practically out on his feet. If he weren't so darned stubborn, this should make him go to sleep."

"Romance!" Ptheela chewed the idea and spat it out. "I've read the stories. All spring budding and no seed. A female should have pride from strong husbands and proven seeding."

Vic let them argue. At the moment, Pat's attention was soothing, but only superficially. His head went on fighting for some usable angle and finding none. The men who were supposed to be experts knew no more than he did. He'd swiped all the knowledge he could from Ptheela, without an answer. Plathgol was more advanced than Earth, but far below the Betz II engineers, who were mere servants of the top creatures of the Council.

No wonder man had resented the traffic with other worlds. For centuries he had been the center of his universe. Now, like the Tasmanians, he found himself only an isolated island of savages in a universe that was united in a culture far beyond his understanding. He'd never even conquered his own planets; all he'd done was to build better ways of killing himself.

Now he was reacting typically enough, in urgent need of someone even lower, to put him on middle ground, at least. He was substituting hatred for his lost confidence in himself. Why learn more about matter transmitting when other races knew the answers and were too selfish to share them?

Vic grumbled to himself, remembering the experts. He'd wasted hours with them, to find that they were useless for anything but argument. The names that had been towers of strength had proved no more than handles for men as baffled as he was. With even the limited knowledge he'd pried from Ptheela, he was far ahead of them—and still farther behind the needs of the problem.

The gun Flavin had insisted he wear was uncomfortable, and he pulled himself up, staring at the crew of men who were working as close to the center of wind as they could get. He hadn't been able to convince them that tunneling was hopeless. All they needed was a one-millimeter hole through the flooring, up which blasting powder could be forced to knock aside the glass shard. They refused to accept the fact that the Betz II shielding could resist the best diamond drills under full power for centuries. He shrugged. At least it helped the general morale to see something being done; he'd given in finally and let them have their way.

"We might as well go back," he decided. He'd hoped that the morning air and sight of the station might clear his head, but the weight of responsibility had ruined that. It was ridiculous, but he was still in charge of things.

Flavin reached back and cut on the little television set. With no real understanding, he was trying to learn tolerance of Ptheela, but he felt more comfortable in front, beside the chauffeur.

Pat caught her breath, and Vic looked at the screen, where a newscast was showing a crowd in Denver tearing down one of the Earth-designed intercity teleports. Men were striking back at the menace blindly. A man stood up from his seat in Congress to demand an end to alien intercourse; Vic remembered the fortune in interstellar trading of levo-rotary crystals that had bought the man his seat—and the transmitter-brought drugs that had saved him from death by cancer. He'd spouted gratitude, once!

There were riots in California, the crackpot Knights of Terra were recruiting madly, and murder was on the increase. Rain had fallen in Nevada, and there were severe weather disturbances throughout the country, caused by the unprecedented and disastrously severe low over Bennington. People were complaining of the air, already claiming that they could feel it growing thinner, though that was sheer hysterical nonsense. The Galactic Envoy was missing.

The editorial of the Bennington *Times* came on last, pointing a finger at Vic for changing the circuits, but blaming it on the aliens who hoarded their knowledge so callously. There was just enough truth to be dangerous. Bennington was close enough to the transmitter to explain the undertone of lynch law that permeated the editorial.

"I'll put a stop to that," Flavin told Vic angrily. "I've got enough muscle to make them pull a complete retraction. But it won't undo all of it."

Vic felt the automatic, and it seemed less of a nuisance now. "I notice no news on Pan-Asia's ultimatum."

"Yeah. I hear the story was killed by Presidential emergency orders, and Pan-Asia has agreed to a three-day stay—no more. My information isn't the best, but I gather we'll bomb it with our own bombs if it isn't cleared up by then."

Vic climbed out at the local station office, with the others trailing. In the waiting room, a vaguely catlike male from Sardax waited, clutching a few broken ornaments and a thin sheaf of Galactic credits. One of his four arms was obviously broken and yellow blood oozed from a score of wounds.

But he only shrugged at Vic's whistled questions, and his answer in Code was unperturbed. "No matter. In a few moments, I ship to Chicago and then home. My attackers smelled strongly of hate, but I escaped. Waste no time on me, please."

Then his whistle stopped at a signal from the routing office, and he hurried off, with a final sentence. "My attackers will live, I am told."

Remembering the talons on the male's hands, Vic grinned wryly. The Sardaxians were a peaceful race, but they were pragmatic enough to see no advantage in being killed. The mob had jumped on the wrong alien this time. But the others races . . .

He threw the door to his little office open, and the four went in. It wasn't until he started toward his desk that he noticed his visitor.

The Galactic Envoy might have been the robot he claimed to be, but there was no sign of it. He was dressed casually in expensive tweeds, lounging gracefully in a chair, with a touch of a smile on his face. Now he got up, holding out a hand to Vic.

"I heard you were running things, Peters. Haven't seen you since I helped pick you for the first-year class, but I keep informed.

Thought I'd drop by to tell you the Council has given official approval to your full authority over the Earth branch of Teleport Interstellar, and I've filed the information with the U.N. and your President."

Vic shook his head. Nice of them to throw it all on his shoulders. "Why me?"

"Why not? You've learned all the theory Earth has, you've had more practical experience with more stations than anyone else, and you've picked Ptheela's brains dry by now. Oh, yes, we know about that; it's permissible in an emergency for her to decide to help. You're the obvious man."

"I'd rather see one of your high and mighty Galactic experts take over!"

The Envoy shook his head gently. "No doubt. But we've found that the race causing the trouble usually is the race best fitted to solve it. The same ingenuity that maneuvered this sabotage—it was sabotage, by the way—will help you solve it, perhaps. The Council may not care much for your grab-first rule in economics and politics, but it never doubted that you represent one of the most ingenious races we have met. You see, there really are *no* inferior races."

"Sabotage?" Pat shook her head, apparently trying to grasp it. "Who'd be that stupid?"

The Envoy smiled faintly. "The Knights of Terra are flowing with money, and they are having a very successful recruiting drive. Of course, those responsible had no idea of what risks they were taking for your planet. I've turned the details over, of course."

There was no mistaking his meaning. The Knights of Terra had been a mere rabble of crackpots, without any financial power. But most of the industries forced from competition by the transmitters had been the largest ones, since they tended to lack flexibility. Some of their leaders had taken it in good grace, but many had fought tooth and nail, and were still fighting. There were enough men who had lost jobs, patent royalties, or other valuables due to the transmitters. Even though the standard of living had risen and employment was at a peak now, the period of transition had left bitter hatreds, and recruits for the hate groups should be easy enough to find for a well-heeled propaganda drive.

"Earth for Earth, and down with the transmitters," Vic summed it up. The Envoy nodded.

"They're stupid, of course. They forget that the transmitters can't be removed without Council workers," he said. "And when the Council revokes approval, it destroys *all* equipment and most books, while seeing that three generations are brought up without knowledge. You'd revert to semi-savagery and have to make a fresh start-up. Well, I'll see you, Vic. Good luck."

He left, still smiling. Flavin had been eyeing him with repressed dislike that came out now. "A helluva lot of nerve for guys who claim they don't interfere!"

"It happened to us twice," Ptheela observed. "We were better for it, eventually. The Council's rules are from half a billion years of experience, with tremendous knowledge. We must submit."

"Not without a fight!"

Vic cut in. "Without a fight. We wouldn't have a chance. We're babes in arms to them. Anyhow, who cares? All the Congressional babble in Hades won't save us if we lose our atmosphere. But the so-called leaders can't see it."

The old idea—something would turn up. Maybe they couldn't turn off the transmitter from outside, and had no way of getting past the wind to the inside. But something would turn up!

He'd heard rumors of the Army taking over, and almost wished they would. As it stood, he had full responsibility—and nothing more. Flavin and the Council had turned things over to him, but the local cop on the beat had more power. It would be a relief to have someone around to shout even stupid orders and get some of the weight off his shoulders.

Sabotage! It couldn't even be an accident; the cockeyed race to which he belonged had to try to commit suicide and then expect him to save it.

He shook his head, vaguely conscious of someone banging on the door, and reached for the knob. "Amos!"

The sour face never changed expression as the corpselike figure of the man slouched in. But Amos was dead! He'd been in the transmitter. They all realized it at once and swung toward the man.

Amos shook off their remarks. "Nothing surprising, just common sense. When I saw the capsule start cracking, I jumped for one headed for Plathgol, set the delay, and tripped the switch. Saw some glass shooting at me, but I was in Plathgol next. Went out and got me a mess of *tsiuna*—they cook fair to middling, seeing they never tried it before they met us. Then I showed 'em my pass, came back through Chicago, took the local here, and went home; I figured the old woman would be worried. Nobody told me about the extent of the mess till I saw the papers. Common sense to report in to you, then. So here I am."

"How much did you see of the explosion?" Pat asked.

"Not much. Just saw it was cracking—trick glass, no temperature tolerance. Looked like Earth color."

It didn't matter. It added to Vic's disgust to believe it was sabotage, but didn't change the picture otherwise. The Council wouldn't change its decision. They treated a race as a unit, making no exception for the behavior of a few individuals, whether good or bad.

Another knock on the door cut off the vicious cycle of hopelessness. "Old home week, evidently. *Come in!*"

The uniformed man who entered was the rare example of a fat man in the pink of physical condition, with no sign of softness. He shoved his bulk through the doorway as if he expected the two stars on his shoulders to light the way and awe all beholders. "Who is Victor Peters?"

Vic wiggled a finger at himself, and the general came over. He drew out an envelope and dropped it on the desk, showing clearly that acting as a messenger was far beneath his dignity. "An official communication from the President of the United States!" he said mechanically, and turned to make his exit back to the intercity transmitters.

It was a plain envelope, without benefit of wax or seals. Vic ripped it open, looked at the signature and the simple letterhead, and checked the signature again. He read it aloud to the others:

"'To Mr.'—dammit, officially I've got a doctor's degree!—'to Mr. Victor Peters, nominally'—oof!—'in charge of the Bennington branch of Teleport Interstellar'—I guess they didn't tell him it's *nominally* in charge of all Earth branches. Umm . . . 'You are hereby instructed to remove all personnel from a radius of five miles minimum of your Teleport branch not later than noon, August 21, unless matters shall be satisfactorily culminated prior to that time. Signed, Homer Wilkes, President of the United States of America.'"

"Bombs!" Pat shuddered, while Vic let the message fall to the floor, kicking it toward the wastebasket. "That's what it has to mean. The fools—the damned fools! Couldn't they tell him what would happen? Couldn't they make him see that it'll only make turning the transmitter off impossible—forever?"

Flavin shrugged, unconsciously dropping onto the couch beside Ptheela. "Maybe he had no choice—either he does it or some other power does it."

Then he came to his feet, staring at Vic. "My God, that's *tomorrow* noon!"

IV

Vic looked at the clock later and was surprised to see that it was already well into the afternoon. The others had left him, Ptheela last when she found there was no more knowledge she could contribute. He had one of the electronic calculators plugged in beside him and a table of the so-called Dirac functions propped up on it; since the press had discovered that Dirac had predicted some of the characteristics that made teleportation possible, they'd named everything for him.

The wastebasket was filled, and the result was further futility. He shoved the last sheet into it, and sat there, pondering. There had to be a solution! Man's whole philosophy was built on that idea.

But it was a philosophy that included sabotage and suicide. What did it matter any . . .

Vic jerked his head up, shaking it savagely, forcing the fatigue back by sheer will. There *was* a solution. All he had to do was find it —before the stupidity of war politics in a world connected to a Galaxy-wide union could prevent it.

He pulled the calculator back, just as Flavin came into the room. The man was losing weight, or else fatigue was creating that illusion. He dropped into a chair as Vic looked up.

"The men evacuated from around the station?" Vic asked.

Flavin nodded. "Yeah. Some of the bright boys finally convinced them that they were just wasting time, anyhow. Besides, the thing is still spreading and getting too close for them. Vic, the news gets worse all the time. Can you take it?"

"Now what? Don't tell me they've changed it to tomorrow morning?"

"Tomorrow hell! *In two hours* they're sending over straight blockbusters, radar controlled all the way. No atomics—yet—but they're jumping the gun, anyhow. Some nut convinced Wilkes that an ordinary eight-ton job might just shake things enough to fracture the glass that's holding the short. And Pan-Asia is going completely wild. I've been talking to Wilkes. The Generalissimo over there probably only wanted to make a big fuss, but the people are scared silly, and they're preparing for quick war."

Vic nodded reluctantly and reached for the Benzedrine he'd hoped to save for the last possible moment, when it might carry him all the way through. What difference did it make? Even if he had an idea, he'd be unable to use it because a bunch of hopheads were busy picking themselves the station as a site for target practice.

"And yet . . ." He considered it more carefully, trying to figure percentages. There wasn't a chance in a million, but they had to take even that one chance. It was better than nothing.

"It might just work—if they hit the right spot. I know where the glass is, and the layout of the station. But I'll need authority to direct the bomb. Flavin, can you get me President Wilkes?"

Flavin shrugged and reached for the televisor. He managed to get quite a ways up by some form of code, but then it began to be a game of nerves and brass. Along his own lines, he apparently knew his business. In less than five minutes, Vic was talking to the President. For a further few minutes, the screen remained blank. Then another face came on, this time in military uniform, asking quick questions, while Vic pointed out the proper target.

Finally the officer nodded. "Good enough, Peters. We'll try it. If you care to watch, you can join the observers—Mr. Flavin already knows where they will be. How are the chances?"

"Not good. Worth trying."

The screen darkened again and Flavin got up. The thing was a wild gamble, but it was better to jar the building than to melt its almost impregnable walls. Even Betz II metal couldn't take a series of hydrogen bombs without melting, though nothing else could hurt it. And with that fury, the whole station would go.

They picked up Pat and moved out to Flavin's car. Vic knew better than to try to bring Ptheela along. As an alien, she was definitely taboo around military affairs. The storm had reached the city now, and dense clouds were pouring down thick gouts of rain, leaving the day as black as night. The car slogged through it, until Flavin opened the door and motioned them out into a temporary metal shelter.

Things were already started. Remote scanners were watching the guided missiles come down, and mechanical eyes were operating in the bombs, working on infrared that cut through the rain and darkness. It seemed to move slowly on the screen at first, but picked up apparent speed as it drew near the transmitter building. The shielding grew close, and Pat drew back with an involuntary jerk as it hit and the screen went blank. Dead center.

But the remote scanners showed no change. The abrupt break in the airmotion where the transmitter field began, outside the shielding, still showed. Another bomb came down, and others, each spaced so as to hit in time for others to be turned back if it worked. Even through the impossible tornado of rotating fury, it was super-precision bombing.

But the field went on working, far beyond the shielding, pulling an impossible number of cubic feet of air from Earth every second. They stopped watching the screen shown by the bomb-eyes at last, and even the Army gave up.

"Funny," one observer commented. "No sound, no flash when it hits. I've been watching the remote scanners every time instead of the eye, and nothing happens. The bomb just disappears."

Pat shook herself. "The field—they *can't* hit it. They go right through the field, before they can hit. Vic, it won't matter if we do atom-bomb the station. It can't be reached."

But he was already ahead of her. "Fine. Ecthinbal will love that. The Ecthindar wake up to find exploding atomic bombs coming at them through the transmitter. They've already been dosed with our chemical bombs. Now guess what they'll have to do."

"Simple." It was the observer who got that. "Start feeding atom bombs into their transmitters to us. We get keyed in to receive automatically, right? And we receive enough to turn the whole planet radioactive."

Then he shouted hoarsely, pointing through a window. From the direction of the station, a dazzle of light had lanced out sharply, and was now fading down. Vic snapped back to the remote scanner and scowled. The field was still working, and there was no sign of damage to the transmitter. If the Ecthindar had somehow snapped a bomb into the station, it must have been retransmitted before full damage.

The Army man stared sickly at the station, but Vic was already moving toward the door. Pat grabbed his arm, and Flavin was with them by the time they reached the waiting car. "The Bennington office," Vic told the driver. "And fast! Somebody has to see the Ecthindar in a hurry, if it'll do any good."

"I'm going too, Vic," Pat announced. But he shook his head. Her lips firmed. "I'm going. Nobody knows much about Ecthinbal or the Ecthindar. You call in Code messages, get routine Code back. We can't go there without fancy pressure suits, because we can't breathe their air. And they never leave. But I told you I was interested in races, and I have been trying to chitchat with them. I know some things—and you'll need me."

He shook his head again. "They'll probably welcome us with open arms—firearms! It's enough for one of us to get killed. If I fail, Amos can try—or Flavin. If he fails—well, suit yourself. It won't matter whether they kill me there or send through bombs to kill me here. But if one of us can get a chance to explain, it may make some difference. I dunno. But it may."

Her eyes were hurt, but she gave in, going with him silently as he stepped into the local Bennington unit and stepped out in Chicago, heading toward the Chicago Interstellar branch. She waited patiently while the controlmen scouted out a pressure suit for him. Then she began helping him fasten it and checking his oxygen equipment. "Come on back, Vic," she said finally.

He chucked a fist under her chin lightly and kissed her quickly, keeping it casual with a sureness he couldn't feel. "You're a good kid, Pat. I'll sure try."

He pulled the helmet down and clicked it shut before stepping into the capsule and letting the seal shut. He could see her swing to the interstellar phone, her lips pursed in whistled code. The sound was muffled, but the lights changed abruptly, and her hand hit the switch.

There was no noticeable time involved. He was simply on Ecthinbal, looking at a faintly greenish atmosphere, observable only because of the sudden change, and fifty pounds seemed to have been added to his weight. The transmitter was the usual Betz II design, and everything else was familiar except for the creature standing beside the capsule.

The Ecthindar might have been a creation out of green glass, coated with a soft fur, and blown by a bottle-maker who enjoyed novelty. There were two thin, long legs, multijoined, and something that faintly resembled the pelvis of a skeleton. Above that, two other thin rods ran up, with a double bulb where lungs might have been, and shoulders like the collar pads of a football player, joined together and topped by four hard knobs, each with a single eye and orifice. Double arms ran from each shoulder, almost to the ground.

He expected to hear a tinkle when the creature moved, and was surprised when he did hear it, until he realized the sound was carried through the metal floor, not through the thin air.

The creature swung open the capsule door after some incomprehensible process that probably served to sterilize it. Its Galactic Code whistle came from a device on its feet and through Vic's shoes from the floor. The air was too thin to transmit sound normally. "We greet you, Earthman. Our mansions are poor, but yours. Our lives are at your disposal." Then the formal speech ended in a sharp whistle. "Literally, it would seem. We die."

It didn't fit with Vic's expectations, but he tried to take his cue from it. "That's why I'm here. Do you have some kind of a ruler? Umm, good. How do I get to see this ruler?" He had few hopes of getting to see the ruler, but it never did any harm to try.

The Ecthindar seemed unsurprised. "Of course, I shall take you at once. For what other purpose is a ruler but to serve those who wish to see it. But—I trespass on your kindness in the delay—but may I question whether a strange light came forth from your defective transmitter?"

Vic snapped a look at it and nodded slowly. "It did."

Now the ax would fall. He braced himself for it, but the creature ceremoniously repeated his nod.

"I was one who believed it might. It is most comforting to know my science was true. When the bombs came through from you, we held them in an instant shield, since we had expected some such effort on your part to correct your transmitter. But in our error, we believed them radioactive. We tried a new negative aspect of space to counteract them. Of course, it failed, since they were only chemical. But I had postulated that some might have escaped from receiver to transmitter, being negative. You are kind. You confirm my belief. And now, if you will honor my shoulder with the touch of your hand, so that my portable unit will transport us both . . ."

Vic reached out and the scene shifted at once. There was no apparent transmitter, and the trick beat anything he had heard from other planets. Perhaps it was totally unrelated to the teleport machine. But he had no time to ask.

A door in the little room where they were now opened, and another creature came in, this time single from pelvis to shoulders, but otherwise the same. "The ruler has been requested," it whistled. "That which the ruler is shall be yours, and that which the ruler has is nothing. May the ruler serve?"

It was either the most cockeyed bit of naïveté or the fanciest runaround Vic had found, but totally unlike anything he'd been prepared for. He gulped and began whistling out the general situation on Earth.

The Ecthindar interrupted politely. "That we know. And the converse is true—we too are dying. We are a planet of thin air, and that little is chlorine. Now from a matter transmitter comes a great rush of oxygen, which we consider poison. Our homes around are burned in it, our plant life is dying of it, and we are forced to remain inside and seal ourselves off. Like you, we can do nothing—the wind from your world is beyond our strength."

"But your science . . ."

"Is beyond yours, true. As is our *average* intelligence. We run from an arbitrary lowest of one to a highest of two relatively, however, while you run from perhaps a low of an eighth to a high of nearly three, as we figure. We lack both your very lows and your genius level—some of you are more intelligent than any of us, though very few. But you are all adaptable, and we are too leisurely a race for that virtue."

Vic shook his head, but perhaps it made good sense. "But the bombs . . ."

A series of graceful gestures took place between the two creatures, and the Ruler turned back to Vic.

"The ruler had not known, of course. It was not important. We lost a few thousand people whom we love. But we understood. There is no anger, though it pleases us to see that your courtesy extends across space to us in commiseration. May your dead pass well."

That was at least one good break in the situation. Vic felt some of his worry slide aside to make room for the rest. "Then I don't suppose . . . Well, then, have you any ideas on how we can take care of this mess. . . ."

There was a shocked moment, with abrupt movements from the two creatures. Then something came up in the Ruler's hands, vibrating sharply. Vic jumped back—and froze in mid-stride, to fall awkwardly onto the floor. A chunk of ice seemed to form in his backbone and creep along his spine, until it touched his brain. Death or paralysis? It was all the same—he had air for only an hour more. The two creatures were fluttering at each other and moving toward him when he blacked out.

V

His first feeling was the familiar, deadening pull of fatigue as his senses began to come back. Then he saw that he was in a tiny room —and that Pat lay stretched out beside him!

He threw himself up to a sitting position, surprised to find that there were no aftereffects to whatever the Ruler had used. The darned fool, coming through after him! And now they had her, too.

Surprisingly, her eyes snapped open, and she sat up beside him. "Darn it, I almost fell asleep waiting for you to revive. It's a good thing I brought extra oxygen flasks. Your hour is about up. How'd you insult them?"

He puzzled over it while she changed his oxygen flask and he did the same for her. "I didn't. I just asked whether there wasn't some way we could take care of this trouble."

"Which meant to them that you suspected they weren't giving all the help they could—after their formal offer when you came over. I convinced them it was just that you were still learning Code, whatever you said. They're nice, Vic. I never really believed other races were better than we are, but I do now—and it doesn't bother me at all."

"It'd bother Flavin. He'd have to prove they were sissies or something. How do we get out?"

She pushed the door open, and they stepped back into the room of the Ruler, who was waiting for them. It made no reference to the misunderstanding, but inspected him, whistled approval of his condition, and plunged straight to business.

"We have found part of a solution, Earthman. We die—but it will be two weeks before our end. First, we shall set up a transmitter in permanent transmit, equipped with a precipitator to remove our chlorine, and key it to another of your transmitters—whichever one you wish. Ecthinbal is heavy but small, and a balance will be struck between the air going from you and the air returning. The winds between stations may disturb your weather, but not seriously, we hope. That which the Ruler is, is yours. A lovely passing."

It touched their shoulders, and they were back briefly in the transmitter, to be almost instantly back in the Chicago branch. Vic was still shaking his head.

"It won't work—the Ruler didn't allow for the way our gravity falls off and our air thins out a few miles higher up. We'd end up with maybe four pounds pressure, which isn't enough. So we both die—two worlds on my shoulders instead of one. Hell, we couldn't take that offer from them, anyhow. Pat, how'd you convince them to let me go?"

She had shucked out of the pressure suit and stood combing her hair. "Common sense, as Amos says. I figured engineers consider each other engineers first and aliens second, so I went to the head engineer instead of the Ruler. He fixed it up somehow. I guess I must have sounded pretty desperate, at that, knowing your air would give out after an hour."

They went through the local intercity to Bennington, and on into

Vic's office, where Flavin met them with open relief and a load of questions. Vic let Pat answer, while he mulled over her words. Somewhere, there was an idea—let the rulers alone and go to the engineers. Some obvious solution that the administrators would try to understand, run into their preconceptions, and be unable to use? He shoved it around in his floating memory, but it refused to trigger an idea.

Pat was finishing the account of the Ecthindar offer, but Flavin was not impressed. Ptheela came in, and it had to be repeated for her, with much more enthusiastic response.

"So what?" Flavin asked. "They have to die, anyhow. Sure, it's a shame, but we have our own problems. Hey—wait. Maybe there's something to it. It'd take some guts and a little risk, but it might work."

Flavin considered it while Vic waited, willing to listen to any scheme. The man took a cigar out and lit it carefully, his first since the accident; he'd felt smoking used up the air. "Look, if they work their transmitter, we end up with a quarter of what we need. But suppose we had four sources. We connect with several oxygen-atmosphere worlds. Okay, we load our transmitters with delayed-action atom bombs and send one sample capsule to each world. After that, they either open a transmitter to us with air, or we really let them have it. They can live—a little poorer, maybe, but still live. And we're fixed for good. Congress and the President would jump at it."

"That all?" Vic asked.

Flavin nodded, just as Vic's fist caught him in the mouth, spilling him onto the floor. The man lay there, feeling his jaw and staring up at Vic. Then the anger was gone, and Vic reached down to help him up.

"You're half a decent guy and half a louse," he told Flavin. "You had that coming, but I should have used it on some of the real lice around. Besides, maybe you have part of an idea."

"'Sall right, no teeth lost—just the first cigar I've enjoyed in days." Flavin rubbed his jaw gingerly, then grinned ruefully. "I should have known how you feel. But I believe in Earth first. What's this big idea of yours?"

"Getting our air through other planets. *Our* air. It's a routing job. If we can set up a chain so the air going out of one transmitter in a station is balanced by air coming in another in the same station, there'd be a terrific draft; but most of it would be confined in the station, and there wouldn't be the outside whirlwind to keep us from getting near. Instead of a mad rush of air in or out of the building, there'd be only eddy currents outside of the inner chamber. We'd keep our air, and maybe have time to figure out some way of getting at that hunk of glass."

"Vic! You honey!" Pat's shoulders straightened. But Flavin shook his head.

"Won't work. Suppose Wilkes was asked to permit us to route through like that for another planet—he'd have to turn it down. Too much risk, and he has to consider our safety first."

"That's where Pat gave me the tip. Engineers get used to thinking of each other as engineers instead of competing races—they have to work together. They have the same problems and develop the same working habits. If I were running a station and the idea was put to me, I'd hate to turn it down, and I might not think of the political end. I've always wanted to see what happened in continuous transmittal; I'll be tickled pink to get at the instrument rolls in the station. And a lot of other engineers will feel the same."

"We're already keyed to Plathgol on a second transmitter in there," Pat added. "They could send to us, though the other four transmitters were out of duty. And the Ecthindar indicated they had full operation when it happened, so they're keyed to five other planets that could trigger them to transmit. But they don't connect to Plathgol, as I remember the charts."

"Bomb dropping starts in about four hours," Flavin commented. "Atomic, this time. After that, what?"

"No chance. They'll go straight through, and the Ecthindar can neutralize them—but one is pretty sure to start blasting here and carry through in full action. Then there'll be no other transmitter in their station. Just a big field on permanent receive."

"Then we'd better find a route from Ecthinbal to Plathgol—and get a lot of permissions—pronto!" Flavin decided. "And we need all the charts we can find."

The engineers at the Chicago branch were busy shooting dice when the four came through the intercity transmitter. Ptheela had asked to accompany the three humans, and her offer was welcome. More precisely, two engineers were playing. There was no one else in the place, and no sign of activity. Word of the proposed bombing had leaked out and the engineers had figured that answering bombs would come blasting back through all Earth teleports. They knew what Earth governments would have done and didn't know of the Ecthindar philosophy. The engineers had passed the word to other employees, and only these two were left, finishing a feud of long standing in the time left.

"Know anything about routing?" Vic asked. He'd already looked in the big barnlike building just outside the main shell, now empty of its normal crew. When they indicated no knowledge, he chased them out on his Teleport Interstellar authority and took over. He had no need of more engineers, and they were cynical enough about the eventual chances there to leave gladly. Vic had never had any use for Chicago's manager and the brash young crew he'd built up; word shouldn't have gone beyond the top level. If it leaked out to the general public, there'd be panic for miles around.

But Chicago's routing setup was the best in the country, and he needed it. Now how did he go about getting a staff trained to use it?

"Know how to find things here?" Flavin asked Pat. He accepted her nod, and looked surprised at Ptheela's equally quick assent. Then he grinned at Vic and began shucking off his coat. "Okay, you see before you one of the best traffic managers that ever helped pull a two-bit railroad out of the red, before I got better offers in politics. I'm good. You get me the dope, Vic can haggle on the transmitter phones, and I'll route it."

He *was* good. His mind could look at the complicated interlocking block of transmitter groups and jump to the next step without apparent thought—and he had to have information only once before engraving it on his mind. It was a tough nut, since the stations housed six transmitters, keyed to six planets each—but in highly varied combinations; each world had its own group of tie-ins with planets. Routing was the most complicated job in the work.

Plathgol was handled by Ptheela, who was still in good standing until her council was informed of her breaking the Law by talking to Vic. There was no trouble there. But trouble soon developed. The Ecthinbal station had been keyed to only two other planets when the accident happened, it turned out. Vromatchk was completely cold on the idea and flatly refused. Ee, the other, seemed difficult.

It surprised Vic, because it didn't fit with Pat's theories of engineers at all. He scowled at the phone, then whistled again. "All right, no matter. Your zeal is commendable. Now put an engineer on!"

The answering whistle carried a fumbling uncertainty of obvious surprise. "I—how'd you know? I gave all the right answers."

"Sure. Right off the Engineer Rule Sheet posted over the transmitter. No real engineer worries that much about them—he has more things to think of. Put the engineer on."

The answer was obstinate. "My father's asleep. He's tired. Call later."

The connection went dead at once. Vic called Ecthinbal while clambering into the big pressure suit. He threw the delay switch and climbed into the right capsule. A moment later, an Ecthindar was moving the capsule on a delicate-looking machine to another transmitter. Something that looked like a small tyranosaurus with about twenty tentacles instead of forelegs was staring at him a second later, and he knew he was on Ee.

"Take me to the engineer!" he ordered. "At once."

The great ridges of horny substance over the eyes came down in a surprisingly human scowl. But the stubbornness was less certain in person. The creature turned and led Vic out to a huge shack outside. In answer to a whooping cry, a head the size of a medium-large car came out of the door, to be followed by a titanic body. The full-grown adult was covered with a thick coat of ropy hair.

"Where from?" the Ee engineer whistled. "Wait—I saw a picture. Earth? Come in. I hear you have quite a problem down there."

Vic nodded. It came as a shock to him that the creature could probably handle the whole station by itself, as it obviously did, and quite efficiently, with that size and set of tentacles. He stated the problem quickly.

The Looech, as it called itself, scratched its stomach with a row of tentacles and pondered. "I'd like to help you. Oh, the empress would have fits, but I could call it an accident. We engineers aren't really responsible to governments, after all, are we? But it's the busy season. I'm already behind, since my other engineer got in a duel. That's why the pup was tending while I slept. You say the field spreads out on continuous transmit?"

"It does, but it wouldn't much, if there isn't too long a period of operation."

"Strange. I've thought of continuous transmittal, of course, but I didn't suspect that. Why, I wonder?"

Vic started to give Ptheela's explanation of unbalanced resonance between the vacuum of the center and the edges in contact with matter, but dropped it quickly. "I'll probably know better when I can read the results from the instruments."

The Looech grumbled to itself. "I suppose you wouldn't send me the readings—we're about on a Galactic level, so it wouldn't strain the law too much."

Vic shook his head. "If I can't complete the chain, there won't be any readings. I imagine you could install remote cutoffs fairly easily."

"No trouble, though nobody ever seemed to think of them. I suppose it could be covered under our emergency powers, if we stretch them a little. Oh, blast you. Now I won't sleep for worrying about why it spreads. When will you begin?"

Vic grinned tightly as they arranged the approximate time and let the Looech carry him back to the capsule. He flashed through Ecthinbal and climbed out of the Chicago transmitter to find Pat looking worriedly at the capsule, summoned by the untended call announcer.

"You're right, Pat," he told her. "Engineers run pretty much to form. Tell Flavin we've got Ee."

But there were a lot of steps to be taken still. He ran into a stumbling block at Noral, and had to wait for a change of shifts, before a sympathetic engineer cut the red tape to clear him. And negative decisions here and there kept Flavin jumping to find new routes.

They almost made it, to find a decision had been reversed on them by some authority who had gotten word of the deal. That meant that other authorities would probably be called in, with more reverses, in time. Once operating, the engineer could laugh at authority, since the remote cutoff could be easily hidden. But time was running out. There were only twenty-seven minutes left before the bombs would be finally ordered dropped, and it would take fifteen to countermand their being dropped.

"Give me that," Flavin ordered, grabbing the phone. "There are times when it takes executives instead of engineers. We're broken at Seloo. Okay, we don't know where Seloo ships." His Galactic Code was halting, but fairly effective. The mechanical chirps from the Seloo operator leaped to sudden haste. A short pause was followed by an argument Vic was too tired to catch until the final sentence of assent. Then Pat took over, to report shortly to Flavin. "Enad to Brjd to Teeni clear."

"Never heard of Brjd," Vic commented.

Flavin managed a ghost of a swagger. "Figured our lists were only partial and we could stir up another link. Here's the final list. I'll get in touch with President Wilkes—now that we've got it, he'll hold off until we see how it works."

It was a maze, but the list was complete; from Earth to Ecthinbal, Ee, Petzby, Noral, Szpendrknopalavotschel, Seloo, Brjd, Teeni, and finally through Plathgol to Earth. Vic whistled the given signal and the acknowledgments came through. It was in operation. And Flavin's nod indicated Wilkes had confirmed it and held off the bombs.

Nothing was certain, still; it might or might not do the trick. But the tension dropped somewhat. Flavin was completely beaten. He hadn't had decent exercise for years, and running from communications to routing had been almost continual. He flopped over on a shipping table. Ptheela bent over him and began massaging him with deft strokes of her arms. He grumbled, but gave in, then sighed gratefully.

"Where'd you learn that?"

She managed an Earth giggle. "Instinct. My ancestors were plants that caught animals for food. We had all manner of ways to entice them—not just odor and looks. I can feel exactly how your body feels in the back of my head. Umm, delicious!"

He struggled at that picture, his face changing color. Her arms moved slowly, and he relaxed. Finally he reached for a cigar. "I'll have nightmares, I'll bet—but it's worth it. Oh-oh, some of the rulers are catching on, and don't like it!"

The minimum staff left in Bennington was reporting by normal televisor contact, but while things seemed to be improving, they couldn't get near enough to be sure. The tornado around the city was abating, they thought, but Earth's weather patterns were slow to change, once thoroughly upset. The field was apparently collapsing as the air was fed inside it, but very slowly.

Ptheela needed no sleep, but Flavin was already snoring. Pat shook her head as Vic started to pull himself up on a table. She led him outside to the back of one of the sheds, where a blanket lay on a cot, apparently used by one of the supervisors. She pushed him toward it. As he started to struggle at the idea of using the only soft bed, she dropped onto it herself and pulled him down.

"Don't be silly, Vic. It's big enough for both, and it's better than those tables."

It felt like pure heaven, narrow through it was. But his body was too tired to respond properly. The tension remained, reminding him that nothing was sure yet. Beside him, Pat stirred restlessly. He rolled over, pulling himself closer to her, off the hard edge of the cot, his arm over and around her.

For a moment, he thought she was protesting, but she merely turned over to face him, settling his arm back. In the half-light, her eyes met his, wide and serious. Her lips trembled briefly under his, then clung firmly. Her body slid against him, drawing tighter, and his own responded, reaching for the comfort and end of tension hers could bring.

It was automatic, almost unconscious, and yet somehow warm and personal, with an edge of tenderness all the cloudiness of it could not dull. Then she lay relaxed in his arms while his own muscles released themselves to the soft comfort of the cot. She smiled faintly, pushing his hair back.

"I'm glad it's you, Vic," she said softly. Then her eyes closed as he started to answer, and his own words disappeared into a soft fog of sleep.

The harsh rasp of a buzzer woke him, while a light blinked on and off near his head. He shook some of the sleep confusion out of his thoughts and made out an intercom box. Flavin's voice came over it sharply as he flipped the switch.

"Vic—where the hell are you? Never mind. Wilkes just woke me with his call. Vic, it's helped—but not enough. The field is about even with the building now. But it's stopped shrinking, and we're still losing air. There's too much loss at Ecthinbal, and at Ee—the engineer there didn't get the portals capped right, and Ecthinbal can't do anything. We're getting about two thirds of our air back. And Wilkes can't hold the pressure for bombing much longer! Get in here!"

VI

"Where's Ptheela?" Vic asked as he came into the communication and transmitter room. She needed no sleep and should have been taking care of things.

"Gone—back to Plathgol, I guess. Said something about an appeal. She was flicking out by the time I really woke up. Rats deserting the sinking ship, seems to me—though I had her figured different. It just shows you can't trust a plant."

Vic swept his attention to the communicator panel. The phones were still busy. They were still patient—even the doubtful ones were now accepting things; but it couldn't last forever. Even without the risk, the transmitter banks were needed for regular use. Many did not have inexhaustible power sources, either.

A new note cut in over the whistling now, and he turned to the

Plathgol phone, wondering what Ptheela wanted. The words were English. But the voice was different.

"Plathgol calling. This is Thlegaa, Wife of Twelve Husbands, Supreme Plathgol Teleport Engineer, Ruler of the Council of United Plathgol, and Hereditary Goddess, if you want the whole routine. Ptheela just gave me the bad news. Why didn't you call on us before —or isn't our air good enough for you?"

"Hell, do you all speak English?" Vic asked, too surprised to care whether he censored his thoughts. "Your air always smelled good to me. Are you serious?"

The chuckle this time wasn't a mere imitation. Thlegaa had her intonation down exactly. "Sonny, up here we speak whatever our cultural neighbors do. You should hear my French nasals and Hebrew rough-breathings. Now that you know we can speak, there's no point in keeping the law against free communication. And I'm absolutely on the level. We're pulling the stops off the transmitter housing. We run a trifle higher pressure than you, so we'll probably make up your whole loss. But I'm not an absolute ruler, so it might be a good idea to speed things up. You can thank me later. Oh—since she broke the law before it was repealed, Ptheela's been exiled. So when you get your Bennington plant working, she'll probably be your first load from us. She's packing now."

Flavin's face held too much relief. Vic hated to disillusion him as the man babbled happily about knowing deep down all along that the Plathgolians were swell people. But he knew the job was a long ways from solved. With Plathgol supplying extra air, the field would collapse back to the inside of the single transmitter housing, and there should be an even balance of ingoing and outcoming air, which would end the rush of air into the station and make the circular halls passable, except for eddy currents. But getting into the inner chamber, where the air formed a gale between the two transmitters, was another matter.

Flavin's chauffeur was asleep at the wheel of the car as they came out of the Bennington local office, but instinct seemed to rouse him, and the car cut off wildly for the Interstellar station. Vic had noticed that the cloud around it was gone, and a mass of people were grouped nearby. The wind that had been sucked in and around it to prevent even a tank getting through was gone now, though the atmosphere would probably show signs of it in freak weather reports for weeks after.

Pat had obviously figured out the trouble remaining, and didn't look too surprised at the gloomy faces of the transmitter crew who were grouped near the north entrance. But she began swearing under her breath, as methodically and levelly as a man. Vic was ripping his shirt off as they drew up.

"This time you stay out," he told her. "It's strictly a matter of muscle power against wind resistance—and a man has a woman beat there."

"Why do you think I was cursing?" she asked. "Take it easy, though."

The men opened a way for him. He stripped to his briefs and let them smear him with oil to cut down air resistance a final fraction. Eddy currents caught at him before he went in, but not too strongly. Getting past the first shielding wasn't too bad. He found the second entrance port through the middle shield and snapped a chain around his waist.

Then the full picture of what must have happened on Plathgol hit him. Chains wouldn't have helped when they pulled off the coverings from the entrances—the sudden rush of air must have crushed their lungs and broken their bones—or whatever supported them—no matter what was done. Imagine volunteering for sure death to help another world! He had to make good on his part.

He got to the inner portal, but the eddies there were too strong to go farther. Even sticking his head beyond the edge almost sucked him into the blast between the two transmitters. Then he was crawling out again.

Amos met him, shaking a gloomy head. "Never make it, Vic. Common sense. I've been partway in there three times with no luck. And the way that draft blows, it'd knock even a tractor plumb out of the way before it could reach that glass."

Vic nodded. The tanks would take too long, anyhow, though it would be a good idea to have them called. He yelled to Flavin, who came over at a run, while Vic was making sure that the little regular office building still stood.

"Order the tanks, if we need them," he suggested. "And get them to ship in a rifle, some hard-nosed bullets, an all-angle vise big enough to clamp on a three-inch edge, and two of those midget telesets for use between house and field—quick."

Amos stared at him, puzzled, but Flavin's car was already roaring toward Bennington, with a couple of cops leading the way with open sirens. He was back with everything in twenty minutes.

Vic motioned to Amos questioningly and received an answering nod. The man was old, but he must be tough to have made three tries inside. Pat was setting the midget pickup in front of the still-operating televisor between the transmitter chamber and the little office. Vic picked up the receiver and handed the rest of the equipment to Amos.

It was sheer torture fighting back to the inner entrance port, but they made it, and Amos helped to brace him with the chain while Vic clamped the vise to the edge of the portal and locked the rifle into it, somehow fighting it into place. In the rather ill-defined picture on the tiny set's screen, he could see the shard of glass, out of line from either entrance, between two covering uprights. He could just see the rifle barrel, also. The picture lost detail in being transmitted to the little office and picked up from the screen for retransmittal back to him, but it would have to do.

The rifle was loaded to capacity with fourteen cartridges. He lined it up as best he could and tightened the vise, before pulling the trigger. The bullet ricocheted from the inner shield and headed toward the glass—but it missed by a good three feet.

He was close on the fifth try—not over four inches off. But clinging to the edge while he reset the vise each time before he pulled the trigger was getting harder, and the wind velocity inside was tossing the bullets off course.

He left the setting and fired four more shots in succession before he had to stop to rest. They were all close, but scattered. That could keep up all day, seemingly.

"Better let me try, Vic," Amos shouted over the roar of the wind inside. "Been playing pool, making bank shots, more than thirty years. And I had a rifle in my hands long before that."

He pulled himself into place, made a trifling adjustment on the vise setting, and squeezed the trigger. Then he leaned against the rifle stock slightly, took a deep breath, let it out, and fired again. There was no sound over the roar of the wind—and then there was a sound, as if the gale in there had stopped to cough.

A blast of air struck them, picking them up and tossing them against the wall. Vic had forgotten the lag before the incoming air could be cut! And it could be as fatal as the inrush alone.

But it was dying as he struck. His flesh was bruised from the shock, but it wasn't serious. Plathgol had managed to make their remote control cut out almost to the microsecond of the time when the flow to them had stopped, or the first pressure released—and transmitter waves were supposed to be instantaneous.

He tasted the feeling of triumph as he crawled painfully back. With this transmitter off and the others remotely controlled, the whole business was over. Ecthinbal had keyed out automatically when Earth stopped sending. And from now on, every transmitter would have a full set of remote controls, so the trouble could never happen again.

He staggered out, unhooking the chain, while workmen went rushing in. Pat came through the crowd with a towel and a pair of pants, to begin wiping the oil off him while he tried to dress. Her grin was a bit shaky, and he knew it must have looked bad when the final counterblast whipped out.

Amos was busy cleaning himself off, and Vic grinned at him. "Good shooting, Amos. I guess it's all solved."

The old man nodded. "Sure. Took a little common sense, that's all."

From the crowd, the Galactic Envoy shoved through, holding out his hands to them and smiling. "Co-operative sense, you mean, and that's not as common as it should be on any world. And, Amos, you'll be glad to know you're not under suspicion any longer. I have been able to furnish your government with a list of the real saboteurs, and they're all in custody. As I told you, I'm only an observer—but a very good observer of all that goes on!"

"Figured I'd be on the list. Common sense when I was closest to the accident and got away," Amos said. He shrugged. "You going to let the guys who did it get regular Earth trials?"

"Certainly," the Envoy answered. "It looks better. Nice work, Pat, Vic, Amos—you, too, Flavin. I wasn't sure you had it in you. You solved it—by finding you could co-operate with other worlds, which is the most mature way you could have solved it. So I consider that Plathgol and Earth have passed the final test, and are now full members, under Ecthinbal's tutelage. We're a little easier at lending a hand and passing information to proven planets. Congratulations! But you'll hear all about it in the news when I make the full announcement. See you around—I'm sure of that."

He was gone, barely in time for Ptheela to come trooping up with six thin, wispy versions of herself in tow. She chuckled. "They promoted me before they banished me, Pat. Meet my *six* strong husbands. Now I'll have the strongest seed on all Earth. Oh, I almost forgot. A present for you and Vic."

Then she also was gone, leading her husbands toward Flavin's car while Vic stared down at a particularly ugly *tsiuna* in Pat's hands. He grinned a bit ruefully.

"All right. I'll learn to eat the stuff," he told her. "I suppose I'll have to get used to it. Pat, will you marry me?"

She dropped the *tsiuna* into Amos' hands as she came to him, her lips reaching up for his. It wasn't until a month later that he found *tsiuna* tasted slightly better than chicken.

A few days after the sale of the novelette to Gold, Scott Meredith called me in to have a long talk with me. He didn't bother to say so, but it was my agent and friend discussing things with me, not my employer. He wanted to go over my affairs with me and see just where things stood.

My earnings for the past few months were quite enough for me to live on, even without the salary from working at the office. And the prospects were even better. I had a contract for a fact book on atomic power. (That turned out to be what is called a critical success. It was widely praised and placed on the New York Public Library's recommended book list. But the publisher never got it out properly, and my final sales came to something like 740 copies!) I'd established myself in a number of fields of pulp fiction, and several editors were beginning to ask for my work. And I was back to doing science fiction, which was a booming market that paid well. Scott assured me that he could sell everything I wrote—a promise which he's kept for all the years since.

So obviously it made no sense for me to treat writing as a part-time job. Writing at night was fine, if I liked to do it that way; but it wasn't fine after a day at the office. It was time I made up my mind that I was a professional writer who didn't need any other job.

We'd discussed that before, but not in detail, and with no date in mind. But now we decided that I should work one more month and then quit.

There were three bits of science fiction written during that final month, and I originally meant to include them. But I've decided against it now. The true cutoff date was the moment when I decided I was a professional, not the time when I finally cleaned up and left the office.

It took me almost exactly twelve years after the publication of my first story to decide that my job was writing, and that it was more than one of my numerous interests. It was a little hard to realize, but my principal feeling was one of relief at having finally made the decision. It's always a good thing to know that one is doing exactly what one should be doing.

So this is the story of twelve years of fumbling along on the road to being a science fiction writer, with those examples which haven't already been collected in volumes of my work.

I left the office in May 1950. And since then, my principal source of income has always been my writing.

I've done other things, but they've been connected with the field, and are by-products of my writing. I've edited magazines (four at one time, for a while), reviewed books, lectured and taught courses in schools. And all of that is good, because I think a man should have at least some experience with every aspect of the field in which he works. I've been well enough recognized by the readers of science fiction to make the job seem properly rewarding, too; I've served as toastmaster and guest of honor at world conventions, and I've been invited to be guest of honor at a number of smaller conventions.

There have been bad times, too—but mostly of my own devising. I went through a very long slump once, where I seemed totally unable to write. But the royalty from the juvenile books and the subsidiary rights to old stories were enough to keep me going. And eventually the slump disappeared one day, as slumps always will, if a writer refuses to panic.

The world of science fiction has been good to me. It has opened up a whole cosmos to me in innumerable marvelous stories. It has granted me a profession I enjoy and a reasonable amount of honor. And from it, I have drawn a large number of friends among editors, writers, and fans—the best and most interesting friends anyone could want. To a very large extent, it has made those friends relate to me as if we were all of one family, sharing our joys and sorrows and uniting in an ever-expanding common interest.

To me, it is the best of all possible—and sometimes impossible—worlds.

APPENDIX

The Fantasy and Science Fiction of the Early Years

	STORY (*Words*)	MAGAZINE *Issue*	COLLECTION
1	THE FAITHFUL (4,000)	Astounding Science Fiction April 1938	The Early del Rey
2	. . . And It Comes Out Here (6,000)	Galaxy Science Fiction February 1951	Mortals and Monsters
3	Ice (12,000)	———	———
4	Helen O'Loy (4,500)	Astounding Science Fiction December 1938	And Some Were Human
5	CROSS OF FIRE (3,000)	Weird Tales April 1939	The Early del Rey
6	The Day Is Done (6,000)	Astounding Science Fiction May 1939	And Some Were Human
7	A Very Simple Man (5,000)	———	———
8	The Luck of Ignatz (12,700)	Astounding Science Fiction August 1939	And Some Were Human
9	Forsaking All Others (5,000)	Unknown August 1939	And Some Were Human
10	The Coppersmith (6,000)	Unknown September 1939	Robots and Changelings

Notes: Stories in CAPITAL LETTERS appear in this volume.
Other collections referred to are those from Ballantine Books.

	STORY (*Words*)	MAGAZINE *Issue*	COLLECTION
11	ANYTHING (5,600)	Unknown October 1939	The Early del Rey
12	The Hands of the Gods (5,000)	———	———
13	HABIT (4,800)	Astounding Science Fiction November 1939	The Early del Rey
14	Glory (5,000)	———	———
15	THE SMALLEST GOD (14,500)	Astounding Science Fiction January 1940	The Early del Rey
16	Fade-Out (3,800)	———	———
17	THE STARS LOOK DOWN (15,000)	Astounding Science Fiction August 1940	The Early del Rey
18	Coincidence (5,000)	———	———
19	The Late Henry Smith (6,000)	———	———
20	DOUBLED IN BRASS (6,400)	Unknown January 1940	The Early del Rey
21	Miracles, Second Class (6,400)	———	———
22	REINCARNATE (11,000)	Astounding Science Fiction April 1940	The Early del Rey
23	The Pipes of Pan (6,000)	Unknown May 1940	Robots and Changelings
24	Dark Mission (6,400)	Astounding Science Fiction July 1940	And Some Were Human
25	CARILLON OF SKULLS (6,400)	Unknown February 1941	The Early del Rey
26	DONE WITHOUT EAGLES (6,400)	Astounding Science Fiction August 1940	The Early del Rey

	STORY (*Words*)	MAGAZINE *Issue*	COLLECTION
27	The Boaster (5,000)	————	————
28	Milksop (6,400)	————	————
29	Hereafter, Inc. (4,500)	Unknown Worlds December 1941	And Some Were Human
30	The Wings of Night (6,500)	Astounding Science Fiction March 1942	And Some Were Human
31	MY NAME IS LEGION (10,000)	Astounding Science Fiction June 1942	The Early del Rey
32	THOUGH POPPIES GROW (12,600)	Unknown Worlds August 1942	The Early del Rey
33	Nerves (30,000)	Astounding Science Fiction September 1942	Nerves
34	LUNAR LANDING (20,000)	Astounding Science Fiction October 1942	The Early del Rey
35	FIFTH FREEDOM (8,000)	Astounding Science Fiction May 1943	The Early del Rey
36	WHOM THE GODS LOVE (4,300)	Astounding Science Fiction June 1943	The Early del Rey
37	Misdirection (6,200)	————	————
38	The Renegade (6,400)	Astounding Science Fiction July 1943	And Some Were Human
39	THOUGH DREAMERS DIE (8,000)	Astounding Science Fiction February 1944	The Early del Rey
40	Kindness (5,700)	Astounding Science Fiction October 1944	Robots and Changelings

	STORY (*Words*)	MAGAZINE *Issue*	COLLECTION
41	FOOL'S ERRAND (2,100)	Science Fiction Quarterly November 1951	The Early del Rey
42	THE ONE-EYED MAN (8,000)	Astounding Science Fiction May 1945	The Early del Rey
43	Into Thy Hands (8,000)	Astounding Science Fiction August 1945	Robots and Changelings
44	AND THE DARKNESS (7,000)	Out of This World Adventures July 1950	The Early del Rey
45	SHADOWS OF EMPIRE (6,500)	Future/Science Fiction Stories July–August 1950	The Early del Rey
46	UNREASONABLE FACSIMILE (6,300)	Future Science Fiction July 1952	The Early del Rey
47	Uneasy Lies the Head (6,500)	Ten Story Fantasy Spring 1951	Robots and Changelings
48	CONDITIONED REFLEX (6,600)	Future/Science Fiction Stories May 1951	The Early del Rey
49	OVER THE TOP (5,000)	Astounding Science Fiction November 1949	The Early del Rey
50	The Monster (5,000)	Argosy June 1951	Robots and Changelings
51	WIND BETWEEN THE WORLDS (17,500)	Galaxy Science Fiction March 1951	The Early del Rey